S0-AYS-255

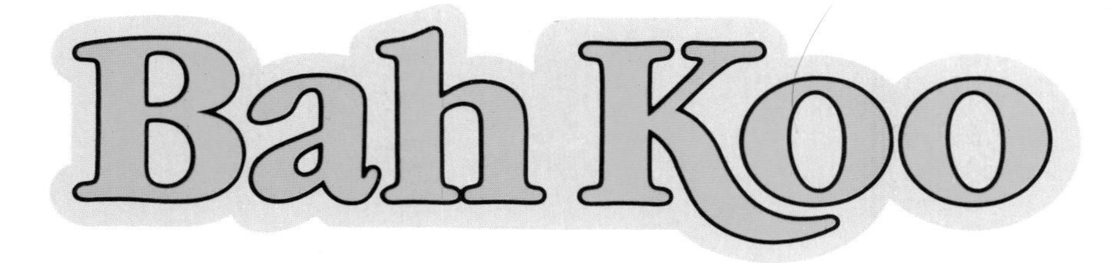

Bah Koo

By Robert V. Rhodes

Illustrated by Gary Patterson

St. Martin's Press New York, New York

The author would like to give
special recognition and thanks
to his friend Michael H. Ruggles
for the introduction to the "baku"
of Oriental mythology and
to the talented illustrator
of this book,
Gary Patterson.

Library of Congress Cataloging-in-Publication Data

Rhodes, Robert (Robert Voorhis)
Bah Koo—chaser of bad dreams.

Summary: Bah Koo leaves his forest home, where the other animals laughed at him for being different, and goes to live with a human family where he discovers he possesses a magical gift that can help all humans.
[1. Animals—Fiction. 2. Dreams—Fiction]
I. Patterson, Gary, ill. II. Title.
PZ7.R34766Bah 1987 [Fic] 87-16444
ISBN 0-312-01001-X

First Edition
10 9 8 7 6 5 4 3 2 1

There is a friend in this world for us all—but he is a special friend to children. Until now, however, he has not been very well known—at least, that is, to many of the people that I know. You see, Bah Koo (for that is his name) was born in a far-off part of the world and does not look like anything anyone has ever seen before. He has a short little trunk, the mane and the body and the tail of a lion, the ears of a cow, and three toes on each of his feet. Bah Koo is very soft when you hold him, but when he fights to protect a friend, Bah Koo *changes!* He gets very large and grows fangs. Another toe appears on each of his feet and four white claws extend, long and sharp and clean.

But, before we get into all of that, it's important for you to know the story of Bah Koo, and how all of this began . . .

Bah Koo was born many, many years ago in an ancient and faraway land. There he grew up and, like all the other animals, he lived and played in the meadows and forests and hills—but Bah Koo, alas, was different. He did not look like the other animals in his land. Not only did he look different, but he also had a strange and mysterious feeling that there was something he was meant to do . . . but just what it was, he did not know.

When Bah Koo was very small, he did not know that he was different from all the other animals. As he grew older, the other animals began to make fun of him and the way he looked, and Bah Koo soon learned the loneliness that comes from being "different."

One day Bah Koo became very sad. He became so sad, in fact, that he began to feel that he no longer belonged anywhere in his land, and he decided to run away! He planned to live all by himself where none of the other animals would ever find him. And so, the next morning, before anyone was up, Bah Koo, in deepening sadness, left his home.

Bah Koo wandered for many, many days. He was tired and hungry and cold and wet and all the things that make any of us sad when we are alone and far from home. Then, all of a sudden, he came upon the strangest sight he had ever seen. There were people—and there were houses.

The people looked very strange to Bah Koo—for he had never seen anything like them before. They looked even stranger to him, in fact, than his own reflection, which he had often seen in the little pond at home.

The houses also looked strange to Bah Koo—for he had never seen a house before either. There was a big house, painted red, with huge doors. And there was a smaller house, painted white, with odd shiny windows. But the strangest of all was the little house . . .

—for the little house was sitting in a *tree!*

PRIVet

Bah Koo stopped and stared at all the strange things around him and suddenly he was afraid.

Just then two little people, a large four-legged animal, and what appeared to be a furry ball with huge eyes all came bounding and tumbling and shouting out of the little house in the tree. They were jumping and running and waving their arms in the air, and they were all heading straight for him.

Bah Koo was so afraid that he could not move—he just shut his eyes in fear and waited for the charging pack of wild animals to leap upon him.

But the little people scooped him up and, still making an awful racket, carried him, dirty, wet, and shaking, back to the little house with the odd shiny windows, which he heard one of them call "home."

The two larger people, who had been working in the fields, came back to the house to see what all the shouting was about. When they saw how dirty and wet and cold and afraid Bah Koo was, they felt sorry for him.

They warmed some water on the stove and poured it into an old wooden tub. Then, gently, with loving hands, they placed him into the water and the children washed him clean from the top of his head to the tip of his tail.

Bah Koo soon learned that his friends were people, that what they lived in was a house, and that the large four-legged animal, who was always bumping into things, was a dog.

And the fussy, furry ball, who was always licking and cleaning its fur, was a cat.

He learned that the little people who had found him were called "children." And although he loved everyone who lived in the house, Bah Koo found that he really loved the children the most.

For the first time in his life Bah Koo felt wanted. Feeling wanted was a very nice feeling. It was as nice as the feeling he had felt that first day when he had been bathed, warmed by the fire, fed, wrapped in a blanket, and placed in a little wooden box by the stove.

The people loved Bah Koo and were proud of him, for he never bothered the cat or the dog or the birds or the mice or anything else, for that matter. He played and made noises, didn't eat too much, never complained, and never made a mess or a fuss about anything. The people were so proud of Bah Koo, in fact, they even showed him off to all their friends.

Bah Koo, in turn, loved the people and the children. He longed to find a way to repay all the love and kindness that they had given him, but no matter how hard he tried, he could not seem to do enough.

He also tried to share with everyone the two little friends he had made since coming to live with the family. But, alas, Bah Koo could not speak, so there was no way he could tell them. No one seemed to be able to see his little friends either. For whenever he pointed excitedly at them, everyone would look, then shrug, pat Bah Koo gently, and walk away shaking their heads in wonder.

One of the friends was a lovely little fairy. Her name was Flossyna and she came every night to see if either of the children had lost a tooth. If she found one, she took it from where it had been placed and put it in the magic purse that she wore at her side. In an instant the tooth would change, and from the magic purse, Flossyna would pluck a wonderful surprise that she would carefully place where the tooth had rested only moments before.

The other friend was a little old man. His name was Mr. Fortywink, and he visited every night, too. He had a marvelous twinkling lantern and a bag of magic sand. Mr. Fortywink told Bah Koo that he was the Sandman, and that he quietly sprinkled a little of his magic on everyone to help them fall asleep.

Bah Koo loved Mr. Fortywink, the Sandman, with his funny stocking cap, funny fuzzy pajamas, and long funny beard. And Bah Koo loved Flossyna, the Tooth Fairy, too, for she was very beautiful. He loved to watch her as she floated sparkling in her long flowing gown with all the twinkling bright little stars in her long golden hair. He knew that Flossyna and Mr. Fortywink were very special and, as the days passed, the feeling he had always had that he was special too seemed to grow even stronger in his heart. He knew that there was something that he and he alone was meant to do, but, alas, he did not know what it was.

Bah Koo's discovery of his mysterious and wondrous gift came to him late one night when the house was very still . . . and very quiet . . . and very, very dark.

Everyone was sound asleep . . . everyone, including Bah Koo. Then . . . upstairs in the dark and quiet little house, one of the children slowly began to stir.

And, suddenly, downstairs in the little wooden box by the stove, Bah Koo was awake! . . .

Awake as he had never been before, and he felt different. He felt strong—very, very strong and . . . yes, as strange as it was for him, Bah Koo . . . felt fierce and angry!

The little child began to moan, and Bah Koo was suddenly halfway up the stairs before he even knew what was happening. He stopped at the top of the stairs and suddenly he felt *bigger* than the house, although he was not, and *stronger* than anything in the whole wide world. And he may have been. The child began to cry out, and in a flash . . .

Bah Koo was in the room and it was filled with a strange light coming from somewhere behind him, but, at that moment he could not turn around to find its source. For there, hovering like an awful, horrible, ugly being, was the child's Bad Dream, and Bah Koo knew right then what it was that he was meant to do. The Bad Dream was his foe! It was something Bah Koo had to destroy!

He did not understand what happened next, because it was the first time it had ever happened. Suddenly, Bah Koo *was* large and filled with power and strength! His mane stood up. His eyes grew red and mean, and his claws and fangs grew long and sharp and strong. Then, with one mighty, angry, and snarling leap . . .

Bah Koo leapt right on top of the swirling Dream . . .

. . . and the ugly, awful, horrible thing was gone!

In one split second . . . in one-half of one instant! . . . the Bad Dream had been completely gobbled up and Bah Koo's great power and strength began to melt away. His eyes cleared. His fangs and claws disappeared. His mane grew smooth and soft and he was no bigger than he had ever been before. He took a deep breath and let out a long sigh.

The parents had also heard the child moan in his sleep and they had gotten up to see what was wrong. Just as they had reached the open door to the room they had stopped in shock! For in that moment Bah Koo had changed! He had attacked and swallowed the child's Bad Dream.

The child awoke! His parents were talking excitedly and Bah Koo was sitting quietly on his bed. The parents quickly explained to the child what, to their amazement, they had seen, and the child picked up Bah Koo and hugged him for a long, long time.

In the days that followed Bah Koo seemed to grow restless, and the children began to wonder if he really belonged to them like all the other animals that they had taken in. The children's mother and father knew now that Bah Koo was very special, and so they told the children that one day soon they would all have to say good-bye to him. They

explained that Bah Koo should be free to go anywhere in the world to fight and destroy Bad Dreams wherever he found them, and that they were very sure, in their hearts, that this was indeed what Bah Koo was truly meant to do.

In order to make it easier for everyone on the day when Bah Koo would no longer be with them, the children's mother made two little dolls out of stuffing and brightly colored cloth and gave one to each of the children. The plump little dolls looked just like Bah Koo, and everyone including Bah Koo took great delight in them.

Although he felt sad about his thoughts of leaving, Bah Koo also felt peace in his heart. For at last he knew what it was that he was meant to do. . . . He, Bah Koo, was the destroyer of Bad Dreams! And because of this, no one now, no matter how big or how small, or how brave or how shy, would ever have to be afraid of a Bad Dream again. And Bah Koo knew something else, too.

He knew that the great light that had filled the room when he had fought the child's awful Dream was the presence of the Great Creator, supporting and protecting him. And he knew that the light would always be with him whenever he faced and fought one of his horrible foes.

The days came and went until one day, just as suddenly as he had come, Bah Koo was gone! He had left the little house, and the people and the animals who were his friends. For he had found his real home. The home he found was everywhere, with everyone who loves and needs him. But his special home . . . the one that Bah Koo loves the most . . . is in the hearts of children everywhere!

. . . OH! by the way, if you watch some clear and starry night with a keen and patient eye, you may catch a glimpse of Bah Koo racing across the sky. . . . But then, that's another story to be told. . . .

Here is an uncommon history of the commonplace—a compendium of extraordinary facts about all kinds of things you use and see every day: automobiles, locks, bathtubs, bicycles, cats, coffee, asparagus, eyeglasses, hamburgers, pianos, safety pins, etc.

Hundreds of fascinating and unusual pictures enliven the sprightly text, and make the reading of this volume a real enjoyment.

Mammoth Book of

Fascinating Information

Richard B. Manchester

A HART BOOK

A & W VISUAL LIBRARY • NEW YORK

CONTENTS

PUBLISHED BY
A & W PUBLISHERS, INC.
95 MADISON AVENUE
NEW YORK, NEW YORK 10016

LIBRARY OF CONGRESS
CATALOG CARD NO. 80-80792

ISBN: 0-89104-191-5

MANUFACTURED IN THE UNITED STATES OF AMERICA

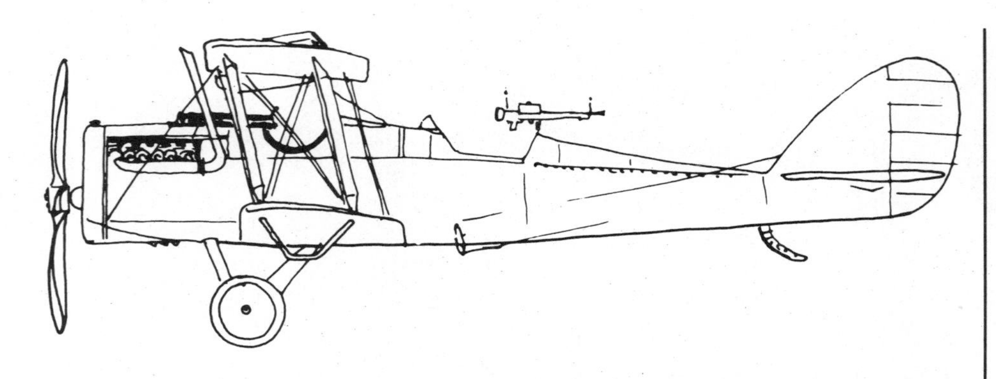

Aircraft

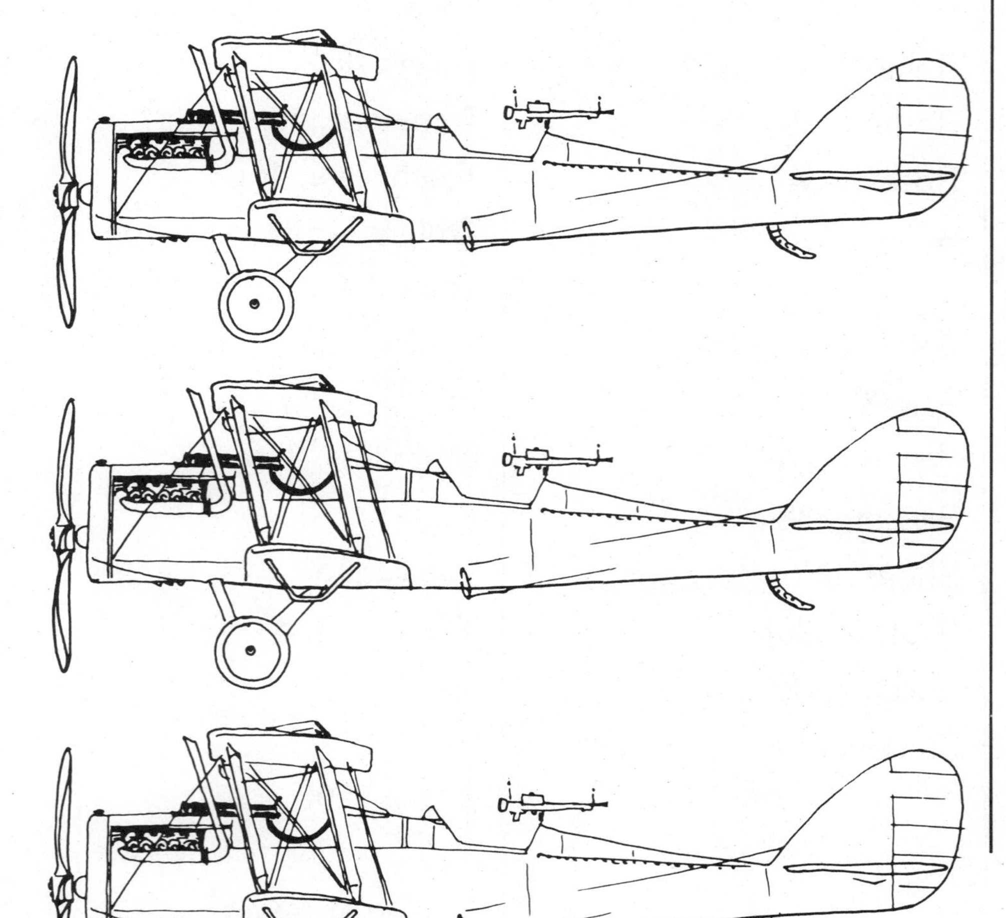

Twenty miles was about the farthest a primitive man could hope to travel in a day, using the only means of transportation he had available—his feet. When recorded history began, a good day's journey by horse might cover as much as 80 miles. A few thousand years passed before the railroad lengthened the distance a man could travel in eight hours to about 150 miles. By 1925, the automobile had doubled that distance.

Then, about 25 years later, the distance that could be traveled in eight hours skyrocketed to over 4,500 miles. By today, it has doubled again. Man can now travel literally halfway around the earth in the time it took his primitive ancestors to trek just 20 miles. The entire world is within reach of a day's journey. How did this come about? Man left the earth and took to the air!

Flying has been man's dream ever since he first watched birds soaring through the air. But for a long time man relegated flight to the realm of the gods, who in the Egyptian, Minoan, and other ancient cultures were often depicted in birdlike form. Greek and Roman gods were thought capable of flight, though only the winged Mercury bore any visible means of support. The angels of Hebrew and Christian lore, on the other hand, were always depicted with wings. In order to strengthen their claims to divinity, kings in Persia, China, and other lands sometimes had their magicians and historians create legends suggesting the monarchs were capable of flight. But myths such as the Greek story of Icarus show what would happen to a mortal who dared imitate his divine superiors.

Most of man's early scientific writings on human flight attempted to show, not how it could be achieved, but why it was impossible. However, beginning in the Middle Ages, writers and scientists such as Francis Bacon, Isaac Newton, Roger Bacon, and others began to seriously speculate on human flight, and the first "science fiction" authors anticipated it. Jules Verne forecasted a manned flight to the moon aboard a rocket launched from Florida a century before this became a reality.

Ascension of the Montgolfiere balloon in a Parisian park on September 18, 1783.

EARLY VISIONS OF FLYING

Flying machine invented by Signor Ignazio of Milan, Italy.

Degroff's flying machine.

Zaphaniah Phelps, a Connecticut inventor, attempting his first aerial trip.

W.J. Lewis' flying machine.

ABOVE: *Leturr's flying machine.*
BELOW: *Marriott's aerial steam carriage, the "Avitor."*

A biplane built by Wright in 1904.

In the 17th century, English writer John Wilkens suggested that there were four ways in which man could hope to fly: with angels, with the aid of birds, with wings, or in a flying chariot. The last, of course, would prove the only feasible way. But for a long time man's admiration of the birds, and his belief that in order to fly man would have to imitate them, hindered early attempts at flight. In the 19th century, most designs for flying machines included some form of flapping wings, like the devices Leonardo da Vinci had sketched earlier.

Man's earliest successful flights came not in a winged flying machine, but in the basket of a simple hot-air balloon. The first balloon of which we have a record was the invention of a Portuguese priest. In 1709, he succeeded in raising a hot-air balloon a few feet off the ground at an indoor exhibition. But it was the work of the French Montgolfier brothers, Joseph and Etienne, that first turned the attention of the world toward manned balloon flight.

Ascension of a balloon in Paris in 1784.

Noticing that smoke always floats upward, in June 1783, the Montgolfier brothers constructed a bag 30 feet in diameter, held it over a fire until it had inflated with smoke, and watched it rise high into the air above Annonay, France.

As word spread of the Montgolfiers' balloon flight, another pair of French brothers, the Roberts, set out to build their own balloon. Not knowing what gas the Montgolfiers had used to fill their balloon, the Roberts chose hydrogen, which had been isolated 17 years earlier. The Roberts' 15-foot balloon was launched into the rainy skies above Paris. It drifted 15 miles before settling down near the village of Gonesse, where frightened peasants attacked the "apparition" with scythes and pitchforks and tore it to pieces.

In September, 1783, the Montgolfiers repeated their earlier balloon success before the court of Louis XVI at Versailles. A crowd that included Benjamin Franklin watched while a sheep, a rooster, and a duck rose into the air in a basket attached to the

Many people believe that Charles Lindbergh was the first man to achieve aviation's great milestone, the transatlantic airplane flight. Lindbergh was actually the 81st person to fly across the Altantic Ocean, but he was the first person to do it alone.

smoke-filled balloon. When the balloon touched ground, all three creatures were in perfect health. If animals could survive flight, it was reasoned, so could man. But who would be foolhardy enough to be the first man to climb into the balloon basket?

Initially, it was proposed that condemned criminals be used as guinea pigs in the first manned balloon flight. Then Jean-François Pilâtre, arguing that the honor of man's first flight should not be squandered on criminals, stepped forward to volunteer. Together with the Marquis d'Arlandes, François Laurent, Pilâtre climbed into the basket of a Montgolfier hot-air balloon in the Bois de Boulogne, Paris on November 21, 1783. The first manned balloon climbed 3,000 feet into the air while its two occupants fueled a fire on board to keep the balloon filled with hot air. After a 23-minute flight, the two pioneers touched down 10 miles away. The world was abuzz with the sensational news.

Other balloonists quickly joined the race to the heavens. In 1784, a 13-year-old boy made the first recorded balloon flight in America, riding a 30-foot hot-air balloon over Baltimore, Maryland. Nine years later, Jean-Pierre Blanchard soared skyward in a balloon before a thrilled crowd that included President George Washington. By then, the hot-air balloon was already giving way to the hydrogen-filled model. Among its other advantages, the hydrogen balloon did not require a continually fueled fire to remain aloft.

Once man had succeeded in ascending into the air, he turned his attention to finding a way of getting back to earth. Leonardo da Vinci had sketched a parachute in the form of a cloth pyramid, but no one was certain such a device would work until the Montgolfiers dropped a sheep bouyed by a seven-foot parasol from a tower in Avignon, France. In 1797, André Garnerin performed one of the most daring feats in aviation history when he rose above Paris in a balloon basket attached to an umbrella-like parachute, and at more than 2,000 feet above earth, cut the basket loose from the balloon. The parachute worked, and Garnerin went on to give a number of parachuting exhibitions from even greater heights.

It was a mere 163 years later that Joseph Kittinger survived a record-setting plunge from a considerably greater altitude. Carried aloft in a balloon, the American was 19 miles above earth when he dove into the rarefied, 90-degrees-below-zero air. Kittinger dropped an amazing 84,700 feet—more than 16 miles—free-falling for about four-and-a-half minutes before opening his chute.

In 1942, a Russian pilot set a far less enviable record when he survived a fall from a plane at an altitude of 21,980 feet—without a parachute!

With or without parachutes, early balloonists faced another major problem in their attempts to conquer the skies: a balloon can neither be steered nor set down at will, and instead relies on the vagaries of the wind. To control their flight, balloonists needed both a way of steering and a means of propulsion independent of the wind. Thus the airship, or self-propelled balloon, was born.

On September 24, 1852, Henri Giffard took off from Paris in a steam-powered, propeller-driven airship lofted by a cigar-shaped gasbag 144 feet long, achieving man's first controlled navigation of the air. But 32 years passed before airship engineers could design a machine with enough steering control to enable it to return to its point of ascent. The feat was first accomplished by Charles Renard and A.C. Krebs aboard an electric-powered airship christened *La France*.

During the 1890s, while the Wright Brothers and other airplane pioneers were hard at work on their flying machines, most aviation headlines were garnered by the airship, or dirigible. Playboy-aviator Albert Santos-Dumont created quite a stir in Paris by paying social calls in a one-man, gas-filled airship. As early as 1897, August André and two companions attempted a daring airship flight over the North Pole, but the three men vanished in the frozen Arctic. In 1930, their bodies and equipment were found by explorers—and some 33-year-old photographic plates left by the tragic mission provided excellent pictures when developed!

In 1900, Ferdinand von Zeppelin, the German who gave his name to the rigid-framed airship, launched his first hydrogen-filled craft above Lake Constance. By 1914, the Zeppelin Company was offering the first regularly scheduled air flights between German cities. Despite the dangerously volatile nature of hydrogen, Zeppelin's airships achieved a remarkable safety record on their commercial flights. By 1936, airships were carrying as many as 117 people on transatlantic flights.

In 1937, disaster struck. The 803-foot-long jewel of the Zeppelin fleet, the *Hindenburg,* had crossed the Atlantic 21 times when it landed in Lakehurst, New Jersey. For a reason never fully understood, the airship suddenly exploded, killing 36 people. The dangerous hydrogen-filled airship soon gave way to airships filled with nonexplosive helium.

By that time, the airplane had already become a reality. While many early aviators had turned their attention to balloons and airships, other forward-looking individuals had toiled on flying machines that could offer a more practical solution to the problem of manned flight. The 19th century saw hundreds—perhaps thousands—of ill-fated attempts at airplane flight.

In 1857, a French monoplane, a single-winged craft, succeeded in moving along the ground, but not above it. In 1875, a British engineer managed to lift his flying machine a few inches above the ground before it succumbed to the law of gravity. Nine years later, a Russian aeronaut constructed a steam-driven monoplane that managed to remain airborne for a few seconds when launched from a ski jump.

German inventor Otto Lilienthal carried out aviation research that was to heavily influence the work of the Wright Brothers. Concentrating on the sheer dynamics of flight rather than the problems of self-propelled aircraft, Lilienthal constructed the world's earliest successful gliders. By 1896, when he perished in a crash, Lilienthal had experienced over 2,000 successful glider flights—including one of 1,000 feet.

By the turn of the century, most of the equipment and technology necessary for powered flight was already available. In fact, an internal-combustion engine had already been used to power an airship. By 1903, Samuel Pierpont Langley and his assistant, Charles Manley, had developed an internal-combustion engine light enough to power an unmanned aircraft. Though Langley's invention later proved to be the first successful design for a heavier-than-air, gasoline-powered aircraft, it never left the ground. A test vehicle launched from a boat in the Potomac River plunged immediately into the water upon takeoff, just nine days before the Wright Brothers' first successful flight.

The Wright brothers working on one of their early planes.

Raised in Dayton, Ohio, Wilbur and Orville Wright tried their hands at publishing and bicycle repair before turning their attention to aviation. After reading of the experiments of Lilienthal and other aviators, the Wrights began their own research, first testing kites, then tethered gliders, then free-flying gliders. Even before they'd begun work on self-propelled aircraft, the Wrights had developed such innovations as the curved wing that was to form the core of their subsequent patent claims.

Contrary to a popular notion, a desire for privacy was not the Wrights' motive in transferring their operations to Kitty Hawk, North Carolina. Rather, the brothers preferred the seashore

The world's shortest scheduled flight takes passengers between two neighboring Orkney Islands in Scotland. The scheduled flight time is two minutes, although with a good wind the trip has been made in as little as 69 seconds.

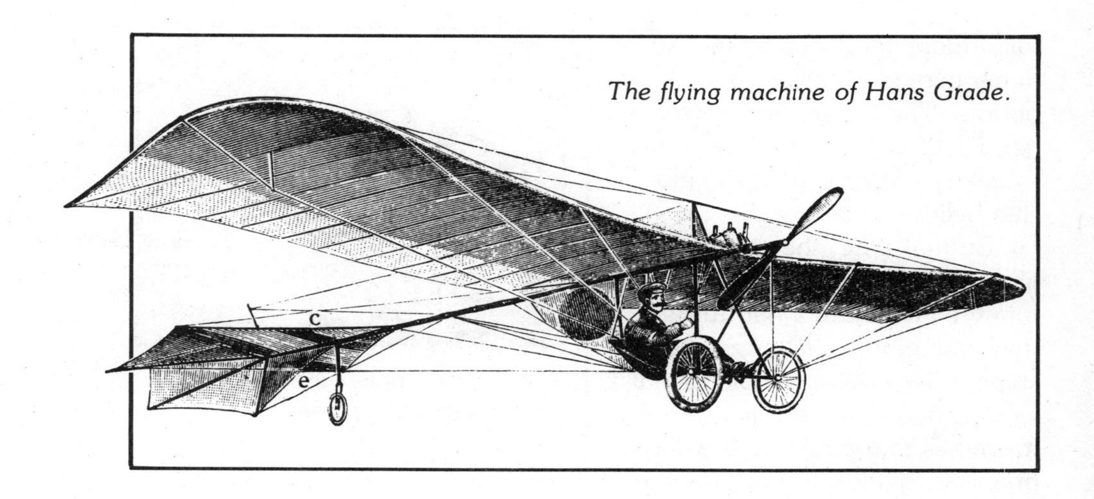

The flying machine of Hans Grade.

area because of the reasonably constant winds and the availability of sand dunes to soften landings. But their first attempts at manned glider flight at Kitty Hawk proved less than encouraging.

Returning to Dayton, the Wrights carried out extensive wind-tunnel tests on their glider designs, at one point coming quite close to giving up their efforts in desperation. Then, in 1902, they returned to Kitty Hawk and successfully flew the first practical glider in history. Now they were ready to construct the first airplane capable of powered flight.

On December 14, 1903, Wilbur Wright won a coin toss and climbed onto the bottom wing of *Flyer I.* The aircraft was fitted with a gas-powered engine and twin 40-foot wings, and was launched by a dolly moving along a 60-foot monorail track. At the first launch, the aircraft plowed into the sand at the end of the track. Three days later, it was Orville's turn. At 10:35 A.M., *Flyer I* moved along the track and took off into a 20-mile-an-hour wind, remaining aloft for 12 seconds before touching down. Man's first powered airplane flight had become history.

Though the Wrights were able to duplicate their initial success with three more flights that morning, including one of a 59-second duration, few people at the time took note of their achievement. Most magazine and journal editors regarded the Wrights' story as so much science fiction. It was close to five years before the American public was ready to believe the Wright Brothers had actually flown at Kitty Hawk. Amazingly, the first eyewitness account of a Wright Brothers flight was published in a magazine called *Gleanings in Bee Culture,* after its editor witnessed a flight of the Wrights' second machine, *Flyer II.*

By mid-1905, the Wrights had logged 49 flights in *Flyer III,* the first of their machines designed with an upright engine and a seated pilot. The longest flight was over 24 miles, and the average speed of the craft was 38 miles per hour. In 1906, an airplane patent was issued to the Wrights, and within two years, they were negotiating with the U.S. War Department for the construction of a military plane.

Soon after the success of *Flyer III,* Wilbur Wright had gone to Europe. Wilbur amazed European aviators with flights as long

Surprisingly, private planes in the United States carry about 50 times as many passengers per year as all American-owned scheduled airlines combined!

as 77½ miles. On December 31, 1908, he remained aloft for a record-setting two hours, 20 minutes. Spurred on by the demonstrations, European inventors hurried to build their own powered aircraft.

Orville remained in America to work on the military aircraft. He succeeded beyond anyone's wildest dreams. Slowly, the public began to awaken to the Wrights' achievement. But on September 17, 1907, Orville crashed while testing his new plane, and sustained serious injuries. A passenger named Thomas Selfridge perished, becoming the first man to die in a powered airplane.

Seven years later, aviator-showman Glenn Curtiss obtained the flying machine designed by S.A. Langley and demonstrated that this plane, rather than *Flyer I*, was the first airplane capable of powered flight. The Smithsonian Institution in Washington recognized the claim, and installed Langley's machine as "the first airplane capable of sustained free flight with a man." Orville Wright, who survived his brother by 36 years, remained bitter over the decision until his death in 1948, and refused to give *Flyer I* to the Smithsonian. In 1928, the machine was placed in the Science museum in South Kensington, London. Twenty years later, on the 45th anniversary of man's first flight, *Flyer I* was returned to the United States and formally installed in the Smithsonian Institution.

In 1909, Frenchman Louis Bleriot became the first man to fly across the English Channel. A year later, Jorge Chavez became the first man to fly across the Alps, though a prize offered by the Italian Aviation Society remained uncollected when Chavez was killed on landing.

On this side of the Atlantic, air shows and races quickly became a sensation. In 1910, a massive airplane meet in New York City included a race around the Statue of Liberty. The following year, C.P. Rogers became the first man to fly from coast to coast, traveling from New York to Los Angeles in 68 hops. Still, few people could see beyond showmanship to the long-range possibilities of airplanes for transportation and military use. Then, World War I changed everything.

The idea of using aircraft for military purposes had occurred to Napoleon, who considered using balloons to invade England. In 1794, observation balloons were used for the first time during the Battle of Fleurus, Belgium. The Union army employed reconnaissance balloons during the American Civil War. In 1870, the *Balloon Poste* carried mail and passengers in and out of besieged Paris.

Wilbur Wright had naively written that the airplane would make war impossible, since air observation could expose an army's movements. In 1911, the Italians demonstrated the use of aircraft equipped with bombs during the Italo-Turkish War in North Africa. Nevertheless, French commander Ferdinand Foch declared that aircraft would never be more than sporting devices. At the beginning of World War I, military aircraft were used almost exclusively for reconnaissance, with pilots carrying no more than an occasional pistol or rifle to fire on enemy reconnaissance planes.

LEFT:
Orville Wright (1871-1948).
RIGHT:
Wilbur Wright (1867-1912).

Then, in 1915, the Germans perfected the synchronized machine gun, timed to fire through spinning propeller blades without striking them. For a time, German aircraft such as the Fokker triplane flown by the Red Baron, Manfred von Richthofen, ruled the skies. The French countered with the Nieuport, the British with the Sopwith Camel and other planes. The Americans, who had not a single plane ready for combat at the outbreak of the war, soon had their first ace, Capt. Edward Rickenbacker—though Eddie's 26 kills were far outshadowed by the 80 credited to the Red Baron.

By the end of the war, hundreds of thousands of people were employed in the aircraft industry. Every nation now recognized the grim potential of armed aircraft. In 1918, the British had even constructed the world's first aircraft carrier, the 560-foot-long *Argus*, four years before the first U.S. carrier, named after aviator S.P. Langley.

After the war, the airplane was largely returned to the showman. Air circuses abounded as aviators converted hundreds of leftover warplanes for civilian use. In the United States, it was airmail service that provided the foundation for later commercial aviation. By 1920, transcontinental airmail service had been inaugurated in the United States. Four years later, the first regular night flights in the world were instituted for airmail delivery.

Many people believe that Charles Lindbergh was the first man to achieve aviation's next milestone, the transatlantic airplane flight. Actually, the feat had been accomplished many times before Lindbergh's historic journey. In 1919, a crew of six U.S. Navy flyers had crossed the Atlantic in a Curtiss hydroplane, landing in the Azores before continuing on to England. Later that year, two Englishmen accomplished the first nonstop crossing, traveling from Newfoundland to Ireland in just over 16 hours. Their gear included two stuffed black cats. Including airship crews, Lindbergh was actually the 81st person to fly across the Atlantic Ocean. But he was the first person to do it alone.

The first solo nonstop transatlantic flight began at Roosevelt Field, Long Island, when Lindbergh took off in a Ryan monoplane named the *Spirit of St. Louis,* which he'd flown from San Diego to New York just days before. Lindbergh took to the air at 7:52 A.M., May 20, 1927, and touched down at Paris's Le Bourget airport shortly after 10 o'clock the following night, having covered 3,610 miles in 33½ hours. The flight won a prize of $25,000 offered by Raymond Orteig, and the attention of the world.

Eddie Rickenbacker may have been America's most well-known ace, but a pilot named J.H. Hedley was surely the luckiest. On January 6, 1918, Captain Hedley was flying over German territory in a plane piloted by a Canadian named Makepeace, when the plane was attacked by German fighters. To evade the enemy, Makepeace took his plane in a vertical dive that pulled Hedley right out of his seat and into the ozone. Makepeace continued his descent for several hundred feet, *sans* co-pilot, then leveled off. Incredibly, the plunging Hedley landed smack dab on the tail of the airplane, then pulled himself back into his seat and landed safely!

The excitement generated by Lindbergh's feat did much to spur the development of commercial aviation in the United States. Within a few years of the historic flight, investors had poured over a half-billion dollars into the commercial aviation industry. In 1927, the first scheduled night service in America was inaugurated between Boston and New York. The same year, Pan American Airlines began service between Key West, Florida, and Havana, Cuba. By 1939, Pan Am was operating flights from the United States throughout South America, and across the oceans to England and Manilla as well.

In Europe, regularly scheduled commercial flights had begun almost immediately after World War I. Like their American counterparts, early European airplane travelers rode unconverted warplanes with unheated, uninsulated, open cabins. The flights were noisy, uncomfortable, and dangerous. By 1930, when Europe was crisscrossed with commercial air routes, aircraft manufacturers had begun constructing airplanes for passenger use. Passengers were soon riding inside soundproof cabins shaped much like those of today's jets, with streamlined planes like the Boeing 247D, Douglas DC-2, and Lockheed 10 leading the way.

Early in the 1930s, commercial airplane passengers num-

The flying machine of Bleriot.

bered just a few thousand per year. Accidents were not rare—the death rate for airplane travel stood at about one fatality per eight million passenger-miles. By the early 1940s, when millions of people were flying annually, the rate had plummetted to one fatality per 100 million passenger-miles. Future European giants such as Air France, KLM, Lufthansa, Swissair, and Imperial Airways (later BOAC and BEA) had already been founded, and international transatlantic flights had been instituted by Pan Am and Imperial Airways.

Airplane daredevils, meanwhile, were still hard at work. In 1931, Wiley Post and Harold Gatty flew around the world, departing from New York and returning eight-and-a-half days later. In 1933, Post accomplished the feat on a solo flight, returning in just over seven-and-a-half days. Even future billionaire Howard Hughes got into the act. In 1938, Hughes and a crew of four left New York and circled the globe in three days, 19 hours, covering 15,500 miles.

In 1957, the record for the fastest circumnavigation of the globe was set by three U.S. Air Force B-52's when they returned to their starting point in California after a flight of just 45 hours, 19 minutes. The record for the fastest round-the-world trip by a commercial airliner was not set until 1976, when a Pan Am 747 returned its 98 passengers to New York City after a flight of 46 hours, having stopped for refueling only twice.

Why would anyone want to fly a commercial jet around the world? Well, Pan Am's record-setting flight was actually a publicity stunt calling attention to the company's New York to Tokyo flight, the world's longest scheduled nonstop flight. Inaugurated in 1976, the thrice-weekly flight covers 6,754 miles in less than 14 hours.

At the other end of the scale, the world's shortest scheduled flight takes passengers between two neighboring Orkney Islands in Scotland. The scheduled flight time is two minutes, although with a good wind the trip has been made in as little as 69 seconds. Fare on the twin-engine eight-seater is about $10, but neither movies nor food are offered aboard.

Incidentally, on-board movies are not a recent innovation. On October 8, 1929, a milestone

The Boeing 747 is a full 23 times as long as the smallest manned airplane ever to leave the ground, the Stits Skybaby. Flown in 1952, the midget craft measured just 9 feet, 10 inches in length, but achieved speeds of up to 185 miles per hour.

A Rumpler-Eindecker of 1913.

in modern transportation was reached when a newsreel and two cartoons were shown on a Transcontinental Air Transport plane.

The propeller-driven aircraft that took early aviators into the skies are quickly becoming historic relics as we continue into the jet age. As early as 1930, an American named Frank Whittle had patented a jet engine. But the first successful gas-turbine engine to successfully fly an airplane was built nine years later in Germany. In 1942, a Bell XP-59A craft powered by a General Electric engine became the first American jet to reach the skies when it took off successfully from Muroc Lake, California. By the end of World War II, jets were in full production in both England and the United States.

America's first jet transport was the four-engine Boeing 707, launched in 1954. The 707 began regular commercial service four years later. By 1969, there were 2,200 turbine-jet craft in operation among American commercial airlines, and just 300 prop planes.

No sooner had airline companies finished replacing their prop planes with jets than a new type of jet appeared that threatened to make many of the earlier craft obsolete—the wide-bodied jetliner. In 1970, Boeing unveiled the 747, the largest jet airliner in the world with a capacity of up to 500 passengers. The wide-bodied Douglas DC-10 and Lockheed Tri-Star L-1011 followed quickly on the heels of the Boeing craft. By the mid-70s, wide-bodied jets were the rule rather than the exception on most long-distance commercial flights.

The Boeing 747 is a full 23 times as long as the smallest manned airplane ever to leave the ground, the Stits Skybaby. Flown in 1952, the midget craft measured just nine feet, 10 inches in length, but achieved speeds of up to 185 miles per hour.

The fleets of most airlines now include an assortment of jet aircraft, assigned to various flights according to distance and passenger demand. Some of the more common commercial jets in use today, along with their maximum passenger capacity and speed, appear in the adjacent box.

Pilots now average about $50,000 in salary per year, working a three-day week.

Type of Airplane	Passengers Carried	Speed (m.p.h.)
Boeing 707	219	600
Boeing 727	131	600
Boeing 737	130	580
Boeing 747	500	640
McDonnell-Douglas DC-8	176	580
McDonnell-Douglas DC-8 S	259	600
McDonnell-Douglas DC-9	90	565
McDonnell-Douglas DC-10	380	597
Lockheed Tri-Star L-1011	400	620
Sud-Aviation Super Caravelle	118	498
Sud-Aviation/BAC Concorde	128	1,320

The last plane listed in the box, the Concorde, has opened up a new frontier in commercial aviation: supersonic flight. Jets faster than the speed of sound (660 miles per hour) have been a reality, officially, since 1955. But the French- and English-built Concorde is the first jet to offer travel at supersonic speeds to commercial passengers. In 1977, the Concorde began regular flights from Paris and London across the Atlantic and to the Middle East. London to New York trips that once took seven hours can now be made in half that time. In the Concorde, passengers can ride at altitudes of up to 60,000 feet, high enough to view the curvature of the earth!

The Concorde is not the fastest jet in the world, however. That honor goes to the Lockheed SR-71, a reconnaissance aircraft capable of speeds up to 2,200 miles per hour. Nor is the Concorde the fastest commercial aircraft in the world, for the Russian Tupolev TU-144 can reach speeds up to 1,520 miles per hour. Despite a crash in 1973, the Russian jet is already in service on selected domestic routes. America also had a supersonic jet on the drawing board. But in 1972, the Federal Government cut off development funds for the craft, called the SST.

Nevertheless, Americans remain the most airborne people on earth. In 1975, American-owned airlines accounted for more than half of the miles flown by commerical aircraft throughout the world. Airline travel is growing at a furious pace worldwide, too. In 1952, scheduled airline flights carried 46 million passengers; in 1962, 121 million. By 1975, the world's airlines were carrying some 433 million passengers annually—not including Russian and Chinese airline passengers.

The last 20 years have also seen a sharp improvement in the airlines' safety records. In 1960, U.S. air carriers suffered 90 accidents, resulting in 499 fatalities. In 1975, there were 42 accidents and 124 fatalities. The rate of fatal accidents has plummetted from one per 100 million miles flown to just one per one billion miles.

Worldwide, the fatality rate has dropped from one per 50 million miles to about one per 250 million miles over a similar period of time. The worst year for aerial mishaps was 1974, when 1,301 passengers died as a result of air accidents—including the 346 people who perished in the crash of a Turkish jet near Paris, the worst air disaster of all time.

A look at the fatality rates of various world airlines confirms that, on the whole, American-owned carriers are safer than foreign airlines. Among the safest airlines have been Delta, American, TWA, Continental, United, Eastern, National, and Braniff—all American carriers—along with Qantas, SAS (Scandinavian), Japan, and Lufthansa. The highest safety award goes to TAP of Portugal. The most dangerous airlines, judging from past performance, include Royal Jordanian, VIASA of Venezuela, Egyptair, Turkish, Middle East, Air India, and a number of carriers from Eastern Europe.

The world's largest airline is state-owned Aeroflot of the U.S.S.R., with some 1,300 craft and 400,000 employees. The largest commercial carrier in the world is United Air Lines, with 365 aircraft. United now carries about 30 million passengers annually. But surprisingly, private planes in the United States carry about 50 times as many passengers per year as all American-owned scheduled airlines combined! Only 10 percent of American cities are served by regularly scheduled flights, making a private craft a necessity for the globe-trotting executive. There are now an estimated half-million licensed pilots in the United States, of whom but 20 percent own their own planes.

Speaking of pilots, the men who fly for American air carriers

Santos Dumont early model.

The record for the fastest round-the-world trip by a commercial airliner was not set until 1976, when a Pan Am 747 returned its 98 passengers to New York City after a flight of 46 hours, having stopped only twice for refueling.

are members of the second highest-paid profession in the nation, after physicians. Pilots now average about $50,000 in salary per year, working a three-day week. In 1934, the average pilot earned just $7,000 a year.

The plight of the stewardess has also changed drastically in recent years. During the 1960s, stewardesses were required to wear girdles, white gloves, and hats, and forbidden to marry. As a result of loosening restrictions, the average age of an American stewardess has risen from the low 20's to nearly 30, and the attrition rate has dropped from 36 percent to just four percent. More and more men are becoming air stewards, lured by the prospect of free air travel.

Aviation has changed a great deal at ground level, too. The first international air station in the United States, Meacham Field in Key West, Florida, consisted of one small frame building beside a runway, with maintainance facilities housed in an old fort nearby. Beginning in 1927, the station served Pan American's first international flights between Florida and Cuba.

Excluding runways, the entire air station probably could have fit inside a single large hangar at the Dallas/Fort Worth Airport in Texas, presently the world's largest. Opened in 1974, the Dallas-Fort Worth Airport extends over nearly 28 square miles. Eventually, the $810-million airport will include nine runways, 13 terminal buildings, and 260 boarding gates, with a capacity of 60 million passengers per year.

But the Texas facility is likely to enjoy a short reign as the world's largest airport. The Montreal airport will cover about 29 square miles when completed. Yet even that airport will be dwarfed by one planned for Jidda, Saudi Arabia.

When completed around 1982, the Jidda airport will sprawl over 41 square miles of desert land outside the city, which is located on the Red Sea. By contrast, Manhattan Island is 22.6 square miles in area. The airport complex will include a year-round commercial terminal, a royal pavilion for the Saudi ruling family and guests, a cargo terminal, an air force base, a hospital, a quarantine area, a hotel, seven mosques, a maintainance plant, housing for airport staff, and a desalination plant—with all concrete surfaces faced with marble! The three runways will be among the longest in the world.

But the most spectacular feature of the Arabian facility, which may cost as much as eight billion dollars when completed, will be an immense haj (pilgrimage) terminal. This terminal alone will cover 10 million square feet, more space than the two World Trade Center towers in New York combined. Yet the terminal will be open for only one month each year! The facility is designed exclusively to handle the three million Moslems who converge on Jidda during the holy month on their pilgrimage to Mecca, 30 miles away.

In terms of total passenger traffic, the world's busiest airport is Chicago's O'Hare. About 38 million persons embark or disembark at O'Hare during an average year. That's about 10 million more passengers than the world's second busiest airport, Atlanta International, and almost twice as many as the John F. Kennedy Airport in New York City. Thirteen of the world's 20 busiest airports are in America.

But if we rank airports solely on the basis of airplane traffic, some lesser-known airports come to the fore. Chicago's O'Hare remains America's busiest airport, handling close to 700,000 takeoffs and landings each year. But the second busiest of America's 7,000-plus airports is located in Santa Ana, California. Van Nuys Airport is third, followed by Long Beach Municipal. Much of the operational volume at these three airports—all located in the Los Angeles area—is accounted for by private planes or test vehicles flown by nearby airplane manufacturers. Surprisingly, John F. Kennedy airport in New York ranks 16th in the nation in takeoffs and landings; although at peak hours, the facility can handle more than 80 planes an hour.

The International Federation of Airline Pilots recently singled out Los Angeles International as the nation's most unsafe airport. Since the airport is located in a residential area, all night flights must approach from and take off toward the west, over the ocean, to reduce noise levels in the surrounding area. Pilots claim these restrictions make the airport particularly hazardous.

The future of commercial aviation is difficult to predict. The engineers who designed propeller-driven transports surely felt their planes would be the last word in aviation—until the appearance of the jet. Then, early jetliner designers watched their craft made old hat by the appearance of the wide-bodied jet. Now, supersonic jets threaten to change the face of commercial air travel. Small STOL (Short Takeoff and Landing) vehicles could someday make the sprawling airport obsolete. Even the airplane pilot is losing some of his importance. By the 1980s, commercial flights may be pre-programmed from take-off to landing, with computers directing the jet on the safest, fastest, and most comfortable route. Many jets already have the capability for a fully automatic landing.

But perhaps the biggest changes in aviation will take place at the ticket counter. Despite inflation, the cost of some airplane tickets has actually gone down over the past 20 years. In 1939, a one-way ticket on Pan Am's New York to Marseilles flight cost $375. Today, a charter airline passenger can fly *round-trip* from New York to Europe for less than $300.

The lowering of transatlantic fares has resulted in a curious anomaly in the rate structure of commercial airlines. A passenger may now purchase a ticket on a charter airline for a 3,500-mile journey across the Atlantic for significantly less than it would cost for a 2,500-mile flight from New York to California.

The initiation of "no-frills" service on some domestic air routes has already brought down the minimum cost of a flight between American cities. If we subtract the cost of a no-frills ticket for a flight between, say, New York and Miami, from the price of a coach seat on the same plane, we find that a passenger pays close to $45 for the drinks and food the no-frills passenger must do without—and the first-class passenger pays much more. That makes the New York to Miami jet one of the most expensive restaurants in the world!

If we look at international passenger traffic alone, Heathrow Airport in London is the world's busiest. Heathrow processes about 16 million international travelers annually, and 20 million passengers overall. John F. Kennedy in New York is second, with 10 million international passengers, followed by Orly in Paris, Frankfurt-Main in Germany, Schiphol in Amsterdam, Kastrup in Copenhagen, and Fiumicino in Rome. Miami International is America's second busiest airport in international traffic, processing about four million passengers each year.

ALPHABETS

If one man could be credited with the invention of the alphabet, he would probably stand as the greatest inventor of all human history. For its long-reaching importance, the alphabet is the most significant of all cultural inventions. Writing would be possible without an alphabet, but hardly as accessible as it is today, and hardly as precise. The effects of widespread literacy and precise written languages have touched in some way on almost every other invention and cultural advance.

An alphabet is a code, a shorthand for human speech sounds. The alphabets of the world range from 11 letters to 72 letters, with the average in the 20s. Those letters cover the entire range of sounds in a language, yet are simple enough to be learned by a first-grader.

But the alphabet was not, of course, the invention of a single person. The alphabet was produced by a gradual evolution of written language from primitive picture drawings. Despite the invention of printing and typing, that alphabet has undergone relatively few important changes in 3,000 years.

There are three fundamental kinds of writing systems: logographic, syllabic, and alphabetic. They differ from one another in the kinds of units their symbols represent. Basically, the three systems evolved one from the other in that order, but all three are still in use.

In a *logographic* writing system, each symbol represents a word. Logographic writing systems developed directly from the oldest form of written communication: pictures representing objects or actions. Unlike a letter of the alphabet, a logographic symbol has no phonetic value, though the word it represents has a pronounciation. Our symbol *3*, for instance, has no phonetic value, in itself, but does stand for a word pronounced *three*.

Chinese is the most familiar example of a contemporary logographic writing system. For the most part, each Chinese character stands for a single word rather than a sound. Learning to write Chinese requires memorizing many thousands of characters, a skill well beyond any first-grader. And the number of characters makes Chinese a difficult language to reproduce with a printing press.

But Chinese does have one advantage: the written language can be understood by people all over China, even though they speak dialects that are not mutually intelligible. The sign for "house," for instance, is understood by all Chinese to mean a dwelling, no matter how the word for "house" is pronounced in the speaker's dialect.

In a *syllabic* writing system, each symbol stands for a single syllable. A syllabic transcription of our word *alphabet* would require three signs: one for *al*, one for *pha*, and one for *bet*. Since the number of different syllabic sounds in any language is often less than a hundred, a syllabic written language is much easier to learn than a logographic system with its thousands of characters.

Japanese is an example of a written language that is basically syllabic. In the fifth century, the Japanese adopted Chinese script and selected 47 Chinese characters to represent 47 syllabic sounds of the Japanese language.

In one corner of the world, the neighboring countries of China, Japan, and Korea, we find all three kinds of writing systems in current use: the Chinese logographic, the Japanese syllabic, and the Korean alphabetic—the Koreans adopted an alphabet from Sanskrit forms.

By far the most common form of writing system around the world is the *alphabetic*, in which each symbol represents a single sound element. The number of single sound elements in a language is lower than the number of syllabic sounds, and so an alphabetic system can be learned easily at a young age. Our own alphabet makes do with just 26 letters; other alphabets have fewer.

The development of our alphabet—the Roman—follows an evolution from logographic to syllabic to alphabetic writing systems. Writing systems developed independently in the Far East and the Americas, but writing as we know it took shape in the Near East, beginning with the cuneiform writing of the Sumerians and the hieroglyphics of the ancient Egyptians—which may have themselves evolved from Sumerian writing.

The cuneiform writing of the Sumerians and Babylonians was in use by 3,000 B.C. Originally, Mesopotamian tongues were represented by pictures carved in stone. But the picture forms evolved into a syllabic shorthand of some 150 symbols, consisting of lines ending in the wedge-shaped marks that gave cuneiform its name. (The word comes from *cuneus*, Latin for "wedge.") The change may have been due in part to a move from the stone tablet to the clay tablet as a writing surface. Carving intricate pictures with a stylus is difficult with clay; pressing in wedge-shaped marks is far easier.

The hieroglyphic writing system of ancient Egypt originally consisted of word signs alone. Gradually, some of these symbols came to represent word sounds instead. A symbol standing for the word *ray*, for instance, could come to stand for the sound "ray," and thus could be joined with the sign for the word *sing* to produce *racing*.

With only word sounds to represent rather than the individual words, the Egyptian written language was reduced to a system of about 80 characters. Since each symbol no longer had to look something like the object or action it represented, and was less likely to be confused with another sign, writing could be executed much more quickly and carelessly. These hieroglyphic symbols, as written hastily by ordinary Egyptians, became the hieratic and demotic scripts of Egypt, and perhaps the syllabic symbols of other Near Eastern languages, such as Aramaic, Phoenician, and Early Hebrew.

We know that the Greek alphabet was derived from one or more of the Semitic alphabets, for the Greek and Semitic alphabets employed similar names for the letters, and listed the letters of their alphabets in basically the same order. Also, the names of the Semitic letters had some meaning in the Semitic tongues—*aleph*, the first letter, meant "ox," while *beth*, the second letter, meant "house"; the Greek names for those two letters, *alpha* and *beta*, had no meaning in Greek. Our word *alphabet*

This is one of the pages of a book published in Magdeburg, Germany in 1689. Four alphabets are presented: UPPER LEFT, *Black letter;* BOTTOM LEFT, *Roman;* UPPER RIGHT, *Hebrew;* BOTTOM RIGHT, *Greek.*

is formed from the names of the first two letters of the Greek alphabet, though it was the Romans who coined the word, not the Greeks.

But the exact origins of the Greek alphabet are still open to question. According to one theory, simplified Egyptian hieroglyphics evolved into an alphabet used in the Sinai Peninsula around 1,500 B.C., which later evolved into the various Semitic alphabets that fathered the Greek. Another theory holds that these Semitic alphabets developed independently of the Egyptian writing system somewhere in the Near East. Two alphabets in this area during the first millenium B.C. were those of the Phoenician language and those of the Aramaic, the region's most common language of the time. The Greek alphabet probably evolved from one or both of these scripts.

It's possible that the Greeks first came in contact with a form of the Aramaic alphabet that was used by Semitic peoples in Asia Minor before 1,000 B.C. A second borrowing of a Semitic alphabet may have come through Phoenician traders who roamed the Mediterranean in the earliest days of Greece. The Phoenician writing system was used in ancient Carthage, and formed the basis of the modern Berber alphabet. By the fourth century B.C., a number of Greek scripts had merged into a uniform Greek alphabet.

The earliest surviving Greek writing dates from the eighth century B.C., and was written right-to-left, as are Semitic tongues, or with alternating rows of right-to-left and left-to-right. All Greek writing wasn't left-to-right until the fifth century B.C. The Greeks directly borrowed some signs of the Semitic alphabet and adopted some of the unused symbols for use as vowels, since the Semitic scripts did not have vowel forms.

It was the Greeks, then, who first employed a truly alphabetic writing system like the one we use today. Originally, the Greek letters, like the Semitic, stood for syllable sounds: the letter *t*, for example, stood for either *te, ti,* or *ta*. To distinguish between the syllable sounds, the Greeks added vowel symbols after the *t*, and these vowel signs came to represent the vowel sound itself; the *t* then came to represent the consonant alone.

The Roman alphabet was derived directly from the Greek. It may have reached Italy with the Etruscans who settled there in the ninth century B.C., bringing with them a Greek alphabet from Asia Minor, or with Greeks who settled in southern Italy a century later. A number of languages and alphabets were in use in Italy for a time. But as the Romans gained predominance, their alphabet and language, called Latin, replaced all others. The oldest surviving example of Latin writing dates from the sixth century B.C., and was written right-to-left.

The Romans borrowed 16 of the 24 letters of the Greek alphabet, discarded other Greek letters that stood for sounds absent in Latin, and invented or adapted other letters for Latin sounds that did not exist in Greek. For instance, the Romans developed both the *c* and the *g* from the Greek letter *gamma*, and changed the Greek symbol for a long *a* to our *h*.

The Romans had no use for the sixth letter of the Greek alphabet, the *z*, since that sound did not exist in the language. It was reinstated in the first century B.C., along with the *y*, to transcribe Greek words, and placed at the end of the alphabet. The Romans introduced the letter *f*, taking the form from an old Greek symbol for a *w* sound. Initially, the *f* sound was represented in Latin by the letter combination *fh*. The Romans also used the letter *v* to stand for three sounds: the *u*, the *v*, and the *w*.

Three Greek symbols that the Romans did not incorporate into their alphabet were adopted for use as numerals. The Greek *theta* became the *C*, standing for 100; the Greek *phi* became the M, standing for mille, or 1,000; the Greek *chi* became the *L*, standing for 50.

Thus Latin was written with an alphabet of 23 letters. Around the 10th century, the *v* split into two letters, *u* and *v*. Soon after, the letter *w* entered the alphabet. The last of our 26 letters, the *j*, didn't appear until the 15th century; previously the *i* had stood for both the *i* and the *j* sound. The oldest letter in our alphabet is the *o*, which has remained unchanged since its use in the Semitic alphabets.

The Semitic scripts that evolved into our Roman alphabet also produced many of the world's other alphabets. Semitic traders brought an alphabet to India that was to become the Brahmi script, the parent of all Indian alphabets. The Aramaic alphabet became Persian script. The Aramaic alphabet as used by peoples in Arabia also evolved into the modern Arabic script, now the second most common in the world, after the Roman. Looking at a page of modern Arabic, it's hard to believe these symbols evolved from the same source that produced our own alphabet!

The Runic alphabet, used by Teutonic peoples in Northern Europe during the Roman Empire, was probably derived from either the Greek alphabet employed in the area close to the Black Sea, or the

Some characters from the Runic alphabet.

Latin alphabet of the Romans who colonized the area. The Slavic alphabets used today by many people in Eastern Europe were invented by the ninth-century missionary Cyril to transcribe the Slavic tongues; the forms were adopted from a Greek alphabet of the time. Two scripts developed, the Glagolithic and the Cyrillic, but since the 17th century only the Cyrillic has been used.

Not all Slavic languages use the Cyrillic alphabet, however. Missionaries who worked among the Poles and Czechs introduced the Roman alphabet instead of the Greek. In Yugoslavia today, we find two alphabets in use to transcribe the same language: the Serbians use a Cyrillic alphabet for Serbo-Croatian, while the Croatians use a Roman alphabet.

There are now about 65 alphabets in use around the world. The alphabet with the most letters is Cambodian, which has 72. Naturally, the logographic Chinese system has many more characters than there are letters in any alphabet: one Chinese dictionary listed almost 50,000 signs, including 92 for a single sound! And the most complex Chinese character has 52 individual strokes!

The alphabet with the least letters is Rotokas, a South Pacific tongue, which has 11 letters and only six consonants. Two Caucasian alphabets include just two vowels, while another Caucasian tongue, Ubyx, has 80 consonant sounds, the most of any language on earth. A Vietnamese language called Sedang can claim the most vowel sounds, 55.

Our alphabet has 26 letters, of course, but if you examine modern script you'll find that we really have two different alphabets: the lower case and the capitals. Look, for instance, at the upper and lower case forms *A* and *a*, or *G* and *g*, *D and d*, or *R* and *r*. You'd have little reason to guess that these symbols are different forms of the same letters!

The Roman alphabet consisted solely of capitals for many centuries. But the large, angular Latin letters that were suitable for carving in stone were less suitable for quick everyday writing. By the fourth century, scribes had adopted a set of letters, called *uncials*, that were developed from the capital forms, but were more rounded and easier to write quickly. These uncials later contributed to the formation of the *minuscule* alphabet, forerunner of our lower case letters. Minuscules were far easier and quicker to write with a pen than the older majuscules, or capital forms.

By the eighth century, a "perfect minuscule" alphabet had been developed in Western Europe. This script, called the Carolingian, later became the model for the modern lower case alphabet. At the time of Gutenberg, around 1450, the Gothic or black letter script was the most common in Europe. Black letter remained in use through much of Europe until the 17th century—and in Germany, into the 20th century.

Early in the renaissance period, scribes in Florence developed a script, based on the earlier Carolingian minuscule, that was more sloping and cursive than black letter. This writing gradually became the modern Italian script you undoubtedly use today, as well as the modern *italic* type.

Our alphabet hasn't necessarily seen its last change, either. Many people are eager to see a reform of English orthography, or spelling, that would bring the written language more into line with the spoken language. In some modern tongues—Spanish, Italian, and German, for instance—the spoken language is fairly accurately transcribed by the written language. But in English, due to the retention of archaic forms, there is often no correlation between the way a word is spelled and the way it is pronounced—which makes the spelling bee a distinctly English or American activity.

The English words *cite, site,* and *sight* are all pronounced the same, but spelled differently. And the letter combination *ough* has a different pronunciation in each of the words *through, bough, cough, rough, brought, hiccough,* and *dough*. It's not that far-fetched to think that, a few centuries from now, those words might be spelled *thru, bow, cawf, ruff, brawt, hikup,* and *doe*—or perhaps with letters that aren't even in our alphabet today.

George Bernard Shaw, for one, proposed an alphabet of 40 symbols, in which each sound in our language would be represented by one letter. As Shaw pointed out, according to contemporary orthography, the word *fish* might be spelled *ghoti*—taking the *gh* from *enough*, the *o* from *women*, and the *ti* from words such as *nation*.

Our spelling is not, after all, as simple as *abc*.

Apples

An old-fashioned apple peeler and corer.

Nothing may be as American as apple pie, but there's really nothing American about the apple at all. This familiar fruit is now grown in every state, and eaten in some form by almost all of us. Yet when Columbus set foot in the New World, there wasn't a single apple tree on this side of the Atlantic!

The apple is actually native to parts of Europe and western Asia, and may have originated in the area of present-day Iran. The fruit has been eaten by man since earliest times. How early? No, it wasn't necessarily the apple that Adam and Eve tasted in the Garden of Eden.

The Bible tells us only that Adam and Eve sinned by eating the fruit of the "tree of knowledge of good and evil." The word *fruit* came into our language as *apple*, which was formerly used to mean any fruit. Nowhere does the Bible claim that the forbidden fruit was actually what we now call the apple. In similar legends from the East, the forbidden fruit was the *banana!*

The word *apple* was also used in past centuries for the pupil of the eye, a translation of the Latin *pupillam*. The Latin phrase "apple of the eye" thus meant simply the pupil of the eye. But the phrase has been used to refer to something precious.

The Apple of Discord in Greek mythology also was not necessarily an apple. According to the myth, Eris, sister of Ares, was angered at a group of wedding guests, and tossed an apple among them, intended for the most beautiful woman in the group. There were three claimants: Hera, Athena, and Aphrodite. The Trojan prince Paris was chosen as the judge. To win his favor, Hera offered him power; Athena promised him wisdom; Aphrodite promised him the most beautiful woman in the world. Paris chose Aphrodite, and she assisted him in carrying off Helen, beginning the Trojan War.

But it was surely the real apple that was flourishing in Europe by the third century B.C., when Roman censor Cato described seven varieties. The Romans did a great deal to spread the apple through the Empire, although certain species were probably growing earlier in Europe. The Druids of Britain, for instance, venerated the apple prior to the arrival of the Romans. Perhaps they knew that, centuries later, one of the fruits was to fall on the head of Isaac Newton and help man gain his first insight into gravity.

Apples were cultivated largely in monasteries until the 16th century, and thereafter in small private orchards. Over 100 varieties of apple were known in medieval Europe. The fruit continued to spread, to North America, to South America, to Australia, even to the Orient: Japan is currently one of the top apple-producing nations! And the apple in all its varieties is now the most widely cultivated tree fruit of the temperate climes.

The first apples to reach America arrived from England in 1629, along with seeds and propagating wood. Ten years later, the first apples grown in the United States were plucked from trees planted on Beacon Hill, Boston. By 1741, New England was producing apples for export, and apple cultivation was sweeping westward across America.

One of the men we might thank for spreading the apple tree in America was Jonathan Chapman, better known as Johnny Appleseed. Many people think Johnny was merely a legendary figure, but he lived, indeed. Born in Massachusetts around 1775, Chapman set out alone into the unexplored wilderness that is now Ohio, Indiana, and western Pennsylvania, with a sack of apple seeds he'd collected from cider mills. Wherever he went, he planted apple seeds, and retraced his paths to prune the trees he'd planted. Before he died in 1846, he covered more than 100,000 square miles with apple trees!

The fruit that gave Jonathan Chapman his nickname is known in botanical circles as *Malus* pumila. The apple is a pome, or fleshy fruit, like the pear and quince. The *Malus* genus, which includes about 25 species, owes its name to the Latin word for "evil," due to its Biblical reputation.

The only apple we might dub truly "evil" is an apple with a worm in it. These pesky critters do not crawl inside the apple that provides their home—they're born there. Fruit flies stab holes in the skin of a ripening apple and release eggs into the fruit. The eggs hatch into white worms, which feed on the apple tissue as they grow. When the apple falls to the ground, the worms crawl out and burrow into the earth; the following summer, they emerge as fruit flies and begin searching for a likely apple for their eggs.

Another apple that might deserve the name *malus* is the crab apple—which owes its name not to a crustacean, but most likely to a Scottish word for a wild apple. Crab apples comprise a number of *Malus* species, whose high acid content and sour taste make them unsuitable for eating. Crab apple trees are often used as ornamental plants, and some of the fruits find their way into jelly or apple cider.

In the United States, we use the word *cider* for both the fermented and the unfermented juice of the apple. But in France, *cidre* always packs a punch of at least 3.2 percent alcohol. More than three-quarters of all French apples are used for cider—France produces over 40 million gallons a year! Most cider comes from Normandy and Brittany, from apples that would make poor eating fruits.

Some 900 million bushels of apples are currently harvested around the world each year, and more than a quarter of them find their way into cider. Worldwide apple production has almost doubled in the last 40 years. The largest apple growers are France and the United States, both of whom harvest more than 100 million bushels a year. Apples are grown in quantity in all of Western Europe, and in Japan, Australia, Argentina, and Canada.

In America, apples are grown from coast to coast, but the Pacific Northwest accounts for about 35 percent of the annual apple harvest, and the Northeast about 25 percent. Washington is the number-one apple growing state. New York, Virginia, Michigan, Pennsylvania, Oregon, and California are also large producers. Perhaps some of those Pennsylvania apples are relatives of the trees Johnny Appleseed planted!

Over 7,000 varieties of apple have been recorded in the United States, only a handful of which have become commercially important. Apple trees do not grow true to type by seed, and therefore are propagated by budding and grafting. Most varieties arose from chance seedlings that produced trees with good qualities, including resistance and high yield. A good tree can produce over 30 bushels of fruit each harvest. That means that when an Oregonian set the current world's record for apple picking—270 bushels in eight hours—he must have stripped the fruit from at least nine trees!

The *Delicious*, grown largely in the Northwest, is the most common variety of apple in the United States, accounting for about 20 percent of the annual production. The *McIntosh,* widely grown in the Northeast and in western Canada, accounts for about 10 percent. Other popular varieties are the *Winesap,* grown largely in the Northwest; the *Jonathan,* popular in the Midwest; the *Rome Beauty,* another Midwestern favorite; the *Baldwin,* grown in the Northeast and especially suited for apple juice; the *Northern Spy, York Imperial, Stayman Winesap,* and *Grimes Golden.*

More than half of the apples grown in the United States are eaten fresh, while about one-fifth are used for vinegar, juice, jelly, and apple butter, and one-fifth for canned pie stock and applesauce. In Europe, a far higher percentage of the apple production is used for cider. The average American consumes from 20 to 25 pounds of apples a year, in one form or another.

How much of the American apple harvest is currently used for good old-fashioned American apple pie is unknown. Also unknown is the origin of the phrase "apple pie order," for there's nothing particularly orderly about the apples in an apple pie. Some etymologists have suggested the phrase may have originated in the French *cap-à-pie*—"head to foot"—or *nappes-pliées*—"folded linen."

Other popular apple phrases include "apple polisher," a person who curries favor with gifts—like a student who brings his teacher an apple. "To upset the apple cart" requires no explanation. "Applesauce" connotes nonsense.

Then there's "an apple a day keeps the doctor away"—it might also keep the dentist at bay—and of course, the "Big Apple," one of the more kindly epithets for America's largest city, New York.

But the most profound comment on *Malus pumila* can be credited to William Shakespeare. "There's small choice," the bard wrote, "in rotten apples."

Asparagus

Today, asparagus may well be considered the "prince of vegetables," for the delicious green shoots—even the canned variety—are higher in price per pound than almost any other common vegetable. The high price and peculiar appearance of asparagus might suggest an exotic origin for the vegetable, but the fact is, asparagus is grown and eaten today, as always, almost exclusively in Europe and the United States.

Botanically, asparagus is a genus of the lily family, comprising some 120 species growing widely in the temperate zones of Europe and America. *Asparagus officinalis,* the popular edible variety, is a native of the temperate zones of the Old World, and grows naturally in southern England and the Russian steppes. Though the plant produces a flower and a small whitish berry, we eat only the stem, or shoot, of the plant.

Asparagus has been cultivated around the Mediterranean for many centuries, and there is evidence of the vegetable in Egypt as long ago as 3000 B.C. The Greeks and Romans were both fond of asparagus, and by the second century B.C. the green shoots were already considered a luxury food. The Romans cultivated asparagus in trenches, vying for the biggest shoots, and served it often in pureed form at banquets. We know that Cleopatra entertained Marc Antony with asparagus at such a feast. The Roman expression "You can do it in less time than it takes to cook asparagus" was the Latin equivalent of "two shakes of a lamb's tail."

Asparagus cultivation lapsed for centuries, then reappeared in the 16th and 17th centuries in France and England. French monarch Louis XIV took great pride in serving his guests forced-grown asparagus in January.

"Asparagus" is a second-century Latin word based on the Greek word for "sprout" or "shoot." In 18th-century England the vegetable was known as "sparagus," "sparage," or "sparagrass," and later—somewhat tongue in cheek, perhaps—as "sparrow-grass."

Thomas Jefferson was one of the first farmers to cultivate asparagus in the United States, growing the vegetable in his greenhouse with seeds imported from Europe. Cultivation on a large scale began here in the 1850s. Today asparagus is grown in 15 states from Maine to Virginia; from California, well over 120,000 tons reach the market each year. In some places the plant has escaped cultivation and can be found growing naturally in salt marshes and along roadsides.

There are four basic varieties of asparagus in widespread cultivation today. The French *Argen-*

Asparagus steamer. In this upright copper pot with brass handles, asparagus may be cooked to perfection. This 10-inch high contraption is lined with tin.

teuil has a thick stem and a purple head. The English *Green* is, not surprisingly, green, smaller, thinner, and more flavorful than the Argenteuil. The Genoa variety—called *asperge violette* in France is, as you might have guessed, purple. (Mildly flavored white asparagus is also grown in Europe, chiefly for canning.) The most popular edible variety is the *Lauris*, a French hybrid developed from the English Green and now grown extensively in southern France. And other species—mainly African climbing varieties—are used as decorative plants.

The asparagus spears we eat are actually shoots growing out of the soil from submerged roots, and if not picked before maturity, would eventually blossom into flowers and fruits. Each plant formerly produced less than a dozen shoots, but with modern cultivation techniques one plant can now furnish as many as 70. They're in season, by the way, from January through September—don't expect anything but canned spears at most other times.

Asparagus presents a problem in cooking, since the tender tips will cook much sooner than the fibrous stem bottoms. Chefs recommend that you cook the spears upright in a pan, with water reaching slightly more than halfway up the spears, so that the submerged bottoms are boiled, and the tips merely steamed. They also suggest that undercooked asparagus is preferable to overcooked spears, and warn against using strongly flavored sauces or wine with asparagus, since the vegetable contains high amounts of sulfur that can ruin a wine.

Well, now that you know where "sparrow-grass" comes from, the available varieties, and the best way to prepare it, the only question remaining is: how can you afford it?

Asparagus is higher in price per pound than almost any other common vegetable.

Automobiles

Around the turn of the century, New York's equine helpmates were depositing some two-and-a-half million pounds of manure on the streets each day!

Crushed-velour upholstery. Air conditioning. Power brakes and steering. Leather-padded dashboard. Quiet, cushioned ride. AM/FM radio, CB unit, and tape deck.

To the owner of an automobile 50 years ago, these features would probably seem fit only for the most expensive of limousines; today, we're apt to find them in many ordinary family cars. If we insist on comfort as much as speed and reliability in the automobiles we drive, it's not without good reason: in the age of the automobile, an American can spend up to 10 or 15 percent of his waking hours in the well-appointed confines of his home-away-from-home, the car.

Without doubt, the automobile ranks among the two or three most important inventions of our age. The car has determined the shape of our cities and the routine of our lives, made almost every inch of our nation easily accessible to everybody, ribboned our country with highways, cluttered the landscape with interchanges, gas stations, parking lots, drive-ins, and auto junkyards, and covered over 50,000 square miles of green with asphalt and concrete!

Considering that there is now one automobile in this country for every two persons (compared to, say, China, with over 14,500 persons per car), it's certainly easy to agree with a writer who described the American as a "creature on four wheels."

The technological revolution that has produced our mobile, car-oriented society has taken place almost entirely in the last 70 or 80 years. But the idea of a self-propelled vehicle had been on man's mind for centuries before the first automobile cranked into gear. As long ago as the 13th century, Roger Bacon predicted the use of vehicles propelled by combustion.

In 1472, a Frenchman named Robert Valturio described a vehicle combining wind power and a cogwheel system for propulsion.

If, in 1600, you happened to be walking along a Dutch canal, you might have been surprised to see a two-masted ship bearing down on you. Not in the canal—on the road! There was one such ship that was said to have reached a speed of 20 miles per hour while carrying 28 fear-striken passengers. In his notebooks, Leonardo da Vinci had envisioned some sort of self-propelled vehicle; and some Dutchman, quite naturally, had modeled such a vehicle after a sailing vessel.

About 1700, a Swiss inventor mounted a windmill on a wagon. It was hoped that as the windmill wound up a huge spring, the vehicle would lope along under its own power.

In the early 18th century, another Frenchman designed a

machine run by a series of steel springs, similar to a clock movement, but the French Academy had the foresight to declare that a horseless vehicle "would never be able to travel the roads of any city."

No single man can be termed the inventor of the automobile. Rather, advances on motor cars were made by many men working in various countries around the same time. But credit for the first mechanically propelled vehicle is generally given to the French engineer Nicholas Cugnot, who, in 1769, built a three-wheeled steam-propelled tractor to transport military cannons. Cugnot's machine could travel at speeds of up to two-and-a-half miles per hour, but had to stop every hundred feet or so to make steam.

Through much of the 18th century, steam-driven passenger vehicles—both with and without

On of the earliest steam automobiles, this one was built in 1884. It developed into the gorgeous Stanley Steamer of 1902.

tracks—were in regular operation in England. The early steam engine, however, was found to be impractical on ordinary roads, for it required great engineering skills on the part of the driver. Numerous fatal accidents stiffened resistance to the new machines, and beginning in 1830, Parliament passed a number of laws greatly restricting their use. One such regulation, called the Red Flag Law, stipulated that horseless cars must be preceded by a person on foot with a red flag in hand, or a red lantern at night, to warn of the car's approach. Another law limited the speed of horseless vehicles to a blinding four miles per hour. The limit was not raised until 1896, when English motor club members celebrated with an "emancipation run" from London to Brighton, initiating what was to become an annual event.

These early restrictions naturally limited interest in automotive research in England. Other sources of power were investigated elsewhere. Over the latter years of the 19th century, various electric cars were introduced with some frequency, but these never quite caught on with the public because they had to be recharged regularly. Most work on the internal-combustion engine was performed on the continent, especially in France and Germany. The internal-combustion engine, like the auto itself, had no single inventor. But in 1885, Gottlieb Daimler of Germany became the first to patent a high-speed four-stroke engine.

Around the same time, Karl Benz, another German, was building an internal-combustion tricycle that could reach a speed of 10 miles per hour. The general public remained largely unimpressed. A German newspaper, reporting on Benz's work, asked the question: "Who is interested in such a contrivance so long as there are horses on sale?"

Daimler and Benz worked independently for years, but later joined to form what is now the Mercedes-Benz Company—the name Mercedes having been borrowed from the daughter of a Daimler associate.

The first practical gasoline-powered car with a modern-type

The Benz Second Motor Tricycle Carriage (left), produced in 1886, ran at a maximum speed of 10 mph.

The original "Benzine Buggy" was patented in 1895.

chassis and gears was the work of a Frenchman named Krebs, who designed the Panhard in 1894. In the early years of the industry, France led the world in automobile production. The still-flourishing Renault company was founded before 1900. But around the turn of the century, Americans began to take the lead in automotive innovation.

The first successful internal-combustion car in the United States was the work of the Duryea brothers, Charles and J. Frank, bike manufacturers from Springfield, Massachusetts. The Duryeas had read of Karl Benz's work in Germany, and they built their first car in 1893. Two years later, the brothers formed the Duryea Motor Wagon Company, the first automobile manufacturing firm in the nation. They later went on to win one of the most important races in automobile history.

Racing and sport motoring were then considered the primary uses of the automobile. Few people could see the future of the car as a common means of practical transportation.

The first automobile race ever held was won by a car that was powered by a steam engine. On June 22, 1894, Paris was bubbling with excitement as 20 horseless carriages lined up for the 80 mile race from Paris to Rouen and back again to the big town. Could these newfangled things run at all? And if they did, would they prove as fleet and as durable as a few changes of horses?

Less than five hours later, a De Dion Bouton lumbered down the boulevards of gay Paree. The steamer had covered the distance at the daredevil rate of 17 miles per hour.

The first auto race in America was held on Thanksgiving Day, 1895, over a snowy 55 mile course stretching from Chicago to Waukegan, Illinois. Sponsored by the *Chicago Times-Herald,* the event included about 80 entries. But only six vehicles managed to leave the starting line.

Only two finished—the victorious Duryea, and a rebuilt electric Benz that had to be pushed over a considerable part of the route. The victory of the gasoline-powered Duryea did much to

this picture shows some of the starters in the first automobile race ever run. The race from Paris to Rouen on July 22, 1894.

establish the internal-combustion vehicle as the car of the future.

At the time, American cities were certainly in desperate need of horseless carriages—and horseless streets. Around the turn of the century, New York City's equine helpmates were depositing some two-and-a-half million pounds of manure and 60,000 gallons of urine on the streets each day!

This restored Duryea automobile is now on display at the Smithsonian Institution in Washington, D.C. Smithsonian Institution. Photo No. 34183

In the early 1900s, if you were lucky enough to own a sports model deluxe automobile, the chances were you had a chauffeur to drive you around.

American engineers and inventors rose to meet the challenge with great advances in automotive technology in the later years of the 19th century. In 1899, over 2,500 cars were produced by 30 different American companies. By 1904, there were over 54,500 cars on the roads here. But even then, poor roads and high costs made the automobile chiefly a sporting vehicle. It remained for an American industrial genius to bring the car within reach of the average citizen.

Henry Ford is usually credited with introducing mass-production techniques to automobile manufacture, but Ford actually adapted innovations made earlier by Ransolm E. Olds. Olds was but 30 years old when he designed his first internal-combustion vehicle in 1897. Later, Olds was forced to seek financial help from a friend, who agreed to advance the needed capital if Olds would locate his plant in Detroit, then a city of less than 300,000 people.

By 1902, Olds was turning out 2,500 cars annually with assembly-line techniques, and the "Motor City" was born. Today, the Detroit-Flint corridor in Michigan produces about one-fourth of all American cars.

Henry Ford began his motor company in 1903 with capital of only $28,000, twelve workers, and a plant only 50 feet wide. Additional funds were supplied by the Dodge brothers, themselves auto manufacturers. The Dodges' initial $20,000 investment was eventually worth $25 million.

Soon afterward, Ford improved on Olds' mass-production

CAR OF THE FUTURE

Ford Motor Company has developed a car which will be called the Mercury Antser. This 1,200-pound electric-concept car will seat four passengers.

Among other features, the dashboard will contain a computer controlled map which can be programmed to give detours and alternate routes around accidents and other traffic problems.

As a safety measure, the highly sophisticated electronic instrument panel continuously displays the computer-calculated average distance required to stop the car under the current operating conditions.

The top picture shows the entire car.

By 1902, the year this advertisement appeared, Oldsmobile was producing 2,500 cars annually.

The most expensive standard car now on the market is the Mercedes 600 Pullman. One of these six-door beauties will set you back $90,000—less your trade-in, of course.

ideas and introduced the conveyor-belt assembly line. Ford's first successful mass-produced car was the Model N, brought out in 1906 for $500. (From the very beginning, Ford used letters of the alphabet to identify his models.) But the car that made Henry famous was the Model T.

Preparation for the Model T's production brought Ford so close to bankruptcy that he had to borrow $100 from a colleague's sister to pay for the car's launch. That $100, by the way, was eventually worth $260,000 to the generous donor. The first "Lizzie" rolled off the line in 1908, with a four-cylinder, 20-horsepower engine capable of speeds of 40 miles per hour. It carried a price tag of $850.

Mass-production innovations continued to lower the price of the Lizzie. In 1916, a new Model T sold for just $360.! Each vehicle finished its turn around the assembly line in just 90 minutes, compared to the earlier day-and-a-half assembly-line run.

Today, most plants can turn out 50 to 60 cars an hour. The Chevrolet plant in Lordstown, Ohio, the nation's most modern, can produce over 100 vehicles an hour.

Sales of the Model T rose to 734,811 in 1916, accounting for half of all American car production. Eventually, some 15 million

Lizzies were produced before the car was discontinued in 1927. The Ford Company offered its Lizzies in any color, "so long as it is black."

In 1908, there were over 500 car companies in the United States, but that year marked the beginning of General Motors' eventual domination of the automobile market. The corporation was largely the work of William Crapo Durant, the millionaire grandson of a Michigan governor. Durant gained control of his first car company, Buick, in 1904, and moved his plant to Flint, Michigan. In 1908, Durant took over the Olds Company. Durant now began to absorb a number of ailing car and accessory companies under the corporate umbrella of General Motors. The Cadillac Company—named for Antoine de la Mothe Cadillac, the founder of Detroit—joined GM in 1909. Durant even approached Ford with an offer to join General Motors, but Henry turned him down.

The roller coaster career of W.C. Durant took a turn for the worse shortly after General Motors was formed, and he eventually lost control of the corporation he had founded. Durant's new car firm, the Chevrolet Company, named after a race driver who had designed engines for Durant, was such a success that the new leaders of GM were forced to take Durant, and Chevrolet, into the firm. By 1918, Durant was again at the helm of the corporation. But the founder of what is presently the largest manufacturing corporation in the world, with sales of $35 billion in 1975, declared bankruptcy in 1936, claiming over a million dollars in debts and assets of just $250—the clothes on his back!

The first decades of this century saw bankruptcy and merger greatly reduce the number of American car firms. In 1920, Walter Chrysler, a former vice-president at General Motors, joined the Willys-Overland company, once the number-two car producer after Ford, and laid the groundwork for the Chrysler Corporation. Chrysler absorbed Maxwell-Chalmers and the Dodge brothers' company, and introduced the Plymouth in 1929. The Lincoln Company became part of the Ford Corporation in 1921, and the Mercury was introduced in 1939.

The Studebaker and Packard, both introduced before 1902, eventually merged, and the Nash Company—founded by Charles Nash, who had replaced Durant at General Motors—joined the Hudson Company in the 1950s to form the American Motors Corporation. As early as 1914, 75 percent of all American cars were manufactured by the 10 largest companies.

The Rolls-Royce Corporation was founded in 1904 by two Englishmen named—you guessed it, Rolls and Royce.

The familiar Volkswagen "beetle" was first produced in 1938. By the 1950s, Volkswagen was the largest car producer in Europe; and in 1972, the "beetle" surpassed the Model T in total sales for a single model, with over 15 million sold throughout the world.

Vehicles in vogue during the first decade of the 20th century.

TOP:
The Extension-front Brougham.

MIDDLE:
The Torpedo-type Touring Car.

BOTTOM:
The Electric Victoria-phaeton.

The United States has been the leader in automobile production for many years. Over a million cars were produced here in 1916, and over three million in 1924, when there were some 15 million cars registered in America. In 1952, about four million American passenger cars rolled off the line, 10 times the number produced by the second-ranking nation, Great Britain. At the time, there was a car on the road here for every 3.5 persons alive, compared to, for example, one car per 564 persons in Japan. The second-ranking nation in car use was, surprisingly, New Zealand, with six persons for each car.

American dominance of the automobile market has slipped somewhat in recent years, yet the United States still ranks first in total production, with 6.7 million passenger cars turned out in 1975. Japan ranked second that year with 4.5 million cars, followed by West Germany and France with just under three million each, Great Britain and Italy with about 1.4 million each, Canada with one million, and the Soviet Union with 670,000.

What is the most popular car in America? For years it's been the Chevrolet. In 1975, 1.6 million new Chevies left the assembly line, while the Ford ranked second with 1.3 million cars, followed in order by the

Famed British speed king, Sir Malcolm Campbell, was the first man to drive a car 300 miles an hour over a measured mile course.

BREAKING 300

It wasn't enough for Sir Malcolm Campbell to be the first to drive a car faster than 250 miles an hour; his goal was 300!

And so on September 3, 1935, the flying Englishman and his mighty 2,500-horsepower Blue Bird, *stood at the starting mark of the Bonneville Salt Flats at Great Salt Lake, Utah.*

Adjusting his goggles, Sir Malcolm hopped aboard. He had six miles in which to pick up speed before hitting the timing tape. Screaming along at 280 with two miles to go, he closed his radiator front to streamline the car—and got into trouble.

Blotches of oil blacked out his windshield as the Blue Bird *snapped the timing tape. In his rocketing prison, Campbell continued to torture the accelerator, and covered the required mile in 12 seconds. But as he slowed down to 280 miles, the left front tire blew and the* Blue Bird *went crazy. Campbell spun the wheel furiously in order to right the skidding car, and five miles later he stopped—with flames eating up the bad tire!*

But Campbell had done only half a day's work. To establish a record he had to make the return trip.

Squirting out the fire, his mechanics threw on new wheels, and before he waved goodbye again the timers informed him he had run the course at a bit over 304 miles an hour. He could already see the newspaper headlines!

Only this time he had to let the car breathe. The radiator was left open, to push against a brick wall of wind; the speedometer read 290. Feeling his blood becoming a part of the car's circulation, he begged more speed out of it . . . and was timed at just under 296 for the return trip.

His average was 299.9—a tenth of a mile short!

He was already starting to think about next time as he walked unhappily away from the car. Suddenly an official shouted, "Wait, there's been a mistake!"

Sir Malcolm actually hit 298.013 on the second trip. His average speed was a neat 301.1291 miles per hour!

Oldsmobile, Buick, Pontiac, Plymouth, Mercury, Dodge, and Cadillac. Among American auto manufacturers, General Motors was far and away the leader, with 3.6 million cars produced; Ford was second with 1.8 million, Chrysler third with 900,000 and American Motors fourth with 320,000.

There are now about 107 million passenger cars registered throughout this country, and 125 million licensed drivers. Car registration began here in 1901, in New York State. The first license plates appeared in France in 1893.

England's first license plate, A1, was purchased in 1903 by Lord Russell, after an overnight wait outside the license bureau office—and that plate was reportedly sold to a collector in 1973 for $35,000! As late as 1909, driving licenses were required in only 12 American

A taxi was creeping slowly through rush-hour traffic, and the passenger was already late.

"Please," he asked the driver, "can't you go any faster?"

"Sure I can," the hack replied. "But I'm not allowed to leave the cab."

Willie Menkenn of Hillsboro, Oregon, surely built himself a car. Aptly named "Hash," it was made up of a motorcycle engine, an airplane propeller, and auto steering wheel, and only three wheels.

A proliferation of new items for the car trade are developed each year. Some of the latest are shown on these pages.

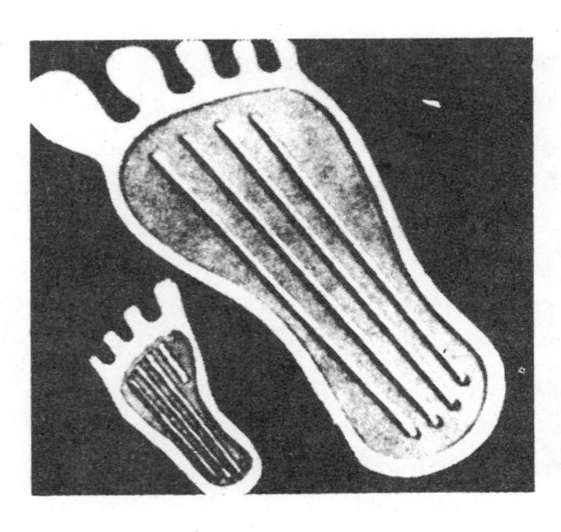

PHONY FOOT PEDALS: *Do you like to drive barefoot? These cast-aluminum phony pedals clamp right over the existing pedals.*

PORTABLE ELECTRIC VACUUM: *Has no cord, will travel! This portable cleaner goes anywhere, and weighs a mere 1½ pounds.*

The Lamborghini Countach or the Ferrari BB Berlinetta Boxer, the fastest regularly produced cars now available, can both reach speeds of 186 miles per hour.

states, when there were few traffic laws of any kind.

The first modern traffic light, in fact, did not appear until 1914, on Euclid Avenue, Cleveland, Ohio. And in England driving tests were not required for would-be drivers until 1935!

Which should bring us to the subject of automobile accidents. The first traffic accident in the United States was recorded in 1896, when a Duryea Motor Wagon collided with a bicycle in New York City, sending the cyclist to the hospital and the driver to jail. Three years later, a 68-year-old real estate broker named Henry Bliss became the first American to die as a result of an auto accident, when he was run over while stepping from a New York streetcar. By the early 1920s, traffic fatalities were already topping the 20,000 mark annually—not to mention an estimated 700,000 auto injuries each year.

In the mid-1950s, close to three million Americans were killed or injured each year in automobile accidents—about 570 deaths for every 10 billion miles driven, compared to 14 deaths for every 10 billion airplane miles, 13 deaths for the bus, and just five for the train.

But Americans are far from the world's most reckless drivers. That honor belongs to the Austrians, who in a recent year suffered 386 auto deaths per one million population. That year, drivers in West Germany, Canada, and Australia also suffered more fatal accidents than their American counterparts, with the United States in fourth place with 272 deaths per million persons. The lowest rate among major car-using nations belonged to Mexico, with just 83 deaths per million persons.

Surprisingly enough, the death rate per vehicle mile has actually declined here since 1941, due in large part to the proliferation of divided highways. The Interstate Highway System, the largest single construction job ever undertaken by man, will, when complete, include about

FOG-PROOFING STICK: *For foggy or rainy nights, one application of this fog-proofing stick will clear your windshield and windows. Smear a line every couple of inches across the glass; then buff with soft dry cloth.*

AUTO ALTIMETER: *Up, up, and away! This auto altimeter measures from zero to 15,000 feet, telling you how high you are as you motor along.*

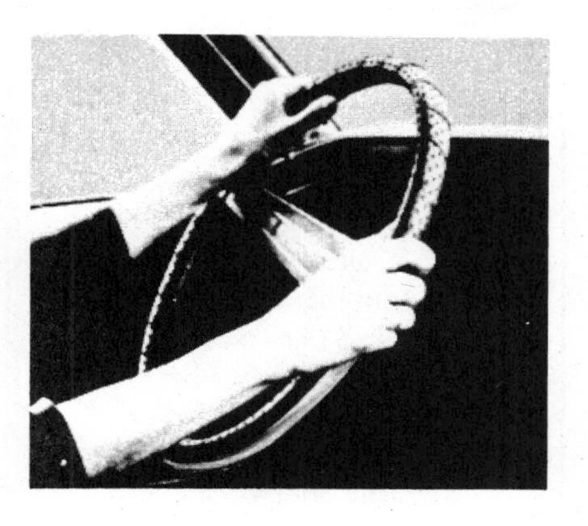

WHEEL COVER: *With this textured-vinyl steering-wheel cover, your hands will cease to slip and slide while you drive. The grip is warm in winter and cool in summer.*

42,500 miles of divided highway, accommodating an estimated 25 percent of all United States traffic. The system was 80 percent complete in the mid-70s.

Automobile design and usage have changed a great deal since the days of Daimler, Benz, and Duryea, but almost all cars, past and present, compact and luxury, have one thing in common: the internal-combustion engine. (A present exception is the Mazda, which operates with a rotary, or Wankel engine.) The internal-combustion engine converts heat generated by the burning of gasoline to the motive power required to turn the car wheels.

Basically, the internal-combusion engine works like this: fuel and air first mix in each cylinder of the engine. The piston in the cylinder, rebounding from its previous stroke, compresses the fuel and air mixture. At this point, a hot electric spark ignites the compressed mixture. The rapid combustion of the gasoline and air mixture speeds up the motion of their molecules, increasing the pressure they exert on the top of the piston. This pressure forces the piston down the cylinder. Each downward stroke of the piston turns the crankshaft, which in turn spins the drive shaft. The drive shaft turns the gears in the differential, the gears turn the rear axle, and the axle rotates the rear wheels. Unless the car is equipped with four-wheel drive, the front wheels are not connected to the engine-driven mechanism.

A car runs more smoothly at night or in damp weather simply because the air is cooler, not because it contains more oxygen: the amount of oxygen in the air is constant. Cool air is more dense than warm air; and therefore, an engine takes in a greater weight of air when it is damp and chilly. This accounts for the increased power and the freedom from engine knock which so many motorists notice when they drive at night or in the rain.

Most cars today are equipped with either a four-, six-, or eight-cylinder engine—but a 1930 Cadillac was powered by a 16-cylinder engine! And speaking of Cadillacs, the largest automobile ever constructed was a special limousine built for King Khalid of Saudi Arabia in 1975, measuring 25 feet and two inches in length, and weighing 7,800 pounds.

The largest car ever produced for regular road use was the 1927 "Golden Bugatti," which measured 22 feet from bumper to bumper. Only six of these cars were made, and some of these survive in excellent condition.

Automobiles over 20 feet in length are built for more comfort than speed, of course, but compared to the earliest automobiles, even the most cumbersome of today's limos are virtual speed demons. The first auto race in Europe, held in France in 1895, was won by a car averaging but 15 miles per hour. The Duryea brothers' car won the Chicago-to-Waukegan race that year, with an average speed of only seven-and-a-half miles per hour. By 1898, the record automobile speed stood at a mere 39.3 miles

Here is the first fiberglass car that General Motors ever put out. This Chevrolet Corvette, made in 1953, was the result of experiments in building bodies of plastic reinforced with glass fiber. In the picture, a worker shows the light weight of the body shell by lifting it over his head with one hand.

The zinc-nickel oxide battery pack is seen here installed in the rear of a General Motors experimental electric car called the Electrovette. The company hopes to offer electric-powered vehicles in the mid-1980s.

A woman was trying to maneuver her car out of a parking space. She first crashed into the car ahead, then banged into the car behind, and finally struck a passing delivery truck as she pulled into the street.

A policeman who had watched her bumbling efforts approached her. "All right, lady," he demanded, "let's see your license."

"Don't be silly, officer," she replied. "Who'd give me a license?"

per hour. A little over 65 years later, Craig Breedlove became the first person to drive a car over a mile course at an average speed in excess of 600 miles per hour. The record for the highest speed ever attained by a wheeled land vehicle was set on the Bonneville Salt Flats in Utah in 1970, when Gary Gabelich drove a rocket-engined car at an average speed of 631 miles per hour over a distance of one kilometer.

With the current 55 mile-an-hour limit on all American roads, you certainly won't need such horsepower. But if it's sheer velocity you're interested in, you might take a look at the Lamborghini Countach or the Ferrari BB Berlinetta Boxer, the fastest regularly produced cars now available, which can both reach speeds of 186 miles per hour.

If price is more important to you than speed, you might want to test-drive a Mercedes 600 Pullman, the most expensive standard car now on the market. One of these six-door beauties will set you back $90,000—less your trade-in, of course. And if used cars are your preference, you might be interested in a Rolls-Royce Phantom, once owned by the Queen of the Netherlands, that sold in 1974 for a record $280,000!

Speaking of used cars, the most durable car on record was a 1936 Ford two-door model that in 1956 logged its one-millionth mile—with the odometer showing zero for the 11th time. Today, a car is considered well into old age by the time it reaches 75,000 miles.

But surely, the most incredible automobile record ever achieved belongs to Charles Creighton and James Hargis who, in 1930, drove a Ford Model A roadster from New York City to Los Angeles *without stopping the engine once.* The two men then promptly drove back to New York, completing the 7,180-mile round-trip in 42 days.

Oh, one more thing: on both coast-to-coast journeys, the car was driven exclusively *in reverse!*

The Packard Model F of 1903, built in Warren, Ohio, to sell for $2,500.00.

Backgammon

Backgammon is much older than craps, ranking as the oldest dice game still widely played.

Just 20 years ago, most Americans probably regarded backgammon—if they knew the game at all—as an exotic, unfamiliar game whose board often turned up, quite uselessly, on the back of checkerboards. Times have changed, and the games we play have changed as well. While checkers has lost a good deal of its popularity, "exotic" backgammon is now the fastest-growing game in America, with millions of dedicated players, hundreds of backgammon clubs, and an international circuit of major tournaments. Today, backgammon experts command lesson fees of up to $150 an hour!

But the current backgammon craze is hardly a phenomenon unique to our age. The popularity of backgammon has not risen steadily to its present peak, but rather has surged and ebbed through the ages. After a period of obscurity, backgammon is now riding the crest of a new wave of interest. Who knows? If backgammon continues to grow at the present rate, it might even become as popular as it was 2,000 years ago!

Historians have traced the origins of backgammon to many sources. The fact is, the game was never "invented." Instead, backgammon evolved from a number of old games, including the earliest known board games enjoyed by man.

In the 1920s, during British archaeologist Sir Leonard Woolley's excavation of the ancient Sumerian city of Ur, he found five game boards in the royal cemetery that bore a resemblance to early backgammon boards. The 5,000-year-old Sumerian game was played on a board of 20 squares, with six dice and seven pieces for each player.

A game board similar to those unearthed at Ur was found among the treasures in the tomb of the Egyptian king Tutankhamen, dating from 1500 B.C. Egyptian wall paintings show that the board game, called *senet,* was popular among the common people as well as among royalty. The Egyptians even had a sort of mechanical dice cup, a machine that shook and threw the dice to protect against dice cheats, who seem to be as ancient as dice themselves.

Oddly enough, the Spanish explorer Ferdinand Pizarro found the Aztecs in Mexico playing a game, *patolli,* that bore a remarkable similarity to the games enjoyed by the ancient Egyptians. Nobles in the court of Montezuma played *patolli* for high stakes, using semiprecious stones as game pieces. Some anthropologists view the similarity between the Aztec and Egyptian games as proof that the people of the Americas migrated to the Western Hemisphere from Africa or Asia.

The still popular Persian game of *parcheesi* may have been a remote ancestor of backgammon. In parcheesi, as in backgammon, the object of the game is to remove all of one's pieces from the board. Single pieces left on the parcheesi board may be "hit" by an opponent and sent back to the beginning of the board. Two or more of a player's pieces on a single square, or point, capture the point in parcheesi as well as in backgammon. Parcheesi also includes bonus provisions for a player rolling doubles.

Games far closer to modern backgammon were widely enjoyed by the ancient Greeks and Romans. Plato commented on the popularity of these games, and Homer mentions them in the *Odyssey*. The Greeks, by the way, had names for various dice throws reminiscent of our *snake eyes*. A six was known as *aphrodite;* a one was called a *dog*.

In ancient Rome, we find the first game board featuring 12 points on each side, like the backgammon board. The Romans' *ludus duodecim scriptorum,* or "12-line game," is thought to have been adapted from earlier board games similar to the one found in Tutankhamen's tomb. But the Roman game board included *three* rows of 12 points. A later Roman game, called *tabulae,* reduced the number of points to 24, with 12 on each side, as in the modern game. The Romans played both games with three dice rather than two.

Tabulae was very popular among the Roman aristocracy. In the ruins of Pompeii, we find a *tabulae*-board table top in the courtyard of almost every villa. Nero was known to play the "sport of emperors" for as much as $15,000 a point, and the Emperor Commodus sometimes dipped into the royal treasury to pay off his *tabulae* gambling debts. But Roman paintings tell us that the game was popular among plebians as well. One painting depicts a fight

A Dutch backgammon set of the 17th century.

in an inn arising from a game of *tabulae*. Another suggests that the Romans used *tabulae* to play a form of classical "strip poker."

The beginning of the Christian era did little to stamp out *tabulae* in Europe. A marble slab game board dating from the early days of Christian Rome bears a cross and the inscription: "Christ grants aid and victory to dicers if they write His Name when they roll, Amen." Modern backgammon gamblers have been known to utter the name of the diety in a slightly different vein.

Roman legionnaires spread *tabulae* throughout the Empire. In England, the game became known as *tables,* a term which persisted well into the 17th century. But *tabulae* and similar games gradually waned in popularity in Europe until revived by Crusaders returning from the Mideast.

At the time of the Crusades, the Saracens enjoyed a game called *nard* that they'd learned from the Persians. The Persians, in turn, may have developed *nard* from earlier Mesopotamian or Indian games, or from parcheesi, or from the board games of Greece and Rome. *Nard* employed black and white pieces on a checkered game board with 12 divisions, and unlike *tabulae,* was played with two dice. By the time of the Third Crusade in the 12th century, backgammon-like games were so popular among the Crusaders that Kings Richard I of England and Philip II of France issued a joint edict prohibiting all gambling games among their troops.

A number of games similar to backgammon have been enjoyed for centuries in the Orient. The Chinese play *shwan-liu,* the Japanese enjoy *sunoroku,* the Koreans *ssang-ryouk,* and the Thais, *len sake.* But most historians believe that these Oriental equivalents of backgammon were imported from the West, and therefore played no part in the development of backgammon itself.

Tables, which included elements from both *tabulae* and *nard,* was widely played by the aristocracy through the Middle Ages, and the game eventually found its way to the lower classes as well. Medieval innkeepers customarily kept boards and dice on hand for their patrons. The Church opposed the game, as it did all gambling pastimes. In 1254, Louis IX outlawed it in France. Suppression of the game continued right up into the 16th century, forcing diehard players to disguise their boards as books, the hinged game board masquerading as the book cover and the dice and pieces hidden inside.

As many as 25 different versions of tables existed in medieval Europe. The modern backgammon board has existed since at least the 14th century, when the game was already quite popular in England. Chaucer mentions tables in the *Canterbury Tales,* with the line "They daucen, and they playen at ches and tables." James I of Scotland was said to have spent the night before his murder in 1437 "playing at Chess and Tables." A psalter dating from 1499, considered one of the earliest illustrated books ever printed, contains a picture of a man and a woman playing tables. Shakespeare acknowledged the game in *Love's Labour Lost,* when the character Biron says:

This is the ape of the form, Monsieur the Nice,
That, when he plays at tables, chides the dice
In honourable terms.

A story is told that the Duke of Albany, the brother of James III of Scotland, used tables to win far more than cold cash. While imprisoned in Edinburgh castle in the 1480s, the Duke invited the captain of the guard into his cell one night to play tables. In the morning, the captain was found dead in the cell, and the Duke had made good his escape.

The 17th century saw the first wide use of the word *backgammon* in place of *tables,* along with a number of other innovations. For the first time, doubles entitled the roller to play the roll twice, as in the modern game. The concept of the *backgammon* victory was also introduced, although as used at the time a *backgammon* was actually the modern *gammon*—a victory in which the winner succeeds in bearing off all his men from the board before his opponent can remove any of his men.

The word *backgammon* itself has been traced to a number of sources. Some etymologists point to the Welsh *bach cammaun,* "small battle." But most favor the Middle English *baec gamen,* or "back game," traced by some to the medieval custom of constructing a backgammon board on the back of a chessboard, as is often done today. Thus, tables became known as the "game on the back" of the chessboard, and later, "back game."

On the Continent, the game was known as *tavole reale* in Italy, *tablas reales* in Spain, and *trictrac* in France. The French term is thought to owe its origin to the sound made by tumbling dice on a wooden board. A number of *trictrac* boards were

The game of backgammon was a favorite during the 18th century.

used by the French court at Versailles. One elaborately decorated board belonging to Marie Antoinette was reputed to have cost over a quarter-million francs.

For some reason, backgammon became very popular among 18th-century clergymen. During the same era, physicians also seem to have favored the pastime. One doctor wrote that backgammon was "an anodyne to the gout, the rheumatism, the azure devils, or the yellow spleen." Even Thomas Jefferson was a backgammon fancier, playing the game in his off hours, while drafting the Declaration of Independence.

Edmond Hoyle has been credited with formulating the rules to many popular games, but actually Hoyle never heard of most of the games for which he is supposed to have codified the rules. In the case of backgammon, however, Hoyle rightly deserves recognition. In 1743, Hoyle wrote a treatise on the game laying down many of the rules we follow today.

Backgammon waned in popularity during the 19th century, although Mississippi riverboat gamblers frequently included a backgammon board in their bag of tricks. Then, in the 1920s, interest in the game was suddenly revived when an unknown American player devised the concept of "doubling"—a rule by which a player can double the stakes in an attempt to force his opponent to concede the game. Doubling did away with long games that had to be played to a finish even after the eventual winner was already fairly obvious.

The concept of redoubling was added shortly thereafter, by another unknown genius. After a few thousand years of evolution, backgammon had become the game we know today. But the modern rules weren't completely codified until 1931, when Wheaton Vaughan of the New York Racquet and Tennis Club prepared the first universally recognized rulebook for the modern game. Backgammon has undergone few changes since then.

The most recent backgammon rage had its beginnings in 1964, when Russian Prince Alexis Obolensky of Palm Beach, Florida, founded an international tournament in the Bahamas for jet-set backgammon buffs. The tournament has been held there every year since then. The maiden 1964 tourney included just 32 players; by 1968, the number had swelled to 128, with additional tournaments for beginners and "consolation flights" for first-round drop-outs. The number of backgammon players in the United States, meanwhile, soared from about 200,000 in 1969 to over two million today. In 1973, game board producers sold more backgammon sets than they had sold in the previous 20 years combined!

Prince Obolensky went on to found similar tournaments in Las Vegas and other places. Since 1966, an annual international backgammon tournament has been held in the London Clermont Club. The 1978 tourney included 100 players competing for $100,000 in prizes. And private gambling matches, played for up to $25 a point, have been known to cost unlucky participants as much as $100,000!

Despite the current backgammon boom, there are certainly millions of Americans without the slightest notion of how the game is played. Though a great deal of strategy and calculation go into an expert game of backgammon, the basic rules of the game are not complex.

The backgammon board contains 24 triangular segments, called *points,* with 12 points on each side. Two players each begin with 15 pieces, arranged on the board as shown in the accompanying diagram. Each player moves his pieces in the direction indicated, according to the throw of two dice. The object of the game is to bring all of one's pieces into the appropriate home board, and then to *bear off* or remove the pieces with suitable throws of the dice.

A player with two or more of his pieces on a point is said to have *made* that point. His opponent's pieces may not come to rest on that point. A single piece remaining on a point is a *blot.* If an opponent's piece comes to rest on a point occupied by a blot, that blot is *hit* and placed on the *bar,* the line between the two halves of the board. A hit blot must then re-enter the game in the opponent's home board, and continue around the board toward the player's own home board.

In each turn, a player rolls two dice. He may move one piece a number of points corresponding to the number rolled on one die, then move a second piece a number of points corresponding to the second die. Or he may use both moves to advance just one piece. A throw of doubles entitles a player to four moves, each the number of points corresponding to the number shown on one die. For example, a pair of three's allows the roller to make four moves of three points each.

The first player to bear off all his pieces wins the game. A player who bears off all his pieces before his opponent can bear off any of his pieces wins a *gammon.* If he succeeds in bearing off all his men

Seagram's 1974 American Championship Tournament of Backgammon at the Plaza Hotel in New York City. Prince Alexis Obolensky, the doyen and arch promoter of backgammon, is seated in the center with arms folded.

while his opponent still has one or more pieces in the winner's home board, the player wins a *backgammon.* Gammon winners collect double the stakes; backgammon winners collect triple.

No one can be expected to play a game of backgammon using only the rules sketched above. But if you've never played before, you might have some idea now what all the fuss is about. Backgammon is far more than a simple racing game in which both players move their pieces around the board as quickly as possible. Backgammon players attempt to make points to hinder their opponent's play, and to move their pieces forward without leaving a blot that can be hit by the opponent. Backgammon strategy is intricate enough so that some newspapers, including the *New York Times,* now carry a backgammon column, as has been traditional for bridge or chess.

Backgammon can be played easily enough with just a pair of dice, a makeshift board drawn on a piece of cardboard, and a few checkers. But that hasn't stopped some buffs from shelling out hundreds, or even thousands, of dollars for more elaborate equipment. Stores devoted exclusively to backgammon equipment display such luxurious equipment as a pearl-and-onyx inlaid board rimmed with gold, with pieces made of jade or ivory. Backgammon fanciers have coughed up over $600 for sets that include elephant-hide boards and sterling silver doubling cubes. And one backgammon board, made from batik leather, sells for well over $2,000!

One of the incarnations of Chiquita Banana.

Bananas

"Yes, we have bananas" may not be as humorous nor as rhythmic as "Yes, we have no bananas," the well-known words to the once-popular song, but it's certainly closer to the truth. Americans do have bananas—billions of them! Our ever-growing taste for the fruit has made the United States the world's largest consumer of this yellow-skinned wonder. If Americans continue to consume bananas at the present rate, this country may soon earn the sobriquet of "banana republic."

The banana is now America's favorite fresh fruit. More apples and oranges are consumed here than bananas, but both these fruits are frequently enjoyed in juices and other processed products. Bananas are almost always eaten fresh. Americans now devour over 12 billion bananas each year—close to 19 pounds per person. Yet, virtually no bananas are grown within this country—and the fruit was almost unknown here until just a century or so ago!

A recent survey disclosed that about half of all American shoppers buy bananas at least once a week.

A recent survey disclosed that about half of all American shoppers buy bananas at least once a week. And with good reason, for the banana is one of the most compact, inexpensive, and nutritious foods available. Bananas are high in potassium, iron, and various vitamins; and low in sodium. They are 99.8 percent fat free, and devoid of cholesterol. The fruit is so easily digestible that it's often the first solid food fed to babies. But most important, bananas are delicious. It's hard to disagree with British statesman Benjamin Disraeli who, writing from Cairo in 1831, called the banana "the most delicious thing in the world."

The banana has also been called the most ancient fruit on earth. Most botanists believe bananas first grew in southeast Asia, perhaps on the Malay Peninsula. Primitive people there considered the fruit so important that they took banana rootstocks with them wherever they migrated.

The fruit undoubtedly reached India and China at a very early date. The Chinese scholar Yang Fu, in a second-century work called *Record of Strange Things,* extolled the banana as having "a very sweet-tasting pulp, like honey or sugar. Four or five of these fruits are enough for a meal," he noted, "and after eating, the flavor lingers on among the teeth." The neighboring Koreans, however, considered the banana, rather than the apple, the forbidden fruit of the Garden of Eden.

Alexander the Great and his conquering Macedonians were probably the first Europeans to savor bananas in India during the fourth century B.C. We are told by the Roman historian Pliny that the Macedonians found wise men in India sitting in the shade of a banana tree, eating the fruit and discussing philosophy. Many centuries later, when the Swedish botanist Linnaeus classified the plant kingdom, he called the banana *Musa sapientum*, "fruit of the wise men."

The first banana recipe in history appears in the writings of the 10th-century Arab poet Masudi. He described a dish of bananas, almonds, honey, and nut oil that was all the rage in Damascus, Cairo, Constantinople, and other eastern cities. By the year 1000, the banana plant was a familiar sight throughout much of the Mideast.

During the 15th century, the Portuguese brought bananas from the Guinea Coast of Africa to the Canary Islands. It was the Portuguese who coined the word we use today to identify the fruit. The Indians of Alexander's time called the fruit *pala;* while in Africa, it was termed in various languages *banna, abana, gbana,* and *funana*. The Portuguese combined a number of these African words into the easily pronounceable *banana*.

Bananas first arrived in the New World in 1516, just 24 years after Columbus's first journey. A Spanish priest named Fra Tomas de Berlanga brought dry rootstocks from the Canary Islands to Santo Domingo, the first colonial city in the Americas. Bananas were found to grow well in the American tropics, and were soon placed under cultivation in South and Central America, Cuba, Jamaica, and "all other islands peopled by Christians."

One story has it that Puritan settlers in North America sampled bananas during the 1690s, and found them unpalatable—probably because they boiled them, skin and all. But the first recorded appearance of the banana in this country dates from 1804, when a ship brought 30 bunches of the slender fruits from Cuba. Bananas remained rare and expensive items here through most of the 19th century.

Many Americans caught their first glimpse of the banana at the 1876 Centennial Exposition in Philadelphia. Bananas were still so unfamiliar to most Americans that the fruit and the telephone became the two most popular exhibits at the Exposition. The fruits sold for 10¢ apiece, a high price at the time. Each banana was wrapped in tin foil, although the fruit was naturally protected by its thick skin.

The high price of the fruit was perhaps due to the fact that up to half of each banana cargo was lost to spoilage en route. Then, in 1899, the plantations of Minor Keith, the ships of Lorenzo Baker, and the sales network of Andrew Preston were combined to form the United Fruit Company, which soon became the largest importer of bananas to America. Using modern farming techniques and refrigerated ships, the firm set up a network that brought fresh bananas to market within a month of harvest. This process eliminated the large-scale spoilage that had plagued earlier importers.

Banana tree.

It was the United Fruit Company (now the United Brands Company) that devised the advertising campaign featuring the now familiar Chiquita banana. Beginning in the early 1940s, the lively banana with high-heeled shoes, ruffled dress, and fruit-bowl hat served as spokeswoman for the firm's principal product. Chiquita sang clever calypso jingles on radio, and later appeared in animated form on television. Chiquita is the official logo and trademark for bananas sold by United Brands.

The most prolific of all food plants, the banana "tree" is actually not a tree at all, but a giant herb—the largest plant on earth without a woody stem. The "trunk" of the banana plant is not a trunk at all, but is made up of thick leaves furled one upon another in overlapping layers, combining to form a shoot that can reach heights of up to 30 feet. And the palmlike leaves themselves often grow up to 10 feet long!

A banana plant will bear fruit only once, but each rootstock of the plant can, in turn, produce an unending series of plants, assuring a continuous crop. Cultivators allow one plant from each rootstock, or rhizome, to mature and bear fruit. Then, they cut down the plant and nurture another shoot from the rhizome.

Each plant bears about 10 bunches of fruit, called *hands,* and each hand contains from 10 to 20 bananas, or *fingers*. Thus, one banana plant will produce an average of 150 bananas, weighing about 85 pounds altogether.

A new banana plant sprouts quickly, producing leaves in

A banana plantation.

as little as three weeks. Some old-time banana plantation workers claim they can "hear" the plants growing in the dark. After about eight months, a single bud pushes through the center of a leaf cluster. Small flower clusters then appear, which eventually bend outward and upward as they turn into the hands. Thus the fruits actually grow upside-down. As soon as the fruits begin to form, plantation workers place plastic bags over each hand to protect the bananas from insects, birds, and scarring by wind-battered leaves.

Within a year, the bananas are ready for harvest. Unlike most other fruits, bananas are picked green and ripen later. If the fruits were allowed to ripen on the plant, they would split open and lose much of their sweet flavor.

At harvest time, the fruits are cut from the plants in their plastic bags, then sent by overhead cable or truck to nearby boxing stations. At the boxing station, the bananas are washed, cut into clusters, labeled, boxed, and sent by rail to port.

The boxed bananas are loaded quickly aboard refrigerated ships—banana boats are often in and out of port within 12 hours—and delivered to ports in the United States. Before being shipped to markets, the fruit is stored in ripening rooms for a few days until the green color changes to a golden yellow. The entire trip from plantation to consumer's shopping cart can take as little as 10 days!

Bananas undergo their final ripening in the home. For best results, the fruits should be stored at room temperature until fully ripe, then placed in the refrigerator. Many Americans are reluctant to store bananas in the refrigerator, lessoned by an earlier Chiquita banana song that warned:

Bananas like the climate of the
very, very tropical equator,
So you should never put bananas
in the refrigerator.

Actually, however, refrigeration will cause the skin to turn brown, but the fruit itself will remain unspoiled for a few days inside its natural shell. The browner the banana's skin, the sweeter the fruit. As Chiquita banana sang:

When they are flecked with
brown and of a golden hue
That's when bananas are the
best for you.

There are over 100 varieties of banana now in cultivation. The two most common varieties are the Gros Michel and the Cavendish. The Gros Michel, grown in large quantities in Jamaica, Panama, and Costa Rica, was for many years the overwhelming favorite in this country. But the tall Gros Michel is particularly susceptible to wind storms. Winds of just 20 to 30 miles per hour can devastate an entire plantation in minutes. The shorter, sturdier Cavendish has therefore become the most popular variety on most plantations.

The *plantain*, a short, green banana is usually cooked, since its fruit is starchy rather then sweet. Many Caribbean and Central American dishes use the plantain in much the same way that we use the potato.

Incidentally, banana oil does not come from the banana, for banana plants produce no commercial oil of any kind. Banana oil is actually a synthetic compound, so-named because its aroma was thought to resemble the banana's.

The soft, sweet fruit of the banana is usually eaten raw in this country, but bananas can be broiled, baked, sauteed, grilled, or even frozen. Bananas make a delicious ingredient in dips, drinks, salads, breads, pancakes, fritters, and a variety of desserts. Innumerable recipes derive their special flavor by using the banana as a major ingredient. Bananas are cheap as well as versatile, costing no more today than they cost 20 years ago.

For a quick, nutritious drink, try a banana shake: mix a cup of milk, a banana, and a teaspoon of vanilla in an electric blender, turn on the switch, and enjoy.

If you prefer a more potent banana beverage, there's always the frozen banana daiquiri. You can make a banana daiquiri in your blender, too: just fill the container with a jigger of rum, an envelope of daiquiri mix, ice cubes, and a ripe banana. Then turn on the machine, and let the blender do the rest.

For those who really love bananas, there's even a "bananawich," made with sliced bananas and peanut butter, with or without ham.

The ubiquitous banana split is surely one of this country's most popular dishes. A classic recipe calls for a banana sliced lengthwise and topped with vanilla, chocolate, and strawberry ice cream, whipped cream, nuts, and marshmallow, chocolate, and pineapple or strawberry sauce. A special dieter's banana split substitutes cottage cheese for ice cream—and, of course, omits the whipped cream and sauce. Presumably, few dieters could be found in the vicinity of the largest banana split in history, a mile-long feast concocted in St. Paul, Minnesota, in 1973. That record-breaker included 10,580 bananas, and 33,000 scoops of ice cream!

Fetish banana trees near the river Ogowe, Gabon.

Basketball

The first intercollegiate basketball game was played in 1896, with a seven-man Wesleyan University team defeating Yale 4 to 3.

Baseball may be our "national pastime," and football may draw the largest crowds per game, but surprisingly enough, it's basketball that claims the honor as the largest sport in America. A 1950s survey showed that basketball attendance at all games was, at least at the time, larger than the combined annual attendance totals of baseball, football, hockey, and six other major sports.

More teams are organized each year to play basketball than any other sport, and no American playground or gymnasium is complete without at least two basketball hoops. And basketball, now the third largest sport worldwide, is the only widely played game with an exclusively American origin.

You may have heard that the ancient Aztecs of Mexico played a game similar to basketball, and thus were the real originators of the sport. True, 16th-century Aztecs did play a team game called *tlachtli* or *ollamalitzli*, but the Indian games actually resembled soccer more than basketball. The object of the Aztec game was to propel a ball through vertical stone rings placed at each end of the court, about eight feet above the ground. The rubber ball was about the size of a cantaloupe, and the opening in the ring slightly larger. Players could use various parts of the body to strike the ball, but could not touch it with their hands, *a la* soccer. Spectators at *tlachtli* matches frequently took to their heels the moment a player scored a goal, since a goal earned the scoring player the right to collect clothing and jewelry from the crowd. The captain of the losing team was often beheaded. Talk about pressure games!

The game of basketball, as played today, is actually less than a hundred years old, the brainchild of Canadian-born James A. Naismith. In 1891, while working as a physical education instructor at the International YMCA training school in Springfield, Massachusetts, Naismith sought to invent a new indoor game to relieve the boredom of contemporary gym classes, which were usually limited to less-than-thrilling calisthenics, marching, and apparatus work. After much trial and error, Naismith borrowed and modified elements from football, soccer, hockey, and other sports to produce his new ball game.

Naismith's original plan was to set up square boxes as targets at opposite ends of the gym, nail-

ing them to the overhead board track. When the square boxes were unavailable, Naismith substituted two half-bushel peach baskets, and the new game immediately became known as basketball.

Naismith first tested his game with a gym class of 18 boys, dividing the class into two teams of nine. The first basket in the sport's history was scored by young William R. Chase, who led his team to a 1-0 victory. The game was an immediate sensation among the boys at the school, and the word spread among their friends at other schools and YMCAs. Soon, gym instructors from around the nation were writing to Naismith for the rules of the game.

Naismith first published his rules in a local paper, *Triangle Magazine,* in 1892, and later that year brought out the rules in booklet form. Naismith's booklet contained only 13 simple rules, including four principles that are still the basis of the game: (1) The goal is to be elevated and horizontal; (2) No running with the ball is permitted; (3) All players may handle the ball at any time; (4) No personal contact is allowed.

Unlike most other sports, which develop slowly and gradually attain popularity, basketball was an instant success throughout the United States. The ranks of YMCA members swelled as boys flocked to their gyms to learn the new sport. As early as 1893, one year after Naismith published his rules, an issue of the *YMCA Review* noted that "Ministers, lawyers, bankers, editors, merchants, clerks, mechanics, boys, young men, older men, yes, everybody plays basketball now."

But various organizations, including the YMCA, soon banned the sport, claiming that a game allowing only 10 or 20 boys in a class of perhaps 50 to participate created too much ill-will among the non-players. Banishment of the game led to a huge decrease in YMCA members; many basketball players were forced to rent gyms for their games—and therefore charge admission, a practice that eventually resulted in the professionalization of the sport.

As the game continued to catch on, basketball rules slowly evolved, with the rules for each game somewhat dependent upon the court it was played on. In 1896, the first basketball rules committee was formed to coordinate the various sets of regula-

The first hoop and basket sets sold by the Narragansett Company were closed-bottomed, and a ladder had to be used to retrieve the ball after each basket.

tions, and the first college basketball rules committee was founded in 1905. By 1913, there were five complete sets of rules for the game, and teams sometimes switched from one set to another at halftime. It wasn't until 1915 that the rules of the game were standardized for the first time.

In the early years, the size of the basketball court and the number of players on each team varied widely from game to game. A Cornell University class once tried a game with 50 players on each side, but the experiment failed dismally as all 100 players converged on the ball. For a time, teams consisted of either five, seven, or nine players, depending upon the size of the court, until the five-man team became the rule in 1897.

Some early basketball courts were irregularly shaped, twisting around pillars or other impediments. In some courts, balls going out of bounds were considered in play, forcing players to dash into the stands and fight with the spectators for the ball, while in other courts ropes were strung around the playing area as boundary lines, with players rebounding from the ropes like boxers in a ring. It wasn't until 1903, that straight, marked boundaries became part of the standard court.

With early baskets, balls that were thrown past the goal often ended up in the stands, where a fan could throw the ball in bounds to the favored team. So, beginning in 1895, a screen was usually placed behind the basket to serve as a rudimentary backboard. Glass was first used as a backboard in 1908, and the now popular fan-shaped backboard was legalized in 1940. Since 1946, most good courts have been fitted with transparent rectangular backboards.

There are now more than 20,000 high school basketball teams from coast to coast in the United States. Attendance at these games is something like 125 million people each season.

On April 6, 1935 the Amateur Athletic Union held a contest in Madison Square Garden. In the foul shooting contest, Harold Levitt started heaving foul shots into the basket at seven o'clock. By midnight, he had dunked 499 consecutive free throws.

The basket itself has changed a great deal since the early days. Naismith's peach baskets were quickly discarded. Lew Allen of Hartford, Connecticut developed a cylindrical basket of heavy woven wire in 1892, and the following year, the Narragansett Machinery Company of Providence, Rhode Island, marketed the first iron hoop basket. But it seems odd today that early players and basket makers were so slow to see the advantages of a basket with a hole at the bottom. Even the first hoop and basket sets sold by the Narragansett Company were closed-bottomed, and a ladder had to be used to retrieve the ball after each basket. Later, a small hole was cut in the bottom of the basket—not for the ball, but for a pole the referee used to dislodge the ball. Incredibly enough, it wasn't until 1912—20 years after Naismith's rulebook—that open-bottomed baskets were placed into official service on the court.

At first, Naismith had considered using both the oval rugby ball and the soccer ball before deciding on the round ball. In 1894, the Overman Wheel Company of Chicopee Falls, Massachusetts, a bike manufacturer, marketed the first "basketball," four inches larger in circumference than the soccer ball. In

1948, the circumference of the ball was reduced to 30 inches, and the laceless ball was declared official.

Even the players' dress varied greatly in the early days. Players on one court might opt for knee-length football trousers, other players for jersey tights like those worn by wrestlers, still others for short padded pants and knee guards. The latter uniform evolved into modern basketball dress.

The rules of the sport were changed many times this century to combat early basketball's biggest drawback: the slow pace of the game. Even after the introduction of the open-bottomed basket—and the farewell to the ladder—basketball games were for the most part dragged-out affairs, with the winner rarely scoring over 30 points, and stalling was the major weapon of the team with the lead. The pace was speeded up somewhat in 1932, when a rule was passed allowing a team only 10 seconds to advance the ball past midcourt, and again in 1936, when the three-second rule was put into effect. The following year, the time-consuming jump ball after every basket bit the dust. The 24-second clock was put into use in professional basketball beginning with the 1954-55 season.

The entry of the "big man" in basketball has also necessitated a number of rules changes. Goaltending—interference with the ball on its final arch toward the basket—was declared illegal in 1944. The appearance in 1967 of seven-foot, two-inch Lew Alcindor—later Kareem Abdul-Jabbar—forced the NCAA to outlaw the dunk shot.

Basketball is the number-one college sport in the United States. Football is bigger at some of the larger universities, but most smaller schools that can't afford a football team still field a basketball squad. Where did it all begin? It depends upon whom you ask.

Some sports historians say that the first college basketball team to be organized represented Geneva College of Beaver Falls, Pennsylvania, while others claim it was the University of Iowa or Mount Union College of Alliance, Ohio that first fielded a basketball squad. In any case, all three schools formed teams in 1892. The first intercollegiate basketball game was played in 1896, with a seven-man Wesleyan University team defeating Yale, 4-3. According to whom you believe, the first intercollegiate game with five-man teams was played between either the University of Pennsylvania and Yale in 1897, or one year earlier between the University of Chicago and the University of Iowa.

The first University of Chicago team was organized by Amos Alonzo Stagg, the school's athletic director, who'd learned the game from a student from Springfield, Massachusetts. The squad won its first five-man game against the University of Iowa, 15-12, with the coach of the Iowa five acting as referee. Although the majority of the spectators at the game hadn't the foggiest notion of basketball rules, it's recorded that many vociferously expressed their disapproval of the referee's calls.

National basketball tournaments have been held since 1897, when the 23rd Street YMCA of New York won an AAU competition, but the first national college tourney took place in 1937 in Kansas City, Missouri. The National Invitational Tournament (NIT) was organized by a group of New York sports writers in 1938, and the following year the NCAA organized its first national championship tournament. College basketball became front-page news in the early 1950s, when two investigations uncovered widespread game-fixing by gamblers. Ultimately, 49 games in 17 states were declared fixed, and 30 persons were arrested in all.

Women's basketball has been around since the 1890s, when Clara Baer introduced the game at a New Orleans college using Naismith's published rules (although another claim traces the first women's basketball to Smith College in 1892). But Clara misinterpreted some of Naismith's diagrams, assuming that certain dotted lines Naismith had drawn to indicate the best area for team play were actually restraining lines to be drawn on the court. Thus, for many years, women's basketball was played under different rules than the men's game, with each player limited to movement only within certain parts of the court. Today, women's games are played under men's rules, and the old game is now called "rover" or "netball."

Basketball has become a big-money professional sport only in the past few decades, but professional basketball teams have existed almost from the very beginning of the game. A team from Trenton, New Jersey became the nation's first professional five in 1898, when the squad rented a Masonic Hall for a game and charged admission to pay for the $25 rental.

The first widely-known professional basketball team was the Original Celtics, begun in 1915 by a group of New York City youngsters. During the 1920s, older, more skilled players were gradually added to the team, and

In 1946, Rhode Island was playing Bowling Green in Madison Square Garden. Rhode Island was behind two points. There were only three seconds left to play. Ernie Caverley of Rhode Island threw the ball from back court with all his might. The 55-foot shot went in, and tied the game. Rhode Island won it in the overtime by 82 to 79.

by 1928, when the squad disbanded, they were considered invincible. The team was regrouped in the 30s as the New York Celtics, before permanently disbanding in 1936. At the height of their popularity, the Celtics played a game every night, and two on Sunday, and were almost continually on the road—yet during the 1922-23 season the Celtics amassed a whopping 204 wins against just 11 defeats!

The first professional basketball association, the National Basketball League, was formed in 1898 to protect players from unscrupulous promoters. The league was disbanded and re-organized many times over the years, with the last NBL established in 1938. A rival organization, the Basketball Association of America, was founded in 1946, and after two years of "war" the leagues combined to form the National Basketball Association, with 17 member teams. A rival league, the American Basketball Association, was founded in 1967, but disbanded after the 1975-76 season, with four teams joining the NBA. The NBA now includes 22 teams in four divisions.

The professional basketball player of today probably logs more travel miles than the politician or business executive. Unlike baseball teams, who usually play three or four games on each trip to another city, basketball teams play single-game series, with more than 40 road games each season. Cities with basketball franchises now range from Boston in the East all the way to Portland and Seattle in the West, and to New Orleans and San Antonio in the South.

Even college basketball teams now play coast-to-coast schedules. By 1970, more than 30 college fives were traveling over 10,000 miles and playing to more than 200,000 fans in an average season. The 1968-69 UCLA team logged some 22,500 travel miles and played before almost 400,000 fans.

There are now about 20,000 high school basketball teams from coast to coast, and attendance at these games is said to approach 125 million in a season! In areas such as Indiana, where basketball has become a way of life, many small communities have built high school gymnasiums with a seating capacity larger than the population of the town.

Canada was the first country outside the United States to adopt basketball, with a men's college team from Toronto playing in open competition as early as 1893. The game reached France the same year, and England, Australia, China, India, and Japan soon after. The sport grew rapidly on an international scale after World War II, and today basketball ranks as the third most popular sport worldwide after soccer and cycling. Since 1936, basketball has been a part of the Olympic competition, with the United States dominating the sport.

Despite the popularity of school, professional, and international basketball, the honor of playing before the largest crowd in basketball history belongs to the Harlem Globetrotters, who drew 75,000 people to a Berlin stadium in 1951. The zany club, combining real basketball talent with comic relief, was formed by Abe Saperstein in 1927, and played its first game in Hinckley, Illinois. Over the years, the Globetrotters have become virtually an international institution, and now play before two or three million fans each year. At one time, three separate Globetrotter teams barnstormed at the same time to satisfy the demand for the club. By 1970, the Globetrotters had played in 57 nations on all five continents, amassing 6,569 wins against only 303 defeats during the first 33 years of their existence!

Like all sports, basketball has produced its moments of greatness. One of the high points of college basketball was reached in the 1949-50 season, when the underdog City College of New York became the first—and only—team to win both the NCAA and NIT championships in the same year. The Beavers had finished their schedule that year without ranking among the top 20 teams, and had been the last squad to be invited to both tournaments. Yet they went on to victory in both competitions, in the process defeating the teams ranked one, two, three, five, and six.

Perhaps the most breathtaking clutch shot in college basketball history occurred during the 1946 NIT games in New York. An underdog Rhode Island State team was trailing the Bowling Green Five, 74-72, with only three seconds left to play. Taking possession of the ball under their own basket, the Rhode Island team managed to get the ball to five-foot, 10-inch Ernie Calverley, who lofted a desperation shot from well behind the midcourt line. As the buzzer sounded, the Madison Square Garden crowd of 18,548 rose in astonishment—Calverley's shot had whisked through the mesh without even touching the rim! Rhode Island had tied the score, and went on to win in overtime, 82-79. Observers have estimated that the distance Calverley's shot traveled was somewhere between 55 and 65 feet!

Then there's the incredible streak of the UCLA teams, who won seven straight national championships during the late 1960s and 70s, and 10 championships in 12 years. And let's not forget the fantastic professional career of Wilt "The Stilt" Chamberlain, regarded by most aficionados as the best basketball player of all time. As a pro, Chamberlain became the career leader in almost all offensive departments, finishing his 13-year career with a lifetime average of 30.1 points per game! Chamberlain is still the only professional player ever to score 100 points in a game, accomplishing the feat on March 2, 1962, during a 169-147 rout of the New York Knickerbockers.

Another enviable scoring record was set on February 28, 1975, when an amateur player named Ted St. Martin sank 1,704 consecutive free throws without a miss.

John T. Sebastian of Illinois accomplished a similar feat in 1972 when he sank 63 consecutive free throws—blindfolded!

But surely the most peculiar game of basketball ever played took place in Sweden in 1974, when a boys team defeated its rival by the incredible score of 272-0! And get this: a 13-year-old named Mats Wermelin scored *all 272 points* for his team!

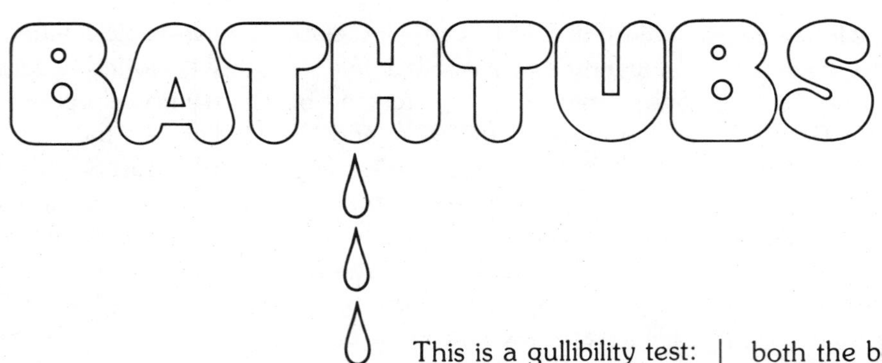

This is a gullibility test:

The bathtub was introduced in England in 1828. The first tub in America was used by a Cincinnati resident named Thompson in 1842. After an argument among medical authorities concerning the benefits and hazards of bathing, the bathtub was banned in Boston in 1845. Six years later, the first bathtub was installed in the White House for Millard Fillmore.

Believe it? Well, this capsulized history of the bathtub appeared in the *New York Evening Mail* in 1917, and was immediately accepted as fact by many readers. But the article was actually the devious work of humorist H.L. Mencken, and was—as Mencken readily admitted—a "tissue of absurdities, all of them deliberate and most of them obvious." Yet, much to Mencken's amazement, more than one lazy writer subsequently published this information as the gospel truth.

Although the porcelain tub is now indispensable in every home, it is a rather recent innovation. However, the institution of bathing is much older than Mencken facetiously suggested. The fact is, regular bathing has periodically gone in and out of fashion over the centuries.

From time immemorial, the act of bathing has been regarded as a sacred rite in many cultures. The ancient Egyptians bathed before worship, in the belief that both the body and soul should be pure in the presence of the gods. Christian baptism is a bathing rite, symbolizing the washing away of original sin. To the devout Hindu, a bath is a once-yearly rite, taken only in the sacred waters of the Ganges.

The ancient Greeks are thought to have introduced the bathtub, or at least the wash basin. The Greek vessels were used to hold water for rinsing, but were too small to accommodate a bather. The ruins of the palace at Knossos, Crete, reveal a number of bathrooms that were apparently supplied by a relatively advanced plumbing system. Vase paintings suggest that the Greeks used some form of shower as well. Most early Greeks, by the way, washed only with cold water —warm water was considered effeminate.

In later periods, the Greeks built public baths; but it was the Romans who made the bathhouse the center of their social lives. In the early days of the Roman Republic, wealthy citizens often installed private baths in their homes, similar to the modern Turkish bath.

Later, the public bath came into vogue in almost all cities and towns of the Empire. Huge baths, or *thermae*, became the recreation centers of the Imperial City itself, providing not only bathing

Queen Elizabeth I of England reportedly bathed once a month, "whether she needed it or not."

facilities but gyms, libraries, theaters, gardens, and assembly halls.

The Roman baths were masterpieces of architecture and engineering, and the epitome of imperial luxury. The walls were usually covered with marble; the high, vaulted ceilings were decorated with colorful mosaics. The water taps were made of silver. Statues were everywhere, with small cubical lockers set in the niches between them. Hot water, provided by furnaces, was piped into the bath. The rooms were kept warm by smoke and by hot air circulating under the floors and in the hollow walls.

The first large Roman public bath was built by Agrippa in 27 B.C. Others were constructed by Nero (65 A.D.), Titus (81 A.D.), Domitian (95 A.D.), Trajan (100 A.D.), and Commodus (185 A.D.). Diocletian built baths in the year 302 that were large enough to accommodate 3,200 bathers at one time!

The Roman's bathing ritual consisted of a series of baths, each taken in a different room. The bather began in the undressing room, then moved to another room where he was anointed with oil, then to the gym for exercise. After the gym came the *calidarium*, or hot bath; then the steam room, the *tepidarium*, or lukewarm bath; and finally, the *frigidarium*, or cold bath which was usually a sort of swimming pool. Sounds much like our modern health spa, doesn't it?

Until the second century, men and women bathed together in Rome. Then emperor Hadrian ordered segregated bathing. However, Hadrian's decree was frequently overlooked during the more decadent eras of the Empire. In most cities outside Rome, men and women used the bathing facilities at different hours, but it was always considered immoral for a woman to bathe at night.

The Roman baths were the social centers of the time, combining the modern barroom, health spa, and community center. They were open continually except for religious holidays and times of national crisis. Customarily, a Roman would bathe before the principal meal of the day, but some of the more idle—and cleaner—citizens went through the entire bathing ritual as many as six times a day.

As the Empire waned and barbarian invaders destroyed the Roman aqueduct systems, most baths were shut down. But the public bath lived on in the Eastern Empire, and was eventually adopted by the Arabs, who liked vapor baths. The Turkish bath is a direct descendant of the Roman bath, via Constantinople.

The Teutonic tribesmen who overran Europe bathed for the most part in cold rivers or streams. During the Middle Ages, among some communities, bathing was considered a sin and an act of pride. Probably, the Church's opposition to bathing stemmed from the excesses of the Roman public bath.

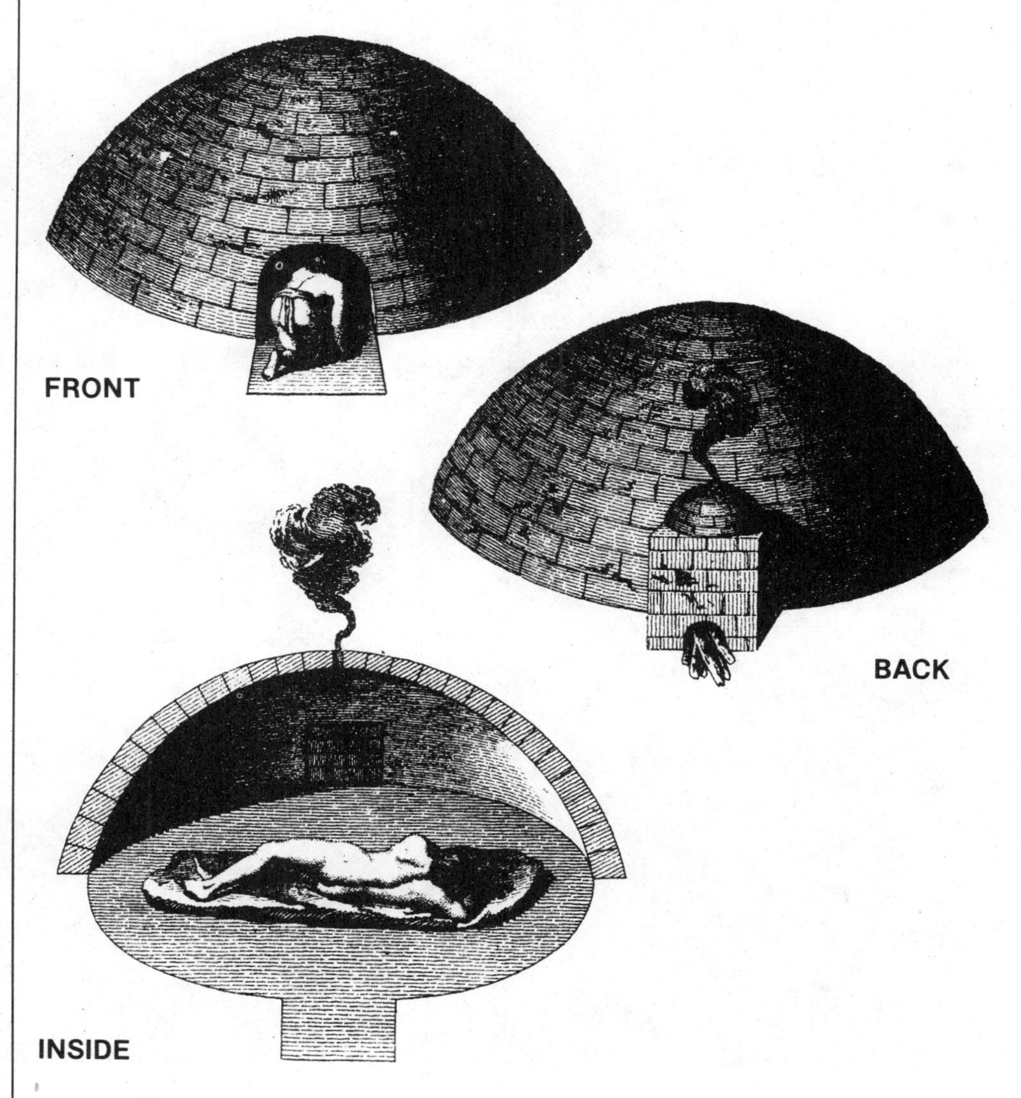

Among the medieval landed classes, the lack of a need to bathe was considered a sign of wealth and leisure. Many an aristocrat bragged of never having taken a bath. Consequently, the demand for perfume and aromatic oils was very high, and the need for spices helped spur the explorations of the 15th century which led to the discovery of America. By the way, Queen Elizabeth of England reportedly bathed once a month, "whether she needed it or not."

After the institution of bathing was revived by the Crusaders' contact with Eastern bathhouses, the common people took frequent public baths. Public baths were common in France as early as the 12th century, and were reputedly as notorious for their promiscuous activities as had been their Roman precursors. By the 17th century, no decent citizen would consider entering a public bath, and the Church frequently decried the excesses of the institution.

Because of the aristocracy's aversion to bathing, many of the more famous palaces surviving today are completely without sanitation facilities. Although many people dispute it—and others refuse to believe it—there were evidently no toilets of any kind in either the Louvre or in the palace at Versailles. Members of the court were expected to relieve themselves before they entered the palace; the rows of statues that lined the garden promenades provided convenient niches for an undisturbed tinkle.

The Meshlakh, or cooling room, was one of the features of the Jermyn Street baths.

In Europe, the medicinal spring bath has been popular for centuries. During the 18th century, the English city of Bath—so named after an ancient Roman spa built there—became the most fashionable resort in all Europe, thanks chiefly to the restorative work of Beau Nash. Such luminaries as Pitt, Nelson, Gainsborough, Garrick, Gay, Pope, Steele, and Fielding came to enjoy the social life and the hot, radioactive waters of the natural spring. Like earlier baths, however, the resort at Bath eventually became associated with debauchery and the spread of disease.

The word "spa," incidentally, comes to us from the Belgian town of Spa. A mineral spring discovered in 1326 helped make the town a very fashionable resort during the 18th century. Today, the most famous spas in the world are at Baden-Baden in Germany (*bad* means "bath" in German), Carlsbad in Czechoslovakia, Vichy in France, and Hot Springs in Arkansas.

The earliest bathtubs in America were simple wooden tubs, lined with metal and the water was poured in by hand. The first public bath was opened here in 1852. An 1895 law ordered all municipalities in New York State to provide free public baths for their citizens, many of whom had no other means of washing.

In the early decades of this century, many apartments in American cities were equipped with a bathtub in the kitchen. When European immigrants arrived here, many considered the bathtub an unnecessary luxury, and used the tub as a planter for flowers and vegetables.

Traditionally, in Japan, the bath was a large wooden tub placed outside in the garden and filled with very hot water. The entire family bathed together at the same time. In Japanese baths, both public and private, there is rarely an attempt to achieve privacy. Public baths often have large unprotected openings through which people passing in the street can observe the bathers. But nowadays, bathing in Japan—especially in the cities—is becoming westernized.

America easily leads the world today in bathtubs per capita. Many American homes are equipped with two or three or even four tubs. The shower has recently replaced the bath as the preferred washing ritual. A shower, by the way, uses up only about half as much water as a tub bath.

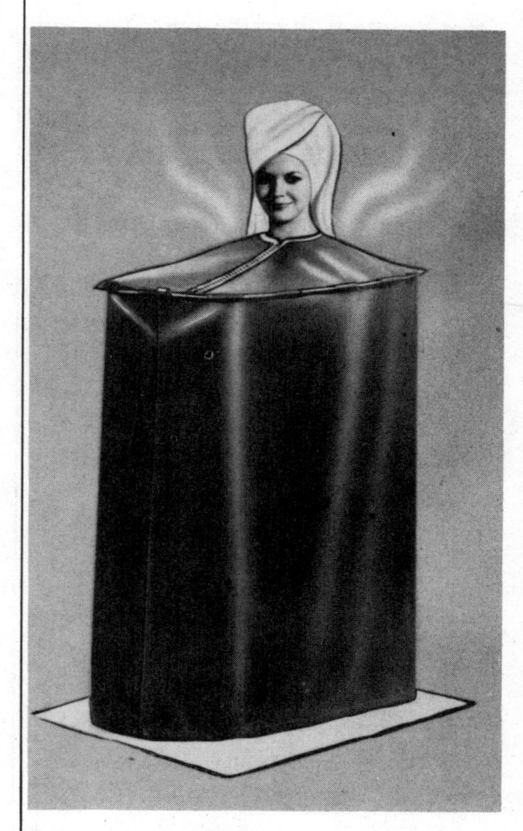

This vinyl fold-up steam bath is billed as the "poor girl's sauna."

Of all the common objects examined in this book, there is none you're more likely to use on a day to day basis, or take more for granted, than the bed. You might drive your automobile for an hour or two a day, you might watch television for as many as four or five hours daily, but you probably spend about one-third of your life stretched out on a mattress of some kind. Yet we devote a woefully small part of our budget to bedtime comfort. A recent poll disclosed that the average American spends 120 times more money each year on tobacco products than on beds and bedding!

Eight hours of sleep daily may be considered the average, but side by side with the proverb "Early to bed, early to rise, makes a man healthy, wealthy, and wise," we must mention: "Six hours of sleep for a man, seven for a woman, and eight for a fool." Naturally, some people spend a good deal more time in bed than others—for sleeping as well as for sundry other pastimes. Noted authors who often worked in bed include Cicero, Horace, Milton, Voltaire, Jonathan Swift, Alexander Pope, Mark Twain, and Marcel Proust. And speaking of bona fide lovers, British writer Max Beerbohm once declared that his ideal of happiness was "a four-poster in a field of poppies."

Considering the length of time man has been sleeping, the bed, as we know it, is a rather recent development. The first bed in history was a patch of earth where a tired caveman laid himself down to rest. We know little of the sleeping gear of primitive man, since all wooden objects from prehistoric times have vanished—not to mention piles of leaves, grass, moss, or feathers. The simple stone slab beds that do remain cannot be regarded as proof that all primitive peoples slept on stone. Our ancient ancestors probably slept much the way people in India, Africa, and other places do today, for the bed as an item of furniture is primarily a Western predilection.

Beds are virtually unknown in much of India, though one Indian maharajah of recent times boasted a one-ton bed complete with four life-sized nudes that automatically began fanning and playing music the moment the monarch put his weight on the mattress. Wealthy Arabs sometimes sleep on elaborate tentlike beds, but most people in the Mideast still slumber on simple piles of rugs. The Japanese customarily catch their shuteye on a mat, called a *tatami,* spread over the floor. Many Japanese do not even have a bedroom—in the morning, they roll up their *tatami* and their *futon,* or quilt, and use the sleeping quarters as a dining room.

The Chinese, on the other hand, have a long tradition of bed slumber. Wooden beds similar to those made in ancient Egypt were in use in China as early as 2,000 years ago. Even the four-poster bed is not unknown in China. But, by our standards, old Chinese beds would not be very comfortable, with matting substituting for a mattress, and pillows made of wood or stone, carved to fit the head or neck.

In the West, the history of the bed begins in ancient Egypt. To our eyes, Egyptian beds look more like couches. And well they should, for Egyptians made no distinction between a day bed, or couch, and a night bed; they used the same item for both lounging and sleeping. The earliest known models were made of palm sticks or palm leaf wicker, lashed together with pieces of cord or rawhide. Later, Egyptian bed-makers introduced mortise-and-tenon constuction and wood bed frames veneered with ivory or ebony. In the royal household, beds made from naturally curved timbers were sometimes sheathed in gold. Most mattresses were made of woven cord, interlaced like the modern chaise lounge or beach chair.

The Egyptian bed was equipped with a footboard, but not with a headboard. Egyptian pillows would seem appallingly uncomfortable by modern standards: most were raised headrests, curved to fit the head or neck, made of wood, ivory, or alabaster, and sometimes inlaid with ivory or colored stones. Many beds, especially those in the poorer quarters, were fitted with a canopy of some kind from which mosquito netting could be hung. The Greek historian Herodotus claimed that contemporary Egyptians used the nets by day to catch fish.

Even in wealthier households, the Egyptian bedroom was starkly furnished, with just a bed and perhaps a chair and a small table. In many houses, there was but one bedroom, for the master of the house; the servants slept in the hall. The ruins of one aristocratic Egyptian home suggest that younger children sometimes slept in their parents' bedroom.

Most ancient peoples of the Mideast slept on beds similar to those in Egypt. Phoenician beds often sported foot panels with erotic ivory carvings—the Bible, you'll recall, equated "beds of ivory" with sinful luxury. Sardanapalus, the last great king of Assyria, evidently had quite a thing for beds, right to the end. According to an aprocryphal Greek fable, the Assyrian king committed suicide, along with his wives and concubines, on a pyre fueled by his 150 beds.

Since almost all the beds of ancient Greece were made of wood, none survive today. But artwork from the period shows that the Greeks slept on beds very similar to those of Egypt. The earliest models consisted of a wood frame and a mattress of lashed rawhide bands. Later, the wood frames were veneered with ivory, bronze, or silver. For some reason, the Greeks dropped the footboard in favor of the headboard.

As described in *The Odyssey*, Penelope's couch was fitted with a stuffed mattress, a purple linen sheet, and blankets made from fleeces and rugs. Considerably less fortunate, and less comfortable, were the men of Sparta, who were required to sleep in a tent along with 15 other compatriots, while their wives remained at home. Even married men were not permitted to sleep away from their tents until the age of 30!

The Greek sleeping chamber, called a *thalamos,* was small and windowless, with light reaching the room only through the large doorway. The master bedroom, which was often in the women's quarters, usually contained a bed and perhaps a few coffers and chairs. The Greek's idea of bedroom luxury was a bed of roses with "no rooster within earshot."

Although the bedrooms in most large Roman homes were arranged around an open central court, the average bedroom, or *cubiculum,* was as small and dark as the Greek *thalamos,* with glassless windows shuttered during sleeping hours to keep in heat and shut off light. A *cubiculum* customarily contained a bed, or *lectus,* along with a chair, chest, floor mat, and chamber pot. Although the Romans used both single and double beds, only in the poorest homes would you find two beds in the same room. In larger homes, curtains divided the bedroom into a space for attendants, a dressing room, and the sleeping area proper. Some of the homes found in the ruins of Pompeii contained sleeping alcoves set in wall niches behind curtains or sliding partitions.

Roman bedsteads were often mounted on a platform, and many were fitted with a canopy from which curtains or mosquito netting was hung.

The Romans, like the Greeks, customarily went to their tomb on their bed. Many *lecti* also doubled as couches for dining, and some could hold as many as six people. Wealthy Romans were evidently quite proud of their elegant bedding. The author Martial wrote of a rich man who feigned illness so that he could show off his bed coverings to visiting well-wishers. The poor, on the other hand, usually slept on masonry shelves along the walls of their *insulae,* or tenements. Others had to make do with a simple wood plank covered with a bug-ridden pallet.

This bedstead of English metal work was constructed during the 19th century.

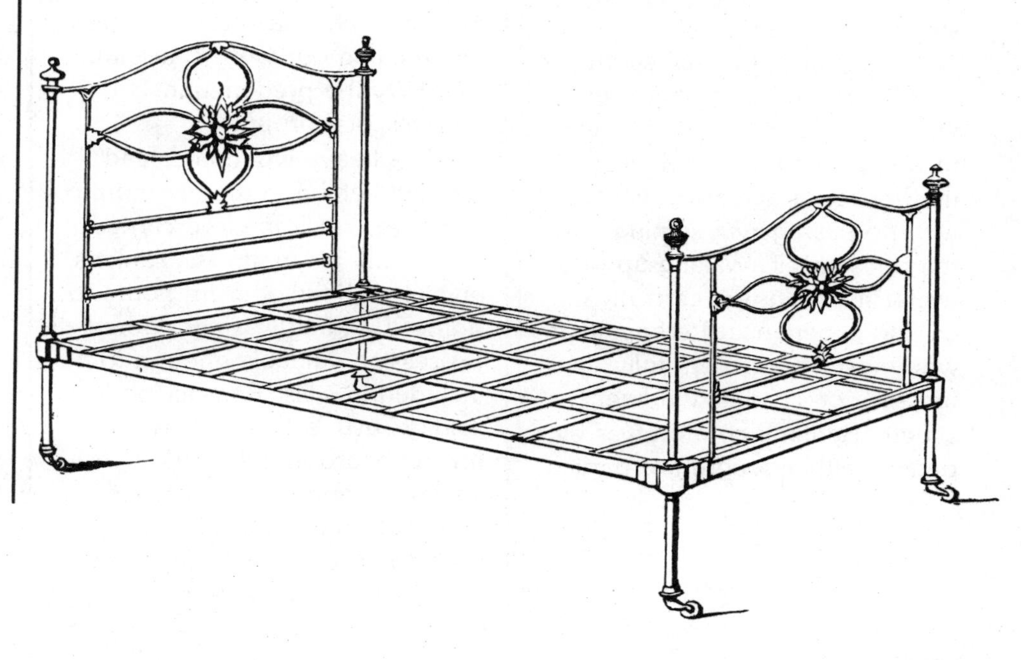

No matter what their social class, Romans rarely owned special sleepwear. Men removed their toga and climbed into bed in their undergarments, while women went to bed laden with their *capitium, mamillare,* and *strophium*—corset, bra, and panties. Bedtime was usually between seven and nine o'clock, and the dawn crowing of the rooster provided the only alarm clock. A breakfast of more than plain water was rare, as was a morning wash-up, since most Romans included a trip to the public baths as part of their daily routine.

Like many other luxuries, the comforts of the Roman boudoir, vanished with the end of the Empire. The Germanic tribes that overran Europe were accustomed to sleeping on the ground, atop piles of leaves or skins. During the early Middle Ages, many peasants slept in the barn along with their animals, or on the earth floor, or on a wooden bench in the hall, the only room in the house with a fireplace. Some enjoyed the luxury of mattresses stuffed with feathers, wool, hair, or straw. The Old English expression for "make a bed" literally meant "prepare straw."

In England, the earliest medieval bedroom, called a *bower,* was no more than a simple lean-to set against the outside wall of the house, or against a fence, with no passageway joining it to the house itself. Waking up on a winter morning was certainly a chilling experience. Perhaps that's why most people slept fully dressed, or swaddled in linen sheets. Bedtime comfort was evidently neither sought nor particularly missed, for the 10th-century English ruler Edgar banned "warm baths and soft beds" as effeminate.

In feudal days, only the lord and lady of the house were afforded the luxury of a bedroom. The servants still slept in the hall on piles of straw. Most bedrooms contained a bed, chest, chair, bench, and a clothes rack called a perch, with walls whitewashed or covered with curtains. The bed was usually made of wood fitted together with nails or pieces of iron, with a headboard or footboard decorated with crude carvings. Many beds were fitted with bolsters that raised sleepers to a nearly sitting position.

Aristocratic Europeans of the period moved frequently from one manor to another, carrying their furniture with them rather than furnishing each home. Therefore, many beds and couches were portable. The French word for furniture, *meubles,* and the German word *Mobel* are both derived from words meaning *movable.* And since a family's belongings had to be continually transported from house to house, furniture was kept at a minimum. A single chair was usually reserved for the lord of the house—from this tradition came our word *chairman,* to signify the predominant member of a group.

The heavy wood bedstead was left behind in the bedroom, however, while the lord carried along only his mattress, blankets, and other bedding from home to home. Bedding was considered a possession valuable enough to be included in wills. Ransacking soldiers usually headed straight for the bedroom when they entered a home, claiming bedding as booty. And it was not uncommon for a man to name his bed, as he would a pet!

Among his other idiosyncracies, English monarch Richard III carried along his heavy wooden bedstead when touring his domain. After King Richard's death, the bedstead remained in the inn where he'd last slept. A century later, the landlord of the inn took apart the bedstead and found a double bottom filled with Richard's stash of gold coins.

In wealthier homes, the simple bed of the early Middle Ages gradually gave way to a curtain-enclosed bed so large that it formed a room within a room. A canopy, called a *tester,* was suspended over the bed on rods or chains to form the ceiling. Beneath the canopy hung curtains, which completely enclosed the bed, holding in heat. The warm space between the bed and the wall, called the *ruelle,* was sometimes used to receive intimate guests. Bedding now included silk or leather-covered cushions, and velvet, silk, and—ouch!—pearl-studded pillows. By the end of the Middle Ages, bedrooms were roomy and well-lit, with glass windows, fireplaces, and hand-crafted beds and bedding. Gradually, the comforts worked their way down to the common man.

Elizabethans attached great ceremony to the marriage bed. Often, an entire wedding party accompanied the bride and groom to their bedroom for music, games, and the official blessing of the bed by a cleric. When the bride began to remove her wedding dress, she customarily tossed one of her stockings to the revelers, and the person who caught the garment was deemed the next in the room to marry—thus, our wedding custom of "tossing the garter."

Speaking of the nuptial bower, the marriage bed of Philip, Duke of Burgundy, and Princess Isabella of Portugal was probably the largest bed of all time, measuring 19 feet by 12½ feet. Constructed in 1430, in Bruges, Belgium, the bed has long since been dismantled. The largest bed still in existence is the Great Bed of Ware, built around 1580 for the Crow Inn in Ware, England. Now on exhibit at the Victoria and Albert Museum in London, this ponderous bed measured about 11 feet square and close to nine feet tall. Compare that with the largest bed now on the market, the nine- by-nine foot Super Size Diplomat, which sells for well over $2,000.

Camp beds were in use as early as the 15th century for traveling gentry. The camp beds of the era were hardly cots, though, and some of the heavier four-posters must surely have required a wagon all their own for transport. The trundle bed also appeared during the era, originally for servants who slept in their master's room. (Queen Elizabeth herself had a bedroom guard of 18 persons.) By day, the beds were rolled under the master's four-poster.

The familiar lullabye "Rock-a-bye Baby" is at least as old as the Elizabethan period. The lyrics may harken back to an earlier epoch when a mother might place baby's cradle in the branches of a tree to be rocked gently by the wind.

In France, the king's bed—known as the "Bed of State"—was treated with a reverence that sometimes surpassed that accorded the throne. Persons entering the king's chamber were expected to genuflect in front of the bed, even if the king was not in the room. A railing separating the sleeping area from the rest of the room was originally intended to keep dogs from the bed. The king's bed was also known as the "Bed of Justice," where from the period of Louis XI on, *le roi* customarily reclined while parliament was in session.

An ornate bed, 19th century, exhibited at the London Crystal Palace show.

The age-old custom of laying a deceased relative to rest in his or her bed through the mourning period prompted the families of many beheaded aristocrats to have their dear ones' heads sewn back on, so that the body could be more decorously displayed. A nobleman fortunate enough to keep his head, and perhaps a bit wary of losing it, often ordered servants to remain in his bedroom for as long as he might nap. One English duke insisted that his two daughters stand beside his bed during his afternoon nap. When he awoke one day to discover that one of the young women had had the audacity to sit down, he promptly sliced 20,000 pounds off her legacy.

The 17th century is sometimes known as "the century of magnificent beds," in tribute to the elaborate furniture of the period. In England, most beds retained the full tester, though in France the half-tester became more popular. Beds of the time were large enough to serve as mini-parlors, where the lord or lady of the house could grant audiences without surrendering the warmth of the blankets. Women at the Palace of Versailles regularly received visitors—male and female alike—in bed, without raising eyebrows, for the bed was deemed the proper place to accept congratulations or condolences. In fact, the idea that sitting on another person's bed was somehow improper did not occur to anyone until the mid-17th century.

Louis XIV owned an estimated 413 beds in his various palaces. Louis's favorite bed at Versailles was fitted with crimson velvet curtains so heavily embroidered with gold that the crimson was scarcely visible. A ribald painting called "The Triumph of Venus" originally adorned the king's bed, but his second wife, a woman of a more religious bent, had it replaced with "The Sacrifice of Abraham."

The 18th century saw the appearance of the first metal bedsteads since the days of ancient Rome. Metal beds had one large advantage over wooden beds: they were less likely to be infested with "sleep's foe, the flea, that proud insulting elf." Feather pillows became common during the era.

Across the ocean in America, simple wood beds and straw mattresses were still the rule in all but the wealthiest homes. American inns of the period offered little more in the way of comfort—an innkeeper would think nothing of asking a guest to share his bed with a stranger when accommodations became scarce.

Speaking of cheap accommodations, Parisian flophouses of the 19th century offered their more indigent guest a place at the "two-penny leanover," a long bench with a rope stretched in front of it, which the sleeper could lean over during his sit-up slumber. In the morning, an inappropriately named "valet" rudely awoke the guests by cutting the rope.

During the 19th century, English manufacturers began to turn out cast-iron bedsteads in quantity. Gradually, mattresses stuffed with feathers, leaves, hair, moss, wool, or seaweed gave way to the spring mattress, which had been patented in the late 18th century. The first spiral mattress—similar to the one you may sleep on—appeared first in 1826, intended for use aboard ship as an aid against seasickness. In 1857, the first box springs, one foot deep, reached the shores of America from France.

Victorian publications never dared show a bed in any of their advertisements. When illustrations of the bedroom were required, the bed itself was decorously hidden by curtains. At the same time, advertisers began to peddle inventions we now call alarm clocks, but which the class-conscious Victorians preferred to call "servant regulators."

Victoria herself could boast a few peculiar bedtime habits. Even after the death of her husband, Prince Albert, the queen always slept in a double bed, and had her servants lay out the deceased Prince's bedclothes each night. A picture of Albert's corpse hung continually above her bed.

With sturdy bedsteads and spring mattresses at their disposal, 19th-century Europeans began to turn their attention to the amenities of bedroom comfort. Tin hot-water bottles had been in use since the 17th century, but the rubber models were surely a vast improvement. Belly-warmers were also popular for a time, complete with a concave depression for the stomach. Electric blankets have made such devices obsolete, although the earliest warming blankets were a

This Spanish bedstead was made during the 19th century.

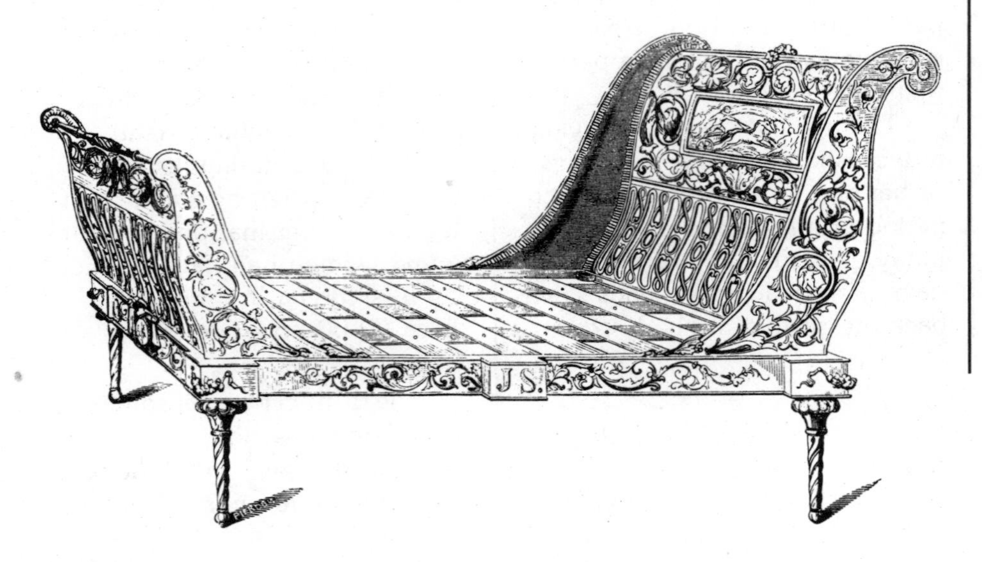

A four-poster bedstead of the Renaissance style.

dangerous proposition—electric blankets caused an estimated 2,600 fires during the first three years of their sale here.

The first railroad sleeping car in this country appeared in 1836, on the Cumberland Valley Railroad. In 1858, George Pullman introduced the sleeping car that was to make his name synonymous with railroad comfort. When introduced on the Chicago and Alton Railroad, Pullman's simple, practical vehicle cost but $1,000. By 1865, luxury Pullmans including everything *and* the kitchen sink were selling for 20 times that amount.

The first Murphy bed appeared in 1909, manufactured by the Murphy Door Bed Company of San Francisco. Initially called "in-a-door beds," the Murphy's were designed to fold back on a pivot behind a door or closet.

The foam rubber mattress is the most familiar slumbertime development of the 20th century, but the water bed is probably the most controversial. Some people now maintain that the water bed is unequaled for a slumber par excellence, while others warn that the watery bower leads only to seasickness, cold feet, and the threat of a bedroom deluge.

In 1975, a furniture company and a chemical engineer combined to bring out a new kind of water bed that might eliminate most critics' objections. Called a Gel-bed, the bed is filled with a plastic substance called Flo-lok that can't leak in quantity from the bed, doesn't make waves, and remains warm enough to eliminate the need for the heater found on other water beds. A Gel-bed mattress can presently be purchased for under $200—and a frame is not required!

The phrase "bedtime sports" may have illicit connotations, but there are indeed a number of athletic contests involving the bed. The Australian Bedmaking Championships are one example. The record time for bedmaking under the stringent rules of the tournament is 35.7 seconds, but we're not sure what kind of bed, or bedding, was used in that monumental performance. Since 1966, the annual Knaresborough Bed Race has thrilled participants in Yorkshire, England, with the record time for the two-and-a-half-mile course now standing at just over 14 minutes.

The record distance for bed pushing was achieved in 1975, by 12 young people in Greensburg, Pennsylvania, who wheeled a hospital bed a total of 1,776 miles in 17 days. A group of students attempting to match that feat once fitted a wheeled bed with a 197-cc. engine—and accumulated 52 traffic summonses during their maiden voyage.

Speaking of motorized beds, the late billionaire Howard Hughes designed a bed for himself that employed 30 electric motors, to move himself and various parts of the bed. The bed was also equipped with piped-in music and hot and cold running water!

The weirdest of all bed sportsmen are surely those human beings who subject their tender flesh on a bed of nails. The record for nonstop endurance of such an inhospitable bower was set in 1971, in Wooster, Ohio, when Vernon E. Craig lay atop a bed of nails for 25 hours, 20 minutes. And unverified claims for bed-of-nails endurance range as high as 111 days!

Some bed of roses!

Bicycles

In the United States, where the automobile is king of the road, it's easy to underestimate the importance of the bicycle. To many Americans, cycling may mean cruising around Central Park in Manhattan, or along Lake Shore Drive in Chicago, or pedaling lazily over surburban streets on a modern 10-speed. But while in America the bicycle is chiefly a sporting vehicle or a plaything for children, in much of the world, the bike remains man's primary means of transportation.

It should come as no surprise that the bicycle is the principal vehicle in the Orient, in parts of Africa, and the Near East. But even in the developed nations of Europe, the bicycle retains an importance wholly out of proportion to its use in America. The streets of Amsterdam, Brussels, and Paris teem with bicycles, and during working hours many European squares become forests of parked bicycles. Though exact figures are impossible to come by, there's little doubt around the

OPPOSITE PAGE:

An indoor bicycle race in Liverpool held in 1869. Evidently a rider must catch a ring with his pennant and remove it from the bar while racing.

world that bicycles vastly outnumber automobiles.

Even in America, surprisingly enough, more bicycles are manufactured each year than automobiles. During the five years ending in 1977, over 68 million bikes were sold in the United States, compared to 60 million automobiles during the same period. In 1973, bicycle sales in America reached a peak of over 15 million, but the year 1977 still showed a healthy total of about nine-and-a-half million new bikes. Some 100 million Americans—almost half the population—now ride bikes.

What kind of bicycles are Americans buying these days? Increasingly, they're turning to lightweight 10-speed models. In 1970, lightweight, narrow-wheeled bikes accounted for only 20 percent of the market; they now account for more than half. A decade ago, the sale of 10-speed bikes stood at just five percent of total bike sales, with an overwhelming 73 percent single-speed, coaster-brake models in use. By 1977, 10-speeds accounted for 36 percent of the market and three-speeds for 11 percent, while single-speeds had dipped to 52 percent.

Men's bikes continue to outsell women's models by almost two-to-one. Bicycles imported from more than 20 foreign nations continue to account for about 20 percent of all American sales.

The popularity of the bicycle is well deserved. An extremely efficient machine, the bicycle is light but strong, capable of supporting a load over 10 times its weight. Bicycles are inexpensive to purchase, simple to maintain and repair, easy to store both at home and away, and relatively safe to drive. The estimated one million cycling injuries and 1,000 cycling deaths that occur yearly in America usually involve an automobile. The bike does not pollute the environment, and is an excellent instrument for promoting physical fitness. Over shorter distances, in fact, the bicycle is actually more efficient—and convenient—than the automobile.

The bicycle commonly used in most of the world is a far cry from the elaborate 10-speed models that now fill American bikeways. As late as the 1960s, three-speed "racers" were considered the epitome of biking pleasure. Today, 10-speeds make uphill pedaling a breeze. But even the crudest of today's bikes would look like streamlined speedsters compared to the heavy iron-wheeled contraptions that began the curious history of the bicycle.

Suggestions of wheeled vehicles propelled by the muscle power of their riders are found among the artifacts of various ancient cultures, including the bas-reliefs of Egypt and Babylonia and the frescoes of Pompeii. A design for a wheeled machine propelled by cranks and pedals was found among the writings of Leonardo da Vinci, dating to about 1493. The so-called "cycle window," made in Italy in 1580 for a church in Stoke Poges, England, shows an angel astride what appears to be a wheeled vehicle made of wood. A trumpet attached to the front handlebars suggests a horn used to warn

In 1891, the first of the legendary six-day bicycle races was held in Madison Square Garden, New York. The maiden race included 40 entries, of which only six finished, with Bill Martin winning on a highwheeler.

The Royal Salvo Tricycle, designed by James Starley, attracted the attention of Queen Victoria who ordered two of the machines and thereby established the respectability of the new fad of cycling. This model was considered particularly well suited for female riders.

The smallest working bicycle of all time, a two-pound vehicle with two-and-one-eighth-inch wheels, was ridden regularly by a full-grown Las Vegas showman, Charlie Charles.

pedestrians of the vehicle's approach. But we find no reference to such a vehicle in the writings of the period.

The earliest prototypes of the bicycle of which we have a record appeared in France and England late in the 18th century. These simple vehicles consisted of two wheels linked by a wooden "backbone" upon which the rider sat, propelling the machine by pushing with his feet against the ground. The backbones often took the shape of snakes, lions, horses, and other animals, leading to the name of "hobby horse." But these vehicles were virtually useless until 1816, when Baron von Drais of Karlsruhe, Germany, introduced a pivoted front wheel that could be turned by a handle, enabling the rider to steer his hobby horse for the first time.

Though photography pioneer J.N. Niepce has been credited with constructing a similar vehicle which antedated von Drais's by a few years, it was von Drais's machine that spurred the English hobby horse craze of 1819-1821.

Known under such names as the *draisine*, the *celeripede*, the *patent accelerator*, the *bivector*, the *bicipede*, the *swiftwalker*, and the *pedestrian curricle*, the pedalless vehicle of the time was propelled by pushing along the ground with the feet. To climb a hill, a rider had to carry the 50-pound vehicle on his shoulders. And downhill riding could be treacherous, since draisines were not equipped with brakes!

English magazines began satirizing the new craze with cartoons depicting English dandies cavorting on their draisines, tumbling head over heels as their wheels struck a hole or a stone in the road. One cartoon showed a group of blacksmiths chasing a rider and smashing his "dandy horse," while their smithies remained boarded up for lack of business.

On the other side of the Atlantic, Americans lost no time either in adopting or damning the new vehicle. In 1819, the Common Council of New York City passed a law to prevent the use of these early bikes "in the public places and on the sidewalks of the city of New York."

The dandy horse craze came to a rapid demise in England and America as many riders sustained ruptures and other injuries caused by their uncontrollable iron-wheeled playthings. Then, in 1838, a Scotch blacksmith named Kirkpatrick Macmillan built the first draisine-type vehicle that allowed the driver to ride with both feet off the ground. Propulsion was furnished by two pedals connected by rods to the rear axle. Though Macmillan's machine may be considered the world's first bicycle, the vehicle attracted little attention at the time, due to public contempt for the hobby horse of earlier years. In fact, Macmillan himself was arrested a number of times for running down pedestrians.

Twenty years passed before the next major development, the rotary crank, was introduced by Frenchmen Pierre Lallement and Ernest Michaux. Their vehicle, called a velocipede, operated on a principle similar to the child's

Some English bicycles of 1887.

A cartoon of 1895 has a heading, "If the country roads are not improved."

tricycle of today, with pedals directly attached to the front axle.

Early velocipedes were very heavy. Their wooden wheels fitted wtih iron tires vibrated so furiously over the rough roads of the time that the vehicle quickly earned the nickname "bone-shaker." Nevertheless, during the 1860s, a velociped craze swept both England and America. Within three months in 1869, 50 velocipede riding schools were opened in New York City alone—bearing names such as *Amphcyclotheatrus* and *Gymnocyclidium*. Newspapers derided the craze by dubbing the heavy vehicles "wood locomotives." Like the earlier hobby horse craze, velocipede mania vanished as quickly as it had appeared.

But bicycle innovators had not given up. The year 1868 saw the introduction of rubber tires. In 1869, the word *bicycle* itself was patented in England by one J. Stassen. Meanwhile, the size of the vehicle's front wheel grew to outlandish proportions. Since one revolution of the pedals turned the front wheel once, the larger the wheel, the further each revolution would propel the cycle. So, front wheels with 54-inch or even 64-inch diameters were common, while the rear wheel shrank to as little as 12 inches.

These asymetrical vehicles, known as ordinaries or high-wheelers, made cycling easier on the legs, but harder on the head. Since the rider sat high above the huge front wheel, he could not reach the ground with his feet when the vehicle began to tumble. A rider striking a stone or hole in the road could easily be thrown forward on his face. Serious injuries, even death, were not rare among avid cyclists. Still, the ordinary's popularity gained steadily. By 1878, 50,000 highwheelers were in use in England alone, not to mention thousands of tricycles for the less daring.

The American bicycle industry had been born the year before, when Colonel Albert A. Pope of Boston commissioned the Weed Sewing Machine Company to make 50 "Columbia" bikes in a corner of their shop in Hartford, Connecticut. Bicycle manufacture quickly became one of America's leading mass production industries. By 1892, applications for bicycle patents had grown so numerous that the U.S. Patent Office had to establish a special department for cycles and their parts.

The growth of the American bicycle industry played a large part in the development of both the automobile and the airplane. Almost every mechanical improvement in the early automobile can be traced to the bicycle, including ball bearings, the pneumatic tire, speed transmission, shaft drive, and brakes. Automotive pioneers Charles Duryea, Elwood Haynes, and Alexander Winton were all involved in the bicycle business before turning their sights to the horseless carriage. Wilbur and Orville Wright were bike repairmen in Dayton, Ohio, before they made their historic flight at Kitty Hawk.

It wasn't until around 1880, with the introduction of the safety bike, that the two-wheeler began to resemble the modern bicycle in general outline. Invented by Englishman H.J. Lawson, the safety bike reduced the size of the front wheel and set the seat lower over the bar so that the rider could stop his bicycle with his feet when a fall was imminent.

Then, in 1879, came another major development: the chain-driven *Flying Dutchman.* Now the pedals, instead of turning the front wheel, moved a rope that turned a grooved pulley on the rear axle. The *Rover,* an early safety bicycle built by J.K. Starley of England, included chain drive, direct steering, brakes, cushion tires, and a diamond-shaped frame, all features of the modern bicycle. The year 1887 saw the introduction of the curiously named *Psycho,* with a lamp and a bell fitted to the frame. Other bikes with less than inviting names included the *Broncho* and the *Kangaroo.* By 1893, the highwheeler had gone the way of the hobby horse and velocipede.

The ensuing bicycle craze of the 1890s reached unbelievable heights in both England and the United States. Bicycles of the time were not the utilitarian vehicles they are in many parts of the world today, but sheer playthings. Everyone had to own one.

By 1895, English and American bicycle manufacturers could scarcely keep up with the demand as bike riding became *the* warm-weather pastime. Streets and roads were filled with sporting bikers of both sexes. Bicycle cops appeared, on the lookout for "scorchers" who dared to race their bikes on public thoroughfares at speeds of up to 20 miles an hour. "Wolves a-wheel" jockeyed for position behind female riders for a glimpse of their seated derrieres. Bicycle paths began sprouting up in many cities.

The most famous bicycle path in America was probably the Coney Island Bikeway in Brooklyn. Opened in 1895, the route stretched five miles between Prospect Park and the amusement area of Coney Island. The road, known as Coney Island Boulevard, consisted of two crushed bluestone pathways on either side of a central boulevard reserved for carriages. Each

During the 1950s, bicycle racing as a gambling sport was the rage in Japan, topping all other forms of entertainment, including the movies. In a typical year, Japanese gamblers bet over $150 million on bicycle races—and that figure accounts only for legal wagers.

This two-wheeler appeared in the late 1880s. It was brought to America in 1896, and was used as an advertising medium.

pathway took bikers in a different direction, making the bike paths perhaps the first one-way streets in the nation. The entire route was lined with trees. The road still exists, renamed Ocean Parkway, though the two bike lanes have long since become service roads for the central boulevard.

One of the oddest bikeways in the nation stretched between Pasadena and Los Angeles in Southern California. Called by some the predecessor of the modern superhighway, the Pasadena Cycleway consisted of a narrow elevated road, similar to a boardwalk, wending its way between houses and over empty fields. Lamps were provided for night riding. Bike rental and repair shops stood at each end of the cycleway, and toll booths appeared sporadically along the nine-mile route.

Incidentally, the era of the bikeway is far from over. The Federal Government has already approved $120 million for bikeway facilities all across the country.

Tandem bicycles also enjoyed a vogue during the Gay Nineties. Successful tandem bikes had been built as early as 1869, but the vehicle remained a curiosity even during its heyday, and never achieved the widespread popularity legend might suggest. The words of a well-known 1890s song were probably more humorous at the time than the modern listener might realize:

Daisy, Daisy, give me your
answer, do.
I'm half crazy, all for the love
of you!
It won't be a stylish marriage,
I can't afford a carriage.
But you'll look sweet,
upon the seat
Of a bicycle built for two!

Like the single-passenger vehicles of their time, tandem bikes took many shapes. Some placed the riders side by side, others positioned the rear rider higher than the front rider so that both could enjoy the view. Three-seaters began to appear, then four-seaters, culminating in the monstrous 10-seat *decemtuple*, a 23-foot-long curiousity that toured Europe and America late in the decade. But even the *decemtuple* would seem a mere child's trike compared to the 72-foot-long, 34-seater built in 1876 by a Danish manufacturer.

Other curiosity bicycles appeared on the scene as European and American inventors attempted to make the bike a more utilitarian vehicle. Traveling professionals took their shops on wheels, with bicycling barbers, cigar dealers, ice cream peddlers, lawn mowers, and hurdy-gurdy men among them. In 1899, a water bike was constructed with paddles fitted to the pedals. Ice bikes appeared, fitted with skates and propelled by a spiked wheel. One enterprising inventor from Germany even constructed a bicycle that ran on dog-power, with two pooches running on treadmills fitted to the bicycle frame!

The so-called *Eiffel Tower* bicycle lofted its rider 10 feet above ground atop a metal framework that did indeed resemble the Parisian landmark. In 1897, a Boston manufacturer constructed an eight-man tricycle that weighed close to 3,000 pounds with its riders. The 17-foot-long trike was fitted with two 11-foot-diameter rear wheels and 18-inch tires! The front wheel was a mere six feet in diameter.

Nilsson crossed the United States on a unicycle.

At the other end of the scale we find *midget* bikes, complete in every detail, that measured as little as nine inches from axle to axle. As early as 1869, P.T. Barnum had ordered a custom-built velocipede for the midget Tom Thumb. The bike is now on exhibit in the Henry Ford Museum in Dearborn, Michigan. The smallest working bicycle of all time, a two-pound vehicle with two-and-one-eighth-inch wheels, was ridden regularly by a full-grown Las Vegas showman, Charlie Charles.

The armed forces took advantage of improved bicycle technology by constructing special vehicles for their "bicycle corps." Troops were equipped with lightweight folding bikes that could be carried on the back when the

In 1971, Englishman Ray Reece set the record for round-the-world cycling by circling the globe in just 143 days.

During the five years ending in 1977, over 68 million bikes were sold in the United States, compared to 60 million automobiles during the same period.

roads were muddied. The frames were fitted with special attachments to hold a rifle. During World War I, bicycles were used extensively to lay telegraph wire. There was even a tricycle fitted with a mounted gun!

While many bike enthusiasts of the time were content to laze along on a sunny afternoon on a shady cycleway, other bikers took to racing. Bicycle racing had begun in the days of the high-wheeler, but with the advent of the safety bike, racing reached unprecedented heights in Europe and America. In 1896, bike racing was included in the reinstituted Olympic games. For a time, bicycle racing outdrew even baseball in this country. During the 1950s, bicycle racing as a gambling sport was the rage in Japan, topping all other forms of entertainment, including the movies. In a typical year, Japanese gamblers bet over $150 million on bicycle races—and that figure accounts only for legal wagers.

Bicycle racers of the 1890s achieved speed records that would startle the modern cyclist. In 1899, Charles "Mile-a-Minute" Murphy earned his nickname by covering a mile in just under 60 seconds on a board track laid over the tracks of the Long Island Railroad. Murphy had help in his feat—he pedaled behind a train fitted with an enormous windshield so that the cyclist was riding in a near vacuum.

In 1941, Alf Letourner also had the benefit of a windscreen when he achieved a mark of 108.92 miles per hour on a California highway. Alf followed a midget auto racer. In 1973, Dr. Allan Abbott pedaled in a near vacuum when he set the modern record for bicycle velocity, 140.5 miles per hour, racing behind a car over the Bonneville Salt Flats in Utah. One old record that remains unbroken is the mark set in 1926 by Leon Vanderstuyft. Racing behind a motorcycle, but without a windscreen, the Belgian cyclist started from a dead stop and covered 76 miles, 604 yards in one hour on a bike track in Montlhéry, France. Modern cyclists might find it difficult to achieve such a speed even on a downhill incline.

In 1891, the first of the legendary six-day bicycle races was held in Madison Square Garden, New York. The maiden race included 40 entries, of which only six finished, with Bill Martin winning on a highwheeler. The event became an immediate spectator sensation, attracting close to 100,000 persons over the course of a week. The race remained a one-man event until 1899, when two-man teams first appeared. The record for six-day marathon racing is an impressive 2,093 miles.

Today, the most important bicycle race in the world is the annual Tour de France. Begun in 1903, by a publisher as a circulation stunt, the race is now one of Europe's major sporting events. Originally 3,560 miles long, the present course stretches about 2,780 miles through France, Spain, Switzerland, Italy, and Belgium. Bikers average 200 miles per day over the near month-long race, and stop riding at sunset. An estimated 15 million people in France alone turn out to watch the bikers as they wend their way over hill and dale, and climb over mountain passes as high as 8,000 feet. In some towns, petty criminals are released from jail for the day

World's largest bicycle, built in 1968 in England, seated 21 riders.

so that they can take in the spectacle. One observer has calculated that if one-third of all the Frenchmen lose one-third of a day's work due to the race, the Tour de France takes a toll of close to two billion dollars on the French economy!

There is no comparable event in the United States, but American cyclists have proved quite adept at cross-country biking—literally cross-country, that is. In 1940, Raymond Bryan rode from New York to San Francisco in 27 days, 11 hours. By 1973, Paul Cornish had lowered the record coast-to-coast time to a mere 13 days, five hours, averaging 225 miles per day. The year 1973 also saw a pair of young Americans pedal around the country on a tandem bike, covering 4,837 miles in four months.

In 1934, a vaudeville performer named Walter Nilsson set an unenviable record when he pedaled from coast to coast on and eight-and-a-half-foot-high unicycle! Nilsson covered 3,306 miles in just 117 days on the single-wheeled vehicle without falling once, an achievement that earned Robert Ripley's award for "The Most Unbelievable Feat of the Year." Speaking of unicycles: in 1967, Steve McPeak of Tacoma, Washington, climbed atop a 32-foot-high unicycle and pedaled between two towers 100 feet apart.

But all bicycle records seem to pale when compared to the feats of a number of individuals who have taken it upon themselves to pedal around the world. As early as 1897, Mr. and Mrs. H. Darwin McIlrath accomplished the feat on a pair of safety bikes. In 1971, Englishman Ray Reece set the record for round-the-world cycling by circling the globe in just 143 days. Itinerant lecturer Walter Stolle has pedaled an estimated 270,000 miles in his lifetime, traveling through 140 nations—and suffering 26 robberies en route.

But surely the most incredible feat of bicycle daring in history was the round-the-world journey of American Thomas Stevens. Beginning in San Francisco, Stevens pedaled across America, sailed across the Atlantic, cycled through Europe, the Middle East, India, and the Orient, then boarded a ship for San Francisco, completing the round-the-world journey in under three years. What makes Stevens's feat so remarkable was its date: 1884 to 1887, *before* the development of the safety bike. Stevens actually circled the globe on a high-wheeler with a 50-inch-diameter front wheel! Since John Dunlop was not to invent the pneumatic tire until 1894, Stevens's "vicious cycle" was equipped with rough-riding solid tires. Ouch!

Billiards

Billiards at a fashionable gathering during the 1890s.

Games such as croquet, archery, and lawn bowling are usually considered pastimes of the upper classes, while many gambling and team games find their most avid players at the other end of the social scale. Billiards has historically been one of the few games to find its greatest popularity at *both* ends of the social spectrum.

The first professional billiards championships were played by English gentlemen dressed in black tie and tails. Even today, the game is sometimes referred to as the "aristocrat of sports." Yet for many years, the pool hall was considered a house of ill fame, the hangout of juvenile delinquents, hustlers, and petty criminals. Politicians and clergymen decried the game, blaming the pool hall for everything from truancy to alcoholism.

Today, billiards and pool seem to find their fans closer to the middle of the social spectrum. Experts predicted that the advent of television would spell the doom of billiards in this country, but middle-class Americans are now taking up the game in increasing numbers. An estimated 20 million Americans play pool each year. Over a half-million homes in North America are now equipped with a billiard table of some kind. The game is booming in many other countries, too. During the 1960s, close to 9,000 new billiard parlors were built in Japan each year!

The Japanese learned billiards when they captured Singapore from the British during World War II. Shorter in stature than the British, the Japanese found the billiard tables too high for comfortable play. So they cut off six inches from each table leg, and took to billiards with a passion.

We don't know what the Japanese call the games, but Americans often use the words *billiards* and *pool* interchangeably. Actually, the terms refer to two entirely different games. Let's have a look at both, and a few of their cousins.

Billiards—sometimes known as English billiards in this country—is played on a table measuring 12 feet by six-and-a-half feet, with six pockets. Only three balls are used: a red ball, a white ball, and a spotted white ball. A line, called the balk line, is drawn across the table 29 inches from one of the shorter cushions. A semicircle 11½ inches in radius is drawn around the midpoint of the balk line.

Each white ball serves as the "cue" ball for one of the players—one player must always strike the plain white ball with his stick, the other the spotted white ball. A player continues to shoot as long as he makes a scoring play. His opponent takes over when he fails to make a score.

There are three scoring plays in billiards: the winning hazard, the losing hazard, and the cannon. The word *hazard* originally referred to a pocket, possibly because the pockets were themselves descendants of the hoops and other obstacles used on the earliest billiard tables. *Cannon* is a corruption of *carom,* from the French equivalent, *carambole.*

A player scores a winning hazard when his ball drives either his opponent's ball or the red ball into a pocket. Two points are awarded for pocketing the opponent's ball, and three points for pocketing the red ball.

A player scores an ineptly-named losing hazard when his ball is pocketed after striking either his opponent's ball or the red ball. He scores two points for pocketing his ball after it has struck his opponent's ball, and three points for pocketing his ball off the red.

A cannon is scored when the striker's ball hits both his opponent's ball and the red ball, either simultaneously or successively. If no balls are pocketed, the cannon scores two points. If the striker's ball is pocketed after scoring a cannon, the striker gains an additional two or three points, depending on which ball, opponent's or red, was struck first by the striker's ball.

There's much more to billiards than the rules we've briefly outlined. Special regulations govern balls lying in the balk area. A player can score points when his opponent is the striker. But it should be clear that the game of billiards is much different from the game Americans usually enjoy on a billiard table: pool.

As every red-blooded American should know, pool, or pocket billiards, is played with 15 numbered balls and one white cue ball. The table measures five feet by 10 feet, significantly smaller than the table used for billiards. Players score by pocketing one of the numbered balls after contact with the cue ball, the only ball the player may strike with his stick. The striker must indicate before the shot which ball he intends to pocket, and which pocket he is aiming at.

There are many variations of pocket billiards. One of the most popular is *Eight Ball.* In this game, the first player to pocket one of the striped or solid-colored numbered balls must then attempt to pocket the other six similar balls, and then the eight ball. His opponent must pocket the other seven balls, striped or solid-colored as the case may be, and then the eight ball. A player pocketing the eight ball prematurely loses the game. Thus, if the eight ball is between the cue ball and the next ball that the striker must pocket, the striker is in a very difficult position—"behind the eight ball."

In the game of *Rotation,* the balls must be played in numerical order, with points awarded to the striker according to the numerical value of the pocketed ball. Since the 15 balls add up to 120 points, 61 points are required to win a game. 15-ball pocket billiards is similar to *Rotation* in that points are awarded for pocketing a ball according to its number. But in this game, the balls need not be pocketed in numerical order.

Nine Ball is played with—you guessed it—nine balls, the first eight of which must be pocketed in numerical order. A player wins the game by pocketing the nine ball after the first eight balls have been pocketed, or off a combination shot with the "on" ball—the ball that must be pocketed next. In *One-Pocket,* each player chooses a pocket and scores a point only for a ball sunk in that pocket, either by himself or by his opponent.

Snooker, which is now more popular in Britain than billiards itself, combines elements of both billiards and pool. The snooker table is identical in size to the large English billiard table, and includes a balk line and semicircle, as in billiards. In America, the game is sometimes played on the smaller pool table. Twenty-two balls in all are used: a cue ball, fifteen red balls, and six colored balls.

During each turn, the player must first pocket one of the red balls, then one of the non-red balls, then a red-ball, and so on. Pocketed red balls remain off the table; pocketed non-red balls are replaced on the table. When all red balls have been pocketed, the players must then attempt to pocket the non-red balls in ascending order of value: the yellow, green, brown, blue, pink, and black balls are worth two, three, four, five, six, and seven points, respectively. Players are awarded the appropriate points for a non-red ball whenever one is pocketed, and receive one point for each red ball pocketed.

The term *snooker* refers to a lie in which the "on" ball—the non-red ball that must be pocketed next—is obstructed by another ball. The cue ball must not strike any ball without first hitting the "on" ball. So a snookered player must attempt a carom shot that takes the cue ball around the obstructing ball or balls and into contact with the "on" ball. The term comes from either a slang word applied to first-year cadets at an English military school, or another word meaning "to ambush" in parts of England.

Snooker was developed from pool and billiards late in the 19th century. One story has it that the game originated among English troops in India. Tiring of ordinary billiards, the soldiers added a black ball from a set of pool balls to spice up their game. Then they added a pink ball, then a blue, and eventually all seven of the solid-colored balls. But the game may well have originated instead from *Pyramids,* a game similar to pool that some historians claim was played in Persia as long ago as the 12th century. In any case, by the 1880s, snooker had reached England. In 1916, the first official champion was crowned.

Carom billiards in its various forms is played on a pool table without pockets, with a red ball, a white ball, and a spotted white ball. To score in simple carom billiards, a player must drive his cue ball against both of the other balls. In three-cushion carom billiards, a scoring player's ball must strike the cushions three times, as well as both of the other balls.

There are dozens of other billiard games, some widely known, others common only in a particular area. But all are offspring of the age-old game we now call English billiards.

The exact origin of billiards itself is obscure. The Scythian philosopher Anacharsis wrote of a game similar to billiards that he observed being played in Greece during the sixth century B.C. The English, French, Chinese, Irish, Italians, and Spanish have all claimed credit for inventing the game. But most historians conclude that billiards evolved from a variety of old games played with balls and a stick of some kind.

It may be that billiards evolved from the game of bowls, or lawn bowling, which was quite popular in England during the late Middle Ages. According to some accounts, avid English bowlers became so fed up with rainy weather and wet grass that they took their game indoors. But the size of the indoor bowling "alley" was limited by the size of the rooms in which the game was played. The smaller courts were less challenging. To make the game more difficult, bowlers began propelling their bowls with sticks instead of rolling them. Gradually, hoops and other obstacles were added to the alley. Then, at some unknown date, the court was raised to a table top, and *viola*—billiards was born.

Another interesting, though apocryphal, tale traces the origin of the game in England to a 16th-century London pawnbroker named William Kew. The Englishman allegedly took down the three balls identifying his pawnbroker's shop and used a yardstick to push the balls around in the street. Eventually, young canons from nearby St. Paul's Cathedral joined in the game. *Bill's yard*-stick became *billiard* stick, and later, *billiard cue,* from Kew. Of course, the clergymen invented the *cannon* shot.

We don't know for sure where billiards was invented, but it was in France that the game first achieved widespread popularity. The 15th-century monarch Louis XI played some form of the game. A century later, Henri III installed a primitive billiard table in his residence at Blois. Disregarding the tale of William Kew, the word *billiards* itself is probably French in origin, perhaps from *bille,* (stick or ball), or from *billart* (curved stick). By the 16th century, the word billiards was in use in both France and England.

Like their French counterparts, English monarchs seem to have taken a shine to billiards. During her captivity in 1576, Mary Queen of Scots complained that her billiard table had been removed. Thirty years later, James I ordered a "billiarde bourde, twelve foote longe and fower foote broade."

Shakespeare would have us believe that the ancient Romans enjoyed billiards. But the line, "Let us to billiards," which appears in *Antony and Cleopatra* is surely anachronistic. Oddly enough, the game had already appeared in America by the time the Bard composed the line! In 1565, Spanish settlers in St. Augustine, Florida, listed billiard equipment among their baggage, and presumably played the first game of billiards on this side of the Atlantic.

Early billard games employed only two balls. A third—the "neutral red ball"—was added to the French game during the reign of Louis XIV, who played the billiards on the advice of his physicians. The cannon shot, which requires three balls, did not become part of the game in England until late in the 18th century. By 1800, the game was played basically as it is today.

French drawings of early billiard players show a table with a hoop near each end, and cues resem-

Louis XIV playing billiards. After an engraving by Réouvain.

bling short hockey sticks. At some point, the hoops gave way to pockets, one at each end. Later, the pockets were moved to the corners and side pockets were added. Slender cues began to replace thicker maces. In 1807, a French political prisoner named Captain Migaud invented the round leather cue tip, which provided considerably more ball control than earlier cue tips. But leather tips slide easily off the ball. An abrasive of some kind was needed.

For a time, players roughened the cue tip by rubbing it against a whitewashed ceiling. Then, an Englishman named Jack Carr discovered the chalk would fill the bill nicely. Carr toured Europe and demonstrated a billiards dexterity previously unknown, using his chalked cue tip to put spin on the ball. Thus the *masse* shot entered billiards, and the word *English* entered billiard terminology, referring to backspin placed on any kind of ball. Carr peddled a "special-formula twisting chalk" that he credited for his great skill, but actually Carr's magic substance was chalk, pure and simple.

To one John Thurston we owe the invention of the rubber table cushion, which replaced the crude felt-stuffed cushions previously in use. In 1845, Thurston patented the use of vulcanized rubber for billiard cushions. A year later, he patented the slate table bed that replaced the wood bed.

A billiard room was considered *de riguer* in fashionable Victorian homes. Architects of the era took great pains to design the room so that persons entering or sitting in the raised spectator section would not disturb the players. Even the fireplace was carefully positioned to avoid distraction. A billiards etiquette book from the period advised that persons about to enter a billiard room should listen through the door until they heard the balls click, so that their entrance would not disturb a player about to shoot.

During the 19th century, billiard balls made of ivory were in vogue. Since the billiard cue strikes its ball with the smallest surface area of any implement used in ball games, billiard balls have long demanded delicate manufacture. Traditionally, the finest tusks were reserved for billiard balls.

In 1880, crystalate balls made of nitrocellulose, camphor, and alcohol began to appear. In 1926, they were made obligatory by the Billiards Association and Control Council, the London-based governing body. Billiard equipment had now evolved basically into modern form. But the game itself was fast being superceded by its cousins: in the United States, by pocket and carom billiards; and in England, by snooker.

The term, *U.S. billiards* is sometimes used to designate the games of carom billiards and pocket billiards, or pool. Forms of pocket billiards were probably played on billiard tables from the time these tables first began to sport six pockets. Authorities date the real start of U.S. billiards from the year 1859, when the first American championship match was played in Detroit. The game was carom billiards, and the table measured six feet by 12 feet.

Within 10 years of that match, U.S. billiards championships were being played on a table measuring five-and-a-half feet by 11 feet. By 1876, the now standard five-by-ten-foot table was the rule. Four-ball and three-ball carom billiards in their varied forms remained the predominant billiard games here until well into the 20th century, when pocket billiards began its rise to eventual domination.

When the rules of pocket billiards were standardized around the turn of the century, Thomas Hueston and Alfredo DeOro were the premier players in this country. Ralph Greenleaf, called by many the greatest pocket billiards player of all time, dominated the game in the 1920s and early 30s. Until 1945, Walker Cochran was the premier three-cushion billiards player. By that time, carom billiards maestro Willie Hoppe had already become a legend.

Hoppe was an accomplished billiards player by the age of five. In 1906, he won the world title from Frenchman Maurice Vignaux at the age of 16—still wearing kneepants. Hoppe went on to dominate championship play for 46 years, capturing 51 titles in four different carom billiards games.

During World War II, Hoppe and pocket billiards ace Willie Mosconi exhibited their skills for the American armed forces. Mosconi first won his pocket billiards world title in 1941. He went on to 12 more championship victories until his retirement from title play 16 years later.

Willie's prowess with the pool cue has long been legendary. In 1956, Mosconi was matched against Jimmy Moore in a world championship tournament match in Kingston, North Carolina. Moore took the table for the break and played a safety. That was a mistake—Moore's *last* mistake. Mosconi took the table and proceeded to pocket 150 consecutive balls for the victory. Moore never got a chance to shoot again.

Noted pool sharp Luther Lassiter was another victim of Mosconi's selfish control of the green baize table. In a 1953 world championship match in San Francisco, Willie won the crown by running the

Welker Cochrane (left) posing before a match with Willie Hoppe.

game in only two innings. One year later, Willie set the world record for consecutively pocketed balls by running 526 balls in an exhibition match in Springfield, Ohio. That's better than 37 racks without a single miss!

Consecutive runs in English billiards are considerably easier to accomplish, as the world records for the longest billiards runs—or "highest breaks"—can attest. In 1907, an Englishman named Cook set the official record by racking up 42,746 points without a non-scoring shot. The same year, English billiards champ Tom Reece accomplished an amazing break of 499,135 during a London match. But, alas, the mark was not recognized as official, because no member of the press or public bothered to remain on hand for the 85 hours it took Reece to accomplish his feat.

Modern pool parlors are a far cry from the seedy, crime-ridden establishments of earlier notoriety. Today's pool parlors are often air-conditioned, with thick rugs, excellent lighting, and the finest pool equipment available. But pool has now become most popular as a bar game in the U.S.. Many taverns devote more of their space to the pursuit of pool pleasure than to the enjoyment of the grape. Though exact figures are unavailable, the prevalence of pool as a bar game has probably made *Eight Ball,* the most commonly played bar game, the reigning favorite of all pool games in this country.

Whether a championship match played under the glare of television lights or a friendly game in a local tavern, the age-old game of billiards remains one of man's most diverting pastimes. And pool-table banter must rank as one of the game's most appealing features, as this ditty from a decades-old issue of *Punch* suggests:

Oh! the man of the cue has but little to do,
If you listen to popular rumour;
From daylight to dark, he's as blithe as a lark,
And he sparkles with wit and good humour!

BOOKS

"Of making many books, there is no end."

Are those the sentiments of a browser in a modern bookstore? Or a worker at the U.S. Copyright Office, besieged by thousands of new books and manuscripts each year? A librarian? A printer?

No, those words were written thousands of years ago, by the author of the Old Testament Book of Ecclesiastes!

There are now over 4,000 publishers "making many books" in the United States, and some 80,000 stores that sell books of some kind. A list of books currently in print might contain more than 400,000 titles, and in an average month about 3,000 new titles join the list. Some works are printed in editions of a few hundred, others in many thousands—and each year about 40 books will be printed in a million or more copies!

Remember: these figures pertain only to the United States. West Germany, with a population a quarter as large as the United States, has a bookstore for every 10,000 persons, and publishes more books annually than the United States!

How many books there were in the Old Testament world, or in any other ancient civilization, we can't be sure of. Most of the written material of former times has long since disintegrated or disappeared—just as centuries from today, most of our books will have vanished, too.

But we do know that the making of "books" began with the clay tablets of ancient Mesopotamia. The oldest surviving writing dates from 3500 B.C., in Sumeria, while the oldest Egyptian "book" is a papyrus scroll of maxims from 2500 B.C.

The ancient Greeks traded and sold manuscripts regularly. In Rome, where private libraries were popular among the wealthy, new and second-hand manuscripts were sold from stalls in the Forum. Some contemporary authors could be read throughout the Empire.

The ancients wrote on scrolls of papyrus, made from the papyrus reed, or *biblos,* that grew in the Nile Delta. In the second century B.C., the craftsmen of Pergamum, in Asia Minor, learned how to produce parchment from the skins of calves, goats, sheep, and other animals. Parchment did not crack when folded, and could accept writing on both sides. While a papyrus manuscript was constructed of overlapping squares of papyrus pasted together, then rolled up, a parchment manuscript could be arranged in folded leaves.

So the introduction of parchment led to the *codex,* or parchment-leaf book, which was already in use during the Roman Empire. Apparently the codex was first adopted for law books, since the pages of a codex could be added or deleted easily as laws changed.

Not a single scroll or codex from the golden ages of Greece or Rome has survived until modern times. The oldest Latin work we possess dates from the fourth century. Libraries were established in the ancient world to preserve written works, but these libraries were plundered or destroyed centuries ago. Among the largest ancient libraries were those in Pergamum and Ephesus in Asia Minor, and in Alexandria, Egypt. At its height, the Alexandria library contained some 750,000 scrolls—all of which were destroyed by various invaders.

Libraries have not fared well anywhere in the world. In the 1560s, the Spanish Bishop of Yucatan, in Mexico, burned the entire native literature of the Mayan Indians, claiming that the writing contained only "superstition and lies of the devil."

After the collapse of the Roman Empire, the copying and preservation of written works in Europe was carried out almost entirely by monks in their isolated monasteries, especially in the British Isles. In the 12th century, vendors called *stationarii* began to peddle books near the Universities of Paris and Bologna, beginning what we might call the bookseller's trade. The following century saw the introduction of paper-making, and with it, the flourishing of books in many parts of Europe.

Babylonian spelling book written on clay in 442 B.C.

Of the 200 or so "Gutenberg Bibles" printed, only 48 survive, and one of these recently fetched $2.5 million at auction—making it the most expensive book ever purchased!

Around 700, the Koreans had allegedly produced books by wood block printing, but the first printing press in Europe did not appear until almost eight centuries later. In 1455, a German named Johann Gutenberg became the first to produce a book by means of movable type. Of the 200 or so "Gutenberg Bibles" printed, only 48 survive, and one of these recently fetched $2.5 million at auction—making it the most expensive book ever purchased!

England's first printer, William Caxton, began his work in 1476; by 1500, there were printing presses in some 250 European

The Milbank papyrus of the Egyptian Book of the Dead. *The document is in the form of a roll which is about 40 feet in length. (Date uncertain.)*

cities and towns, and 40,000 titles in print.

In the earliest codices, single sheets of vellum were folded once and sewn together along the fold. Later, books were formed from larger sheets folded a number of times, with their outer folds cut, as they are today. Thin pieces of wood were placed at the front and back of the codex to keep the pages flat, and later were attached by a leather spine. The leather eventually covered the wood to form a binding as we now know it.

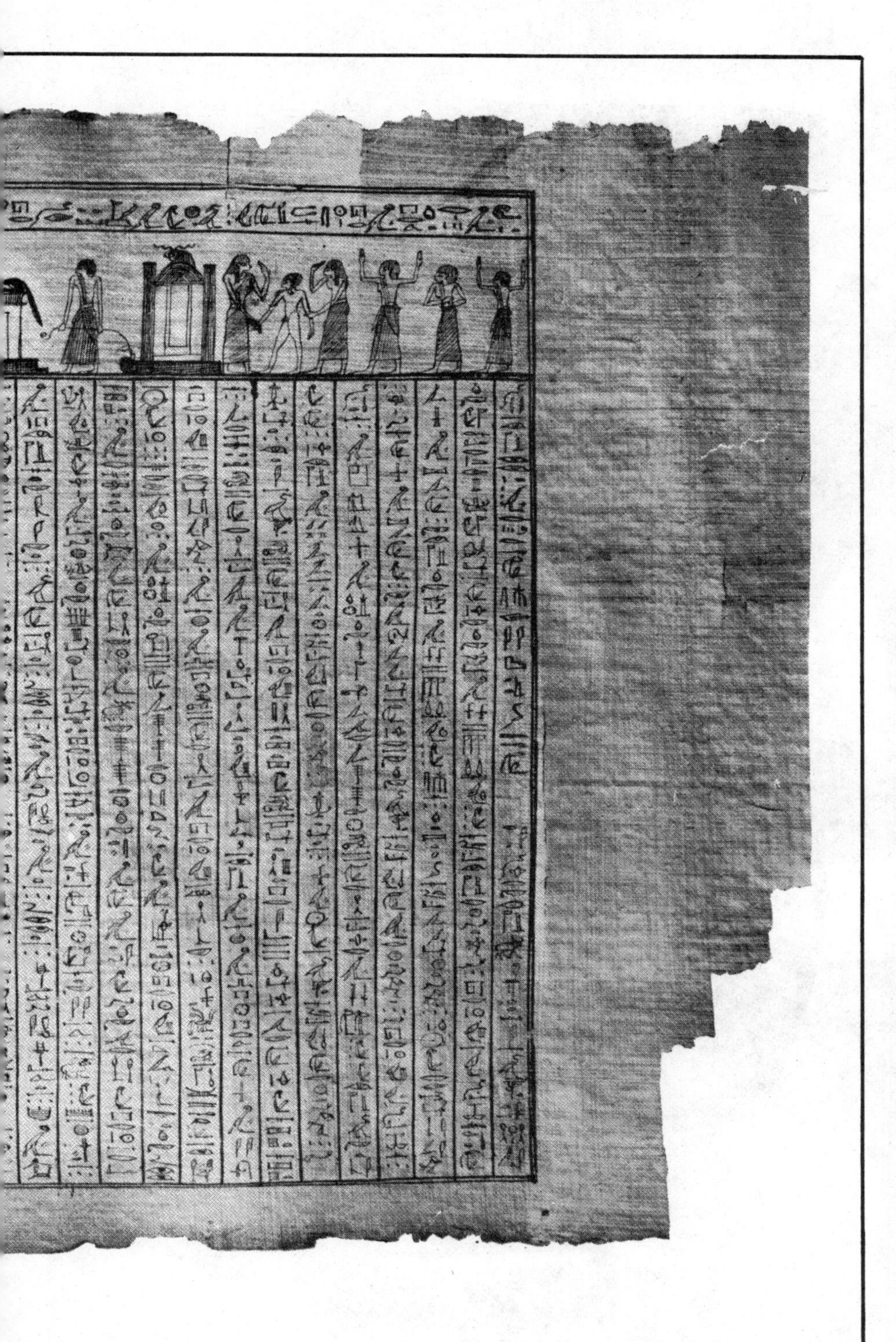

The first book to be copyrighted in the United States, *The Philadelphia Spelling Book,* was printed in 1790.

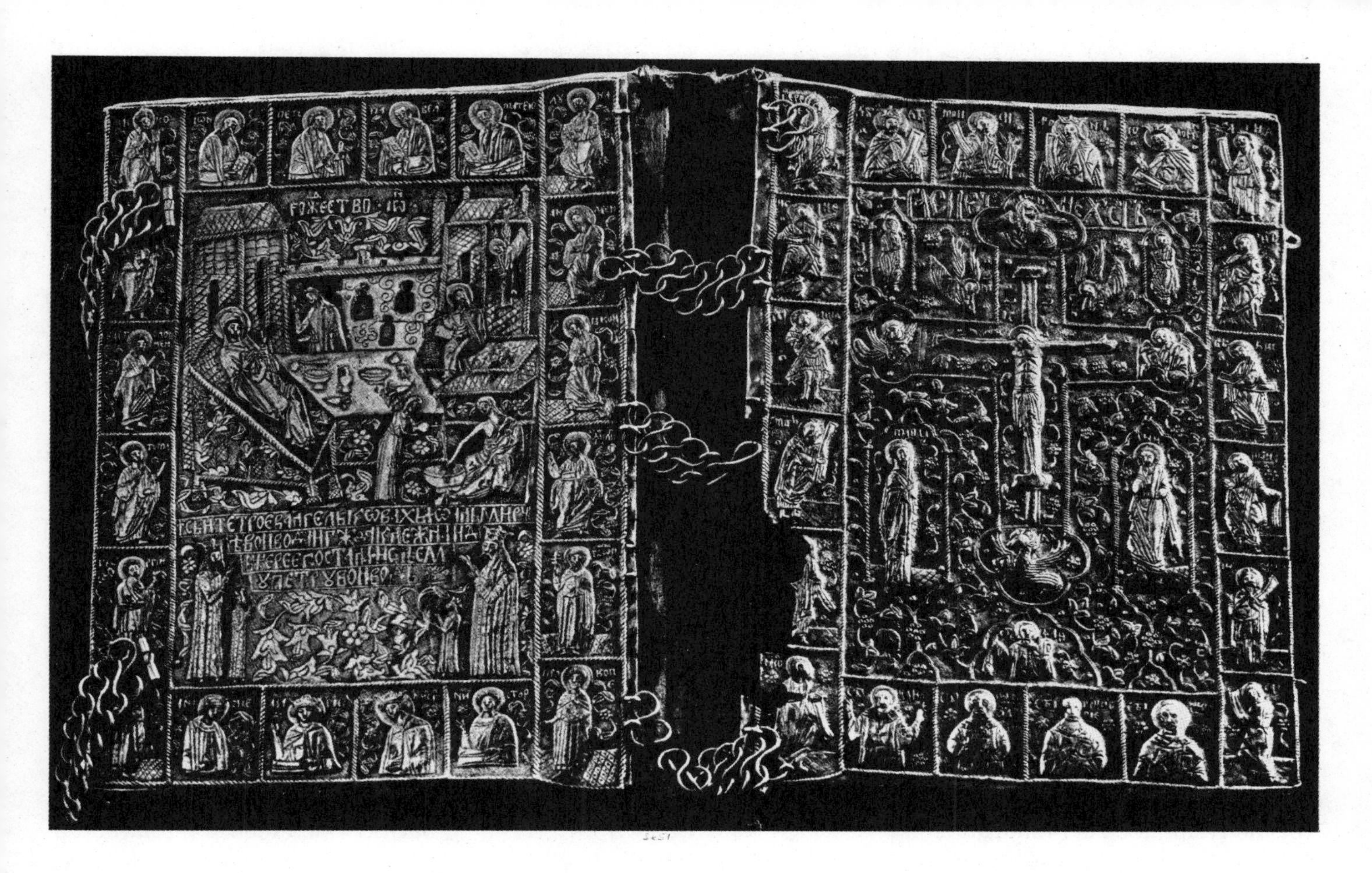

The Gospel of Prince Tchiobanu, 16th century. This book is located in the Monastery of Dionisiu, Mount Athos, Greece.

Books intended for the nobility were bound in leather ornamented with jewels, ivory, enamel, and precious metals. The oldest surviving book of this kind is a seventh-century Gospel.

Until the 17th century, books were often displayed without a binding—the buyer could select his own binding when he purchased the book. And as long ago as ancient Rome, the author Seneca complained that book buyers were paying more attention to a book's cover than they were to its contents!

Indonesian books being sold by a 20th-century vendor. Books are made of strips of bamboo decorated with all kinds of symbols.

Speaking of bindings, the mistress of French novelist Eugene Sue dictated in her will that a set of Sue's books be bound in her own skin!

After printing began in Europe, books remained in appearance very much like their handwritten ancestors. Printers designed type faces to resemble the handwriting styles then in vogue, hand-lettered the chapter headings and initials, and added their own illustrations. Pagination wasn't common until the 15th century, and the title page, not until the 16th century. Printers at the time also sold their own books. Only in the 19th century did publishers and booksellers take on separate roles.

The first European book to reach America was an almanac carried by Columbus. But the first book printed in America was the work of Cambridge, Massachusetts printer Stephen Day, who turned out a 1639 edition of Psalms. In 1642, Hezekiah Usher of Boston opened America's first bookshop—or at least, the first shop to sell books, for most Colonial "bookshops" also peddled an assortment of items from sealing wax and cough medicine to lemons and chocolate. The favorite reading matter of the colonists included Greek and Roman classics, almanacs, current English works, Bibles in various languages and copies of sermons—some of which were produced with paperback covers. By 1711, there were some 30 booksellers in Boston alone.

The first book to be copyrighted in the United States, *The Philadelphia Spelling Book,* was printed in 1790. The first American novel that could be called a "best-seller" was *Charlotte, a Tale of Truth,* published four years later. Over 200 editions have been printed to date. And the first erotic novel to be published and sold in the United States was John Cleland's *Memoirs of a Woman of Pleasure,* better known as *Fanny Hill,* which has been bringing a blush to cheeks since 1786. Another popular erotic novel of the time masqueraded as *Aristotle's Masterpieces.* Attempts have been made to censor these and other books since before the United States was formed, but most of these works have survived, even flourished, in spite of the restraints. As Montaigne wrote, "books being once forbidden become more saleable and public."

By 1850, the publishing business in the United States was centered in New York, and many of today's publishing giants were already in existence. These firms initially sold their books only at their own stores. Before World War I, however, 90 percent of American books were not sold by stores at all, but by mail order and itinerant book hawkers.

The book club—a German idea—first appeared in America in 1926, with the Book-of-the-Month Club and the Literary Guild. By the way, the first work offered by the Book-of-the-Month Club was *Lolly Willowes, or the Loving Huntsman,* by Sylvia Townsend Warner. By the late 1940s, the book clubs of America could list three million members, accounting for about 30 percent of all American book sales.

Gutenberg and friends examine the first printed page.

Today, the largest publishing companies in America include McGraw-Hill of New York, and Time, Inc., whose net revenues, including publishing, are over a billion dollars annually. But the largest publisher in the world is actually the U.S. Government Printing Office in Washington, D.C., which disperses about 150 million items each year!

Though books with paper covers are age-old, the paperback boom in the United States really began in 1939, when Pocket Books first offered its smaller, cheaper books at newsstands and bookstores. By 1946, when Bantam Books was founded, paperbacks still cost but a quarter. Bantam is now the number-one paperback publisher in the United States, accounting for 18 percent of the market, while Dell Books is number two.

Paperback books are currently sold in two forms: mass-market and trade. Mass-market paperbacks, which measure four-and-a-quarter by seven inches, are sold in drugstores, supermarkets, and other places as well as bookstores; trade paperbacks, which are usually larger, are sold almost entirely in bookstores, at an average price higher than the mass-market paperback.

American best-seller lists have been kept since before the turn of the century. A book could make the earliest lists with sales of just 100,000 or more copies—and remember, there were no paperbacks! Popular works included a good deal of historical fiction, and many English imports. In 1895, the best-selling book in America was *Beside the Bonnie Brier Bush,* by Ian Maclaren, and in 1900, it was *To Have and To Hold,* by Mary Johnston.

In 1909, Mary Roberts Rinehart's *The Man in Lower Ten* became the first American detective novel to reach the best-seller lists. The following year, *The Rosary*, by Florence Barclay, was such a success that its publisher, G.P. Putnam, could build a new office building with the profits; it is called the "Rosary Building" in the trade.

In 1919, the best-seller list was first divided into fiction and nonfiction categories. Among the works that have since topped the nonfiction list, we might mention Emily Post's *Etiquette* (1923), George Dorsey's *Why We Behave Like Human Beings* (1926), and of course, Mortimer Adler's *How to Read a Book* (1940).

Eleanor H. Porter's *Pollyanna* topped the fiction list in 1913, while Zane Grey was number one in 1920, with *The Man of the Forest.* The following year, Sin-

A page from an original Gutenberg Bible.

The first erotic novel to be published and sold in this nation was John Cleland's *Memoirs of a Woman of Pleasure,* better known as *Fanny Hill,* which had been bringing a blush to cheeks since 1786.

clair Lewis first reached the best-seller list with *Main Street,* which sold almost 300,000 copies in its first year. Lewis made the list again with *Babbit,* and again with *Arrowsmith,* and yet again with *Dodsworth,* and in 1927, topped the list with *Elmer Gantry*.

In 1928, Erich Maria Remarque's *All Quiet on the Western Front* became the first book from outside America or England to top the list. F. Scott Fitzgerald never made it to the top of the list, but *The Private Life of Helen of Troy* was the best-seller of 1926.

A number of books have topped the best-seller list for two years in a row. Pearl Buck's *The Good Earth* was number one in 1931 and 1932, Hervey Allen's *Anthony Adverse* in 1933-1934, and Margaret Mitchell's *Gone with the Wind* in 1936-1937. *The Robe,* by Lloyd C. Douglas, was number one in 1943, and number two the next year, then became the number one best-seller all over again in 1953, upon the release of a movie version.

In 1938, Daphne Du Maurier's *Rebecca* became the first best-selling Gothic novel in America. The next year, John Steinbeck's *The Grapes of Wrath* was the top seller, and in 1940, Ernest Hemingway first reached the list with *For Whom the Bell Tolls*—though number one that year was *How Green Was My Valley*, by Richard Llewellyn.

Norman Mailer first made the list in 1948, with *The Naked and the Dead,* but the number one book of that year was Lloyd C. Douglas' *The Big Fisherman*. In 1958, Boris Pasternak's *Doctor Zhivago* became the first Russian novel to head the best-seller list.

Irving Stone's *The Agony and*

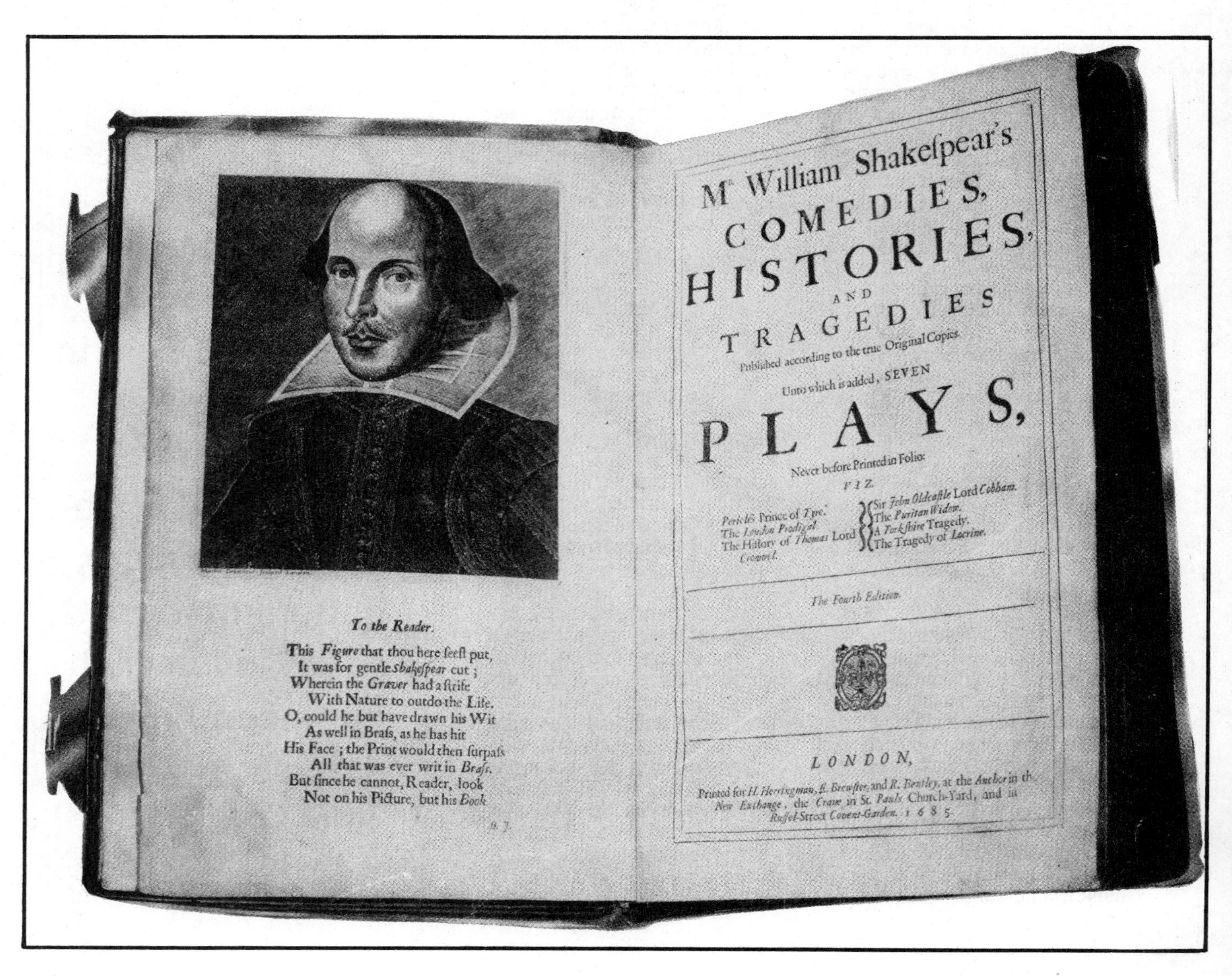

The Lord Carnarvon copy of The Plays of Shakespeare, *the only one extant in the original vellum binding with the original clasps.*

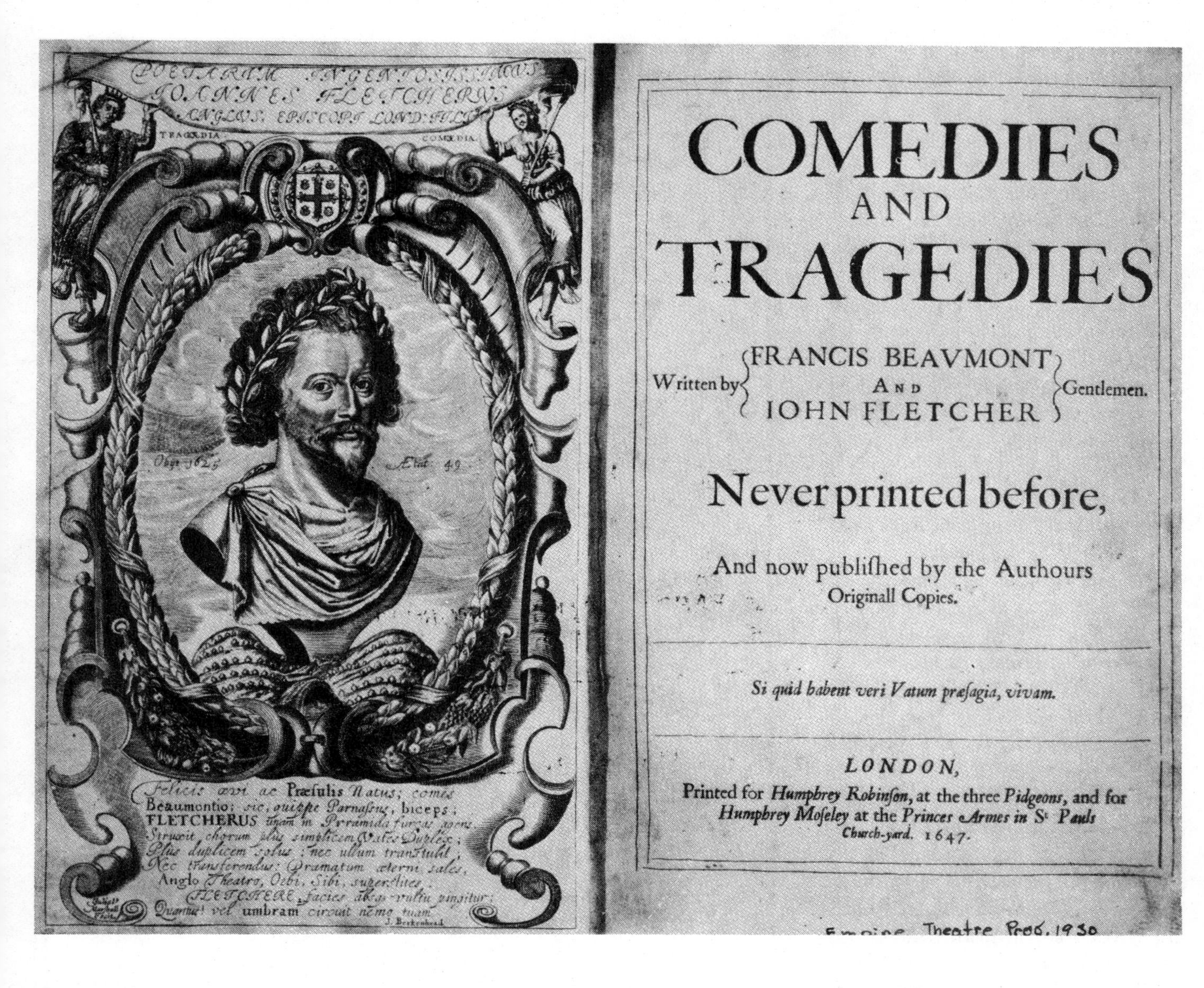

COMEDIES
AND
TRAGEDIES

Written by { FRANCIS BEAVMONT AND IOHN FLETCHER } Gentlemen.

Never printed before,

And now publiſhed by the Authours Originall Copies.

Si quid habent veri Vatum præſagia, vivam.

LONDON,

Printed for *Humphrey Robinſon*, at the three *Pidgeons*, and for *Humphrey Moſeley* at the *Princes Armes in St Pauls Church-yard*. 1647.

The title page of Beaumont and Fletcher's Comedies and Tragedies, *as it appeared in 1647.*

the Ecstasy was number one in 1961, with J.D. Salinger's *Frannie and Zooey* as number two. Believe it or not, there was one Latin book on the best-seller list that year: a Latin translation of A.A. Milne's *Winnie the Pooh*, titled *Winnie Ille Pu*. In 1964, *The Spy Who Came in from the Cold*, by John Le Carré, became the first thriller to top the best-seller lists, and Ian Fleming, creator of James Bond, first made the list with *You Only Live Twice*. Fleming also topped the paperback lists that year, with *On Her Majesty's Secret Service*.

James A. Michener first topped the list in 1965, with *The Source*, and repeated the feat nine years later with *Centennial*. In 1966, *Valley of the Dolls* by Jacqueline Susann was number one. It went on to become the best-selling novel of all time, with sales of over 20 million copies. Arthur Hailey made the top of the list in 1968, with *Airport*, and again in 1971, with *Wheels*. In 1970, Erich Segal's *Love Story* was the best-selling novel, while nonfiction honors went to David Reuben's *Everything You Ever Wanted To Know About Sex, but Were Afraid To Ask*.

In 1973, *Jonathan Livingston Seagull*, by Richard Bach, became the first book since *Gone with the Wind* to top the list two years running. The book was also the number-one paperback that year. A recent best-seller, *The Silmarillion* by J.R.R. Tolkien (1977), was one of the fastest-selling hardbounds in publishing history, selling over one million copies in two-and-a-half months!

An 18th-century title page of Joe Miller's Joke Book.

The first two paperback bestseller lists, in 1957-1958, were headed by Grace Metalious' *Peyton Place.* Ian Fleming dominated the list in the mid-60s, selling 16 million copies of 12 titles in a single year! By 1965, over 22 million paperback copies of Charles Schultz's *Peanuts* had found their way to a buyer. *Love Story* was number one in 1970 and 1971, but the 1972 winner was Xaviera Hollander's *The Happy Hooker.* In 1974, William Blatty's *The Exorcist* garnered top honors, with sales of over seven million copies.

Without question, the best-selling book of all time is the Bible. No one knows for sure how many copies of the Good Book have been printed through history, but a good guess would be around three billion. Trailing far behind in second place is *Quotations from the Works of Mao Tse-tung,* with some 800 million copies in print. Sales of *The American Spelling Book* by Noah Webster may approach 100 million, and Dr. Spock's *The Common Book of Baby and Child Care* has sold about 24 million copies. Other books that have topped the 20-million mark include the works of Marx, Lenin, Stalin, *The World Almanac,* and *The Guinness Book of Records.*

The best-selling author of all time is either the Belgian Georges Simenon, whose crime novels and other works have sold over 300 million copies, or Agatha Christie, who penned 80 crime novels.

Currently, about 35,000 new titles are brought out each year in the United States, about three-quarters new and the rest re-

Joe Miller's *JESTS:*

OR, THE

WITS

VADE-MECUM.

BEING

A Collection of the moſt Brilliant JESTS; the Politeſt REPARTEES; the moſt Elegant BONS MOTS, and moſt pleaſant ſhort Stories in the *Engliſh* Language.

Firſt carefully collected in the Company, and many of them tranſcribed from the Mouth of the Facetious GENTLEMAN, whoſe Name they bear; and now ſet forth and publiſhed by his lamentable Friend and former Companion, *Elijah Jenkins,* Eſq;

Moſt Humbly INSCRIBED

To thoſe CHOICE-SPIRITS *of the* AGE,

Captain BODENS, Mr. ALEXANDER POPE, Mr. Profeſſor LACY, Mr. Orator HENLEY, and JOB BAKER, the Kettle-Drummer.

LONDON:

Printed and Sold by T. READ, in *Dogwell-Court, White-Fryars, Fleet-Street.* MDCCXXXIX.

(Price One Shilling.)

prints. Nonfiction accounts for the overwhelming majority. But general fiction is the largest-selling single category among paperbacks, followed by religious books, mysteries, cookbooks, and science fiction. And the largest single chunk of the $4 billion or so spent each year on books goes to textbooks.

A number of nations produce more new books, in relation to their population, than the United States. The United Kingdom, with 56 million people, brings out over 30,000 new titles a year. Denmark, with five million people, and Switzerland, with six million, both bring out about 6,000 books annually. West Germany publishes 45,000 in an average year, and the U.S.S.R., as many as 85,000.

These figures, and the best-seller lists, indicate how many books are published and bought, but don't tell us how many are *read*. For one thing, lists don't reflect book borrowing. "Books," noted Isaac D'Israeli, "are subject to certain accidents besides the damp, the worms, and the rats;

Poster promoting "Uncle Tom's Cabin" which appeared in the 1850s.
New York Historical Society.

135,000 SETS, 270,000 VOLUMES SOLD.

UNCLE TOM'S CABIN

FOR SALE HERE.

AN EDITION FOR THE MILLION, COMPLETE IN 1 Vol., PRICE 37 1-2 CENTS.
" " IN GERMAN, IN 1 Vol., PRICE 50 CENTS.
" " IN 2 Vols., CLOTH, 6 PLATES, PRICE $1.50.
SUPERB ILLUSTRATED EDITION, IN 1 Vol., WITH 153 ENGRAVINGS,
PRICES FROM $2.50 TO $5.00.

The Greatest Book of the Age.

By the late 1940s, the book clubs of America could list three million members, accounting for about 30 percent of all American book sales.

one not less common is that of the borrowers, not to say a word of the the purloiners." And then there are the libraries. A single copy of a book in a library may be read by hundreds—even thousands—of people.

In 1747, the first public library was opened in Warsaw, Poland. America's first public library was opened in 1895, in New York City. The New York Library, now the world's largest public library, presently contains over eight million volumes, plus millions of manuscripts. But the largest library of any kind in the world is the Library of Congress in Washington, D.C., which houses over 75 million volumes and manuscripts—including a copy of every book ever copyrighted in the United States!

Books you no doubt won't be able to borrow from your nearest lending library include *The Little Red Elf,* a verse tale by William P. Wood, which is the largest book in the world: seven feet, two inches in height and 10 feet across when opened. You're also not likely to get your hands on the world's smallest book, a type catalogue recently published in Scotland, measuring less than three millimeters on a side!

The longest novel ever written is *Men of Good Will* by Jules Romains, brought out between 1932 and 1946 in 27 volumes. But the largest publication in existence is a set of *British Parliamentary Papers* of 1800-1900, which comprises 1,112 volumes and weighs 3.64 tons. You can pick up a copy for about $70,000. Perhaps the largest publication of all time was a Chinese Encyclopedia, written in the 15th century, of 22,937 volumes!

The world has indeed seen a good many books come and go, yet not even those people responsible for them, the writers, have agreed on their merits. Seventeenth-century author Thomas Fuller, for one, declared that

Workers in an American book bindery during the 1890s.

Cover of The Pony-Express Rider, *which was sold in the 1890s at five cents a copy.*

"learning hath gained most by those books . . . which the printers have lost." And Benjamin Disraeli went further, declaring that books "are the curse of the human race. Nine-tenths of existing books are nonsense, and the clever books are the refutation of that nonsense. The greatest misfortune that ever befell man was the invention of printing."

It was Voltaire, we think, who was most succinct: "It is with books as with men: a very small number play a great part, the rest are lost in the multitude."

The largest publisher in the world is actually the U.S. Government Printing Office in Washington, D.C., which disperses about 150 million items each year!

cameras

You may have heard the expression "in camera," meaning "in secret," and chuckled over the image of a meeting or conversation held within the dark, hidden confines of your Kodak or Polaroid. Amusing, perhaps, but *camera* happens to be the Italian word for "room." Well then, how did our picture-taking devices come to be known as "rooms?" Quite simple: *camera obscura,* literally "darkened room," was the term applied to the earliest image-focusing devices of Renaissance days.

The history of photography begins with the camera obscura, a darkened "room"—actually, a darkened box—with a small hole that projected an image of the scene outside onto a sheet of white paper. The earliest attempts at producing a picture-taking device were aimed at aiding the portraitist or landscape painter rather than driving him out of business. For the camera obscura was used chiefly by artists, who sketched the outlines of the projected image and later painted in the colors.

The invention of the camera obscura is usually ascribed to one Giovanni Battista della Porta in 1553, although other men had written of similar devices some 400 years earlier, and Leonardo da Vinci described and sketched a camera obscura early in the 1500s. In 1568, Danielo Barbaro fitted a convex lens to the camera obscura aperature for greater sharpness in the projected image, and an Italian named Danti further refined the process by fitting a mirror behind the lens to correct the reversed image. By the beginning of the 18th century, the portable camera obscura was widely used by artists to sketch scenes from nature.

In the 1720s, J.H. Schulze of Germany proved that the blackening of silver salts was caused by light. (All photography is based on this simple principle,

A camera obscura of 1769. This massive four-drawer telescoping instrument was intended for serious work.

A table camera from around 1770. In this camera the image was produced by means of mirror reflection. The lens was under the table near the floor.

and all photographic films contain silver.) Schulze's discovery led Thomas Wedgwood—son of the great potter Josiah Wedgwood—to find a "method of copying paintings on glass and of making profiles by the agency of light upon nitrate of silver." Even at that date, then, photography was seen chiefly as an aid to the painter, rather than as potential competition.

Sir Humphrey Davy experimented with Wedgwood's findings, discovering that silver chloride was more sensitive to light than silver nitrate. But all photographic processes of this era failed to produce a fixed image. The pattern of light and dark recorded on plates coated with silver compound was obliterated upon exposure to light.

During the early 1800s, Frenchman Joseph Niepce was experimenting with various materials for use in lithography. Since Niepce could not draw, his son Isaac provided the artwork for Niepce's experiments. When Isaac was drafted by the army, his father was spurred to invent a way of producing images by photographic process.

At first, Niepce experimented with coated metal plates in a camera made from a cigar box and a lens from a solar microscope. In 1822, he obtained a fixed photograph image on glass. Four years later, he captured the courtyard of his country home on a pewter plate after an exposure of about eight hours. Either picture, or *heliograph,* may be considered the first permanent photograph on record.

In 1829, Niepce formed a partnership with Louis J.M. Daguerre, a painter who had been carrying out his own photographic research. Daguerre discovered that an image could be recorded on an iodized silver plate fumed with mercury vapor. The discovery came about by accident. The artist left an exposed photographic plate in a cupboard overnight, and in the morning found that the plate bore a visible image. Daguerre traced the fortuitous accident to a quantity of mercury stored in the cupboard, whose vapor had condensed on the plate.

The first pictures produced with Daguerre's techniques, called *Daguerreotypes,* were not reproducible, and could be viewed only by tilting the picture a certain way. Furthermore, early Daguerreotypes required expo-

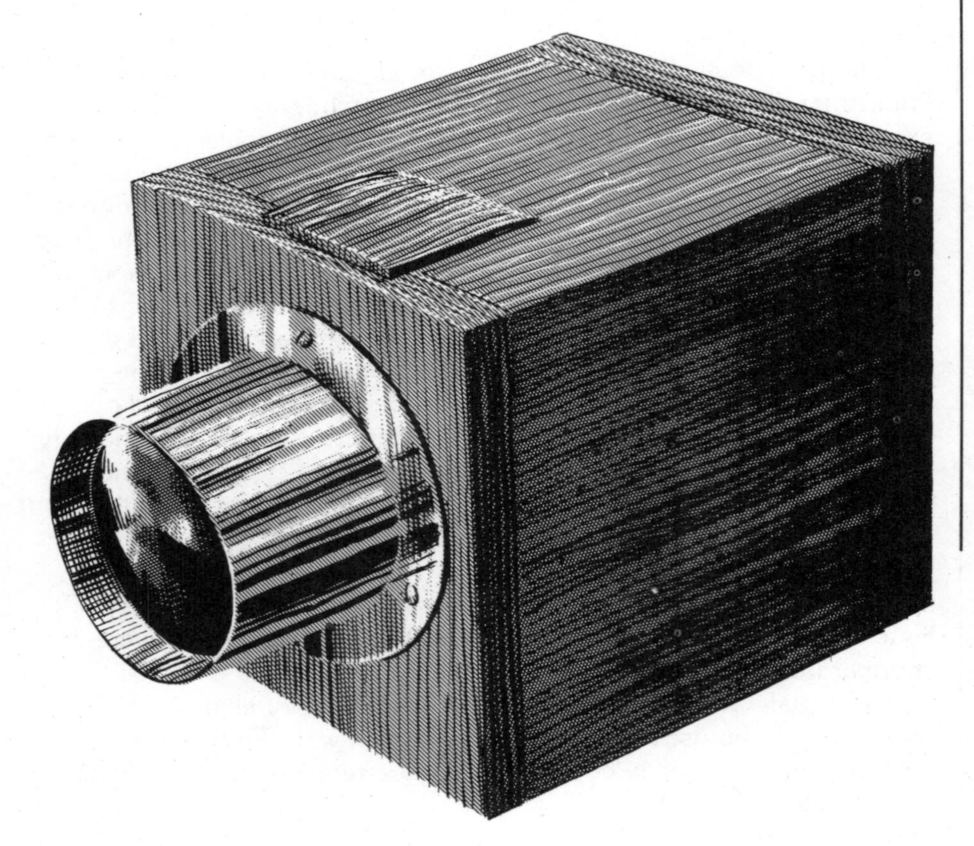

TOP LEFT:
The official Daguerre camera produced by Daguerre's brother-in-law, Alphonse Girous, carried a label that says: "No apparatus guaranteed if it does not bear the signature of M. Daguerre and the seal of M. Giroux."

BOTTOM LEFT:
A Fox Talbot experimental camera of 1835 was a simple-looking instrument. It produced the very first photograph ever to be made on paper.

sures of an hour or more, ruling out the shooting of scenes with moving objects. Yet the entire world applauded Daguerre's work—with the exception of a few portrait artists who could read the writing on the wall. In 1839, Daguerre sold the rights to his invention to the French government for a lifetime annuity, and his photographic process, called *Daguerreotypy*, flourished until replaced by better processes developed in the early 1850s.

The English scientist William Fox Talbot, often called the "real father of photography," began work in 1834 on a photographic process involving a negative and positive print. This process, patented in 1841, had the overwhelming advantage of furnishing a reproducible print, the "negative" from which any number of positive prints could be made. Talbot's *calotypy* produced fixed,

TOP RIGHT:
Johann Zahn's reflex camera was built in 1685. The principle of this early camera is exactly that of the modern reflex.

BOTTOM RIGHT:
A Gay 90s beach photographer as portrayed in the Police Gazette *of those days.*

The earliest Kodak cameras were preloaded at the factory with film for 100 pictures—each round in shape and just two-and-a-half inches in diameter.

This head clamp for a camera studio was in use in 1851. This picture shows how great, great-grandmother managed to keep her head still in the days when a snapshot took many, many seconds.

The Imacon 600, a camera made in England for use in physics research, can take 600 pictures per second.

reproducible images that were less sharp than Daguerreotypy, but its advantages made it the basis of most of the later experimentation that eventually led to modern photography. By the way, some of Talbot's negatives still exist, and yield excellent prints!

Amateur photographers were responsible for most advances in camera design and photographic processes during the mid-19th century. But in the 1880s, experimental work was largely taken up by photographic equipment companies. In 1884, George Eastman and an associate literally developed the first roll film, greatly simplifying photography for amateur shutterbugs. Four years later, Eastman's company, Eastman Kodak, marketed the first portable roll-film camera, with fixed focus and aperature. Photography was now accessible to everyone, with or without technical expertise—or a darkroom—and amateur photography quickly became a popular pastime in Europe and the United States.

The earliest Kodak cameras were preloaded at the factory with film for 100 pictures—each *round* in shape and just two-and-a-half inches in diameter. After the film was completely exposed, the camera itself was returned to the factory, where the film was developed and a new roll inserted in the camera for return to the photographer.

Professionally, the camera was first used for portraiture.

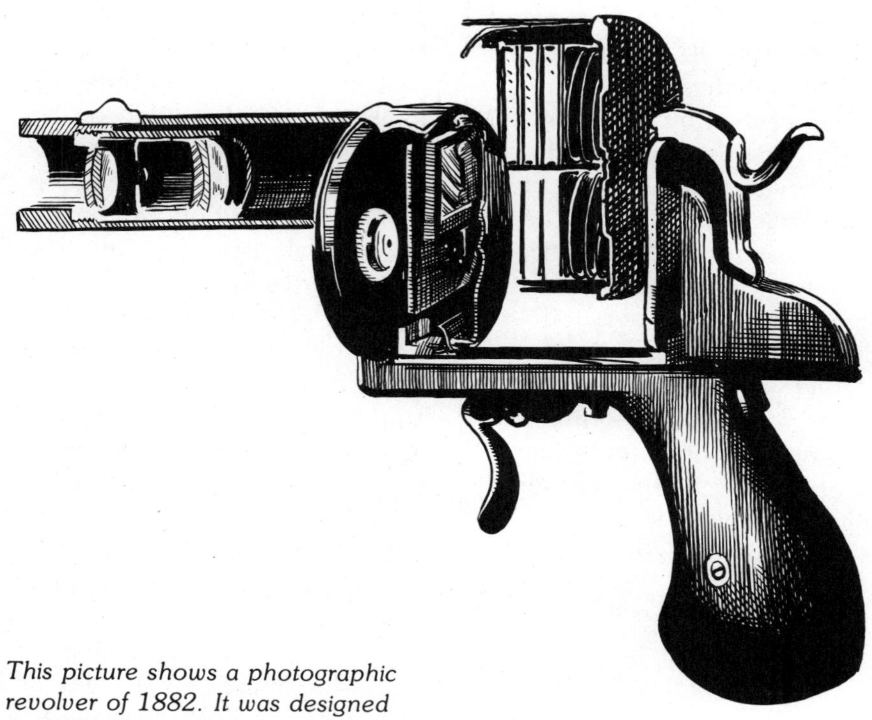

This picture shows a photographic revolver of 1882. It was designed for ease of use.

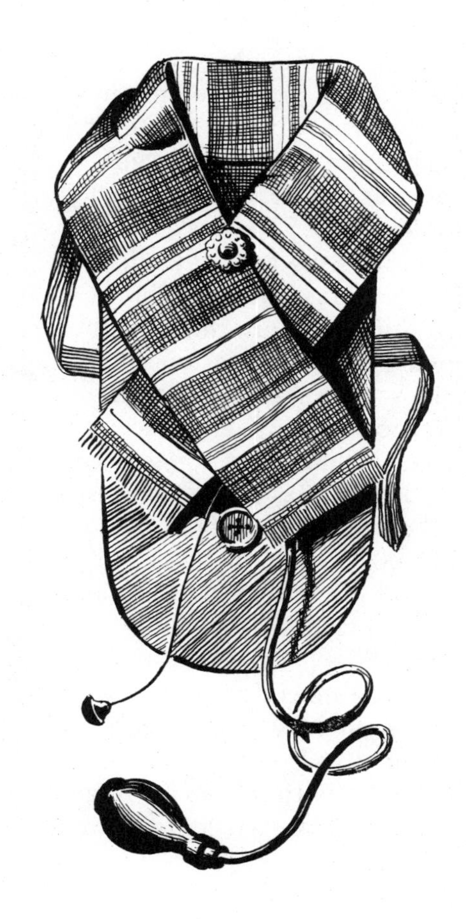

In this detective camera the lens was disguised as a cravat pin, and the magazine of six glass plates was fed past the lens. The cable was hidden in the wearer's pocket. So was the pneumatic shutter bulb.

While previously only the wealthy could afford a painted portrait, now everyone could, and did, have a good portrait taken by Daguerreotypy or later processes. The long exposure time necessary for an adequate shot in the earliest portrait studios required the photographer to attach a head clamp to the sitter to prevent movement and a blurred image. This clamp did much to produce the rigid, artificial facial expressions typical of most early photo portraiture.

The 1920s saw the introduction of *miniature* cameras, the light, compact cameras most amateurs and professionals use today to shoot 35-mm. film. Almost all still photography and motion-picture cameras now employ film of the same 35-mm. width, for the miniature camera was originally designed to test 35-mm. motion-picture film. The term *miniature* is now applied only to a camera utilizing film less than 35-mm. wide.

The first successful commercial model of the lightweight modern camera was the Leica, marketed by the German Leitz optical firm. The flash bulb popped onto the photographic scene in 1925—before that, the photographer used burning magnesium or flash powder for added illumination. In the later 1930s, reversal color film became generally available. Improvements in photographic techniques have continued without interruption since then, toward simplification as well as precision.

Among the latest products of photographic simplification is the Kodak Instamatic, complete with built-in flash, fixed focus, and fixed aperature, a camera so simple and foolproof it practically takes pictures by itself—or as

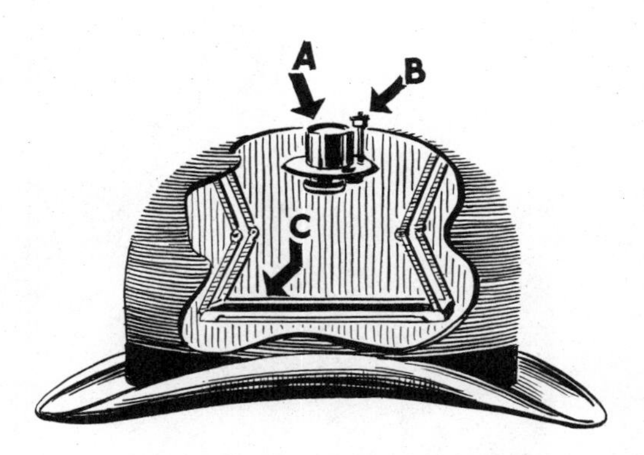

The Adams hat-camera was designed to make every man his own detective. In the diagram, "A" is the camera lens, "B" the shutter release plunger. Two small holes had to be made in the hat for these.

George Eastman boasted in 1888, "You press the button, we do the rest." Even more remarkably, some modern "instant" cameras are now on the market for less than $20, while even in the 1880s the earliest Kodak roll-film cameras sold for $25!

If you're more serious about your shutterbugging, you might take a look at the Nikon system, the most expensive available, which with all accessories, including 19 cameras and 62 lenses, will set you back more than $110,000. You might also take a look at the F-1 35-mm. Canon system, with 40 lenses and more than 180 available accessories.

But a newer camera, made by Canon—the electronically powered A-1, could someday make the F-1 and similar cameras obsolete. The A-1, introduced in 1978, has the capacity to automatically select either shutter speed or aperature, or both, in 41 milliseconds. Its aperature range can be adjusted continuously rather than by increments, or *stops*. These and a host of other innovations make this precise, versatile camera almost as simple to use as the Instamatic. How much will such a modern photographic marvel cost you? Under $350, plus lenses.

Along with Canon, the other major producers of top-of-the-line photographic equipment include the German Leica firm, whose cameras sell chiefly in the $700-$1,200 range, and the Japanese Nikon and Minolta companies—Minolta is presently the second largest-selling camera in the world, after Canon.

Though Japanese firms now dominate camera production, most of the world still relies on film produced at Kodak Park, in Rochester, New York, and at other Kodak plants, making the United States the world's largest producer of photographic goods. In one recent year alone, the estimated 2,500 film laboratories in America boasted a film-processing business of some $850 million! About 90 percent of that figure was spent on color film. And about 40 percent of all film materials are purchased by amateurs!

Not included in these film-processing figures are the photos taken with the Polaroid camera, which are developed in the cam-

J.L. Daguerre (1789-1851) was the inventor of the Daguerreotype, the first commercially successful photographic process.

Lead illustration for an article which appeared in the Century Magazine *of July, 1885.*

era, rather than at the lab. Polaroid cameras utilize a process called diffusion-transfer to produce positive prints within a minute after the picture is taken. Invented in 1939 in Europe for use in office copying machines, the diffusion-transfer process was first adopted for use in a camera in 1947, by American inventor Edward Land, who went on to found the Polaroid Corporation.

Black-and-white Polaroid film consists of two sheets, a positive and a negative. The positive carries pods of jellied processing solution. After the image is recorded on the negative sheet, the negative and positive sheets pass between rollers, and the pressure ruptures the jelly pods and spreads the processing solution over the positive sheet. Ten seconds later, the negative sheet is peeled away, leaving a completely developed positive print. Polaroid color film, available since 1963, works on a more complicated process, utilizing six layers of active chemicals.

While the earliest Daguerreotypes required exposure times of close to an hour, exposure times of a mere 1/125th or 1/250th of a second are now the most common. The Imacon 600, a camera made in England for use in physics research, can take 600 pictures per second. Movie cameras have reached speeds of 11 million pictures per second. If such a camera photographed a bullet traveling at the speed of 1,900 miles per hour, three minutes of normal-speed projection would be required to show just one foot of the bullet's travel!

Miniature cameras include a Japanese model called the "Petal," which is just 1.4 inches in diameter and only a half-inch thick. Various cameras used in cardiac surgery and espionage are even smaller. At the other end of the scale, we find a Rolls-Royce camera built in England in 1959, which occupies 2,470 feet and weighs about 27 tons—one of these babies will set you back a clean $240,000! The largest camera of all time, though, was constructed around the turn of the century to photograph railroad equipment, and was itself the size of a railroad boxcar!

CANNING

Despite popular belief to the contrary, most vitamins are unaffected by long-term preservation.

ODE ON AN EMPTY TIN CAN

Consider this dismal tin can:
Once contained a mess of good fare,
It may have held prunes, or soup, or fried loons;
But now its insides are bare.

This bathetic lament could well serve as a paen to one of the more ubiquitous products of technology—the tin can. There is now scarcely a person on earth who has not eaten canned food at one time or another. Despite the advent of frozen foods, there is little chance that the use of canned foods will decrease in the future.

The explanation should be obvious. Frozen foods require continual refrigeration. Canned foods require no upkeep, and unlike frozen foods, will remain edible almost indefinitely. Incredibly, a recently discovered tin of rations dating from the Civil War was fed to a dog, and the pooch found the century-old victuals quite delicious!

Foolproof food canning is a result of 20th-century technology, but the history of commercial food canning actually begins in Revolutionary France. In 1795, while France was torn by revolutionary strife at home and at war with several nations, the government offered a prize of 12,000 francs to anyone who could devise a method for preserving food for the embattled French army and navy. But it wasn't until 1809, 14 years later, that a confectioner named Francois Nicholas Appert stepped forward with a satisfactory food-preservation plan.

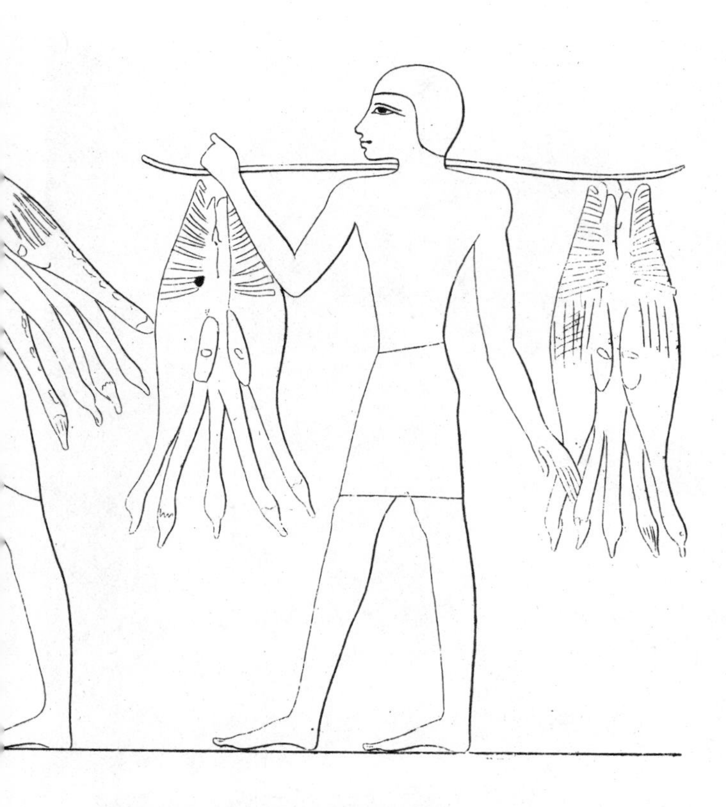

Preparation of geese which were to be conserved in jars. This drawing from ancient Egypt illustrates the early beginnings of canning and preserving.

Appert found that food would remain fresh much longer if it was sealed in airtight glass bottles and immersed for a time in boiling water. Through trial and error, the inventor finally succeeded, but was totally unaware of the scientific reasons for his method's success, for bacteria were then unknown. But Appert received the government prize, and published his findings in a treatise entitled *The Book for All Households or the Art of Preserving Animal Substances for Many Years.* Thus, Napoleon had enough fresh provisions to boast that his army "marched on its stomach."

The Dutch began preserving fish in metal containers as early as 1800, and the English likewise preserved bully beef beginning in 1810, but none of the earliest canning techniques could preserve food indefinitely.

The next major figure in the history of canning, then, is William Underwood, an English pickler who arrived in the United States in 1817. Underwood had read Appert's treatise while in England, and upon reaching America began his own experiments in food preservation. By 1829, his firm was bottling food in Boston—most bearing the label "Made in England," since Americans at the time were more likely to trust preserved foods shipped over from the Old Country than native products.

According to some accounts, it was Underwood

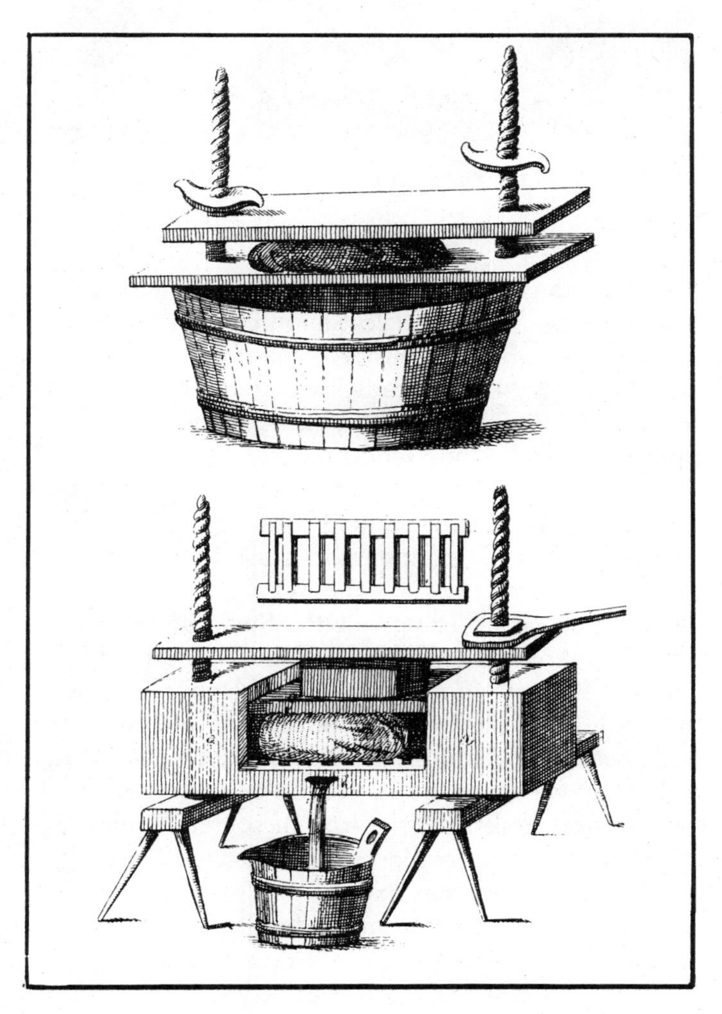

Fruit presses used in canning during the beginning of the 19th century.

Peeling fruits at the Del Monte plant.

himself who gave us the word "can"—though the dictionary favors the Anglo-Saxon *canne* as the source. The word "cannister"—from the Greek *kanastron,* "basket of reeds," was regularly applied to the reed baskets used to hold tea, coffee, fruits, and vegetables. Underwood merely shortened the word to "can." The first gold to reach the Atlantic coast from the California gold rush was reputedly brought across the continent in a used Underwood tin can!

The can began to replace the bottle in 1839, when Underwood and a New York rival named Thomas Kensett adopted tin-coated steel containers for use in food packaging. Underwood and Kensett's early cans were hand-assembled by factory workers, then filled with food through a hole left in the top of the can and sealed with a drop of solder. Even the most adroit canner could not be expected to fill more than 60 cans per day.

Until the 1860s, the major problem faced by all canners was the inordinate amount of time required to heat the sealed containers in boiling water. But in 1861, a Baltimore canner named Isaac Solomon, drawing on the work of the English scientist Sir Humphrey Davy, found that the addition of calcium chloride could raise the boiling point of water from 212 to 240 degrees. Food heated at the higher temperature, Solomon discovered, required a sterilization period of only 30 minutes, compared to the earlier one of four or five hours. Canneries that had been limited to a production of about 1,500 cans per day could now turn out more than 20,000 daily.

The needs of the Union army during the Civil War brought about a sharp increase in the production of canned foods in the United States. The United States soon became the world's leader in canning technology and production. In 1898, George Cobb of Fairport, New York turned out the first double-seamed solderless cans. The first decade of this century saw the advent of the "open-top" can, the

OPPOSITE PAGE:
Sorting asparagus in the Del Monte plant preparatory for canning.

C.P.C. 139

one we're most familiar with, which had a double-seamed top and bottom, assuring a perfect closure. Canning soon became completely mechanized. Early in the 20th century, the two giants of the industry were founded, the American Can Company in 1901, and the Continental Can Company in 1927.

Meanwhile, the science of bacteriology had been born. By 1860, Louis Pasteur had shown that all food spoilage was the result of invisible organisms called bacteria. Canners now knew why their sterilization methods worked: heat kills bacteria, and sealing prevents re-infection.

In an 1898 report to a canners' convention, W.L. Underwood, grandson of William, showed that the occasional spoilage of canned foods was due not to air penetrating the can, but to spores present in the food that were not killed by the sterilization process. From then on, canners were careful to apply heat sufficient to kill spores as well as living bacteria in the food, and to make sure that the heat reached all the way to the center of the can.

A canner exceedingly canny,
One day, remarked to his granny;
"A canner can can
Anything that he can—
But a canner can't can a can, can he?"

Did you ever wonder why most canned foods are packed in water or syrup? In 1927, American Can Company researchers found that preserved foods surrounded by liquid rather than air were less likely to spoil or lose their vitamins. Foods that could not be packed in liquid were henceforth vacuum-packed—sealed in cans from which all air has been excluded. Food canning was now considered virtually foolproof.

During World War I, American canners produced some 500 million cans of food annually for the military alone, and the canned rations the doughboys distributed to their allies helped spread interest in canned foods throughout Europe. By 1935, America was producing about eight billion cans of fruits, vegetables, fish, and processed meat each year, and by the 1950s, more than 12 billion cans annually.

The notion that food should not be stored in opened cans in the refrigerator is simply an old wives' tale.

The names of many of the pioneers in canning technology and the food preservation industry can still be found on the labels of canned food today. Gilbert Van Camp began canning fruits and vegetables in the back room of his Indianapolis grocery in

Peeling tomatoes at a Del Monte plant in California in 1942.

1861. Gail Borden—not Elsie—received a patent for canned milk in 1856. By 1880, the Borden Company was canning over 13 million pounds of milk yearly. Joseph Campbell of Camden, New Jersey found that the then high cost of packaging and shipping soup could be lowered significantly if the soups were condensed before packing, and the first Campbell's soups began appearing on American tables in 1873.

Modern fruit and vegetable canneries are located as close as possible to the farm. Some foods are canned just three or four hours after picking. Basically, the canning process works like this: the fruits or vegetables are first cleaned with water or blasts of air. Then the food is trimmed, husked, sectioned, sliced, diced, peeled, cored, or pitted, to prepare it for packaging. Some products are then blanched in hot water to drive out gases and shrink the food to its desired size.

The prepared food is packed into cannisters made from sheet metal with a thin tin coating—"tin" cans were never made wholly from tin. Some canning machines can fill up to 300 containers per minute. Then the can is vacuum-sealed, heated, cooled in water or air, and finally labeled and packed in crates for shipping.

For the most part, canned foods suffer no loss of nutritive value. Despite popular belief to the contrary, most vitamins are unaffected by long-term preservation. The notion that food should not be stored in open cans in the refrigerator is simply an old wives' tale. Food will spoil no faster in an open can than it will in any other kind of open container, and the occasional discoloration of the can after opening does not affect the food.

Often praised and sometimes cursed, the tin can now brings us a major portion of the food we eat and the beverages we drink. Today, the problem posed by canning is not to find ways to safely preserve foods, but to discover an adequate means of disposing of the can afterward, since the aluminum increasingly used for canning does not decompose naturally. Think of it—the aluminum can of soda that you opened today may well be around long after your bones have crumbled to dust!

Cattle

The dog may be man's best friend, but from a strictly utilitarian point of view, the most important of man's allies in the animal kingdom is without doubt a group of large, docile creatures known collectively as cattle. The single genus to which these animals belong, *Bos*, provides man with his number-one draught animal, supplies half of his meat, 95 percent of his milk, and 80 percent of his leather. Civilization as we know it today might not exist without domesticated bovines.

And in no other country are cattle more important than in the United States. The milk of the cow is the most popular single food item in this nation, with the average American consuming 291 pounds per year. Americans also produce and consume about 35 percent of the world's beef, while comprising only five percent of the world's population.

Cattle herds contribute about 85 billion pounds of meat to the world's larder each year, and American cattle account for about 25 billion pounds of that total. But the United States ranks second in overall cattle ownership, with about 115 million head, while the U.S.S.R. and Brazil can both claim close to 100 million. Then which country ranks number one? Of the estimated 1.1 billion head of cattle presently on earth, the largest number—about 176 million—are to be found in India, a nation which does not eat beef!

Beef is now the third most popular food item in the United States—the average American consumes 89 pounds per year. Among the top dozen most popular home-cooked dishes in the United States, five are beef dishes: roast beef, beef stew, meat loaf, pot roast, and swiss steak. The ground beef patty known as the hamburger is far and away the most popular eating-out dish—the McDonald's Corporation alone sells over four billion hamburgers a year!

Still, the American is not the greatest meat-eater in the world. New Zealand leads all countries with a per capita annual consumption of 224 pounds, followed by Uruguay, Australia, Argentina, and the United States.

And let's not forget the cows. Each year, the females of the *Bos* genus donate some 200 billion quarts of their milk to the world's food supply. We should be thankful indeed that, in the words of Ogden Nash:

The cow is of the bovine ilk;
One end is moo, the other milk.

The word "cattle" is often used for all members of the ox family, as well as the particular species we in America call cattle. The ox family includes, in addition to our cattle, the buffalo, bison, yak, and zebu of Africa, and the gaur, gayal, and bantin of India. All but the bison, gaur, and bantin have been domesticated, and all members of the genus can interbreed with one another.

The buffalo was thought to be an exception until recently, when breeders succeeded in crossing cattle with buffalo. In 1974, one of the hybrid creatures, called "beefalo," sold for $2.5 million, the largest sum ever paid for a single bull!

Bovines were without doubt one of the first animals to be domesticated. Early man found that the cow produces milk far in excess of that needed for its offspring, and that the male can be made docile enough for work as a draught animal. Also, the digestive system of these creatures enables them to subsist on roughage and other plant parts that might otherwise be useless to man. For thousands of years, cattle were employed as work animals and raised for their milk; raising cattle for meat is a relatively recent development. There are still parts of the world, like India, in which beef is never eaten, despite an abundance of cattle.

Cattle were probably first domesticated in India and Central Asia, perhaps as early as over 11,000 years ago, and brought by Neolithic migrators to Europe and Africa. There they interbred with native cattle, which are thought to have evolved from an extinct wild ox. The earliest known domestication dates from 6000 B.C., in Greece and Crete.

The ancient Egyptians raised cattle for their milk and for use as draught animals, and hunted wild cattle for sport. Domesticated cattle were also used to trample grain on the threshing floor. By Roman times, cattle markets were common sights in many cities—and so were Imperial meat inspectors.

From ancient times through much of the Middle Ages, cattle and wealth were virtually synonymous. Our words "capital" and "chattel" are both derived from the word for cattle—or rather, from the Latin *caput*, "head," from "head of cattle." In the language of the Aryans who invaded India centuries before the Christian era, the word for war literally meant "desire for more cattle." In Europe, cattle were used as the standards of exchange as late as the eighth century.

Cattle came to the New World almost as soon as the Europeans themselves, for Christopher Columbus brought a few head to the Americas on his second voyage. As early as 1611, English settlers at Jamestown were raising cattle; by 1624, the colony could claim 20,000 head. By the mid-18th century, America was already beginning to export its cattle.

The cattle-raising land of the United States has been moving westward ever since then. Around 1800, the cattle industry in the United States was centered around Ohio and Kentucky. By 1850, it had moved to Illinois and Missouri, and by 1870, to the states of the Great Plains and the Southwest. Most American breeds are descendants of the British breeds brought from Europe and the longhorn breeds brought to Mexico by Spanish colonists.

To a great extent, cattle settled the American West. Much of our Wild Western lore centers around the cattle ranch, the cattle trail, and the cowboy. Initially, cowboys not only tended cattle herds, but drove them long distances over cattle trails to cities for slaughter. Beginning around 1850, Western cattle took to the railroad for the ride to the slaughterhouse, and cowboys thereafter drove their herds only to the nearest rail depot. Thus Dodge City, Abilene, and other famous Western "cow towns" were born.

Today, American cattle are raised for beef in the sparsely populated rangeland states of the West, while dairy farming predominates in Midwestern and Eastern states close to urban centers. Texas leads all states in the

Names of the several joints of beef, as depicted in Household Management *by Mrs. Beeton, published in London in 1899.*

HIND QUARTER.

1. Sirloin.
2. Rump.
3. Aitchbone.
4. Buttock.
5. Mouse-round
6. Veiny piece.
7. Thick flank.
8. Thin flank.
9. Leg.

FORE QUARTER.

10. Fore rib (5 ribs).
11. Middle rib (4 ribs).
12. Chuck rib (3 ribs).
13. Leg of mutton piece.
14. Brisket.
15. Clod.
16. Neck.
17. Shin.
18. Cheek.

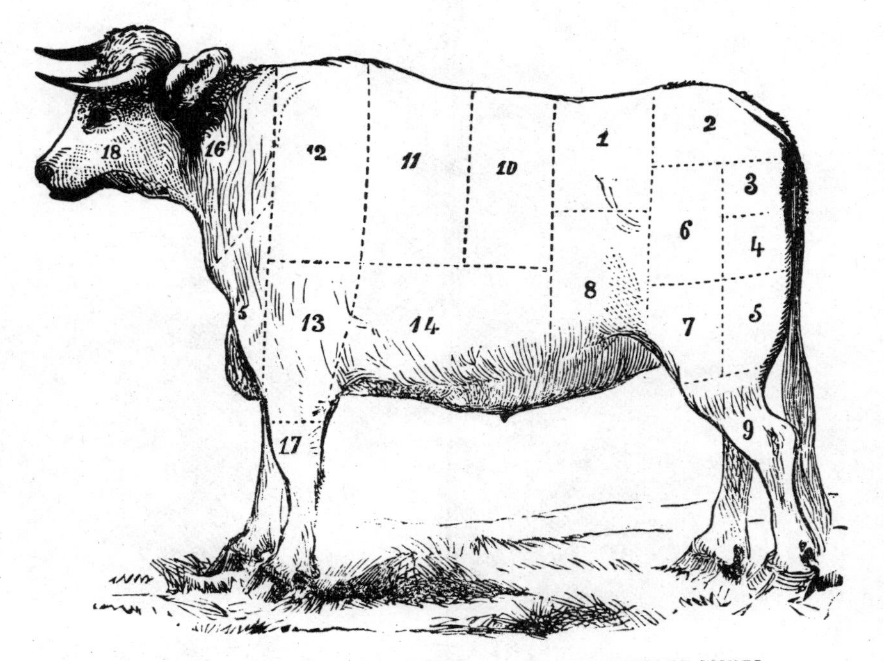

OX, SHOWING THE MODE OF CUTTING UP THE VARIOUS JOINTS.

number of cattle, and most of these are beef cattle. The American "dairy belt" stretches from New England through New York and Pennsylvania to Michigan, Minnesota, and Wisconsin. Southern Wisconsin can claim the heaviest concentration of cows per square mile in the United States.

There are now some 280 recognized breeds of cattle, of which 33 are beef breeds. Generally, cattle breeds were developed to produce animals good for either their meat or their milk, but rarely for both. In the United States, there are about 10 times as many beef cattle as there are milk-producing cows, and about 30 percent of all dairy cows eventually find their way into the meat freezer as low-grade beef.

The most popular beef breeds in the world are the *Shorthorn* and the *Hereford*. Both were originally developed in the British Isles, and are favored for their hardiness and rapid maturation. Henry Clay is credited with introducing the first Herefords to the United States, in 1817. The Hereford is generally the heaviest of all breeds: a cow may weigh up to 1,700 pounds, and a bull may weigh a ton. The largest bull on record, in fact, was an American-raised Hereford-Shorthorn that tipped the scales at a prodigious 4,720 pounds!

The *Angus,* another beef breed, was originally developed in Scotland. In the United States, the *Angus* was crossed with the *Brahman,* the humped cattle of India, to produce a new breed, the *Brangus.* In the 1930s, breeders at the King Ranch in Texas crossed the Brahman and the Shorthorn to produce the *Santa Gertrudis* breed, which rivals the Hereford for sheer size.

The King Ranch is popularly regarded as the largest cattle ranch of all time. Actually, the largest cattle range in the world

Indian humped cattle.

today is in Australia, covering some 6,500 square miles. Another Australian ranch, now partitioned into smaller units, once covered 35,000 square miles—about the size of the state of Indiana!

The world's most popular dairy breed is by far the *Holstein,* originally developed in Northern Europe and known as a fine milk-producer for over 2,000 years. A Holstein cow can produce up to 14,000 pounds of milk a year, while the average dairy cow of other breeds produces about 11,000 pounds. One Holstein raised in America claims the all-time milk producing record: 50,000 pounds in one year! And it was a Holstein that set the record for the largest amount of money every shelled out for a single cow: $122,000.

Other popular dairy breeds include the *Ayshire,* the *Jersey*, and the *Guernsey*. The latter two breeds were developed on the English Channel islands that bear those names, while the Ayshire was developed in Scotland. All three are now raised almost around the world. The Guernsey is noted for its yellowish milk, due to a pigment in the cow's skin.

A Jersey cow.

A Holstein cow.

Many American city-dwellers would probably have as much trouble distinguishing a steer from a stag as they would a Guernsey from a Hereford. What do those terms mean? Most male cattle are castrated, and become *steers*. In two or three years, they would grow into an *ox*. If left uncastrated, they become *bulls*. A bull, castrated after mating, is called a *stag*. A female is called a *cow* only when it reaches maturity; an immature female is a *heifer*.

Surely a more familiar cattle terminology is that used to identify beef in the supermarket. All beef sold in the United States is graded for quality, and there are eight basic grades. *Prime* is the best—the meat is flecked with fat, or "marbled," and is very flavorful and juicy. Beef of the *Choice* grade is also top-quality beef, though it's generally less marbled than *Prime*-grade beef. *Choice* beef accounts for about 40 percent of all the beef sold in the United States. *Good* and *Standard* are the other grades of beef from young animals. *Commercial, Utility, Cutter,* and *Canner,* the lowest grades, are generally from mature animals, and are used mostly for processed foods such as salami and sausage.

The terminology used to identify cuts of beef may vary from

supermarket to supermarket, but generally the porterhouse, tenderloin, filet mignon, and T-bone, all cut from the short loin, are the most expensive cuts. Sirloin steak is usually not cut from the short loin, but from the loin end section of the beef carcass. The story that King Charles II of England liked loin end steak so much that he dubbed it "Sir Loin" is, though quaint, a complete fiction. The "sir" in "sirloin" is actually derived from the French word *sur*, "over."

Our supermarkets probably wouldn't be filled with beef products at all if it weren't for the peculiar digestive system of cattle. Bovine creatures have four stomachs; the first two are the *rumen* and the *reticulum*. Food is partially digested in these two stomachs, then coughed up in "cuds" a few times so that the animal can chew over, or "ruminate," the partially digested food before swallowing it again. A cow may spend up to nine hours a day ruminating. Later, the food passes to the other two stomachs for further digestion.

This hardy digestive system, and the many kinds of bacteria present there, enable cattle to subsist on roughage that human beings could not digest. Therefore, man has historically been able to keep cattle without surrendering part of his vegetable diet. In most of the world today,

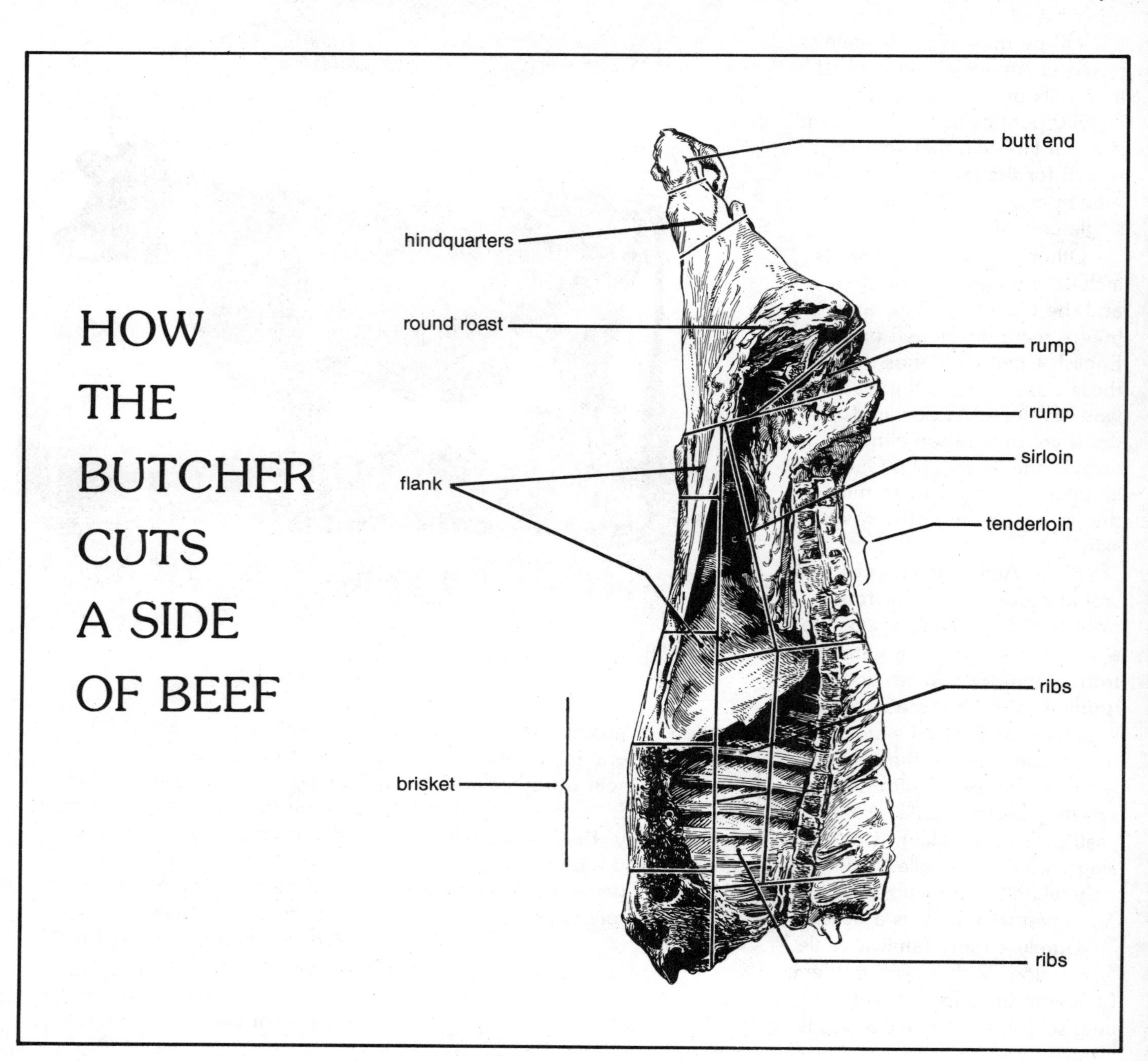

A Friburg bull.

cattle feed on grass, hay, and other roughage, but in the United States, they're fed grain for fattening. In a single year, American cattle will consume the equivalent food energy of 240 million tons of corn!

In return for this grass and grain, each head of cattle rewards the rancher with about 450 pounds of beef suitable for the retail market, along with 150 pounds of by-products and 150 pounds of low-value salvage. By-products include the hide (for leather), hair (felt, brushes), suet (margarine), and inedible fats (soap), along with the bones used for glue and gelatin, and the blood that in a dried form is used as animal feed.

But it is beef, of course, that is the most prized product of the steer. Beefsteak is regarded by many as the premier meat, especially in England and the United States, and a "thick, juicy steak" is most Americans' idea of gustatorial perfection. The rest of the world by and large does not agree. As late as the 19th century, beefsteak was regarded even by Europeans as primarily an English specialty. French writer Alexander Dumas wrote that beefsteak "must be eaten in an English tavern, with wine or anchovy butter, served on water cress."

The Beefsteak Club was one of the most well-known London social clubs of the 18th and 19th centuries, including among its members such luminaries of the art and theater worlds as William Hogarth, John Wilkes, and David Garrick, plus the Prince of Wales. The club reportedly was so named because its original members met to enjoy a steak dinner. Members were later called "Steaks," and the club the "Sublime Society of Steaks."

Also in England, the ceremonial royal guard—called yeoman of the guard—have long been nicknamed "beefeaters." In 1669, the grand duke of Tuscany noted the size and stature of the guard members during a trip to England, and wrote: "They are great eaters of beef, of which a very large ration is given them daily at the court, and they might be called 'beefeaters.'"

Aside from vegetarians, there are probably few Americans today who don't qualify for that nickname. But if you are a member of that tiny minority, you might take heart in the words of William Shakespeare: "I am a great eater of beef, and I believe that does harm to my wit."

CATS

The oldest domestic cat on record, a tabby owned by a woman in England, died on November 29, 1939, at the ripe old age of 36 years!

Are you an ailurophile or an ailurophobe? In plain English: Do you love or hate cats? Either way, you're in large company.

Ever since the domestication of the feline, the cat has been variously regarded as a representation of the gods or an embodiment of the devil. Even today, there seems to be no middle ground. The dog may be loved, hated, or tolerated, but the cat—well, choose your side.

Dogs and cats are far and away the most popular pets in the world today. But the dog has been a friend of man for much longer, having been domesticated some 50,000 years ago. On the other hand, the cat was not tamed to any extent until just

5,000 years ago. Yet the dog, as we know it today, is in evolutionary terms a rather recent development. The cat family, on the other hand, evolved into its present form some seven million years ago, long before most surviving mammals. During the intervening ages, it has undergone little change.

Over the ages, the feline species spread to all parts of the earth, with the exception of Australia and a few islands. The original ancestors of the cat evolved into two general families. One family, called the *Hoplophoneus,* included the Smiladon, or saber-toothed tiger, and other extinct animals. The second group, the *Dinictis,* produced all our modern cats.

There are many ways of classifying the members of the cat family, but the most commonly accepted divides the felines into three genera. The *Panthera* genus includes the great cats, such as the lion, tiger, leopard, and jaguar. The lion is the only gregarious member of the cat family. Its nickname—"king of the jungle"—is something of a misnomer. The tiger is generally larger and stronger than his unstriped cousin. Fortunately, the two creatures rarely meet—there are no tigers in Africa, and few lions anywhere else.

"Ligers and Tigons" may sound like a classic spoonerism, but these animals actually exist. They are the hybrid offspring of the lion and tiger, and there are about a dozen of these creatures in captivity today. When the father is a lion, the cub is called a liger; when the sire is a tiger, the cub is a tigon. And if a liger and tigon mate—well, you figure it out.

The *Acinonyx* genus includes only, since ancient times, the cheetah, a sleek, spotted cat that has been domesticated and used in hunting in Egypt, India, and other Asian lands. The cheetah has been called the fastest animal on earth, and can race along at speeds of 60 miles per hour—though some claim to have clocked this quick-footed cat at close to 75 miles per hour!

The third genus, *Felis,* includes the puma, ocelot, bobcat, serval, lynx, and of course, the common house cat, known rather plausibly in zoological circles as *Felis catus.*

There is no record of domesticated cats before 3,000 B.C., though by that time the kitty was already regarded as sacred in some Near Eastern cultures. The Egyptians tamed a species of wild African cat, *Felis lybica,* an animal about the size of the modern house cat, and put him to work protecting grain supplies from rodents. Egyptian artwork also depicts small cats killing snakes.

Rodent-hunting cats proved so valuable that the Egyptians considered them representations of the gods—a designation that conveniently helped protect the cat from ancient ailurophobes. The Egyptian cat-god *Bast,* was a symbol of the kindly powers of the sun, as opposed to *Sekmet,* the lion-god, who represented the destructive forces of nature. The cat was also worshipped or in some way connected with religious observance in Babylonia, Burma, Siam, Japan, and China, where the domesticated cat first appeared around 500 B.C.

The Egyptians went so far in their ailurophilia as to embalm cats, as they would a member of the royal household. Thousands of cat mummies have been found in Egyptian ruins—along with even more mouse mummies, presumably entombed to provide food for the resurrected cats. In the 1890s, 180,000 mummified cats found near Cairo were auctioned off in England, where many were used as fuel. The auctioneer used a mummified cat as a gavel to peddle the cats in ton lots.

Legend had it that cats led to the defeat of the Egyptian army in 525 B.C., through a stratagem of the Persian invader Cambyses. The Persian king placed a row of cats in front of his troops, and the Egyptian archers refused to shoot their arrows across the sacred animals, for fear of killing them.

The domesticated African cat spread from Egypt to Europe, where it interbred with a European wild cat known as *Felis silvestris,* literally "forest cat." The Greeks kept few cats which they used as household mousers. Phoenician traders brought the domesticated cat to Italy long before the days of the Roman Empire, and cats were not uncommon as household pets among aristocratic Romans.

The cat would eat fish,
and would not wet her feet.
—John Heywood, *Proverbs*

The first record of domesticated cats in Britain dates from around year 936, when a law was enacted in Wales for their protection. Throughout the Middle Ages, in most countries, cats—especially black cats—were suspected of sorcery, perhaps due to their stealth, independence, and nocturnal habits.

Even today, you find an occasional individual who's convinced the cat has some supernatural powers. As Sir Walter Scott wrote, "Cats are a mysterious kind of folk. There is more passing in their minds than we are aware of."

Today, some ailurophiles entertain the idea that mass cat slaughter during the Middle Ages led directly to the spread of the Black Death, because of the consequent rise in the rat population. Actually, considering the unsanitary conditions of the day, rats, fleas, and the plague would have flourished with or without the intervention of the feline.

Speaking of mousers, you've no doubt heard the one about the traveler who came sadly to the front door of a farmhouse to report an unfortunate accident. "I hate to tell you this, ma'am," he said, "but I just ran over your cat on the road. I'm terribly sorry. Of course, I'll replace him."

"Well, don't just stand there!" the woman snapped. "There's a mouse in the kitchen!"

Domesticated house cats fall into two broad groups: short-haired and long-haired. The long-haired variety developed in Persia and Afghanistan, and the two prevalent types of long-haired cat are now called the Persian and the Angora. As a pet, the Persian has replaced the Angora in most Western countries.

The Abyssinian, a beautiful short-haired feline, developed entirely from the African wild cat.

The tailless Manx cat is common in the Far East, where few long-tailed cats are found. The name comes from the Isle of Man off England, though it is unknown whether the cat was brought there or developed there by mutation.

The Manx cat.

The Siamese cat, a much favored pet, first reached the United States in 1895 and has flourished ever since. Incidentally, almost all Siamese cats are cross-eyed.

The number of cats extant throughout the world today is anybody's guess. The United States ranks first among ailurophilic nations. There are an estimated 20 to 25 million cats in American households today, but with the inclusion of all alley cats and other strays, the total cat population could well top the 40 million mark, which is the population figure estimated for American dogs. The popularity of cats in this country continues to grow. The cat-care business is now a multimillion-dollar industry, providing cat food and accessories, cat hospitals, kennels, and even kitty cemeteries. Pedigreed cats sell for upwards of $200.

The precise origin of our word "cat" is uncertain, but similar words designate the feline in many unrelated languages. One Latin word for the feline was *catus*, and the Anglo-Saxons dubbed the creature *catt* or *cat*. In French, we find *chat*, in Italian *gatto*, in Spanish *gato*, and in German *Katze*.

The origin of "puss" is unknown, but "kitty" comes from *chaton*, a diminutive of the French *chat*. Since at least 1450, "Tom" has been used to designate a male. A polecat, by the way, is not a cat at all—in the United States, the term designates a skunk.

According to some accounts, the expression "to fight like Kilkenny cats" dates back to a somewhat ailurophobic custom among Hessian soldiers stationed in Ireland: tying two cats together by the tails and hanging them over a fence or clothesline. One day, the story goes, an officer approached a group of soldiers thus occupied. To hide their deed, one soldier cut off the tails of both tormented animals. The officer was then told that the cats had fought so hard that they'd devoured each other, leaving only the tails.

The notion that a cat can fall from a great height and survive is not an old wives' tale, and may have contributed to the idea that a cat has nine lives. One cat fell from the 20th floor of a Montreal apartment building in 1973 and suffered only a pelvic fracture.

The story of a cat that fell from the Washington Monument and survived has been batted about for years. According to some, the facts are these: during construction of the Monument, workers came across a cat lurking in the framework near the top of the structure. The cat panicked, and leaped from the scaffolding. Incredibly enough, the cat survived the 500-foot-plus fall—but, even more amazingly, the stunned creature was pounced on and killed almost immediately by a wandering dog.

We have no idea how old that unfortunate feline was when it lost its ninth life, but on the average, a house cat can be expected to live from eight to twelve years, with one year in a cat's life equivalent to about seven years in a man's life. However, many cats have survived for considerably longer, and life spans of over 20 years are not at all uncommon. The oldest domestic cat on record, a tabby owned by a woman in England, died on November 29, 1939, at the ripe old age of 36 years!

The average household kitty weighs from eight to twelve pounds, but the largest puss on record, a tom from Connecticut, weighed in at a hefty 43 pounds. And the most valuable cat on record is, depending upon how you look at it, either a tabby inappropriately named "Mickey" who killed more than 22,000 mice during a 23-year career with an English firm, or a pair of house cats which, in 1963, inherited the entire estate of their ailurophilic owner, a California doctor. The estate was valued at $415,000!

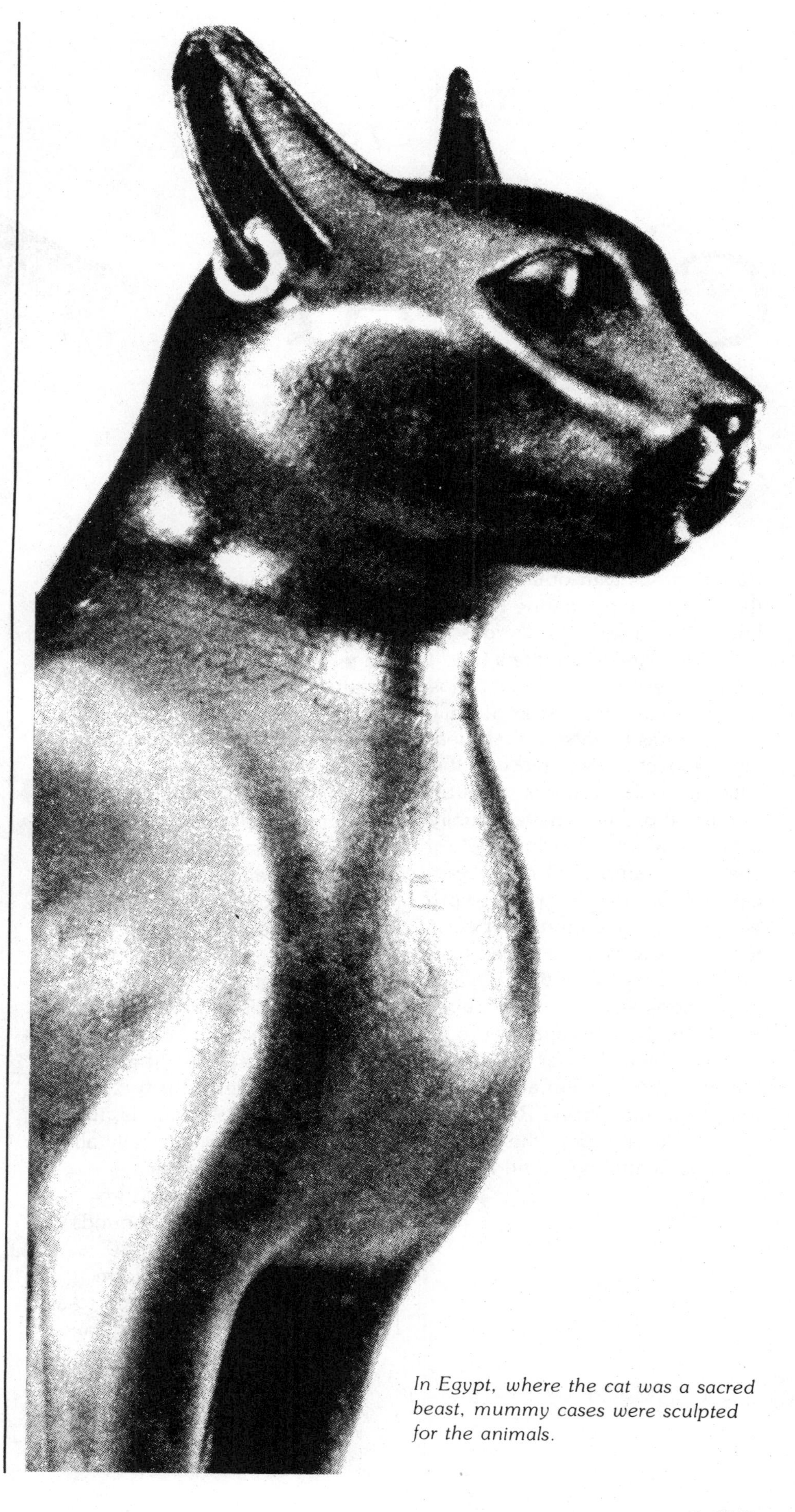

In Egypt, where the cat was a sacred beast, mummy cases were sculpted for the animals.

CAVIAR

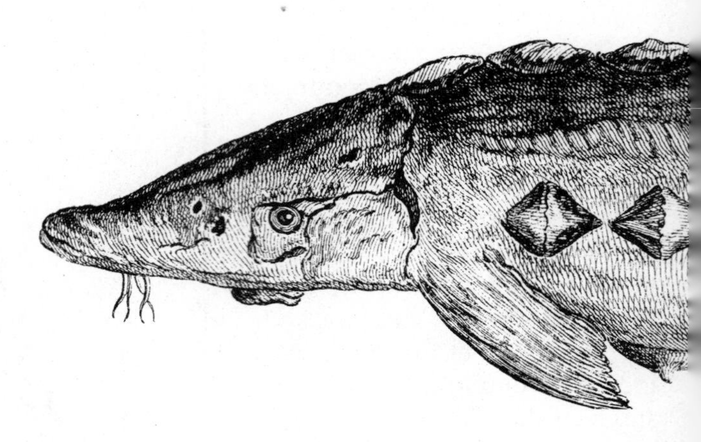

Synonymous with opulence is that salty, lumpy marine delicacy known as caviar. The word is rich with princely connotations for almost everyone—including those with no idea what caviar actually is. For it has been said that those who respect caviar's place in the elite of epicurean treats far outnumber those who have actually tasted it. Many who do have a chance to sample the delicacy can only wonder why it is so prized. But as any connoisseur can testify, caviar is an acquired taste that—for reasons of the pocketbook—is best not acquired.

Caviar is the prepared roe, or eggs, of the *acipenser,* a fish found in the Caspian and Black Seas, and the Girond River in France. At one time, the *acipenser* could be found in many European rivers, and even in some North American lakes; but since the onset of the industrial age, that fish's habitat has been reduced to portions of Russia, Iran, and Rumania. Today, virtually all caviar is produced in those three countries.

There are three kinds of *acipenser* that most graciously donate their eggs for the benefit of man's palate, and thus there are three kinds of "true" caviar. The Beluga is the largest fish of the three, growing up to twelve feet in length and weighing up to a ton! One Beluga can produce up to 130 pounds of caviar.

Another species, the Sevruga, is much smaller; four feet long and weighing 60 pounds, the Sevruga can produce only about eight pounds of caviar.

The Ocietrova, or sturgeon, may weigh up to 400 pounds and will produce about 40 pounds of caviar. The term "sturgeon" is often applied to all three kinds of caviar-producing fish, but the Ocietrova is, in fact, the only true sturgeon.

The taste for caviar flourished in the Middle Ages, when sturgeon roe was prepared as a feast for kings. The Cossacks of Russia organized massive caviar- hunting expeditions twice each year, with every member of the community taking part in the two-week campaigns. Among other things, the Cossacks used cannons to stun the fish in the water!

Today, the gathering of roe is somewhat more scientific. The fish live in the salt water of the Caspian and Black Seas but spawn in fresh water, depositing their roe at the bottom of river beds. The fish are caught as they prepare to spawn: the roe, at that time, is barely edible.

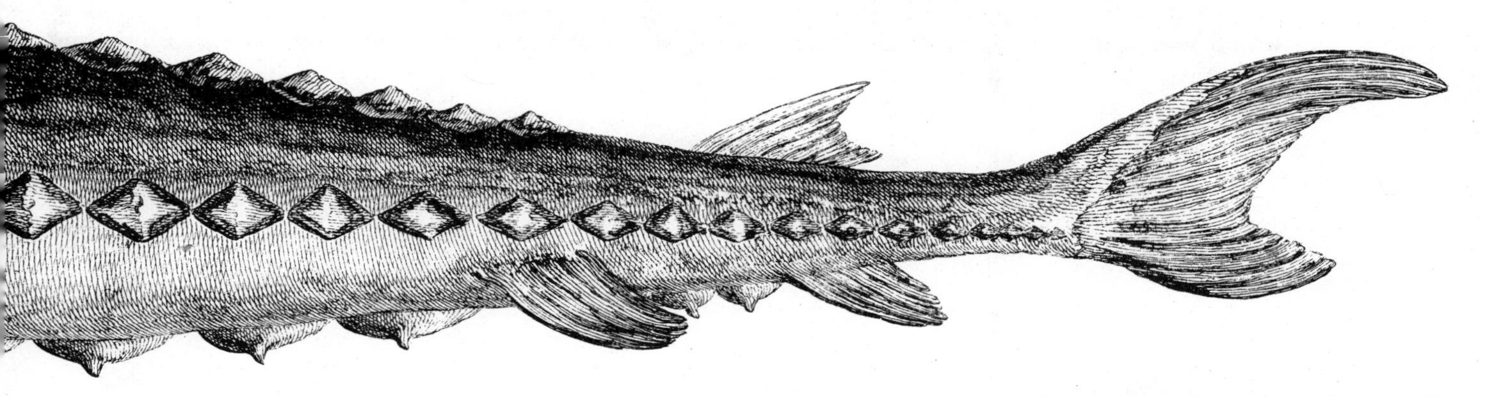

Caviar is produced from the roe of the sturgeon fish.
Drawing courtesy of Romanoff Caviar.

The captured fish are placed in submerged floating cages, where due to the lack of food, they are forced to use up the reserve nourishment stored in their roe. When the roe is fit for consumption, the fish are killed and the eggs extracted.

The roe is then pressed through a sieve to remove membranes from the eggs, and then steeped in a brine solution. The production of caviar requires only 15 minutes, but must be carried out with great skill.

The best caviar is sold by weight, is slightly salted, and extremely nourishing. Malossol caviar contains up to 30 percent protein. Due to its salt content, caviar will remain fresh for a long time. But never place it in a freezer or you'll end up with a worthless lumpy broth!

The roe of various fish have been enjoyed as a delicacy by the rich for thousands of years. "Red caviar," however, is a cheap imitation made from salmon roe.

The French have been connoisseurs of caviar from medieval times on. Rabelais speaks of the delicacy in *Pantagruel,* calling it *caviat.* In Shakespeare's day, caviar was recognized as a food for the more discerning, as Hamlet suggested when he said: "The play, I remember, pleas'd not the million; 't was caviare to the general." In other words, the play, like caviar, was pleasant only to a trained palate.

The Czar Alexander I is often credited with introducing caviar to the social elite of Paris. The word "caviar," however, is not Russian in origin (the Russians call it *ikra),* but comes from the Italian *caviola,* derived from the Turkish word *khavyah.*

Today, you can expect to pay anywhere from six to sixteen dollars for an ounce of the prized delicacy—and an ounce is considered scarcely a portion.

Until recently, about 35,000 pounds of fresh caviar were consumed yearly in the United States; a current caviar shortage has reduced American consumption to 20,000 pounds. Sixty-five long tons of caviar were imported into the United States from Iran each year, and the total American retail market for caviar is $6 million annually. But if the treat is beyond your pocketbook, or if you've already tried caviar and have been ashamed to admit that you can't stomach it, take heart. The epicurean chronicler Thomas Mouffet had this to say about the costly treat: "As for caviar, or their eggs being poudred, let Turks, Grecians, Venetians, and Spaniards celebrate them ever so much, yet the Italian proverb will ever be true: *Who eats caviar eats flies, dung, and salt.*"

Cellophane Tape

"Held together with Scotch tape" is hardly a complimentary description of any item, but our use of the cliché does suggest the extent to which Scotch tape itself has become part of the American household. You might forget from time to time that "Scotch" is merely a brand name, and owes nothing at all to Scotland—but did you realize that the word *cellophane,* too, is regarded as a brand name in most of the world?

First of all: what is cellophane? Despite common belief, neither the product nor its name originated in the United States, and both are a good deal older than you might imagine.

Cellophane is a thin film made from cellulose, the chief constituent of a plant's cell walls. In 1892, three British chemists discovered viscose, a solution of cellulose; and six years later another Englishman was granted a patent for producing films from viscose. But the cellophane industry was launched in 1911, when a Swiss chemist, named J.E. Brandenburger, invented a machine for the mass production of a strong, transparent viscose film. He named the new product *cellophane,* combining the French words *cellulose* and *diaphane,* "transparent."

The French firm La Cellophane began making the product in 1920; and three years later, sold the U.S. manufacturing rights to E.I. DuPont de Nemours & Company. Dupont built the first American cellophane plant in Buffalo, New York, in 1924, selling the transparent wrapping at $2.65 a pound.

The 1927 invention of moistureproof cellophane by two American chemists soon made the product the premier protective wrap for food. By 1950, America was producing about 250 million pounds annually, or half the world's supply, with over 50 varieties of the wrap on the market. Cellophane is widely used today for food and cosmetic wrapping—it's strong, attractive, moistureproof, odor-proof, grease-proof, gas impermeable, and transparent.

The word *cellophane* is still considered a brand name in England, France, and many other nations, where the term is traced legally to the La Cellophane firm. But a court decision declared cellophane a generic term in the United States, the name of the substance rather than a particular product.

Cellophane was still in its infancy when cellophane tape was born in the laboratories of the Minnesota Mining and Manufacturing Company. The first seeds for the new product were sown in 1925, when a 26-year-old lab assistant named Richard Drew invented a new kind of masking tape for painters in the auto industry. Drew perfected a rubber-based adhesive that allowed the tape to be wound on a roll without sticking to itself, and christened his creation "Scotch Brand Masking Tape"—complete with its now familiar red and yellow plaid tartan.

Why Scotch? That depends upon whom you ask. One apocryphal tale suggests we owe the name to a grumbling painter. When the masking tape was first being tested by painters, adhesive was applied to only the outer edges of the tape, leaving the center of the two-inch strip clear, and one painter complained: "Why so Scotch with the adhesive?"

"Scotch" masking tape was a multimillion-dollar seller by 1935, and led to the development of over a hundred other products—including cellophane tape. At the time the masking tape was introduced, cellophane was just coming into widespread use as a food wrap. But cellophane wrapping presented a problem—how to seal the cellophane wrapping itself with an equally transparent tape.

In 1929, Drew was presented with another problem: a St. Paul, Minnesota firm manufacturing insulation for refrigerator cars asked the 3M Company for a tape to seal the wrappings of their insulating material, which had to remain waterproof against refrigerator moisture. At the same time, one of Drew's assistants proposed that 3M use cellophane to package their Scotch masking tape. On June 18, 1929, Drew had a brainstorm: why not coat cellophane itself with an adhesive and use it as a tape for cellophane wrapping? After all, it's transparent and waterproof!

Drew ordered 100 yards of cellophane from DuPont and began experimenting with various rubber-based adhesives. At first Drew found that his adhesives turned the cellophane a "dirty amber" color. Experimentation continued, but by the time the 3M Company was ready to market the new tape, the product was far from perfect—it curled near heat, split easily, and failed to adhere evenly, and was amber-colored to boot.

Success came in 1930, when Drew found a stronger, more transparent adhesive. The first roll of the new product was sent to the Shellmar Products Corporation to seal cellophane-wrapped bakery goods. The tape was an instant success—it was adhesive, cohesive, elastic, and proved reliable at great temperature extremes. And it was—well, *almost*—transparent, a pale amber color.

Initially, the 3M Corporation hesitated to invest heavily in the new tape, for the Depression had clouded the United States' entire economic outlook. Yet, in a way, the Depression helped to popularize the tape when it was introduced—in hard times, people were more likely to mend an older item than replace it. The new product, called Scotch Brand Cellophane Tape, was used industrially at first; but within a few years, it had found its way into many American homes and classrooms.

Today, the amber-colored Scotch tape has, to a great extent, given way to another 3M product, called Scotch Brand Magic Transparent Tape, which is, magically enough, transparent. And the old red and yellow plaid wrapper has been replaced with green and yellow plaid.

We've neglected one milestone on the road to Scotch tape perfection: the dispenser. As you know, Scotch tape in a simple roll demands the tedious effort of first searching for the end, and then gingerly detaching it. But for saving the wear and tear on your fingernails—and your nerves—you can thank Joseph A. Borden, who designed the Scotch tape dispenser we use today.

These are the huge storage tanks in which the liquid is stored for the manufacture of cellophane.

CHAIRS

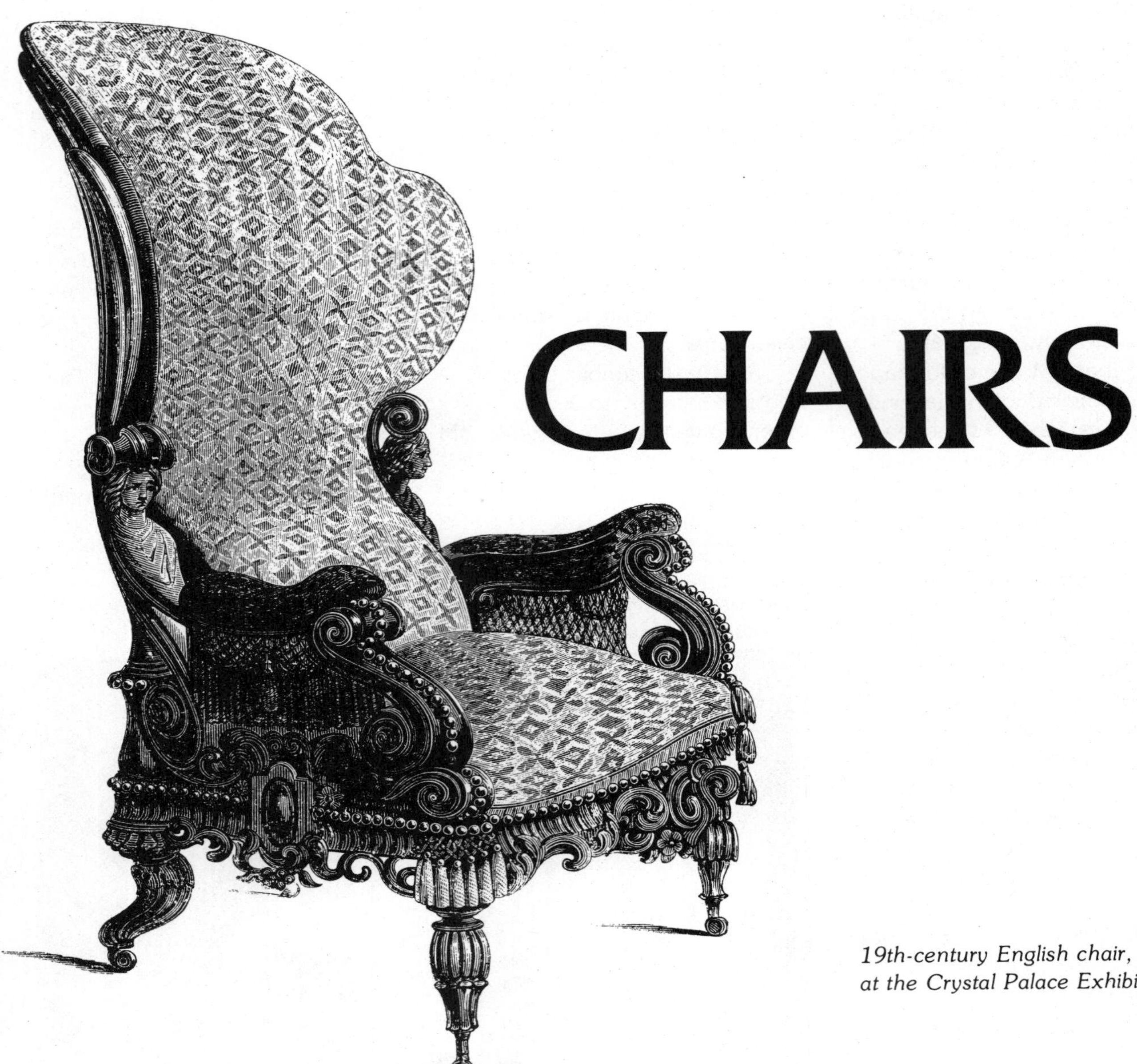

19th-century English chair, exhibited at the Crystal Palace Exhibition.

The chair is such a simple, necessary, and ubiquitous piece of furniture today, it might seem natural to assume that man has been making chairs for as long as he's been sitting. But there are many material elements of modern life whose present importance belies their relatively late appearance in the household, and the chair is one of them. For this familiar piece of furniture was not common anywhere in the world until just 300 years ago!

That may seem hard to believe, until you remember that there are still parts of the world where the chair remains a rarity. The fact is, your city or town probably contains more chairs than there were in all of ancient Egypt.

If the chair has been popular only for a few centuries, you might wonder what people did sit on for thousands of years. The most common articles of furniture for sitting were the bench, the stool, and the chest.

The bench, a simple plank of wood with two supports, was easy to make and could accommodate a number of people. The stool was also simple to construct, usually being fashioned from untrimmed forest timber. The chest was simply a storage box that could, when closed, double as a seat. You might recall that ancient Romans of means ate their meals at a low table while reclining on couches, so even in the dining room the chair was hardly a necessity.

Ancient peoples did have chairs, but these were almost

always reserved for the rich and powerful. As a throne, the chair served for ages as a symbol of authority, an emblem of the state or the seat of religious dignitaries.

In the Middle Ages, even aristocratic households usually owned but one chair, and that chair was reserved for the lord of the house. The historical status of the chair is preserved in our use of the word "chairman" for the head of a group, or in phrases such as "the judgement seat."

Our word "chair" itself was ultimately derived from the Latin *cathedra*. The Romans used that word especially to refer to a teacher's seat, and later it became associated with the seat of a bishop or other religious figure. The word also provided the term "cathedral," which was originally used for the bishop's chair itself and later transferred to the church that contained it, the "seat" of his power.

Few chairs have survived from ancient Egypt, but we know from Egyptian art that the chair was used only by the rich, and especially by political and religious leaders. Egyptian chairs were carved from wood, ebony, or ivory, and many were covered with costly fabrics. The backs were slanted, as they are today, while the legs were often carved to resemble the feet of beasts.

Some of the oldest chairs of which we have a record were depicted on a monument found in the ruins of the Assyrian capital of Nineveh. These were backless chairs with legs carved in the form of lions' claws or bulls' hooves, or supported by caryatides—columns in the shape of human figures.

The art of the ancient Greeks often depicted gods sitting on thronelike chairs. Visitors to the Parthenon, for instance, will find on the frieze of that building a representation of Zeus, seated on a chair ornamented with winged sphinxes. Many chairs depicted in Greek art had legs in the shape of animals' feet, and straight backs that did not conform to the shape of the human spine—but then these chairs may have been designed for gods instead of men.

Ancient Roman households might have included a number of couches and benches, but only the richest had the luxury of a chair. Expensive marble was a favorite building material for these chairs which, like their Greek and Egyptian predecessors, were often elaborately carved and ornamented with costly materials. An early type of Roman chair was the *currule*, a backless folding chair with curved legs that may have originally been reserved for use in a magistrate's chariot. The word itself comes from *currus*, the Latin word for chariot, and is used even today to mean "of the highest rank."

The most famous chair of antiquity is the so-called chair of St. Peter, housed in St. Peter's church at the Vatican. The chair is made of acacia wood with ivory carvings depicting the labors of Hercules, and is actually a Byzantine work of the sixth century A.D. with a few pieces of oak taken from an earlier piece of furniture. This chair is popularly thought to be contained within the bronze chair of Lorenzo Bernini, who designed portions of St. Peter's. But St. Peter's chair is kept under triple lock at the Vatican, and exhibited only once every century.

After the fall of Rome, the Byzantines retained the currule chair, often with a back in the

The chair was not common anywhere in the world until just 300 years ago!

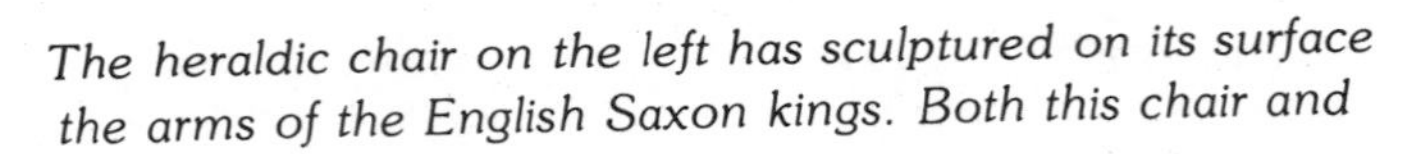

The heraldic chair on the left has sculptured on its surface the arms of the English Saxon kings. Both this chair and its rustic cousin on the right were shown at the Crystal Palace Exhibition during the 19th century.

shape of a lyre, a design common in modern chairs. The rigid, high-backed chairs of the later Middle Ages, or Gothic period, featured pointed arches and carved ornamentation in the form of foliage and geometric designs. In medieval France, chairs were customarily made from stone, while the English preferred wood.

At this time, the chair was still monopolized by aristocrats and religious leaders, and was the seat of authority in both the literal and figurative senses. At the lord's manor, the chair was kept at the head of the dining table, while the rest of the household sat on benches. Some of the thronelike chairs of the period were large enough to seat both the lord and his lady, and might include arms, a high back, a canopy, and a locked storage area underneath the seat. The lord was said to sit "in his chair"; as a result, we still sit "in" an armchair but "on" an ordinary chair.

It was during the renaissance period that the chair came into general use in all households. Since then, the chair has varied more with fashion than has any other item of furniture, and an expert can usually tell from exactly what period an old chair originates simply by examining its stylistic elements.

Until the middle of the 17th century, the majority of chairs in all European countries were made of oak, without upholstery or other cushioning. Gradually, oak was replaced by lighter, more easily carved woods, like walnut. Leather came into use for cushioning, then expensive materials such as silk and velvet. The Louis XIII period saw the introduction of cane backs, decorative gilt ornamentation, inlay, and painting.

In the early 18th century, chairs of the Queen Anne style came into fashion in England. These chairs were smaller, narrower, and lighter than the older oak chairs of that country, and featured less decorative carving. Shell motifs became especially popular. Gradually the high-backed chair faded away, and the chair began to look very much like the modern variety.

But in France, the rococo Louis XV style came into vogue, featuring elaborate detail, sweeping curves, gilded woodwork, and tapestried upholstering. Lacquerwork became fashionable, as did upholstered sides, which previously had been rare. Popular decorative elements included flowing scrolls, cupids, doves, wreaths, and shells.

Toward the middle of the 18th century, chairs began to take the form that was later to be called Chippendale, after the English furniture designer Thomas Chippendale. These chairs stressed practicality over ornamentation, and were solid and sturdy, yet gracefully formed. Mahogany came into wide use for the frames, the backs took on a flowing, interlaced form, and the legs ended in ball and claw feet.

A mahogany Chippendale chair holds the current record as the most expensive chair ever purchased. In 1972, this corner chair dating from the mid-18th century sold at auction for a neat $85,000.

Other English furniture designers, such as George Hepplewhite, Thomas Sheraton, and the Adam brothers, lent their talents to a gradual lightening and refinement of the Chippendale chair, and each gave his name to a distinct style of furniture. The Chippendale with its sturdy, practical construction, and the Hepplewhite with its delicacy, grace, and rounded or oval backs, together determined what might be called the modern chair.

Chair design in America was from the beginning based on the imitation of current European styles, with occasional native adaptations. The first chair factory in the United States actually didn't make its appearance until 1818, in Connecticut. One purely American innovation was the writing-arm chair, typified by the addition of a pear-shaped desk section that could often be raised from the arm. This type of chair, still common in some American schools, is called a "desk" rather than a chair.

But surely the most important and familiar American contribution to chair design was the rocking chair, reputedly invented by Benjamin Franklin. The Boston rocker, with its rounded back and curved seat, has been called the most popular chair ever made.

The largest chair in existence was built in Reykjavik, Iceland in 1977. This chair is indeed fitting for a god of Greek mythology: it stands 24 feet, four inches tall and weighs 12.32 tons!

Since the 18th century, no new style of chair has lasted for any length of time. For the most part, chair design has moved out of the hands of original artists and into the hands of designers who resurrect or recombine older styles to produce the ordinary chair of today—with occasional exceptions such as the sweeping "modernistic" designs of Mies van der Rohe and others.

No matter what kind of chair you prefer, you surely have a few around the house. For in recent centuries, everyone has become a "chairman"—or a "chairperson"—and the ordinary chair is no more a symbol of authority and position than the kitchen table. Even an impoverished recluse like Henry David Thoreau could claim a number of chairs in his forest hut: "One for solitude, two for friendship, three for society."

A Canadian chair exhibited at the Crystal Palace, 19th century.

Cheese

Cheese has been called "milk's leap to immortality." To those who consider cheese merely a colorful addition to a hamburger, the scientific expertise and tender loving care that go into the production of fine cheese may well seem extravagant. But to connoisseurs, who savor above all else a perfectly ripened piece of creamy Camembert, tangy Gorgonzola, or pungent Limburger, the world of *belle fromage* truly marks man's most ambitious effort in the pursuit of gustatory pleasure.

Cheese is, prosaically enough, the consolidated curd of milk. The cow, and to a lesser extent, the goat and sheep, are by far the most common providers of milk for cheese. But the milk of the buffalo, camel, horse, llama, yak, reindeer, ass, and zebra have also been used to make cheese in various parts of the world.

There are many ways to make cheese, some simple, some quite complex. Most cheese-making begins with the coagulation and separation of milk into two components, curds and whey. Untreated milk will coagulate naturally, but the separation of the curd from the whey is usually aided by the addition of bacterial cultures or rennet, an enzyme found in the stomachs of calves.

When the milk has separated, the watery whey is removed, leaving the semisolid curd, or fresh cheese. Heat is sometimes applied to aid in the coagulation. The curd is pressed into shape, coated with wax or other wrapping, then cured and ripened in any of hundreds of different ways. About 10 volumes of milk are required to produce one volume of cheese, but cheese contains almost all of milk's fat, protein, and calcium.

For the most part, cheese-making techniques have been developed independently in various parts of the world. Some of these techniques have been kept secret by cheesemakers since well before the Christian era began. There is good reason for this secrecy, for the making of fine cheese is an extremely delicate operation.

Minute changes in the processes or ingredients used to make cheese will produce marked differences in the final product. Cheese, like wine, is very much a product of the area in which it is made. Just as wine grapes from, say, Burgundy, which are replanted in California will never produce a wine identical to French Burgundy, a cheese made in a particular area cannot be exactly duplicated anywhere else.

The kind of milk used—cow or goat, whole or skimmed—plays a large part in determining the taste and texture of a cheese. But elements, such as the types of grasses and herbs common in an area, and the mineral content of the soil, will also influence the cheese produced there. The milk-producing animal's diet will determine the amounts of acidity and butterfat in the milk. The types of bacteria or molds used in ripening the cheese also play a part in determining the final product, as do the amount of salt and other seasonings added and the methods used in coagulating and curing the cheese.

The story of Liederkranz cheese illustrates the delicacy of cheese production. In 1892, a cheese maker named Emil Frey set out to duplicate a certain German cheese at a plant in Monroe, New York. Instead, he produced an entirely new cheese. Frey named his cheese after a choral group he belonged to in New York City: *Liederkranz*, or "wreath of songs."

In 1929, the Borden Company took over production of Liederkranz, and shortly after decided to move the cheese factory to Van Wert, Ohio. In an attempt to duplicate the environment for Liederkranz production as closely as possible, Borden moved every last piece of cheese-making apparatus to Ohio, and continued to use precisely the same ingredients. But the Ohio Liederkranz simply did not taste the same as the New York variety.

Finally, the cheese makers brought a quantity of old Liederkranz made in the New York plant to the new facility, and smeared the cheese over the tile walls of the plant. Thereafter, the Ohio Liederkranz was virtually identical to the New York product. Why? The first time around, the cheese makers had neglected to take into account the effect of airborne

An old cheese press.

It would probably surprise most Americans to learn that the United States is the world's largest producer of cheese.

bacteria on the final product—bacteria growing on the cheese-smeared walls!

There are an estimated four to five hundred different names for the cheeses produced around the world, but many of these names are merely different terms for one cheese commonly produced in the area. *Limburger* cheese, for example, may be called *Algau, Lanark, Marianhof, Morin, Tanzenberg, Briol,* or *Lindenhof* when produced in the town bearing those names. Actually, there are but 18 or 19 distinct varieties of cheese. Furthermore, all cheeses fall into one of six general categories.

Unripened cheese, such as cottage cheese, cream cheese, *ricotta,* and *mozzarella* is eaten fresh, without curing or ripening.

Soft ripened cheeses are ripened by bacterial cultures that begin growing on the surface of the cheese and progress from the rind to the center. Popular cheeses in this category include *Brie, Camembert,* and *Limburger.*

Semisoft ripened cheeses such as *Bel Paese, Munster,* and *Port du Salut* ripen from the interior as well as from the surface.

Firm ripened cheeses such as *Cheddar, Emmenthaler,* and *Edam* are generally ripened for considerably longer than the softer cheeses.

Very firm ripened cheeses like *Parmesan* and *Romano* are ripened for an even longer period, and are usually used for grating. The Swiss *Saanen* is the world's hardest cheese, requiring about seven years to fully ripen.

In blue-vein mold ripened cheeses, curing is aided by a characteristic mold culture that grows throughout the interior of the cheese. The most popular blue-veined cheeses include *Roquefort, Gorgonzola,* and *Stilton.*

The earliest cheeses made by man were probably unripened cheeses, similar to modern yogurt or cream cheese. One such cheese, the Arabian goat cheese called *kishk,* is the oldest cheese still made today. Ripened cheeses such as *Parmesan* and *Brie* were developed during the Middle Ages, while many semisoft chéeses appeared much later. Most of the cheeses produced today were developed only within the last few centuries.

Cheese-making began well before recorded history, possibly among shepherds in the Indus Valley or in Mesopotamia. One legend tells us that cheese was "discovered" by a young shepherd boy in the Middle East who carried milk in a pouch made from a sheep or goat's stomach. Since the stomachs of these animals contain rennet, milk stored in such a pouch would coagulate into cheese. But it seems more likely that the cheese-making process was readily discovered by a number of ancient cultures soon after they began drinking the milk of domesticated animals. Cheese was important among ancient peoples because it provided a way of preserving milk, thousands of years before refrigeration.

As long ago as 4000 B.C., cheese-making was well known to the Sumerians of Mesopotamia. Cheese molds found among the ruins of the Egyptian and Chaldean civilizations show that cheese was a common food there before 2000 B.C. The Old Testament mentions "cheese of the herd," and tells

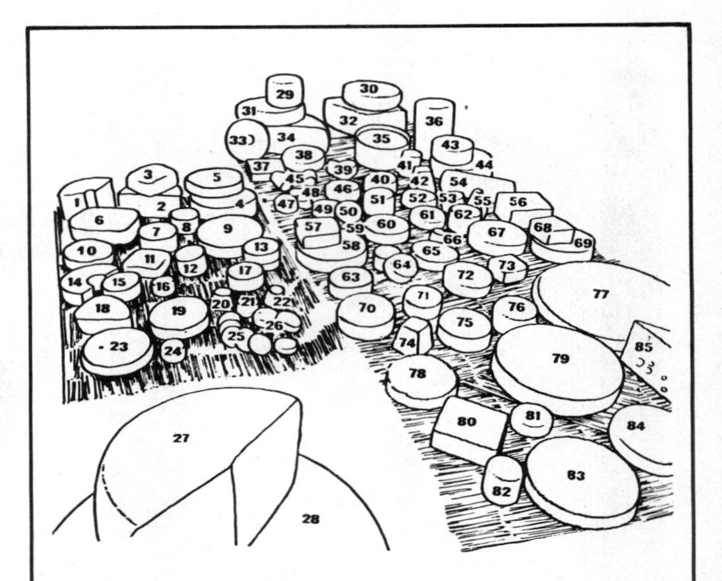

THE CHEESES OF FRANCE:
France produces more varieties of cheese than any other country in the world: the official census lists 327. The samples pictured on the facing page can be identified from the numbered keys below.

1. Bleu des Causses. 2. Roquefort. 3. Nillo. 4. Fondu aux raisins. 5. Citeaux. 6. Tomme au marc. 7. Chaource. 8.Aurore. 9. Munster au cumin (caraway seeds). 10 and 11. La Mothe-Saint-Heraye. 12. Chaumont. 13. Duc. 14. Dauphin. 15. Rollot. 16. Tomme de Crest. 17. Langres. 18. Boulette de Cambral. 19. Soumarintrin. 20. Bressant. 21. Rigotte de Condrieu. 22. Chabichou. 23. Coulommiers brie. 24. Crottin de Chavignol. 25. Rocamadour. 26. Picodon. 27. Cantal. 28. Beaufort. 29. Persille de Savoir. 30. Saint-Nectaire. 31. Port Salut. 32. Gex. 33. Murol. 34. Laruns. 35. Vacherin. 36. Fourme d'Ambert. 37. Pont-l'Eveque. 38. Brillat-Savarin. 39. Gournay. 40. Bourgogne. 41. Double Bondard. 42. Valencay. 43. Livarot. 44. Tomme de Savoie. 45. Neuchatel. 46. Epoisses. 47. Les Aides. 48. Bouton de Culotte. 49. Vendome cendre. 50. Poivre d'ane. 51. La Bouille. 52. Vendome bleu. 53. Saint-Marcellin. 54. Baguette lyonnaise. 55. Pouligny. 56. Puant marece. 57. Recollet. 58. Munster. 59. Banon. 60. Saint-Florentin. 61. Fin de siecle. 62. Bleu de Bresse. 63. Livarot. 64. Mr. Fromage. 65. Cendre d'Olivet. 66. Maconnais. 67. Lucullus. 68. Maroilles mignon. 69. Tamie. 70. Port Salut. 71. Montpezat. 72. Camembert. 73. Cure. 74. Levroux. 75. Chevrotin. 76. Chambarand. 77. Brie de Meaux. 78. Pithivier au foin. 79. Brie de Melun. 80. Maroilles. 81. Pelardon. 82. Charollais. 83. Feuille de Dreux. 84. Roblochon. 85. Comte du Haut-Jura.

us that David was delivering cheese to Saul's camp when he encountered Goliath. The long-suffering Job complained: "Thou hast poured me out as milk and curdled me as cheese."

Unripened cheese was a staple food among the ancient Greeks, who dubbed the god Aristaeus "the giver of cheese." In Homer's *Odyssey*, Ulysses discovers "a drying rack which sagged with cheeses" in the Cyclops' cave. The diet of Greek athletes consisted largely of cheese, for they believed that cheese increased endurance. Coins minted on the island of Delos bore a representation of cheese, while the island of Samos was noted throughout Greece as the home of great cheesecake. The Greeks' wedding cake, incidentally, was almost always a cheesecake covered with honey.

Cheese-making was an extensive industry among the ancient Romans, who also imported cheeses from various parts of the Empire. The historian Pliny the Elder tells us that Roman legions in Britain favored a sharp, *Cheshire*-like cheese, while Roman gourmets were particularly fond of *caseus helveticus*, a Swiss cheese much like the modern *Sbrinz*. The homes of Roman aristocrats often included special kitchens for cheese-making, while plebeians visited public smokehouses to cure their farm cheese.

The cheeses of France.

The Roman army subsisted largely on cheese—as did the hordes of Genghis Khan—for cheese is nutritious, long-lasting, and concentrated. Like the Greeks, the Romans used the phrase "little cheese" as a term of endearment. The modern "big cheese," meaning someone or something of importance, is probably derived not from the word *cheese,* but from the Persian *chiz,* meaning *thing.*

The Latin word *caseus,* however, is the basis of our word *cheese,* as well as the German *kase* and the Spanish *queso.* The Greek word *formos,* applied to the wicker baskets used for draining cheese, became *forma* in Latin, *formaggio* in Italian, and *formage* in French before it evolved into the modern French *fromage.*

Many of the cheese-making advances of the Middle Ages were the work of cloistered monks who were among the few people of the era with the time to experiment and the literacy required to write down and evaluate results. Outside the monasteries, cheese-making remained basically a family industry until the 15th and 16th centuries, when cheese-makers began joining together to form cooperatives. Road taxes actually played a part in the change to community cheese-making. At the time, carts were assessed a tax for using a highway according to the number of cheeses they carried, rather than the total weight of the cheese. Thus cheese-makers who joined together to produce large cheeses could transport their product much more cheaply.

During the Renaissance, cheese eating fell out of fashion among the upper classes, partly as a result of physicians' warnings that it was an unhealthy, indigestible food. Shakespeare usually referred to cheese with distaste. For example, in *The Merry Wives of Windsor,* Bardolph insults Slender by calling him "You Banbury cheese!" A contemporary writer named Thomas Muffet wrote that cheese "lieth long in the stomach undigested, procureth thirst, maketh a stinking breath and a scurvy skin." Some people even believed that cheese had certain occult powers.

The main reason for the poor opinion of cheese among Renaissance Europeans was the belief that cheese was impossible to digest. But the view was also held that cheese aided in the digestion of other foods. As John Ray noted in a 1670 poem:

Cheese, it is a peevish elf
It digests all things but itself.

This belief certainly contributed to the custom of eating cheese after a meal. In any case, by the 19th century, cheese had regained its popularity. Ever since then, cheese consumption has been on the rise.

Some of the cheeses we enjoy today take their name from special ingredients included in their manufacture, such as *Grappe,* whose surface is covered with grape seeds, and the German *Nagel,* literally *nail,* which is studded with naillike pieces of clove or caraway. Other cheeses take their name from their characteristic shape. *Provolone,* for example, comes from the Italian word for *oval,* while the American *brick cheese* is shaped like a brick. *Ost* is cheese in Scandinavia, and many cheeses from this region, including *Mysost* and *Gjetost,* end with those three letters. German cheeses often end in *-kase,* while many Danish cheeses end in *-bo.* But most of the world's cheeses simply bear the name of the abbey or town where they were first made or sold.

France, third after the United States and Italy in total cheese production, can boast the most varieties of cheese—some 240 in all. Among the most popular is *Camembert,* produced by inoculating ripening cheese with the *Penicillium candidum* mold. Legend has it that Camembert was first produced around 1780, and made famous by Napoleon, who was so pleased with his first taste of the cheese that he kissed the waitress who served it.

Another French cheese of ancient vintage is the butterlike *Brie,* which may have been developed as long ago as the 12th century. Brie is sometimes known as the "cheese of kings," since it has earned the praise of so many monarchs.

The "cheese of kings" is not to be confused with the "king of cheeses," *Roquefort,* by far the most popular sheep's milk cheese in the Western world. According to a legend, this blue-vein mold ripened cheese was discovered many centuries ago by a shepherd boy who left a lunch of bread and sheep's milk cheese in a cave. Returning weeks later, he found that his cheese had been miraculously transformed into the marbled delicacy so popular today.

Roquefort is now ripened with the aid of *Penicillum roqueforti,* a mold-producing substance made from rye breadcrumbs. By law, the term Roquefort may be applied only to cheeses ripened in damp limestone caves near Roquefort in southeastern France. The precedent for this stricture was set in 1411, when Charles VI decreed that the term Roquefort could not be applied to "bastard cheese made in bastard caves."

Port du Salut, a semisoft cheese popular in both

This statue in Normandy commemorates the first maker of Camembert cheese.

Europe and the United States, was first made early in the 1800s by Trappist monks at the monastery of Notre Dame de Port du Salut in Entrammes, France. In 1873, Port du Salut cheese made its debut in Paris, and became an instant favorite. Trappist monks supervise production of the cheese in many places, and the monastery at Entrammes still turns out 200,000 cheeses each year. But this cheese is not to be confused with Trappist cheese, a similar product made in Yugoslavia and very popular in Austria and Hungary.

Maroilles is another French cheese developed by monks. First produced in 960 at the abbey of Thierache, Maroilles is bathed in beer during the ripening process. Frenchmen call Maroilles *vieux puant*—"old stinker."

Pont L'Eveque, another ancient French favorite, owes its distinctive taste to a fungus found only in a certain area in northern France.

France can also boast the world's most expensive cheese. *Laruns,* a cheese made from sheep's milk in the Bearn area of southern France, sometimes sells in Paris for close to four dollars a pound, making it the costliest of all cheeses in its country of origin. But many cheeses are considerably more expensive as imports. French Brie, for example, can sell in America for over six dollars a pound.

Gorgonzola is the most popular Italian import in the United States. Named after the town near Milan where it was first produced in the ninth century, this blue-veined cheese is ripened with the aid of a certain fungus found in caves in the area.

Italian ricotta, Romano, and mozzarella are all very popular in the United States, but for the most part we eat American imitations of these cheeses. In Italy, ricotta is made from sheep's milk; in America, it is usually produced from whey left over from Cheddar cheese production. Similarly, Italian Romano is made from sheep's milk, American Romano from cow's milk. Interestingly, mozzarella was originally made from buffalo's milk, as it is today in some parts of Italy. In the United States, tons of the chewy, unripened cheese are devoted to the art of pizza-making.

The next time you enjoy a bowl of pasta, you'll likely season your dish with grated Parmesan cheese. But in Italy, the word Parmesan—from the city of Parma—is virtually unknown. Italians call the cheese *Grana,* in reference to its granular appearance. First made during the Middle Ages, Parmesan is one of the hardest cheeses in the world, requiring a considerable ripening period and the occasional rubbing of its surface with oil during the curing period.

Provolone, like its other popular Italian cousins, is widely produced in the United States. Americans are no doubt less familiar with *Manteca,* a solid whey butter ripened in carved-out areas inside Provolone cheeses.

Belgium has given us the notoriously pungent Limburger, but most of the Limburger consumed in America is now produced domestically. American Limburger once led to an incident referred to in Wisconsin as the Limburger Rebellion. According to the tale, residents of a town in Green County became enraged when a caravan containing Limburger cheese was parked in front of a local bank to ripen in the summer sun. After threatening a variation on the Boston Tea Party, the locals were appeased when a farmer agreed to remove the offending cheese to his cellar.

A storeroom for aging Parmesan cheese in a cheese factory located in Parma, Italy.

A controversy also arose in Wisconsin when a mailman refused to handle a particularly pungent shipment of Limburger, claiming that the smell made him ill. A court decision upheld the right of cheesemakers to ship their odiferous product in the U.S. mails.

In 1877, a Dodge county, Wisconsin, cheesemaker named John Jossi set out to make Limburger and instead ended up with the savory, semisoft product we now call brick cheese. Aside from Liederkranz, brick cheese is the only cheese native to the United States.

Switzerland has given the world one of its finest cheeses, *Emmenthaler,* known in the United States simply as Swiss cheese. Originating during the 15th century in the Emmenthaler Valley, Swiss cheese is now produced in almost every Western country. A French variation is known as *Gruyère.* Emmenthaler requires three different species of bacteria in ripening—including one culture that produces the characteristic holes. These holes are initially small, and grow when the cheese is allowed to "rise" during the curing process.

Highway taxes induced Swiss cheesemakers to combine their produce into the massive wheels we now associate with Swiss cheese. Before 1800, most Emmenthalers weighed less than 100 pounds. Exported Emmenthalers now weigh 160 pounds on the average. The largest wheels, which can tip the scales at 220 pounds, require over a ton of milk! The Swiss Cheese Union, considered the strictest cartel in the world, scrutinizes Emmenthaler production in Switzerland. First produced here around 1850, Swiss cheese now ranks second in production among all our domestic cheeses.

The number-one honor goes to Cheddar cheese, first produced near the English village that bears its name. By law, English Cheddar is no longer permitted in this country. The American product, called *Cheddar, American, Monterey,* or *Jack* cheese, accounts for an amazing 85 percent of all the cheese produced in this country—due largely to its traditional use atop cheeseburgers. Cheddar may range in flavor from blandly mild to very sharp. Mellow Cheddar is aged just a few months, while the sharper varieties may be left to ripen for up to two years.

Another English cheese, *Cheshire*, may have been made in Britain before the arrival of the Romans. Dr. Samuel Johnson was said to be particularly fond of this cheese, though contrary to popular belief he never frequented a tavern called the Cheshire Cheese—no such establishment existed in London at the time.

Mold-ripened *Stilton* is considered by many the premier English cheese. First made at least as early as 1730, Stilton was first served at the Bell Hotel in the town of Stilton. In flavor, it is slightly milder that its blue-veined cousins, Roquefort and Gorgonzola.

The English, large consumers of cheese, now produce less than 40 percent of the cheese they consume. Compare that with New Zealand, which exports about 20 times as much cheese as it consumes. Italy, also a country of cheese consumers, exports just five percent of its annual production.

The English language, by the way, seems somewhat ambiguous in its opinion of cheese. The expression *cheese it* means "to be quiet" as well as "to look out or scram," while a *cheese-eater* is an informer. An Englishman who is *cheesed off* is quite ruffled, while *cheese down* is a verb meaning "to form into a tight coil." And though *big cheese* is complimentary, *cheesy* certainly is not.

We're unaware of any Dutch expressions employing the word *kaas,* but we're quite familiar with two popular Dutch exports, *Gouda* and *Edam*. Each owes its name to the town of its birth. Dutch immigrants in East Prussia were also responsible for *Tilsit* cheese, now widely produced in Germany.

Unripened *feta,* made from goat's or sheep's milk, is the favorite in Greece. *Domiati,* called "pickled cheese" because of its heavy salt content, is the premier *fromage* in Egypt. You're more likely familiar with Danish cheese, especially Danish blue, or *Danablu,* now the most popular imported cheese in America. The Danes began producing their own cheeses on a large scale—or rather, copying the cheeses of other nations—when normal supplies of imports were cut off during World War I.

It would probably surprise most Americans to learn that the United States is the world's largest producer of cheese. Annual production here now hovers around the billion-pound mark, accounting for about one-quarter of all the cheese produced in the world. About one-tenth of all milk produced in the United States is devoted to cheese-making.

When it comes to consumption, however, Americans are far from the world's greatest cheese-lovers. The average American consumes from 10 to 12 pounds of cheese annually, including about four pounds of cottage cheese. The average Frenchman, on the other hand, consumes some 30 pounds of *fromage* each year.

Stacking "globes" of cheese on wooden trays at an outdoor market in Alkmaar, Holland.

Greek shepherds watch while whey drips from the cheesecloth in the cheese-making process.

A modern-day, fast-food cheeseburger.

Cheese began to be exported from America as early as 1790, when 150,000 pounds were shipped abroad. Cheese-making in early America was basically concentrated among English settlers in New York State and Swiss immigrants in Wisconsin. But the first cheese-making cooperative was founded, appropriately enough, in Cheshire, Massachusetts. In 1802, the year after its founding, the cooperative presented President Thomas Jefferson with a 1,235-pound cheese as a New Year's gift. Six horses were required to transport the cheese to Washington.

In 1851, Jesse Williams of Rome, New York, founded the first large cheese-making factory in America, buying excess milk from neighboring dairy farmers for the production of cheese. Within 15 years, there were more than 500 cheese-making factories in New York State alone, and more than half of all American-made cheese was being made in the factory rather than the farm. Today, Wisconsin is far and away the major cheese-producing state, accounting for about half of all American production.

Incidentally, the American favorite known as *pineapple cheese* has nothing whatsoever to do with pineapples. First produced in 1808, in Troy, Pennsylvania, pineapple cheese is actually Cheddar cheese hung to drain in net bags that mold the cheese into the shape of a pineapple. The netting provides the cross-hatching so reminiscent of the prickly fruit.

Most of the cheeses we've discussed so far are known as "natural" cheeses. But a large percentage of the cheese produced in America today is "processed" cheese—cheese that has undergone further treatment after ripening. Most processed cheese is first pasteurized, then blended with other ingredients or other cheeses, seasoned, poured into molds, and sold as slices, bricks, or wedges. Pasteurized process cheese keeps well, and melts easily when reheated.

Processed cheese was actually first produced in Switzerland in 1912. A year later, a Chicago cheese dealer named James L. Kraft began experimenting with processed cheese, laying the groundwork for the massive Kraft Foods Corporation that now provides America with a large part of its domestic cheese. About three-quarters of all American-made cheese now undergoes some kind of pasteurization process before packaging. But the rest of the world is hardly rushing to follow in our footsteps—the United States produces more processed cheese each year than the rest of the world combined.

Further down the road to cheese adulteration, we find pasteurized process cheese *food*. If you look on the dairy shelves of your supermarket, you'll find that sliced American cheese is sold as both processed cheese and processed cheese food, with the latter slightly cheaper. Cheese food contains less cheese than processed cheese, with nonfat dry milk or whey solids added.

Going one step further, we find pasteurized process cheese *spread*. Most spreads are packaged in jars or loaves. Many contain additional flavoring ingredients, such as pimentos, peppers, or meat. Cheese spread is higher in moisture and lower in milk fat content than cheese or cheese food.

Processed cheese food and spread hardly seem an appropriate place to end our look at the world of *belle fromage*. Instead, let us take a peek at the world of *grande fromage*. In 1840, English cheesemakers delivered a half-ton Cheddar as a bridal gift for Queen Victoria. Little did they suspect that, 124 years later, the Wisconsin Cheese Foundation would produce a mammoth Cheddar tipping the scales at 34,591 pounds! The Cheddar was delivered for exhibition at the 1964 World's Fair in New York City aboard a specially designed, 45-foot-long refrigerated trailer called the "Cheese-Mobile." Now *that's* a big cheese!

In 1837, President Andrew Jackson invited the public to partake of an extraordinarily smelly 1400-lb. cheese.

Chewing Gum

"Does your chewing gum
lose its flavor
On the bedpost overnight?"

The title of this 1960s song may not tickle your funny bone if you don't chew gum, but those who do indulge will certainly get the picture. The sight of a dried up, mouldering piece of chewed gum stuck to the underside of a desk won't strike the non-chewer as very appetizing, but to the gum-chewer—well, a piece of gum is a piece of gum.

And there are gum-chewers galore in this country, male and female, young and old, from every stratum of society. No one knows for sure how many people chew gum, but some 35 *billion* sticks will find their way into American mouths this year. That's about five billion packets, or 25 packets for each man, woman, and child in the United States. At, say, 20 cents a throw, Americans will spend about a billion dollars on gum this year. And you thought gum-chewing was on the wane?

The urge to masticate seems to be quite strong in the human animal, for gum-chewing has been popular in many cultures over the last 2,000 years. The ancient Greeks chewed a gum obtained from the resin of the mastic tree. Our words "mastic" and "masticate" are both derived from the Greek word for "chew."

Over a thousand years ago, the Mayans and other American Indians chewed chicle-based gums. But the first gums American colonists encountered were spruce gums introduced to the Pilgrims by the Wampanoog Indians in the early 17th century. Made from wads of resin the Indians found stuck to the bark of spruce trees, spruce gums were waxy and tough, more cordial to the teeth than to the taste buds.

Yet spruce gums were to remain the only chews available in the United States for close to 200 years, until the introduction, in the 19th century, of paraffin gums. The first spruce chewing gum to be commercially manufactured in this country was the "State of Maine Pure Spruce Gum," brought out in 1848 by a Bangor, Maine, entrepreneur named John Curtis. Curtis later sold spruce gums under such names as "American Flag" and "200 Lump Spruce." He also sold paraffin gums dubbed "Licorice Lulu," "Sugar Cream," and "Biggest and Best."

Pioneers settling the American West found the Osage Indians chewing a chicle-based gum made from the hardened sap of the sapodilla tree. The Osage, who'd been chewing chicle for many hundreds of years, had apparently obtained their first chews from Indian tribes living south of the Mexican border, where the sapodilla grows.

The Mexican General Antonio Lopez de Santa Anna—yes, the same Santa Anna of Alamo notoriety—thought that chicle could be used in the manufacture of

Beeman's— THE ORIGINAL Pepsin Gum

CAUTION.—See that the name **Beeman** is on each wrapper.

The Perfection of Chewing Gum

And a Delicious Remedy for Indigestion and Sea Sickness.

Send 5c. for sample package.

Beeman Chemical Co.
28 Lake St., Cleveland, O.
Originators of
Pepsin Chewing Gum.

In the days of unregulated advertising, chewing gum manufacturers often made extravagant claims for their product.

rubber. So in 1839, he brought some sapodilla sap to the American inventor Thomas Adams. Attempts to manufacture rubber from the tree sap failed, but by the 1870s, Adams's company was marketing the nation's first commercial chicle- based chewing gums.

Chicle, Adams found, lasted much longer than paraffin or spruce, and carried flavors better than the earlier gums. Adams was soon selling such treats as *Peppermint, Spearmint, Black Jack* (licorice, of course, still popular), *Clove, Pepsin,* and *Cinnamon.* Today, the Adams Company and the William Wrigley, Jr. Company are the nation's largest manufacturers of chewing gums.

Thirty-year-old William Wrigley, Jr. moved to Chicago in 1891 and set up the Wrigley Company with just $32 of his own money and a $5,000 loan. The firm initially sold soap, then branched out into baking powder. In 1892, Wrigley ordered some chewing gum from the Zeno Manufacturing Company to offer jobbers as an inducement to buy his baking powder. Wrigley's salesmen dispensed two packs of gum with each 10-cent package of baking powder, and the jobbers soon reported that they found it much easier to sell the gum than peddle the powder. It didn't take Wrigley long to see the possibilities.

By the turn of the century, Wrigley's gum was being sold, coast to coast, in stores and vending machines. Chewing gum factories were soon springing up in a number of foreign countries, including Canada, England, Germany, Australia, and New Zealand. By the end of World War II, the taste for Wrigley's product in America, Europe, and Asia was so great that his factories could barely keep pace with the demand.

Today, most chicle comes from Mexico. Sapodilla trees are tapped with grooved cuts and the latex is collected in small receptacles, as in the gathering of

A stick of sugarless gum contains but 6 or 7 calories—while a regular stick contains a whopping 8 calories!

maple syrup. Most productive sapodilla trees are over 70 years old. For best results, each tree is tapped only once every six to eight years. The collected sap is then boiled, coagulated, and molded into blocks.

At the manufacturing plant, the chicle is kneaded into a hot sugar and corn syrup mixture, then flavored and rolled into thin strips. Most modern gums contain 20 percent chicle, 60 percent sugar, 19 percent corn syrup, and one percent flavoring. Of course, after a few hours of chewing, the wad in your mouth isn't likely to contain anything but the gum itself. Some gum manufacturers now use synthetic products to give their gum its chewiness.

Americans spend more money on chewing gum than on books; if you want to know the reason why, read some of the books.

The largest collection of baseball cards in the world—200,000 cards—belongs to the Metropolitan Museum of Art in New York.

Gumdrops are made not from chicle, but from gum arabic, a substance obtained from exudations of certain types of acacia tree. Gum arabic products were used as medicaments for many years, since the slow solution of gum in the mouth allowed a steady release of the active ingredients.

Many gum specialties have come and gone over the 100-year history of chewing gum marketing. For decades, the Adams Company has been selling Chiclets—pellets of gum wrapped in a sugar candy. The 1970s saw the introduction of "squirt" gum, wads of chewing gum with liquid centers that "explode" into the mouth upon the first chew. And the sweet, pink chew known as bubble gum needs little identification.

Bubble gum first appeared in 1933. But it wasn't until 1947, when the Topps Chewing Gum Co. began to offer the familiar Bazooka penny piece, that bubble gum became the ubiquitous source of oral gratification it is today. Later, Topps included baseball cards with slabs of gum.

The earliest baseball cards appeared during the 1880s in packets of cigarettes and tobacco. Candy companies began to issue cards in 1913, and bubble gum manufacturers included cards with their product beginning in 1933. Topps entered the baseball card field in 1951, and has since become the giant of both the bubble gum and baseball card industries, distributing some 250 million cards each year.

The Topps company estimates that there are now more than 100,000 serious baseball card collectors in the United States. Enthusiasts will pay surprisingly high sums for a valuable specimen. The largest collection of baseball cards in the world—200,000 cards—belongs to the Metropolitan Museum of Art in New York, and the most prized Topps card in existence is the 1952 Mickey Mantle, valued as high as $100.

During baseball's spring training period, Topps signs and photographs all rookies and established players whom they believe have a chance to make the major league rosters in the upcoming season. Each player is photographed both wearing a cap and bareheaded. If the player is traded to another club after his picture is taken, the bareheaded photo is used on the player's card. In case you were wondering, a player *is* paid for the use of his picture—$250 each year a new card appears.

The baseball card trade is not without its lighter side. A number of right-handed practical jokers have posed for the Topps photographer wearing a left-handed glove, or vice versa, and more than one player has appeared on a card bearing another player's name. In 1969, California Angels'

In 1975, Kurt Bevacqua of the Milwaukee Brewers won the Topps World Series Bubble-Blowing Contest with this 18" bubble. The prizes were a $1,000 donation to the charity of the winner's choice, a giant-sized baseball card of the player, and a year's supply of Bazooka bubblegum.

third baseman Aurelio Rodriguez duped Topps into photographing the team batboy in his place, and thousands of cards bearing the batboy's image over Rodriguez' name were distributed before Topps caught the error.

Few people buy Topps baseball cards for the slab of bubble gum included in each package. Bubble gum addicts are more likely to get their fix from a piece of Topps Bazooka gum. Bazooka was introduced in 1947, and owes its name to the resemblance between the early five-cent size and the bazookas used in World War II.

Each piece of Bazooka gum comes with a premium of sorts—a Bazooka Joe comic. Topps first included the comics with their gums in 1953; and in the years since, the firm has developed a repertoire of close to 700 different comics. The company tries not to repeat a title for about seven years so that the comics are fresh for each new generation of bubble gum chewers.

Sugarless gums have been with us since the 1940s, and now account for 10 percent of all chewing gum sales. A stick of sugarless gum contains but six or seven calories—while a regular stick contains a whopping eight calories!

Gum makers have also developed gums that won't stick to dentures, and they are presently working on such earth-shattering innovations as a bubble gum whose bubbles glow in the dark.

In the early days of chewing gum marketing, gum companies tried to sell their products by stressing their value to dental health. Advertisements pointed out that primitive races whose diets demand a great deal of chewing usually have excellent teeth. When the Wrigley Company began to market its chewing gum in England around 1911, the firm's ads pointed up the values of gum to dental *and* mental health, claiming that gum eased tension and thereby improved concentration.

Wrigley faced an additional challenge in convincing the Englishman to chew gum: to rid gum-chewing of its lower-class connotations. When Wrigley began to advertise heavily in English magazines, he surprisingly chose those publications most read by the social elite. Sure, the ads read, gum may be out of place at the opera or in Buckingham Palace, but gum-chewing can be both proper and highly beneficial at most other times. The results of the ad campaign? Sales of Wrigley's products in England doubled over the next 20 years.

In the Soviet Union, where the manufacture of chewing gum is prohibited by the State, foreign tourists are frequently accosted by young Russian boys clamoring for "tchewing gum! tchewing gum."

Why do people chew gum? Ask the average gum-chewer why he uses gum and you'll most likely receive in response, a shrug of the shoulders. But the answer is simple: gum-chewing uses up excess nervous energy.

Studies have shown that the use of gum rises in periods of social tension, and falls in more tranquil times. For instance, the use of gum in this country soared from a per capita 98 sticks in 1939 to 165 sticks by the early 50s, duplicating a similar rise during World War I. Today's per capita consumption of chewing gum stands at 175 sticks per year. So, as if you needed any further confirmation, the chewing gum barometer suggests that we once again live in troubled times.

Chickens

"A chicken in every pot" is no longer a dream or an idle campaign slogan: it's a reality. The chicken, the most abundant of all domesticated creatures, now numbers over four billion, or one for every person on earth. And the expression "an egg on every plate" might be equally apt, for each year the world's chickens produce some 390 billion eggs—enough to provide every human being with a hundred eggs a year!

That's a lot of chickens and a lot of eggs, considering that the chicken was once no more plentiful than any other jungle bird!

The chicken is such a common creature today that we have more than a half-dozen words for the bird, and the terminology might be confusing to anyone who didn't grow up on a poultry farm. *Chicken* itself usually refers to any member of the *gallus domesticus* species, male or female. The word comes from the Old English *cycen,* which was in turn derived from *kukin*, "little cock."

A *cock* is a male chicken, or a *rooster.* The word *hen,* which designates a female chicken, usually one of egg-laying age, is also derived from an Old English word for rooster, *hana.* A *pullet,* meanwhile, is a hen less than a year old. The term comes from the French word for hen, *poule,* from which our *poultry* is derived. A *capon* is a castrated male chicken, and a *springer* is a female chicken a few months old.

The chicken of today, rooster, hen, pullet, springer, and capon alike, is the product of many centuries of domestication. The wonderful fowl that now graces so many of our dinner plates is believed descended from *gallus gallus,* a jungle bird of India and Southeast Asia. The chicken may not have been domesticated on any large scale until as recently as 1500 B.C., in contrast to the cow and sheep, which were domesticated well before recorded history began.

But the chicken was a common fowl in Europe by the time of the Roman Empire. The Romans may have been the first to raise chickens in batteries, roosts in which large numbers of birds can be raised together cheaply. To improve the flavor of the meat, the Romans sometimes treated their chickens to a diet of barley and milk; to improve their chicken dishes, they often stuffed the bird with sausages, eggs, peas, and other delights. One story has it that the Emperor Didius forbade Romans from stuffing their "hens or roosters" in order to stretch the Empire's food supply. To circumvent the law, Romans castrated roosters and stuffed them, since the castrated birds could not legally be termed either "hens" or "roosters"—and so the capon was born.

The Romans, by the way, ate a great number of birds in addition to the familiar chicken, duck, and goose, and many of these feathered delicacies might seem rather odd dishes to us today. Roman banquets often included such avian treats as the parrot, flamingo, thrush, peacock, pigeon, lark, blackbird, nightingale, partridge, and dove. Hosts sometimes prepared birds'-tongue pie to impress their guests, and we have record of one feast that included a pie made solely from the tongues of songbirds.

During the Middle Ages, European serfs raised chickens for both meat and eggs. Often they turned over a number of chickens each year to their lord as rent for the land they worked. American president Herbert Hoover is frequently credited with the expression "a chicken in every pot," and indeed the phrase was used as a Republican campaign slogan for the 1932 election. But the saying is actually much older: around the year 1600, French King Henry IV used those words in reference to his agriculture plans for France: "I hope to make France so prosperous that every peasant will have a chicken in his pot on Sunday."

Napoleon was an avid chicken fancier. While campaigning, he had his cooks prepare a fresh chicken every half-hour so that one would always be ready when he decided to eat. Napoleon's chef is credited with the invention of one of the most familiar and delicious of all chicken dishes. During the battle of Marengo in Italy, the Little Corporal's chef found himself without butter, so he obtained some native olive oil in which to fry his chicken. To mask the flavor of the oil, he added tomatoes, mushrooms, wine, and herbs. Napoleon loved the dish, and *Chicken Marengo* entered the world of chicken cookery.

In the United States, the chicken didn't become as popular a food item as it is today until the 1930s, when Americans began to raise chickens in batteries, employing scientific feeding systems. Chicken farmers were soon raising birds as plump in seven weeks as they had formerly been in three months, making chicken farming more lucrative.

Today, the chicken population of the United States at any given time is usually around 380 million. About four-fifths are used for meat and the remainder for eggs. The average American consumes 45 pounds of the fowl annually, compared to 88 pounds of beef and about 41 pounds of pork. The U.S.S.R. owns more chickens than any other nation—there are some 565 million chickens in Russian barnyards—while other large chicken producers include China, England, Australia, Ireland, Denmark, Canada, and France.

Pound for pound, chicken is a more economical, nourishing meat than either beef or pork. A hundred grams of chicken meat (about three-and-a-half ounces) contains from 150 to 200 calories, while a like quantity of beef contains 273 calories and pork about 450. Chicken is twice as rich in protein as an equal portion of pork, and contains only a fraction of the fat (from seven to 12 grams per 100) in either beef (22 grams) or pork (45 grams).

To a city slicker, it might seem like a good idea to raise chickens for their eggs and then sell them for meat when their egg-laying days are over. The fact is, most chickens are raised exclusively for either meat or eggs. Generally, egg-layers do not provide good meat, and chickens that are raised as fryers and broilers for the most part do not produce eggs for the commercial market.

Today, there are five classes of chicken: English, Asiatic, Mediterranean, American, and Continental European. Each of these classes includes a number of breeds—there are some 100 breeds and varieties altogether. Only Mediterranean chickens lay white eggs; the others lay mostly brown eggs. But Mediterranean chickens are generally not good for meat.

The most popular breeds of chicken in the United States and Europe include the *Leghorn*, a

A Black-tailed Japanese bantam male.

A Dominique male.

A Black Java male.

A single-comb white leghorn male.

Mediterranean breed raised for its eggs; the *New Hampshire,* an American breed noted for its rapid growth that is usually raised for meat; the *Plymouth Rock,* another American chicken raised most often for its meat; the *Rhode Island Red,* an American breed bred for egg-laying and sometimes for its meat; and the *Cornish*, an English breed that makes a fine roaster.

The average chicken weighs from three to six pounds, but some older hens have been known to attain a weight of over 20 pounds. The largest chicken on record, a California native nicknamed "Weirdo," weighed 22 pounds at age four. This fowl, obviously not chicken-hearted, killed a rooster and two cats, and injured a dog as well as its owner.

As long as people continue to enjoy chicken meat and eggs, chicken raising can be a profitable occupation. A single farmer can care for as many as 50,000 chickens at one time, and can bring his flock from egg to market in only three months. In the largest chicken farm in the world, the so-called "Egg City" of Moorpark, California, four-and-a-half million chickens are housed on a mere 600 acres, and turn out over two million eggs each day!

On chicken farms that produce primarily eggs, the male chickens are sold for meat soon after birth, while the females begin laying about 150 days after birth. Normally, a hen would lay about 15 eggs per month during her first year, and about 20 per month in her second year. But chickens are hardy eaters: it takes at least five pounds of chicken feed to produce just a dozen eggs. As a 17th-century Englishman noted, "Children and chickens must be always picking."

A redoubtable egg-laying record was achieved by a Rhode Island Red of recent acclaim that laid 20 eggs in seven days, including seven in one day. At that rate, the prolific hen would have smashed the all-time annual egg-laying record: in 1930, a New Zealand fowl laid 361 eggs in a single year!

While we're on the subject of eggs, the size classifications of the eggs in your supermarkets aren't merely descriptive. U.S. Department of Agriculture regulations specify that to qualify as "Extra Large," a dozen eggs must weigh 27 ounces. A dozen "Large" eggs should weigh 24 ounces; a dozen "Medium" eggs should tip the scales at 21 ounces; and "Small" eggs should weigh 18 ounces per dozen. "Jumbo" eggs are 30 ounces to the dozen.

Egg grades refer not to the size, but to the quality of the egg. The best grade is AA; these eggs should have a firm, high yolk and a thick white. Grade A eggs are slightly thinner, but still are fine for baking and other uses where the appearance of the egg is not important.

We have no idea of the grade of an egg laid by a Jersey hen, in 1965, that tipped the scales at close to a pound! The record-setting egg had two yolks and a double shell. And speaking of egg yolks, many eggs contain more than one; the record is nine, set by a hen in New York State.

Crossing the supermarket from the dairy aisle to the meat department, we'll find chickens under such names as *broiler, fryer, roaster, capon,* and *game hen.* All are young birds with tender flesh. Older, mature birds are usually marked *hen, stewing chicken,* or *fowl,* and are certainly no spring chickens. A trip to the frozen foods aisle and its host of prepared chicken dinners, pies, and other dishes will show that we've come a long way since the 17th century, when English philosopher Francis Bacon died while trying to freeze a chicken by stuffing it with snow.

Almost every cuisine in the world includes a number of chicken dishes, and America is certainly no exception. Fried chicken is now the most popular single dish in the United States, far surpassing the runners-up—roast beef, and spaghetti. In sheer poundage, chicken ranks number eight among all food items consumed in the United States—and that's not including the 263 eggs consumed yearly by each American!

New dishes for the versatile chicken are probably being invented every day, and will continue to appear as the number of chickens in the world rises steadily. Since there are now about as many chickens in the world as there are people, and the population of the world in the year 2000 is projected to be around eight billion, we might anticipate that there will be some eight billion chickens around by that time!

But then again, that would be counting our chickens before they're hatched.

That expression has been credited to a 17th-century English poet named Samuel Butler, although it was also used by Cervantes, Erasmus, and Aesop, and is surely much older. Coincidentally, it was another Englishman by the name of Samuel Butler, a 19th-century author, who offered the cleverest answer to the age-old question: "Which came first, the chicken or the egg?"

"The hen," Butler wrote, "is only an egg's way of making another egg."

A Bearded Silver Polish male.

A Bearded Silver Polish female.

Chocolate

The fruit of the cacao tree, from which chocolate is produced.

At the market in the Mayan city of Chichen Itza, 10 cacao beans could purchase a rabbit, four beans a pumpkin. A slave was a real steal, at just 100 cacao beans.

It's difficult to imagine a confectionery industry in the West without chocolate. Cocoa and chocolate are virtually unknown as a popular food outside Europe and the United States. Just five nations—the United States, England, West Germany, the Netherlands, and France—now account for four-fifths of all world imports. Ten nations account for over 95 percent. But chocolate is actually a native of Central America, and was totally unknown in Europe less than 500 years ago—and little known outside of Spain until the 17th century!

When Spanish explorer Hernando Cortés arrived in Mexico in the early 16th century, he found the Indians drinking a dark, frothy beverage called *chocolatl,* brewed from the beans of a native plant. The Aztecs regarded the plant as a divine gift brought to earth by the god Quetzalcoatl. Chocolate was so highly prized in the area that both the Aztecs and Mayans used cacao beans as currency. At the market in the Mayan city of Chichen Itza, 10 beans could purchase a rabbit, four beans a pumpkin. A slave was a real steal, at just 100 cacao beans.

The Aztec king Montezuma, who introduced Cortes to the Chocolatl, was said to drink no other beverage than chocolate, consuming some 50 pitchers a day. Over 2,000 pitchers of chocolate were prepared daily for the royal household, usually mixed with honey, vanilla, or peppers, and cooled with ice from nearby mountains. Montezuma consumed a golden goblet of chocolate beverage before he entered his harem, then tossed the cup into the lake beside his palace. Indians were still diving for the golden goblets years after the Spanish began to colonize the area.

An Indian legend maintains that the word *chocolatl* originated when confectioners mixed *atl,* water, with ground cacao beans and stirred the mixture over a flame in huge vats. The bubbling mixture made a sound similar to "choco-choco." But the word more likely comes from the Aztec word *choqui,* "warmth." Today, we use the word *cacao* when referring to the raw bean, *cocoa* for the pulverized bean, and *chocolate* for the solid manufactured product.

Christopher Columbus may have brought cacao beans to Spain. But it was Cortés who first turned the attention of his countrymen to the New World product, writing to Emperor Charles V that he'd discovered a "divine drink . . . which builds up resistance and fights fatigue."

By 1520, cacao had made its first appearance in Spain, where thick, sugared, chilled chocolate beverages became an instant sensation. By 1525, cacao plantations were flourishing on Trinidad. Within a century, large quantities of chocolate were being exported from Venezuela.

The clergy took an immediate distaste to chocolate, as was their wont with any new foodstuff. The churchmen declared chocolate "the beverage of Satan" and "a provocative of immorality," since it was thought that chocolate was an aphrodisiac. The idea did not die easily. As late as 1712, the English magazine *The Spectator* warned that men "be careful how they meddle with romance, chocolate, novels, and the like inflamers."

Chocolate remained popular in Spain for more than a century before it caught on elsewhere in Europe, for the Spanish carefully guarded the methods of manufacturing drinkable chocolate. Late in the 16th century, when the Dutch captured a Spanish ship laden with cacao beans, they considered the unfamiliar cargo so worthless that they tossed the beans into the sea.

In 1606, an Italian named Antonio Carletti introduced chocolate to his country after a trip to Spain. Some historians believe that chocolate then made its way over the Alps to Austria, and was brought to France by Anne of Austria, the queen of Louis XIII. But it's more likely that chocolate was brought to France by the Spanish Infanta, Maria Theresa, when she moved to Paris to become the bride of Louis XIV.

As had been her custom in Spain, the new queen had her maid prepare a cup of chocolate for her each morning. Soon, other women of the court were clamoring for the queen's "naughty beverage." Louis himself enjoyed chocolate as his breakfast drink. And Louis's war minister, the Marquis de Louvois, invented the still popular *Café Louvois,* a mixture of semisweet chocolate, coffee, and whipped cream.

Around the mid-17th century, chocolate houses began to appear in many European capitals. The price of chocolate was still high enough to make the houses fashionable retreats for the wealthy. In 1657, the first London shop opened, selling the exotic beverage Samuel Pepys called "jocolatte." Spurred by doctors' reports claiming chocolate was an effective medicine, with one ounce equal in nutritive value to a pound of meat, chic Londoners began flocking to their chocolate houses, making such establishments as the Cocoa Tree Club and the St. James Club centers of social intercourse and political discussion.

A quaint tale from the early 18th century tells of an Austrian nobleman named Prince Dietrichstein who ordered a chocolate beverage in a Vienna chocolate house and was so enraptured by the waitress who served him that he wooed and eventually married her. The Prince commissioned the noted Swiss portraitist Jean-Etienne Leotard to paint a portrait of his wife, Anna Beltauf, in her waitress garb. Titled *La Belle Chocolatière,* the painting soon found its way to a museum.

In 1872, an American executive of the Walter Baker Chocolate Company saw the painting of Anna Beltauf during a trip to Europe, and purchased it for use as the firm's emblem. Baker chocolate products still bear a reproduction of the Leotard portrait.

The Walter Baker Chocolate Company was manufacturing chocolate in this country as long ago as the 18th century. In 1765, the first chocolate factory in the United States was established in Dorchester, Massachusetts, by one John Hannan. Fifteen years later, Hannan sold the plant to Dr. James Baker, the founder of the Walter Baker firm.

Eating chocolate as we know it today was a fairly recent development. For centuries, chocolate was enjoyed as a beverage, rather than an edible snack. Breakfast cocoa was introduced in 1828, when Dutchman Coenraad Van Houten invented a machine for removing oil from the fermented cacao bean. Milk chocolate was not perfected until 1876, when a Swiss chocolatier named M.D. Peter combined chocolate with milk solids. Today, American chocolate manufacturers use close to 3,500,000 pounds of whole milk daily in the production of milk chocolate candy.

Switzerland and the Netherlands, now the world's foremost producers of quality chocolate, did not begin making chocolate products on a large scale until early in the 18th century.

Assorted filled chocolates of the type now sold by such giants as Fanny Farmer and Barricini's first appeared in 1870, when chocolatiers began covering fresh cream with chocolate liquor as a way of preserving and selling cream. In 1903, the industry received a big lift when a Frenchman invented a machine called the enrober that could mechanically coat candies with chocolate.

The chocolate bar is a 20th century innovation. In 1903, a chocolatier from Lancaster, Pennsylvania, named Milton Snavely Hershey established a chocolate plant on undeveloped property near Harrisburg. The community that grew up around the plant—named, not surprisingly, Hershey—was built entirely by the chocolate company itself, complete with homes and gardens for the workers, streets, sewers, schools, a power plant, a post office, a bank, and a 75-acre park. The plant, the world's largest chocolate factory, now sprawls over two million square feet of floor space, turning out some hundreds of million chocolate bars each year. In 1973, more than a million tourists visited Hershey's chocolate world.

To Americans, the chocolate bar and the Hershey bar are virtually synonymous. Other chocolate manufacturers began large scale production of the candy bar during World War I. At first, the chocolatiers shipped blocks of solid chocolates to GI's in training camps around the nation. Since the weighing and cutting of smaller blocks became too time-consuming on the bases, manufacturers began wrapping chocolate "bars" individually for shipment to the soldiers, and the candy bar—as we know it—was born.

The Nestlé Company, another major chocolate producer, cornered a large chunk of the American market with the introduction of "morsels" for use in chocolate chip cookies. During

The shape of Hershey's chocolate kisses must be exact for wrapping by automatic equipment.

As late as 1712, the English magazine *The Spectator* warned men to "be careful how they meddle with romance, chocolate, novels, and the like inflamers."

An ad for Metcalf's Coca Wine in the latter part of the 19th century.

the 1940s, a Massachusetts restaurant called the Toll House Inn earned a local reputation by serving cookies studded with especially delicious bits of chocolate. When cookie lovers discovered that the "secret" ingredient in the cookies was a certain semisweet chocolate sold in local stores, they quickly wiped out all supplies. So the Nestlé Company introduced their Toll House cookie morsels to satisfy the demand, and homemade chocolate chip cookie lovers have been grateful ever since.

Today, few Americans are more than a short walk from the nearest chocolate bar. But chocolate itself travels a long road from the tree to the candy store.

Cacao beans come from a tropical plant known as *Theobroma cacao*. The first word literally means "food of the gods." A cacao tree can grow 30 or 40 feet high, but most cultivated trees are pruned to a height of about 20 feet to facilitate harvesting.

Cacao trees begin to bear fruit after three or four years, and reach full production after about eight years. Most trees remain productive for up to 40 years, and some have been known to bear fruit for almost a century.

A cacao tree bears about 20 pods, each about 10 inches long and four inches in diameter. Each pod in turn contains from 20 to 40 beans. Ripe pods are picked by hand and slit open to remove the beans, which are then fermented in their own pulp and dried in the sun.

At the manufacturing plant, the cacao beans are cleaned, roasted, shelled, and broken into smaller bits known as nibs. The nibs are cleaned and ground into

Chocolate for candy comes from a tree that looks like this. This cocoa tree stands in Trinidad.

Today, the annual worldwide production of cacao tops the million ton mark—that's over two *billion* pounds of cacao each year!

a paste, liquifying the fat known as cocoa butter that makes up about 55 percent of the bean. Different processes then produce either cocoa or eating chocolate.

Cocoa is produced by squeezing about half of the cocoa butter from the chocolate paste, then grinding, cooling, and sifting the resultant powder. Eating chocolate is produced by grinding the paste for days, pouring it into molds, and mixing with additional cocoa butter and flavorings.

On the average, eating chocolate contains about 42 percent chocolate, an equal percentage of sugar, and about 16 percent cocoa butter.

For many years, Central America, Ecuador, and Venezuela were the major producers of raw cacao beans. Today, about 75 percent of the world's supply comes from Africa. The nation of Ghana, which did not begin cacao cultivation on a large scale until 1879, presently accounts for about 30 percent of the African crop. But most African cacao is considered "base" grade, inferior to the "flavor" grades now produced in Central America, Ecuador, and Brazil.

In 1850, the total world production of raw cacao stood at a mere 20,000 tons. By the turn of the century, chocolate lovers were consuming close to 100,000 tons of the bean, and by 1925, the figure had skyrocketed to almost a half-million tons. Today, the annual worldwide production figure tops the million ton mark—that's over two *billion* pounds of cacao each year!

The United States is the largest consumer of chocolate products, accounting for about one-quarter of world imports. About half of the 450-million-pound annual American import of chocolate is used in the production of sugar confectioneries, including ice cream, about a quarter in candy bars, 10 percent in chocolate coverings, seven percent in assorted chocolates, and only seven percent in the production of cocoa. Chocolate byproducts are also used to make cosmetics, and cacao shells provide animal fodder.

About half of all confectionery products in America contain chocolate. All told, America consumes about eight billion pounds of candy each year, making confectionery the eighth largest food processing industry in this country. But per capita, Europeans are far ahead of Americans in chocolate consumption. The average American gobbles up about 16 pounds of candy each year, including about two-and-a-half pounds of chocolate; the average Englishman, about 28 pounds of candy annually.

Western Europe as a whole accounts for up to 60 percent of world chocolate imports, with England, Germany, and the Netherlands the leading consumers.

Without doubt, chocolate must rank as one of the most delectable taste treats ever developed by man. But chocolate is also useful as a source of quick energy, since most chocolate products are high in sugar. Also, cacao beans contain *theobromine,* a mild stimulant, and caffeine. Chocolate's low bulk and high calorific content make it an excellent food for soldiers' ration kits. Queen Victoria sent a half-million pounds of chocolate to English soldiers fighting the Boer War in South Africa, and American GI's helped popularize the candy bar in Europe during World War II. The Hershey Company, the manufacturer of the Ration O bar, reached a peak production of 500,000 bars a day. Wiley Post, the first man to fly solo around the world, ate chocolate bars throughout his journey to keep himself awake.

You may have seen Mole sauce on the menu of a Mexican restaurant. No, the sauce owes nothing to the burrowing animal of that name. Mole sauce is actually a chocolate sauce commonly used with fowl, an invention of nuns in Mexico.

Chocolate is more often consumed in the United States in confectionery items, sold as bars, blocks, morsels, powder, and small candies in an untold number of shapes. Egotistic chocolate lovers might prefer their confections in a more personal form. For $350, Kron Chocolatiers in New York will shape a bust of your head from solid chocolate. Even Montezuma never had it so good!

The average American gobbles up about 16 pounds of candy each year, including about two-and-a-half pounds of chocolate.

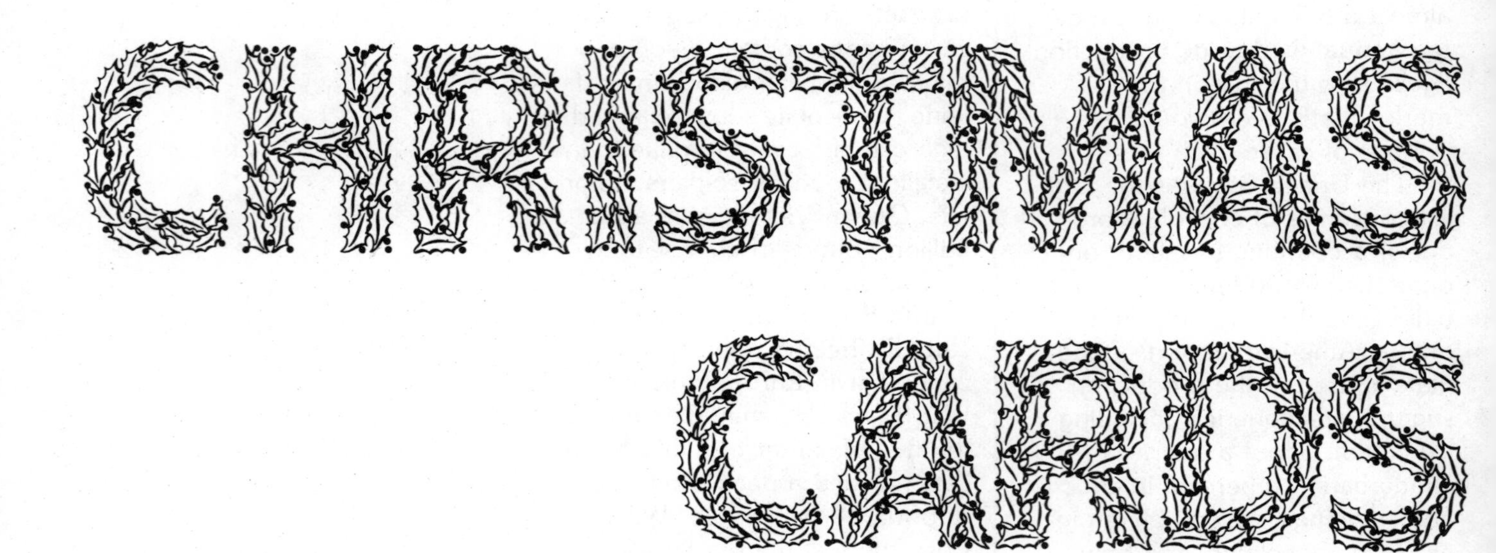

No one could fail to notice that most Christmas cards today have nothing whatsoever to do with Christ or Christianity—but did you know that Yuletide greeting cards were secular from their inception? Sanctimonious individuals may annually decry the deluge of cards and bewail the "loss of religious spirit," but the fact is that few of the customs we now associate with Christmas have anything at all to do with religious commemoration—and some of these customs are a good deal older than Christianity itself!

The date of Christ's birth is purely conjectural—there is no historical evidence that Christ was born on December 25. Mention of a December 25 celebration of Christ's birth first appeared around the year 353, but it wasn't until 440—more than four centuries after his actual birth—that the Church proclaimed that day as the official date for the festival. Conveniently, December 25 already marked a holiday among many Europeans—the celebratory rite of the winter solstice, marking the beginning of lengthening days and the expectation of spring and rebirth. Due to changes in the calendar, Christmas no longer falls exactly on the solstice.

As the celebration of a mid-winter Christmas spread with Christianity, people in various cultures retained many of their pagan solstice customs and incorporated them in the

The first Christmas card was designed by John Horsley in 1843.

Christmas rite. At that time of year, the ancient Romans had exchanged gifts to mark the feast of Saturnalia. Celtic and Teutonic tribes kept many customs of their 12-day Yule celebration. Mistletoe, for instance, was prominent in midwinter Druid rites, and holly was similarly used by the Anglo-Saxons. The evergreen tree had long been regarded as a symbol of survival by Scandinavian peoples—though the Christmas tree proper did not find its way to England until 1840, introduced by Queen Victoria's German-born husband, Albert.

By the middle of the 19th century, Christmas was being observed throughout the Christian world very much as it is today—with the notable absence of the Christmas card. The idea, if not the custom, of pictorial representations of seasonal greetings dates back to the Middle Ages. An engraving by one "Master E.S." depicting the infant Christ stepping from a flower has been dated to around 1466, and is thought to be a copy of an even earlier design. Similar works from the 15th century refer to both Christmas and New Year. Calendars in the 17th and 18th centuries often carried Yuletide greetings, with domestic winter scenes, sailing ships, and red-cheeked goddesses among the favored motifs.

As to the first legitimate "Christmas card," there is some controversy. According to many accounts, the idea of a Christmas greeting card sprang from the fertile brain of Sir Henry Cole, the first director of the Victoria and Albert Museum in London. In 1843, Cole commissioned John Collcott Horsley, a fashionable artist of the time, to design his first card. Horsley was well known not only for his artwork, but for leadership of a campaign against the use of nude models by artists—work that earned him the nickname "Clothes-Horsley."

The artist's first card consisted of one unfolded sheet, oblong in shape, with a rustic bower

This 19th-century Christmas card is one of the 70,000 unusual cards in the Hallmark Historical Collection.

forming a frame for three illustrations. The central scene depicted a typical middle-class Victorian family gathered around a sumptuously laden table, drinking to the health of an absent friend—the card's recipient. The card also showed a moralistic scene depicting a charitable soul feeding the hungry at Christmas. The card also contained a representation of another good Samaritan clothing the naked—though Horsley, true to form, depicted the naked indigent as fully clothed. Above the tableau, appeared the word "To" followed by a space for an inscription; on the bottom of the card, the word "From" followed by a picture of an artist with a palette and the date "Xmasse 1843." A banner stretching across the bottom of the central scene carried the greeting "A Merry Christmas and a Happy New Year to you." Christmas cards haven't changed much, have they?

Horsley became the world's first Christmas-card sender when he presented Cole with a signed copy of his original design, bearing the brilliantly original inscription:

"To his good friend Cole
Who's a merry young soul
And a merry young soul is he:
And may he be for many years
to come! Hooray!

Cole had a thousand copies of the original card printed and issued by Summerby's Home Treasury Office. Only a dozen are known to exist today. Two of these can be found in the

70,000-card Hallmark Historical Collection, the largest and most representative museum of greeting card art in existence.

Initial reaction to the distribution of Christmas cards was hardly favorable. Some critics claimed Horsley's card was too secular, and accused him of encouraging intemperance and alcoholism. Others criticized the idea of cards as a foolish extravagance. In fact, certain Protestant sects refused to condone the Christmas card until the turn of the century.

But Yuletide cards caught on quickly among the general population, and within 20 years were well entrenched in Victorian Christmas celebrations. At first, cards were generally not mailed or signed, but delivered by messenger with a calling card. The penny post, introduced in England in 1840, did much to popularize Yuletide greetings by mail; and by the 1850s, Christmas cards began to appear on the European continent as well.

Victorian Christmas cards were considerably more elaborate than today's, often adorned with layers of lace, silk fringes, tassels, ribbons, dried flowers, satin, or mother-of-pearl. Some were glass frosted. One surviving Victorian card consisted of 750 pieces of material stitched together.

The Christmas card first appeared in the United States in 1874, brought out by Bavarian-born Boston lithographer Louis Prang. Prang's card was designed by Mrs. O.E. Whitney, and based on an English card signed *Charles Dickens* that Prang had brought back from Europe. At first, the cards were produced for export to England, since the custom of sending greeting cards at Christmas had yet to appear in America. But Prang's cards—among the first to depict religious scenes—went on sale in the United States the following year. Christmas-card fever soon became a permanent American ailment.

Through the years, Christmas-card design has often changed to reflect the feeling of the times. During the Depression, many cards spoofed poverty to make light of temporary hard times. Santas carrying flags were popular during World War II, as were inscriptions such as "Missing You" and "Across the Miles." The Cold War years saw an increased demand for humorous cards.

Today, Christmas cards are a multimillion-dollar industry in most English-speaking countries. Hallmark Cards, the largest American greeting card company, boasts annual sales of $400 million. In 1954, Americans sent about two billion Christmas cards; now, the yearly figure stands at close to four billion, for an average of 20 cards per person.

Of course, many Americans send considerably more than 20 cards. One Werner Erhard of San Francisco sent 62,824 cards in a single year. This is believed to be the largest outpouring of Christmas-card generosity in history.

Critics continue to lay the blame for an outlandish waste of time, money, and paper at the feet of overzealous Christmas-card senders. The English magazine *Punch* hit it on the head when, in a 1900 editorial, it declared: "We deprecate the absurd habit of Christmas cards and presents—we refer, of course, to those we have to *give!*"

In 1954, Americans sent about two billion Christmas cards; now the yearly figure stands at close to four billion, for an average of 20 cards per person.

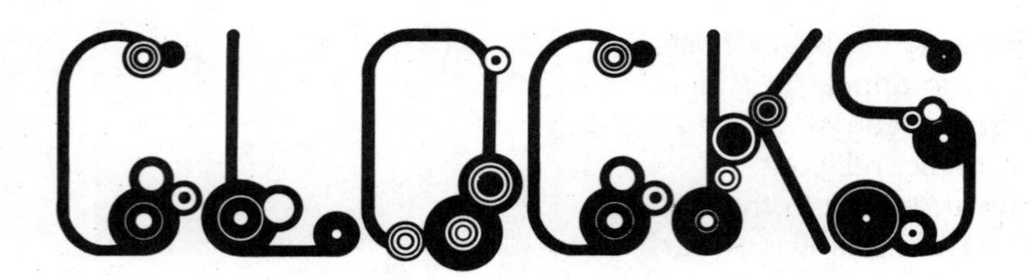

More than any other single facet of modern technology, timekeeping devices and the importance we attach to them illustrate the steadily increasing pace of civilized life. Ask anyone in the street for the time today and you're likely to receive a reading from an electronic digital watch down to the exact minute. Yet just a few centuries ago, knowledge of the exact time was thought to be so unimportant that clocks of the day were constructed without hands—the hourly striking of a bell was all the enlightenment anyone thought was necessary. And the idea of a portable clock reading the hour, minute, and second—how preposterous!

Six hundred years ago, the few existing clocks were accurate to within only about an hour per day. Until 1582, even the calendar in use was 10 days out of line with the seasons. In contrast, we now have atomic clocks—utilizing the oscillations of individual cessium atoms for time measurement—that are accurate to within one second every 60,000 years. And, as if that weren't quite sufficient, a time-measuring device installed in the U.S. Naval Research Laboratory in 1964, which utilizes hydrogen masers, is reputedly accurate to within one second per 1,700,000 years!

Modern man, then, is certainly time conscious. But is our preoccupation with the exact time due solely to the availability of the means to measure it? Not likely. If ancient man was without the means to closely measure time, it's also true that for the most part he simply didn't need to.

A Frisian clock.

The ancient Babylonians, who used a calendar with 12 30-day months, were apparently the first to apply the number 12 to a system of telling the time of day. They were also the first to divide the day into 24 segments, a custom later adopted by the Greeks.

The earliest timekeeping devices depended upon the movement of the sun to provide an approximation of the hour. In Egypt, the sundial—the oldest scientific instrument in continuous use—told time by day; the water clock, similar in principle to the sandglass, was used at night. Lamp clocks or simple candles were later employed to count the hours. The sandglass itself was popular right up into the 16th century, when it was often used in church to measure the length of a sermon.

Speaking of ecclesiastical timepieces, medieval monks invented the world's first alarm clock. Monks sometimes slid a lit candle between their toes before dozing, so that the flame would rudely awaken them at the desired hour. For obvious reasons, the hot-foot alarm clock did not catch on elsewhere.

The invention of a mechanical

clock has been attributed to the Chinese of the eighth century, but the first mechanical timekeeping devices appeared in Europe in the 12th and 13th centuries. Almost all of the earliest clocks were turret clocks built into church towers to help the faithful get to church on time. A bell and striker system provided the hour—there were no hands. The word "clock" comes from the French *cloche,* "bell." Originally, the word was applied only to those timekeeping devices that struck the hour with a bell or gong.

Among the most famous medieval church clocks were those of the Cathedral of Strasbourg in France and St. Paul's Cathedral in London. The astronomic clock in the Strasbourg church, called the most elaborate clock ever built, was not installed until 1842, replacing an earlier model. St. Paul's clock, built in 1286, contained mechanical figures that struck a bell on the hour. The gong clock in the Cathedral of Notre Dame in Dijon, France, has struck the hour every hour since 1383. In 1950, an ambitious mathematician computed that by then the gong had tolled the hour 32,284,980 times.

When the dial did appear on timekeeping devices, there was only one hand, with the perimeter of the dial calibrated for the hour and the quarter-hour. In some early clocks, the hand revolved; in others, the hand remained stationary and the dial itself revolved. An Italian, Jacopo Dondi, has been credited with designing the first clock dial in 1344. A reconstruction of one of Dondi's clocks is now on display at the Smithsonian Institution in Washington.

A marble and bronze clock of the Louis XVI period.

When Emperor Charles V of Spain retired to the monastery of Yuste, he indulged his mechanical bent by lining up several clocks and trying to make them tick in unison. He finally gave up in despair, observing that if he could not make any two clocks run together in the same rhythm, how could he possibly have believed he was able to make thousands of men think and act alike?

However, William H. Prescott, the noted historian, refused to credit this story. In his book, *The Life of Charles the Fifth After His Abdication,* Prescott wrote: "The difficulty which he found in adjusting his clocks and watches is said to have drawn from the monarch a philosophical reflection on the absurdity of his having attempted to bring men to anything like uniformity of belief in matters of faith, when he could not make any two of his time-pieces agree with each other. But that he never reached the degree of philosophy required for such reflection is abundantly shown by more than one sentiment that fell from his pen, as well as his lips, during his residence at Yuste."

The chief companion of Charles V at his retreat was one Torriano who was reputed to be highly skilled in the manufacture of time-pieces and who had made many elaborate clocks to adorn his monastic apartments.

All early clocks were weight-driven, and therefore quite large. But around 1500, the German Peter Henlein's invention of the mainspring eliminated the need for heavy clock mechanisms, and timekeepers could be made portable. Some historians maintain that Henlein himself made the world's first watch shortly after his invention of the mainspring, but recently other experts began making a case for an Italian origin for the watch.

The earliest watches were large and unwieldy, often four or five inches in diameter and up to three inches thick, certainly too large for the pocket. Some watches were worn around the waist on a belt, while the wealthy had their servants lug around their portable timekeepers.

Like the clocks of their time, early watches struck the hour and were equipped with only one hand. (The word *watch* in this sense is derived from *watchman*, since in England the town watchman, the caller of the hours or town crier, was among the first to carry a portable timepiece. The minute hand was not to appear on the watch until 1670 in England—and much later in Europe! The Roman numbers I through XII marked the hours, and some watch faces also showed the numbers 13 through 24 beneath the lower numbers for Italians and Bohemians who favored the 24-hour system. But early watches were predominantly jewelry pieces, and few of their owners actually expected them to tell the correct time.

The accuracy of clocks and watches improved steadily during the 16th and 17th centuries, but the basic mechanism of timekeeping devices remained the same. All mechanical watches link a device performing regular movements—a balance and spring, for example—to a counting mechanism capable of recording the number of those movements. The mainspring stores energy imparted by winding and transmits the energy to the balance and spring. The oscillations of the balance and spring trigger—after a few dozen intermediate steps—the movement of the hands. If it sounds fairly simple, it isn't: hundreds of years and thousands of refinements were necessary before the clock and watch could be called truly accurate.

The Germans completely dominated watchmaking until the early 17th century, when Germany was ravaged and the industry was destroyed by the Thirty

Watch backs, enameled and set with jewels.

Years War. The French then took over the watchmaking leadership, with their industry centered around Blois. Most French watches were oval, not circular, their faces covered either by glass or a metal lid that had to be opened for a peek at the time.

A "banjo" clock.

French watch cases were often elaborately decorated with engravings of figures, foliage, and domestic or religious scenes, and rank among the most finely crafted objects of their time.

When the English developed a watchmaking industry in the 17th century, they concentrated on the mechanism of the watch rather than its aesthetic design—the inside rather than the outside—and thus English watches soon surpassed their fancier French counterparts in accuracy. By 1800, England reigned supreme as the watchmaker for the world, with over 70,000 people involved in an industry centered around London's Clerkenwell district.

The English reign lasted only until the middle of the 19th century, when Swiss watchmaking began its ascendancy. According to legend, an Englishman passing through the Swiss town of Le Locle in the late 17th century brought a broken watch to a Monsieur Jean-Richard for repairs. The device so intrigued Jean-Richard's son, Daniel, that the boy decided to make one for himself—and did so in 18 months. Later, Daniel's five sons followed their father into the trade to help establish the Swiss watchmaking industry. A statue of a boy in blacksmith's robe stands today in a square in Le Locle, a tribute to Daniel Jean-Richard, the "father of Swiss watchmaking."

A less quaint explanation attributes the rapid development of Swiss watchmaking to French Huguenot craftsmen forced by religious persecution to flee France for Geneva, a Protestant city, during the late 17th century. Another points to religious reformer John Calvin's decree to end the manufacture of all jewelry and other "vanities" in Geneva. Swiss jewelers then turned to watchmaking, which Calvin did not condemn. In any case, watchmaking fit in perfectly

A grandfather clock.

A contemporary sundial by the French artist, Maurice Djian. Sundials must be custom-made for each latitude and for the direction which the sundial faces.

with the Swiss way of life. Since most Swiss were farmers, watchmaking at home provided an excellent source of income during the otherwise unproductive Alpine winter. By 1800, entire families in French-speaking Switzerland were engaged in making watch parts. The components were usually assembled in factories.

The Swiss invested heavily in watchmaking machinery during the mid-19th century, but the English continued to rely on hand craftsmanship. While simple English watches frequently sold for as much as 10 pounds—a great deal of money at the time—a Swiss named Roskopf brought out the world's first cheap, reliable watch in 1865. By 1900, the Swiss takeover was complete, and English watchmaking has never since recovered.

In early 19th-century America, laws restricted the importation of clocks and watches, but the real beginning of the American watch industry didn't come until 1849, when the American Horologe Company was founded in Roxbury, Massachusetts. Until then, watches in the United States were handmade, and each could be repaired only by the craftsman who made it. Aaron Dennison, the founder of the Roxbury firm, introduced mass-produced parts to the American watchmaking industry—an innovation that earned him the nickname "The Boston Lunatic" from

some doubting Thomases. The first American watch to be entirely mass produced was the Waterbury, in 1880. By 1890, the Waterbury Company was producing over a half-million watches per year.

The wristwatch was still a novelty as late as 1900, when almost all watches were carried in the pocket. The English developed the custom of carrying a watch in the vest pocket when Charles II began the fashion of wearing long vests in 1675. During the 18th century, the Englishman carried his watch in a vest pocket at the end of a chain, which was frequently ornamented with dangling seals and charms. For a time, fashion dictated the wearing of a watch and chain in both vest pockets, although one chain was usually attached to a false watch.

This electric clock, which is about 7½ inches in diameter, runs counterclockwise.

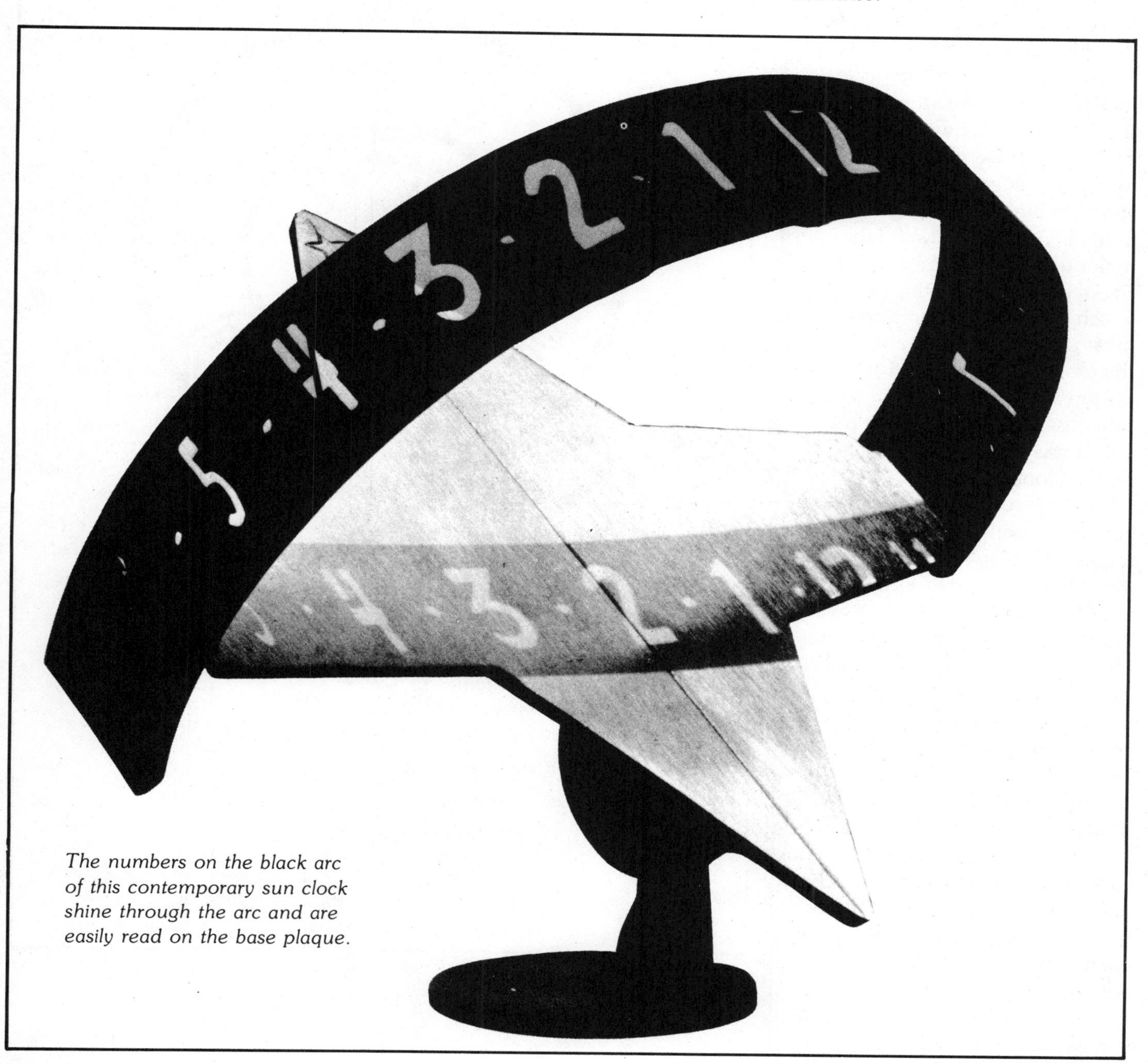

The numbers on the black arc of this contemporary sun clock shine through the arc and are easily read on the base plaque.

The first wristwatch was made in Geneva in 1790, but for the most part the "bracelet watch" was unheard of until the 1880s. According to one story, a watchmaker saw a woman suckling a child on a park bench with a watch and chain wrapped around her wrist, and was struck by the logic of wearing a timepiece on the wrist. At first, the idea of a wristwatch was scorned by the English, so the French took the lead in early production.

The English finally came around to wristwatch production in 1901, and the Swiss began making watches on a large scale in 1914. That year, a wristwatch displayed at the Swiss National Exhibition at Bern was regarded by most viewers as merely a "passing fancy." Passing fancy, indeed! Today, wristwatches make up about 80 percent of all Swiss watches, and the wristwatch has become the single most popular item of jewelry in the world. An estimated half-million womens' watches are purchased annually during the Christmas season in the United States alone.

The next major development in watchmaking was the quartz crystal, developed in America at the Bell Laboratories in the late 1920s, and introduced at retail by the Bulova Watch Company in 1970. The quartz crystal watch depends on the natural vibrations of a pure quartz crystal, and is considerably more accurate than earlier mechanical devices.

The first electric watch was brought out in 1957 by the Hamilton Watch Comapny, an American firm. In most electric watches, an electrically driven tuning fork provides the motive power, with each oscillation of the fork advancing a wheel and in turn moving the hands. The electricity is provided by a small energy

The foliot, the earliest form of mechanical-clock escapement, was mentioned by Dante in 1320 in his Divine Comedy. *This is a contemporary reproduction of a foliot wall clock.*

cell. The watch has no mainspring, and 35 percent fewer parts than a mechanical device.

The first electronic watch placed on the market was the Accutron, produced by the Bulova Watch Company in 1960, although electronic watches had been made as early as 1948. The Accutron's tuning fork vibrates exactly 360 times per second to provide the oscillations formerly furnished by the balance and spring. Electronic watches with a digital readout, rather than a dial and hands, were introduced in 1972. Digital watches now account for over five million watch sales in this country alone. An electronic watch—according to its manufacturers, at least—is accurate to within one minute per month or better.

Even the earth itself is not an entirely accurate timekeeper. The length of time required by our planet to complete one orbit of the sun is, on the average, 31,556,925.9747 seconds. But the earth can take as much as three seconds more or less to complete an orbit—one year is not always the same length as the next!

Today, about 80 million watches and an equal number of clocks are produced annually throughout the world. The Swiss account for about half of the watch production. The United States, Japan, and the Soviet Union each produce about 35 million clocks and watches a year, with the American figure consisting mostly of clocks, the Japanese mostly of watches.

No one has to be told of the tremendous variety of watches available on the market today—electric, electronic, digital, jeweled, illuminated, waterproof, shockproof, self-winding—you name it. When did they originate? A self-winding watch was made in London as long ago as 1780, but a patent was not secured until 1924. The first hermetically sealed, or waterproof watch was produced by the Rolex Company in 1926—although a completely airtight watch still does not exist. For the clock-watching executive, or the occasional cat-napper, the first watch successfully fitted with an alarm was brought out in France in 1947. Other novelty watches include a device with a braille face and gong for the blind, and complex astrological models that calculate the rising and setting of the sun and moon and the position of the stars.

Watches always make great gifts, so if you're shopping for a present you might take a look at the Swiss *Grande Complication*. The most expensive watch in the world without a jeweled case (excluding antiques), this plain-looking timepiece will set you back a mere $60,000! You prefer something in a jeweled case? How about a Piaget men's model, the world's costliest at $67,500? After all, what's more important than the correct time?

This lucite, battery-operated clock, known as a squash clock, projects a rather interesting image of time.

This clock shows the time for all of the world's time zones.

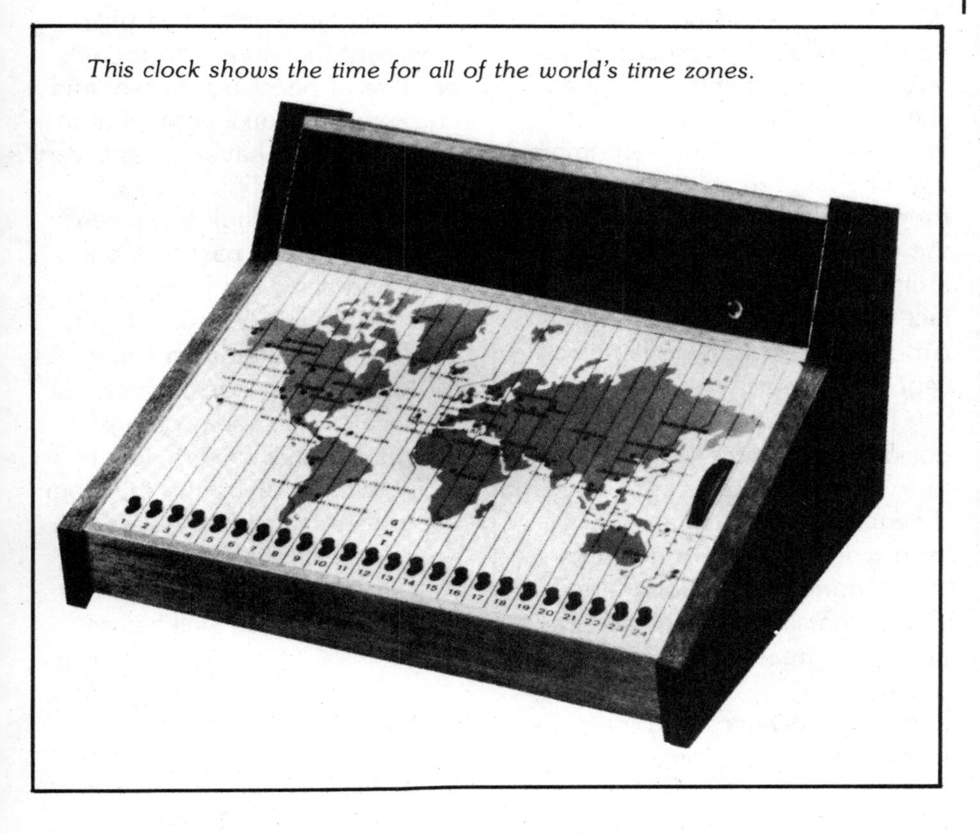

Cocktails

Walk into any American bar today and you'll find dozens of different kinds of spirits lining the shelves. You'll also notice that very few of the patrons are imbibing their favored spirit straight from the bottle. To Americans, the mixed drink may seem quite a time-worn tradition, and the fact is that the cocktail is an American invention—a fairly recent one at that.

The ancient Greeks had a cocktail hour in the late afternoon or evening, complete with hors d'oeuvres. An Athenian gentleman would drop by a neighbor's house during the "happy hour" with a goatskin of wine, and expect to be treated to an outlay of appetizers—the Greeks called them "provocatives to drinking"—that might include caviar, oysters, nuts, olives, shrimp, and paté. Compare that spread to today's bar-fare of peanuts, cheese, and crackers and you'll agree that in some ways we haven't come very far in the last 2,500 years.

The mixed drink is a recent invention. In the past, not only wine and beer, but hard liquor, too, was usually drunk straight, or at most, diluted with water. As for tomato juice, tonic water, ginger ale, club soda, orange juice, and other mixers, few of these had yet made the trip from the grocery store to the barroom as recently as 200 years ago.

Alcohol itself, of course, has been with us since well before recorded history began. Alcohol still ranks as the oldest and most widely used drug on earth. Primitive man probably discovered the first alcoholic drinks by accident, since any sugar-containing mishmash left exposed to warm air will eventually ferment. Studies of alcohol use among various preliterate societies suggest that alcohol was used by prehistoric man primarily in conjunction with war, religious worship, and various rites of passage—baths, marriages, funerals, and feasts.

The Babylonian Code of Hammurabi, dating around 1750 B.C., set down regulations for drinking houses. Egyptian doctors frequently prescribed alcohol as a medicine. By studying the remains of the Egyptian and Babylonian cultures, we can conclude that alcoholism has been a problem for well over 4,000 years.

The Chinese have been distilling an alcoholic beverage from rice since at least 800 B.C., and the Arabs have swilled alcohol from palm sap for many, many centuries. The earliest alcoholic beverage in the West was wine, brewed either from grapes or honey. Mead, a sweet wine made from honey, was widely enjoyed in Poland as recently as the 19th century.

The Greeks made their wine from grapes, but usually drank it diluted with water. Thus, the wine Athenians quaffed during their cocktail hour was probably less than 8 percent alcohol, a weak beverage by modern standards. In fact, most of the wine the Greeks and Romans enjoyed would probably taste rather crude to the modern palate. After all, we live in an age when an avid oenologist paid over $14,000 for a single bottle of 1806 Chateau Lafite-Rothschild!

Hard liquor is a newer arrival in the West. Around the year 300, the Irish brewed up *usquebaugh* from oat and barley beer. Tenth-century Italians began distilling brandy from wine, and 16th-century Scots first made whiskey from malted barley. The first cognac was distilled by the French around 1750. But it wasn't until Louis Pasteur's research in the 1850s into the action of yeasts and molds that Western man developed the controlled fermentation that makes for a consistently good alcoholic product.

Over the years, there were probably scattered incidents of man mixing hard liquor with a sweet beverage, but the cocktail did not become a popular drink until early in the 19th century. The origin of the word *cocktail* is uncertain. One claim maintains that it comes from a French drink served in New Orleans in the 1800s, called a *coquetier*, named for the tiny egg-cup in which the drink was usually served to women.

There are, however, dozens of other theories. According to some, the first cocktail in America was served in a tavern in Elmsford, New York, where cockfights were often held. The story has it that Betsy Flanagan, a barmaid, decorated the bar with tail feathers of some of the deceased combatants, and inserted one in a mixed drink when an inebriate requested "one of those cocktails." Another story tells us that as a publicity stunt, the proprietor of the tavern regularly inserted the tail feathers of fighting cocks in his mixed drinks, the feathers to be used as swizzle sticks.

In any case, the first mention of the cocktail in print appeared in an 1809 issue of the Hudson, New York, *Balance*, which described the concoction as a "stimulating liquor composed of spirits of any kind, sugar, water, and bitters."

Speaking of bitters, angostura, the most popular modern variety, have been with us since 1824, when a German doctor living in Venezuela prepared them as a tonic for his ailing wife. He reportedly learned the recipe from sailors, who frequently added bitters to rum as a cure for seasickness. When angostura bitters became part of the Manhattan cocktail, their place behind the bar was established forevermore.

The cocktail party is thought to have originated as an outgrowth of the aperitif hour before dinner. As the "hour" gradually lengthened, a buffet of some kind became necessary to allay the appetites of the imbibers. Psychologists attribute the popularity of the cocktail party, and the before-dinner cocktail itself, to their function as a separation between the working day and the evening relaxation. In recent years, many other countries have followed the American example and have adopted both the cocktail hour and the cocktail party.

As a rule, tipplers in most countries prefer a beverage produced from a native product—in effect, the "national drink" of that nation. For instance, vodka, an unaged spirit obtained from potatoes or grain and filtered through vegetable charcoal, is the over-whelming favorite in Poland and the Soviet Union, where the raw materials are plentiful. Vodka, by the way, has recently replaced bourbon as the most popular liquor in America.

44 WAYS TO SAY **DRUNK**

Soaked	Polluted
Crocked	Bibulous
Addled	Plastered
Balmy	Reeling
Jug-bitten	Potted
Smashed	Blotto
Soused	Pie-eyed
Hopped up	Muzzy
Nappy	Stoned
Seeing double	Boozy
Corned	Loaded
Besotted	Pickled
Tanked	Canned
In one's cups	Oiled
Fuddled	Stinko
Raddled	Pot-valiant
Shellacked	Swacked
Bagged	Decks-awash
Half-seas over	Sodden
Tipsy	Flying the ensign
Listing to starboard	Stiff

Three sheets to the wind

Under the affluence of incohol

Bourbon, America's contribution to the whiskey world, accounted for about one-fourth of all distilled spirits consumed in this country during the 1960s. But that figure has now decreased to about 15 percent, while vodka consumption has doubled over the same period. Vodka drinking now accounts for about 20 percent of the total American alcohol intake. Consumption of scotch whiskey, meanwhile, has held steady at about 12 percent.

Named after the county in Kentucky which may have been its birthplace, bourbon is distilled from a mash that by law must contain at least 51 percent corn. But Jack Daniel's whiskey, which many people consider bourbon, is technically a sour mash whiskey, or a Tennessee whiskey, and not a bourbon at all. Jack Daniel's, produced for over a century in the small Tennessee town of Lynchburg, is filtered through 10 feet of sugar maple charcoal to remove some of the harsh esters. The Federal government decided that this filtering process changed the whiskey's character so much that the drink could not be called bourbon.

Whiskey is usually distilled from the fermented mash of grain—usually oats, barley, rye, or corn. Whiskey is produced primarily in Scotland, Ireland, Canada, and the United States.

Rum is obtained from fermented sugar cane or molasses, and produced primarily in the Caribbean.

Brandy is distilled from wine or the fermented mash of fruit—grapes, cherries, apples, plums, apricots, peaches, blackberries, or whatever.

Tequila is distilled from the sap of an agave plant indigenous to Mexico, not from the mescal cactus, as so many people believe. Flavored spirits like gin, aquavit, and absinthe are produced by redistilling alcohol with a flavoring agent. Juniper is used to flavor gin; caraway seeds to flavor aquavit.

In the Orient, millet and rice are most commonly used for distilling spirits. *Ng ka py* is how you order a shot in Peking. It's made from millet, with various aromatics added. Saké, a beverage made from rice, is the favorite in Japan.

Spirits differ greatly in alcoholic content. Most wines contain from 8 to 12 percent alcohol, with certain aperitif and dessert wines, like vermouth and sherry, as high as 18 percent. The strength of beer ranges from a weak 2 percent brew, produced in Scandinavia, to about 8 percent. Four or 5 percent is the average in the United States. Most hard liquors contain from 40 to 50 percent alcohol, with cognac as high as 70 percent. Cordials and liqueurs contain from 25 to 40 percent alcohol.

The strongest spirits that can be produced are raw rum and certain vodkas which contain up to 97 percent alcohol. Polish White Spirit Vodka is the strongest liquor sold commercially, packing a wallop of 80 percent alcohol.

Most liquor bottlers identify the alcoholic content of their product by "proof." The term dates back to the earliest days of liquor distilling—when dealers would test the strength of an alcoholic product by soaking gunpowder in the beverage, and then igniting it. Spirits with enough alcohol to permit the ignition of gunpowder were considered to be 100 proof—the idea being that the gunpowder test was "proof" that the juice was strong. In England, 100 proof was established as eleven parts of alcohol by volume to 10 parts of water. In the United States, the proof figure was set as double the alcoholic percentage. Thus, 86 proof whiskey is 43 percent alcohol, and pure alcohol is 200 proof.

Just as nations have their favored beverage, most have a favored toast as well. The term originated in the custom of dunking a slice of toast in a glass of wine, for reasons unknown. Englishmen like to toast with *Cheerio, Cheers,* or *Down the hatch.* Scandinavians say *Skoal. Prosit* is a German favorite, though the word is Latin. Italians clink glasses to the tune of *Cin-cin.* The Spanish favor *Salud,* and the French *Culs secs.* Americans have coined the likes of *Bottoms up, Here's mud in your eye,* and *Here's looking at you*—as well as some more indelicate expressions from the frontier West.

While we're on the subject of word origins: the word *booze* does not, as widely believed, come from a liquor bottler named E.C. Booz. The word is quite old, originating perhaps from the Dutch word *buyzen,* to tipple, or the Middle English *bouse,* to drink deep.

America has nevertheless contributed quite a number of terms to the barfly's dictionary. In the Old West, rotgut whiskey was referred to by such affectionate terms as *old pine top, skull varnish, tarantula juice, Taos lightning, snake water, bug juice,* and *red-eye.*

Today, the names of popular cocktails are somewhat more flattering. The origins of some are obvious; others, lost in history. The *Rickey,* for example, is said to be named after a certain Colonel Rickey. The word *Julep* comes from the Arabic *julab.* The *Black Russian* is named for its primary ingredient, vodka. (It's not black, but it's certainly Russian.) The *Grasshopper,* consisting of green creme de menthe, with creme de cacao, and cream, owes its name to its green color. The *Martini, Tom Collins,* and *Alexander* are named after individuals. The origins of the *Fizz, Sour,* and *Stinger* shouldn't be hard to imagine. As for the *Zombie,* you won't need three guesses—the talk is that three Zombies will turn you into one.

But the names of modern cocktails are certainly not lacking in color. Witness the *Red Devil, Sitz Mark, Bourbon Fog, Hurricane, Barbed Wire Fence, Rhett Butler, Cable Car, Sombrero, Tequila Sunrise, Pink Lady, Pink Elephant, Godfather, Harvey Wallbanger,* and a warm wine-and-brandy concoction billed as the *Instant Cold Cure.*

Among the less exotic—and more popular—cocktails we find the *Old Fashioned,* a mixture of whiskey, sugar, bitters, and club soda. The *Screwdriver* combines vodka and orange juice; the *Bloody Mary,* vodka and tomato juice. A *Daiquiri* includes rum, lime juice, and sugar. A *Mint Julep* usually includes bourbon, mint leaves, sugar, and water. A *Margarita* combines tequila, salt, lime juice, and Triple Sec. A *Manhattan* is made with whiskey, vermouth, and bitters. And the ever popular *Martini* includes gin, a dash of vermouth, and an olive.

Speaking of the Martini, there's the tale about the South Seas explorer whose friend gave him a bon voyage packet containing bottles of gin and vermouth and a jar of olives. A tag attached to the gift said, *for insurance against loneliness.* When on the high seas, the explorer opened the present. Inside the package, a card contained the following: "I have never yet seen anyone start to make a Martini without someone else coming along and telling him how to do it."

And then there's the one about the man who ordered a Martini in a bar, drank down the cocktail in one gulp, and then began biting the glass. When he'd nibbled the glass down to the top of the stem, he left it on the counter and walked off.

"Did you see that?" a man who had been standing next to the Martini drinker exclaimed aghast to the bartender. "He's nuts!"

"Yeah, he must be," the bartender responded. "He left the best part!"

The production of alcoholic beverages in the United States now stands at over 100 million proof gallons per year, with an estimated half-billion proof gallons in stock. Not bad for a nation in which about one-third of the population are teetotalers.

Today, about 77 percent of adult men and 60 percent of women are regular consumers of alcoholic beverages. Studies have shown that the wealthy and better educated are more likely to be numbered among the drinkers. But in France, where there are few abstainers, those who do swear off the grape are more likely to come from the well-educated, monied classes.

France is the nation with the highest per capita consumption of alcohol: 22.66 liters of pure juice per year, more than twice the American figure. Italians are the highest per capita consumers of wine, downing on the average 153 liters to the American's mere eight. West Germans are the number one swillers of hard spirits—barely beating out the Americans in that category. The Germans are also far and away the leading drinkers of beer and ale, with the average German consuming 182 liters of brew per year. There is a claim, however, that the residents of Australia's Northern Territory far outpace the Germans.

We have no reliable figures for the communist nations, but vodka consumption in the Soviet Union is thought to be extremely high, and Czechoslovakia is said by some to surpass all nations in per capita beer consumption. At the other end of the scale, the citizens of Iceland and Israel rank as the smallest consumers of alcohol.

Enters the wine, comes out the secret.
—Hebrew Proverb

If all be true that I do think,
There are five reasons
we should drink:
Good wine—a friend—
or being dry—
Or lest we should be
by and by—
Or any other reason why.
—Henry Aldrich,
Five Reasons for Drinking

I drink on every occasion, and betimes on no occasion.
—Cervantes, *Don Quixote*

The above figures may surprise those who think that "light wine" countries such as France and Italy consume less alcohol than "hard liquor" nations like Great Britain and the United States. Great Britain, famous for its whiskies, is often thought to be high on the list of alcohol imbibers, but Britons actually consume less alcohol per capita than the citizens of any country in the West.

That hasn't stopped jokesters from commenting on the soft spot the Scotch have for their famous export. Perhaps you've heard the one about the elderly Scotsman who, while carrying a bottle of whiskey on his hip, slipped and fell on a path of ice. Climbing to his feet and feeling something wet trickling down his leg, he murmured: "I hope it's blood."

Dewar's incidently, is the best-selling non-premium scotch in America; Chivas Regal the best-selling premium. In Scotland, Bell's is the most popular domestic scotch whiskey.

With all that drinking going on, it's no surprise that alcoholism is a major problem in many societies. In the United States, and estimated five million people are alcoholics, and perhaps another four million are problem drinkers. In France, estimates of alcoholism put the figure as high as nine to 15 percent of the total population!

Religious proscription has done little to thin the ranks of the dipsomaniacs. The Koran forbids alcohol use. Devout Buddhists and Hindu Brahmins also spurn the grape. And many Christian sects have forbidden drinking—with mixed results.

As for legal prohibition, the longest on record is a wee 26 years, in Iceland, from 1908 to 1934. Russia tried to illegalize the grape early in this century, but the attempt lasted a mere 10 years. Our own "noble experiment" lasted only 13 years—much too long in the minds of many people.

For a point of view, regarding man's oldest and most popular intoxicant we may turn to the Bible. The Good Book mentions two drinks: ". . . *wine,* which gladdeneth the heart of man; and *water,* which quencheth the thirst of the jackasses" (Psalm 104).

Spirits, waters, liqueurs, syrups, etc. used in making of cocktails 100 years ago.

SOURCE NOEL
BRUNNEN
FINEST
COUZAN
SYRUP
ROISDORF
VICHY
HAUTERIVE
TABLE WATER
EAU MINERALE NATURELLE
MARCOLS
CONDILLAC
LIME-FRUIT
SYMINGTONS
ESSENCE
COFFEE
CHICORY
VICTORIA
ROYAL SELTSER WATER

COFFEE

No one need be told that human beings are lovers of the grape. But did you realize that the brew of the coffee bean is drunk by more people than any other beverage on earth?

Coffee is regularly consumed by about one-third of the world's population, and consumption continues to rise steadily. At the turn of the century, world imports totaled about one million tons. But by 1950, that figure had doubled. Today, the total stands at about three-and-a-half million tons—making coffee the second largest item of international commerce after petroleum!

Americans presently put away about one-and-a-quarter million tons of coffee each year, more than the entire world drank just 50 years ago. Coffee is, to say the least, an institution in this country, with the average American gulping down two-and-a-half cups daily. You won't have to look far to find someone who insists he couldn't live without it. And speaking of institutions, in many states, the coffee break is not only a fixture in almost all offices and factories, it's dictated by law.

Still, Americans are not the world's heaviest coffee consumers—the average Swede consumes close to 30 pounds of coffee each year! In fact, in much of Western Europe, the word for coffee, *café,* has come to be synonymous with an eating place. Even in this country, we prefer to call our beanery a coffee shop, a coffee house, or a cafeteria—which literally means "coffee store" in American Spanish.

A customer in the cafe called the waiter to his table and asked, "Is this tea or coffee? It tastes like cough medicine."

"Well, if it tastes like cough medicine, it must be tea," the waiter replied. "Our coffee tastes like turpentine."

Americans and Europeans may be avid consumers of the brew, but it's likely that most Western coffee addicts go through their lives without once laying eyes on a coffee bush. The reason: coffee simply won't grow in the climate of Europe or the United States. The coffee plant is a tropical evergreen shrub indigenous to the eastern hemisphere; 25 species grow wild in Africa, Asia, and the Near East. Oh, there is some coffee grown in the United States—but only in Hawaii.

Most coffee shrubs flourish best in year-round temperatures of from 77 to 88 degrees; a temperature dip to around 32 degrees will kill most coffee plants. And many species require more than 60 inches of rain each year.

Two species of the coffee plant are far and away the most common. *Coffea arabica,* the oldest known variety, hails originally from Arabia or Ethiopia, and is now grown extensively in South America. *Coffea robusta* originated in East and Central Africa and is still the major coffee plant of that continent. *Robusta* is not—well, "robuster" than *arabica.* Actually, it's milder in taste and aroma, and is less favored by Westerners; but in recent years, Africa has become increasingly important as a coffee exporter.

The average coffee shrub grows to a height of about 30 feet, with white flowers and red, fleshy fruits. Each fruit contains pulp and two seeds, and it is the seeds—not "beans"—that are used to make the brew. Why? Caffeine, of course.

Caffeine is an alkaloid that mildly stimulates cerebral and cardiac activity—in short, it's a pick-me-up. Try to imagine the difference in American offices and factories if the drug were suddenly to disappear, for caffeine is often the oil that makes the American brain run smoothly. And not without its price: caffeine causes gastric acidity and nervousness as well as heightened cardiac action. But coffee-swillers, take heart. Though theoretically the drug can be fatal in large doses, there is no case on record of a caffeine overdose.

The coffee plant produces delicate blossoms and rich berries.

Oddly enough, though coffee is today a fixture from Titicaca to Timbuktu, the beverage was virtually unknown in most of the world just a few centuries ago. For years on end, the tribesmen of Ethiopia and Central Africa crushed coffee berries and mixed them with animal fat to form balls which they devoured before their war parties. The Africans also made a wine from the coffee fruit, though they never brewed a hot coffee beverage.

According to some historians, the *arabica* shrub was taken to Southern Arabia for cultivation sometime before the year 600, though the Arabs didn't learn how to brew the hot beverage until the 10th or 11th century. The word *coffee,* by the way, comes to us either from the Arabic *qahwah,* or from Kaffa, a province in Ethiopia that is reputedly the birthplace of the *arabica* plant.

Arab legend maintains that the coffee bean was actually discovered by goats. According to the tale, a goatherd named Kaldi, living around the year 850, was puzzled one day by the queer antics of his flock. After watching them cavort around the fields on their hind legs, the goatherd discovered that the animals had been nibbling on the berries of a wild shrub, and decided to sample the fruit himself. The snack produced a delightful sense of exhilaration, and Kaldi went on to loudly proclaim his find.

Once the Arabs had learned to brew a hot beverage from the fruit, coffee became very popular on the Arabian peninsula, especially in connection with long Moslem religious services. Orthodox priests soon pronounced the beverage intoxicating and banned its use, but still the dark brew spread throughout the Near East.

Venetian traders were probably the first to bring coffee to Europe. During the 16th and 17th centuries, the beverage reached one European country after another. In many places, coffee was banned for a while because of religious, political, or medicinal objections. The Italian clergy at first opposed the drink as the beverage of the infidel, but after Pope Clement VIII tasted the brew, he proclaimed it fit for Christians.

Coffee became widely popular in London during the 17th century. The first coffee house opened its doors in 1652. Soon coffee houses became the centers of political, social, literary, and business life in the city. In America, the first popular coffee houses opened as early as the 1680s—and the *Mayflower* listed among its cargo a mortar and pestle to be used for grinding coffee beans.

At that time, almost all European coffee was imported from Yemen and Arabia, since the Arabs had jealously guarded their coffee monopoly by forbidding the export of fertile seeds on pain of death. But around 1700, Dutch traders managed to smuggle some coffee shrubs out of Arabia, sending the embezzled botanica to the island of Java, then a Dutch possession. The growth of coffee plants in Java soon became so prolific that the island's name became synonymous with the brew.

The French, too, managed to get their hands on the coveted shrub, and established coffee plantations in many of their colonies.

The Dutch and French both founded huge coffee plantations in the Guianas of South America; and like the Arabs, tried their best to guard their prize crop. But according to some accounts, a dashing Brazilian officer won the

heart of the wife of the governor of French Guiana. As a token of her affection, she gave him some of the precious beans and cuttings. Brazil began coffee cultivation in 1727, and was to become the largest coffee growing nation on earth.

Coffee is the major export crop of many of the countries between the two tropics. A price drop in coffee can throw the economy of many nations into complete turmoil, as happened in Brazil in the decade between 1925 and 1935.

After Brazil, Colombia is the world's second largest coffee exporter. In 1973, the Ivory Coast ranked third.

Brazil once accounted for 66 percent of all coffee exports, but as African production has continued to rise, that figure has dropped to 40 percent. Today, about 30 percent of all coffee comes from Africa.

The rarest coffee in the world is Jamaica Blue Mountain. That particular coffee is sold in only a few stores in the United States. Only 800 bags, or 100,000 pounds, are produced each year.

Roasted coffee beans can be brewed into a beverage in dozens of ways, but basically, there are two methods: decoction and infusion. In decoction, the brew is produced by boiling the coffee until its flavor is extracted. In infusion, water near the boiling point flows over unheated coffee grounds.

Americans prefer their java brewed by infusion, with either a drip pot or a percolator. The brew is then mixed with milk and sugar. The French prefer *cafe au lait,* an equal mixture of strong coffee and warm milk. Many Europeans prefer *espresso,* a strong infusion drunk without milk.

Cappuccino is a combination of coffee and frothy milk with nutmeg or cinnamon added. Turkish coffee is a heady, usually bitter decoction made from a strong, aromatic bean. Viennese coffee is usually served with a large dollop of whipped cream. And Irish coffee, a mixture of

Coffee beans being ground to powder in the Dutch colony of Surinam.

coffee, whiskey, and whipped cream, can be good to the very last drop—even if you don't like coffee.

Many urban Americans, especially Easterners, are fond of iced coffee, a beverage that is just now being introduced to other areas of the country. And speaking of ice, there's coffee ice cream. Coffee is also used in some chocolates, and caffeine is an important ingredient in another American institution, Coca-Cola.

For those who don't care for caffeine, there's de-caffeinated coffee, a brew made from ground coffee with all but about two percent of its caffeine removed. And for the real caffeine-hater, there are coffee substitutes made from chicory and other herbs. Postum, a popular American drink for more than 75 years, is made from bran, wheat, and molasses.

While we're on the subject of caffeine: the oft-heard idea that caffeine is an effective antidote to inebriation is simply—er, without grounds. Time is the only remedy for excess alcohol in the bloodstream, so coffee is an aid to the intoxicated only insofar as it takes time to drink it.

Instant coffee is actually brewed in the factory and reconstituted in the home. In the spray-drying method of manufacture, a concentrated brew is

Americans are not the world's heaviest coffee consumers—the average Swede consumes close to 30 pounds of coffee each year!

sprayed into a chamber and mixed with hot dry air. The air carries off the moisture, leaving behind the particles you find in your jar of instant.

In the freeze-drying method, a coffee extract is frozen and introduced into a vacuum chamber, where the moisture is sublimed and a solid mass left behind. The mass is then reduced to granules and packaged for those coffee lovers for whom time is more important than taste.

The debate between the instant-coffee connoisseur and the fresh-brewed fancier will probably go on forever. Which makes sense, since among Americans today, there seems to be no middle ground: you either love coffee or you hate it. If you number yourself among the coffee-crazy, drink hearty—and the next time you pour yourself a cup of java, give silent thanks to an Arabian goatherd and his errant flock.

Next time your guest asks for "just half a cup" of coffee, trot out this 3½" ceramic mug, which holds just four liquid ounces.

After-dinner coffee is made quickly with this espresso machine. Water is electrically heated in the chrome center cylinder, then forced through the grounds. Makes up to five demitasse cups of coffee, and puffs the milk for Espresso Cappuccino.

BEEF BRAZILIA

- 3 lbs. chuck steak cut into cubes
- ½ stick of butter
- 1 tablespoon minced garlic, softened in water
- 3 medium onions, sliced thin
- ¼ cup flour
- 1 cup red wine
- 2 teaspoons salt
- ½ teaspoon pepper
- ¼ teaspoon oregano
- 1 cup strong coffee

1. Melt butter in a deep, heavy skillet.
2. Saute steak until all sides are brown.
3. Now add drained garlic and sliced onions. Cook until onions are soft and transparent. When done, remove meat and onions from skillet.
4. Using the same skillet, blend flour with remaining butter.
5. Now add wine, coffee, and seasonings, and stir constantly until the sauce is creamy, smooth, and thickened.
6. Then put back the meat and onions in the sauce. Cover the pot. When the mixture is boiling, reduce heat, and simmer for 1½ hours, or until the meat is very tender.

Serves 6.

CHICKEN FAZENDA

- 2 broiling chickens, quartered
- 1/2 stick butter
- 1/2 cup strong coffee
- 1/2 cup honey
- 1 1/4 teaspoons dry mustard
- 1/4 cup vinegar
- 1/2 cup brown sugar
- 1 can Mandarin oranges

1. Salt and pepper the quartered chickens to taste.
2. In a shallow baking pan, bake chicken at 350° for 35 minutes.
3. Combine butter, coffee, honey, mustard, and vinegar in a small saucepan. Stir this over low heat until the butter melts.
4. Add the brown sugar, and continue to stir until sugar is completely dissolved. Allow to cool.
5. Brush the cool glaze on the chicken pieces, and continue to bake about 15 to 20 minutes, or until the chicken is brown and crispy on the outside.
6. Garnish each serving with Mandarin orange slices.

Serves 8.

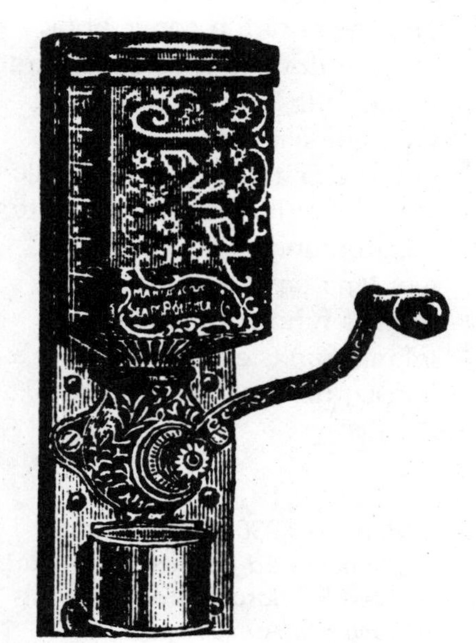

COFFEE OASIS

(As featured at the Oasis Restaurant in Jakarta, Indonesia)

- 1 clove
- 1 long, continuous peel of whole orange
- 1/2 vanilla pod
- 2 inches cinnamon stick
- 3 ounces brown sugar
- 2 1/2 ounces strong black coffee
- 1 ounce cognac
- 1/2 ounce Tia Maria coffee liqueur

1. Heat the coffee in a skillet.
2. Add the clove, the vanilla pod, the cinnamon, and the sugar.
3. Put the orange peel on a fork. The orange peel should be long and in one continuous piece. Hold the orange peel high over the coffee.
4. Ignite the cognac, and pour the flaming cognac from the top of the orange peel down the length of the orange peel, so that there is a fire right down to the coffee. Make sure you have a continuous fire.
5. Now drop the peel in the coffee, and heat for a few moments. (Avoid boiling the coffee.)
6. Remove the clove, the cinnamon stick, the vanilla pod, and the orange peel. Add the Tia Maria.
7. Serve in demi-tasse cups.

Note: This exquisite beverage has all the elements of a fine confection.

Comics

It's the comic strip—not film nor television—that reaches one-third of humanity each day.

ZOWIE! SOCKO! GLUG! WHAP! POW!

Place those words before an American of any age and generally, the reaction will be one of amusement. The comic strip and comic book together form perhaps the largest and the most influential iconographic field in the history of man.

The newspaper comic strip is a relatively new development, but its forerunners are ancient. In the first century B.C., Romans chuckled over tablets with satiric inscriptions sold in the market places of the Eternal City. Chances are, they weren't much different from the editorial cartoons we enjoy today.

Before the invention of the printing press, German artists produced woodcuts arranged in panel form, like the comic strip, dealing chiefly with religious history and current politics. After the printing press came into use, the illustrations took the form of a series of several sheets that could be hung on the wall to form a narrative frieze.

In the 17th century, the Protestant Reformation and the consequent religious wars led to propagandist strips based on political events. A limner by the name of Romeyn de Hooghe was the first artist to devote himself consistently to the narrative strip; he produced pictorial indictments of the persecution of the Huguenots under Louis XIV, and accounts of the accession of William III to power in Holland and England.

German artists began producing crime strips as early as the 16th century. Most strips illustrated, in gory detail, the punishment the perpetrators could expect to receive.

The father of the modern comic strip was Rodolphe Töpffer, a Swiss illustrator and schoolmaster. Töpffer proceeded on the principle that more people can read pictures than can read words. He went on to produce picture-story books and collections of small drawings that were the forerunners of the modern newspaper strip. Töpffer also put out collections of his drawings in oblong albums of about 100 pages. These were the precursors of the comic book.

The dominant comic illustrator in the 19th century was the German Wilhelm Busch, who was the first professional comic-strip artist. His tales of naughty children and pesky animals wouldn't be out of place on today's funny pages. His two infant pranksters named Max and Moritz, his most memorable

During the 1930s, Little Orphan Annie *achieved heights of popularity. Created by Harold Gray, the character of Annie captured the American imagination, and has been reproduced in everything from dolls to a Broadway hit.*

characters, were to form the models for the later *Katzenjammer Kids.* Busch's use of oscillations to suggest movement, and his use of conventional signs to suggest emotions, provided a vocabulary for the comic strip artist that is still in use today.

The newspaper comic strip in this country was born out of the rivalry between two giants of the American press. In 1893, the *New York World* published the first full-color comic page in the nation, depicting a set of humorous characters under the title *Hogan's Alley.* Soon afterward, publisher William Randolph Hearst countered with the first weekly full-color comic

Comic strips are popular throughout the world, and China is no exception.

supplement—eight pages—in the *Morning Journal.*

Hearst's supplement featured *Yellow Kid,* a strip by Richard Outcault, whom Hearst had lured away from the *World. Yellow Kid* was the first continuous comic character in the United States, and standardized the use of speech balloons for comic strip dialogue. Incidentally, the Italian word for comic strip is *fumetto,* "little puff of smoke," so-named after the speech balloon.

Later, Hearst put out Rudolph Dirks's *Katzenjammer Kids,* the first strip fully developed in form, and the most durable comic strip in history. Dirks's strip used speech balloons and a continuous cast of characters, and was divided into panels—unlike *Yellow Kid,* which employed full panoramic scenes.

With the advent of newspaper syndication, comic strips spread rapidly. In 1904, the first daily black-and-white strip, *A. Piker Clerk,* appeared in the *Chicago American.* Actually, the strip was a horse race tip sheet, as was *M.A. Mutt*—later *Mutt and Jeff*—which eventually dropped its racing connections and developed into a general interest strip.

The period between 1907 and 1920 was the golden age for comics. This era saw the birth of dozens of long-running strips and the development of the genres that predominate today. There was the gag strip, *Bringing Up Father,* brought out in 1913, the first American strip to gain international renown; the family saga strip, *Gasoline Alley,* begun in 1919. The career girl strip, *Winnie Winkle,* was started in 1920; the fantasy and parody strips, *Krazy Kat* came into being in 1911, and *Popeye* was inaugurated in 1919. *Krazy Kat* was the first newspaper strip aimed at the intelligent adult.

In the late 20s and 30s, adventure, detective, and sci-fi strips became popular. *Tarzan* began in 1929, followed by *Dick Tracy* and *Flash Gordon.* Nineteen-thirty saw the birth of *Blondie,* perhaps the most successful strip of all time.

The first true comic *book* was marketed in 1933 as an advertising giveaway. The size, glossy cover, and panel format of that first comic book have remained the same right up to today.

At first, comic books were basically reprints of newspaper strips. In 1938, *Action Comics* appeared. *Superman* and the other super-heroes were not long to follow.

By 1943, comics accounted for one-third of all domestic magazine sales. *Superman* alone had a circulation of 1,500,000 copies per month! By the way, the first issue of *Action Comics* now sells among collectors for close to $5,000!

Early comic books were for the most part brutal, sadistic, blood-and-guts affairs that most parents tried to keep out of the hands of their children. In 1951 and again in 1954, Congress investigated the comic book industry, and—simplistically enough—blamed the rise of juvenile delinquency on sadistic comic books. The industry was forced to adopt a code of self-censorship that still exists.

Comics continued to suffer criticism, especially for their racist, militarist, and fascist values.

Partly as a rebellion against this type of politically Neanderthal comic—*Steve Canyon,* for example—a number of newspaper strips appeared in the late 50s that were heavy with sociological and philosophical overtones. Most took their cue from the earlier *Pogo* (1946) and *Peanuts* (1950). Today, the funnies page is a conglomeration of science fiction, fantasy, adventure, slapstick, and subtle humor—something for every taste.

Without doubt, the comic is the dominant graphic mythology of the 20th century. It's the comic strip—not film nor television—that reaches one-third of humanity each day.

In the last 70 years, an estimated 8 to 12 million comic strip pictures have been produced throughout the world.

Over 100 million Americans—virtually half the population—read one or more comic strips regularly. About 300 strips are presently published in American newspapers. *Blondie* can be found in 1,200 papers across the country, and *Dick Tracy* reaches 50 million readers daily in 500 papers.

When Chic Young asked for suggestions for a name for Blondie's second baby, he received 400,000 replies. Al Capp's offer of a prize for the "most gruesome face" for a new *Lil' Abner* character generated over a million replies!

American comics are now read worldwide. *Peanuts*, incidentally, is called *Radishes* in Denmark. In England, a large chain of hamburger stands, the Wimpy Bar, owes its name to a *Popeye* character with a weakness for the burger. Not to be outdone, Texans, in a spinach-growing area in the eastern part of the state, have erected a statue of Popeye in tribute to his appetite for the vegetable.

Surprisingly enough, studies have shown that the more educated a person is, the more likely he is to follow a comic strip. The peak age for Sunday comic strip readers is—no, you'd never guess—30 to 39 years old!

By the time any American has learned to read, he's likely to have his favorite strips. According to a 1960s survey, the most popular strips countrywide are in order: *Blondie, Dick Tracy, Little Orphan Annie, Peanuts*, and *Rex Morgan, M.D.*

Little Orphan Annie began a run as a successful Broadway show ("Annie") in 1977. *Bringing Up Father* has been made into a movie 11 times!

Today, most syndicated strips are the work of an entire staff of writers, calligraphers, artists, and editors. In no other art form is the creator so much the prisoner of his creation, for the characters he invents frequently assume lives independent of their creator—and continue to live on, even after the artist's death!

It would be hard to think of a place in which different periods of history are so intermingled as on the funny page. You'll find *Moon Mullins, Dick Tracy, Gasoline Alley*, and other ancient works side by side with new strips like *B.C.* and *Doonesbury*. But they all have a few things in common:

ZOWIE! SOCKO! GLUG!WHAP! POW!

Chester Gould's Dick Tracy *first appeared in 1931. The name has become a synonym for a cagey cop.*

COMPUTERS

Just a few decades ago, all the money in the world could not buy an electronic computer with half the speed and versatility of the pocket calculator any American can buy today for less than $20. While the earliest computer specialists scarcely imagined uses for their machine outside the office, university, or research center, by the mid-1970s the computer has become such a part of everyday life that technologists can confidently talk of the day when many American homes will be served by their own private computers!

In such a "micro-automated" house, a small computer could regulate the lights, heat, and air-conditioning to maximize efficiency, or warn of impending emergencies, like a leaking water pipe in the basement, or keep trace of pantry supplies, or even water the plants and garden while the owner is away on vacation—in short, take care of everything, without itself needing attention. A home computer could double as a teaching device for children, a phone directory and message center, a menu-planner, or home calculator, and offer a full range of computer video games for every member of the family. Something to look forward to in the distant future? Not at all. Computers and computer kits are now on sale in many electronic stores—some for under $1,000!

What would a home computer look like? Much like a television set with an attached typewriter and cassette recorder. Compare that with the first electronic digital computer ever constructed, the ENIAC, a 100-foot long, 10-foot high monster with 70,000 resistors, 18,000 vacuum tubes, and 6,000 switches!

The history of computers—the realized or the dreamed of—begins much earlier than the 1945 ENIAC. Strictly speaking, man's first computing device was the abacus, first used in the Orient over 5,000 years ago, and popular in ancient Greece and Rome. The abacus performed simple calculations by means of sliding counters arranged along rods. The device is still widely used today not only in the East, but also in the U.S.S.R.

The earliest machines regarded as forerunners of the computer were, in fact, merely calculators, and simple ones at that. In the early 17th century, Scotch mathematician John Napier described a means of mechanically carrying out multiplication and division, and the German Wilhelm Schickard designed a machine with addition and subtraction, but it's doubtful either man actually built his machine. The earliest mechanical calculating machine still in existence dates from around 1644, designed and built by the French philosopher and mathematician Blaise Pascal.

Pascal was only 20 years old when he built a machine to help his father compute his business accounts. The young man's aim was not only to speed up calculating work, but also to assure its accuracy, since at the time, ability in arithmetic was generally rare—even among educated men. Pascal's machine, which could perform only addition and subtraction, employed a series of numbered wheels, each wheel representing a decimal place. When one wheel passed 9, the wheel to its left would advance one digit, "carrying over" the number from the lower wheel.

In the 1690s, German philosopher and mathematician Leibnitz constructed a more advanced digital computer, called the "Stepped Reckoner," capable of multiplying, dividing, and finding square roots. Leibnitz believed a calculator could free the scientist from the tedium of arithmetic, writing "it is unworthy of excellent men to lose hours like slaves in the labor of calculations, which could safely be relegated to anyone else if machines were used."

A copy of Leibnitz's machine was reportedly built for Czar Peter I of Russia, and eventually sent to the emperor of China, but the only copy extant is in the Hanover Library. Though far from speedy or efficient, Leibnitz's machine demonstrated the advantages of the binary number system over the decimal system for mechanical computers, and stimulated many others to experiment with calculating machines.

Around 1835, the English inventor Charles Babbage formulated ideas for a general purpose "Analytical Engine" similar in principle to the modern computer. Babbage's ideas were all but forgotten until the 1930s. In 1886, American statistician Herman Hollerith invented a device using perforated cards to count and classify data for the U.S. Census Bu-

A woodcut of a small portion of Babbage's Difference Engine No. 1. The machine was begun in 1823. The portion seen here was put together in 1833, and the plate shown was printed in 1899.

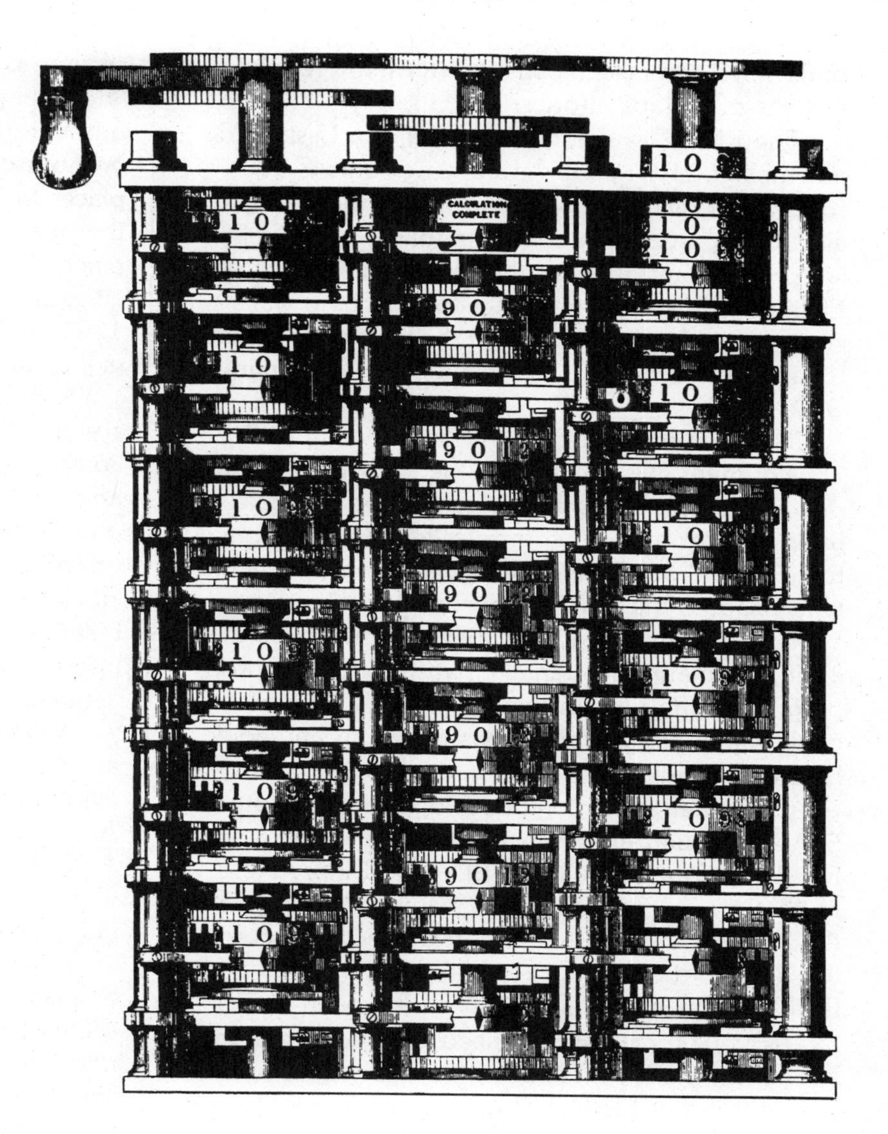

reau, and the machine was actually used in the 1890 census. By the way, a company founded by Hollerith later joined with two other companies to form what became the IBM Corporation, today the largest computer firm in the world.

Close to a half-century passed before Howard Aiken of Harvard University, working in association with a team of IBM engineers, constructed the first fully automatic, electromechanical calculator, the Mark I. Beginning in 1939, Aiken's team worked for five years to build their device, which like its modern electronic cousin used punched paper tape and punched cards. But the Mark I was no speed demon—a multiplication calculation required six seconds, and division 12 seconds.

The first electronic digital computer was, as we've mentioned, the ENIAC (Electronic Numerical Integrator and Computer), built by J. Presper Eckert and John Mauchly at the University of Pennsylvania. Completed in 1946, the ENIAC was a thousand times faster than any earlier computer. Engineers, at last, had their dream: a machine that could—in sec-

The world's most powerful computer, the Control Data Corporation's CDC 7600, can perform 36 million operations in one second. You can pick up a CDC 7600 for about $15 million the next time you need help balancing your checkbook.

onds—perform calculations that formerly required months of tedious effort.

The ENIAC was a huge machine, a U-shaped assemblage of 40 panels occupying some 3,000 square feet, with literally hundreds of thousands of electronic parts. By modern standards it was still fairly primitive, and most of the ideas underlying the ENIAC were abandoned after the machine was completed—but you can view the original machine today at the Smithsonian Institution in Washington, D.C.

The next milestone on the trail of computer development was a big one—the EDVAC machine developed in the late 1940s was to form the basis of most modern computer technology. A major force behind the EDVAC was John von Neumann, who adapted the ENIAC concept to produce a stored-program computer capable of supervising itself. Neumann, incidentally, was a bit of a stored program computer himself—his friends claimed he could repeat verbatim any passage from any book he'd ever read!

Computer technology developed rapidly after the EDVAC. Eckert and Mauchly and the Remington Rand Corporation built the BINAC—Binary Automatic Computer, in case you were wondering—and the UNIVAC, the first commercial electronic computer. Two further advances were the ORDVAC and ILLIAC, built at the University of Illinois in 1952.

As you've no doubt noticed, computer designers like to name their creations with acronyms—words made of the first letters of a series of words. Those who believe scientists do not formulate their acronyms with an eye toward mirth might look at ALGOL, GOMIT, BASIC, SNOBOL, LISP, SLIP, JOHNNIAC, and JOVIAL—that's Jules's Own Version of the International Algorithmic Language!

The earliest mechanical computers were concerned chiefly with rapid, accurate calculation. While the modern computer can perform even the most complex mathematical calculations in a fraction of a second, computers today are more important as information storehouses. An electronic brain can find one piece of datum from among trillions within a mere nanosecond—that's a billionth of a second. In effect, the modern computer is much like an automated file cabinet, locating, organizing, and presenting information from hundreds of different "files" within a split second.

Mathematically, the basis of all computers is the binary number system. The decimal system we use for normal calculations is based on 10 digits; the binary system has only two digits, one and zero. As with our decimal system, each digit in the binary system assumes a value according to its position, or "decimal place," in the number. For instance, in our number 100, the one represents the quantity 100 because of its place in the number—the "hundreds" place. In the binary system's 100, the one represents the quantity four, since we find it in the "fours" place. Counting from one to 10 in binary numbers gives us, 1, 10, 11, 100, 101, 110, 111, 1000, 1001, 1010—that last number actually reads: One eight, no sixes, one two, no ones, for a total of 10.

Simple enough? Well, to the computer the binary system is a breeze. Each piece of information fed the computer can be translated into a binary number, and each binary digit can be reduced to a simple one/zero decision—or in electronic terms, a simple on/off decision. Computer punch cards actually carry binary numbers—a hole in a certain spot represents a one, the lack of a hole, a zero. All the information on your computerized telephone bill can actually be translated into a long binary number!

Newer computers can read magnetic tape or ink as well as punched cards or tape, and some can even interpret printed material or handwriting. And—shades of the computer "Hal" in *2001: A Space Odyssey*—computer technicians are now working on a computer that can be activated by voice input!

How fast is a computer? Modern electronic brains can accept up to 100 million instructions per second, retrieve any piece of information in just 250 nanoseconds, and print data at a top rate of 6,000 lines per minute. The world's most powerful computer, the Control Data Corporations's CDC 7600, can perform 36 million operations in one second. You can pick up a CDC 7600 for about $15 million the next time you need help balancing your checkbook.

At the other end of the cost scale is the electronic pocket calculator that's revolutionized mathematical computation in the last decade. Even the smallest of these devices—in effect, tiny electronic computers—can perform in nanoseconds a difficult square-root calculation that would take the best mathematician minutes to figure out. Some mathematicians predict that pocket calculators will become so widely used in the coming decades, that educators could now do better instructing students how to skillfully use the calculator, than wasting time teaching them how to perform calculations by hand!

Ah, if students now sweating through their mathematics exams could only be sure . . .

Two monumental inventions mark the history of the printed word. The first, Johann Gutenberg's printing press, enabled one man to produce in a few hours what might previously have taken a scribe years to laboriously transcribe by hand. But for five centuries, the ability to reproduce printed matter remained in the hands of a small group of workers: the printers. The second invention, Chester Carlson's copying machine, gave that ability to everyone. It's conceivable that centuries from today, the name of Chester Carlson will be as familiar as Johann Gutenberg's.

Carlson's name is certainly not a household word yet—in fact, you may never have heard it before. But Carlson justly deserves credit as the inventor of the copying machine. Though the Xerox Corporation's name is today synonymous with the copying machine, most of the fundamental discoveries that led to its invention were the work not of a team of corporate research scientists, but of one man working alone in a home laboratory.

Even more surprisingly, Carlson's invention—eventually worth billions of dollars—did not appear in an office until 21 years after the principles of xerography were patented. During that time, it was turned down for production by a host of large corporations.

Chester Carlson was born in Seattle in 1906, and received a physics degree from the California Institute of Technology. Soon after, he moved to New York to work for Bell Telephone Laboratories, then for a patent attorney, and later for an electronics company, earning a law degree "in his spare time." While working as a patent specialist for the electronics firm, Carlson noted that there were never enough copies of patent specifications available, and that there was no easy way to produce them: retyping was time-consuming, and photographic reproduction was expensive. So the young man set out to invent a cheap, quick method of producing copies.

Carlson began his research by studying in his off hours at the New York Public Library. He soon decided to concentrate his efforts in the field of electrophotography, in which electricity is the agent for chemical change, rather than in conventior . photography, in which light is the agent. His earliest research work was carried out in the kitchen of his apartment. Later, he hired an assistant and rented laboratory space above a bar in Astoria, Queens.

Slowly, Carlson made advances in electrophotography—later to be called xerography. He received his first patent in 1937, at the age of 31. Then on October 22, 1938, Carlson and his assistant succeeded in producing the world's first successful xerographic copy, using a sulphur-coated zinc plate. That print, along with some of Carlson's original equipment, is now on display at the Smithsonian Institution in Washington, D.C.

In many ways, Carlson's work had just begun. During the next six years, he tried in vain to interest a company in financing his continuing research. Over 20 corporations, including RCA, IBM, and General Electric, decided there was little future in xerography. Finally, in 1944, Carlson convinced the Battelle Memorial Institute, a nonprofit research laboratory in Columbus, Ohio, to help him develop the xerographic process. But at the time, Battelle wasn't even sure of the practical applications of xerography, and considered using it to produce a

In this 1965 photograph, Chester F. Carlson shows the materials he used to make the world's first xerographic copy on October 22, 1938.

catalogue printer or a child's toy printing machine!

Meanwhile, in Rochester, New York, the Haloid Company was searching for a new product to manufacture. In 1906, the year of Carlson's birth, Haloid had been launched in a loft above a shoe factory, and for decades had manufactured photographic paper. In 1944, an article describing the work in xerography being carried out at Battelle was published in a technical periodical, and came to the attention of Haloid. though neither Battelle nor Haloid was yet convinced of xerography's future, the two organizations came to an agreement giving Haloid a license to develop a copying machine based on Carlson's discoveries.

On October 22, 1948—10 years to the day after Carlson's first successful xerographic print—Haloid demonstrated the process at a Detroit convention. Still, few people could see how the process offered any practical uses.

Around this time, Haloid and Battelle decided that Carlson's word "electrophotography" was too cumbersome, and began to search for an alternative. Ideas such as "Kleen Kopy" and "Dry Duplicator" were tossed around. But the final choice came from a professor at Ohio State University, who suggested a combination of the Greek words *xeros*, "dry," and *graphein*, "to write"—*xerography*.

Later, when Haloid was searching for a name for the copying machine itself, they settled upon XeroX as an unusual, easily remembered term—though there were those who argued that the word was unpronounceable. The capital letter was soon dropped from the end of the word. In 1958, Haloid became Haloid-Xerox, and in 1961, the Xerox Corporation.

In 1949, the company had produced its first copying machine, the XeroX Copier. The machine was slow, the results were dirty, but the invention did find use in the offset printing industry. It wasn't until 1959 that Haloid unveiled the world's first convenient office copier, called the 914 because the machine could copy documents as large as nine by 14 inches. Over 21 years had elapsed since Carlson received his first xerographic patent. And Haloid had spent over $12 million to develop the 914, more than the company's combined earnings over the previous 10 years!

There were other copying machines on the market at that time, but none using the xerographic, or dry process. Other copying processes were costly and slow, or produced copies that darkened with age or had to be dried. The time was ripe for the Xerox machine—more so than its makers ever imagined. The company predicted sales of about 5,000 machines in the first three years. But in two years, the company had already sold 10,000 machines, and was backlogged with orders. The 914 went on to become one of the most successful single products ever made!

There were still a host of problems, major and minor, to deal with before Xerox became a household word. The early copying machines had the nasty habit of occasionally catching fire, and Xerox wanted to provide a fire extinguisher with each machine. Fearing that the term "fire extinguisher" might frighten potential buyers, the company settled upon a more pleasing euphemism, "scorch eliminator." Also, the U.S. government began to question Xerox's claim that their machines could copy on almost any paper. Xerox responded to a government letter by copying their response on a paper bag and sending it to Washington. The claim was never questioned again.

Around this time, Xerox hit upon another scheme that was to make the copying machine much more generally available: instead of selling a machine outright, Xerox would rent it and charge on a per-copy basis. Meters were installed in each Xerox copier to register the machine's usage, and the customer was billed accordingly. Thus, small companies the might not be able to afford to buy a copying machine could rent one.

The story of Xerox's meteoric rise to corporate prominence is legend on Wall Street. In 1959, the company's net income was about two million dollars; in 1963, it was over $22 million. Over one 10-year period, Xerox's revenues increased by an astronomical 4,300 percent! By 1970, Americans were turning out over 20 billion Xerox copies per year, and the U.S. government alone had leased some 100,000 machines. When Chester Carlson died in 1968, his share of Xerox's profits was well over $150 million, though Carlson had given away more than two-thirds of that amount to various foundations and charities. Not bad for a guy who started with a kitchen laboratory!

Carlson's xerographic process might appear so simple that it's amazing no one elso beat him to the punch. It was probably faith and perseverance as much as scientific insight that led Carlson to success, for he had to experiment with thousands of chemicals until he found the ones that would work for xerography. Today's copying machines may include thousands of parts for moving and sorting copies, but the basic principles of xerography are the same no matter how complex the machine. Here's how xerography works.

First, the surface of a plate or drum coated with a light-sensitive metal (selenium) is given a positive electric charge as it passes under electrical wires. Then the document to be copied is projected through a lens onto the light-sensitive surface. The positive charge disappears from all areas of the surface not covered by the image—in the case of a printed document, from all the "white" spaces. The image area remains positively charged.

Negatively charged powder, called toner or dry ink, is then applied to the surface. Being negatively charged, the powder is attracted by the positively charged portion of the plate—the image area—and adheres only to that area. A visual image of the original document is thus created on the surface of the drum.

Paper or other material is then placed over the drum. A positive electrical charge beneath the paper attracts the negatively charged powder from the drum onto the paper, forming a duplicate image on the paper. Heat fuses the image to the surface of the paper. We now have a permanent, exact copy of the original document. The drum can continue to turn out copies of that document, or can be cleaned of electrical charge for reuse.

In the years since Xerox's first copier was introduced, inventors at the corporation have taken Carlson's original process and applied it to a host of new products. In 1963, Xerox introduced the first desk-top copier, the 813. The following year, they brought out the 2400—so named because it could produce 2,400 copies per hour. Later, Xerox introduced the 4000 model, which can copy both sides of a document, and the 9400, which can produce copies at the rate of two per second!

Xerox now sells a line of more than 40 copier models, and manufactures all sorts of related equipment, such as enlargers, microfiche readers and printers, and color graphics printers. Even since 1978, Xerox has turned out 24 new or improved products! And many other companies have followed Xerox into the office copier business, which certainly has not yet witnessed its last major innovation.

Though the printer and typist displaced by the copying machine might not necessarily welcome this new technology, it's not likely that either can be completely replaced by xerography. A copying machine can reproduce any document, but someone has to produce that document in the first place. Xerox and other companies have yet to find a way to translate ideas, in the form of the spoken word, into piles of neatly collated copies.

But they're working on it!

CORKS &

It can be said without the slightest fear of contradiction that were it not for the development of the cork bottlestopper, the corkscrew need never have been invented. But if you were told that the cork was a familiar item by the 16th century, and the corkscrew was not developed until the 17th or 18th century, you might well ask the question: Then how in God's name did anyone open a bottle for one hundred years?

We know that the cork was in common use by the late 16th century, for the works of Shakespeare and contemporary writers indicate that the object was well known to the play-going public of the time. In *As You Like It,* for instance, Rosalind tells Celia: "I pr'ythee take the cork out of thy mouth, that I may drink thy tidings."

But it's unlikely that Celia would need a corkscrew to unstop the flow of her words. The truth is, at the time, cork stoppers were usually set very loosely in the bottleneck, loosely enough to be pulled out by hand. Most corks were shaped with one thin, tapered end that could fit easily into the bottle, and a thicker end to grip when removing the stopper.

Corks like those commonly used in the kitchen for jars and

Busy at the cork harvest. An engraving from the 1880s.

CORKSCREWS

bottles of sauces, vinegars, and other condiments were intended to keep out dust and soot rather than provide an airtight closure. Only wine and ale needed tight corks, so it's likely that improvements in fermenting and bottling techniques requiring tighter corks gradually led to the need for the corkscrew.

The Roman poet, Horace, mentions the use of corks in wine containers, but says nothing of how the corks were removed.

One of the earliest mentions of the corkscrew dates from 1702. A scientific article of the time compared the tail of a tadpole to a corkscrew, describing the tail as a "close spiral revolution like the worm of a Bottle Screw." The comparison is hardly surprising, since we still use the corkscrew to describe coiled tails—the "corkscrew tail" of a pig, for instance. In the mid-19th century, corkscrew curls were the fashion in England and America.

Irish innkeepers of yore used the expression "kettle or screw?" when inquiring about the favored liquid refreshment of their patrons. "Kettle" meant hot punch; "screw" meant wine.

Speaking of Ireland, the city and county of Cork have no etymological connection with the bottle stopper. The word *cork*—or *corcaigh* in Irish Gaelic—signifies a swamp, referring to the fen upon which part of the city was built.

Corkscrews of the 18th century were usually made of brass or steel, with a sheath protecting the screw so that the device could be carried in a gentleman's pocket. Later, the gadget-happy Victorians developed elaborate corkscrew devices that included, in addition to the screw itself, such implements as nail clippers, earpicks, buttonhooks, screwdrivers, cigar piercers, and cigarette-rolling machines.

The first cork manufacturer in the United States reportedly was William King, who in 1850 opened a factory in Brooklyn, New York. In 1860, the first U.S. corkscrew patent was granted for a gimlet screw with a "T" handle.

Today, the corkscrew is an essential implement in any kitchen—except the teetotaler's, perhaps. Varieties of the corkscrew range from tiny penknife models—just try to open a quart bottle with one of those midgets—to intricate cogwheel devices that virtually open the bottle by themselves. Of course, you wouldn't want to unplug a $500 bottle of wine with a 69-cent corkscrew, so there are gold and silver corkscrews available for the oenologist who takes his uncorking seriously.

One modern corkscrew consists of a needle attached to a pellet of carbon-dioxide. The needle pierces the cork, and a pump pushes the CO_2 into the bottle until the pressure inside the bottle ejects the cork. At least, that's the way the device is supposed to work. At times, the pressure will explode the bottle itself instead of the cork.

You may have noticed that some corks stick to the sides of the bottleneck more than others. The longer the cork has been in the bottle, the more likely it is to stick. But the temperature of the wine cellar—or, alas, warehouse—influences the ease of cork removal as well.

Wine aficionados are quick to point out that any old metal coil does not a corkscrew make. As one grape maven writes, a good corkscrew has "just the right spiral and width of flange." A test conducted in the United States concluded that corkscrews vary greatly in gripping power, but that few, if any, were completely reliable in removing tightly sealed corks. As much as 300 pounds of force are required to dislodge the most stubborn corks.

You might well ask: Who would take the trouble to test an item as mundane as the corkscrew? Well, some people do, indeed, take their corkscrews seriously. The current head of a group called the International Correspondents of Corkscrew Addicts has a corkscrew collection that includes over 1,300 specimens, some over 200 years old. Old or rare corkscrews have been sold for as much as $400 at auction.

Corkscrews are manufactured throughout the world, but corks hail mainly from Iberia and North Africa. Cork comes from the bark of the cork oak, which contains a waxy substance that helps make the wood impervious to water and gases. Corks can actually show annual rings just like a tree.

A bale of corkwood ready for shipment. The larger slabs have been placed on the outside, and the whole tightly bound with metal straps.

A one-inch cube of cork contains some 200 million air-filled cells, so that captive air accounts for about half of a cork's volume. The air-filled cells are responsible for cork's bouyancy and elasticity, and contribute to its high degree of imperviousness to air and water.

Today, Spain leads the world in cork production (the word comes to us from the Spanish and Arabic *alcorque)*, followed by Portugal and Algeria. The annual world production, about 300,000 tons, now barely satisfies the demand for cork stoppers. The cost of a champagne bottle cork has already risen to as high as 40 cents. The cork may someday disappear from wine bottles altogether.

The expression "corker," as in "a real corker," originally meant a striking, conclusive statement or fact, an assertion that "corked up" an argument once and for all. The term has gradually come to mean anything or anyone extraordinary.

If you hear someone say a bottle of wine is *corked,* he's not referring to the stopper, but to a peculiar unpleasant taste and odor in the wine due to an offending cork.

And the term *corkage* refers to a nominal charge levied by some restaurants for the privilege of bringing your own wine to dinner—or, as the term suggests, for the aid of a waiter and a corkscrew in opening the bottle.

No discussion of the cork and corkscrew would be complete without mention of the longest recorded flight of a champagne cork from an untreated, unheated bottle: just under 103 feet, achieved at La Habra Heights, California in 1975. And isn't that a real corker!

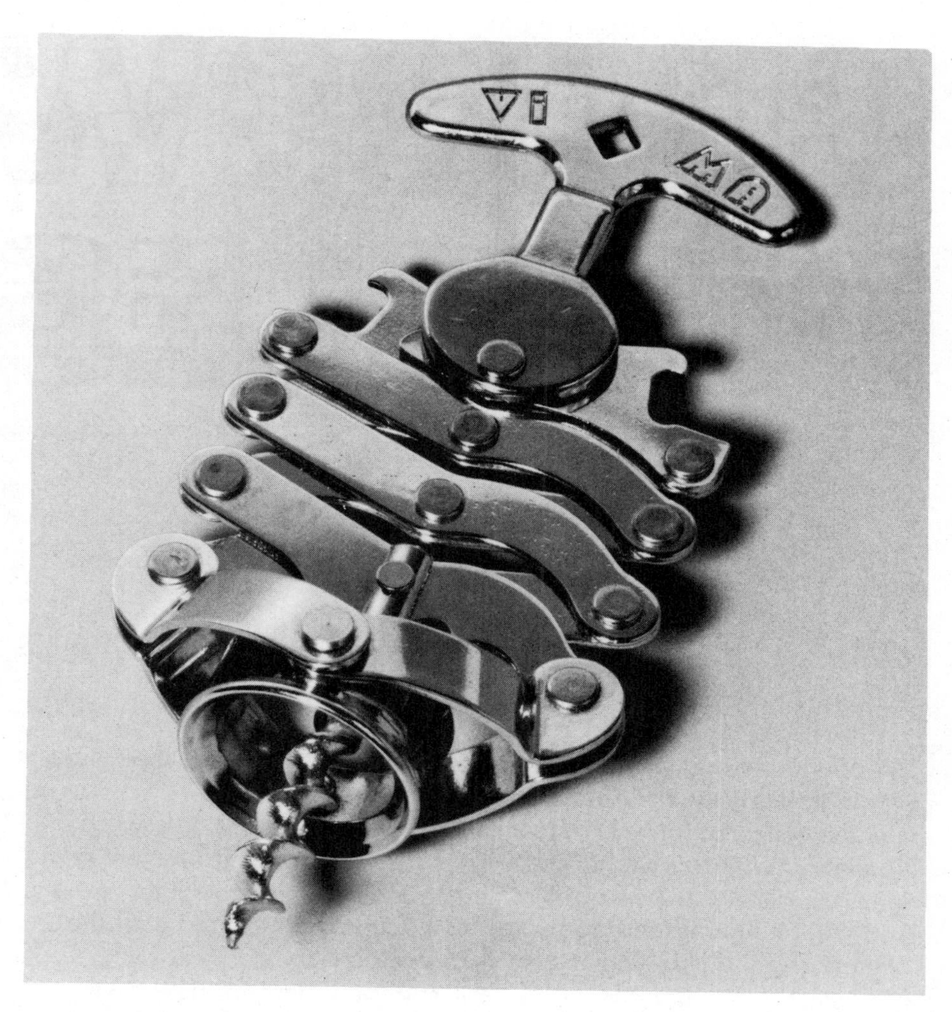

The Accordian Corkscrew is one of the latest types on the market.
Photo courtesy of Hammacher Schlemmer Co., New York.

So much for record-keeping, past and present—we know the longest champagne cork flight, but not the inventor of the common kitchen device the French call *tire-bouchon*, or "corkpuller." The poet Nicholas Amhurst bemoaned this lack of knowledge in an 18th-century tribute to the anonymous inventor of the corkscrew that included these less than immortal lines:

Still unsung in pompous strains
Oh! Shame! The Bottle Scrue remains.
The Bottle Scrue whose worth, whose use,
All men confess, that love the juice.

Old or rare corkscrews have been sold for as much as $400 at auction.

CROSSWORD PUZZLES

Did you know that an *ani* is a South American bird, but an *ana* is a collection of anecdotes? How about *anil?* It's an indigo dye. *Ara?* That's a genus of birds. And if someone asked you for a "diva's forte," would you respond immediately with *aria?* Well, if you were an addict of that ubiquitous indoor sport known as the crossword puzzle, these words would be as familiar to you as *emu, gnu, ort,* and *ait.*

You'd be in rather large company, too. A 1959 Gallup Poll found that matching wits with crossword compilers is the number one indoor game in this country, surpassing such favorites as checkers, bingo, and poker! An estimated 30 million Americans regularly wrack their brains for the name of "an East Indian shrub" or "an African antelope," and in England, an even larger percentage of the population regularly accepts the crossword challenge. In fact, the crossword puzzle is a familiar sight to speakers of every language that uses the Roman alphabet. And speaking of the Roman alphabet, some stuffy crossword buffs have gone so far as to construct their puzzles in Latin!

With all of this crossword construction going on, you might think that sooner or later puzzlers would be confronted with the same crosswords that had stumped them in their novice years. No chance of that. A mathematician once computed the number of permutations possible with a standard 11 x 11-square crossword puzzle; that is, given 122 squares and a 26-letter alphabet, how many different puzzles could be constructed? The answer was found to be a number that would blow the lid off any pocket calculator: 24,873 plus 222 zeroes. That's higher than the number of seconds that have elapsed since the beginning of the universe!

Where did crosswords begin? No, the ancient Greeks and Romans did *not* test their wits against the familiar black and white squares. But the crossword does owe a large debt to two other word games, the acrostic and the word square, both of which date back to classical times.

An *acrostic* is a composition—a verse or a series of words, for instance—in which letters of each line or word, usually the initial letters themselves, form a word or words when arranged in order. For example, the first-letter acrostic of "this heavy elephant" is *the.* The ancient Greeks dabbled with this kind of puzzle, and 12 poems in the Old Testament form acrostics. In Psalm 119, for instance, the first letters of each line form the Hebrew alphabet.

In a crossword puzzle, almost every letter of every word can be thought of as forming an acrostic with letters from neighboring words. Four four-letter words written across, for example, form four words when the letters are read down.

This brings us to the *word square,* a more direct ancestor of the crossword. A word square is comprised of three or more words arranged in a square so that the words read across the same as they read down. For example:

P E A T
E A C H
A C H E
T H E Y

The ancient Greeks and Romans were both familiar with the word square. A pillar built by the Greeks in Egypt bears a word square with 39 letters on a side, with words reading across, down, and diagonally. A true word square comprised of five-letter words was found among the ruins of Pompeii.

Word squares and acrostics were popular in England during the 19th century, especially in children's books. But both were usually presented as *faits accomplis* rather than as puzzles. Then, during the 1890s, newspapers began to carry word square puzzles in which the boxes of the word square were presented, filled with only a few of the letters or none at all. The clues were most often given in verse form.

The shape was not always square; diamond-shaped word squares such as the one below were not uncommon:

T
K E Y
T E N E T
Y E T
T

Though word squares most often included just four-letter or five-letter words, word squares with as many as nine letters have been constructed. But if you can construct a word square with 10 letters on a side, you will be the first to do so.

It's easy to see the relationship between the word square and the crossword. In effect, each corner of a crossword forms a word square, although in a crossword the across words are not the same as the interlocking down words. Yet, the idea of a crossword puzzle did not enter the heads of any word-square compilers until early this century, when Arthur Wynne, an editor of the New York *World*, produced the granddaddy of all crosswords.

The English-born Wynne was busy preparing puzzles for the 1913 Christmas edition of his paper's Sunday supplement, *Fun*, when the idea struck him: why must the words of a word square read the same down as they do across? Wynne sketched a diamond-shaped grid, reached for a dictionary, and within a few hours compiled a new kind of puzzle he called a *word-cross*.

Wynne's maiden crossword appeared in the December 21, 1913 edition of the *World*, among a group of puzzles that included anagrams and rebuses. The crossword contained 32 words, in a diamond-shaped diagram with a diamond-shaped opening in the center, and no black squares. Clues were keyed to the diagram by the number of the last square filled by each corresponding answer, as well as by the first square, as is the case with today's crosswords.

The response to the initial crossword was immediate and overwhelming. Letters began pouring into the *World* demanding more crosswords. From the very beginning, the newspaper received crosswords compiled by readers at the rate of about six per week. The *World* continued to publish crosswords in its Sun-

A pollster riding the trains in 1924 found that 60 percent of all passengers passed their travel time battling crosswords. The B & O Railroad placed dictionaries on all its main-line trains, and the Pennsylvania Railroad printed crosswords on the back of its diner car menus.

The Nazis recognized the English penchant for the crossword when, during World War II, they showered England with leaflets containing crossword puzzles with propaganda messages.

day supplement until the printers working on the paper—who hated the crossword for the typesetting difficulties it presented—convinced the editors to remove it. But a flood of protests following the puzzle's deletion convinced the editors that their readers' hunger for the crossword was more important than their printers' nerves, and the *World* crossword was permanently reinstated.

For 10 years following Wynne's first crossword, the *World* remained the only paper in the nation to offer the puzzles to its readers. In 1920, the paper hired a young woman named Margaret Petheridge to check the crosswords for printer's errors. Miss Petheridge responded splendidly: she went on to become the most renowned crossword editor in the nation.

Soon after Miss Petheridge's arrival at the *World*, the newspaper began publishing the nation's first daily crossword, edited in part by the noted rhymster Gelett Burgess. In 1924, Burgess penned this paean to his crossword fans:

The fans they chew their pencils,
The fans they beat their wives.
They look up words for extinct birds—
They lead such puzzling lives!

By that time, the crossword was already a fixture in many American papers, and a rage throughout the land. A pollster riding the trains in 1924 found that 60 percent of all passengers passed their travel time battling crosswords. The B & O Railroad placed dictionaries on all its mainline trains, and the Pennsylvania Railroad printed crosswords on the back of its diner car menus. Ocean steamers stocked supplies of crosswords for their passengers, along with dictionaries and dozens of copies of *Roget's Thesaurus.*

The crossword craze continued to grow through the mid-1920s, touching almost every aspect of American life. Couples published crosswords in newspapers to announce their engagements. Preachers used crosswords during their sermons to present religious texts. Checked patterns became the rage in the fashion world—one dress manufacturer even included a crossword book with each purchase, offering a discount to any buyer who returned the book correctly filled in.

In 1925, a large crowd filled a hall in New York's Hotel Roosevelt to watch Yale defeat Harvard in the first intercollegiate crossword puzzle tournament.

Some doctors decried the crossword as a cause of eyestrain, while others recommended the crossword to invalid patients as an excellent way to keep mentally alert. The crossword craze reached such heights that many libraries imposed a five-minute limit on dictionary use.

A judge in a New York courtroom had to break up a boisterous gathering of attendants, police, and lawyers battling a stumper crossword in front of his bench. And a Chicago court, faced with a wife's claim that her husband was spending too much time on his crosswords at the expense of providing for his family, decreed that the husband limit himself to just three crosswords a day.

Speaking of crossword court capers: recently, a West German puzzle buff became so frustrated by a particularly difficult crossword, that she woke her husband for assistance three times as she

THE FIRST CROSSWORD PUZZLE

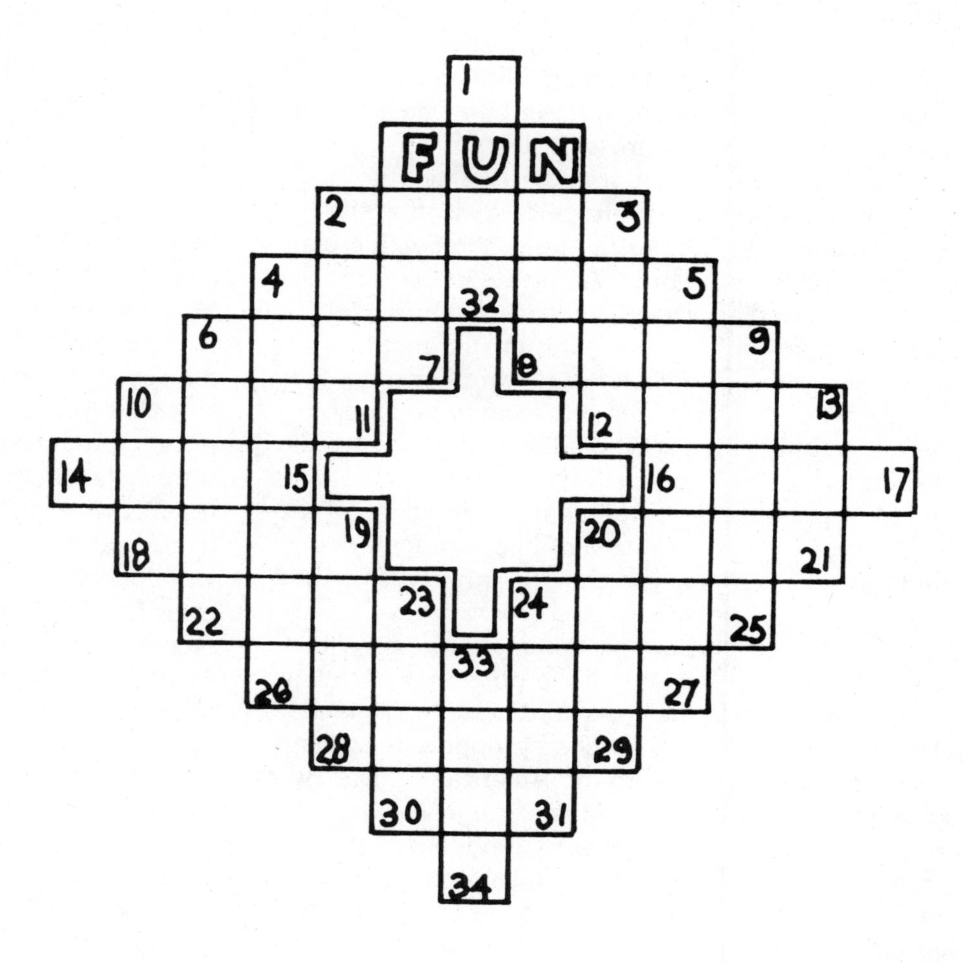

2-3. What bargain hunters enjoy.
4-5. A written acknowledgment.
6-7. Such and nothing more.
10-11. A bird.
14-15. Opposed to less.
18-19. What this puzzle is.
22-23. An animal of prey.
26-27. The close of a day.
28-29. To elude.
30-31. The plural of is.
8-9. To cultivate.
12-13. A bar of wood or iron.
16-17. What artists learn to do.
20-21. Fastened.
24-25. Found on the seashore.
10-18. The fibre of the gomuti palm.
6-22. What we all should be.
4-26. A day dream.
2-11. A talon.
19-28. A pigeon.
F-7. Part of your head.
23-30. A river in Russia.
1-32. To govern.
33-34. An aromatic plant.
N-8. A fist.
24-31. To agree with.
3-12. Part of a ship.
20-29. One.
5-27. Exchanging.
9-25. To sink in mud.
13-21. A boy.

battled the poser through the night. The fourth time the puzzled frau woke her weary consort, he strangled her to death. The court acquitted the husband on the grounds of temporary insanity.

In 1924, two neophyte publishers named Dick Simon and Lincoln Schuster were looking for their newly-formed company's first manuscript when they realized that no book of crossword puzzles had yet appeared in this country. They contacted Margaret Petheridge, who agreed to compile a crossword book along with two of her *World* co-editors. Simon and Schuster presented Ms. Petheridge with a $25 advance, then began searching for a printer who would work for deferred payment. They found one—a crossword addict.

In April of that year, Simon and Schuster brought out *The Crossword Puzzle Book,* an anthology of 50 puzzles from the *World*. On the advice of friends who could see only disaster ahead in the crossword book game, Simon and Schuster omitted their firm's name from the book, opting instead for the Plaza Publishing Company. The book sold for the then rather high price of $1.35, but each copy came complete with a neatly sharpened pencil—provided free by the Venus Pencil Company as an advertising gimmick.

The success of the book was immediate—within three months, 40,000 copies of *The Crossword Puzzle Book* had been sold. A later 25-cent edition was so popular that one distributor placed an order for a quarter-million copies, the largest book order of the time. Volume Two followed later that year, bearing the name of Simon and Schuster, although Plaza Publishing Company was to remain on the firm's crossword collections until their 50th volume. Within a year, the firm had sold 400,000 crossword books, and they were to follow with two crossword collections per year for decades after. Today, Simon & Schuster is one of the largest publishing houses in the world—and it all began with the crossword!

Across the Atlantic, the English were quick to scoff at the American fascination with crosswords. An article in the London *Times*, entitled "An Enslaved America," estimated that five million hours were being wasted daily in this country by employees who fiddled with crosswords during working hours.

Apparently, the editors of the *Times* were unaware that, five weeks earlier, Arthur Wynne had submitted a crossword to the London *Sunday Express*. Within weeks of the puzzle's publication, the crossword craze in England had reached proportions comparable to the American mania. By 1925, American newspapers were able to announce that Queen Mary was a crossword buff, and that the Prime Minister highly recommended the puzzles for their "educational value."

Crossword addicts in England were no less devoted to their sport than their American counterparts. The London zoo was so deluged with questions that they announced they would no longer answer inquiries pertaining to the names of unusual animals. Libraries began to black out the crosswords in all their newspapers to prevent puzzlers from monopolizing the papers. Advertisers had to pay particularly high prices for the spaces next to crosswords. Some advertisers bought the spaces and then left them blank—a small notice at the bottom of the otherwise blank space told puzzlers whom to thank for the doodling room. One Liverpool crossword buff went so far as to black out, in the library's dictionary, a key word needed to complete a puzzle contest that the puzzler was intent on winning for himself.

The crossword contest began to appear almost as early as the crossword. In 1924, the New York *Evening Graphic* became the first American paper to offer a crossword contest, or *pruzzle*, so called from a combination of *prize* and *puzzle*. Most contests were lotteries, in which only contestants who correctly completed a crossword were entered. Many were offered as advertising stunts, or as fund-raisers for charitable organizations. Before long, entire pages of newspapers were being filled with crossword contests, and professional puzzle solvers had gone into business, offering to complete contestant's puzzles for a small fee.

The crossword puzzle frenzy has tapered off somewhat in the United States over the decades since its inception, but the English are as fervent as ever in their dedication to the black and white squares. The Nazis recognized the English penchant for the crossword when, during World War II, they showered England with leaflets containing crossword puzzles with propaganda messages. A typical clue might be *warmonger*, with *Churchill* or *Roosevelt* the answer.

But the English put their crossword skills to use in the war as well, occasionally burying coded secret messages in newspaper puzzles. The Hungarian government had recognized the secret-message capabilities of the crossword in 1925, when they ordered that all newspaper crosswords first be submitted to official censors for approval. One crossword not submitted for government approval was the work of a Budapest man who left a suicide note in the form of a crossword puzzle, with the reasons for his act, and the persons to be contacted, cleverly incorporated into the puzzle.

Today, the weekly crosswords appearing in *The Observer*, a London paper, are generally considered to be among the world's most difficult. The first puzzle composer at *The Observer* was Edward P. Mathers, or "Torquemada," who began work during the 1920s and published 670 puzzles before his death in 1939. Torquemada's puzzles, along with those of his successor at the paper, D.S. Macnutt, or "Ximenes," are generally considered to be among the cleverest, most challenging puzzles ever constructed. The few readers who did complete the puzzles required an average of from two to four hours to do the job, although the compilers needed but an hour and a half to construct them.

The crosswords published by the London *Times* are also considered to be among the world's most challenging. The *Times* began publishing daily crosswords in 1930, despite heavy objections from some of the paper's more stodgy readers. Searching for a writer to compile the paper's first puzzle, the editor charged with the task asked the help of a friend, who then recommended his son, 28-year-old Adrian Bell. Previously, Bell had not only never compiled a crossword, he had never even attempted to solve one! Yet, in 10 days, Bell turned out the *Times's* first masterpiece, and over the next 40 years, contributed a large portion of the paper's 10,000-plus stumpers. Today, the *Times* employs an editor and 10 compilers to toil solely on crosswords.

In America, the puzzles of the *New York Sunday Times* are generally recognized as the most consistently challenging, but most American crosswords are child's play compared to their English cousins. Oddly enough, the *Times* was the last major American paper to include a crossword, publishing its first puzzle in 1942 and its first daily crossword eight years later. Margaret Petheridge (later Farrar), of earlier crossword fame, edited the *Times* puzzles until her retirement in 1969.

Petheridge's distinguished tenure at the *Times* was not without its moments of levity. On one occasion, the compiler was searching for a clue for "wooden leg," and opted for "Ahab's distinguishing feature." A reader's letter quickly pointed out that the captain of the *Pequod* in *Moby Dick* had an ivory, not wooden, leg. But the content of the letter was less surprising than the age of its author—an eight-year-old boy!

Errors are far from rare in crossword puzzles. One compiler tells of the time he misread a word in the puzzle diagram and devised the clue "Catholic chief" for what he thought was "pope." The published answer was "dope," prompting a deluge of letters from Catholic readers. A newspaper once published a set of clues with the wrong puzzle diagram, only to find that many readers had successfully reconstructed the correct diagram from the clues!

In 1970, the first annual crossword puzzle championships were held in England, sponsored

A 1959 Gallup Poll found that matching wits with crossword compilers is the number one indoor game in the United States.

Measuring six feet long by 18 inches wide, this crossword puzzle is printed on a plastic-coated washable fabric so it can be hung on the wall for posterity. Definitions are printed on a separate sheet, as are the answers.

by the Cutty Sark Distilling Company. Puzzle buffs wishing to participate were asked to complete five puzzles and send them to the contest organizers. Over 20,000 persons successfully completed the puzzles! The finals were held in a BBC studio, with a 43-year-old diplomat named Roy Dean taking first prize—the Cutty Sark trophy, a silver cube mounted on a stand. To the embarrassment of the contest organizers, the crossword diagrams on the cube faces bore a pattern of black squares strikingly reminiscent of the swastika.

En route to his victory, Dean set the all-time record for completing a puzzle from the London *Times* under test conditions—an amazing three minutes, 45 seconds! As a rule, even the best puzzlers require half an hour or so to complete the *Times* crosswords. At the other end of the spectrum, in 1966 a woman wrote to the *Times* to announce that she had just completed a puzzle published in the paper's April 4, 1932 issue!

We wonder how that dilatory puzzler might fare with the largest crossword ever published. Completed in 1975, this giant stumper contained 2,631 clues across and 2,922 clues down, and measured over 16 square feet. A Los Angeles man named Robert Stilgenbauer once compiled—but did not publish—a crossword with 3,149 clues across and 3,185 clues down. Stilgenbauer sent out 125,000 copies of the puzzle—which required 11 years to compile—but none was returned correctly completed. Another ingenious puzzler constructed a three-dimensional crossword, 15 squares on a side, with clues given for words across, down, and depth.

The average crossword is a good deal simpler. Crossword puzzles generally fall into four different categories:

1. Square or rectangular puzzles, usually of symmetrical design.
2. Asymmetrical puzzles, in the shape of a heart, cross, hexagon, or other design.
3. Puzzles without black squares; thick lines indicate where one word ends and another begins.
4. Diagramless puzzles, which simply offer clues, with no hint as to how the diagram is shaped.

But there are dozens of variations, and dozens of ways to disguise a clue. Many puzzles contain unclued words or words with identical clues, revolving around a central theme. Some puzzles ask for answers written in reverse, others for puns or anagrams of the clue. Occasionally, a short word must be deleted from all answers before they are written in the diagram; for instance, if the key word is *cat,* the answer *catatonic* would be written simply *atonic* in the diagram, and the answer *ducat* as *du.*

English puzzle compilers like to use narrative clues, with the answers comprising words left out of a story or poem. Puzzles have been constructed requiring algebraic calculations, with the answers written in the diagram as numbers rather than letters. Some puzzles require a symbol such as the heart or diamond as part of each answer, as *heartless* or *Diamond Lil.* Other puzzles require overlapping answers: for example, an answer such as *teasingleambleedit* might require six clues, one each for *teasing, single, gleam, amble, bleed,* and *edit.*

Bilingual crosswords, with clues in English and answers in French, were once common in England, as were English/Yiddish puzzles in New York. One particularly difficult puzzle form provides one set of clues and two accompanying diagrams. Each clue must be used twice, once for each diagram, but no hint is provided as to which answer belongs in which diagram. Sound impossible? Well, English writer Max Beerbohm once constructed what he called the "Impossible Crossword," with nonsensical clues for nonexistent answers. The crossword, published in 1940, came with a warning to readers that the puzzle could not be solved.

You may have seen crosswords that include a number or numbers in parentheses after each clue. These numbers refer to the number of letters in each word of the answer. But at one time, the numbers in parentheses were provided to confirm that a contemplated answer was correct. Each letter was assigned a number (A=1, B=2, etc.). The numbers represented by each letter in an answer could be added together, and the sum checked against the number in parentheses.

Crosswords have spawned a number of related games and puzzles. Scrabble, one of the most popular games in America, was invented in 1948, and the present rules formalized in 1953. If you're a Scrabble fan, read this and weep: during the 1970 national championships, the woman who was to become the eventual winner amassed an eye-popping 1,266 points in a single game!

The double crostic, another puzzle similar to the crossword, was invented in 1934 by Elizabeth Kingsley, whose double crostics appeared in every issue of the *Saturday Review* for 18 years. In the double crostic, the puzzler must first answer a number of clues, then transfer each letter of an answer to a corresponding square in the diagram, according to the numbers that appear under the answers. The completed diagram will then contain a quotation, and the first letters of the answers will also form an acrostic providing the author and work from which the quote was taken.

You'd like to try your hand at compiling crosswords? It's not easy, but here are some guidelines. Margaret Petheridge formulated five basic rules for crosswords she might find acceptable. First, all words in the diagram must totally interlock, with no letter of any word dependent on a single across or down clue. No more than one-sixth of the squares in the diagram may be black. No two-letter words are permissible. The word count should be as low as possible—a long word is preferable to several shorter words. Cliches should be avoided whenever possible—and a hackneyed answer must be balanced by a clever, original clue.

To be a successful crossword compiler, you'll need, in the words of one compiler, "practice and a ragbag of a mind that stores away completely unrelated bits of fact."

If you're wondering what kind of individual spends his time toiling over crossword composition, you might be interested to learn that of 100 regular contributors to two New York puzzle magazines, 25 are currently in prison!

Today, the weekly crosswords appearing in *The Observer*, a London paper, are generally considered to be among the world's most difficult.

DIAMONDS

In size alone, the Cullinan diamond is the granddaddy of all famous diamonds. Discovered in 1905 in the Premier Mine in Transvaal, South Africa, the stone in the rough weighed 3,106 carats—1⅓ pounds.

"A diamond is forever" may sound like an advertising slogan devised by the jewelry industry, but it's not far from the truth. Long after the gold band of a wedding or engagement ring—and the finger that wore it—have vanished into dust, the diamond itself will be as hard and brilliant as ever. There is, quite simply, nothing on earth hard enough to crush or chip a diamond—except another diamond. Unless it is cut by man or burned in a furnace, the diamond will, indeed, last forever.

The ancient Greeks had another expression for the treasured gem: "A diamond is invincible." At least, the Greeks called the diamond *adamas,* "the invincible." The word was first applied to all hard metals, then to corundum and certain other hard stones. However, by the first century B.C., the exclusive meaning of *adamas* was diamond. From *adamas* came the later Latin *diamas,* then the Middle English *diamaunt,* and then our words *diamond* and *adamant.*

The diamond owes its extreme hardness to its tightly-knit crystal structure. Atomically, diamond is identical to coal and graphite, two of the softest minerals—all three are composed entirely of carbon. Each carbon atom in a diamond is firmly linked to four equidistant neighbors, while in graphite the atoms are free to "roll" over one another. Its tight crystal structure makes diamond 90 times as hard as the second hardest substance on earth, corundum. Acids cannot harm a diamond, nor can any but the hottest fires—temperatures over 1,400 degrees, to be exact!

Diamonds may be valuable in industry for their hardness, but it is their brilliance that makes them valuable as gems. The brilliance of the diamond is due to its high refractive powers—much of the light reaching a diamond is reflected back into the stone rather than through it. The best diamonds are transparent and colorless, but diamonds actually range in color from clear to black. The rare pale blue and yellow-tinged diamonds are more highly prized than other "fancy" stones, which may be green, deep blue, pink, or deep yellow in color.

Diamonds are found in four forms, only one of which is used as a gem. *Bort* is a gray or brown crystal, while *ballas* is a powder of minute round crystals. Both are used exclusively in industry, as is *carbonado,* an opaque black or gray mineral. Diamonds are so vital that many industries would come to a complete halt without them. Their many uses include metal-working, stone-cutting, and all kinds of grinding, polishing, and sharpening. Closer to home, diamonds are used for phonograph needles and drill bits—including the one your dentist may use to drill your teeth.

The "Big Hole" in the Kimberly diamond mines of South Africa.

The beautiful gem that might now be sparkling on your finger was formed deep within the earth, where extreme pressures and temperatures forced the crystallization of carbon. Although 4,000 feet is the deepest any diamond has been found, the gems actually originate about 75 miles below the surface of the earth, and are pushed to the surface by volcanic activity. Some are released from the earth by erosion and deposited in river and stream beds. Others remain in the earth, usually in diamond "pipes," funnel-shaped lodes of diamond-rich rock called *kimberlite*. Most diamonds today are mined from pipes, including those found in the world's richest mines, near Kimberley, South Africa.

"'Diamonds in the rough" are usually round and greasy-looking. But diamond miners are in no need of dark glasses to shield them from the dazzling brilliance of the mines, for quite another reason: even in a diamond pipe, there is only one part diamond per 14 million parts of worthless rock. Approximately 46,000 pounds of earth must be mined and sifted to produce the half-carat gem you might be wearing. No wonder diamonds are expensive!

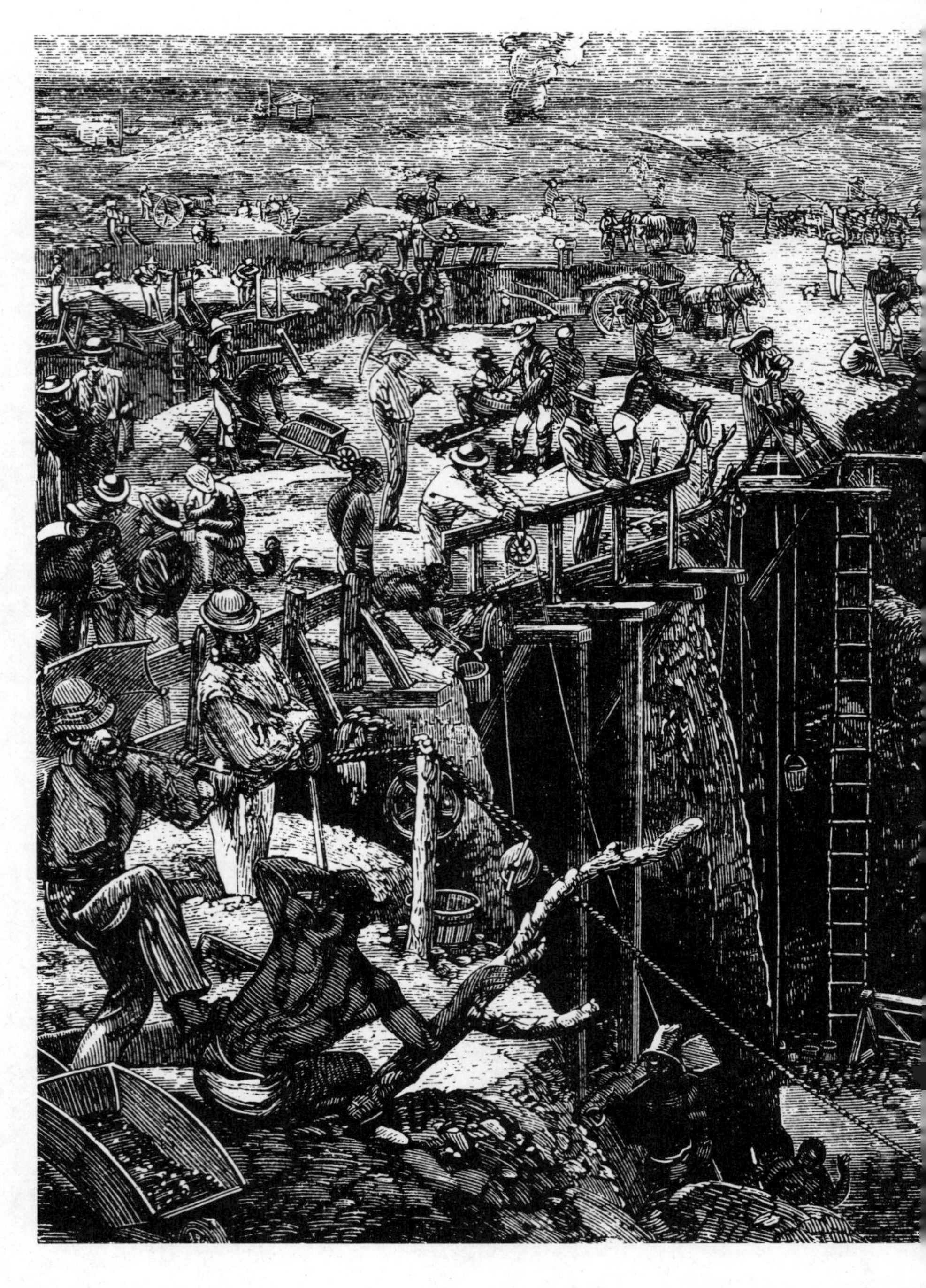

The diamond diggings in South Africa.

After diamond-bearing ore is brought up from the mine, it is crushed into smaller rocks no larger than one-and-a-quarter inches in diameter, then washed to remove loose dirt. At the recovery plant, the ore is spread on tables covered with grease and sprayed with water. The water moves the rocks off the table, but the diamonds adhere to the grease. Then the grease is boiled off, leaving "rocks" of quite another sort.

Diamonds are weighed by the *carat* rather than by the grain or gram. The word comes from *carob*, a bean once used to weigh gems on a balance scale because of its uniform size. A *karat*, meanwhile, is used in reference to the purity of gold—24-karat gold is pure. An English carat is equivalent to 3.168 grains, or 205.3 milligrams, but in most places the metric carat, equivalent to 200 milligrams, is the standard. The differing values of the carat in various places and during various times has resulted in a good deal of confusion as to the weights of some of the

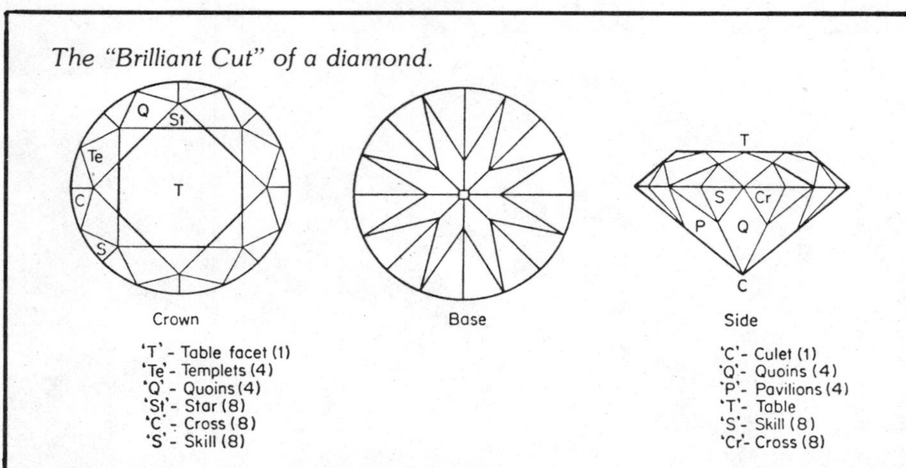

The "Brilliant Cut" of a diamond.

world's more famous gems. The present metric carat wasn't standardized until early this century.

Diamonds as they are collected at the recovery plant are still a long way from your wedding ring. Skilled craftsmen must transform the shapeless, cloudy stone into a delicate, multifaceted gem. Most diamonds are bought in parcels at diamond "sights" held in London or Johannesburg, then brought to diamond cutters in Antwerp, Amsterdam, and other cities.

Diamond cutting is a slow, painstaking process, involving many steps—and failure at any point could destroy or damage a valuable gem. First, a cutter *marks* the stone, scrutinizing its structure and condition until he decides the best way to cut the stone into smaller gems. Due to its octahedral crystal structure, a diamond will always cut cleanly along a plane parallel to one of the crystal's eight faces. The cutter must decide the best angle at which to cut the stone so that the resultant gem or gems will contain a minimum of flaws.

Next, the cutter *cleaves* the stone along the marked lines, cutting a groove—with another diamond, of course—then inserting a steel wedge in the groove and striking it with a hammer. The rough edges of the gem are then *sawed,* smoothed with a rotating disk charged with diamond dust. Then the gem is rounded, polished, and faceted into the desired shape. The most common diamond shape, called the brilliant cut, consists of 58 facets, 33 above the *girdle* or center line, and 25 below. Other popular cuts include the round, with 18 facets, and such fancy cuts as the marquise, emerald, baquette, and pear.

Most of the diamonds of antiquity were found in the gravel of rivers and streams in India, but since the 18th century, most diamonds have come from South America or Africa. In 1740, the discovery of diamonds in Brazil shifted the mining industry from India to South America. But since the discovery of rich kimberlite pipes in South Africa, Africa has become the center of diamond mining. That continent now produces 80 percent of the world's gem diamonds, and 73 percent of all industrial diamonds.

Zaire is the top diamond-producing nation by quantity, but South Africa produces most of the world's more valuable gem diamonds. Twenty-five percent of all South African diamonds are of gem quality, while only five percent of Zaire's diamonds are of similar value. Diamonds were first discovered in South Africa in 1867, on the banks of the Orange River. Two years later, a second lode was discovered—along with the 85-carat Star of South Africa. By 1870, 10,000 prospectors had joined the diamond rush, panning the gravel of South African river beds much the same way as gold prospectors in California did during the same period.

In 1902, work began at the Premier mine near Pretoria, now the world's richest. Over one-and-a-quarter million carats of diamonds, much of them of gem quality, are produced by the mine each year. To suggest the importance of the Premier mine, and the scarcity of diamonds: in an average year, diamond production for the *entire world* stands at about 10 million carats—just four-and-a-half tons!

Today, the price of diamonds is set chiefly by DeBeers Consolidated Mines Ltd., the firm that owns most South African mines and controls much of the diamond production of other African nations. The DeBeers concern was formed largely from claims consolidated by Englishman Cecil Rhodes late in the 19th century. Due, in part, to the DeBeers monopoly, the price of diamonds has not kept pace with inflation over the last 30 years. In 1950, a one-carat gem diamond cost from $520 to $1,000. By the mid-1960s, the same diamond could

Washing for diamonds in 1870 at Cape of Good Hope.

The diamond fields at Colesberg Kopje.

be bought for from $450 to $1,500. The average gem diamond now purchased in the United States weighs a half-carat, and sells for about $225.

Today, most gem diamonds find their way to wedding and engagement rings, but historically, diamonds have been the playthings of the wealthy. The diamond was first mentioned in 800 B.C., in India. By the first century, the Roman historian Pliny could call it the "most valuable of gems, known only to kings." Even in the East, where diamonds were found, valuable gems were usually the property of sultans and maharajas. Tales abound of a nervous rajah watching over the shoulder of an even edgier diamond cutter, as the craftsman cleaved a precious stone. The craftsman's failure spelled instant execution.

Diamonds have long been the symbols of undying love, their unmatched hardness signifying steadfast devotion, their unequaled brilliance and beauty a compliment to the beauty of the beloved. The first recorded instance of a suitor presenting his fiancée with a diamond ring occurred in 1477, when Maximilian, Archduke of Austria, sealed his troth with a diamond. Today, 85 percent of all American couples choose diamonds for their wedding rings.

Incidentally, a judge in this country recently ruled in favor of a man who had sued his fiancée for the return of her diamond engagement ring when the planned marriage went on the rocks. In effect, the judge declared that an engagement ring remains the property of the donor until the marriage takes place, but should be returned only if the receiver breaks off the engagement.

A diamond may be a "girl's best friend," but the history of the world's most valuable diamonds suggests that the gem has long known the friendship of thieves as well. As if cursed, many noted diamonds brought only misfortune and death to their often quite transitory owners.

One of the most legendary gems in the annals of diamond lore was the Great Mogul, an Indian gem reputed to weigh 280 carats when cut from a 787-carat rough stone. Its owners included Shah Jehan, the builder of the Taj Mahal. The gem was last seen by a European during the 17th century, but disappeared mysteriously soon after. Some experts believe that either the Orloff or the Koh-i-Noor, two other renowned diamonds, may have been cut from the vanished Great Mogul.

The Orloff diamond once formed the glittering eye of an idol in a Brahman temple in Southern India, until stolen by a French soldier feigning a sudden affection for the Hindu religion. The soldier sold the gem to a ship's captain for $10,000, and was promptly tossed overboard. The gem eventually found its way to Europe. There it was purchased by the Russian Prince Orloff for $450,000. The Prince presented the diamond to Empress Catherine the Great as a peace offering after an earlier fall from favor; Catherine accepted the offering, but never returned the Prince to her good graces. The 199-carat gem now forms part of the Romanov's royal sceptre, on exhibit at the diamond treasury in Moscow.

The renowned Koh-i-Noor diamond had been in the hands of an Indian royal family for generations, when it was seized by an invading Persian sultan during the 14th century. Legend tells that the Indian rajah hid the gem away in his turban, but the sultan managed to exchange turbans with the Indian monarch during a feast. The sultan later unrolled the turban, and when the diamond appeared, exclaimed *koh-i-noor*, "mountain of light," in tribute to the gem's brilliance.

The legend that "he who owns the Koh-i-Noor owns the world" did indeed appear to be true in 1849, when the conquering English brought the gem to London and presented it to Queen Victoria. The gem then weighed 186 carats, but Victoria had it recut in Amsterdam to 106 carats. The recutting took 38 days. Since 1911, the gem has formed the central stone of the queen's state crown, now on exhibit in the Tower of London along with the other British crown jewels.

The 137-carat Florentine diamond owes nothing to the city of Florence. In 1467, the yellow Indian gem was reputedly worn into battle by the Duke of Burgundy, found by a peasant or soldier after the Duke fell, and sold as presumed glass for a mere florin! The first attempt at recutting the gem in Amsterdam failed; after the successful second attempt, the cutter fainted. For a time, the Florentine formed part of the Austrian crown jewels, but the gem's whereabouts are now unknown.

Three of the world's most famous diamonds disappeared from view when the French crown jewels were stolen shortly after the French Revolution. The 55-carat Sancy, purchased in 1570 in Constantinople by the Seigneur de Sancy, included among its owners Louis XIV, Cardinal Mazarin, and James I of England. Henry IV of France reportedly once sent the gem as security for a loan, only to have his messenger set upon and murdered by thieves. The king ordered the trusted messenger's stomach slit open, and found the diamond where the thieves had not. Stolen in 1792, the gem was recovered in 1828, along with the Regent diamond, and now belongs to an Englishman.

The Regent was found in 1701, by an Indian slave, and eventually found its way into the hands of the Duke of Orleans, the Regent of France. A favorite of Marie Antoinette, the 140-carat gem was cut from a 410-carat rough stone. The diamond was recovered in a Paris garret after its 1792 theft. Later, the Regent was used by Napoleon as security for a massive loan. For most of this century, the Regent has been on display at the Louvre—except for a short period when it was secreted away to hide it from the Nazi occupational forces.

The third member of the pilfered French trio, the 68-carat Hope diamond, met a considerably worse fate. The sapphire-blue gem, once the property of Louis XIV, was never recovered after the 1792 theft. In 1830, a 44-carat diamond that most experts believe was cut from the original gem appeared in London, where it was purchased by Henry Hope for $90,000. Bought by a New York diamond merchant early this century, the gem is now on exhibit at the Smithsonian Institution in Washington.

In size alone, the Cullinan is the granddaddy of all famous diamonds. Discovered in 1905, in the Premier mine in Transvaal, South Africa, the stone in the rough weighed 3,106 carats—one-and-a-third pounds! Named after Sir Thomas Cullinan, who had opened the Premier mine and was visiting there when the gem was found, the diamond was presented to Edward VII as a gift of the Transvaal government. The king had the diamond cut into nine gems. The largest, called Star of Africa Number One, weighs 530 carats—the largest gem diamond on earth—and now forms part of the British crown jewels.

But even that gem might appear a mere trinket compared with the largest raw gem ever mined, a topaz of 1.36 million

The world's largest diamond, the great Cullinan diamond, in its rough state. It weighed better than 3,024 carats.

carats—596 pounds!—that now resides in a glass case in the American Museum of Natural History in New York. The topaz is rather dull-looking, however, and few visitors to the museum pay the huge gem any mind.

The largest stone of true gem quality was a Brazilian aquamarine, discovered in 1910, that tipped the scales at 229 pounds. The hefty stone provided over 200,000 carats of quality aquamarines!

Some diamond owners were more famous than the gems they owned. The Emperor Jahangir of India, who died in 1627, reportedly owned a total of 279,450 carats of diamonds, along with 931,500 carats of emeralds, 376,000 carats of rubies, and two million carats of pearls! The emperor, an avid fisherman, never killed a fish he caught; instead he slipped a string of pearls through the fish's gills and tossed it back in the water.

The Western madam known as Diamond-tooth Lil owed her nickname to a gold front tooth studded with a large diamond. Immortalized by Mae West's portrayal in a movie called *Diamond Lil,* the Austrian-born madam accumulated husbands as easily as diamonds—she married eight times without bothering to go through the formality of divorce.

Another noted diamond owner, railroad equipment salesman "Diamond Jim" Brady, used a collection of diamond jewelry to dazzle prospective clients. Jim commonly sported a 25-carat diamond ring, a diamond tiepin, cufflinks, and glasses case, and a cane fitted with a diamond handle. When asked if a particular gem were genuine, Jim often proved its worth by using the diamond to scratch his name on a pane of glass. After his death, Jim's diamonds were found to be of generally poor quality.

Most of the world's large, storied diamonds are priceless, and many have been insured for millions of dollars. For the largest amount of cold cash ever laid out for a piece of diamond jewelry, we must turn to the 69-carat ring bought at a 1969 auction by actor Richard Burton, and presented to his wife, Elizabeth Taylor. The gem set Burton back a neat $1,200,000! His other gifts to Elizabeth include the $350,000 Krupp diamond, a $38,000 diamond, a $93,000 emerald, and a sapphire brooch valued at $65,000.

Burton's record will undoubtedly be broken someday. And the future may hold in store sad tidings for other diamond fanciers as well. Already, the ruby has surpassed the diamond as the world's most valuable gem, carat for carat. Since 1955, when ruby supplies began to dwindle, flawless natural rubies have sold for as high as $5,000 per carat.

Simulated diamonds are certainly no novelty. But the possibility of synthetic diamonds has intrigued scientists since late in the 19th century, when two Frenchmen claimed to have produced a small diamond by a process that, alas, proved unrepeatable. In 1955, the General Electric Company reported that scientists in their laboratories had succeeded in manufacturing a synthetic diamond by subjecting carbonaceous material to pressures of one-and-a-half million pounds per square inch, and temperatures over 5,000 degrees. The synthetic diamonds, the largest of which was a mere one-tenth of a carat, were of industrial quality.

And now jewelers are shuddering at the appearance of cubic zirconia gems, man-made byproducts of laser technology, that can reportedly pass as diamonds to almost any eye—and cost but $12 a carat!

DICE

Prehistoric man used dice much like ours, played dice games similar to our own, and cheated his opponents with loaded dice!

Comparing the vast, electrified skyline of a modern city with the stark simplicity suggested by an ancient ruin, it's easy to see that man has changed his environment a great deal over the past millennia. But has man's nature changed along with his environment? Not really. Take the institution of dice gambling, for instance. We known that prehistoric man used dice much like ours, played dice games similar to our own, and—to seal the argument—cheated his opponents with loaded dice!

The card catalogue of any large library will illustrate the age-old controversy over dice gambling. Almost as soon as man had developed the printing press, he began to publish treatises for or against the innocuous little cubes—mostly against. The flavor of those early works, is suggested by one 16th-century treatise published in England and entitled: "A Manifest Detection of the Most Vyle and Detestable Use of Dice Play." A bit heavy-handed, perhaps, but you get the idea.

Dice are the oldest gaming implements known to man. Before dice became gaming pieces, numbered cubes were used as magical devices for divining the future. The next time you're searching for a word to stump a self-proclaimed vocabulary know-it-all, try "astragalomancy"—that's the practice of divination by means of dice!

Primitive man probably used cubical knucklebones or the anklebones of sheep for his gaming pieces. The Arabic word for knucklebone, in fact, is the same as for dice. Even today, experienced elbow shakers often call dice "bones" or "devil's bones."

Archaeologists have shown that dice predate the written word, and can be found in almost every culture in the world, including the American Indian, Eskimo, and African. Excavations in Egypt have turned up stone dice dating from 2000 B.C. Archaeologists in China have discovered gaming cubes from 600 B.C. that look remarkably similar to the modern thing.

For his dice, ancient man used, among other things, plum and peach pits, stones, seeds, bones, horn, pottery, pebbles, shells, and beaver teeth.

The Greeks and Romans were heavy gamers, favoring dice of bone or ivory and occasionally of semiprecious stone. Even Plato was not wont to take the art lightly, writing that "nobody can become a skilled dice-player if he has not devoted himself to it from his childhood, but only plays for pleasure."

The Bible mentions that Roman soldiers cast lots for Christ's robe after the Crucifixion. The Emperor Claudius went so far as to publish a book on dice games. And Julius Caesar, at the Rubicon, uttered the famous words: *Jacta alea est*—"the die is cast."

To mark the spots or "pips" of his dice, early man either bored holes in the cubes or carved

This detail from a Greek vase in the Vatican Museum depicts Ajax and Ulysses playing at dice.
Photo: Alinari Brothers, N 35766, Rome.

circular marks on the faces. He was also quite adept at loading dice. The earliest written records of man mention both dice and crooked dice. Dice especially made for cheating have been found in the tombs of Egypt, of the Orient, and of the Americas.

Modern man has improved both the manufacture of dice and the methods of loading them. Today's galloping ivories are usually made of cellulose or plastic. There are basically two varieties: "casino" dice and "drugstore" dice.

Casino dice are handmade, sawed from plastic rods, and perfectly cubical to within one five-thousandth of an inch. Casino dice three-quarters of an inch on a side are most often used for casino games of craps.

The drugstore die is smaller, machine made, and seldom as perfectly cubical as the casino die.

"Peewee" dice are only a quarter-inch on a side.

At various times, dice have been fashioned in the shape of a pyramid, pentagon, and octagon.

In the manufacture of casino dice, each spot is drilled precisely 17/1000 of an inch into the face, then filled with paint weighing exactly the same as the plastic removed for the hole. Thus the die remains balanced on all sides.

So much for honest dice. Through the ages, man has devised a number of ways to improve his odds at "indoor golf." The most familiar way is "loading" the dice—a weight of some kind is placed inside the die against one face, thereby assuring that the opposite face will come up more often than one might mathematically expect.

There are more subtle methods, however. "Shapes" are dice with one slightly sawed-off edge. The longer faces are more likely to come up than the shortened faces—imagine rolling a brick and trying to leave one of the narrow sides up.

"Tops" or "bottoms" are dice with incorrectly numbered faces. Instead of the numbers one through six, a "tops" die might show the numbers three, four, and five, each repeated on two faces. When used in conjunction with a die reading one, five, and six, the pair cannot produce a seven.

You're not likely to be fooled by such a crass trick, you say? Keep in mind that only three faces of the die are visible to you at any one time; a good dice cheat can slip in his "tops" by sleight of hand and withdraw them from play before you can say "Rip-off!"

A good dice cheat can bilk you even with honest dice. There are ways to "spin" the dice to improve the chances of certain combinations. Your best bet is to immediately suspect anyone who suggests a game of craps and just happens to have his own ivories on hand.

That brings us to the subject of craps. The game is American in origin, a variant of an old European game known as "ha-

In the late 19th century, dice games drew crowds at the gambling saloon in Wiesbaden, Germany.

zard" that was popular in London in the 17th and 18th centuries. In fact, the 1-1 and 1-2 combinations in hazard have been known as "craps" since the 16th century.

According to some accounts, the origin of craps can be traced to Bernard de Mandeville, a Frenchman who brought the game of hazard to New Orleans in 1813. Since the nickname for Creoles was Johnny Crapauds, the game became known as Crapaud's game, and later, simply craps. Mandeville, himself, lost a fortune at the game, and was forced to sell his New Orleans property to pay his debts. A street cut through his land was called Craps Street; it later changed to Burgundy Street.

Number of ways of rolling a given number at craps.

2	1 way	8	5 ways
3	2 ways	9	4 ways
4	3 ways	10	3 ways
5	4 ways	11	2 ways
6	5 ways	12	1 way
7	6 ways		

American blacks around New Orleans are often credited with developing the game of craps as it is played today. They also left us with a wealth of dice slang. There's hardly any need to tell you what "Mississippi marbles" or "Memphis dominoes" are. Or "snake eyes," or "boxcars." How about "Little Joe from Kokomo?" Fours, my friend. And let's not forget that time-worn exhortation: "Come on, mama, baby needs a new pair of shoes!"

A New York dicemaker by the name of John H. Winn—that's right, Winn—has been called the first craps banker in history, and is credited with the invention of open craps, that variety of elbow athletics you're most likely to find in an alley or pool hall. Craps was spread by American soldiers during the two World Wars. Today a variant known as "bank craps" is played in casinos throughout the world.

Most experienced casino gamblers consider bank craps the casino game which offers the player the greatest chance to walk away a winner. Some also nominate craps as the most exciting of all casino games. It's certainly the most colorful to watch.

Earlier in this century, many American drugstores and soda fountains offered counter dice games to their patrons. Counter games are still legal in some parts of the country. Some of the more descriptively named games still enjoyed by Americans include Drop Dead, Pig, Heaven and Nine, and Hooligan. When you think of it, craps isn't bad either!

Today, backgammon is rapidly becoming one of the most popular games in America. The fact is, backgammon is much older than craps, ranking as the oldest dice game still widely played. The ancient Romans played a variety of backgammon. And as for the name, etymologists trace it either tothe Saxon expression *bac gamen*—"back game"—or the Welsh *back gammon*—"little battle."

There are literally thousands of other games that employ the timeless cubes. Despite the use of cards and spinners, dice remain, quite simply, the best way of introducing the element of chance into any game, no matter how complex. As Mallarme suggested in the title of one of his most famous poems, "A Throw of the Dice Never Will Abolish Chance."

In some things, then, there is simply no room, or need, for improvement. Long before man had perfected the way he would build or find his home, his food, his weapons, his clothes, or his power, he'd just about perfected the way he would gamble.

DICTIONARIES

"Everything that coruscates with effulgence is not ipso facto aurous" is a rather highfalutin way of saying "All that glitters is not gold," but without a dictionary, you'd never guess it.

"Look it up in the dictionary" is a piece of advice foreign to few ears, but did you realize that until the 18th century speakers of English had no lexicographic authority to consult for the meaning of the thousands of English words now nestled between *aardvark* and *zymurgy?*

The first English work to bear the title "dictionary" (in its Latin form, *dictionarius,* from *dictis,* "saying" or "word" and *dicere,* "to say") appeared around the year 1225. But that first manuscript actually listed Latin words to be learned by rote by students, with only a few English words inserted, here and there, for explanation. Words were not grouped alphabetically, but were arranged according to subject.

English words began to appear regularly in 15th-century dictionaries, but still served only as aids to the study of Latin. One noted dictionary of this era was the charmingly titled *Storehouse for the Little Ones,* or *Promptorium Parvulorum,* brought out around 1440 by a Dominican friar aptly named Galfridus Grammaticus—Geoffrey the Grammarian. The work contained about 12,000 English words and their Latin equivalents. It did not appear in print until 1499 for one rather compelling reason—the printing press hadn't yet been invented.

The *Storehouse* was not the only 15th- and 16th-century dictionary with a colorful title—metaphoric titles were the custom for many years. A work dating from 1500 was dubbed *Ortus Vocabulorum, The Garden of Words,* and a 1573 student's dictionary was somewhat presumptuously named *Alvearie,* or "Beehive."

The first real English dictionary was the *Abcedarium Anglico-Latinum pro Tyrunculis,* a Latin-English work completed by Richard Huloet in 1552. This compendium contained some 26,000 words with their Latin translations. Each word was defined in English. Thus, the *Abcedarium,* though designed as a Latin aid, can be considered a bona fide English dictionary.

The *Abcedarium* was popular in its time, but relatively expensive. So in 1570, a physician named Peter Levins brought out a cheaper version of Huloet's work, entitled *Manipulus Vocabulorum—A Handful of Words.* The entries were arranged—not alphabetically—but according the the spelling of their *final* syllables, making the book, in effect, the first rhyming dictionary in the English language.

Early dictionaries made no attempt to include all English or Latin words, only those that were considered troublesome to students. The title of a 1604 work by Robert Cawdrey explains it best: *A Table Alphabeticall, conteyning and teaching the true writing and understanding of hard usuall English wordes . . . gathered for the benefit and helpe of Ladies, Gentlewomen, or any other unskillful persons.* As for the difference between "Ladies" and "Gentlewomen," you'll have to consult a dictionary.

The more tersely titled *The English Dictionarie* appeared in 1623, compiled by Henry Cockeram, but based to a great extent on Cawdrey's work.

Cockeram's dictionary was hardly the last word in lexicographic precision, as is readily apparent in a definition such as "Hyena: A subtil beast, conterfeiting the voice of a man . . . He is sometimes male and sometimes female."

In 1702, John Kersey—alias "J.K. Philobibl."—issued a wordbook entitled *New English Dictionary* that was the first volume to define words in everyday usage. And in 1721, a schoolteacher named Nathaniel Bailey published the *Universal Etymological English Dictionary*, containing "more words than any English Dictionary before extant."

Another of Bailey's works, *Dictionarium Britannicum*, appeared in 1730, displaying "not only the Words, and their Explications, but the Etymologies." Bailey was also among the first to indicate the pronunciation of words along with their definitions.

In 1791 came the *Critical Pronouncing Dictionary and Expositer of the English Language*, compiled by an elderly actor named John Walker. Walker's book is still considered valuable for its treatment of pronunciation. The phonetician, Isaac Pitman, based his popular shorthand system on Walker's principles.

Perhaps the most remarkable dictionary of the 18th century was the accomplishment of the legendary Samuel Johnson. Johnson's prodigious work—which was completed single-handedly—was brought out in 1755 as *A Dictionary of the English Language*. As Johnson's renowned biographer James Boswell noted: "The world contemplated with wonder so stupendous a work achieved by one man, while other countries had thought such undertakings fit only for whole academies."

Most earlier lexicographers sought to lay down rules for usage and spelling, but Johnson sought more to reflect current usage—to reflect rather than dictate the accepted meaning—explaining in his *Preface* that no scholar "can embalm his language and secure it from corruption."

Said Johnson: "No dictionary of a living tongue can ever be perfect, since while it is hastening to publication some words are budding, and some falling away." Today's dictionaries, likewise, make little attempt to dictate,

In 1755, Dr. Samuel Johnson published a dictionary that was a landmark in lexicography.

From Samuel Johnson's dictionary of the English Language (1755):

Lexicographer: *A writer of dictionaries; a harmless drudge, that busies himself in tracing the original, and detailing the signification of words.*

Oats: *A grain, which in England is generally given to horses, but in Scotland supports the people.*

only to reflect the ever-changing meaning of words.

Johnson was the first to use illustrations of word usage gleaned from "the best writers," as do many modern lexicographers. Because of the extensive research involved in gathering the illustrations, Johnson's work—planned to take three years—eventually required eight.

After his long years of toil, Johnson was piqued by an article written by Lord Chesterfield, the statesman and author, in which the Earl claimed undue credit as the patron of Johnson's dictionary. (Chesterfield had actually sent Johnson a 10 pound subscription for the dictionary in 1747.) "I have been pushing on my work through difficulties, of which it is useless to complain," Johnson wrote in his now-famous letter to Chesterfield, "and have brought it, at last, to the verge of publication, without one wit of assistance, one word of encouragement, or one smile of favour . . . Is not a Patron, my Lord, one who looks with unconcern on a man struggling for life in the water, and, when he has reached ground, encumbers him with help?"

Although English dictionaries had been published in America as early as 1788, the first English dictionary compiled by an American was *A School Dictionary,* brought out in 1798 by a Connecticut teacher named—appropriately enough—Samuel Johnson, Jr.

In 1806, another Connecticut resident, Noah Webster of New Haven, issued *A Compendious Dictionary of the English Language* with some 40,000 words. But the most important milestone in American lexicography came in 1828, when Webster published his masterpiece, *An American Dictionary of the English Language,* with about 70,000 entries. Webster's work was the first American dictionary to gain wide acceptance in both the United States and England.

You may be confused by the plethora of dictionaries on the market bearing the name "Webster's." The fact is none of these books—or at least, very few—are directly derived from the work of Noah Webster. The word "Webster's" has become merely an identifying title, like the word "dictionary" itself, and cannot be copyrighted. Anyone at all can publish a book and call it "Webster's Dictionary," although the G.&C. Merriam

Noah Webster compiled An American Dictionary of the English Language *in 1828. Revised versions of this monumental work are still widely used in the United States today.*

The last words of Noah Webster were probably zyme, zymosis, and zymurgy.

Company of Springfield, Massachusetts, claims that their dictionaries are the legitimate successors to Webster's works.

Many stories have been told about the famed American lexicographer—most of them apocryphal. Witness, for example, this droll tale:

One day Mrs. Webster entered the parlor to find her husband locked in an embrace with the maidservant. "Noah!" she sputtered, "I *am* surprised!"

Noah disentangled himself and quickly regained his professional composure. "No, my dear," he told his wife, "It is *I* who am surprised. *You* are merely astonished."

Many other dictionaries have come and gone since the days of Webster and Johnson, but the greatest English dicitionary on either side of the Atlantic remains the *Oxford English Dictionary*, conceived in the mid-19th century, but not completed until 1928. The *Oxford* lists all recorded English words, and their varying usages from the seventh century through the twentieth. Thus, a simple word such as "place," due to its many uses and its long history of change, might occupy 20 or 25 small-print pages. Compiled with the aid of hundreds of research assistants in both England and America, the *Oxford* remains the largest dictionary in the world. Its 12 volumes contain about 415,000 words, almost two million illustrative quotations, and close to 228 million letters and figures!

A glance at a card catalogue in any large library will suggest the tremendous range of dictionaries now available, covering almost every specialized vocabulary imaginable. Witness, for example, *A Dictionary of the Stitches Used in Art Needlework*, or *Dictionary of the Underworld: the vocabulary of crooks, criminals, racketeers, beggars and tramps, convicts, the commercial underworld, the drug traffic, and the white slave traffic.*

And then there's the *Dictionary of Waste Disposal and Public Cleansing*—published, *naturlich* in Germany.

The number of dictionaries in existence today is difficult to calculate, but in English, there is a dictionary for most of the 5,000 foreign languages spoken throughout the world today.

By the way, the first Bohemian-English dictionary—626 pages long—was brought out in 1876, and the long-awaited Mongolian-English dictionary was published in 1953.

How many words are there in the dictionary? First of all, no English dictionary but the *Oxford* claims to include anywhere near all the words in the language.

The word "unabridged" in a dictionary title does not mean the work contains all the words in the language, but merely that the book includes all entries appearing in earlier editions of the work.

English, the second most commonly spoken language in the world after Mandarin Chinese, contains the largest vocabulary of any language on earth, an estimated 800,000 words—of which the average person uses only about 60,000. *Webster's Third International Dictionary* contains about 450,000 entries.

You'll find more dictionary entries under the letter *T* than under any other, for *T* is the most common initial letter in our language. The most common letter in English is *E*, and the most common words are *the, of, and*, and *to*, in that order.

Schoolboy wisdom holds that *antidisestablishmentarianism* (28 letters) is the longest word in the language, but the *Oxford English Dictionary* includes the word *floccipaucinihilipilification* (29 letters). The word means "the action of estimating as worthless."

Webster's Third International Dictionary lists *pneumonoultramicroscopicsilicovolcanoconiosis* as a lung disease common to miners.

The longest word in common use is generally thought to be *disproportionableness* (21 letters). And the longest chemical term ever used, the name of an amino acid compound, contains some 3,600 letters.

However, as any lexicographer with a sense of humor will point out, the longest word in our language is actually *smiles*—because there's a mile between the first and the last letters!

Incidentally, excluding proper names, the oldest word in the English language still in use in a comparable form is *land*, derived from the Old Celtic *landa*, "heath." This word is thought to have been in use on the European continent well before the beginning of the Roman Empire.

The dictionary is easily the most useful reference work ever created. Yet there are a number of languages in existence today that are not likely to be recorded in a new dictionary. Why? Well, there are now about 20 languages in which no one can converse, for the simple reason that there are only one or two, or perhaps a few, speakers of the tongue still alive. For example, Eyak, an Alaskan Indian language, is certainly one of the most moribund languages on earth—spoken only by two aged sisters when they chance to meet!

Dogs

Depiction of a dog from a Boeotian amphora, 750 B.C.

"He cannot be a gentleman that loveth not a dog," reads an old proverb, and there can be no doubt that the American loveth all things canine. There are now about 1.1 million pedigreed dogs registered in this country—about one pedigreed pooch for every 200 Americans. The number of mongrels extant is anybody's guess. One knowledgeable estimate puts the total number of dogs in the United States as over 40 million!

Americans will spend some one-and-a-half *billion* dollars this year on pet food, close to four times the sum spent on baby food! And there are at present over 400 pet cemeteries in this country!

When did this long and happy relationship between man and dog begin? Far too long ago to estimate a date, for man had domesticated the dog well before recorded history began. The bond between man and his best friend was—and still is—a symbiotic relationship, with both parties benefitting from the alliance.

The word *dog* originally referred to a particular English breed of canine, but is now used generally to refer to all members of the *Canus familiaris*. Other species in the *Canus* genus are the *aureus* (the jackal) and the *lupus* (the wolf). Anthropologists aren't quite sure which species was the first to join forces with his upright fellow hunters.

Most likely jackals and primitive dogs, originally independent hunters and scavengers, found it advantageous to follow nomadic human hunters for the bones and food scraps left behind when they broke camp. Gradually, prehistoric man came to realize that the presence of these beasts surrounding the camp at night could benefit him as well, since the howling canines would warn of the approach of deadly predators. The more the hunter went out of his way to feed his watchguards, the more dependent upon him they became.

Slowly, dog and man began to join forces in hunting, the dog contributing his scent to flushing out game, and man returning the favor by providing the dog with a steady diet of meat. We know that aborigines of Ireland, Switzerland, and the Baltic lands used dogs for hunting—and occasionally partook of dog flesh—long before farming was introduced in Europe. Cave paintings 50,000 years old depict hunters with dogs at their side.

The original domesticated canines—wolf, dog, and jackal—were probably interbred to evolve the modern *familiaris* species. Subsequent breeding by man gradually produced distinct breeds. The oldest records of Mesopotamia and Egypt show that distinct breeds of domesticated dogs had been developed by the year 3000 B.C., including animals much like the modern greyhound and terrier. The breed classifications of the Romans were quite like our own, distinguishing between scent-hunting and sight-hunting dogs, and between *Canes villatici* (house-dogs), and *pastorales* (sheep or herding dogs).

In the 14th century, attack dogs with spears and buckets of fire harnessed to their backs were used to upset cavalry horses. But for the most part, throughout the Middle Ages, dogs were used for hunting and herding. Yet over the centuries, man has come to rely on the dog more for companionship than for anything else.

By the 17th century, the dog

was a ranking member of the household as a note by Samuel Pepys might suggest: "At night my wife and I did fall out about the dog's being put down in the cellar . . . because of his fouling the house . . . and so we went to bed and lay all night in a quarrel." Today, the dog is valued as a guard, a shepherd, a guide, a hunter, a retriever, a soldier, a policeman, and a friend.

Dogs skilled at sniffing out caches of concealed drugs are becoming increasingly popular among many police forces. A few years ago, a Florida policeman demonstrated his dog's sleuthing talents to a group of students. He hid packets of drugs around the room, and then loosed his keen-nosed sidekick to find them. The policeman hid 10 packets; the dog brought back 11.

At last glance, there were 163 recognized dog breeds in the United States. All canines can be broken down into six main groups according to their original use by man.

The Sporting Group includes dogs that hunt by air scent, such as the *pointer*, the *retriever*, the *Labrador*, the *Irish setter*, the *Weimaraner*, and the *cocker spaniel*. These dogs serve primarily as hunters' assistants, finding and retrieving small game.

The pointer (or "bird dog,") first appeared in Britain some time during the 17th century.

The Hound Group is made up of those dogs that hunt by ground scent. This group includes the *Afghan*, the *beagle*, the *basset hound*, the *bloodhound*, the *dachshund*, the *foxhound*, the *saluki*, and the *greyhound*. Dogs similar to the dachshund can be found in Egyptian carvings dated around the 15th century B.C. The bloodhound probably owns the keenest sense of smell of all dogs.

A pair of draft dogs, used to pull a European milk cart.

But the most spectacular canine tracking feat on record was not the work of a bloodhound. In 1925, a Doberman pinscher named "Sauer" tracked a thief 100 miles across the Great Karoo, an arid plateau in South Africa, by scent alone. And a fox terrier lost by a truck driver in Hayes Creek, Australia, rejoined his master eight months later in Mambray Creek—a distance of 1,700 barren miles from Hayes Creek!

The Working Group includes dogs that serve primarily as guides, guards, and herders, such as the *Doberman pinscher*, *German shepherd*, the *collie*, the *great Dane*, the *Newfoundland*, the *St. Bernard*, the *Shetland sheep dog*, and the *Siberian husky*. These dogs probably constitute the most useful group of canines. Eskimos use them for draught animals. In this country, they're valuable as "seeing-eye" and "police" dogs—a term not restricted to German shepherds. The Newfoundland has been used to rescue swimmers, while

Two mountain climbers, trapped in a snow storm in the Alps, had just about given up hope of surviving when one of them spotted a St. Bernard equipped with a brandy keg. "Look!" he shouted joyously to his companion. "Here comes a dog with man's best friend."

A Wire-haired Terrier.

for centuries the St. Bernard has served as a rescue dog for the monks of the Alpine Hospice of St. Bernard.

The Terrier Group—dogs that hunt by digging and flushing out burrowing animals—includes, not surprisingly, most terriers, along with the *schnauzer.* The word "terrier" comes from the Latin *terra,* "earth." Most terrier breeds were developed in the British Isles. The *Airedale terrier,* for instance, was first bred in the Aire valley of England.

The Toy Group consists of dogs that serve primarily as human companions, and includes such favorites as the *Pekinese,* the *Maltese,* the *Chihuahua,* the *toy poodle,* the *Yorkshire terrier,* the *pug,* and the *pomeranian.* Most toys are miniature versions of older larger breeds. The Pekinese has existed in China for over 5,000 years.

The smallest dog on earth, the *Chihuahua,* usually weighs in somewhere between two and four pounds, although some specimens have tipped the scales at a mere 16 ounces.

Small toy dogs became popular in the British Isles when laws were enacted to control poaching pooches. The 11th-century King Canute, for instance, decreed that all dogs kept within 10 miles of the king's forest preserve must have their knee joints cut to hinder them from chasing his game. But exceptions were made for any dog that could fit through a "dog guage," a ring seven inches wide and five inches high.

The sixth group of dogs is known as the Nonsporting Group, a miscellaneous class consisting chiefly of dogs with muscular necks and strong jaws. The *bulldog,* the *Boston terrier,* the *chowchow,* the *Dalmatian,* and the *poodle* are listed among this group. The chowchow is most likely the oldest member, dating at least from 150 B.C. in China. The Boston terrier is one of the few breeds originating in the United States. It was developed by a Bostonian named Robert Hooper in the mid-19th century. Despite its modern association with the French, the poodle is probably of German origin.

Which breed of dog is most favored by Americans? Beagle? Collie? German shepherd? Sur-

SMALLEST DOG: *The ancestors of the Chihuahua date back to the ancient Mexican Toltecs. The modern American Chihuahua weighs from one to six pounds.*

LARGEST DOG: *The powerful Irish Wolfhound is the world's tallest dog. The Wolfhound stands from 30" to 34" high, and weighs about 120 pounds. The record height was 39½ inches.*

prisingly, it's the poodle. With some 200,000 registered dogs, there are more than twice as many poodles as there are German shepherds, the second most popular breed. In fact, almost one in every five pedigreed dogs registered in the United States is a poodle!

A list of registered dogs by breed offers a few other surprises. The large numbers of registered dachshunds, Labrador retrievers, and St. Bernards would startle those who consider these breeds to be mere curiosity pieces. Yet such supposedly populous breeds as the bulldog and bloodhound rank pitifully low in actual registration.

Today, the most popular up-and-coming dog breed in America is the Yorkshire terrier. The Yorky led all breeds in new registrations in 1975, with 14,640. At the other end of the scale, the *Chinese fighting dog* is now the rarest dog breed on earth, with only 23 specimens known to exist in 1976—all of them, oddly enough, in California. Another rare breed is the *Belgian Malinois*, which, in the United States, is limited at an elite 100.

Only eight breeds of purebreed dogs originated in the United States: the *American foxhound*, the *American water spaniel*, the *Boston terrier*, the *Chesapeake Bay retriever*, the *coonhound*, the *Amertoy*, the *spitz*, and the *Staffordshire terrier*.

The British Isles holds the pedigreed pooch title: of the world's 163 recognized breeds, 47 originated in Great Britain.

Few dogs today perform any service aside from friendship, though originally the canine was

Americans will spend some one-and-a-half billion dollars this year on pet food, close to four times the sum spent on baby food.

valuable to man because his senses were strongest where man's were weakest. The dog's sense of smell is among the keenest in the animal kingdom. A trained dog can select an item touched only by his master's finger from among dozens of other objects; a bloodhound can pick up one scent from among hundreds. Some dogs can reputedly pick up a scent that is 10 days old!

The canine's sense of hearing is likewise extremely acute. Dogs have responded from 75 feet to orders unintelligible to men only 10 feet away. The range of sound a dog can hear is much wider than man's: "dog whistles"—too high-pitched to be heard by the human ear—can be picked up by dogs 100 yards away.

Most dogs, alas, have poor vision. As a rule, they're nearsighted, yet they can be particularly sensitive to movement. All dogs are color-blind—their visual world is a drab panorama of black, white, and gray. On the other hand, dogs have "eyeshine," and like cats, can see quite well in the dark.

A Mexican hairless.

But it is not the dog's keen smell or hearing that has endeared him to modern man, it's his uncomplaining readiness to obey and lavish affection on his human friends. "To his dog," an old saying goes, "every man is Napoleon—hence the popularity of dogs." A dog is loyal, loving, and lovable, even if his master can boast none of these qualities. The Prussian monarch Frederick the Great hit it on the head: "The more I see of men, the better I like my dog."

Another saying—reportedly a Turkish proverb—has it that "if dogs' prayers were answered, bones would rain from the sky." But most American canines enjoy a diet considerably better than bones—considerably better than the diet of many impoverished peoples, in fact. Many dog owners will argue as to the correct amount of food a dog requires each day, but most authorities agree that dogs over six months of age should be fed one large

"You'll just have to choose between us, Edward . . ."

meal daily, with perhaps one smaller snack. A half-pound of food will suffice for a toy dog, a pound of chow for a dog weighing from 10 to 20 pounds, and two to four pounds for a dog weighing above 50 pounds.

Speaking of heavier members of the canine set, the largest dog on record tipped the scales at a colossal 295 pounds. And larger unverified claims have been heard.

The largest litter ever born consisted of 23 pups. It was thrown by a foxhound in Pennsylvania in 1944.

The most prolific dog on record, a greyhound in London, sired an amazing 2,414 registered puppies, along with at least 600 other unregistered whelps.

Like baseball fans, dog lovers have been known to argue over obscure items of canine trivia. To clear up a few disputes: the country dog does not live longer than the city dog. The city dog may get less exercise, but as a rule he's more pampered, and survives on the average three years longer than his country cousin. Of course, these urban figures don't take into account stray mongrels roaming the streets.

Municipal licensing of dogs, by the way, was instituted in England in 1735 to reduce the number of strays. The first dog licensing in the United States began in New York State in 1894.

To dispel another myth, the mongrel is not generally any smarter than the purebred dog. Individual dogs differ in intellectual capacity and disposition much the same as individual human beings differ: there are smart as well as stupid dogs in both classes. And finally, the dog does *not* sweat through his tongue—the dog's most important sweat glands are actually on the soles of his feet!

There are many words and phrases based on the name of man's best friend. *Dog-eared, dogleg,* and *doggone* are among them, but *dogma* is not.

The expression "raining cats and dogs" has many reputed origins. The most gruesome holds that during the 17th and 18th centuries in England, a heavy cloudburst would fill the gutters with a torrent of refuse not unlikely to include a number of dead dogs and cats. A poem by Jonathan Swift describing a city rainstorm ends with the lines:

Drown'd Puppies, stinking Sprats,
all drench'd in Mud,
Dead cats and Turnep-Tops come
tumbling down the Flood.

As Robert Benchley wrote, "There is no doubt that every healthy, normal boy . . . should own a dog at some time in his life, preferably between the ages of 45 and 50."

These tombstones at the Hartsdale (N.Y.) Canine Cemetery testify to man's love for his best friend. The Bettmann Archive, Inc.

Eggplants

Imagine a dish by the name of "The Priest Has Fainted." Yet possibly the most famous of all eggplant dishes is that *tour de force* known as *Imam Bayeldi,* which owes its name to the Ottoman Turks of the 16th century.

According to legend, a holy man was making a routine call at the home of a particularly beautiful lady. Out of a spirit of hospitality, she insisted that he partake of an eggplant dish she had been preparing. When she bent over to present the dish, her veil slipped off her face and dress, and for a brief moment, the priest caught a glimpse of her two delectable eggplants. Overpowered by the sight and the aroma of the succulent food, the holy man passed out. From that time on, the dish was christened *Imam Bayeldi,* (The Priest Has Fainted).

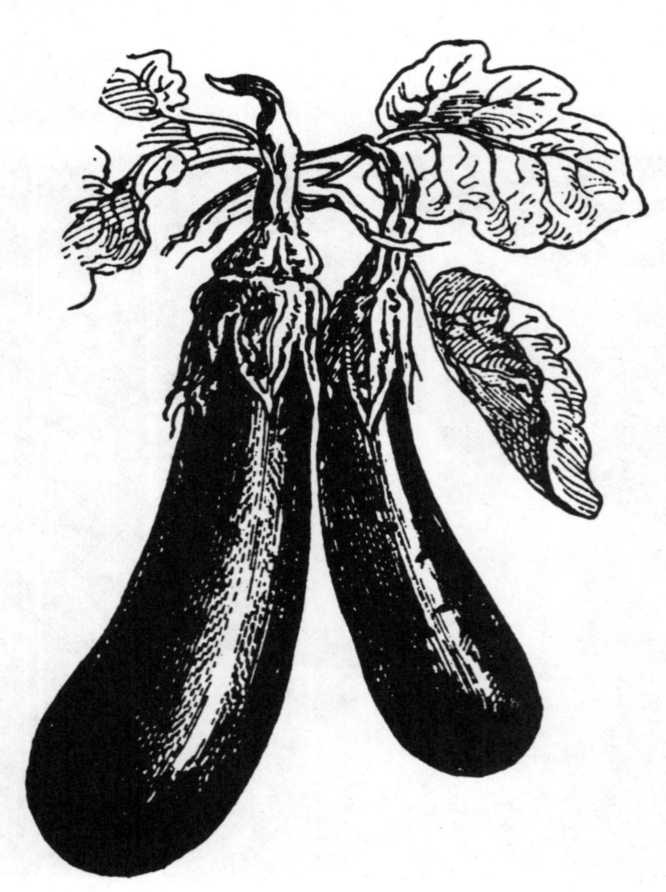

IMAM BAYELDI

3 eggplants
1 12 oz. can tomato puree,
thinned with 1 tablespoon water
1 lb. ground lamb
½ lb. butter
1 onion, chopped
½ teaspoon celery seed
½ teaspoon garlic salt
½ cup pine nuts
⅛ teaspoon nutmeg
⅛ teaspoon cinnamon
⅛ teaspoon ground cloves
⅛ teaspoon pepper

1. Skin eggplants. Cut in quarters lengthwise.
2. Saute eggplants in 3 tablespoons butter, until fairly soft.
3. Slit pieces of eggplant in center, and set aside.
4. Saute ground lamb and finely chopped onion in 2 tablespoons butter, until well browned.
5. Saute pine nuts in 1 tablespoon butter, until slightly browned.
6. Combine all ingredients, and stuff each piece of eggplant.
7. Pour tomato puree over eggplant.
8. Bake for 25 minutes (or so) in 350° oven.

Serves six.

The fact is that there are a number of great culinary expoits that can be performed with the eggplant. This versatile vegetable can be baked, broiled, scalloped, fried, sauteed, stuffed, or marinated. Many countries have their favorite eggplant dishes—Italy, Greece, France, Israel, and Turkey, to name a few. In the Near East and in North African countries, large eggplants are stuffed with meat mixed with onions, tomatoes, garlic, and rice.

The French enjoy a dish which they intriguingly named *Ratatouille*. It is usually baked in a casserole, and consists of eggplant, tomatoes, peppers, onions, and zucchini.

Today, in many Greek restaurants, one of the leading offerings is a dish called *Mousaka,* made from eggplant, lamb, onions, and spices, prepared with an egg sauce. This venerable dish is reputed to have developed in the early Middle Ages.

Most American eggplants come from Florida, Texas, and New Jersey. We produce about a million-and-a-half bushels of the purple fruit each year, and smaller quantities are imported from Mexico. But by and large, the average American isn't very fond of eggplant, and the national consumption comes to about four ounces per year. A pity, because the versatile eggplant has unusual properties, and can be fashioned into a multitude of forms and dishes.

There is a restaurant in Jerusalem whose owner declares he can prepare eggplant in 100 different ways. When the writer questioned him to list his offerings, he only was able to come up with about 16. And yet the statement, "One Hundred Dishes," is really not an exaggeration. There are that many good eggplant recipes around.

Perhaps one of the greatest eggplant dishes ever concocted is a Sicilian specialty called *Caponata*. There are literally dozens of combinations and ways to make this marvelous appetizer. Here is one that never fails to win applause:

CAPONATA

3 eggplants
1 cup olive oil
1 cup shelled walnuts
½ cup pickled melon rind
4 tablespoons garlic salt
½ cup pine nuts
⅛ teaspoon pepper
½ cup drained capers
½ cup finely-chopped sweet mixed pickles
½ cup stuffed green olives, cut in halves
1 cup pitted black ripe olives
1 cup sugar
½ cup cider vinegar
½ tablespoon garlic powder
1 cup finely chopped pimentoes
½ cup small white, sweet pickled onions

---

1. Cut eggplants in 1" slices; then in 1" cubes. Leave skin on. Discard ends.
2. Fry in 1 cup olive oil for about 30 minutes, until fairly soft and brown.
3. Add all other ingredients, and mix all together in a large pot.
4. Add eggplant and oil, and saute 30 minutes longer.
5. Then fill a very large container and place in refrigerator.

Makes enough for 20 or so good-sized portions of appetizer or 30 smaller portions.
Will keep for at least one month.

ELEVATORS

During the 1977 power blackout in New York City, the business and commercial life of the world's busiest metropolis came to a complete halt for an entire day. Though buses were still running to take people to work and many offices had sufficent natural lighting to make some work possible, the blackout shut off one electrical device without which the modern city is completely helpless: the elevator.

With thousands of offices vacant for the lack of a means of reaching them, and hundreds of thousands of people stranded in high-rise apartment buildings, the importance of the elevator in today's city was drawn sharply into focus.

The idea of vertical transportation, if not the means, has been with us for well over 2,000 years. Ruins from a number of ancient civilizations contain shafts; some archaeologists believe that these shafts were actually hoistways in which goods and perhaps people were lifted. But no mention of an elevator-like device appears in any ancient writings until the first century B.C., when the Roman architect-engineer Vitruvius described lifting platforms that utilized pulleys worked by human, animal, or water power. The Roman Coliseum, built in 80 A.D., used crude lifting platforms to raise gladiators and wild animals to the arena level.

Many medieval monasteries were built atop steep cliffs or surrounded by high walls, and some of the more unsociable cloisters depended upon a device known as the basket elevator for entry and exit. A basket elevator was just that—a basket in which the passenger was lifted or lowered by rope along the outside of the monastery walls. Not the most gracious entry, perhaps, but unwanted guests certainly posed little problem.

The elevator in the Convent of St. Catherine on Mount Sinai.

In 17th-century France, the "flying chair" occasionally brought passengers to the upper floors of higher buildings. Similar to hoists used by stablemen to lift bales of hay to a loft, the flying chair was operated by a rope running around a wheel at the top of the building exterior. One end of the rope was attached to the chair, the other end to a counterweight. To rise, a passenger threw off a sandbag attached to the chair—the counterweight would then descend and the much lighter chair and passenger would rise. Not a very pleasant ride, as you might imagine. Even so, at the end of the upward journey, the passenger had to climb in through the window.

In a sense the flying chair was similar in operation to the dumbwaiter, a pulley-and-counterweight device used chiefly to lift food from kitchen to dining room. An apocryphal story credits Thomas Jefferson with the invention of the dumbwaiter; we do know that Jefferson used one of the world's first dumbwaiters in his Virginia home to deliver food from a basement kitchen to the dining room. The dumbwaiter was later used in this country to deliver garbage to the basement of many apartment buildings.

Elisha Graves Otis is often called the inventor of the elevator. Even though he initially contributed only one major safety innovation to elevator design, it was significant enough to make him, in effect, the father of the passenger elevator.

Vermont-born Otis was working in a furniture factory when he was asked to design a machine for lifting lumber and other materials from floor to floor. Otis's invention made its debut at the 1853 Crystal Palace Exposition in New York, where it was billed as "An elevator, or machine for hoisting goods."

Otis's elevator was a simple platform that moved between two guide rails, with a steam-powered windlass at the top of the shaft to raise or lower the cable. The innovation was a safety device that could stop the fall of the elevator in the event the cable broke. The simple device consisted of two metal hooks and a spring, attached to the cable where it met the platform. If tension in the hoist rope was relaxed—in the event of a cable break, for instance—the hooks immediately sprang to a horizontal position, where their ends would catch in teeth cut into the guide rails and stop the

Elisha Otis giving a public demonstration of his safety elevator at the Crystal Palace Exposition, New York City, in 1854.

elevator's descent. Sounds a bit shaky? Well, it's basically the safety device modern elevators rely on today—and it's totally reliable.

According to some accounts, Otis demonstrated the safety of his invention by holding regular cable-breaking exhibitions at the exposition. Spectators would watch in amazement as Otis climbed on the platform, rose to the top of the shaft, and then cut the cable! His expected fall would be checked by the safety hooks.

By 1857, Otis had installed the world's first commercial passenger elevator in the Haughwout Department Store in New York. A steam-driven lift, the elevator rose five stories at a speed of 40 feet per minute—barely faster than a stairway. At first, shoppers were reluctant to risk their lives on the newfangled device, but as more and more people took the—er, plunge, it soon became clear that the passenger elevator was here to stay.

Early steam-driven elevators required a large space for the steam engine, and often spewed thick smoke into the shaft. The next step was obvious: an electric elevator. In 1880, a German named Werner Siemens built a crude electric elevator, with a motor under the platform turning cogwheels that fit into notches in the guide rails.

In 1887, William Baxter built an unsuccessful electric machine in Baltimore. The world's first *successful* electric elevator was installed two years later by the Otis Elevator Company in the Demarest Building in New York—and was in continual use until the building was demolished in 1920.

The Demarest Building elevator's 30-year life span pales next to the endurance record of the world's oldest operating elevators, three hydraulic machines installed in a Gramercy Park, Manhattan apartment building in 1883, and still operating after more than 90 years of service.

By the turn of the century, the problems of speed, safety, and height limitation had been successfully challenged. There remained only improvements in convenience and economy. The push-button elevator, introduced in 1894, was both more reliable and cheaper to operate than the hand-operated manned elevator you can still find in some old city buildings. Automatic leveling, which brings the car to rest precisely at floor level, made its debut in 1915, but the cry of "watch your step" will live on forever. By the middle of this century, automation had rendered the elevator operator nearly extinct.

The Otis Elevator Company, the world's largest manufacturer of elevators, now installs from 20,000 to 25,000 new elevators and escalators each year, and services an estimated 400,000 Otis elevators functioning around the world. As early as the 1890s, Otis was exporting elevator equipment to 31 countries. Nowadays, Otis operates 29 plants worldwide, with over 44,000 employees.

The earliest electric elevators with push-button controls simply carried a passenger from point A to point B without stops—no matter how many people on intermediate floors impatiently watched the car glide by. A modern elevator answers all calls in one direction, then responds to calls waiting in the other direction. Large office buildings with many elevators use group control systems, which keep the cars correctly spaced and send only the closest elevator to answer a call.

Thanks to Otis, elevators are now almost 100 percent safe—five times safer than a staircase, according to the elevator industry. Cable failure is extremely rare, for each of a modern machine's eight woven steel cables can support a load eight times the capacity of the car. Safety devices similar to Otis's assure that even if the cable does break, the car won't fall very far in the shaft. And a device at the bottom of the shaft, called the buffer, will break the fall of an errant elevator in the unlikely event the car does plummet.

An airplane once crashed into a New York office building and struck directly into the elevator shaft, destroying the cables. The car plunged 17 floors—but the buffer saved the life of the elevator's lone passenger!

Modern elevators travel at many times the speed of the earliest machines, with express elevators in some taller buildings speeding along at 1,200 feet per minute—fast enough to require machinery to adjust changing air pressures in the car. And newer elevators, such as those in the Sears Tower and the John Hancock Building in Chicago, travel at speeds of up to 1,800 feet per minute!

One of the largest elevators in the world—an hydraulic model—raises, lowers, and revolves the stage at New York's Radio City Music Hall. But the largest commercial elevator on record was constructed to raise and lower a full swimming pool on

OPPOSITE:
In a Philadelphia hotel elevator.

the stage of the Hippodrome Theater in New York. The device had a capacity of 250,000 pounds—that's equal in weight to 35 hippopotami—and moved at a speed of 12 feet per minute, slower than the most sluggish hippopotamus!

A second means of vertical transportation, the escalator, was developed while the electric elevator was still in its infancy. A patent for an escalator was issued in 1859, but the first working escalator was installed by Jesse Reno in 1896 on a pier in Coney Island, New York. About the same time, Charles Seeburger constructed a similar conveyor with horizontal steps. Seeburger coined the word "escalator" for his invention, combining the Latin *scala* ("steps") with the first letter and ending of "elevator." Seeburger's device forced riders to step on and off to one side—at their own risk. The Otis Elevator Company acquired both inventions. By 1921, Otis had developed the kind of horizontal-step escalator in use today.

Escalators eliminated both the need for an elevator operator and, more important, long waits for an elevator car. Escalators were installed extensively in deep subway stations, transporting a steady stream of riders and thereby eliminating bottlenecks at elevator doors. In fact, the longest escalator in the world can be found in the Leningrad subway, with a vertical rise of 195 feet.

The steps of an escalator are moved by an endless chain powered by electricity, usually at speeds of about 100 feet per minute. The underside of each step is triangular in shape, and mounted on four wheels running in tracks under the steps. When the step begins its ascent, the rear wheels rise to keep the top of the step horizontal.

As anyone who's had to climb to the eighth floor of a department store via seven escalators is well aware, the escalator will never replace the elevator for long distances. As buildings rise higher and increase in floor area, engineers have had to keep pace with constant innovation. The major problem faced by the engineers is how to minimize the space taken up by elevator shafts when many elevators are needed for a building. One answer is the dual elevator—two cars running in one shaft. The first dual elevator was place in service in Pittsburgh in 1931, with the upper car running as an express, the lower car as a local. Another development, the double-deck car, was introduced in 1932, with two attached cars that stop one floor above the other.

Round elevator cars serve a Johnson Wax Company building in Racine, Wisconsin, designed by renowned architect Frank Lloyd Wright. Another Wright creation, the Price Tower in Oklahoma, is served by hexagonally shaped elevator cars.

And who says an elevator can go only straight up? The Eiffel Tower boasts elevators that move along dizzily inclined tracks, as does the George Washington Masonic Monument in Virginia. And the outdoor elevator is now coming into vogue, as demonstrated by the new Hyatt Regency Hotel in Atlanta, served by glass-cab elevators running in rails on the outside of the building.

Beats a flying chair, doesn't it?

The latest word in elegant elevators is the outdoor glass-cab elevator, such as this one at the Hyatt Regency at O'Hare International Airport in Chicago.

Over 100 million Americans, including two-thirds of all adults, now wear eyeglasses. Another 10 million or so regularly don contact lenses. Eyeglass wearers range from the slightly dim-sighted, who slip on specs for reading or driving, to the virtually blind who would be helpless without their lenses.

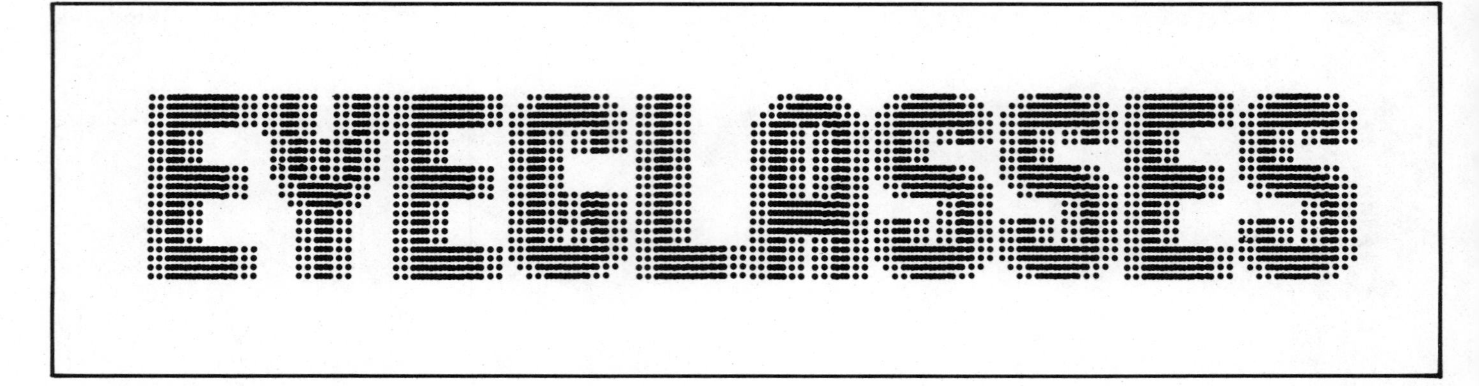

Even those fortunate enough never to need glasses should be grateful for their invention. For corrective lenses rank along with printing, paper, and electric illumination as the major technological milestones along man's road to universal literacy. Today, eyeglasses are considered so vital that it's hard to imagine a world without them. Yet eyeglasses were not commonplace anywhere in the world until about 450 years ago—and precision, individualized lenses date back no further than the 18th century!

What did man do before the invention of eyeglasses? In ancient times, aging scholars often had to give up reading altogether. The more fortunate could afford to pay others to read to them. The Roman dramatist Seneca claimed to have read with the use of a water-filled glass sphere that magnified characters when held just above the page.

Lenses existed even in Seneca's time, but no one seems to have put them to use as vision aids. A rock crystal lens found in the ruins of the ancient Assyrian city of Nineveh was probably used as a burning glass. In *The Clouds,* Greek playright Aristophanes mentioned the use of lenses to burn parchment and to erase writing from wax tablets. Roman historian Pliny wrote that burning lenses were sometimes used to cauterize wounds—though the "emerald" that he claimed the Emperor Nero used to view the gladiatorial games was probably just a curved mirror.

For many Europeans, the Dark Ages must have been quite literally dark—or, at the least, fuzzy. With no eyeglasses of any kind, medieval man had to rely on medicinal remedies of dubious value. One Anglo-Saxon remedy counseled persons with poor vision to comb their heads, eat little meat, and drink wormwood before meals, and perhaps apply a salve made from pepper, nuts, salt, and wine. Fourth-century Italians believed that a person seeing a falling star should quickly begin counting—the viewer would be free from eye inflammations for as many years as he could count before the star disappeared.

For those too slow to catch a falling star, another medieval antidote to eye inflammation required that the sufferer tie a piece of linen around his neck with as many knots as there were letters in his name. White spots before the eyes? Simply catch a fox, cut out his tongue, tie it in a red rag, and hang it from your neck. As for casting out motes, just touch your eyelid, say "I buss the Gorgon's mouth," and spit three times.

An 11th-century Arab work, *Opticae Thesaurus,* mentioned corrective lenses, but as described, the lenses could not have been suitable for improving vision. It wasn't until the 13th century that some scientists began to deal with vision defects more seriously.

Englishman Roger Bacon was the first to suggest the use of lenses for reading, and the first to describe a practical lens, with a thickness less than its radius. In 1268, Bacon wrote that by holding part of a glass sphere over a page, with the convex side up, a reader could magnify the characters and see them more clearly. He also predicted the use of lenses for microscopes and telescopes, hypothesizing that "from an incredible distance we might read the smallest letters and number of grains of dust and sand . . . So also we might cause the sun, moon, and stars in appearance to descend here below."

The next step, naturally, was to move the glass closer to the eye. Historians have been unable to determine the inventor of the first eyeglasses, or the exact date of their appearance, but we do have a number of clues. In 1289, an Italian named Sandro di Popozo wrote: "I am so debilitated by age, that without the glasses known as spectacles, I would no longer be able to read or write. These have recently been invented for the benefit of poor old people whose sight has become weak." So we can conclude that spectacles first appeared shortly before 1289.

In 1306, a Pisan monk delivered a sermon in Florence that included these comments: "It is not 20 years since there was found the art of making eyeglasses which make for good vision . . . I have seen and conversed with the man who made them first." That would date the invention of eyeglasses to around 1287. But who was the man whom the monk conversed with, the man who *invented* eyeglasses?

Some historians believe that man was Alessandro di Spina, a Dominican monk who lived in Pisa. But a document recording Spina's death in 1313 claimed that Spina had seen spectacles on a man who had chosen to remain unknown. Spina merely copied the invention, and distributed it "with a cheerful and benevolent heart."

A tombstone in Florence credits Armato degli Armati, who died in 1317, as the "inventor of spectacles." But the tombstone has been found to be of relatively recent origin; the claim is a fabrication. All we know for certain is that eyeglasses first appeared in the area of Pisa late in the 1280s.

After Marco Polo visited the Orient during the 1270s, he claimed to have found an old Chinese man reading with the use of spectacles. If this is true, then the Chinese invented eyeglasses before any European. At the time, the Chinese claimed to have learned to make lenses from Arabs two centuries earlier. But this claim is regarded as doubtful.

In any case, the appearance of spectacles in Europe caused little furor among the general populace, since at the time few people could read. For a few centuries, eyeglasses were regard-

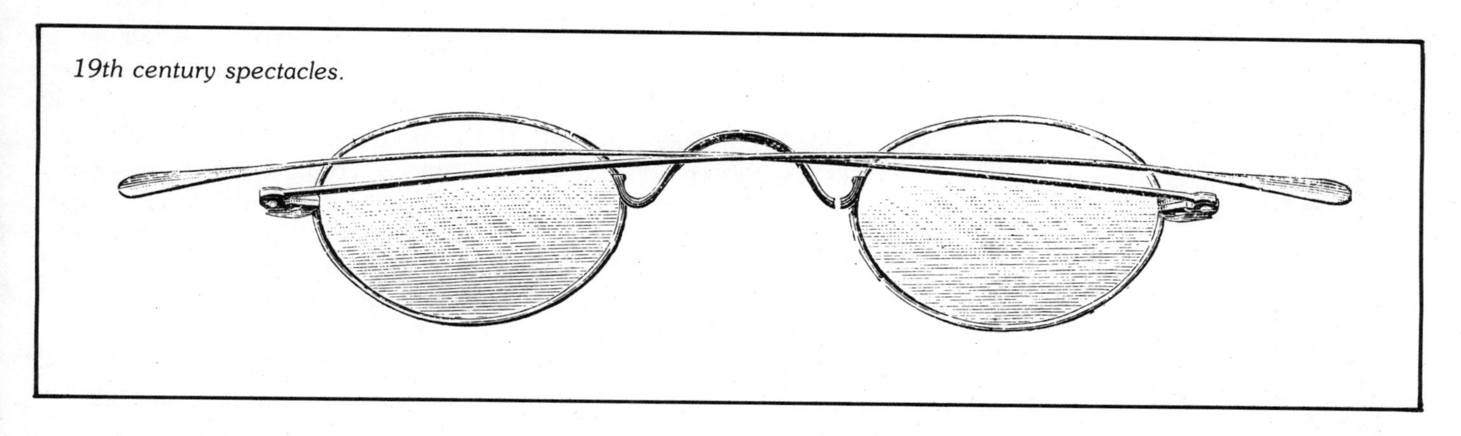
19th century spectacles.

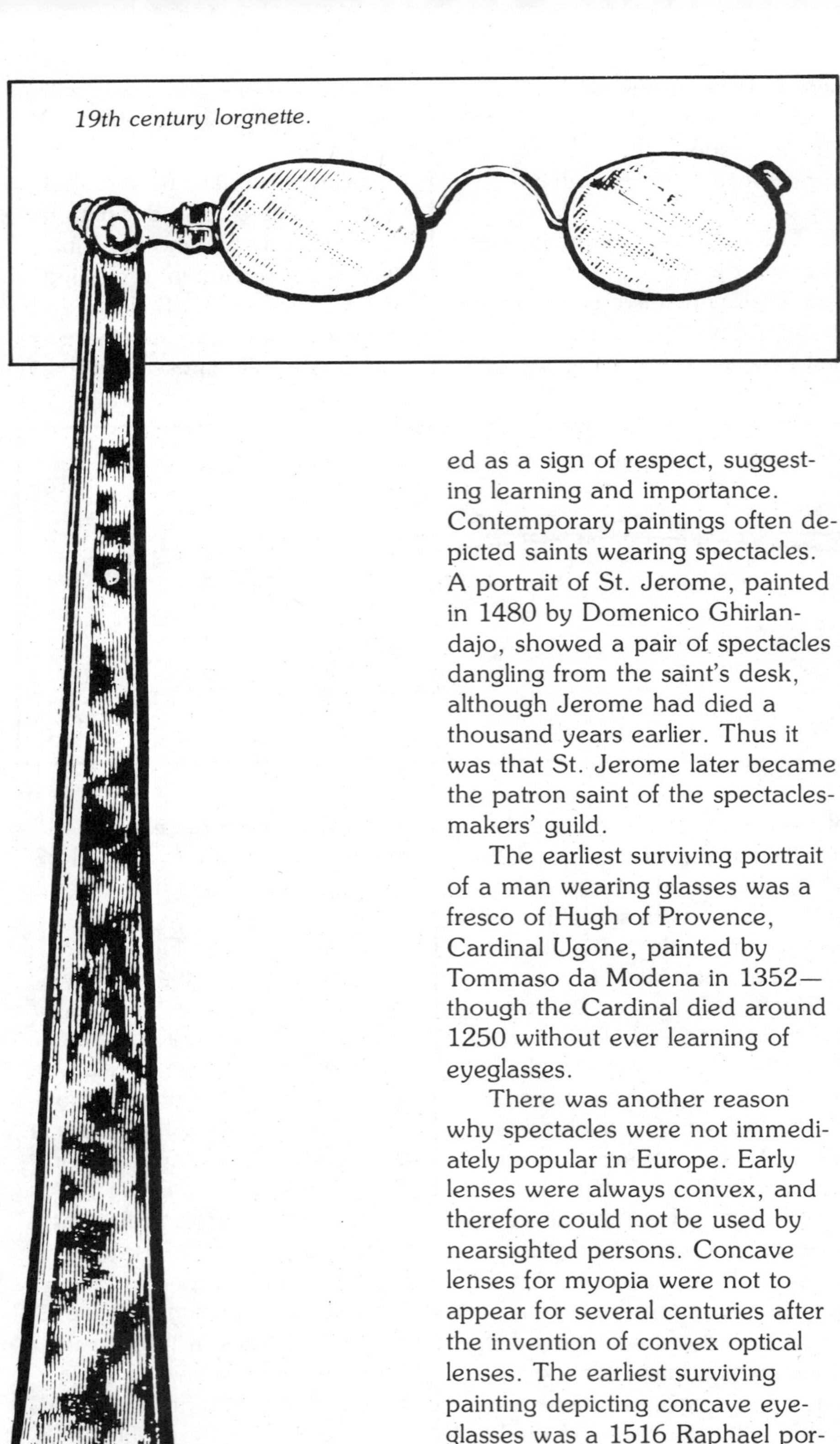
19th century lorgnette.

ed as a sign of respect, suggesting learning and importance. Contemporary paintings often depicted saints wearing spectacles. A portrait of St. Jerome, painted in 1480 by Domenico Ghirlandajo, showed a pair of spectacles dangling from the saint's desk, although Jerome had died a thousand years earlier. Thus it was that St. Jerome later became the patron saint of the spectacles-makers' guild.

The earliest surviving portrait of a man wearing glasses was a fresco of Hugh of Provence, Cardinal Ugone, painted by Tommaso da Modena in 1352—though the Cardinal died around 1250 without ever learning of eyeglasses.

There was another reason why spectacles were not immediately popular in Europe. Early lenses were always convex, and therefore could not be used by nearsighted persons. Concave lenses for myopia were not to appear for several centuries after the invention of convex optical lenses. The earliest surviving painting depicting concave eyeglasses was a 1516 Raphael portrait of Pope Leo X.

The delay in the development of concave lenses was due more to the practical applications of early eyeglasses than to a lack of technical sophistication. Glasses were at first perceived as reading tools only, and no one immediately saw the need to turn a convex lens around for use as a corrective to *myopia*, or nearsightedness. In a myopic person, the eyeball is elongated in such a way that parallel light rays are focused in front of the retina. Concave lenses cause rays to diverge and meet at the retina.

In a person suffering from *hyperopia*, or farsightedness, light rays are focused behind the retina; a convex lens focuses the rays on the retina. *Astigmatism*, caused by an irregularity in the curvature of the cornea, can be corrected with the use of a cylindrical lens—which was not invented until 1827!

The earliest optical lenses were made from beryl or quartz, and set in frames of brass or iron—and later, in bone, horn, gold, or even leather. Single glasses were held in the hand; double glasses were balanced precariously on the nose. Obviously, neither style was suited for continual use, but rather for short periods of reading. Some early spectacles were held on the nose by a hook affixed to the cap. Eyeglass cases, made of decorated wood, metal, or ivory, were usually hung from the belt. One odd eyeglass case from around 1400 was a receptacle built into a book cover, so the reader could leave his specs behind without fear of breakage.

During the 14th and 15th centuries, glass spectacles gradually came into common use. By the 1360s, we can already find references to "spectacles makers." The increased availability of reading matter that followed Gutenberg's printing press gave the industry a major boost. By 1507, a spectacles-makers' guild was firmly established, with Venice and Nuremberg the centers of eyeglass manufacture. Spectacles were now cheap enough that everyone could afford them.

Physicians by and large remained skeptical of eyeglasses, clinging to the older medicinal remedies for poor vision. As late as 1583, Dr. Georg Bartisch of Dresden, one of the most famous oculists of the 16th century, advised patients to do without spectacles. "A person sees and recognizes something better when he has nothing in front of his eyes than when he has something there," the doctor reasoned. "It is much better that one should preserve his two eyes than that he should have four."

In the 16th century, when lenses for myopic persons first appeared, eyeglasses were still selected by trial and error. A person seeking eyeglasses stepped into a spectacles maker's shop, and sampled the wares until he found a pair of specs that seemed appropriate. Spectacles makers scratched a number on each lens they made, to indicate the age of the person they thought the lens would suit. It wasn't until the 18th century that lenses were identified by the radius of curvature.

Toward the later part of that century, spectacles makers began to turn their attention to a means of holding the lenses in front of the eye for longer periods of time. First to appear were spectacles held in place by a strap tied behind the head. Next came glasses with two straps, one to loop around each ear, or spectacles with two weighted cords that were tucked behind the ears and hung almost to the wearer's waist. These latter styles were particularly popular in Spain. The Chinese preferred similar glasses right up to the 20th century, though until recently, Oriental lenses were made from crystal, rather than ordinary glass.

Sunglasses are nothing new in optometry. Tinted lenses were already in common use during the 16th century. By mid-17th century, amber or mica lenses in several colors were available. Samuel Pepys bought a pair of green spectacles in London during the 1660s, and reported their popularity. It wasn't until around 1885, however, that tinted glass spectacles began to appear.

As the use of spectacles became common among all social groups, class distinctions began to arise in eyeglass design. In England, the upper classes preferred the single-lens eyeglass, or *perspective glass,* which was usually left dangling from the neck by a ribbon. The poor opted for double-lens eyeglasses, most often sold by itinerant peddlers. Some peddlers touted their wares with a claim that viewing the sun or moon through colored spectacles would bring both improved vision and good luck. In Spain, meanwhile, spectacles of any kind were considered so chic that no fashionable man or woman would be seen without them—whether they were needed or not!

The early 18th century saw the first appearance of spectacles with the now familiar rigid sidepieces, or *bows.* The English called the bows *temples,* since they pressed against the temple of the wearer, and dubbed the spectacles *temple glasses.* In France, advertisers promoted "English style" spectacles, by promising that wearers would "breathe more easily" than they

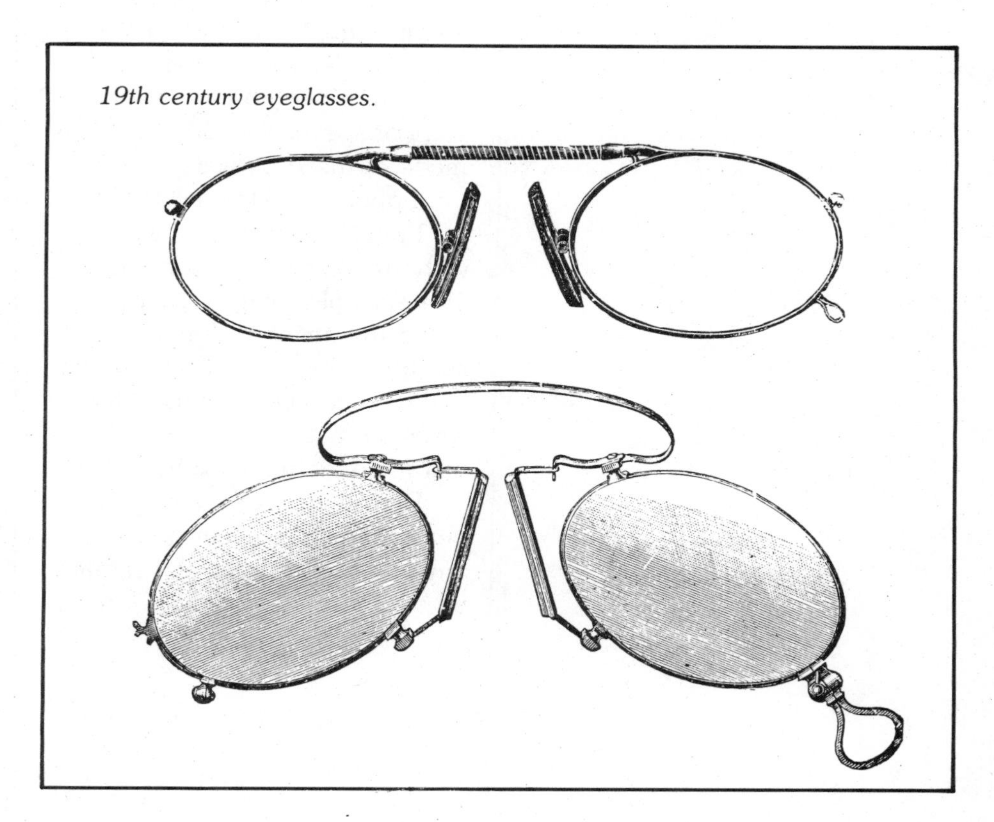

19th century eyeglasses.

would with the older, nose-pinching styles.

Scissor glasses were also popular for a time, serving as a compromise for fashion-conscious Europeans who dared not wear double-lens eyeglasses, yet could not see well enough with the more fashionable single eyeglass. Scissor glasses consisted of two lenses joined by a forked handle. When the glasses were held before the eyes, the handle appeared poised to "scissor off" the nose. The *spyglass,* an earlier invention, also became fashionable—although, for discretion's sake, the spyglass was often hidden in a cane, fan, perfume bottle, or other accessory.

Bifocal lenses were suggested as early as 1716, and may have been first made in London around 1760. However, Benjamin Franklin has generally been credited with their invention. A bifocal lens consists of two semicircular lenses joined together in a frame; the upper portion of the lens corrects for distance viewing, while the bottom half is used for reading. Franklin assembled his first bifocals around 1784, when he tired of carrying around two pairs of spectacles. Bifocal lenses made of fused glass segments did not appear until the 1900s.

Franklin's invention was not without a precedent in nature. The eyes of a tiny tropical fish called the *anableps* function just like a pair of bifocals. The upper half of each eye is focused for water-surface vision; the lower half for underwater sight.

By the 19th century, European men could wear glasses anywhere, but spectacles remained taboo for fashionable women. The spyglass was now more diplomatically called an *opera glass,* due to its nearly universal use at the theater. After the invention of binoculars, in 1823, single and double-lens opera glasses became so popular that a contemporary writer advised: "A bunch of violets, an embroidered handkerchief, a large opera glass, and a bottle of smelling salts—these are the four things a lady of fashion must have at the theater."

The *pince-nez*—literally, "pinch-nose"—first appeared around 1840, and gradually began to supercede temple glasses. By the end of the century, the pinch-nez was in almost universal use among European and American men, though it was almost never worn by women. The *monocle,* long associated with aristocratic snobbery, first appeared in England around the beginning of the century, and became all the rage among the European elite— despite warnings from physicians against their use.

By the 1870s, the United States was the world's largest manufacturer of eyeglasses. The trained vision specialist had taken over from the itinerant peddler—though as late as 1960, some Americans still bought their glasses by mail-order. In 1935, the country could boast 10,000 oculists and 22,000 optometrists, with a total annual outlay for glasses topping the $100-million mark. By now, those figures have more than doubled. One of America's largest eyeglass firms, Bausch & Lomb, had its humble beginnings late in the 19th century, when Mr. Bausch sold Mr. Lomb half interest in a supply of miscellaneous optometry equipment for the sum of $66. By 1961, the Bausch & Lomb company alone was selling glasses to the tune of $68 million a year!

The terms oculist and optometrist are not interchangeable. An *oculist* is a medical doctor who treats the eyes, while an *optometrist* is an eye-care professional without a medical school degree. An *optician,* meanwhile, is a technician who grinds and sells optical lenses, while an *ophthalmologist* is a medical doctor with several years of specialized training in eye care.

The 20th century marks the first time in history that eyeglasses are fashionably acceptable for any man or woman who needs them. In fact, a 1929 poll found that 53 percent of all spectacles wearers considered their glasses "more or less becoming." Beyond mere social considerations, the most important developments of our century are plastic eyeglasses frames and contact lenses.

Contact lenses—small optical lenses worn directly against the eye—were suggested as early as 1845, by Sir John Herschel, an Englishman. But the first pair of contacts was the work of a German, who constructed a pair of protective lenses for a patient who had lost his eyelids due to cancer. The term *contact lenses* was first used in 1887, by a Swiss doctor named A.E. Fick, but the first pair of contacts did not reach the shores of America for almost 40 years.

In 1938, plastic contact lenses began to replace glass contacts. But until 1950, contact lenses were made to fit over almost the entire eye, with a fluid applied underneath the lens to aid against eye irritation. Today's contact lenses fit over the cornea only, floating on a layer of tears and moving with the eye. Contacts can now be worn by any person who wears eyeglasses, and by some for whom eyeglasses would be useless. The biggest problem contacts wearers now face is finding their lenses, for the average contact is under 10 millimeters in diameter, and usually less than a half-millimeter thick. Incidentally, at present, 65 percent of all contact lens wearers are women.

Sunglasses became all the rage in the United States in 1939, and again after 1947, when *Business Week* called them a "definite style item," reporting that "Hollywood turned them into a fad." The latest word in sunglasses is a lens that darkens or lightens by itself according to the amount of light available.

As anyone who has ever visited a modern optician's shop knows, eyeglasses now come in an almost infinite variety of shapes, utilizing a wide range of materials. Checked or leopard-spotted frames are on the market, as are glasses with one-way lenses—the wearer can see through them, but to anyone else the lenses are mirrors. Glasses have been designed with peekhole-shaped frames, and equipped with roll-down awnings. Fishermen can now purchase goggles that enable them to see through reflections on water, and music lovers can buy glasses fitted with a tiny transistor radio. And grapefruit eaters will be happy to learn that they can purchase a pair of spectacles fitted with miniature, battery-powered windshield wipers!

Many people believe that eyeglasses, exotic or plain, are made for the eyes. This, as we all know, is untrue. As Dr. Pangloss points out in Voltaire's *Candide:* "Noses are made for spectacles; therefore we have spectacles."

Here are a pair of sunglasses with wipers. Powered by a standard battery, these wipers really work. And while this pair will probably turn out to be a hilarious party prank, the water skier and snow skier might find these glasses a boon.

FRANKFURTERS

Americans gobble up close to 16 billion weiners each year—about 80 per person.

There is no truth to the notion that frankfurters are unavailable today in Germany, the land of their birth. Stop by a roadside eatery or pop into a quick-lunch restaurant in Germany and you'll have little trouble finding a frankfurter, complete with bread, mustard, and sauerkraut.

But there is one difference between the German frank and the hot dog you'll find at an American stand: in Germany, you'll be served your frank piecemeal, with a sausage, a pile of sauerkraut, and a piece of bread on a plate. The frank-on-a-bun, like its cousin, the hamburger-on-a-bun, is a product of American ingenuity.

The frankfurter and hamburger are both medieval inventions, but the sausage itself predates recorded history. The word comes to us from the Latin *salsus, salted*, or *preserved*. The word *salami* was mentioned often in the pre-Christian period, perhaps associated with the Greek city of Salamis on Cyprus.

Since meat preservation was a problem before the invention of refrigeration, preserved meat was always popular. In the Middle Ages, sausage makers developed individual formulas for seasoning their products, which frequently took the name of the city where they originated. From Frankfurt, of course, came the frankfurter; from Bologna—well, need we say more?

The southern European preferred dry, heavily salted sausage, such as *genoa salami* from Genoa; in northern Europe, cooks preferred fresh and cooked sausage such as *head cheese*, *blood sausage*, and *bratwurst*.

The frankfurter was brought to the United States by German immigrants. Like the hamburger,

The original Nathan's Famous hot dog stand on Coney Island was founded in 1916. This photograph shows the stand in 1920. The little boy in his father's arms is Murray Handwerker, current chairman of the board and president of Nathan's Famous, Inc.

it first became popular in the Cincinnati area. As to why the frank became more popular than any other sausage—well, who's to account for tastes?

Today, frankfurter meat is cured with various combinations of chemicals, such as sodium chloride and sodium nitrite or nitrate, along with sugar. The pork or beef is chopped, seasoned, stuffed into its collagen or intestine skin, and then smoked and cooked. In some frankfurter manufacturing plants, computers select raw materials daily and feed them into a continuous hot-dog processing machine, untouched by human hands. Frankfurter production that formerly required nine hours now takes as little as 45 minutes.

There are over 200 varieties of sausage made in this country, by some 3,000 individual processors. The *frankfurter* is by far the most popular. Americans gobble up close to 16 billion weiners each year—about 80 per person!

Franks with beans were popular on the American frontier, since both would remain fresh for long periods of time. Though refreshment stands at early baseball parks sold such items as tripe, planked onions, and cherry pie, the hot dog eventually became the overwhelming favorite of the bleachers. In fact, the term *hot dog* was coined in 1919 at the Polo Grounds, a major-league ballpark in New York City. Today, a baseball park without hot dogs would be an affront to the sport.

Though the frankfurter remains popular, it certainly is no longer fashionable—except perhaps for the tiny frank-and-bun concoction known as *pigs in a blanket* that are *de rigeur* at so many cocktail parties. And some frankfurter makers now adulterate their product with—your grandparents would shudder—chicken!

We have no idea of the contents of the 20 two-ounce franks that Jimmy Davenport of Kentucky wolfed down in just three-and-a-half minutes in 1976, setting the world's record for hot-dog consumption. But we know that a mammoth weiner exhibited by a California hotel to celebrate the American Bicentennial in 1976 consisted of 40 pounds of pork and beef, and measured 148 inches in length. To our knowledge, no patriot volunteered to single-handedly devour the dog.

GARLIC

Old gag: "They feed the baby garlic, so they can find it in the dark."

Through most of the 19th century, garlic was so little known to most Americans that a cookbook of the era could recommend that "garlics are better adapted to medicine than cooking."

While there are still many who believe garlic has medicinal, even magical powers, the pungent vegetable has by now found its way into many kitchens in the United States, as Americans discover what their European ancestors have long known: garlic is a useful, flavorful addition to almost any dish.

Garlic is a member of the lily family, and specifically of the *Allium* genus, which also includes the onion, leek, shallot, and chive. We eat only the bulb of this perennial plant. A bulb contains about a dozen cloves, or smaller bulbs, each wrapped in an onionskin-like shell that makes garlic both convenient to use and long-lasting.

Garlic probably first grew in southern Siberia, and it is now found naturally in Central Asia and the Mediterranean. Man has eaten the bulb since earliest times, principally as a flavoring. The Israelites of Biblical times cultivated garlic, and during their exile in Egypt longed for a return to the Promised Land with its bounteous flavorful produce.

The ancient Egyptians also cultivated garlic, though among priests it was considered unclean—no one was permitted to enter an Egyptian temple with garlic on his breath. The workers who toiled on the construction of the Pyramids probably ate garlic and onions in large amounts. The Romans fed garlic to their soldiers in the belief that it promoted strength and courage, but the Senate forbade a Roman to enter the Temple of Sybil after eating the aromatic vegetable. In India, too, garlic was condemned by the priestly class while being enjoyed by the masses.

Our word *garlic* is Anglo-Saxon in origin, a combination of the words *gar* ("spear") and *leac* ("leek"), due to its spearlike leaves. But garlic was by and large spurned in England for centuries, and thus it had little place in the cuisine of early America. The later arrival of large numbers of immigrants from Southern Europe made garlic an American staple—try to find a Mediterranean dish that doesn't include garlic!

Today, about 20 million pounds of garlic are produced in the United States each year, principally in Texas, California, and Louisiana. Argentina is now the world's largest producer, while other nations that cultivate it on a large scale include China, India, Iran, Italy, Spain, and the U.S.S.R. Indeed, garlic is one of the few food items that have long been used in cuisines as diverse as Chinese, Indian, and European.

Garlic is usually employed in small amounts as a flavoring, and therefore it's fortunate that it remains fresh for a long time. Garlic stored in the refrigerator may last as long as 200 days. For those who disdain the chore of slicing garlic or mashing it in a garlic press, there are dehydrated garlic chips, garlic powder, and garlic salt.

A host of legends and superstitions have been attached to garlic in many different cultures. In Europe, garlic has been considered an antidote to witches and vampires, and in some places a clove of garlic was rubbed on an infant's lips at the time of christening. In the Orient, garlic is believed to beautify the complexion and improve the intellect, as well as ward off evil spirits. Peoples from the West and East alike have long regarded it as an aphrodisiac. For a time, garlic was also thought to encourage drinking, as evidenced by a line from the 16th-century English poet Thomas Nashe: "Garlicke maketh a man winke, drinke, and stinke."

Actually, there's some truth to the notion that garlic has medicinal value, for garlic contains an antibiotic and has antiseptic properties. It also promotes elimination and sweating.

But garlic is today far more popular among gastronomists than doctors. Some cooks regard garlic as the most indispensable flavoring item in the kitchen. Among the true garlic lovers we might point to French chef Louis Diat, who wrote that "garlic is the fifth element of living, and as important as earth, air, fire, and water."

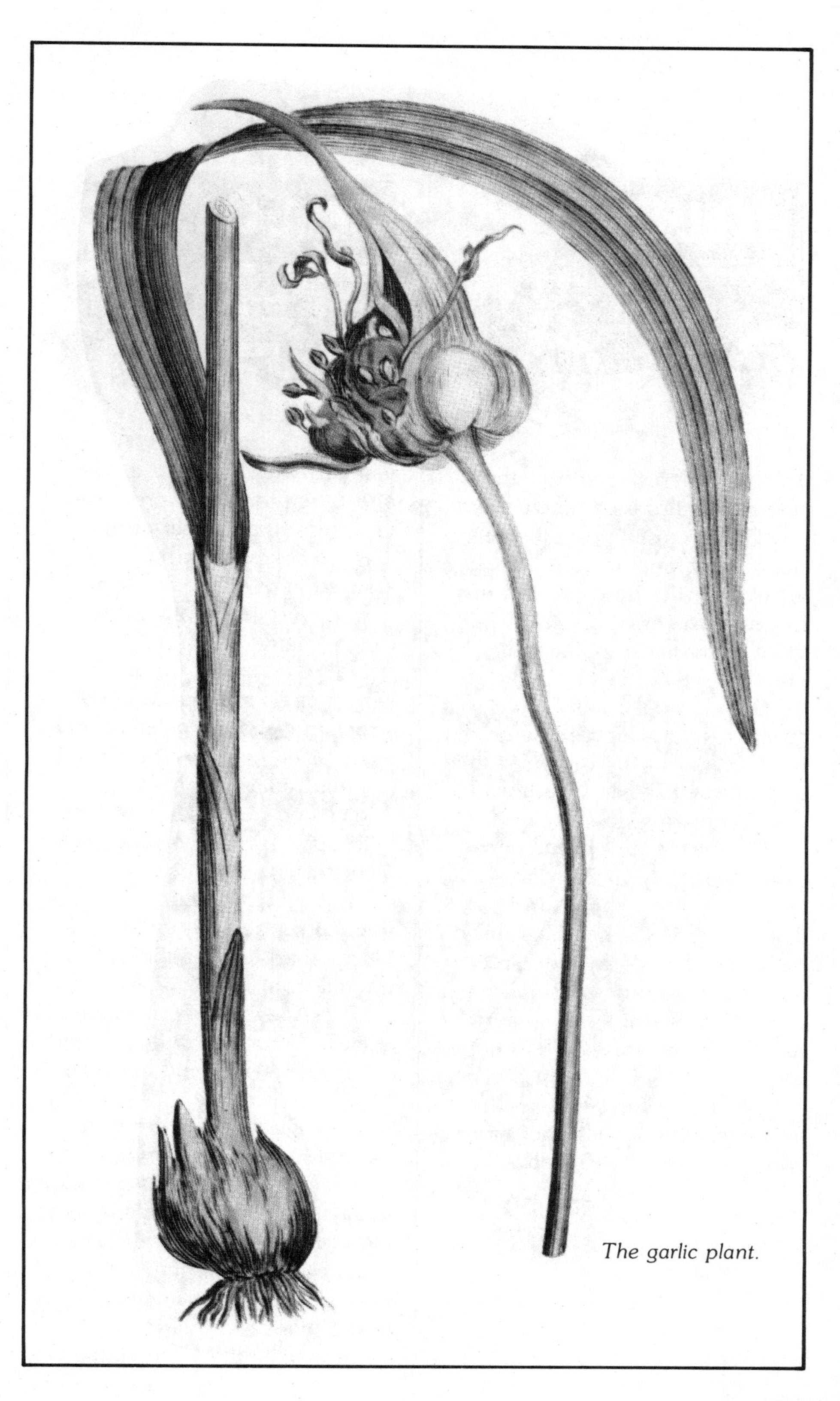

The garlic plant.

Gelatin

To the modern American, the sweet gelatin dessert known as Jell-O is an institution. Just tear open the wrapper, pour boiling water over the powder, and refrigerate in a bowl or mold. Jell-O's a lot easier to make than a pie.

Sure, we take Jell-O for granted, until we realize what our forefathers—or foremothers—had to go through to serve a bowl of the shimmering dessert.

Before the turn of the century, gelatin was a functional food item rather than a treat. Jellies and aspics had been used since the days of ancient Greece to bind, glaze, and preserve other foods. For example: the canned hams packed in aspic you buy today.

We think of gelatin basically as a dessert; but in former times, cooks flavored their gelatins with vinegar, wine, almond extract, and other items that produced a tart rather than sweet product. Those cooks hardly had need of a sweet jelly, since the items they glazed were more often meats than sweets.

As long ago as the Renaissance, chefs took pride in constructing elaborate gelatin molds. In the 19th century, the most popular mold designs were castles and fortresses complete with doors, windows, and crenellated turrets.

Before this century, the glue needed for gelatin—called *collagen*—had to be laboriously extracted from meat bones. In the Middle Ages, deer antlers were a popular source of the glue; and later, calves' feet and knuckles. Housewives in the 19th century used isinglass, made from the membranes of fish bladders.

Gelatin-making was a daylong affair, requiring the tedious scraping of hair from the feet, hours of boiling and simmering with egg whites to degrease and clarify the broth, and careful filtering through jelly bags. The transparent finished product was then dried into sheets or leaves.

Not the easiest process in the world, you'll agree. That's what Charles B. Knox thought, too. In 1890, the Jamestown, New York man was watching his wife make calves'-foot jelly when he decided that a prepackaged, easy-to-use gelatin mix was just what the housewife needed. Knox set out to develop, manufacture, and distribute the granulated gelatin, while his wife invented recipes for the new kitchen staple.

A few years later, a woman named May Wait *didn't* wait for Knox to flavor his gelatin, and concocted a mix of sugar, powdered gelatin, and artificial fruit flavors that she christened Jell-O. But it wasn't until the development of the icebox at the end of the century that America was ready for gelatin desserts.

Wait's product found its way to few American tables before it was bought by the food tycoon Frank Woodward. A genius in packaging, mass marketing, and advertising, within a few years Woodward turned Jell-O into a household word. The 10-cent carton advertised a "delicious dessert" that was "delicate, delightful, and dainty," and the Jell-O trademark of a young girl with carton and kettle in hand soon appeared on store displays, dishes, spoons, and other promotional articles.

To show the housewife how versatile the product was, Woodward's company distributed free booklets with Jell-O recipes. One booklet alone ran to a printing of 15 million copies!

By 1925, Jell-O was a big-money industry. In that year, Jell-O joined Postum to form General Foods, today one of the largest corporations in America. Talk about humble beginnings!

By the 1930s, Jell-O had become a way of life. In the Midwest, no Sunday dinner was complete without a concoction known as Golden Glow salad—Jell-O laced with grated carrot and canned pineapple and served with gobs of mayonnaise.

Knox Gelatine tried to discourage the rush toward Jell-O with ads warning shoppers to spurn "sissy-sweet salads" that were "85 percent sugar." While Knox stressed the purity of their odorless, tasteless, sugarless gelatin, Jell-O highlighted their product's versatility.

Today, you'd be hard put to find a beanery that didn't offer at least one flavor of the fruity dessert. Gelatin is very popular among dieters, especially the sugarless D-Zerta variety, and many restaurants serve elaborate specials of Jell-O, fruit, and cottage cheese. In health-conscious America, Jell-O has become the highly touted alternative to "junk food" desserts.

In the early 1900s, JELL-O salesmen toured the country in special automobiles. They demonstrated the simple preparation of "America's Most Famous Dessert" at fairs, church socials, and picnics.

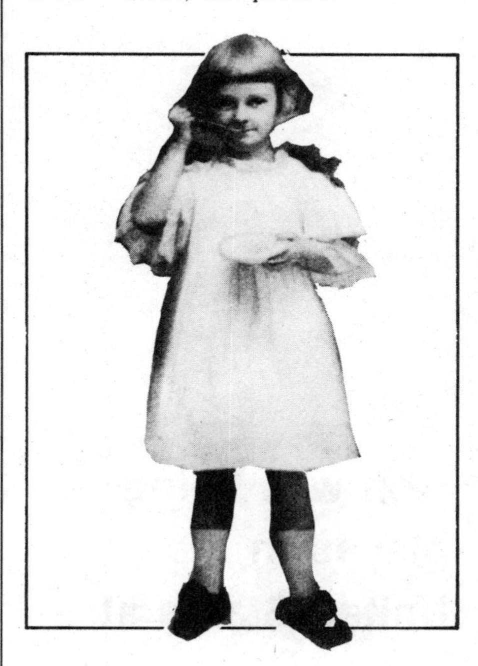

Pictures of Elizabeth King, "the JELL-O girl," appeared in JELL-O advertisements, recipe booklet covers, dessert dishes, and souvenir spoon handles, between 1904 and 1908.

Photo courtesy of General Foods Corp.

GOLF

The early 1970s marked a major milestone in golf history: the opening of the 10,000th golf course in the United States. Figuring conservatively at 6,000 yards per course, we can estimate that some 34,100 miles of this country are regularly traversed by some 10 million golfers.

Assuming a figure of eighty yards as the average fairway width, we can conclude that an area of about 1,550 square miles is now devoted solely to swatting a small ball into a four-and-a-quarter-inch hole—a total area larger than the state of Rhode Island!

The world's most land-consuming game is most often traced to humble beginnings in Scotland, but there is no firm evidence that golf originated in that country. Similar games were played in other nations centuries before golf appeared in the British Isles. In the early days of the Empire, the Romans enjoyed a game they called *paganica,* played with a bent wooden stick and a leather ball stuffed with feathers. The Roman legions may well have brought the game to Britain.

The Dutch played a game called *kolven* on frozen rivers and canals. The players used a wooden club to putt a ball toward a stake pressed into the ice. Sixteenth-century illustrations from Bruges, in Belgium, show players putting a ball at a hole in the ground.

The Soviets recently claimed that golf originated in Denmark in the 15th century, and the Chinese have long claimed that the game was born in the Orient two or three centuries before Christ.

In any case, we first find a reference to golf in Scotland in a 1457 decree ordering that the game "be utterly cryit doun and nocht usit," since it interfered with the practice of archery, a more useful sport to the defense of the realm. Another ordinance of 1471 decried the playing of "golfe and futeball;" and in 1491, yet another decree stipulated punishments for law-breaking linksmen.

This last edict was the work of King James IV, who for a time forbade golf in Scotland, declaring: "It looketh like a silly game." But within a few years of his decree, the king himself became a keen golfer, and entries appear in accounts of James's lord high treasurer, which show the purchase of balls and other golf equipment.

In 1592, the laws against golf were modified. The sport was forbidden only on the Sabbath. That law was later softened to outlaw golf only "in tyme of sermons."

Since the time of James IV, golf has remained a popular royal sport in Britain. Golf has long been officially known as the "royal and ancient game." James's son, James V, was a regular on the links. His daughter, Mary Stuart, was seen with clubs in hand just a few days after the murder of her husband—an indelicacy that should not surprise many of today's more avid linksmen.

Perhaps you've heard the one about the duffer whose partner dropped dead on the golf course? The bereaved player was mournfully sipping his cocktail

Golf was being played in the United States at least as early as 1779.

In the 1700s, the "royal game of golf" was played in the Borghese Gardens in Rome.

at the clubhouse bar when a friend rushed up to offer his condolences.

"I heard you carried poor old Willie all the way back to the clubhouse," the friend said. "That was quite a job. He must've weighed a good 250 pounds."

"Oh, carrying him wasn't difficult," the duffer replied, shrugging. "What bothered me was having to put him down at every stroke, and then lift him up again."

Golf was regularly played in England at least as early as 1603, when King James I—a Scot—appointed an official clubmaker, and budgeted funds for the purchase of golf balls.

Before assuming the English crown in 1685, James II played a challenge match against two Scottish noblemen, choosing for his partner a shoemaker named Johne Patersone. Evidently Patersone was a ringer, for the king won the match, and Patersone bought a house in London with the money he earned from the royal victory.

During the 18th century, golf clubs and associations became popular throughout England and Scotland. The reasons are obvious: anyone can set up a tennis court in his yard, or play soccer in an open field, but even a four- or five-hole golf course requires a vast expanse of well-tended land. Only by pooling their resources, and sometimes their land, could golfers provide themselves with an adequate course.

The first golf club in England, The Royal Blackheath, was founded around 1787, when there were already six clubs in Scotland. The most famous Scottish course, the Royal and Ancient Golf Club of St. Andrews, was founded in 1754, and remains the supreme authority in the sport, framing

Victorian ladies played golf at the "Westward Ho!" Ladies Golf Club in Bideford, Devon.

and revising rules for clubs throughout the world—except for clubs in the United States, which has its own governing body. There are now some 1,800 golf courses dotting the island of Great Britain.

Professional golf began in earnest in the early 19th century. The earliest pros not only played for cash, but lent their talents to the manufacture and design of golf clubs and balls, and instructed beginners as well. The most famous of the early pros was Old Tom Morris, the proprietor of the golf shop at Prestwick, Scotland. Old Tom won the British Open four times between 1861 and 1867 before relinquishing his title in 1868—to his son, Young Tom Morris. Young Tom had entered his first professional tourney at the tender age of 13. He was only 17 when he won the British championship. He won four successive championships and was undoubtedly the premier player of his time.

Golf was being played in the United States at least as early as 1779, when an advertisement for golfing equipment appeared in a New York paper. But the game apparently did not catch on here at the time.

The father of American golf is Robert Lockhart, who returned from Scotland in 1887 with a supply of balls and clubs and laid out a course in a pasture in Yonkers, New York. A year later, Lockhart and his friends founded the first modern American golf club, named St. Andrews after the landmark Scottish course.

Within the next five years, more than two hundred clubs were organized here, among them the Chicago Golf Club, the first American course with 18 holes.

This picture of Britain's early masters was taken in 1902. Left to right are J.H. Taylor, Harry Vardon, B. Sayers, William Auchterlonie, Alexander Kirkaldy, Willie Fernie, and James Braid.

Amy Pascoe, English Ladies' Champion of 1896, demonstrates the finishing stance for the approach shot.

Bobby Jones, one of golf's great immortals, played in his first tournament at the age of 14. The year of the tournament was 1916.

By 1895, there were over 50 clubs, and by the turn of the century, more than 900, with at least one club in each state. A 1901 golfing guide listed 982 clubs, including 66 six-hole courses, 715 nine-hole links, and 92 eighteen-holers.

The 1920s saw a rapid increase in the number of golf courses and players. By 1930, there were over 5,000 courses in operation, with an estimated $830 million in property value and some 2¼ million players—along with 800,000 caddies.

Many Americans considered golf an effete sport until 1913, when a former caddy named Francis Ouimet defeated two British stars to win the U.S. Open. After Ouimet's victory, golf was increasingly accepted by the general public.

Today, there are three types of golf course in the United States: the private course open only to club members; the private course open to the general public (for a price); and the municipal course owned and operated by the city and available to all for a small fee. In addition to the 10,000 regular courses, there are hundreds of small pitch-and-putt courses, and untold numbers of miniature links.

Today, the four major tournaments are the U.S. Open, the Masters, the PGA (Professional Golfers Association) Championship, and the British Open. A victory in all four contests in one year constitutes the "grand slam" of golf. Bobby Jones, perhaps the greatest amateur golfer of all time, is the only man to win "the whole ball of wax."

Jones's four victories in 1930 came in the four major tournaments of *his* time—not the four major tourneys of today.

Today, a modern pro can earn well into six figures in a single year, without winning even one major tourney. Tom Watson, 1977's biggest money-earner, brought home a nifty $310,653 in purses during that season.

Among women golfers, Sandy Palmer was the leading money-winner that year, with over $76,000 in purses. Kathy Whitworth, eight times the leading money-winner among women golfers, has grossed over a half-million dollars in purses during the last 15 years.

But to most minds, Mildred "Babe" Didrikson Zaharias remains the Babe Ruth of women golfers. A star in track and field, tennis, baseball, and basketball before she turned to golf, Babe won more than 50 major golf tournaments in her career, including a streak of 17 straight triumphs. In 1950, the Associated Press voted Babe the greatest female athlete of the half-century.

Golfers, of course, have their own magazines. *Golf Digest,* the leading publication in this field, has a circulation of close to one million copies.

In addition to a hall of fame of great players, golf has certainly produced some marvelous additions to our vocabulary. The word *golf* itself is probably derived from the Dutch *kolf* or *kolven,* or the German *Kolbe.* Some authorities claim that the source is the Scotch *gowf,* "blow of the hand."

The word *caddie* (the youth who carries the golfer's bag and often chooses the club for each shot), comes from the French *cadet,* "young lad." The term *putt,* like the verb "put," is rooted in the Middle English *putten,* which means "push" or "thrust."

The rules of golf, unlike the

rules of many other sports, have changed little over the centuries, but the equipment used in the game has undergone a number of major alterations. The earliest golf sticks were made with thick wooden shafts and long heads. Modern clubs are manufactured with steel shafts and either persimmon wood or chromium-plated steel heads.

Today, we use numbers to designate each club; but until the 1920s, each club had its own name. The woods were numbered from one to five, and were known as follows:

No. 1	**The Driver**
No. 2	**The Brassie**
No. 3	**The Spoon**
No. 4	**The Baffy**
No. 5	**The Clerk**

The irons were numbered one through nine:

No. 1	**The Driving Iron**
No. 2	**The Midiron**
No. 3	**The Mid Mashie**
No. 4	**The Mashie Iron**
No. 5	**The Mashie**
No. 6	**The Spade Mashie**
No. 7	**The Mashie Niblick**
No. 8	**The Pitching Niblick**
No. 9	**The Niblick**

Other clubs include the putter, the jigger or chipper, and various wedges. However, no golfer in tournament play is permitted to carry more than 14 clubs.

Before 1848, golf balls were made of leather, stuffed with "as many feathers as a hat will hold." The leather balls were expensive and virtually useless when wet, so the guttie, a ball of solid gutta percha (a rubberlike substance) caught on quickly in the 1850s. Golfers using the guttie quickly noticed that a new ball tended to hook and slice erratically when hit; but old, pockmarked gutties traveled straight. So the practice began of manufacturing golf balls with small depressions, or dimples, on the outer surface.

Rubber-cored balls appeared in 1898; and at first, were known as "bounding bullies." Since then, golf's governing bodies have legislated the size and weight of the balls to be used in all official play. At present, official U.S. balls are equal in weight, but slightly larger in diameter, than the balls used in Britain and the rest of the world.

By the way, the golf tee was the brilliant invention of one George F. Grant of Boston, who patented a tapered wooden tee in 1899.

Golfing records are difficult to compare, since golf courses vary in difficulty. But the lowest golf score ever recorded for an 18-hole course of at least 5,000 yards was a 55, achieved by E.F. Staugaard in California in 1935, and matched in 1962 by Homero Blancas in Texas.

The longest golf drive on record is 515 yards, by Michael Hoke Austin in Las Vegas, Nevada, in 1974. Prior to that, the record belonged to Englishman E.C. Bliss, who walloped a ball 445 yards during a 1913 match.

Many talented golfers go through life without once tasting that dream of all linksmen, the hole-in-one. But at least 15 players have achieved the remarkable achievement of holes-in-one on successive holes. The greatest of these feats was accomplished in 1964, when Norman Manley recorded back-to-back aces on two *par-four* holes in Saugus, California.

You can be certain that no one will ever score a hole-in-one on the 17th hole of the Black Mountain Golf Club in North Carolina. This par-six hole, the longest in the world, measures 745 yards from tee to cup.

The largest club in the world is undoubtedly the Eldorado Golf Club in California, which includes 15 individual courses!

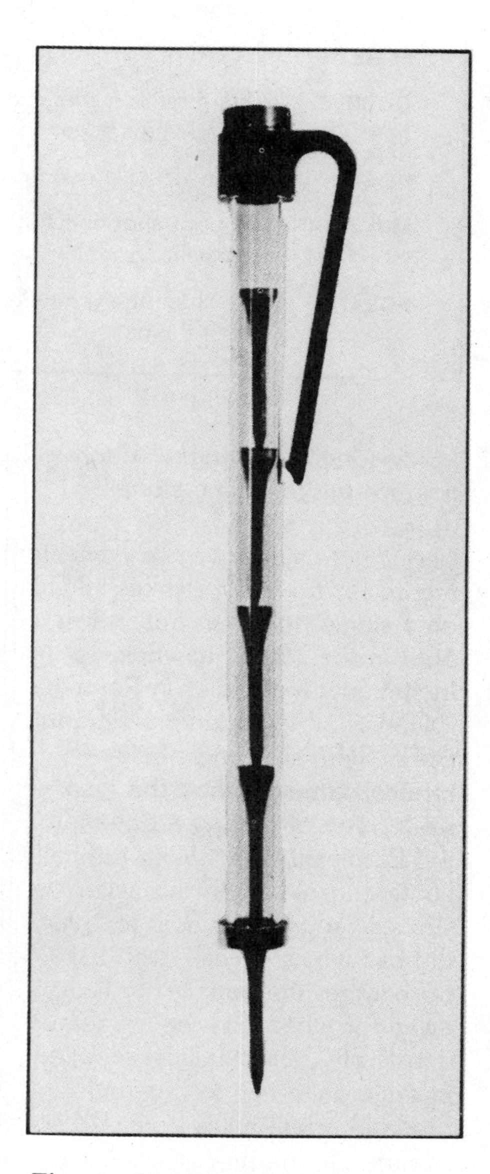

This sturdy, transparent tube clips onto the golf bag and dispenses tees.

GOLF'S MOST COLORFUL TERMS

BIRDIE	Score of one stroke less than the par for that hole.
BISQUE	Handicap stroke that a player may use on any one hole of his choosing, provided he announces his decision to use the stroke before teeing off on the following hole.
BOGIE	Score of one stroke more than the par for that hole.
BUNKER	Sand trap.
DIVOT	Piece of turf cut out of the ground by a player's stroke.
DUB	To hit the ball poorly, or a shot poorly executed.
FORE	A cry of warning to people within range of a shot.
GOBBLE	Hard-hit putt that drops into the cup, but would have traveled far beyond the cup had it not dropped in.
HOSEL	The socket on an iron club into which the shaft fits.
MULLIGAN	A poor shot which a player, by agreement, is allowed to cancel and replay.
SCLAFF	To strike the ground behind a ball before making contact with the ball.

Among the remarkable lore of golf are the following stories:

Let us here set down the enviable record for the most strokes taken on a single hole—an outlandish 166! In the 1912 Shawnee Invitational for Ladies in Pennsylvania, an experienced woman golfer, who shall mercifully remain nameless, had the misfortune of duffing a drive into the Binniekill River. With the ball floating insolently in the water, she set out in a rowboat to "play the ball where it lies," with her husband at the oars. After flailing away for what must have seemed an eternity, she finally succeeded in driving the ball to dry land one-and-a-half miles downstream. By the time she hacked her way back through the woods and holes out on the 16th green, the distraught duffer had taken 166 strokes—all meticulously recorded by her loving husband.

Many a golfer prefers a golf cart to a caddy because it cannot count, criticize—or laugh.

Justice McKenna of the United States Supreme Court was a dedicated golfer, but a rather unsuccessful performer. Hoping that his game might be improved if he took instruction, he engaged a professional for a course of lessons.

One day, while practicing on a course just outside the Capitol, he placed his ball on the tee, swung mightily, and missed. The same thing happened on three successive strokes: each time his club hit several inches behind the ball. The golf pro watched in silence.

The Justice was chafing. Finally, in white heat, he glared at his ball, which hadn't moved a fraction of an inch, and muttered, "Tut! Tut!"

The instructor gravely walked towards the jurist, and said, "Sir, you'll never learn to play golf with *them* words."

An amateur golfer is one who addresses the ball twice—once before swinging, and once again, after swinging.

Lew Worsham leaned over his putter on the 18th green of the Jacksonville Country Club. He needed to sink the ball in 2 to win the 1948 Jacksonville Open Championship, a $10,000 feature. He moved his putter carefully behind the ball. Suddenly, he straightened, dropped his club, and went to the side of the green.

"I touched the ball," he told the tournament official. "Call a penalty stroke."

Worsham then returned to take the 2 putts that now gave him only a tie.

The next day, Lew lost the playoff to Clayton Haefner on the 21st green. But even in defeat Worsham was marked as a great champion—a champion in sportsmanship. Not even his victory in the 1947 National Open earned him the respect he won by calling against himself a penalty nobody else had seen.

Golf: A five-mile walk punctuated by disappointments.

The day was August 19, 1962. Longview, Texas, was agog. Homero Blancas, a 24-year-old graduate of the University of Houston had just completed the first round of the Premier Invitational Tournament in 55 strokes! His card of 27 for the front nine, and 28 for the back, was the lowest round of golf ever played on a course measuring more than 5,000 yards.

Golf is a game in which the slowest people in the world are those in front of you, and the fastest are those behind.

Dave White's round at the Winchester Country Club started fine, but he blew up on the fifth hole and took a horrifying 13! Then the Massachusetts pro settled down with a vengeance. He shot 10 straight birdies to salvage a par round of 72.

The confident golfer teed up his ball, looked toward the next green, and declared to his caddy, "That's good for one long drive and a putt." He swung violently, topped the ball, and watched it roll a few feet off the tee.

The caddy stepped forward and handed him the putter, smugly muttering, "And now for one hell of a putt!"

All seven brothers of the Turnesa family, who were born and reared in Elmsford, New York, became outstanding golfers. Mike Turnesa was a greenskeeper at Fairview Country Club in Elmsford, and he started his kids in the game. They learned fast.

Six of the boys—Mike, Jr., Frank, Joe, Phil, Doug, and Jim—became professionals. The only Turnesa who didn't turn pro was Willie, the youngest. But he, too, was a superb golfer. Willie won the U.S. Amateur in 1938, and again in 1948; and he won the British Amateur in 1947.

Among them, the seven Turnesa brothers won a host of tournaments. In 1952. Jim won the Professional Golfers Association championship.

The seven Turnesa Brothers of Elmhurst, New York were a golfing phenomenon.

McDonald's famous "Big Mac" hamburger.

Sure, everyone knows that the hamburger comes from Hamburg and the frankfurter from Frankfurt. What could be plainer? But it may interest you to know that while the meats themselves are German in origin, the idea of placing a hamburger or a frankfurter on a bun is an American innovation.

The hamburger is a more recent invention than the frankfurter. During the Middle Ages, traveling merchants from Hamburg learned from the Tartars of the Baltic lands how to scrape raw meat and season it with salt, pepper, and onion juice. This came to be known as "Tartar steak." Many restaurants still serve a similar dish known as *steak tartare*.

When the hamburger arrived in America, it was eaten quite raw—the way the French, for instance, still prefer their meat.

The English and Irish were the first to cook their beef patties well-done. The English called the burger *Salisbury Steak* after Dr. James H. Salisbury, who, in the 1880s, recommended to his patients that they eat well-done beef patties three times daily, with hot water before and after, to relieve colitis, anemia, asthma, and other ailments.

Burgers were first popularized in the United States by German immigrants settling around Cincinnati. But the first burger wasn't laid between the halves of a bun until early in this century. Officially, the first *hamburger sandwich* appeared at the 1904 Louisiana Purchase Exposition in St. Louis, Missouri.

As for the modern hamburger, the last decade has seen a huge increase in burger corruption, with soy protein a common culprit. And other scientists with tainted tastebuds have proposed a burger made from cotton.

If the popularity of the frankfurter has tapered off somewhat in recent years, the hamburger is certainly on the rise. Chopped meat now accounts for about 30 percent of all consumer meat sales. As late as the 1920s, many American dictionaries still did not contain the word *hamburger* though most did mention the *Hamburg steak*. Today, it would be hard, indeed, to find a restaurant, a diner, a coffee shop, or a roadside stand that did not serve the burger in some shape or form.

Burger joints have been mushrooming all over Europe, too, led by a British chain known as Wimpy's. And you'll have no trouble in Paris finding a McDonald's for *Le Cheeseburger*.

McDonald's is a story in itself. A chain known as the White Castle was the first to serve cheap, mass-produced hamburgers. Since then, hamburger joints have proliferated. Today, McDonald's is definitely the leader of the pack. Beginning with a stand in Des Plaines, Illinois, which raised its now-famous yellow beams on April 15, 1955, McDonald's has grown into a huge corporation with well over several billion dollars in annual sales. McDonald's sales average a billion hamburgers every three months!

To date, McDonald's has sold 25 billion hamburgers—stack them up and you'd have 20 piles the size of the tallest building in the world, the Sears Tower in Chicago.

The McDonald's Corporation is run from a complex near Chicago called "Hamburger Central." Since 1968, new franchisers have been taught the ABC's of hamburgerology at a school in Elk Grove Village, Illinois, known as *Hamburger University*.

The McDonald's philosophy: in three out of four families, it's the children who decide where to eat. Please the child and you've captured the entire family.

That idea has certainly worked. The McDonald burger has now spread from coast to coast, and through much of Europe and Japan. As of January 9, 1978, there were 4,612 McDonald's stands throughout the world. And, yes, there's a McDonald's in Hamburg!

If the McDonald's burger has lost little in translation, some of the firm's terminology has not fared so well. When McDonald's was laying plans for its first Paris franchise, *Gros Mec* seemed the appropriate translation for the "Big Mac"—until red-faced McDonald's officials learned that *Gros Mec* also meant "big pimp" to the Frenchman.

And McDonald's would be delighted to serve Ronald Sloan, who in 1976 established a hamburger-eating record by devouring 17 burgers, with buns, in a mere 30 minutes—appropriately enough, in Cincinnati.

Today, McDonalds has plenty of competitors. Hamburger chains with scores of outlets have sprouted up all over the United States. The hamburger has become big business.

Nutrition is an inexact science: it cannot explain how teenagers manage to thrive on hamburgers and Coke.

Handkerchiefs

The handkerchief displays a split personality: as an ornamental accessory, it may waft the scent of perfume from a lady's hand or purse. As a utilitarian object, it carries less savory connotations. As you might expect, purely functional usage preceded the handkerchief's entry into the realm of *haute couture*. Yet, among all but the aristocracy, the association of the nose and the handkerchief is a relatively recent development. It took a long time for the handkerchief to become an object of common usage.

The word *kerchief* comes to us from the French *couvrir*, "to cover," and *chef*, "head," since at one time the hanky was used chiefly to cover the head—a use not unknown today. Later, the prefix "hand-" was added, to differentiate the kerchief carried in the hand or pocket from the neckerchief usually worn around the throat.

Primitive man wore woven grass mats over his head for protection from the sun and rain. The mat doubled as a handkerchief to wipe sweat from the face. The head kerchief apparently made its first appearance in China, with silk tissue and paper as the favored materials.

The ancient Greeks and Romans wore simple squares of flax tucked into folds in their robe-like garments. The Romans called their hanky a *sudorium*, from the word *sudor*, "sweat," which leaves little doubt as to its main usage. During the first century B.C., when linen from Egypt was very expensive, the *sudorium* was considered a fashionable luxury. But increases in flax imports lowered the cost of handkerchiefs until they were affordable by all citizens during the later Empire.

The fourth century saw the appearance of the *muscinium*—from the Latin word for "mucous"—whose usage should also be quite evident. During the later years of the Roman Empire, spectators at the gladiatorial arena waved their *sudaria* or *muscinia* to indicate to the Emperor whether they wanted to see a vanquished gladiator spared or slain.

Churchmen were the first to use the handkerchief widely in medieval Europe. Clerical handkerchiefs became part of various Christian rituals. For a time, carrying a hanky was considered a privilege reserved for the clergy.

The handkerchief remained relatively rare right up into the 16th century. We know, for instance, that the 15th-century wife of French king Louis XI had but three handkerchiefs. In those days, hankies were considered valuable enough to be included in wills!

If medieval man rarely carried a handkerchief, what did he use to wipe his nose? The finger and the sleeve—customs not altogether unknown today. In the Middle Ages, when there were no forks, and food was eaten with the hands, etiquette demanded that the cultured individual touch his food only with the right hand, and his nose only with the left. The medieval English *Boke of Curtasye* advised that it was proper to blow one's nose with a finger, as long as the finger was then wiped on the sleeve or skirt.

In the 16th century, when the upper classes were beginning to use handkerchiefs to dab their noses, the peasant still had to make do with his finger or sleeve. The Dutch scholar Erasmus felt compelled to point out that "to wipe your nose on your cap or your sleeve is boorish," though he conceded that it "may be all right for pastry-cooks." A riddle of the era asked: "What is it that the king puts in his pocket but the peasant throws away?"

Incidentally, we can blame Frederick the Great of Prussia for the vestigial buttons still found on men's jacket sleeves. It seems that the monarch was so displeased with the slovenly appearance of his troops, due in large part to their use of the cuffs of their uniforms for nose and sweat wiping, that to discourage this habit, he ordered a row of buttons sewn on the top side of all uniform sleeves. There-

In the late 18th century, the English amused themselves with political caricatures printed on handkerchiefs. The inscriptions underneath each figure read as follows:

'The slap up swell wot drives when hever he likes.'

'The man wot drives the Opposition.'

'The guard wot looks after the Sovereign.'

'The man wot drives the Sovereign.'

'The cad to the man wot drives the Sovereign.'

after, the unmindful soldier would receive a nasty scratch on his face whenever he used his sleeve as a towel. The buttons still survive on men's jackets, though they've been moved from the top of the sleeve to the side.

The ornamental use of handkerchiefs was far more prevalent than its practical use. Embroidered and fringed silk handkerchiefs began to appear in Europe during the 16th century, and quickly became *de rigueur* for all fashionable ladies. In the 17th century, the French developed hanky craftsmanship to a fine art, turning out elegant handwrought laces with delicate threadwork and embroidery. They even ornamented some of their masterpieces with precious gems!

The use of handkerchiefs as love tokens was well established during the Renaissance, perhaps as a continuation of the older European custom of an exchange of handkerchiefs between a betrothed couple. The handkerchief—called *fazzoletto* from the Italian word for "face"—was no mere trinket at the time, but an expensive personal item.

A handkerchief given as a love token plays a most crucial role in Shakespeare's *Othello*. The Moor gave his wife Desdemona a "handkerchief spotted with strawberries" as his "first remembrance."

He conjur'd her she should ever keep it,
That she reserves it evermore about her
To kiss and talk to.

The treacherous Iago managed to obtain the treasured handkerchief, and used it to convince Othello that his wife had been unfaithful. To Othello, this was proof positive:

To lose't or give't away were such perdition
As nothing else could match.

The French monarch Louis XVI can be credited for the uniform shape of today's handkerchiefs. At one time, handkerchiefs came in almost any size and shape—round, square, oval, or whatever. According to one tale, Queen Marie Antoinette told the king she was tired of seeing hankies in all kinds of extravagant shapes. The king quickly decreed that "the length of the handkerchief shall equal the width throughout the kingdom." Since French hanky makers dominated the industry for centuries, Louis's dictum became unwritten law throughout Europe.

The popularity of snuff during the 17th and 18th centuries made the handkerchief indispensable to

A LA
GLOIRE IMPERISSABLE
DE L'EMPEREUR NAPOLEON
LE GRAND

Handkerchief printed by Renault of Rouen in the middle of the 18th century. This ornate handkerchief depicts the tomb of Napoleon.

men or women of breeding. The hanky functioned as both a wipe for the itchy nose and a shield to cover the sneeze. European aristocrats developed great skill at elegantly hiding their snuff-induced sneezes. Most hankies of the era were quite large—about 30 inches square on the average—and darkly colored, to hide the brown tobacco stains.

The pocket handkerchief made its appearance during the 18th century, when middle-class Europeans adopted the hanky to emulate the aristocracy. The invention of the power loom and other advances in textile production in the 1780s ushered in the mass-produced handkerchief, and its artistic design has suffered ever since.

The use of the handkerchief as an ornamental accessory died out in Europe for a time, and in France, any reference to the item was considered the height of vulgarity. But the Empress Josephine reintroduced the lace-bordered *mouchoir* among polite society, reputedly so that she could raise the hanky to her lips when she smiled and hide her imperfect teeth.

Mass-produced hankies of the late 18th and 19th centuries frequently bore illustrations, with satirical cartoons and commemorative tableaus the most popular. Other hankies were imprinted with calendars, almanacs, or railroad timetables.

Today, the handkerchief has to a great extent been superseded by the throwaway tissue. Oddly enough, at their inception, facial tissues had nothing to do with handkerchiefs and were originally manufactured as gas mask filters during World War I. Then, Kleenex was used primarily by women to remove their makeup and cold cream. Finally, it came into general use as a convenient, dispensable substitute for the handkerchief. The familiar Kleenex dispenser was invented in 1959.

In the age of the Kleenex, the handkerchief has almost disappeared from use, but as a piece of costume ornamentation, it periodically falls in and out of fashion. Most recently, it found its place neatly folded and protruding from a man's jacket pocket. Who knows? Tomorrow we may see the perfumed, fringed, and embroidered lace handkerchiefs back among the accoutrements of high fashion.

Hats

Where did you get that hat?
Where did you get that tile?
Where did you get that hat?
Is that the latest style?

It should come as no surprise that the ditty above is the product of another age—the 1890s, in fact. If there is a "latest style" of hat in contemporary America, it's no hat at all. For the first time in centuries, the hat has lost its place in the well-dressed man *and* woman's wardrobe.

That's not to say that Americans don't wear hats to keep themselves warm, or that hats of many styles are not still worn regularly by people around the world. But as a fashion requisite in the Western world, the "tile" has, at least for the time being, fallen into limbo.

Naturally, the hat was worn simply for protection from the rain, sun, and cold long before it became a fashion accessory. But the headdress has also long been a symbol of authority and position—the warrior's helmet, the bishop's mitre, the king's crown. The significance of the crown is ancient, harkening back to sun worship, for the pointed crown may have originally been a solar emblem.

The first headgear used by primitive man was probably a simple band worn around the head to keep hair from falling in front of the eyes. Ancient peoples in the Mediterranean area wore plaited straw or rushes on their heads to shield them from the sun and rain. In Egypt, ordinary workers wore caps or kerchiefs against the sun, while the wealthy often donned wigs, or curled or braided their hair with beeswax, and wore helmets ornamented with symbols of their rank.

Hats used near the headwaters of the Senegal and Gambia rivers in Africa.

Headdress of Chinese woman, Swatow 19th century.

The art of ancient Mesopotamia depicts gods and rulers with tall headdresses, and ordinary men wearing simple caps or no hats at all. By the way, the *beret*, so popular in many countries today, was actually worn in Mesopotamia thousands of years ago. Ninth-century Frankish ruler Charlemagne owned some 500 berets!

European men wore their hair long from the earliest days of recorded history until about the fifth century B.C., then wore their hair short until the end of the Roman Empire, about a thousand years later. Yet neither men nor women in ancient Rome and Greece regularly wore hats. A typical hat of the period was the *petasos*, a flat, circular hat of felt, fur, or leather, similar to the beret. Most of these hats had a band at their edge to keep the hat snuggly on the head; bits of material that protruded from under this band eventually became the hat brim.

In ancient Rome, men's hats were worn mainly by plebians, over short hair. Male slaves were forced to wear their hair long, and a freed slave was often presented with a hat when his hair was shorn. The wealthy wore hats only for hunting and travel, though the Emperor Augustus set a fashion for wearing a lid by always wearing one outdoors.

In military dress, the plumed helmet was common in many parts of the ancient world. Greek helmets often bore horsehair crests, and plumes marked the helmet of the Roman centurion and other officiers. In pre-Columbian Mexico, priests and warriors wore elaborate feather headdresses. North American Indians wore feathered war bonnets, perhaps due to earlier contacts with their southern neighbors. As late as the 18th century, military dress in Europe often featured a tall hat, perhaps ornamented with plumes, to make a soldier appear more formidable to his enemy. A familiar example is the cylindrical *shako*.

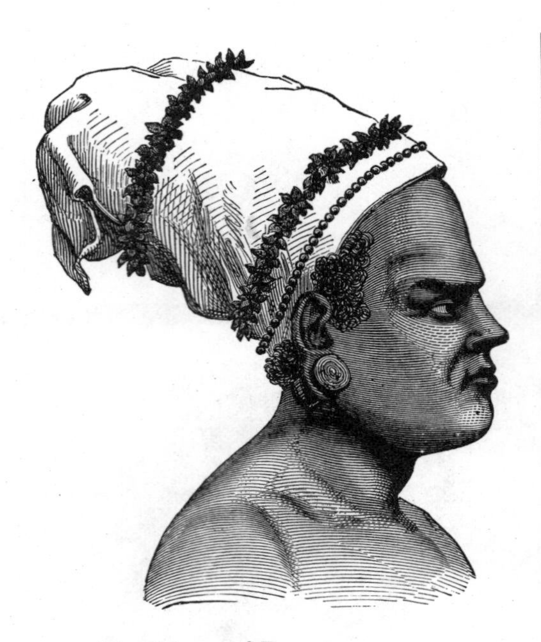

Headdress of Papuan.

The expression "a feather in your cap" was first recorded in the 17th century, but feathers in the cap were a sign of nobility more than 500 years earlier. The phrase may be related to the custom of sticking feathers in a soldier's cap to indicate the number of enemy slain.

The Teutonic tribesmen who overran the Roman Empire brought with them round hats edged with fur from the colder regions of Northern Europe. But the hat was still little worn by men and women in the early Middle Ages. Men favored hooded cloaks, while women swaddled their heads in the cloth *wimple* that completely hid their hair. The wimple may owe something to the custom of covering a woman's head in church. (The Christian man bares his head in a place of worship, but the Jewish man covers his.)

The hat remained very much a symbol of rank. Medieval students who had completed a certain portion of their studies could wear a hat to show that they were no longer subject to their master's rod. In the 13th century, Pope Innocent IV had his cardinals don the scarlet hats they wear today—the color represents the willingness to shed blood for the faith.

Only in the 14th century did the hat truly become part of fashion. Men of the time wore hats shaped like the fez, or brimmed hats remarkably similar to the top hat. The beaver hat first appeared in Flanders, and spread around Europe. Wo-

Fashionable hats of 16th-century Europe.

The most common hat in the world today is the so-called ''coolies hat'' of China, which is worn by one-third of the people on earth.

men's headgear took on fantastic shapes—the tall, conical hat with attached veil, or the "butterfly" headdress with folds of gauze raised above the head on long pins.

In the 16th century, women's hats grew lower, and men's hats regularly took on a brim. But the hat had surely lost some of its association with status; in England, there was a short-lived attempt to force all apprentices to wear wool caps, and in France, an equally abortive effort to force bankrupt merchants to wear a green hat as a warning to prospective customers.

A century later, hats became so chic that they were worn indoors as well as outdoors. Hats with big, floppy brims and feathered plumes came into fashion for men—though Puritans wore hats with stiff, round brims. Styles came and went so quickly that an exasperated King Charles II of England declared no further changes in hat fashion would be permitted at his court.

But of course, that declaration had no effect on fashion. Hats continued to grow and change, reaching the height of their vogue in the 18th century. After that, the gradual shortening of men's hair was eventually to bring in smaller, simpler headgear. One hat of the era was a tiny tricorn worn atop a wig—the smallest we have record of measured just two inches by four inches!

In 1764, a group of dapper English gentlemen formed the Macaroni club, in tribute to the Italian fashions they considered the finest in Europe. The word "macaroni" became associated with English fops in their powdered wigs and fancy hats, and

Elaborate hats, 19th century U.S.A.

found its way into that familiar American ditty, *Yankee Doodle.*

Yankee Doodle came to town
Riding on a pony
Stuck a feather in his cap
And called it macaroni.

Italy also gave us the word *millinery,* which now refers to the women's hat industry. The term originally came from *Milaner,* a resident of Milan, since many women's hats were then imported

Ninth-century Frankish ruler Charlemagne owned some 500 berets!

from that city. The term *haberdashery,* which refers to the men's hat industry, probably came from *hapertas,* a kind of cloth used for hats in England and France.

The three-cornered hat, or tricorn, was the universal men's hat in Europe for most of the 18th century. But after the French Revolution, the tricorn was abolished in France in favor of smaller, round hats. These new hats were considered so subversive in the rest of Europe that Russian Czar Paul I gave their wearers a paid vacation in Siberia.

In the 19th century, the shiny black top hat became *de rigueur* for the well-dressed gentleman.

Ladies' bonnets of the 19th century.

A ten-gallon hat, in case you've wondered, can hold about three quarts.

Scene inside a hat factory as pictured in Harper's *in the 1880s.*

Women's hats grew large and showy, with jewels and flowers for occasional ornament. King George III of England helped things along by decreeing that all hats must bear on their linings the name of their maker. By 1850, a writer could confidently declare that the hat had reached its "ultimate degree of excellence."

It may have also reached its ultimate degree of uniformity. Modern hats are made from all kinds of materials, in all kinds of styles, from all around the world—but no single style predominates. Most of the hat styles of today are from another land or another age.

For instance, you wear a bit of history when you don a fedora, a bowler hat, or a derby. The soft felt, creased *fedora* owes its name to a 1882 production of French playright Sardou's *Fedora,* in which a Russian princess wore such a hat. The *bowler* owes nothing to the kegler. It was named after William Bowler, the English hatter who, around 1850, introduced it as a hard-shelled headgear for horsemen. In the United States, the hat came to be known as the *derby,* after a famous horse race held in Derby, England.

The *shapka,* the Russian fur hat, originated in the Cossacks' sheepskin hat. Early in the 16th century, it was introduced in England by a Russian ambassador. The felt *Homburg* owes its name not to Hamburg, but to a German town called Homburg where it was first made. The *Panama* hat, made from the leaves of the jijippa plant, has never been made in Panama. Most are manufactured in Ecuador, Colombia, or Peru, but the hat originally reached America through distributors in Panama.

Another South American hat, the *chola derby*—popular among the Indians—may have originated when a bankrupt hat dealer dumped his derbies on the Indians, after other South Americans had spurned them. The Mexican *sombrero,* usually made of felt or straw, owes its name to the Spanish word *sombra,* "shade," for reasons obvious to anyone who's been south of the border. The Spanish *mantilla,* or woman's scarf, probably evolved from the Moorish headscarf.

The colorful *tam-o'-shanter* with its center tassel became popular in Scotland during the 19th century, and was named after a character in a poem by Robert Burns. It's actually a form of an old Celtic hat. The Scottish *glengarry,* creased lengthwise and ornamented with ribbons in the back, was named after a valley in Scotland. The expression "hold on to your hat" may also have originated in Scotland. In the 18th century, Scottish soldiers were exhorted to keep their hats on in battle so that they would recognize one another.

In the East, the *turban* has been the customary headgear for many centuries. The color and shape of a turban has historically indicated rank or occupation. The longest turbans may contain more than 20 feet of material. Some Hindu turbans also contained a circular metal blade that could be hurled at an enemy.

Headdress of South America near Lake Titicaca.

Indian turbans, 19th century.

Among Arabs, the common headdress is the *kaffiyeh,* a piece of cloth folded in a triangular shape and secured to the head with a round cord. Another hat from the Near East, the *fez,* was popular as long ago as the 11th century. Most fezes are made from red felt. In a 1920s attempt to Westernize Turkey, the fez was abolished as part of that country's national dress; tradition-conscious Turks who insisted on wearing the hat changed their minds after a few fez wearer's were led to the gallows.

The most common hat in the world today is the so-called "coolies hat" of China, which is worn by one-third of the people on earth. The wide-brimmed hat is made from bamboo, with leaves as padding. The oldest hat in the world may well be the familiar "chef's" hat, which was worn in ancient Assyria as a badge of office in the kitchen. And the most expensive headdress in the world is a hat worn by Napoleon, which recently sold at auction for a handsome $30,000.

French ladies' hats around 1900.

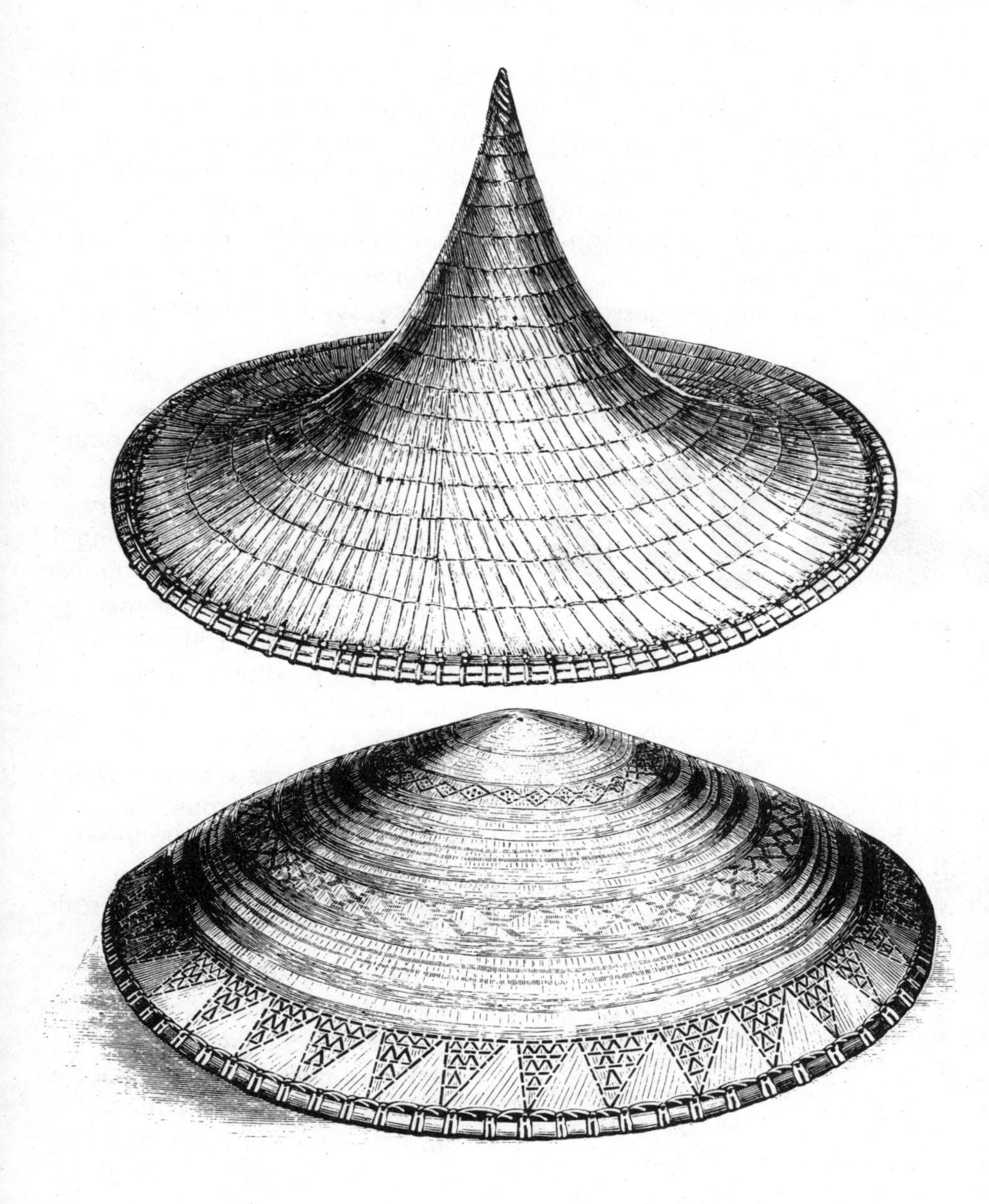

Hats of the Malay Archipelago.

The straw hat was first produced in America in 1798, by a 12-year-old girl in Rhode Island. The first hat factory in the United States, opened in Connecticut late in the 18th century, produced crude fur caps. One kind of hat that is distinctly American is the broad-brimmed ten-gallon hat still popular in the Southwest. A ten-gallon hat, in case you've wondered, can hold about three quarts.

If you're thinking of buying a ten-gallon hat in Kentucky, you might be advised that a law still on the books in that state forbids a man to buy a hat without his wife along to assist in the selection.

Who can tell if the hat will make a comeback on the American fashion scene? For hat styles, like all others, rarely remain popular for long—even if that style is no hat at all. As Shakespeare noted, "as the fashion of his hat, it ever changes."

Besides, as an old ballad points out:

Any cap, whate'er it may be
Is still the sign of some degree.

The *Panama* hat, made from the leaves of the jijippa plant, has never been made in Panama.

Ice Cream

True or false: (1) Ice cream will cool you off on a hot summer day; (2) Americans invented the dessert; (3) Since mechanical refrigeration techniques were not developed until late in the 19th century, ice cream is obviously a recent arrival to man's dessert table.

Americans presently consume over a billion gallons of ice cream, ices, and sherbet each year—enough to completely fill the Grand Canyon.

If you answered "false" to all three of the above statements, you've proved you really have the scoop on man's favorite frosty confection. In fact, three answers of TRUE would place you among the majority of Americans, who are ice-cold when it comes to the finer points of ice cream lore.

First, ice cream is not a cooler. Oh, it may cool your taste buds momentarily, and its psychological effect may convince you that you're cooling off. But ice cream is chock-full of calories, the unit of measurement of heat. So the ultimate effect of a bowlful of ice cream is to make you warmer, not cooler!

Modern American refrigeration techniques and ice cream infatuation notwithstanding, the frozen dessert is neither a recent concoction nor a product of Yankee ingenuity. Most historians would trace the first bowl of ice cream to 15th- or 16th-century Italy, or perhaps England, but the story of ice cream's rise to gustatory prominence is a good deal more interesting than a simple date.

In ancient Rome, the Emperor Nero had snow transported from nearby mountains to cool his wine cellar, and reportedly concocted some of the first water-ice desserts by mixing the snow with honey, juices, and fruit. But the first frozen dessert made from milk didn't reach Europe until the 13th century, when Marco Polo returned from the Orient with a recipe for a milk-ice, presumably similar to sherbet.

Improvements in ice- and sherbet-making probably led to the invention of ice cream some time in the 16th century. We know that early in that century Italian noblemen were enjoying a frozen milk product called "flower of milk." Yet Anglophiles may proudly point to a 15th-century manuscript reporting on the coronation of Henry V that mentions a dessert called *creme frez.* If creme frez was indeed ice cream, then the manuscript proves that the reputedly Italian invention was actually being made in England before the 16th century.

Italian ice cream arrived in France in 1533, along with Catherine de Medici and her retinue of chefs, when the 14- year-old Florentine moved to Paris to marry King Henry II. For many years, the chefs of various French noblemen tried to keep their recipes for ice cream a secret from other chefs—and from their masters, who were frequently astounded by their cooks' talent for serving a cold dessert even in the warmest weather.

Ice cream remained a treat for the rich and regal until 1670, when Paris's first café, the *Procope,* opened its doors and made the frigid dessert available to the masses for the first time. Other cafés quickly followed— including the *Café Napolitain,* whose proprietor, a Monsieur Tortoni, concocted the creamy delight that still bears his name.

The first mention of ice cream in America occurs in 1700, but the dessert was not made here in any quantity until much later in the century. Both George Washington and Thomas Jefferson were known to be ice cream fanciers. Jefferson, who had learned how to make French ice cream during a visit to France, was one of the first officials to serve the confection at a state dinner. Jefferson once served a dessert of crisp, hot pastry with ice cream in the middle, perhaps the first ice cream sandwich in America.

Ice cream remained an expensive dish until the early 19th century, which saw the invention of the insulated icehouse and the hand-crank ice cream freezer. By the 1820s, the dessert was being sold by street vendors in New York City, who beckoned passersby with shouts of "I scream ice cream."

By the middle of the century, ice cream was so popular that a magazine editor was moved to write: "A party without ice cream would be like a breakfast without bread or a dinner without a roast."

The father of the American ice cream industry was Jacob Fussell. Beginning in 1851 with a small ice cream store in Baltimore, Fussell was soon selling his wares in shops from Boston to Washington. During the Civil War, Fussell sold huge quantities of ice cream to the Union army. By the end of the century, ice cream could be bought almost anywhere in the nation. New inventions such as steam power, mechanical refrigeration, electricity, and the homogenizer made the ice cream plant virtually as modern as it is today.

In the early decades of this century, the popularity of the soda fountain made ice cream an American institution. Temperance preachers urged listeners to give up the grape in favor of the cool confection. Baseball star Walter Johnson—no relation to Howard—boasted that all he ever ate on the day he was to pitch was a quart of ice cream.

Beginning in 1921, officials at the Ellis Island immigration station in New York, intent on serving the newcomers a "truly American dish," included ice cream in all meals served at the station.

By that time, the three mainstays of the ice cream parlor—the soda, the sundae, and the cone—were already popular from coast to coast. The first to appear was the ice cream soda. In 1874, a soda-fountain manufacturer by the name of Robert M. Green was busily vending a cool drink made of sweet cream, syrup, and carbonated water (now known as the egg cream) at the semicentennial celebration of Philadelphia's Franklin Institute. One day, Green ran out of cream and substituted vanilla ice cream. The new treat quickly became a sensation. Green went on to make a fortune selling ice cream sodas. His will dictated that "Originator

Ice cream freezer, circa 1870.

The American Cream Freezer.

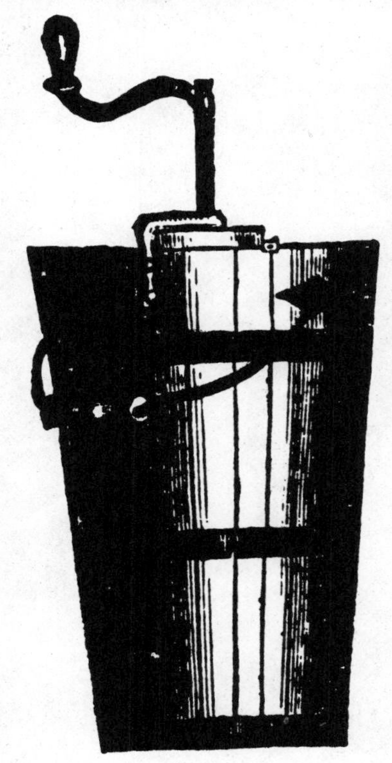

This Freezer possesses all the essentials necessary to freeze cream perfectly. It agitates the ice, scrapes the cream from the sides of Cylinder, mixes and beats it all at the same time, by simply turning the crank. Warranted to freeze cream in as brief a time as any other in the market.

Send for Circulars to

Fraser, Bell & Loughran,
51 Cliff Street,
New York,
Manufacturers.

of the Ice Cream Soda" be engraved on his tombstone.

The ice cream sundae emerged during the 1890s, and there are many claims for its invention. Contemperary laws forbade the sale of soda on Sunday, and this, undoubtedly, had a hand in popularizing the dessert. The first sundaes were sold in ice cream parlors only on Sunday, and thus were called "Sundays" or "soda-less sodas." The spelling change to "sundae" was made later by ice cream parlor proprietors eager to see the dish shed its Sunday-only connotation.

The best-known explanation for the invention of the ice cream cone traces its origin to the 1904 Louisiana Purchase Exposition in St. Louis. According to the tale, an ice cream salesman by the name of Charles E. Menches gave an ice cream sandwich and a bouquet of flowers to the young lady he was escorting. She rolled one of the sandwich wafers into a cone to hold the flowers, then rolled the other wafer into a cone for the ice cream.

Ice cream parlors were an integral part of American life early in the 20th century. In these emporia, busy soda jerks developed a lingo all their own. *Adam's ale,* for instance, was water, while *belch water* meant seltzer. *A pair of drawers* could mean only two cups of coffee.

Fortunes were made in the ice cream trade during the heyday of the soda fountain. Louis Sherry, a Frenchman from Vermont, began his career as a famed restauranteur when he was granted the ice cream concession at the Metropolitan Opera House in New York.

In 1925, Howard Johnson—the father of American franchisers—opened his first ice cream store in Wollaston, Massachusetts. Johnson, incidentally, once sold 14,000 ice cream cones in a single day at his Wollaston Beach stand.

In 1921, the *Eskimo pie* was introduced in Des Moines, Iowa, by the same Russell Stover who was to go on to fame and fortune in the candy trade. The *Good Humor,* meanwhile, was the handiwork of one Harry Burt, and ice cream parlor owner from Youngstown, Ohio. Before starting out in the ice cream business, Burt had sold a lollypop he called the *Good Humor Sucker.* The

In 1898, the first Schrafft's Ice Cream and Candy Shop was opened on Broadway in New York City.

Photo courtesy of Schrafft's Ice Cream Co., Ltd.

"Peaches and Cream" was the title of this drawing by illustrator James Montgomery Flagg.

bright idea to mount a chocolate-covered Eskimo pie on a lollypop stick led to ice-cream-on-a-stick, and the familiar white wagons that still ply our streets with their tinkling bells. Good Humor bars are now sold in most supermarkets as well.

Today, the manufacture of ice cream is, of course, mechanized. Factories first produce a liquid product made of 80 percent cream or butterfat, milk, and nonfat milk solids, and about 15 percent sweeteners. Next they pasteurize, homogenize, whip, and partially freeze the mixture. Then flavoring is added, and they freeze the product in its containers at temperatures of about 240 degrees below zero. The finished product is frequently as rich in vitamins as an equivalent amount of milk.

Frozen mousse is a cold dessert made from sweetened whipped cream, flavoring, and gelatin. *Sherbet* consists of milk, sweeteners, and fruit flavoring, while *Italian Ices* is made from fruit juices, water, and sweeteners. *French ice cream* is definitely different from other varieties: in this country, only ice cream made with eggs can legally be sold as "French."

The quality of ice cream products differs greatly from brand to brand, due to such factors as the amount of fresh milk, cream, or eggs used, the naturalness of the flavoring ingredients, and the presence of preservatives and synthetic flavor and texture enhancers.

Americans presently consume over a billion gallons of ice cream, ices, and sherbet each year—enough to completely fill the Grand Canyon. Americans are by far the world's largest consumers of ice cream. The average person in the United States puts away about 23 quarts each year—that's roughly equivalent to a cone per person every other day. Only Australians, Canadians, and New Zealanders eat even half that much. Compare that figure with the average yearly consumption of 100 years ago—about one teaspoon per person!

Only in America, then, could you expect to find the largest ice cream sundae of all time. The 3,956-pound monster, concocted in McLean, Virginia in 1975, contained 777 gallons of ice cream, six gallons of chocolate syrup, over a gallon of whipped cream, and a case of chocolate

"The Soda Fountain" by William Glackens.
Courtesy of the Pennsylvania Academy of Fine Arts.

sprinkles. The world's largest popsicle, meanwhile, was a paltry 2,800 pounds.

The largest banana split ever thrown together—measured one mile in length and contained 33,000 scoops of ice cream and over 10,000 bananas! This whopper was the pride and joy of a St. Paul, Minnesota ice cream parlor.

Most ice cream stores today point with pride, not to the size of their wares, but to the sheer length of their flavor list. The Baskin Robbins company lists over 300 flavors in its repertoire, and the number is still climbing—though you'll have a tough time finding half that many in any one store. The winner of the Baskin Robbins America's Favorite Flavor Contest, by the way, was Chocolate Mint ice cream.

The modern ice cream maker will go to any length to outdo the competition with bizarre new taste treats, and novelty flavors such as *iced tea, bubblegum, root beer,* and *mango* ice cream. The newcomers occasionally outsell the old standbys—*vanilla* and *chocolate*.

But don't think that exotic flavors belong solely to the modern ice cream maker. A recipe book dating from 1700 shows that even at that date, French confectioners were turning out such tempting ice cream flavors as *apricot, violet,* and *rose!*

These are just a few of the ice cream concoctions offered by The Flick Ice Cream Parlor *in New York City in 1978.*

PARTIAL MENU OF "THE FLICK"

SUNDAES

Large Sundae / $2.25
Your choice of 2 flavors ice cream, topping, nuts, whipped cream and cherry

Extra-Large Sundae / $3.95
4 scoops ice cream, topping, nuts, whipped cream and cherry

Gibson Girl / $3.95
4 scoops mixed ice cream, butterscotch sauce, wet walnuts, whipped cream and burgundy cherry

A Sherbet Delight / $3.95
Fresh fruit topped with Flick orange and lemon sherbet

Fresh Fruit Flick Delight / $3.95
Giant bowl of fresh fruit, your choice of 2 flavors of ice cream, whipped cream and cherry

Flaming Desire / $3.95
4 scoops of ice cream of your choice, topping, whipped cream and burgundy cherry. Set aflame and served to delight you

Mission Impossible / $4.25
Egg nog, rum raisin and burgundy cherry ice cream topped with hot fudge, marshmallow, butterscotch, crushed pineapple, whipped cream and cherry

Virgin's Delight / $3.95
Vanilla, cherry-vanilla, and cocoanut ice cream with a blanket of marshmallow sauce, whipped cream and red cherry

Lobsters

Soft-hearted cooks have long bemoaned the fact that the preparation of fresh lobster demanded boiling the innocent critter alive. More than one diner has shown a reluctance to partake of a dish that just an hour or so before may have been crawling, quite alive, across the kitchen floor. Modern science and culinary art still have not devised a better method of putting the dinner-to-be to rest. But tests have shown that there is a more humane way to dispose of the lobster—and improve its taste in the bargain.

The tests compared the lobster's reactions to two different methods of cooking. In the first case, the shellfish was plunged alive into boiling water. In the second, it was submerged in cold water that was then slowly brought to a boil. The lobster plunged rudely into boiling water perished within 58 seconds, squeaking and moving about in the pot in apparent pain. But the second lobster remained quite passive as the water heated up, eventually swooning and passing on gracefully—without squeaking. The tests are of interest to the diner as well as the lobster, for lobsters boiled slowly were found to have tenderer, tastier flesh than those put to a speedy death.

Diners with a squeamish bent may refuse to partake of lobsters for another reason: the lobster and related shellfish are, in a manner of speaking, "insects of the sea." Lobsters are arthropods, a group which includes the insects, and crustaceans, a class that also includes shrimps and crabs. Crustaceans, like insects, have a horny exoskeleton, jointed appendages, and segmented bodies. In short, if a lobster a half-inch long were crawling across your wall, you'd probably swat it.

Lobsters live on the rocky bottom of shallow sea waters. They can usually be found at a depth of about 120 feet, but lobsters have been found at depths up to 1,350 feet. For the most part, they are sedentary creatures, swimming only in an emergency or at night, when they seek the small shellfish that form their diet. A hardy specimen can live as long as 50 years—but thanks to hungry diners, few ever get the chance.

Lobsters are so small at birth that hundreds can fit in the palm of a hand. As the creature grows, it must continually shed its shell and replace it with a new one to fit the enlarging body. Young male lobsters molt twice a year, young females once every two years, while a mature specimen will shed its shell once every three or four years. After molting, the lobster will remain unprotected for months until its new shell has formed, during which time the defenseless lobster must, indeed, "lay low."

After about eight years, the lobster reaches full adulthood, usually measuring from 12 to 14 inches in length and rarely weighing more than 10 pounds. The largest lobster on record measured three feet from mouth to tail, and tipped the scales at 42 pounds! The giant crustacean is now on exhibit at the Museum of Science in Boston. There have also been unverified claims of lobsters four feet long caught off the coast of New Jersey, and of a 48-pounder and a 60-pounder caught off New England.

Before your mouth begins watering, we might point out that large lobsters are not very palatable, for their flesh grows quite tough as they age.

Like their insect cousins, crustaceans are well equipped with legs. The lobster has five pairs of legs, the first three equipped with pincers. Each of the lobster's pairs of legs serves a different function. One grasps food, another crushes it, another passes it to the mouth, another flaps to provide a current to aid in respiration.

"As red as a lobster" may be a cliché, but uncooked lobsters are actually dark blue or green in color. The shell turns red or orange only when boiled, as English writer Samuel Butler noted:

And like a lobster boiled, the morn
From black to red began to turn.

In America, we are apt to apply the word *lobster* to a number of different crustaceans. The French are more precise in their terminology, as they usually are in most matters gustatorial. If you discover *langouste* on the menu of a French restaurant, then find the word translated as "lobster" in your pocket dictionary, you're in for a surprise when the dish arrives. *Langouste* is the French word for the sea crawfish, or rock lobster, and not the crustacean we commonly enjoy in America. But the sea crawfish, which is smaller than the lobster and lacks claws, is preferred by most Frenchmen to the true lobster.

Langoustine, meanwhile, is the French word for the large prawn often used in the Italian dish *Scampi. Ecrevisse* refers to the crayfish, or freshwater lobster, which is often referred to simply as a lobster in this country. Actually, the crayfish is a small shellfish found in the muddy banks of rivers in many parts of the world. Then how do you say "lobster" in French? Only the word *homard* refers to the creature we commonly know as the lobster.

"Rock lobster tails" found in the frozen foods compartment of many supermarkets are actually the tails of sea crawfish. Rock lobster has become popular in this country only within the past 40 years. In 1936, a South African firm could not sell a 1,000-pound shipment of sea crawfish here. Ten years later, South African fishermen could barely satisfy the American demand. About 10 million pounds of South African rock lobster tails are now imported here each year.

Lobsters have been eaten for thousands of years by people on both sides of the Atlantic, including the Mayans of Central America. Lobsters were once so plentiful near Plymouth, Massachusetts, and other parts of New England that they were gathered for use as fertilizer when washed ashore during a storm.

Massachusetts provided the bulk of the lobster catch in this country until 1840, when lobstermen began fishing the waters off Maine in great numbers. By 1880, over two million pounds of Maine lobster was being canned each year. The state of Maine now accounts for about 25 million pounds of lobster yearly, although the term "Maine lobster" is also applied to much of the shellfish caught off the Maritime Provinces of Canada. Much of the Canadian catch ends up in the United States which imports over 20 million pounds each year.

Initially, lobstermen used hooked staffs to snare their prey from the sea bottom. Later, they lowered nets to the sea bottom, raising them every so often to see if a lobster had clambered aboard for the small piece of bait inside the net. Now, lobstermen use pots, called *creels,* baited with dried herring or cod. The lobster slips through a funnel-shaped opening for the bait, but cannot escape through the opening without entangling in the net. The lobstermen merely pull up their creels in the morning to count their catch.

The shellfish then end up on dinner plates in a number of different guises. Lobsters may be baked, boiled, or broiled, served au gratin, devilled, creamed, scalloped, or stuffed with crab meat. Lobster meat makes excellent salads, omelets, and croquettes, as well as a creamy soup called lobster bisque. But boiled or broiled lobster served with drawn butter is by far the favorite in this country.

Drawn butter, by the way, is not simply melted butter. Melted butter is prepared over a flame, drawn butter melted over hot water. Drawn butter can not burn.

No matter what the dish, lobsters must be cooked alive for full flavor. If killed first and placed in boiling water later, they will be decidedly inferior in flavor and tenderness. But what about ready-boiled lobsters? There's a simple way of finding out if the ready-boiled lobster you're looking at was cooked dead or alive. Just straighten the critter's tail

Lobstering in Maine, according to a print which appeared during the late 1800s in Harper's.

The largest lobster on record measured three feet from mouth to tail, and tipped the scales at 42 pounds!

and release it. If the tail springs back quickly, the lobster was probably boiled alive. If it sags back—well, good luck.

If you buy your lobsters live, you can store them together in the same tank without fear they'll attack one another. But if one of the lobsters is injured—missing a claw, for instance—the healthy lobsters are likely to destroy it immediately. Which brings to mind the old joke about the diner who was served a lobster with only one claw.

"I'm sorry, sir," the chef explained to the complaining diner, "but it must have been in a fight."

"Then take it back," the diner replied, "and bring me the winner."

If you live far from the seashore, you can still buy live lobsters. A Maine firm will ship you 10 one-pound-plus lobsters, live, for about $50.

Once you've received your mail-order lobsters, you might try your hand at two of the more elaborate lobster dishes, *Homard a l'Américaine* and *Lobster Newburgh.* Some French chefs will tell you that Homard à l'Américaine owes its name, quite simply, to the dish's American origin. But other chefs contend that the dish was invented by a French chef from Nice, who substituted lobster for crayfish in a dish made with tomatoes and white wine. Still others insist that *Américaine* is a corruption of *Armoriquaine*, from *Armorica*, the ancient Roman name for a part of Brittany where the dish was first prepared.

Lobster Newburgh, on the other hand, is definitely an American invention. During the mid-19th century, a regular diner at the famous New York restaurant, Delmonico's, told the proprietor of a dish made with lobster and cream that he'd enjoyed in South America. The next night, the diner was presented with a lobster cooked in a chafing dish with sherry, thick cream, and egg yolks. The invention was promptly installed on Delmonico's menu, christened Lobster Wenburg—after the diner, a shipping magnate.

But fame is indeed short-lived. Loster Wenburg remained on Delmonico's menu until the night its namesake became embroiled in a drunken brawl that ravaged the restaurant. Wenburg was ejected from the restaurant, and from the menu as well—Lobster Wenburg became Lobster Newburgh forevermore.

Getting ready for summer lobster fishing at New Harbor, Maine.

LOCKS

Along with the many other advances that have paralleled the evolution of civilization, the progress of man's history has seen a continual improvement of the resourcefulness of two professionals: the locksmith and the burglar. Almost every advance in the locksmith's craft has been matched by a corresponding refinement in the trade of those who covet their neighbor's goods—or vice versa, depending on your point of view.

And the battle of wits between the locksmith and the burglar is far from over: though the former might maintain that many a modern lock is foolproof, and many a haven totally safe, every year burglaries abound.

The use of a lock of some sort probably dates from the time man first acquired goods he wanted to safeguard. But the use of locks among ancient peoples was limited, for a number of reasons.

First of all, most families had few valuables to guard, and had little reason to leave their home untended for any length of time. Most ancient peoples lived in small communities of friends and relatives, where theft was easily detectable and swiftly punished. Since most homes were one-story, and windows lacked glass, a locked door would accomplish little in deterring a determined thief. Even if a strong lock could be attached to a door, the door itself was often so flimsy that it could be battered down easily, whether locked or not.

Early locks were used mainly by the rich, or by officials to prevent unauthorized entry of a temple or government building. From earliest times right up until today, the essential element of most locks is the *bolt,* the metal or wooden bar that fixes the door to the doorpost and prevents the door from opening. All advances in the locksmith's craft have been primarily in strengthening that bolt, and improving the mechanism that opens and closes it.

The oldest surviving locks were found in the ruined palace of Khorsabad, built by the Assyrians in the eighth century B.C. But locks of similar design were used by the Egyptians more than 4,000 years ago, and may be much older, for their counterparts have been found in places far from the Middle East, among them Norway and Japan. This Egyptian lock was simple in design, and made entirely of wood, but was in principle remarkably similar to the pin tumbler locks we rely on today.

The Egyptian lock consisted of a vertical wooden bar, or *staple,* affixed to the doorpost, and a wooden crossbar, or bolt. The bolt fit into a groove in the staple to lock the door. Pins pro-

The simplest of all true locks.

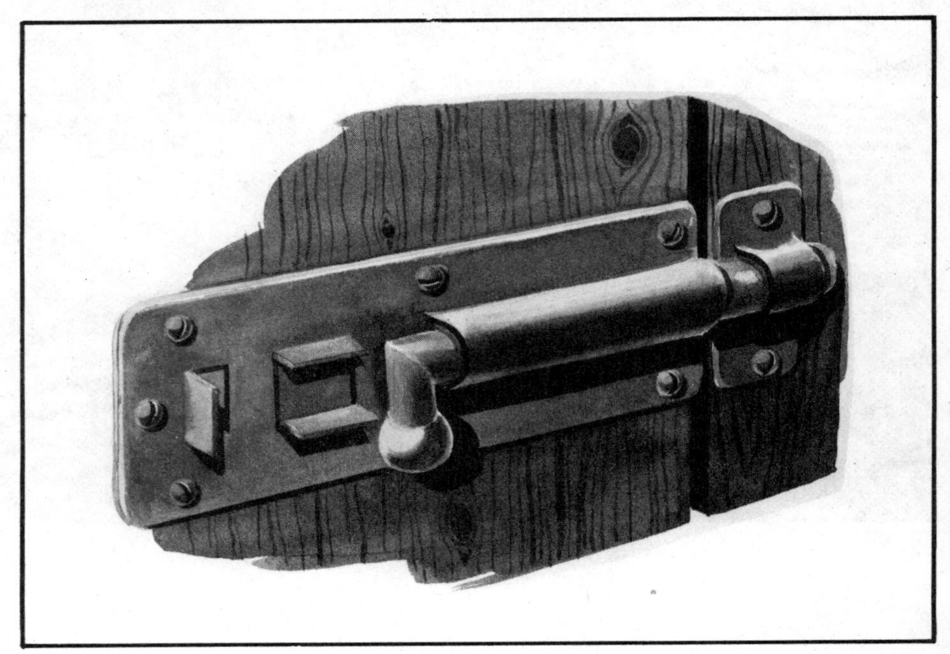

The key to an ancient Egyptian lock and an X-ray picture of an Egyptian lock with the key inside it.

jecting downward from the staple fit into holes in the bolt, and held it firmly in place.

To open the lock, the Egyptians used a huge wooden key, shaped like a toothbrush with a set of wooden pegs in place of bristles. These pegs corresponded to the pegs of the staple. The key was inserted through a hole in the bolt; when the key was levered upward, its pins passed through the matching holes in the bolt and pushed the staple's pins upward and out of the holes, thereby freeing the bolt.

In the homes of the anicent Greeks, as in those of the earlier Mesopotamian peoples, doors and windows usually faced inward on an open courtyard, with only one outer door providing access from the street. To protect this door from would-be thieves, the Greeks designed locks that were intended more for the detection of thievery than for its prevention. One lock of this type consisted of a bolt that was tied to the doorpost with a rope in an intricate knot. A thief could never hope to untie the knot and retie it in exactly the same way, so the owner would always know when the lock had been tampered with.

And in those days, discovery meant certain death to the culprit.

Another type of Greek lock utilized a key the size and shape of a sickle, and featured the first known use of the keyhole. The hooked key was inserted through a hole in the door so that the end of the hook fit into a groove in the bolt. A simple twist of the key's handle would turn the hooked end and slide open the bolt. The heavy key, which was up to three feet long, had the added advantage of doubling as weapon.

The Romans were the first to use a metal lock, fabricating the key from bronze and the locking mechanism from iron. The iron has long since disintegrated, leaving us only the keys. Roman keys were sometimes cut with *wards,* notches that align with corresponding ridges inside the lock. In the days before the pocket, the Romans also invented ring keys that could be carried on the finger. Many Romans used the older Egyptian-style wooden locks; these ancient devices are still in use today in some parts of the Middle East. Duplicate Roman keys, by the way, were called "adulterous," probably for more than one reason.

The Romans, along with the Hindus, Chinese, and others, developed the earliest portable lock, or *padlock.* Many padlocks were adorned with elaborate designs of animals and geometric figures, and inlaid with precious metals. The word "padlock" has been linked to the footpad, or highwayman, whose sticky fingers might delve into an untended saddlebag. But the word probably comes directly from *pad,* a Dutch word for a path or road, since the padlock was most often used to safeguard goods while traveling.

In medieval Europe, the doors of most peasant huts were secured by a simple latch that could be opened by sliding a finger or lever through a hole in the door. These latches might secure a door against the wind, but were no proof against thievery. Medieval castles relied more on the brute strength of their locks than on their complexity. The main gates of most castles were secured by a huge wooden latch that required several men to set in place and remove. In many castles, it was easier to scale the walls than to batter down the doors.

Inside the castle, the door to almost every room was fitted with a lock, as were many chests and strongboxes. So, a special attendant was required to guard all the keys—including those to the dun-

The latch on these great doors is a huge hand-hewn plank, weighing hundreds of pounds.

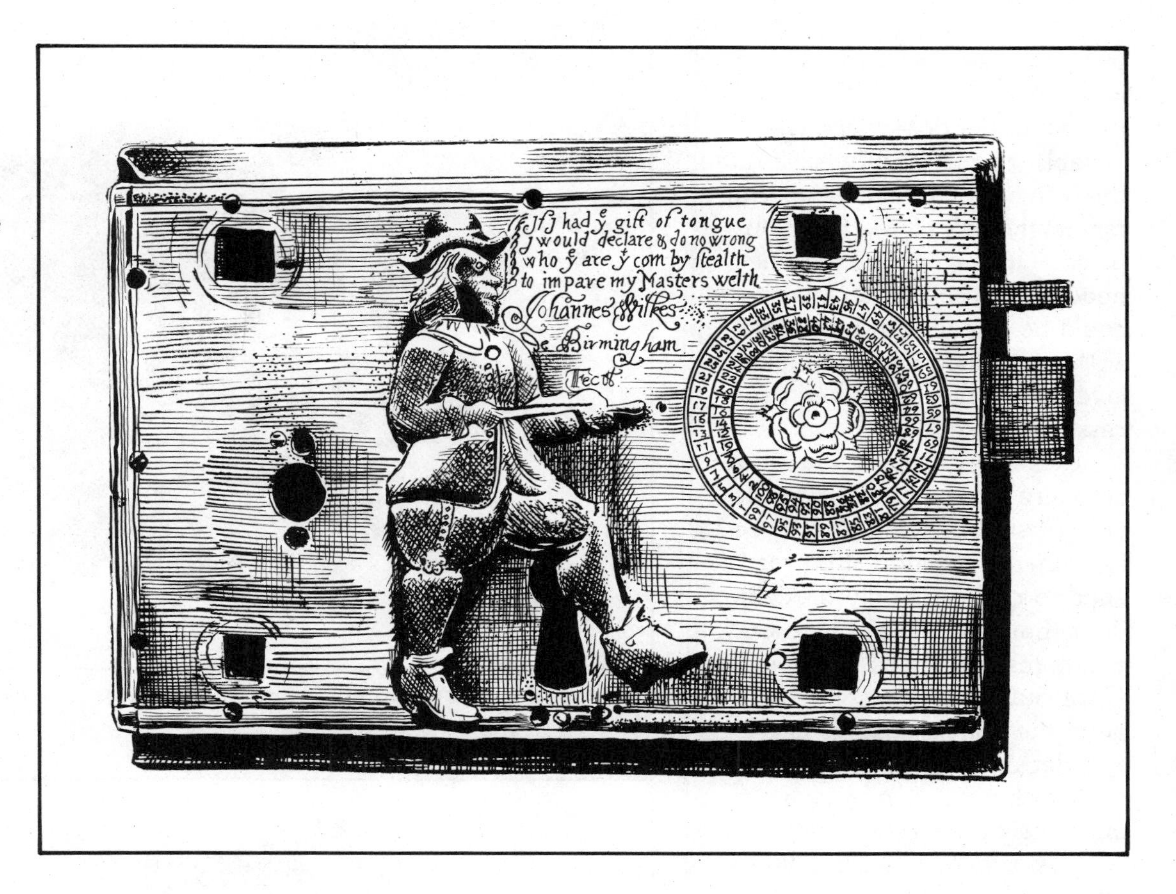

The sign on this lock reads:

"If I had the gift of tongue / I would declare and do no wrong / Who they are that come by stealth / To impare my master's wealth."

geon. This attendant was called the "keeper of the castle" or *chatelain*. The feminine form of the word, *chatelaine*, is still used for a woman's ornamental chain, especially one worn around the waist.

Locks of the Middle Ages and Renaissance often offered more in the way of decorative beauty than security. Most locks employed intricately designed keyways and obstructions around the keyhole to prevent opening with a pick or false key. Since these locks were often undependable, some featured other discouragements to unauthorized opening: sharp blades inside the keyhole, bullet-firing mechanisms activated by the opening bolts, or knives that sprang toward an intruder. From the East came the puzzle lock, with hidden keyholes and buttons to foil the thief. Other locks were fitted with counters that recorded the number of times the lock had been opened. Such a lock couldn't prevent a burglary, but would indicate readily enough if one had been attempted or committed.

English King Henry VIII included a massive gold-plated lock among his traveling baggage. Whenever the wary monarch stopped for the night, he had a carpenter screw the lock to his bedroom door. In the morning, the lock was removed. The king's precautions evidently paid off: his bedroom remained inviolate and he died at the age of 56 from "a surfeit of quinces."

The history of the modern lock began in the 18th century with the invention of the lever tumbler, which made the lock-picker's work much more difficult. With a lever tumbler lock, the key disengages one or more spring-actuated safety devices that fit into notches in the bolt. Still, burglars kept pace with their gimlets, hacksaws, drills, pass-keys, and picks. And too often, they succeeded.

In 1817, British authorities were so fed up with thievery at the Portsmouth Dockyard that they offered a sizeable cash prize to anyone who could invent a cheap unpickable lock. The winning design was the work of one Jeremiah Chubb. To test Chubb's lock, the government presented it to an imprisoned locksmith and lock-picker, and offered him a pardon if he succeeded in opening the lock. After 10 weeks of effort, the convict had to admit defeat.

Chubb's lock employed six control levers that had to be raised to an exact height by the key. The lock was considered

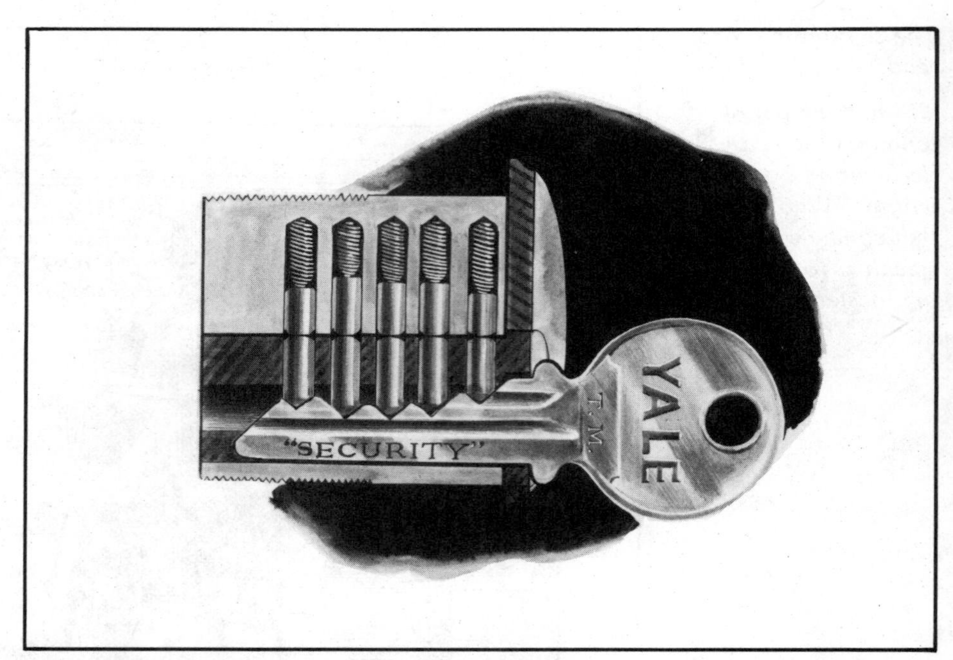

Compare this modern tumbler lock with the large lock used in ancient Egypt.

To open up this padlock, you must line up the four code letters properly.

pickproof because if one of the levers was raised too far by a thief's tampering—which was inevitable no matter how skillful the thief—a set of springs would immediately lock all the levers in place. The key would then be needed to reset the lock before it could be opened. In more than 150 years since Chubb's lock was invented, it has never been successfully picked!

Evidently, not all locks of the era were fitted with Chubb's device. A skilled lock-picker jailed in London's Newgate Prison managed to open not only his cell door, but four additional doors and gates that led to freedom. Once outside the prison, however, the convict lost his nerve and decided to return to his cell—picking all five locks a second time on his return trip!

The first lock and key that we would recognize as modern was the work of the American Linus Yale—whose name is still to be found on keys. Invented in 1861, the device was called the pin tumbler cylinder lock, or more simply, the cylinder lock. It consisted of a cylinder with an attached bar that passed through a hole in the door and activated a bolt on the inside. The cylinder itself consisted of two cylinders, one inside the other. Pins of various lengths in the outer cylinder fit into holes in the inner cylinder, preventing it from turning.

The key for a cylinder lock was cut with ridges that lifted the pins out of their holes, and allowed the inner cylinder to turn and thereby open the bolt. By varying the lengths of the pins, and the corresponding heights of the key ridges, over 36,000 variations could be obtained. In other words, only one key in every 36,000 was identical!

Linus Yale was also credited with reintroducing the combination lock, which had been used in China for many centuries. The older combination lock consisted of a series of numbered or lettered rings revolving around a bolt. Openings within the rings had to be aligned perfectly by the "combination" before the bolt could be withdrawn. But burglars developed a skill for opening these locks with a delicate touch and a sensitive ear. In 1947, Harry C. Miller invented a combination lock that was considered manipulation-proof. In the modern combination lock, revolving wheels are hidden inside the lock, and turned by a single outer wheel marked with numbers or letters.

Modern locks are basically of six kinds. The *rim* lock fits directly on the surfact of the door, with the bolt on the inside and the keyhole on the outside. The modern drop-bolt lock is one example.

The *mortise* lock fits into a cavity within the door, and its bolt slides into an opening in the door frame.

The *key-in-doorknob* lock features, not surprisingly, a keyhole set in the doorknob.

A *cabinet* lock is the kind of simple lock often fitted on cabinet doors or jewelry boxes.

An *electric switch* lock completes an electric circuit when the key is turned; an automobile ignition cylinder is one example. And a *padlock* is familiar to almost anyone who's owned a bicycle or utilized a locker room. The largest padlock in existence, by the way, is manufactured by an English firm, and weighs 100 pounds!

Burglars have shown an equal disregard for all six types of lock, forcing locksmiths to design a number of other kinds for places where security is paramount. Safe-deposit boxes in banks are protected by a lock that requires two keys, one provided to the box holder and the other kept by a security guard. Similar in principle is the master key lock, which employs a separate set of pin tumblers that can be opened by a master key. This kind of lock is often used in hotels, where a chambermaid needs access to a room when the occupant is out.

Banks, naturally, employ the most sophisticated locking mechanisms. The doors of some bank vaults are actually huge locks, equipped with a number of combination dials that must each be opened by a different person. The odds against guessing the correct combination of just one dial are about 100 million to one. And if you're thinking about lifting one of these vault doors off its hinges, you might keep in mind that such a door may weigh 20 tons!

This streamlined padlock and bar offer no starting place for a burglar's tools.

In 1874, the first *time* lock was installed on the vault of a bank in Morrison, Illinois, and time locks have been widely used in banks ever since. A time lock is fitted with a series of watch movements, and will open only at a predetermined time—no matter how dire the threats of a would-be bank robber and how shaky the knees of the bank employees.

Still, the burglar has not admitted defeat. If the lock of a vault or safe is foolproof, there's always the option of blowing the door away with explosives, or using an acetylene torch to remove the entire locking mechanism. Locksmiths and safe manufacturers have responded by building safes encased in a metal alloy that can resist even the flame of an acetylene torch!

But few of us can afford the kind of locks used by banks, jewelry stops, and other storehouses of valuables. So most people have decided, like their Greek forefathers, that detection is as good as prevention: more money is now being spent on burglar alarms than on locks.

Fortunately, the best lockpicker in history was not a burglar, but a magician. Harry Houdini, the renowned escape artist, sometimes had himself bound in chains and manacles, placed inside a locked chest, and dropped into water. But he always managed to unfasten the chains and manacles, open the box, and emerge smiling. No locksmith who examined Houdini's equipment ever claimed that the magician used trick locks. To this day, no one knows how Houdini opened his locks, and no one likely ever will.

If nothing else, Houdini proved that, no matter the circumstances, no matter the lock, anything that can be locked with a key can be opened without one.

MONEY

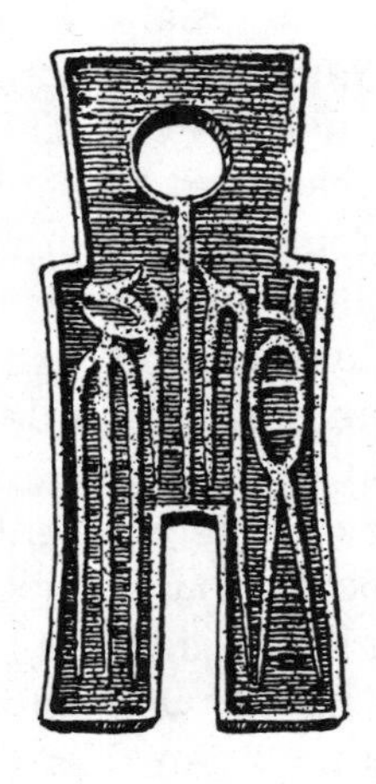

Cloth money served as legal tender in ancient times in the Orient.

The Aboo Bekr *was an ancient Egyptian coin.*

An old fable tells of a miser who buried his gold in the forest. Each day, he crept into the woods, dug up the trove, counted his coins, and buried them again. But one day, another man spied him counting his gold, and returned that night to steal it. The next morning, the miser discovered that he had lost everything.

A friend tried to comfort him. "Take a pile of stones and bury them in the hole," he suggested, "and make believe the gold is still there, for when it was, you did not make the slightest use of it."

The fable cleverly points up the real nature of money. Coins and bills are almost worthless in themselves. Their only worth is the value in acquiring other things. The long history of money has actually been a steady movement away from the immediately useful toward the symbolically valuable. That movement is continuing.

One writer has termed money "the poor man's credit card," for the well-to-do have the luxury of receiving their income by check, depositing it, purchasing items and services with credit cards, and then paying their credit card bills by check, perhaps without ever laying eyes on a dime of cold cash! The movement of wealth, which once dealt solely in the transfer of land, animals, or metal, has become largely a simple movement of paper.

Until the seventh or eighth century B.C., money per se did not exist. Early man's commerce was built on the barter system, involving a simple exchange of goods. A craftsman, for instance, might trade a tanned hide or a carved icon for a supply of grain or milk. But the barter system presented a number of problems. First of all, a successful barter deal depended upon a double coincidence: the man who needed the hide had to have a supply of grain to spare, and the man who tanned the hide had to need and want the grain. Many bartered goods were not partitionable; for example, a man making a coat in the hope of receiving two bushels of wheat could not trade half a coat for one bushel.

In a limited way, the barter system has continued right into the present day. A servant or laborer will often accept food and lodging in partial payment for his services, and sharecropping farmers trade in a portion of their crop for the use of the land they till. But standards and mediums of exchange began to appear well before recorded history.

> *He was subject to a kind of disease which at that time they called lack of money.*
> —Francois Rabelais

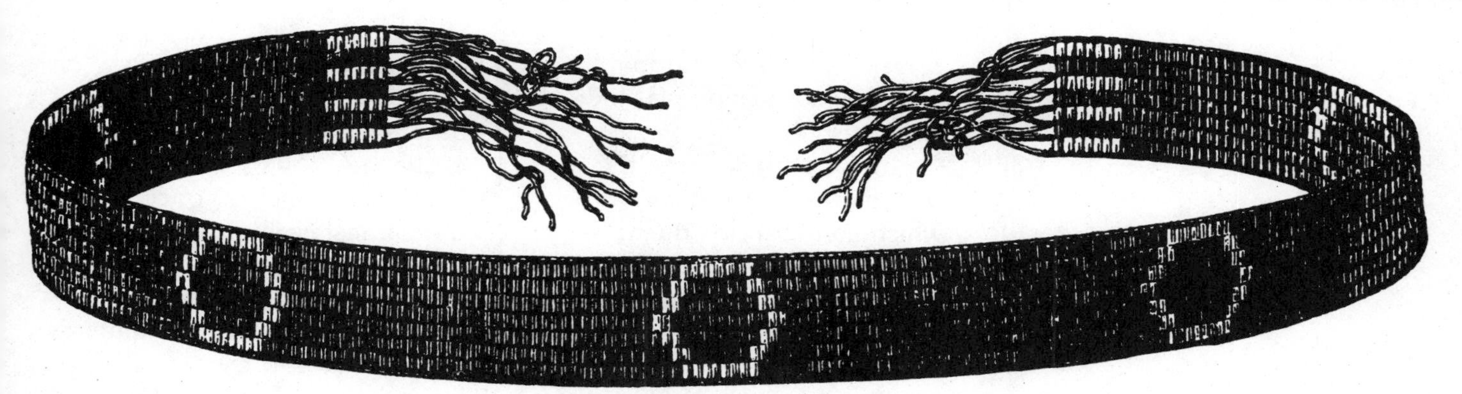

The Onondaga Indians used wampum belts for money.

Among early hunters, tanned hides were useful as a medium of exchange, for everyone could put the hides to use for clothing—and hides, unlike grain or meat, would keep almost indefinitely.

Leather money was used in Russia right up until the 17th century, as was tea money in China. Hundreds of other items have served for a time as legal tender, including slaves, tobacco, gunpowder, pig jawbones, and glass beads. Manhattan Island, you recall, was bartered for 24 dollars worth of glass trinkets. Salt once passed for specie in Ethiopia, and skulls were hard cash in Borneo.

In Western cultures, cattle became a favored standard of exchange at a very early date, since cattle, to a great extent, already formed the basis of wealth. Cattle were generally owned by rich and poor alike; land, only by the aristocracy. Our words *capital* and *chattel* come from "cattle," or rather from "head of cattle," based on the Latin *caput,* "head."

You might conjure up the image of a shopper walking to the store with four head of cattle shuffling behind him as his "pocketbook." But cattle were used more as a *standard* of exchange than as a *medium* of exchange. The value of bartered goods was determined by relating their worth to cattle; most often the cattle themselves did not serve as money. In our modern monetary system, coins and bills are the *mediums* of exchange, and gold, at least until recently, the *standard* of exchange.

But even as a standard of exchange, cattle presented problems, for one steer might be well fed and another scrawny. As actual items of exchange, cattle required upkeep—although they had the happy advantage of occasionally multiplying. The use of metals, then, certainly offered a number of advantages. First of all, metal required neither upkeep nor extensive storage space, and precious metals were valuable in themselves for decorative use.

Iron money was used for a time in ancient Sparta. According to some accounts, Spartan monarchs cleverly minted coins so large they could barely be carried—to prevent the citizens from leaving the country.

At first, metals had to be weighed and assayed at each transaction, but later, pieces of uniform size were stamped to indicate their weight and purity. And that is exactly what a coin is: a piece of metal whose worth has been guaranteed. The first metal coins were minted in the kingdom of Lydia, in Asia Minor, around the year 650 B.C., although there is evidence of silver money in Iran as early as 760 B.C.

By the time of the Roman Empire, land and cattle speculation were already common—thus, these items were valued not for their immediate usefulness, but for their value in metal currency. The Romans adopted a form of gold standard, and stored their reserves in the Temple of Juno Moneta. Moneta became the mint, and Juno was regarded as the goddess of money. Such was the origin of this almighty word.

During the early Middle Ages, the coinage of the Eastern Empire at Byzantium, and later, the coinage of the Arabs, became the most important species in the eastern Mediterranean. In Western Europe, in the late eighth century, Charlemagne sanctioned the abandonment of the gold standard and established a monetary system based on silver. A silver penny, or *denarius,* was the basic unit, with 240 pennies to a pound of silver. The words *livre, lira,* and *pound* as used in British currency, date from this era. The Pound Sterling was originally 240 sterlings, or silver pennies, and literally weighed one pound.

Gold came back into use during the 13th and 14th centuries, with the *florin,* from Florence, among the more important coins. But the older silver system remained in use, so that through the Renaissance two basic monetary systems were current in most of Europe. Financial calculation was indeed a laborious job.

In the 15th century, the Venetian gold ducat—a word which comes from "duchy"—became the most valued coin in much of Europe. Although bills of exchange had been in use since 13th-century Italy, the first bank notes were not placed in service until 1661, in Sweden. Paper money is a Chinese invention, dating from the seventh century.

Why are gold and silver so appropriate as mediums of exchange? First of all, the metals were always highly prized for their sheen and utility in personal adornment and religious statuary. Gold and silver will neither deteriorate nor rust. And the supply of these metals, while large enough to fill the need as a medium of exchange, is not *so* large that the metals become worthless.

But through the ages, metal money has presented its own problems. European monarchs frequently debased their currency—reduced the gold or silver content of the coins—to pay for expensive wars, and many avaricious individuals were wont to clip their coins to steal a few grains of precious metal. The wide variety of money standards in use in medieval and Renaissance Europe often made business transactions difficult—and made the moneychanger an absolute neccessity. Gradually, the moneychanger came to fulfill many of the functions now performed by banks. And with the rise of moneylending and capital accumulation, paper money, otherwise worthless, became reliable as a medium of exchange.

Paper money is, of course, the hardest cash throughout the world. But many of terms we still use when discussing matters monetary reflect earlier standards and mediums of exchange. As we mentioned, *pound, livre, lire,* and also *ruble,* refer to weight. The Greek *drachma* originally meant "handful."

"Pecuniary" comes from the Latin *pecus,* which means "cattle." "Coin" comes from the Latin *cuneus,* which indicates "stamp" or "die;" and "fee" derives from the Anglo-Saxon *feoh,* or "cattle." "Finance" is related to *final,* since a money transaction was regarded as the "final act" of a deal.

The English *guinea* comes from the African area where gold for the coin was originally mined. *Franc* is an abbreviated *Francorum Rex,* "King of the Franks." And the word *money* itself is the legacy of the Roman goddess Juno Moneta.

During the 16th century, when heavy silver coins were widely used throughout Europe, Bohemian coins minted in St. Joachimsthal were considered the purest. They therefore formed the standard of excellence. From Joachimsthaler comes the older words *thaler* and *daler,* and, of course the *dollar.*

In the early days of our nation, English, French, and Spanish monies all circulated through the American colonies, with a concomitant confusion of trade. In 1785, the dollar was adopted by Congress as the unit of exchange, and the decimal system as the method of

Broad *of James I.*

reckoning. The U.S. monetary system was established in 1792: the first mint began operation in Philadelphia the following year.

Many coin and bill denominations have come and gone since then. Among the coins no longer in use are the *half-cent,* the *two-cent,* the *three-cent,* the *twenty-cent,* and the *silver half-dime*. The nickel was not introduced until 1886. Today, gold coins are no longer minted, and you may be surprised to learn, no bills larger than $100 are now placed in circulation.

> *Money isn't everything, but it's way ahead of whatever is in second place.*

The money we use in America was originally based on the gold standard. A bill was, in effect, a promise to pay the bearer on demand the dollar amount of gold stated on the note. But our money no longer has a gold or other commodity backing, and you cannot turn in your bills for gold. A person is willing to accept otherwise valueless paper money because he knows that others will accept these bills from him. Coins, too, are symbolic in value: a dime, for example, doesn not contain 10-cents' worth of metal.

As long as monetary systems were tied to a gold or a silver standard, there were self-imposed restraints on the system: the amount of gold or metal in a nation's reserves limited the

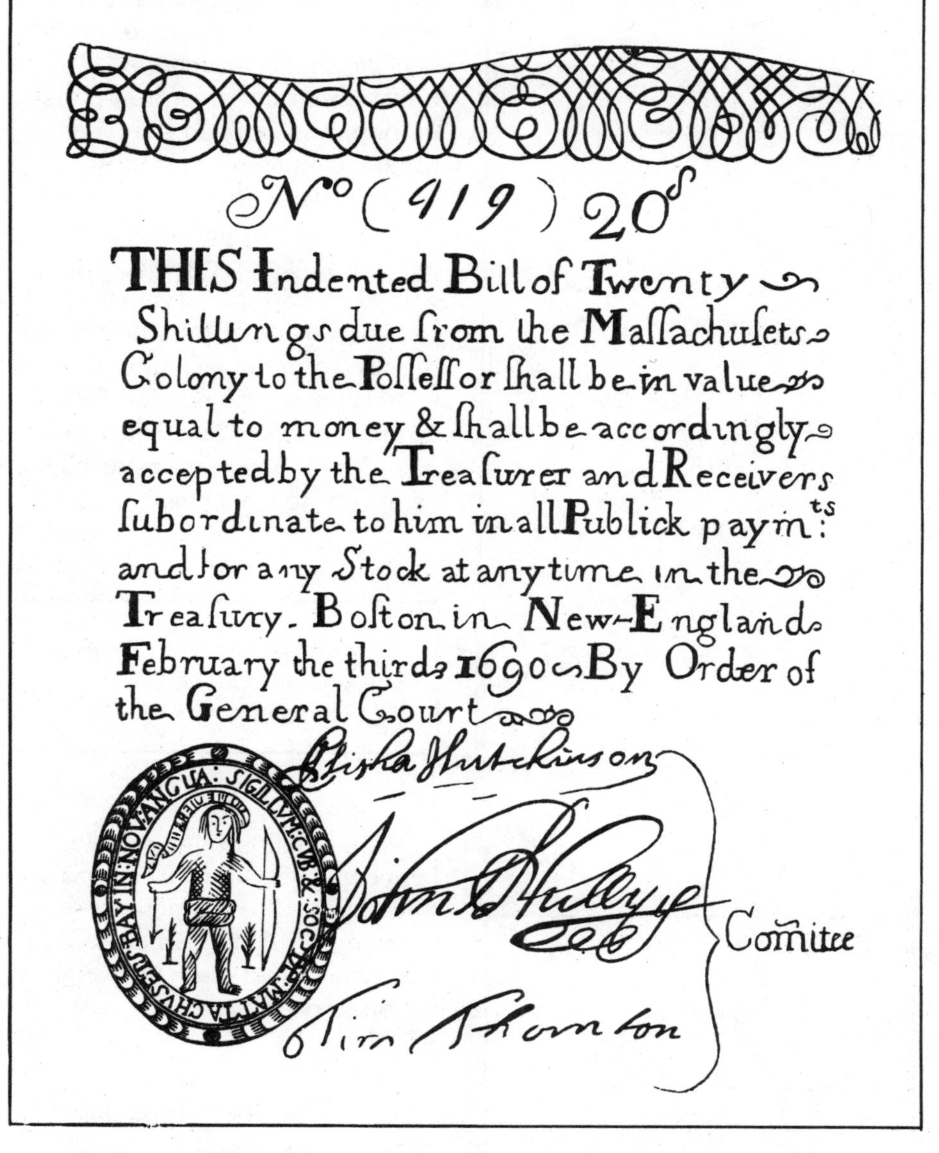

No (919) 20s

THIS Indented Bill of Twenty Shillings due from the Massachusets Colony to the Possessor shall be in value equal to money & shall be accordingly accepted by the Treasurer and Receivers subordinate to him in all Publick paym:ts and for any Stock at any time in the Treasury. Boston in New-England February the third 1690 By Order of the General Court

Elisha Hutchinson
John Walley
Tim Thornton
Comitee

This document passed for a $20 bill in Colonial America.

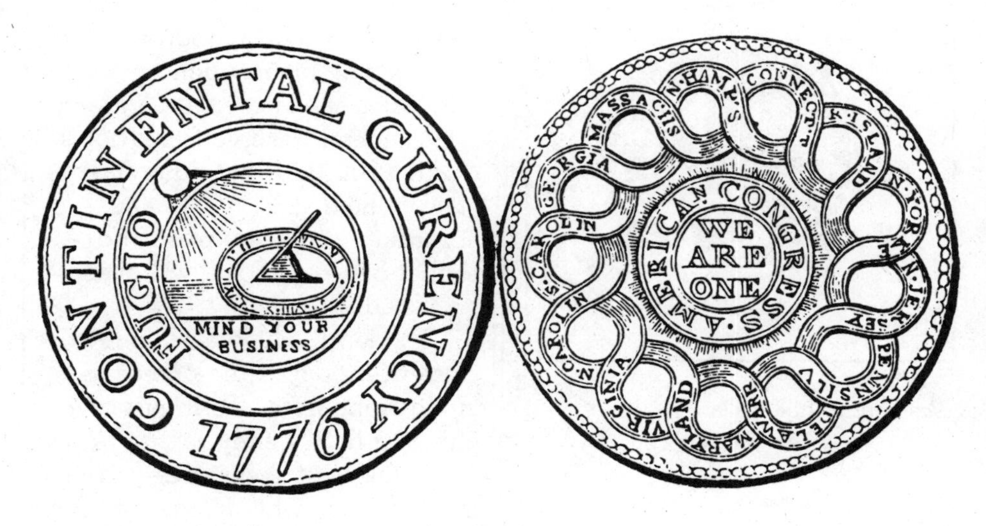

The first money coined in the United States.

amount of money that could be minted. But without a commodity backing to its currency, a government can overprint paper money, and problems such as runaway inflation often arise.

The worst inflation in history occurred in Hungary in 1946, when a single gold pengo was valued at 130 trillion paper pengos! A simple purchase might require so many bills that a wheelbarrow was needed for a trip to the store, and notes were issued in denominations as high as 100 trillion pengos!

> *Sell your pants, if you have to, but you must be rich.*
> —Hungarian proverb

Washington half-dollar.

The inflation rate in Chile, between 1950 and 1973, was an outlandish 423,100 percent—meaning, in American currency, that what could once be bought for one dollar eventually cost $4,231!

Speaking of high denominations, the highest valued paper currency ever printed were U.S. gold certificates issued in 1934, worth $100,000. In case you've never seen one, the bill bore the head of President Woodrow Wilson. The highest denomination notes still in circulation are U.S. Federal Reserve Bank notes worth $100,000, but none has been printed since 1944; and according to present plans, no further bills over $100 will ever be issued.

The least valuable bill in existence today is the *one-cent* Hong Kong note, worth just one-fifth of a U.S. penny.

In terms of sheer size—which matters not a whit in legal tender—the largest and smallest

A 19th-century Chinese coin from the reign of Emperor Hien-Fung (1851-1861).

bills in history are, respectively, the *one-kwan* note of 14th-century China, which measured nine by thirteen inches, and the 1917 *ten-bani* note of Rumania, barely more than an inch-and-a-half square.

As for coins, the smallest in size was the Nepalese silver *quarter-dam* of 1740—you'd need some 14,000 to equal an ounce.

At the other end of the scale, the Swedish copper *ten-daler* coin of 1644 weighed up to 43.4 pounds. And natives of the Yap Islands in the South Pacific at one time used stone coins some 12 feet wide, weighing up to 185 pounds!

The lowest denomination coin in existence today is the *five-aurar* piece of Iceland, which when issued in 1971, had a face value of only .1311 of a U.S. penny—you'd need 762 aurars to equal a dollar.

And the highest denomination coin was the 1654 gold *200-mohur* coin of India, worth the equivalent of $1,400 at that time. Even considering the current skyrocketing of the price of gold, the *200-mohur* is not the most valuable coin in history—that honor goes to an Athenian silver

CURRENCY VALUES

Nation	*Currency Standard*	*Value per U.S. $1.* *
Argentina	peso	1624.50
Australia	dollar	.9098
Austria	schilling	12.64
Belgium	franc	28.64
Bolivia	peso	24.26
Brazil	cruzeiro	45.11
Britain	pound	.4373
Canada	dollar	1.1470
Chile	peso	39.00
Colombia	peso	43.38
Denmark	krone	5.4890
Egypt	pound	.6925
Ecuador	sucre	27.20
Finland	mark	3.7475
France	franc	4.1250
Germany, West	mark	1.7570
Greece	drachma	38.70
Holland	guilder	1.9390
Hong Kong	dollar	4.9480
India	rupee	7.9500
Indonesia	rupiah	625.00
Ireland	punt	.4768
Israel	shekel	3.936
Italy	lire	816.25
Japan	yen	248.32
Jordan	dinar	.2970
Kuwait	dinar	.2737
Lebanon	pound	3.3225
Mexico	peso	22.84
New Zealand	dollar	1.0288
Norway	krone	4.9020
Peru	sol	256.55
Philippines	peso	7.3500
Portugal	escudo	47.80
Saudi Arabia	riyal	3.3625
Singapore	dollar	2.1610
South Africa	rand	.8084
Spain	peseta	66.94
Sweden	krona	4.1965
Switzerland	franc	1.6640
Turkey	lira	70.00
Uraguay	peso	8.4300
Venzuela	boliva	4.2900

* As of Wednesday, February 27, 1980

drachma, sold to a coin collector in 1974 for $314,000!

How much money is there in the world today? It's almost impossible to estimate, since the value of various currencies changes from day to day. But there's an estimated $49.7 billion in gold bullion in the central banks of the world, with the largest single chunk in the Federal Reserve Bank in New York City: $17 billion.

The United States is the nation with the largest gold reserves, but we're not the world's largest gold-producing country. American mines produce an amount equal to the entire production of Asia or Latin America and three times the total European figure. Yet the United States ranks third in gold production, behind Canada. South Africa is far and away the leader.

With all of this money floating around, you may wonder why more of it hasn't found its way into *your* pocket. Don't be ashamed if you feel an uncontrollable hankering for more of the green stuff. After all, *money* is not the root of all evil. The Bible actually says that "the *love* of money is the root of all evil." And that's quite a difference.

Abe said to his friend Willie, "Willie, lend me $20."

Willie took out his wallet and handed Abe a 10 dollar bill.

"Willie," said Abe, "I asked you for $20."

"Yes, I know," said Willie. "This way you lose $10 and I lose $10."

Neckties

The clothing of other periods often looks amusing to us, and current fashions always appear stylish and dignified. Yet future periods may judge the clothes we wear today as foolish-looking as we find a 16th-century man's doublet, leotards, and ruff. If our clothes are supposedly designed for comfort and practicality, how can you explain high-heeled women's shoes? Or skin-tight slacks? Or that completely useless and often uncomfortable piece of apparel without which no man can be considered well-dressed: the necktie?

How did the custom of wearing a necktie arise? Did the tie once have a function? Not really. The scarf and neckerchief have long been used to keep the neck warm. Even the ancient Romans wore a chin cloth, called a *focalium,* to protect their necks and throats. Orators especially favored the *focalium* to keep their vocal cords warm. But the necktie of today really evolved from a series of neckwear items whose function was almost always purely decorative.

Before the first appearance of what we might call the necktie, tie, or cravat, fashionable European men wore various kinds of collars, ruffs, ribbons, bows, and other finery around their necks. In the 16th century, the frilly material at the neck developed into a pleated ruff that completely encircled the neck. Later in the century, the full ruff was opened in front to form more of a recognizable collar, and by the end of the century, the ruff was being replaced by the falling collar.

The falling collar was still the fashion when the cravat was born out of an incident in French history. In 1660, a regiment of soldiers from Croatia (part of modern-day Yugoslavia) visited Paris, and paraded before their French allies wearing brightly-colored handkerchiefs around their necks. The fashion caught on immediately in France, then spread to England after Charles II had returned from France to assume the throne.

At the time, the coat and vest—usually very long—were emerging as distinct garments in men's dress, and colorful neckwear quickly found a place in the wardrobe of fashionable men. But in place of the ordinary handkerchief of the Croatians, European nobles opted for neckwear of rich lace and other expensive materials—English King James II bought three neckerchiefs for $600! These early neckties came to be known as *cravats,* from *cravate,* a French corruption of "Croatian." A regiment of French soldiers was even renamed the Royal Cravates!

Another neckwear item that was named after a military incident was the *steinkirk.* In 1692, according to one story, French soldiers encamped near Steinkirk, Belgium, were surprised by an English attack. In their haste to dress, the soldiers tied their cravats very loosely around their necks, and dashed off into battle. The French won the battle of Steinkirk, and a new neckwear fashion became the rage in Paris the following year. Men began to tie their cravats loosely, leaving long, flowing ends, sometimes threading the two ends through a ring. The official uniform of the Boy Scouts of America still includes a ring-secured steinkirk.

Various neckwear fashions came and went during the 18th century, when cravats with ruffles, pleats, layers, or tasseled strings had their heyday. Jeweled stickpins came into vogue, and so did cravats stiffened with wire or stuffed with cushions. Some cravats were tied so high on the neck that the wearer could barely turn his head, or were thick enough to stop a sword thrust!

French monarch and style-setter Louis XIV favored brightly-colored satin cravats, while his successor Louis XV brought in lace cravats whose ends often reached as far as the waist. Later in the century, cravats of starched linen or cambric came into fashion. Louis XVI, who was to suffer the guillotine during the French Revolution, wore starched muslin cravats around the neck.

The Revolution brought in simpler garments of all kinds—including men's pants. The *stock,* a wide, stiff cravat that encircled the neck, replaced the neckwear finery of earlier periods, and was presented to French soldiers as part of their military dress. According to a tale, Frenchmen of the time believed that a red-faced soldier was a healthy soldier. Men tied their stocks so tightly around their necks during military parades that their faces turned red and their eyes bulged—and so was born the epithet "froggie" for a Frenchman.

By 1840, the stock was still the universal cravat in Europe and America. Extensions to the stock led to a cravat with a slip-knot and hanging ends, called the "four-in-hand" because the wearer described a figure 4 when tying it. A stock with bows on each side evolved into the modern bowtie, while the four-in-hand became the ordinary necktie of today. Both were in fashion by the beginning of this century.

In the United States, almost all cravats were imported from Europe until around 1865, when the cravat was already a must for the well-dressed man. Many books and pamphlets were published advising men how to tie their cravats, including one from 1829 that warned: "In all cases of apoplexy, fainting, or illness in general, it is requisite to loosen or even remove the cravat immediately." The book also advised that "those who are accustomed to sleep in the cravat, should be careful in examining whether it be loose." And regarding the affront of grabbing a man by his cravat, which had long been considered a great insult, the writer declared that "only blood can wash out the stain upon the honor."

The necktie of today was really born in the 1920s, when manufacturers began to turn out stronger ties that would not rip easily and would spring back to shape after untying. Silk knits were the fashion during the 20s, and ties with all-over patterns came into vogue during the 30s, when Americans were already spending $70 million a year for neckties. Average price: 60¢.

During the 1940s, wartime shortages of silk and other expensive materials helped introduce ties of wool and rayon. Wool, silk, and various cotton blends are presently the favored materials for neckties, though manufacturers have produced ties made from such unlikely materials as alpaca, cashmere, fur, glass, and leather!

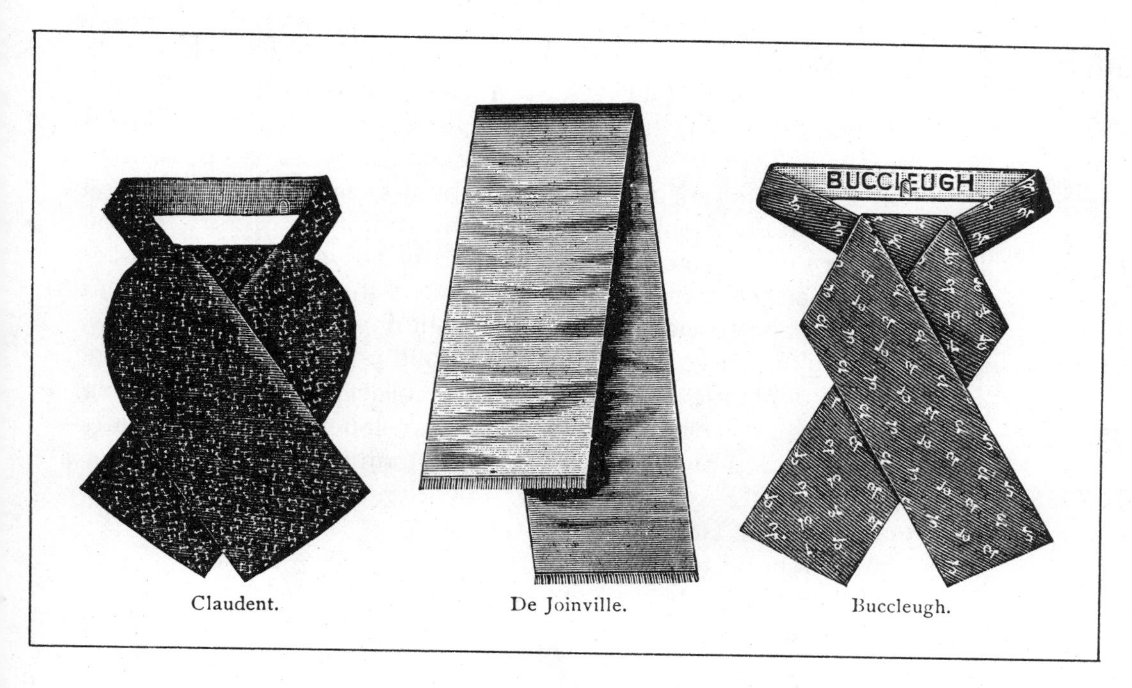

Stylish neckwear from a Jordan Marsh catalog in the early 1900s.

A son gets a birthday present from his mother of two neckties. One of them is blue, and one of them is red. He comes to visit her, and he puts on the blue necktie. She looks at him and says, 'So the red one you don't like?'

After World War II, the vest faded as part of the well-dressed man's wardrobe, and the necktie consequently became more visible and important. Colorful, decorative neckties became the rule, and so did wider, longer ties. Today, necktie fashions seem to change every few years, with necktie width often following the widening or narrowing of the jacket lapel.

In 1946, the Men's Tie Foundation was formed to propagate the wearing of ties in America, with the slogan: "Wear a tie to look your best." By the end of that decade, the Foundation could report that Americans were spending $191 million a year on neckwear, with the average tie selling for from $1.50 to $2.50, and the average man owned four ties. Any necktie up to five dollars, the Foundation declared, was simply a "tie;" if it cost more than five dollars, it deserved the name "cravat." And if it cost more than $15, well, then it was a "creation."

In 1949, the Tie Foundation reported that the American necktie industry used some 34 million yards of material, not including linings and labels—enough to encircle the globe three times! The bowtie accounted for five percent of necktie sales, while about 85 percent of all ties purchased in the United States were bought by women for men! How did American men respond to the selection of their ties by their wives, daughters, and girlfriends? Less than one percent of all ties purchased that year were exchanged!

The Foundation even provided a breakdown of the nation in terms of the favored colors and designs of particular areas. Chicagoans favored green ties. Bostonians purchased far more red ties, while men and women in Dallas seemed to have a liking for blue ties. We don't known what color fashion plates from Omaha favored, but we do know that one Omaha man owned a collection of neckties that would warm the heart of any tie manufacturer: 7,000 ties, cravats, and creations.

The cornhusker's necktie collection surely must have included some of the so-called novelty ties that make their appearance regularly to commemorate an event. Most of the presidential campaigns of this century have produced a collection of commemorative neckties, all of which presumably had a short wearing life. There was even a necktie commemorating the dropping of the atomic bomb on Hiroshima, in production less than 24 hours after the explosion! This necktie attracted far less attention, though, than a tie bearing the reproduction of a painting of a nude woman—authorities raided the tie manufacturer and confiscated the offending neckties!

The future of the necktie is anyone's guess. It's possible that the necktie might be obsolete by the end of the century, so you might as well begin your collection of these fashion curiosities right now. But no matter how proud you might be of your necktie collection, don't ever accept an invitation to a necktie party—the term is American slang for a lynching!

Chicagoans favor green ties. Bostonians purchase far more red ties, while men and women in Dallas seemed to have a liking for blue ties.

NEWSPAPERS

As you may have heard, the famous Battle of New Orleans, won by Andrew Jackson and his troops over the British during the War of 1812, was fought on January 8, 1815—15 days *after* the war had ended. A treaty ending the conflict had been signed in Europe, but the news failed to reach either Jackson or the British troops before the battle. Moreover, Jackson's superiors in Washington were unaware of both the battle *and* the treaty!

It's no surprise that news traveled slowly before the introduction of electronic media and the up-to-date newspaper. But before you laugh too hard, you might consider the results of a 1969 poll taken in Morocco, revealing that only 56 percent of those asked knew that a man had set foot on the moon. And of these, more than half thought the story was a hoax!

The modern newspaper could only be the product of the best printing processes and news-gathering networks, both developments of the 20th century. But written news reports, undependable as they were, date back to classical times. Romans of the fifth century B.C. distributed newsletters with reports from the capital for those residing nearby on the Italian peninsula.

Upon assuming the consulship in 60 B.C., one of Julius Caesar's first acts was to establish a daily bulletin of government announcements, the *Acta Diurna*, to post in the forum. Posted proclamations and the announcements of town criers—and the grapevine—provided the news to many city residents for centuries, but it wasn't until the 17th century that newspapers proper began to spring up around Europe on a regular basis.

Though the Chinese claim the world's first newspaper, a court gazette first published in the seventh century B.C., Chinese newsletters were actually printed by hand or from blocks until movable wood type was introduced in China in the 17th century. Thus, the printed newspaper can properly be termed a European development.

One of Europe's first printed news reports was the work of Englishman Thomas Raynalde who, in 1549, translated German news pamphlets documenting recent political events, murders, and marvels—a style of journalism not unknown today. Early English news reports, translated from German or Dutch, came to be known as *corantos*, a term related to "current."

The early corantos reported news only from the Continent, and were for the most part prohibited, or at least hindered, from relating domestic events. But in 1641, with the abolition of the tyrannical court, the Star Chamber, freedom of the press in England took a major step forward. That year saw the publication of *Diurnal Occurences* (a title identical to Caesar's), the first news pamphlet to contain domestic news, written in London by Samuel Pecke.

Most 17th-century news publications were partisan, printed with the approval, or direct sponsorship, of either the monarchy or parliament. Despite their titles, these journals of "diurnal" occurences were published weekly. The first bona fide *daily* newspapers in England were not published until 1702.

Between 1704 and 1713, Daniel Defoe, best known for his novels, published a weekly entitled *The Review*. At various

Novelist Daniel Defoe was also a crackerjack newspaper editor and major figure in the evolution of modern journalism.

times a paid political pamphleteer, a secret agent, and a hack, Defoe was wont to take his political point of view from the highest bidder, and often switched sides when it suited him. The author of *Robinson Crusoe* once edited a Tory newspaper actually sponsored by the Whigs, and a Whig publication sponsored by the Tories—both at the same time! Nevertheless, Defoe is considered the first important journalist in England, and the originator of the serial story.

Most early English newspapers were political in nature, devoted mainly to domestic and foreign news and commerce reports. The famed journalists Sir Richard Steele and Joseph Addison were among the first to introduce social commentary to the newspaper. The pair began with the *Tatler* in 1709, then, beginning in 1711, brought out the *Spectator*, a daily. Between them, they wrote about 90 percent of the papers themselves. The *Spectator* eventually ran to some 555 issues, and reached a circulation of over 3,000. It was read by many times that number.

Addison and Steele's papers were to have many imitators in England, including the *Idler* and *Rambler* of Samuel Johnson, brought out in the 1750s. By 1753, English newspapers had passed the seven million mark in annual circulation; by 1760, nine million; and by 1767, 11 million. In 1776, there were 53 newspapers in London alone—presumably, most of them made reference to a burgeoning conflict in England's far-off American colonies.

> *Three hostile newspapers are more to be feared than a thousand bayonets.*
> —Napoleon I

Most 18th-century English newspapers were designed for the well-educated. Many of the essays from the *Spectator* or *Rambler* are considered among the finest English writing in this form. Taxes kept the newspaper out of the hands of many people until late in the century, when William Cobbett first tried to reach the masses with a cheap weekly paper.

The *London Times* was begun in 1785 by John Walter, who promised his readers the paper would have no part in political partisanship or scandalmongering. Walter spent a few sojourns in Newgate prison for his journalistic independence. But by the middle of the 19th century, the *Times* was the pre-eminent British newspaper, with a daily circulation of about 50,000. Even at that late date, each issue contained but 12 pages.

> *Were it left to me to decide whether we should have a government without newspapers, or newspapers without a government, I should not hesitate a moment to prefer the latter.*
> —Thomas Jefferson

The first American publication that could justifiably be termed a newspaper was brought out in 1690 by Benjamin Harris, a bookseller who had been forced to flee England after publishing a seditious news pamphlet. Harris called his Boston paper *Publick Occurences Both Foreign and Domestick*, and promised it would be issued "once a moneth (or if any Glut of Occurrences happen, oftener)." Harris's four-page paper was suppressed after only one issue for certain comments found distasteful by Massachusetts governor Simon Bradstreet.

In 1704, a postmaster named John Campbell brought out the *Boston News-Letter*, the first continuously published newspaper in America. Printed by one Bartholomew Green in a back room of his house, the paper was published in some form right up until the Revolution, and was without competition for 15 years—reaching the astronomical circulation figure of 300! By the way, one of the first printers of the *Gazette* was James Franklin, and his apprentice was a certain 13-year-old brother named Benjamin—perhaps you've heard of him?

Benjamin Franklin later moved to Philadelphia to work as a printer and occasional writer; and in 1728, bought a paper begun the previous year by Samuel Keimar. Franklin shortened the paper's 11-word title to the *Pennsylvania Gazette*, and published the sheet successfully for 19 years—by which time Franklin probably had a number of more pressing matters to attend to.

You might have heard that Benjamin Franklin founded the recently defunct *Saturday Evening Post* in 1728, for the claim appeared directly on the cover of each issue. The fact is,

MORNING HERALD.

NEW YORK, WEDNESDAY MORNING MAY 6, 1835.

PRICE ONE CENT.

The first copy of the New York Herald, *May 6, 1835.*

Franklin had nothing whatsoever to do with this magazine, which first appeared in 1821—not 1728. The magazine's publishers fabricated the claim in 1899, and never abandoned it even when the claim was proved patently false.

The first New York newspaper was the *New York Gazette,* brought out by William Bradford in 1725. The *Gazette* was basically an organ of the Colonial government, and gave impetus to patriot Peter Zenger's opposing paper, the *New York Weekly Journal,* which he began publishing in 1733. Zenger was eventually jailed for his work. The court case that followed, exonerating Zenger, did much to establish the principles of freedom of the press in America.

Many claims have been heard for the first daily newspaper to be published in the United States, but it's generally accepted that the honor goes to the *Pennsylvania Packet and Daily Advertiser,* which first appeared as a daily in 1784. Newspapers were not widely read here until the 1830s, when the penny press began to appear. These papers—costing, as you might imagine, one cent, when the going rate was six cents—were the first to be available to people at all economic levels.

The first successful daily in this genre was the *New York Sun,* launched in 1833. In 1841, Horace Greeley founded a rival paper, the *New York Tribune.*

As the founder of New York's highly successful newspaper, the Tribune, *Horace Greeley expanded the concepts of news coverage and developed a high-caliber staff. A dedicated journalist, he had one peculiarity: he was convinced that the word "news" was plural. His staff disagreed, but Greeley was adamant.*

Once, while traveling, Greeley sent a telegram to the home office, asking: "ARE THERE ANY NEWS?"

A reporter responded: "NOT A NEW."

Ten years later, three publishing entrepreneurs issued the first copy of the *New York Times,* today generally regarded as the premier American newspaper. The paper was failing in 1896 when it was taken over by Adolphe Ochs, previously the publisher of a Tennessee paper. Och's early years saw the

IF YOU SEE IT IN
THE SUN
IT'S SO
READ IT

adoption of the slogan: "All the news that's fit to print," along with a slogan that promised: "It does not soil the breakfast cloth"—a reference to the so-called yellow journalism of the day.

The term *yellow journalism* originated in the 1890s when San Francisco publisher William Randolph Hearst invaded the New York market and instituted an all-out rivalry between competing papers. When the *New York World* published the first color comic strip in 1893—"The Yellow Kid" by Richard Outcault—Hearst lured the artist away and published the strip in his own New York paper, the *Journal*. The continuing rivalry between the various New York papers pandering to lurid tastes soon took on the name "yellow journalism." Many papers of this era were much like the modern tabloid or scandal sheet, featuring large banner headlines, plenty of pictures, and sensationalist features.

The 20th century has seen the gradual consolidation of American newspapers and the founding of the newspaper chain. Hearst himself bought or estab-

OPPOSITE:
Advertising poster for the New York Sun, *circa 1895.*

Whitelaw Reid (1837-1912) was a brilliant reporter who took over the New York Tribune *after the death of Horace Greeley. He also served in government in various diplomatic positions.*

BELOW:
English journalists of the Victorian era would rush from the estate of the Prince of Wales in Sandringham, England, to get stories of the future Edward VII's activities to press.

lished some 40 daily papers. The peak year for American papers—in terms of sheer numbers—was 1916, when 2,461 dailies were published across the nation. By 1944, consolidation and bankruptcy had brought that figure down to 1,744.

New York City once had dozens of papers; but by the 1950s, most remaining papers were combinations of earlier publications—the *New York Herald Tribune* and the *New York World Telegram and Sun*, for instance. Today, there are but three daily publications that can be called New York daily newspapers: the *Times*, the *Post*, and the *Daily News*. The latter was founded in 1919 by three Chicago publishers. Within six years, the *Daily News* had become the largest newspaper in the United States, a title it still holds by virtue of selling some two million copies daily.

James Gordon Bennett (1841-1918) took over and expanded the New York Herald, *establishing London and Paris editions.*

A familiar night scene at 34th Street and Broadway in 1899. Bypassers gather to watch the great presses of the New York Herald Tribune.

Joseph Pulitzer (1847-1911) bought and built-up the New York World *through aggressive newspaper coverage, which included the use of illustrations, cartoons, and anti-corruption crusades.*

Much of the news coverage now provided by the daily newspaper is the work of the wire agencies, which maintain a news correspondent in almost every large or capital city in the world. The Associated Press was founded in 1848 by six New York papers to divide the cost of transmitting news by telegraph. By 1950, the agency had some 300,000 miles of wire in operation in the United States alone. The other major American news agency, United Press International, was founded in 1907 by E.W. Scripps, uniting three older news agencies.

Close to one-fourth of the

newspapers published in the world today are brought out in America—1,768 in 1975—with a total paid circulation of close to 62 million copies daily.

But the single newspaper with the largest daily circulation is the Russian *Pravda*, with a reputed circulation of 10 million copies. *Pravda* (which means "truth" in Russian) was begun in 1912. After the 1917 revolution, it became the leading organ of the Russian Communist party.

Izvestia, the official daily newspaper of the Soviet government, is the second newspaper in the world in terms of circulation, with eight million copies sold per day. Those who believe that the high figures attributed to the Soviet papers are due to the fact that there are no other papers published in that country might be surprised to learn that there are some 7,200 papers published altogether in the Soviet Union, though there are only about 650 dailies.

The Japanese daily, *Asahi Shimbun*, ranks third in circulation, at just over seven million copies per day, and two other Japanese papers claim a circulation in excess of five million.

The largest paper in England is now the *London Daily Mirror*, with some four million copies sold per day, and both the *Daily Sun* and the *Daily Express* own circulations close to the three million mark. And the *Evening News*, with an average circulation of over a half-million copies, is the world's best-selling evening newspaper.

After the *New York Daily News*, the *Los Angeles Times* is the nation's best-selling newspaper, with about one million copies sold per day. The *New York Times* follows in the number-three position.

Rounding out the top 10 are, in order, the *Chicago Tribune*, *Detroit News*, *Detroit Free Press*, *Chicago Sun-Times*, *Philadelphia Bulletin*, *New York Post*, and *Washington Post*. But the *Wall Street Journal*, published around the nation rather than in one particular city, officially ranks as the number-two American daily, with a circulation of some one-and-a-half million copies.

In all, American advertisers will spend about eight-and-a-half billion dollars this year on newspaper advertising!

Americans are far from the world's greatest newspaper readers, however. That honor goes to the Swedes, who pore through about 564 papers for every 1,000 persons. (In the United States, the figure is 300 papers per 1,000 persons.) And the newspaper that comes closest to total national saturation is the *Sunday Post*, published in Glasgow, Scotland and read by about four-and-a-half million people each Sunday—more than 77 percent of all Scots of presumed newspaper-reading age.

No one who has carried home a copy of the *New York Sunday Times* could entertain any doubt as to the world's largest newspaper in sheer bulk. The largest Sunday *Times* ever published, on October 17, 1965, consisted of 946 pages in 15 sections, and weighed a whopping seven-and-a-half pounds! Let's see—if the Sunday *Times* has a circulation of about one-and-a-half million copies, we can calculate that the average issue of that paper comprises a total of some 10 million pounds of paper. Now, that's a small forest!

The single newspaper with the largest daily circulation is the Russian *Pravda*, with a reputed circulation of 10 million copies.

ONIONS

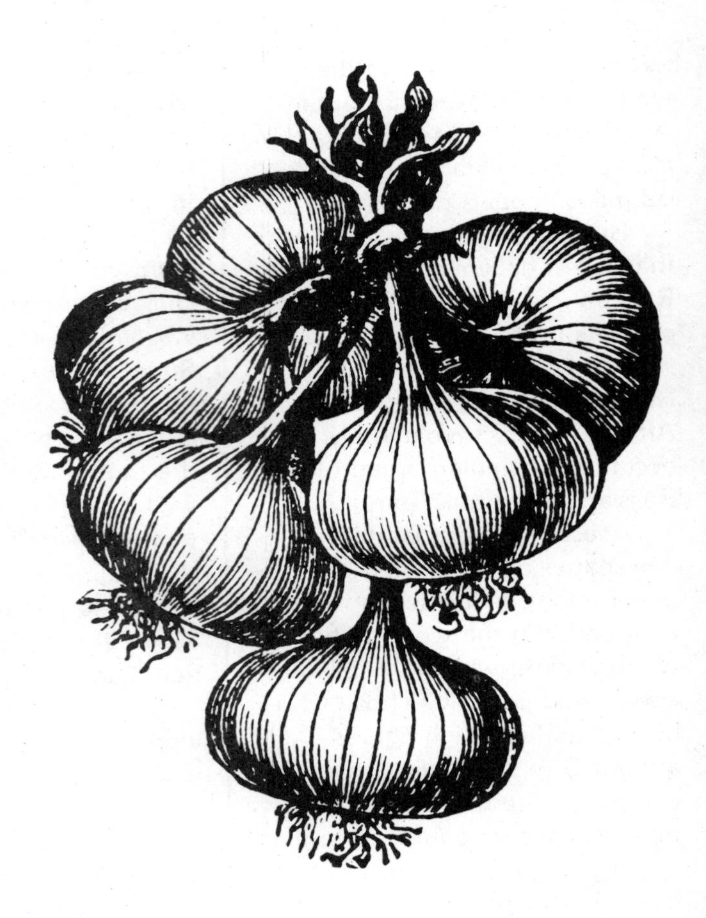

If you were asked to guess the most widely used vegetable in the world, you might think first of corn or potatoes, or perhaps lettuce or tomatoes. Because it is most often used in the United States as a flavoring to other foods, the plant that rightly deserves the award for culinary prevalence might not even come to mind as a vegetable at all. We're talking, of course, about the odorous, oft-derided vegetable that is so essential to any chef, and so unessential to any chef's eye—the onion.

In total production, both the potato and tomato surpass the onion, but neither is used in such a wide variety of cuisines as the onion. The list of recipes, Western and Oriental, that require the services of the onion or its cousins would probably fill a small library. And since it appears both as a flavoring in much *haute cuisine,* and as a staple in much peasant cookery, the onion has traditionally been one of the few vegetables popular with both commoners and kings.

The onion is not only the most widely-used vegetable on earth, it is also one of the oldest. In the book of Numbers in the Bible, chapter II, verse 5, the Israelites bewailed "We remember the fish, which we did eat in Egypt freely, the cucumbers, and the melons, and the leeks, and the onions, and the garlic," to a harassed Moses. A native of Western Asia, probably Pakistan or Afghanistan, the onion has been grown and eaten for so long it no longer exists in a wild state. By the time the ancient Egyptian civilization began to flourish some 5,000 years ago, the onion was already a staple food throughout the Mideast.

It's been said that the Pyramids owe their existence to the onion, since the workers who constructed them subsisted largely on the vegetable. The Roman historian Herodotus claimed to have seen an inscription on the Great Pyramid at Giza that listed the amounts of onions, garlic, and radishes eaten by the workers who built the monument. For some reason, Herodotus also maintained that the onion was good for sight, but bad for the body. Many a tearful cook might disagree.

The upper classes in Egypt also ate onions, though more often as a complement to other foods than as a staple in itself. The historian Pliny wrote that the Egyptians invoked the onion when taking an oath, and one variety was considered divine. The vegetable was depicted on a number of Egyptian monuments as a symbol of eternity, due to its layer-upon-layer formation within the shape of a sphere. Similarly, our word *onion* comes from the Latin

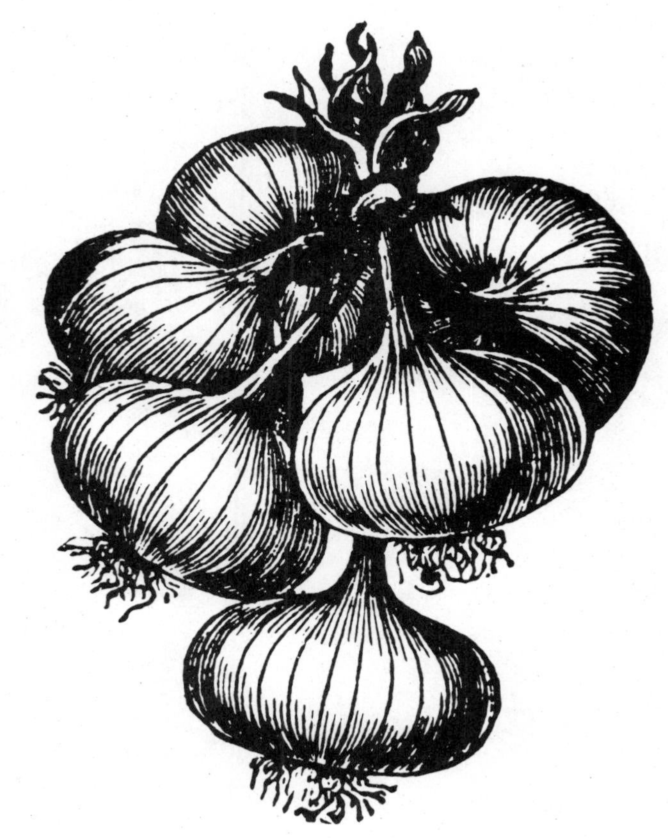

term *unio,* which has also given us *union* and *united.*

The ancient Greeks and Romans cultivated onions extensively, as do the people of Greece and Italy today. The Romans fed onions to their soldiers, believing the vegetable would make them brave. The Emperor Nero favored the leek, a member of the onion family eaten in the Mediterranean area since Biblical times, because he thought it would improve his singing voice.

Phoenician traders had brought leeks to the British Isles before the arrival of the Romans. The leek has been the national emblem of Wales since the year 640, when victorious Welsh soldiers pinned leeks to their caps so that they would not inadvertently bludgeon one another instead of the enemy. But some historians discount the tale, pointing instead to a confusion by English writers between the Welsh words for the daffodil, *cenine,* and the leek, *cenin,* for the daffodil was another Welsh national symbol. In any case, the Welsh still pin leeks to their hats on the feast day of St. David, their patron saint.

Medieval Europeans who did not fancy onions had a difficult time putting vegetables on their table. Meat, fish, game, and baked goods comprised most meals of the time, and among the vegetables, only onions and leeks were widely used. Onions mixed with chopped flowers were the staple food at many medieval monasteries.

The Spanish first brought the onion to the New World, planting the vegetable in their West Indian colonies. Onions had become a staple in America before the Revolution.

Today, New York and Texas are the primary suppliers of the American onion crop, which usually stands somewhere around the three-billion-pound mark annually. Europe produces about twice that amount each year. Even without taking into account the mammoth onion production of the Soviet Union, the worldwide figure is usually over 20 billion pounds a year!

The onion is a species of lily known as *Allum cepa. Cepa* and the Italian word for onion, *cipolla,* come from *caepa,* one of a number of Latin words for the vegetable. Onions contain volatile oils heavy with sulphur compounds that account for the pungent fumes so familiar to onion peelers. These oils disturb the eyes, which tear in order to wash away the offending fumes.

If you've been finding your onions a bit too lachrymal for comfort, try chilling them before you begin cutting. You can remove onion odors from your hands by rubbing them with lemon juice before washing. If onion aroma clings to your knife, just run the blade through a raw potato.

Onions are sensitive to the length of day in the area in which they're grown. Varieties that thrive in northern latitudes are usually grown in the summer, when the days are long, and will not produce large bulbs if transplanted in southern regions. Conversely, onions grown in southern areas are usually grown through the winter. If transplanted in the north during the summer months, the onion will stop growing and ripen before it can produce a large bulb. Onions grown in the north, such as the familiar globe, are usually harder and more sugary and the white onion and others grown in southern regions.

The onion family consists of two main branches, the *dried onion* and the *green onion*. We eat the bulb of the former, and the green top and unformed bulb of the latter. But there are hundreds of individual varieties, for onions grow in the widest range of types among all vegetables.

The globe onion, round, yellow-skinned, and pungent, is the most commonly used dried onion in America. The Grano-Granex onion, better known as the "new" onion, is milder and sweeter than the globe. The new onion is best used raw, while the globe is best suited for cooking. The red onion is another sweet variety often served raw in salads, but it disintegrates when cooked.

White onions, which contain a high percentage of water, often taste best when creamed, pickled, or boiled. The pearl onion is not a separate variety, but a white onion harvested when small. The Gibson, a martini with a pearl onion instead of an olive, is named after New York artist Charles Dana Gibson, though the drink was invented not by Gibson, but by his bartender.

The Bermuda and Spanish onions are the largest members of their family. Both are mild, with a yellow to red skin, and are best eaten raw in salads or atop hamburgers. The Spanish onion, often used for fried onion rings, hails from Central Spain, while the Bermuda onion originated in the Canary Islands.

Green onions are harvested before their bulbs have had time to enlarge, though some green onions are harvested from non-bulbing varieties. Green onions include the scallion, leek, shallot, and chive. All are most often used as flavorings in the United States, although in some parts of Europe the leek is eaten as a vegetable. In France, the leek is known as "the poor man's asparagus."

If you've been finding your onions a bit too lachrymal for comfort, try chilling them before you begin cutting. You can remove onion odors from your hands by rubbing them with lemon juice before washing. If onion aroma clings to your knife, just run the blade through a raw potato.

ONION SOUP

Slice three large onions and brown in three tablespoons of butter or oil. Sprinkle in a tablespoon of flour, and heat for another 10 minutes, stirring occasionally.

Meanwhile, heat a quart of rich beef stock or bouillon. Add the onion mixture and simmer until tender.

Spread grated Parmesan cheese thickly over slices of toasted bread and melt the cheese under a grill.

Pour the soup in tureens and add a slice of toast to each bowl.

Or you can cover each bowl with Swiss, Gruyere, or Mozzarella cheese and bake for 15 minutes.

Onions can be stored for longer periods of time than any other fresh vegetable. But cooks looking for shortcuts—or protecting their tear ducts—can resort to an array of even longer-lasting onion products, including dehydrated minced or flaked onions, onion powder, and onion salt.

The proportions of sugar and water in onions determine the taste of particular varieties. But the way in which an onion is cut or cooked will also influence its taste. A finely-cut onion will more easily lose its oils in cooking, resulting in a milder flavor. Onions cooked in liquid quickly lose water, increasing the proportion of sugar and resulting in a sweeter-tasting, less odorous onion. As Jonathan Swift noted:

But lest your kissing should be spoil'd
Your onions must be thoroughly boil'd.

All types of onion are relatively low in nutritional value, and thus are seldom eaten alone like most green leafy vegetables. As a tribute to its flavoring power, the onion has been called "the vegetable whose absence spoils the stew." But too many onions can spoil the stew just as easily. English writer Sydney Smith advised moderation:

Let onion atoms lurk within the bowl,
And, scarce suspected, animate the whole.

The versatile onion may be boiled and combined with other vegetables, sauteed and piled atop steak or liver, stewed, or made into soup. And speaking of onion ingenuity, one recipe calls for large Spanish onions stuffed with—yes, pearl onions.

French onion soup is considered a gourmet treat in this country, but during the Middle Ages, onion soup was the poor man's staple. If you'd like to try your hand at onion soup, there's a recipe above.

If you'll believe a number of old wives' tales, your homemade onion soup might provide more than a pleased palate and a full belly. The onion has been used medicinally since the days of ancient Egypt. It was thought to ward off evil spirits, and because it induces perspiration, to cure colds. It's also been called into action against such maladies as earaches, insect stings, and warts. A medieval superstition holds that to remove a wart, simply cut an onion in half, rub the exposed inner flesh against the wart, tie the onion back together and bury it. When the onion has decomposed, the wart will have disappeared.

Most likely it's the onion's pungent aroma that has contributed to its place in legend and superstition. Many writers have advised judicious use of the vegetable, especially by lovers. A character in Shakespeare's *A Midsummer Night's Dream* warned: "Eat no onions nor garlic, for we are to utter sweet breath."

Indeed, for pungent aroma the onion's reputation towers above that of all its vegetable relatives—with the possible exception of garlic, which can be considered another member of the onion clan. An old poem correctly ranked the offending vegetables in the order of their olfactory powers:

If Leekes you like, but do their smelle disleeke,
Eate Onyons, and you shalle not smelle the Leeke;
If you of Onyons would the scente expelle,
Eate Garlicke, that shall drowne the Onyon's smelle.

The author obviously "knew his onions."

Ah, hapless wretch! condemn'd to dwell
For ever in my native shell;
Ordain'd to move when others please,
Not for my own content and ease;
But toss'd and buffeted about,
Now in the water and now out.
'Twere better to be born a stone,
Of ruder shape, and feeling none,
Than with a tenderness like mine,
And sensibilities so fine!
—William Cowper,
The Poet, The Oyster and Sensitive Plant

Oysters and Clams

"He was a bold man that first ate an oyster," wrote Jonathan Swift, in homage to the first human being who deigned to swallow the pulpy meat of that slippery mollusk. No, we don't know the name of the fearless individual, but we can conclude that he lived thousands of years before the written word, and—judging from the popularity of oysters forever after—that he probably found the morsel quite delicious!

Oysters, and their bivalve relatives, clams, have always been popular food items in the West. The clam retains its popularity, but oysters were much more widely enjoyed in the past than today, when the hard-shelled critter is considered an expensive delicacy by most people. There's no evidence that the Egyptians ate oysters, and no mention of the food in the Bible, but archaeologists excavating in Denmark have found oyster and mussel shells among pottery shards dating from 8000 B.C.

Oysters and clams are members of the family of mollusks known as bivalves, so named because they consist of two valves, or shells, enclosing a soft body. The word *oyster* is used to designate a particular genus of bivalves. But the word *clam* is a generic term used to designate some 12,000 species of bivalves. In Scotland, the word refers to the scallop. In the United States, *clam* usually refers to the *quahog,* or hard-shelled clam, and the *steamer,* or soft-shelled clam, though the two sea creatures belong to two entirely different genera of bivalves.

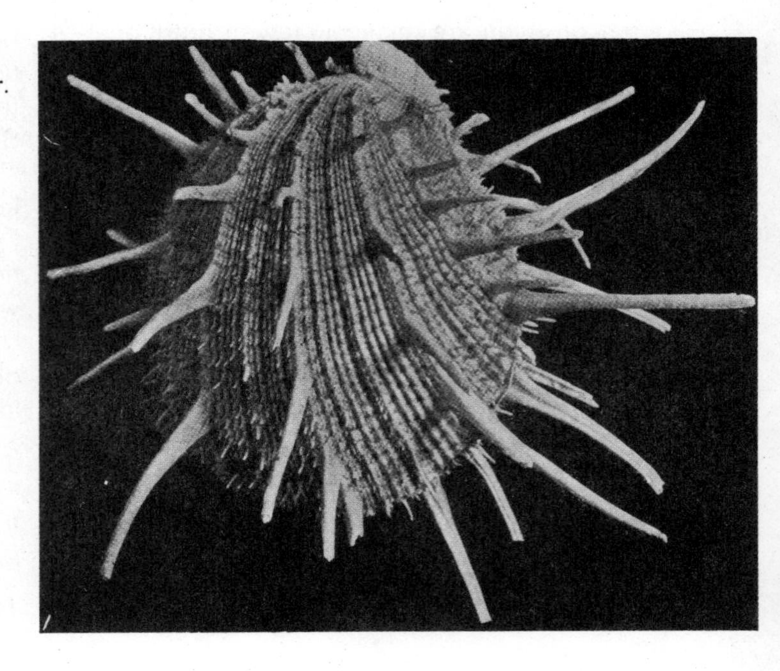

The Royal Thorny oyster.

Hard-shelled clams, found along the Atlantic coast of North America, are the clams you're likely to enjoy on the half-shell. Also called the *quahog*, the hard-shelled clam belongs to a genus of mollusks named *Venus* because of the beauty and symmetry of its shells. The most popular eating clam is that northern quahog, or *cherrystone*. Young quahogs are sold as *Little Necks*.

The ancient Greeks—who gave us the word *oyster* from their *ostreon*—feasted regularly on mollusks. They also used oyster shells for casting votes, scratching the name of the chosen candidate on the inner shell—making Greek politics a real shell game. Greek juries also used the shells in recording their verdicts. Thus a person condemned to exile was "ostracized."

The Romans, too, were voracious oyster eaters. The Romans went so far as to establish a colony at Camulodunum (present-day Colchester, England), where oysters could be gathered and sent back to the Roman dinner table. The first known oyster bed in Italy itself was established by Sergius Aurata in 102 B.C. The famed Roman epicurean and cookbook author Apicius hosted orgiastic banquets featuring oysters. Apicius invented a system to keep his oysters fresh—he stored the mollusks in pewter vessels treated with pitch and vinegar. Eventually, Apicius committed suicide rather than face the poverty that resulted from his largesse.

For a time, the French considered oysters a brain food. King Louis XI feted the Sorbonne professors on oysters once each year "lest their scholarship become deficient." The girthsome gourmet Brillat-Savarin customarily consumed two dozen oysters before breakfast—tuning up, most likely, for the 45-course dinners he regularly attended—and one of Napoleon's marshals devoured over 100 oysters each morning!

Oysters were considerably cheaper in Napoleon's day, but modern oyster-eaters need not hang their head in shame. In 1975, a 48-year-old Florida man gulped down 588 in just 17½ minutes, and in 1977, a man devoured 212 in five minutes. And clam-eaters, take heart: in 1975, in Washington, a man slid 424 of the slimy critters down his gullet in just eight minutes.

In medieval England, an entire bushel of oysters could be bought for about four pence. As late as the mid-19th century,

[illegible] liquor in the kitchen of a gourmet restaurant of the Old South." (1872)

oystermen peddled their wares from wheelbarrows on the streets of London for about four pence a dozen. Dr. Samuel Johnson bought oysters regularly for his pet cat, Hodge. Presumably, he shelled them, too. In fact, oysters were so cheap that the saying arose: "Poverty and oysters always seem to go together." How times do change!

Clams and oysters were long popular among American Indians, who used the shells of a certain hard-shelled clam for *wampum*, or money. The Indians were the first to enjoy a clambake, burying clams along with lobsters and corn in sand pits lined with seaweed and hot coals.

New England colonists quickly made the clambake a culinary custom in that part of the United States. And settlers moving from New England to Ohio were not inclined to surrender the custom simply because there were no clams in Ohio. They buried chickens along with corn instead, but continued to call the feast a clambake. "Chickenbake" just doesn't have the same ring.

Oysters baked in the shell were served at the first American Thanksgiving feast, and oyster roasts were common in Thomas Jefferson's day, with hundreds of the savory sea critters roasted in hot ash until their shells popped open. As early as 1779, the state of Rhode Island set aside part of the public domain for oyster beds. Oyster fishing soon became a big industry on the Atlantic coast, particularly around Long Island—the inlet and town called Oyster Bay attest to this.

German immigrants settling around Cincinnati further popularized oyster eating in the United States. For a time, "oyster parlors" were common meeting places in the city. A rail and river network known as the "oyster express" transported fresh shellfish from Baltimore to Cincinnati. By the 1870s, oysters were a status symbol at dinner parties throughout the nation, and their price had begun to rise.

Oysters planted in tributary of Maryland bay.

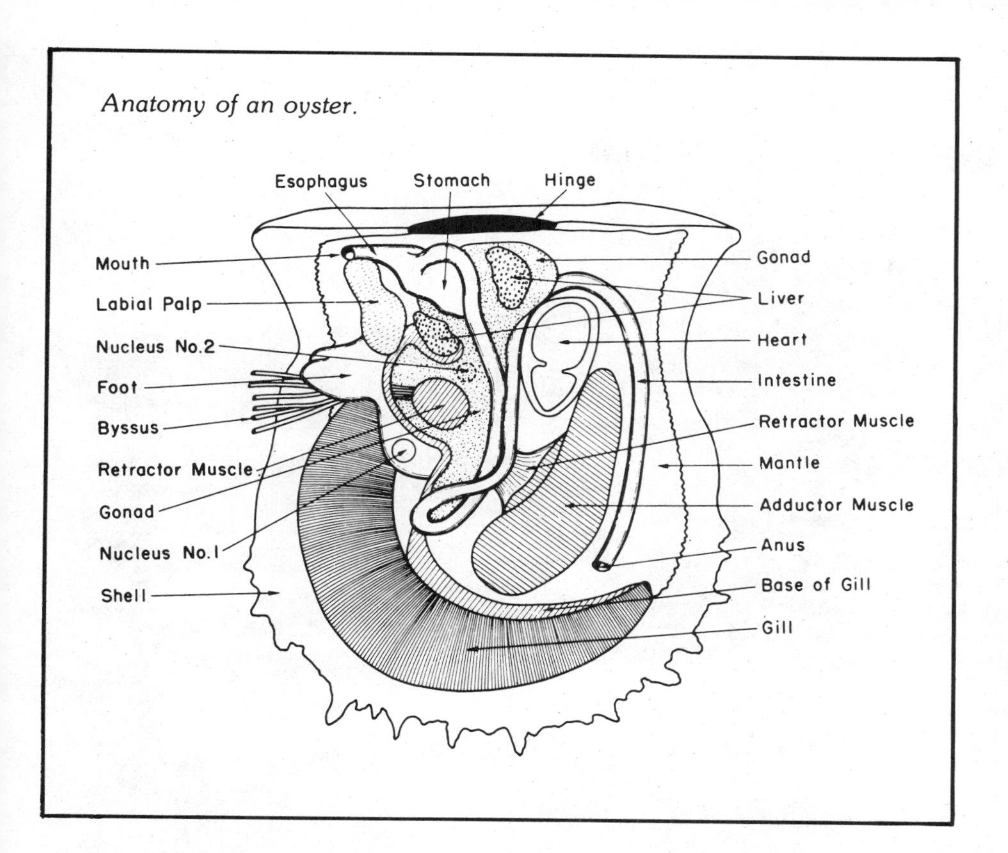

Anatomy of an oyster.

Oysters are cultivated in farms at sea, then transported to beds near the mouth of a river. Many kinds of oyster actually change sex four times each year, alternating between male and female, and each full or part-time female will release two million eggs in the summer—of which only about 50 will survive.

Bivalve larvae are parasites, hooking onto the fins and gills of fish and feeding on the fish's tissues. After a few months of freeloading, the larvae let go of the fish and settle into the mud wherever they land. A newborn oyster will grow from one to four years before it's ready for the dinner table.

A clam can live as long as 10 years if not disturbed by a human or other predator. But clams and oysters see little of the briny deep during their life span, spending their adult lives buried in the mud at the bottom of the water.

Bivalves are equipped with two tubes, called *siphons*, that reach into the water from the creature's half-buried shell. Water flowing through one siphon provides the bivalve with oxygen and food before it flows out the other siphon. An average-sized clam can filter more than 6,000 gallons of water each year through its siphons.

Clams and oysters *can* move, however, pushing along with a small hatchet-shaped foot protruding between the two shells. When danger threatens, the bivalve simply withdraws its foot and siphons and "clams up," closing its shell so snugly only a chisel can pry it open.

Clams are considerably safer from their human enemies at high tide than at low tide, when clam beds are more easily accessible to clammers. The expression "happy as a clam" is actually a shortening of "happy as a clam at high water."

The record for oyster devouring was set in 1975, when a 48-year-old Florida man gulped down 588 in just 17½ minutes. And clam-eaters, take heart: the same year, a Washington man slid 424 of the slimy critters down his gullet in just eight minutes.

Oyster beds in Brittany, France.

The clamshell's gripping power is merely a nuisance to the clam opener, but it could be quite treacherous if you happen to be a pearl diver in the area of the Great Barrier Reef. That's the domain of the *Tridacna gigas*, the world's largest bivalve, which grows to an average of four feet in diameter and weighs about 200 pounds. The largest known specimen, now preserved in the Museum of Natural History in New York, had a body weighing 20 pounds encased in a shell that weighed a quarter of a ton!

Speaking of superlatives, the largest oyster farm in the world is—as any gastronomist might expect—in France, in the Arcachon Basin off the Bay of Biscay. The development of the Arcachon beds came about by complete accident. A Portuguese cargo ship carrying oysters was shipwrecked off the coast of France, and the surviving mollusks founded a colony in the nearby Basin.

The French soon began devouring *huitres* at such a pace that, in 1750, a law was passed that forbade the gathering of mollusks in the Basin for four years. Afterward, oyster gathering was declared illegal from May to October—a law which, coupled with the false rumor that a breeding oyster is inedible, may have led to the belief that oysters are taboo in any month without an "r" (May, June, July, August). Actually, oysters may be eaten at any time of the year.

Another mistaken belief holds that a lucky oyster-eater will occasionally find a small pearl lodged inside his dinner. The fact is the edible oyster does not produce pearls. Pearl oysters are found only in tropical waters, and are not considered fit for consumption. The beautiful iridescent jewel is composed of carbonate of lime, or mother-of-pearl, secreted by the shell lining.

Today, oysters are served raw, grilled, fried, deviled, and in oyster soup. Smoked oysters are imported from Japan and sold as a canned delicacy. Then there's *Oysters Rockefeller*, a gustatory treat created by New Orleans chef Jules Alciatore, which combines oysters with chopped bacon, scallions, spinach, parsley, and bread crumbs. The dish has nothing at all to do with the Rockefellers—the name was selected to suggest the opulence of the dish.

The invention of the oyster cocktail is credited to a California miner of the 1860s, who ordered a glass of whiskey and a plate of oysters and then used the emptied whiskey glass to mix the oysters with Worcestershire sauce, catsup, and pepper sauce. The enterprising bartender thereafter began selling glasses of "oyster cocktail" at 50 cents a throw.

Clam chowder was invented by a group of Breton sailors shipwrecked off the coast of Maine. The venturesome seamen gathered clams and mixed them with salvaged pork, crackers, and potatoes in a large cauldron, or *chaudiere.* Milk was added to the recipe later to produce New England clam chowder, and tomatoes to produce Manhattan clam chowder.

The famed Marennes oyster owes its origin to a peculiar incident that took place during the 17th-century religious wars. At the siege of La Rochelle—described in Dumas' *The Three Musketeers*—the Huguenot defenders began tossing oysters from the parapets of the city when they ran out of more potent ammunition. Some of the missiles landed in the nearby salt marshes. Peasants who later found the oysters discovered the meat had turned an odd green color. The characteristic Marennes green proved to be the result of diatoms (algae) living in the marsh water.

An oyster dredger of the 19th century.

Oyster culture in France.

But the most curious oyster anecdote of all comes to us from 19th-century London. A tavern owner was frightened one evening by a peculiar whistling sound emanating from his storage cellar. Fearing a thief, he tiptoed into the cellar and began gingerly trying to locate the source of the plaintive wailing. What he found was so remarkable that he invited a number of his usual patrons to a special dinner the following night—when Charles Dickens, William Thackeray, and other London notables were delighted by the performance of a singing oyster!

PAPER

Egyptian papyrus was so vital to the Roman Empire that a papyrus crop failure during the reign of Tiberius nearly brought all official and commercial business in Rome to a complete halt.

A Chinese man by the name of Ts'ai Lun is considered by some to be among the 10 most influential persons in all history.

You ask: "Who on earth is Ts'ai Lun? Though his name is unfamiliar to most Westerners, Ts'ai Lun has been credited with the invention of a most important item, without which many other products—including this book—would be impossible—Tsai Lun invented paper.

Before the appearance of paper in the second century, Chinese culture was generally inferior to that of other contemporary civilizations in the West, at least in literacy and technology. But with paper as a tool, Chinese civilization leapt forward to a prosperity unmatched in the West. Then, around the 15th century, Western technology once again gained the ascendancy. The new Western hegemony was due in large part to two new tools: Gutenberg's printing press and, equally important, cheap and plentiful paper to replace expensive papyrus and parchment.

The papyrus reed, or *biblos*, was cultivated in the Nile delta at least as early as 3500 B.C. The Egyptians used the reed for food and fuel, utensils, boats, and ceremonial garlands, but the membranous tissue of the plant's stem was reserved for use as a writing material. Papyrus sheets were made by laying strips of stem tissue together in a crosshatch pattern, and sealing them together with a paste most likely made from bread crumbs soaked in boiling water. The Roman historian Pliny claimed that the Egyptians made their paste solely from the water of the Nile.

Egypt supplied papyrus for the entire ancient world, for the *biblos* has never been grown in any quantity outside that country. Egyptian papyrus was so vital to the Roman Empire that a papyrus crop failure during the reign of Tiberius nearly brought all offi-

cial and commercial business in Rome to a complete halt. Most papyrus documents in Europe vanished long ago due to fire, vandalism, war, or dampness, but the arid climate of Egypt has preserved a number of ancient papyrus scrolls. Arabs continued to use papyrus as a writing material until the eighth or ninth century, but by the 12th century, papyrus had been completely superseded by parchment.

Parchment, made from the skins of calves, goats, sheep, rabbits, and other animals, was competing with papyrus in Europe as early as the second century. A king named Eumenes, who ruled the city of Pergamum in Asia Minor during the second century B.C., is sometimes credited with developing the technology of parchment production. Our word *parchment* is derived from the name of his city. From the very beginning, the finest parchment was made from the more delicate calves' skins, and the word *vellum,* designating the finest parchment of medieval times, is derived from the French word *veau,* "calf."

While the papyrus supply was limited by the size of the crop in the Nile Delta, the supply of parchment was limited by the expense of animal skins. Consequently, both papyrus and parchment remained quite costly through much of their history. In ancient times, wax tablets were used for everyday writing. Characters were pressed into the wax with a sharp stylus, and the wax was melted and was reused afterwards. Medieval monks frequently erased writing from older scraps of parchment and reused them. Fortunately, many of the older writings are visible today under ultraviolet light.

During the Middle Ages, the royalty and clergy were among the few to afford parchment in any quantity. Medieval monarchs published their proclamations on

In the year 105, a privy counselor named Ts'ai Lun presented Emperor Ho Ti with samples of a new writing substance made from some combination of bamboo, mulberry, and other vegetable fibers, along with fish nets and rags—the substance we now call paper.

MAKING PAPER

FROM LEFT TO RIGHT:

(1) Cut bamboo is washed and steeped in a water pit to prepare material for making paper.

(2) Digesting the bamboo pulp.

(3) Making a sheet of paper.

(4) Pressing the sheets of paper.

(5) Drying the sheets of paper.

parchment dyed royal purple, as had been the custom in Rome and Constantinople. The finest Bibles were written in gold or silver on precious stained vellum.

The use of parchment ultimately made possible the replacement of the written scroll by the book, as we know it. A papyrus scroll was constructed of overlapping squares of papyrus pasted together, with the text written in columns across the eight to 15-inch breadth of the scroll. Standard length was from 15 to 20 feet, but a single scroll containing *The Odyssey* or *The Iliad* could stretch up to 150 feet. The Greeks called the scroll a *biblion,* the source of *Bible, bibliography,* and other common words. The Latin word was *volumen.*

To examine a scroll, a reader had to unwind it from the left roller to the right, then rewind it completely when he'd finished. Quick references were, of course, impossible. The difficulty of unwinding and rewinding scrolls has been cited as a reason for the frequent inaccuracy of ancient writers when quoting other authors. Many writers chose simple to rely on their memory rather than take the trouble of dealing with a cumbersome scroll.

Parchment had two advantages over papyrus. First of all, it could be folded without cracking, and therefore could be organized into folded leaves instead of merely being rolled up. Parchment could also be prepared for writing on both sides, an essential quality for any writing material arranged in leaves. The introduction of parchment led to the use of the *codex,* or parchment-leaf book, that was already replacing the scroll by the time of Jesus.

Neither papyrus nor parchment was used at any time in China for a very simple reason: from the second century on, the Chinese had a far better writing material at their disposal. Prior to that, the Chinese had relied on books made of bamboo, which were extremely heavy, and silk, which were very expensive. In the year 105, a privy counselor named Ts'ai Lun presented Emperor Ho Ti with samples of a new writing substance made from some combination of bamboo, mulberry, and other vegetable fibers, along with fish nets and rags—the substance we now call paper.

Alas, Ts'ai Lun's paper profited the rest of humanity far more than it profited its inventor. The eunuch Ts'ai Lun enjoyed a brief period of wealth before becoming involved in a palace intrigue that resulted in a summons to the imperial judges. Instead of appearing in court, Ts'ai Lun retired to his home, took a bath, wrapped himself in his best robes, and and drank poison.

Some historians doubt that Chinese paper manufacture was the achievement of one man alone. But those who extol the accomplishments of Ts'ai Lun point out that, unlike many other inventions, the discovery of paper

was not inevitable even if its inventor had never lived, but rather the work of one gifted individual. Indeed, Europe, which could not boast a Ts'ai Lun of its own, was not to begin manufacturing the paper until 1,000 years after the Chinese inventor had been at it, and then only because Europeans learned the secrets of its production from others.

The use of paper had spread to Korea and Japan by the year 600, but the Chinese continued to guard the secrets of its manufacture from foreign traders and visitors. Then, in 751, Arabs who had occupied the city of Samarkand in Central Asia were attacked by a Chinese army. The Arabs repelled the attack, and captured a number of Chinese skilled in the art of papermaking.

The use of paper made from linen, cotton, and other substances spread quickly throughout the Arab world. We find mention of a paper document in 11th-century Greece, but paper did not reach Europe on any scale until the following century, when the Moors introduced its manufacture to occupied Spain. The Arabs also brought paper to Sicily, and it is on that island that we find the oldest European document written on paper, a deed of King Roger of Sicily that dates from the year 1102.

During the 13th century, the first great paper mills of Europe appeared in the area of Fabriano, Italy, and it is there that we also find the first known watermark. By the 15th century, paper was the most common writing substance in Europe, ousting papyrus completely and relegating the use of parchment to official documents. And just in time: the invention of a practical mechanical printing press by Gutenberg around the middle of the century resulted in a sharp rise in the demand for writing materials. By 1500, close to 40,000 volumes had been printed in 14 different European nations, the majority in Italy and Germany.

The use of the watermark to identify the manufacturer of a piece of paper was unknown in China. Watermarks were used in Fabriano during the 1290s, but the oldest surviving watermark, a circle surmounted by a cross, dates from the year 1302. Watermarks are formed by pieces of wire or wax set in the frame in which the pulp dries. Since less pulp can settle along the outlines of the watermark figure, the paper will be thinner along those lines, rendering the figure visible.

The first watermark in the United States, the word *company*, appeared on paper produced by a mill near Germantown, Pennsylvania, the first paper mill in America. Erected in 1690 by William Rittenhouse and William Bradford, the mill turned out handmade linen paper on the order of 250 pounds per day. Less than a century later, disruptions caused by the American Revolution resulted in a paper famine that spurred the construction of many new mills. By 1810, there were over 200 paper mills in the United States.

N°. 1. Atélier ou l'on délisse les Chiffons.
N°. 4. Fabrication des feuille.
N°. 3.

Paper manufacture in early 19th century.

About one-third of the 18 million volumes in the Library of Congress, the world's largest book and manuscript repository, are too brittle to be handled!

Until the 19th century, most paper was made from substances derived from old linen and cotton rags, and later, from straw. In 1799, a Frenchman named Louis Robert obtained a patent for the manufacture of paper by mechanical means. The resultant increase in paper production, along with a steadily rising literacy rate, created the need for a cheaper, more plentiful raw material for paper manufacture.

Inventors experimented with a number of substances, including hemp, from which the familiar Manila paper has been made here since 1843. By the middle of the 19th century, several processes had been patented for the production of paper from wood pulp. Paper makers at last had an inexpensive, seemingly inexhaustible supply of raw materials for their product, and the forest fire became the single most dangerous threat to world literacy.

World production of paper and paperboard now stands at an astounding 140 million tons per year. How much paper is that? Well, if the entire supply were used to produce standard 20-pound bond typing paper, the yearly world production figure would exceed 40 trillion sheets—10,000 sheets for every person on earth!

And how many trees must be felled to produce that prodigious figure? The answer is difficult to calculate, but 1,000 pounds of pure pulpwood paper require about one cord of wood, or 128 cubic feet.

The United States now leads all other nations in the manufacture of paper and paperboard, producing over 47 million tons a year. (Paperboard is the term applied to any wood pulp product more than .012 inches thick.) Japan ranks a distant second, at about 13 million tons, with Canada and the U.S.S.R. rounding out the top four. The United States is also the home of the world's largest paper mill, the Union Camp Corporation's plant in Savannah, Georgia, which turns out over a million tons of paper annually—an amount equal to 10 percent of the total Canadian production!

As forest land dwindles and paper production soars, wastepaper and other non-pulp materials are becoming increasingly important in paper manufacture. Wastepaper now accounts for about 19 percent of all the paper produced in this country. In West Germany, where the supply of pulpwood is more limited, 45 percent of all paper is made from waste; in forest-rich Finland, only three percent of the paper is made from waste.

Paper is now produced in a nearly infinite variety of kinds and sizes. Bond paper, with or without rag content, is most commonly used for typing paper and stationery. Kraft paper is the coarse, brown substance you see most familiarly in brown paper bags. Blotting paper dates back to at least 1465, and was in common use in Europe by the 16th century. On a more exotic note, handmade Finnish writing paper with a watermark in the form of the buyer's portrait sells for as much as $80 per sheet. More exotic, no doubt, are writing materials from pre-Columbian Peru and Mexico, now in the Vatican Library, which were made from human skin!

Sheet paper is customarily sold by the *ream*. Originally, a ream consisted of 480 sheets, or 20 *quires*, but today, a ream usually contains 500 sheets. The thickness of the paper is indicated by a figure designating the weight of a ream of that paper cut in two-by-three-foot sheets. For example, with "20-pound bond," 500 sheets measuring two-by-three feet will weigh 20 pounds.

If you've ever read the publishing history of an old work of literature, or examined a library card catalog, you may have come across terms such as *folio, octavo,* and *foolscap,* and dismissed them as the esoterica of the bookbinder's craft. These terms refer to the dimensions of the leaves of a book, and the manner in which the pages were folded for binding.

A folio (f) is a book assembled from sheets of paper each folded once, producing two leaves and four pages from each sheet.

A quarto (4to) is a book made from sheets of paper folded twice, producing four leaves and eight pages from each sheet.

An octavo (8vo) is comprised of sheets of paper folded three times, each sheet producing eight leaves and 16 pages.

Foolscap, crown, and *demy* refer to the dimensions of the original sheet of paper. A *foolscap,* for example, is a sheet of paper measuring about 13½ by 17 inches. A *foolscap quarto* is an edition made from foolscap sheets, each folded twice. Each foolscap quarto page will therefore measure about 8½ by6¾ inches.

The term *foolscap* may be derived from the Italian *foglia,* "leaves." But a more interesting derivation traces the term to the period of the English Civil War. Charles I declared that all paper manufactured in England should bear the royal arms as a watermark. When Oliver Cromwell toppled the monarch in 1649, he ordered that a fool's cap and bells be substituted for the royal arms on all English paper. Most of the other terms referring to paper size, such as *demy, crown,* and *royal,* were also derived from a customary watermark.

There is no term for the size of a sheet of paper produced in 1830 by the Whitehall Mills in Derbyshire, England, that measured four feet in width and three miles in length!

The introduction of pulpwood paper has made writing material affordable to all persons, but modern paper does have one major drawback. Pulpwood paper is less durable than paper made from linen or cotton, and the alum-rosin compounds used to coat pulpwood paper produce acids that eat away at the paper. While many parchment manuscripts from the Middle Ages remain in good condition, books printed today are not likely to survive more than 40 to 50 years without turning yellow and brittle.

It would cost an estimated 50 cents per book to use paper durable enough to survive more than a century, compared to over $300 to restore a book once it has suffered the effects of old age. The additional expense might be well worth considering. Already, about one-third of the 18 million volumes in the Library of Congress, the world's largest book and manuscript repository, are too brittle to be handled!

World production of paper and paperboard now stands at an astounding 140 million tons per year. How much paper is that? Well, if the entire supply were used to produce standard 20-pound bond typing paper, the yearly world production figure would exceed 40 trillion sheets—10,000 sheets for every person on earth!

Peanuts

The peanut might seem to be a plant that can't quite make up its mind where it belongs in the world of botanical classification. What's your guess? A nut, you say? Nope—the goober is actually more a pea than a nut. The tasty morsel we call the peanut is the pod or legume—not the nut—of the *arachis hypogea* plant.

But the peanut is an unusual member of the pea family, since its pods have the peculiar habit of ripening underground.

After the plant's flower is pollinated, a stalklike structure called a *peg* begins growing from the base of the flower toward the soil. Only when the tip of the peg is below the surface do the fertilized ovules begin to develop their characteristic pods.

The one to three "nuts" found inside the shell are the seeds of the plant, and the tiny morsel found inside the nut when it's split open is the only part of the seed with reproductive powers.

The peanut is a native of tropical South America. Spanish conquistadores exploring the New World found South American Indians eating what many called *cacohuate,* or "earth cocoa."

The goober was gradually transplanted in West Africa as a food and fodder crop. Slave traders found that the peanut could provide cheap, nutritious food for Africans being carried across the ocean on slave ships. Eventually, some African peanuts were brought to Virginia and planted for livestock fodder. Thus, the peanut made two transatlantic journeys before becoming a North American crop.

Peanuts were used in Virginia as fodder for pigs, and the soft, juicy ham made from peanut-fattened hogs has ever since been known as *Virginia Ham.*

The peanut has also been called *groundnut* and *earthnut,* both aptly suggestive of the plant's peculiar subterranean habits. The word *goober* is reputedly of African origin, from the Bantu *naguba.*

George Washington Carver is the man most responsible for wide-spread cultivation of peanuts in the United States. Carver's work in the early part of this century showed that the peanut could help free the South from its dependence upon cotton, and restore needed nitrogen to soil depleted by cotton cultivation. When Carver began his research in the 1890s, the goober was not even recognized as a crop; by 1940, the peanut ranked as one of the six leading crops in America, and the largest crop in the southern United States after cotton.

Carver, the son of a slave, not only demonstrated the ecological advantages of peanut cultivation, but found new uses for the crop after it had become over-abundant in the United States as a foodstuff. Carver discovered some 300 derivatives of the goober, including cheese, milk, flour, coffee, ink, dye, plastics, soap, wood stains, linoleum, cosmetics, and medicinal oils.

Peanut butter is one peanut derivative we can't thank Carver for. That great favorite of the schoolboy was introduced by a St. Louis doctor in 1890 for patients who needed an easily digestible form of protein. Today, about half of the United States' annual peanut harvest of some four billion pounds is used for peanut butter, with the remainder going to salted nuts, candies, oil, and livestock fodder. Only about 10 percent of our crop is used to manufacture peanut oil.

Planters Peanuts, the world's largest dealer in peanut products, was founded in 1906 by Amadeo Obici, an Italian immigrant who had journeyed alone to America as a 12-year-old boy. Starting as a peanut vendor in Wilkes-Barre, Pennsylvania, Obici built Planters into a 10 million dollar a year business within a quarter-century.

These peanuts are grown in Red Level, Alabama

Photo courtesy of USDA and photographer Steve Wade.

"The Nickel Lunch"

IT'S not a real beach unless equipped with sand, sea, sunshine and Planters Pennant Salted Peanuts. When once you've tasted these flavory, golden peanuts you'll see how necessary they are. You just can't resist them. The biggest, plumpest peanuts in the whole crop—fresh and crisp as a sea breeze—roasted to a healthy tan and with the salty tang that adds to appetite. You can eat all you want of them. They're as wholesome as all out doors. "The Nickel Lunch".

Even though taken from the Planters can, and sold in the Planters jar, they are not Planters Salted Peanuts unless they are in the glassine bag with the "Planters" name and "Mr. Peanut" on it.

Planters Nut & Chocolate Co., Wilkes-Barre, Pa., Suffolk, Va., San Francisco, New York, Chicago, Boston, Philadelphia

MR. PEANUT
REG. U.S. PAT. OFF.

Planters
PENNANT SALTED
PEANUTS

Remember the days of the "nickel lunch?" Today this small bag of peanuts costs a quarter.

"Mr. Peanut," the company's trademark, began his association with Planters in 1916, when the firm offered a prize for the best trademark suggestion. A 14-year-old Virginia boy submitted a drawing for an animated peanut, another artist added the familiar cane, hat, and monocle, and "Mr. Peanut" was soon appearing promoting Planters peanuts everywhere.

The peanut requires at least five months of strong sunshine and 24 inches of rain annually, and thus is restricted to the warmer regions of earth. India is the largest peanut-producing nation, followed by China and West Africa, with the United States fourth in total production.

As a food, the goober is one of the most concentrated sources of nourishment known to man. Pound for pound, the peanut provides more protein, minerals, and vitamins than beef liver, more fat than heavy cream, and—dieters beware—more calories than sugar. Recent experiments in Africa have shown that the discarded shells of the peanut can also be used as animal fodder!

Peanuts may be basically a snack food in the United States, but in many parts of Africa and Asia the goober is an indispensable part of the diet. To demonstrate the importance of the peanut in other nations, we might note that the first American to be honored with a monument in India was none other than George Washington Carver. In 1947, the peanut growers of India unveiled a monument in Bombay to commemorate the American's outstanding work.

PEANUT SOUP

- 1/4 cup margarine or butter
- 1/4 cup minced onion
- 1/2 cup peanut butter
- 1/4 cup chopped celery
- 1 tablespoon flour
- 4 cups beef bouillon
- 2 teaspoons lemon juice
- 1/2 cup chopped roasted peanuts
- 1 tablespoon chopped parsley

1. Melt the butter or margarine.
2. Sauté the onion and celery in the shortening until tender.
3. Put these ingredients into a double boiler. Add peanut butter, flour, beef bouillon, and lemon juice, and blend well.
4. Bring the water in the bottom of the double boiler to a boil, and cook for 20 minutes. Stir the mixture occasionally.
5. Before serving, sprinkle the soup with chopped peanuts, and a dash of very finely chopped parsley.

Serves eight.

PEANUT PIE

- 1 cup sugar
- 1/4 cup light corn syrup
- 1/2 cup margarine
- 3 eggs
- 1/2 teaspoon vanilla extract
- 1 1/2 cups roasted peanuts
- 1 nine-inch pastry shell

1. Combine sugar, corn syrup, melted margarine, eggs, and vanilla in a large mixing bowl. Blend thoroughly.
2. Stir in the roasted peanuts.
3. Turn the mixture into the unbaked pastry shell.
4. Bake in 375° oven for 45 minutes.

Serve warm as is. If you serve the pie cold, garnish with large dollops of whipped cream.

Pianos

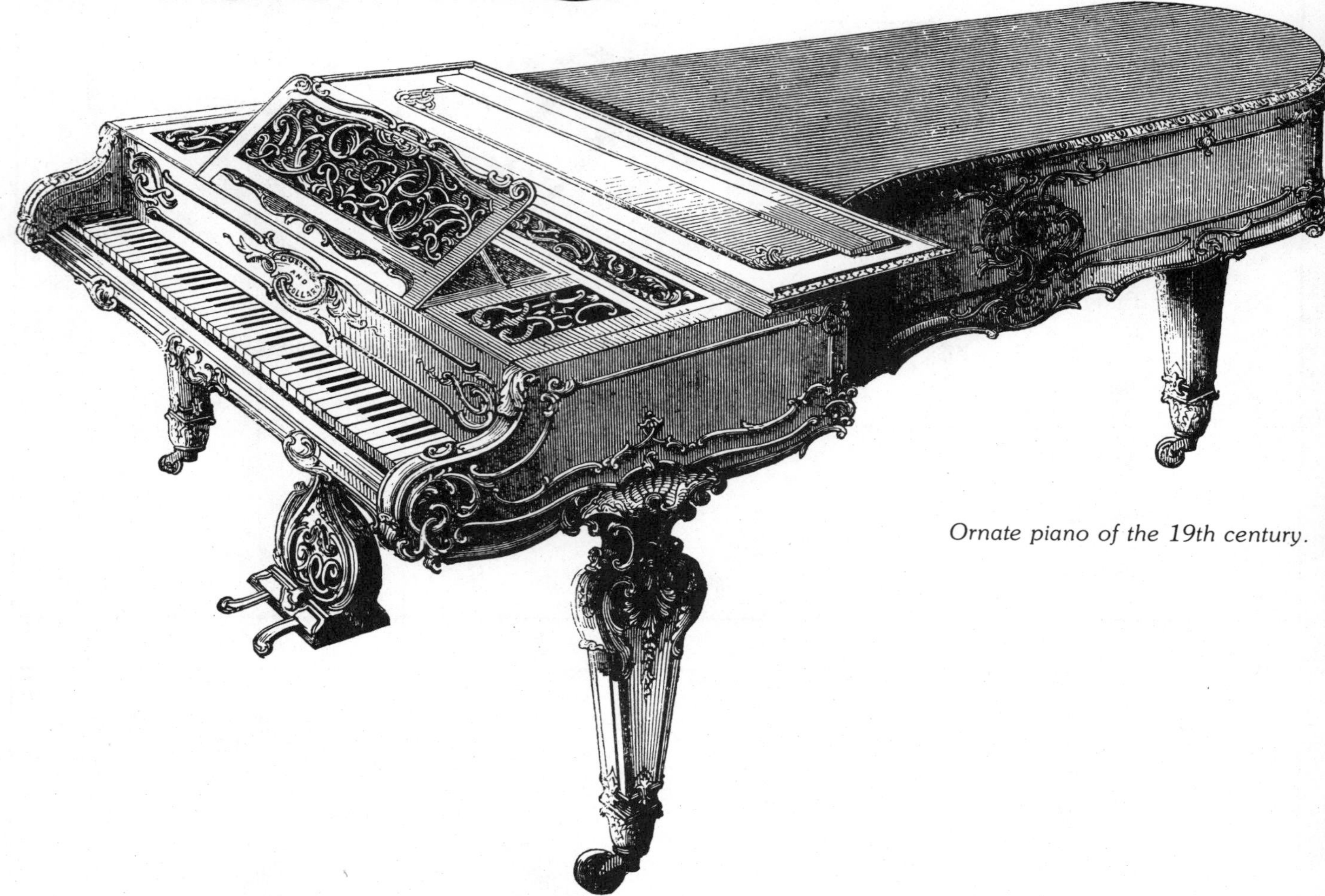

Ornate piano of the 19th century.

Most pianos are harmless things, if people would only let them alone.

Twenty-one million Americans— about one of every 10—now play the piano, more than the number who play all other musical instruments combined.

About 180,000 new pianos are sold in the United States each year, close to double the annual total for the 1930s. We have no idea how many of those pianos are played regularly, and how many merely occupy space in a living room. But there's no question that the piano, though less than 300 years old, is the most popular musical instrument throughout the Western world. If the present trend continues, the piano may someday be No. 1 in the Orient as well!

About 750,000 pianos are produced worldwide each year. What manufacturer would you guess to be the world's largest piano producer? Steinway? Baldwin? Another old, distinguished European firm? Well, only about 60,000 pianos are currently produced in Europe each year—in addition to the 170,000 manufactured in the Soviet Union. In fact, since 1960, the largest piano manufacturer in the world has been Yamaha, a Japanese firm that turns out close to 190,000 pianos a year! Japan is presently the largest piano producing country, manufacturing over 280,000 pianos annually. Even more surprising, most of those pianos are sold *in* Japan, which by and large was not introduced to the instrument until this century!

The Japanese did not invent the piano, of course. Traditional Oriental music cannot be played on any of the popular Western keyboard instruments. The piano and its precursors—the clavichord and harpsichord—directly embody the structure of Western music, and their design was altered as that music evolved from medieval plainsong to the tonal music familiar to our ears today.

There are two basic ways to produce musical tones: with wind or with vibrating strings. Wind was first employed by a keyboard instrument as early as the third century B.C., Ctesibius of Alexandria built a hydraulic pipe organ activated by a keyboard. A keyboard may have been applied to a stringed instrument as early as the 10th century, but the keyboard instruments that led to the invention of the piano did not appear in Europe until four centuries later.

The immediate precursor of the first stringed instrument with a keyboard was the *monochord.* This instrument consisted of a wooden sounding box with a single string and a movable bridge. The bridge could be shifted at fixed intervals to determine the length of the string, and hence, its tone. The ancient Greek philosopher Pythagoras used the monochord to investigate the nature of musical sound. In later centuries, monochords were constructed with more than one string. Then, during the 14th century, an unknown inventor devised a stringed instrument in which the length of the strings was fixed by hammers activated by a keyboard. This was the clavichord.

The word *clavichord*—formed from the combination of the Latin *clavis,* "key," and *chorda,* "string"—was first mentioned in 1404, but the instrument probably appeared during the preceding century in England, France, or Spain. By the 15th century, the clavichord was well known by musicians throughout Europe. In some ways, the clavichord was closer in function to the piano than the harpsichord and other later keyboard instruments.

The rear end of each clavichord key was fitted with an upright metal tangent. When the key was depressed, the tangent rose to strike one or more metal strings. In early clavichords, the strings were of equal length; the tangent itself formed a second bridge when it struck the string, thus determining the length of the string and its tone. The harder the key was struck, the harder the tangent's impact, and hence, the louder the sound. But the clavichord's sound was generally small, making the instrument unsuitable for play with an ensemble.

The *harpsichord,* which marks the next stage of keyboard evolution, provided a louder, more resonant sound, and therefore was commonly used along with other instruments. While the clavichord sounded a string by striking it with a hammer, the harpsichord plucked the string with a short quill called a *plectrum.* The rear end of each harpsichord key was fitted with an upright jack bearing a plectrum made from crow quill or leather. When the key was depressed, a felt damper was lifted from the string to be sounded, the jack rose, and the plectrum plucked the string. When the key was released, the jack fell back into place, while the plectrum swung away on a pivoted tongue so that it could not again pluck the string.

Like the organ, the harpsichord offered no dynamics—no matter how hard the key was struck, the plectrum plucked the string with the same force. Composers writing for the instrument had to provide their own dynamics, adding or subtracting tones to thicken or thin the texture.

The harpsichord—so called because its strings were thought to resemble a prostrate harp—appeared in Europe before 1425, and for a time developed, side by side, with the clavichord. While the organ was retained in church, the harpsichord became the predominant keyboard instrument in the theater or concert hall. At home, cheaper harpsichordlike instruments called the *spinet* and the *virginal* were most common. The rectangular virginal, a favorite of Queen Elizabeth, was often small enough to be placed on a table or in the lap. The term is derived from the Latin word for *girl,* since a small keyboard instrument was largely conceived of as feminine, in contrast to the manly lute.

Early in the 18th century, when the piano first appeared, Western music was undergoing fundamental changes that made most earlier keyboard configurations obsolete. The predominant form of music from the days of ancient Greece up through the Middle Ages was *modal,* built on seven scales called *modes.* Thus, the earliest keyboards contained only seven tones in various octaves: *A* through *G,* with no chromatics (black keys). Since there was no way of otherwise distinguishing the keys, the letters *A* through *G* were often marked directly on the keys.

Then, through the Renaissance period, music gradually evolved from modality to *tonality*, with only two modes or keys, major and minor. Tonality created the need for *chromatics*, or intervals between the *A* through *G* notes— the black keys. First to appear on a keyboard was the B-flat key— the flat symbol was originally just a small *B*. Most 15th-century keyboards contained nine tones per octave: seven white keys plus a B-flat and an F-sharp. Full chromatic keyboards had appeared on organs by the 14th century, but the earliest full chromatic keyboards to appear on stringed instruments contained a separate black key for each sharp and flat—the B-flat was not equivalent in tone to the A-sharp.

Then, beginning around 1690, the *tempered scale* was gradually adopted. It's difficult to explain the tempered scale without delving into mathematics and acoustical physics, but basically the tempered scale equalized the intervals between a black key and its neighboring white keys—B-flat and A-sharp became identical tones. Frequent key changes were possible, and keyboards now matched the modern piano—seven white keys and five black keys within each octave. Early in the 1770s, Bach demonstrated the versatility of the tempered scale by composing his *Well-Tempered Clavier*, which consisted of two pieces of music in each of the 12 major and 12 minor keys.

Through the 18th century, *polyphonic* music, consisting of two or more independent melodies, gave way to *homophonic* music, in which a predominant melody was played over a chordal accompaniment. Hand in hand with the development of homophonic music came the need for keyboard instruments with dynamics—the capability of playing a note loudly or softly. As the composer Couperin wrote in 1713: "The harpsichord is perfect in its compass and brilliant in itself; but as one cannot increase or diminish its sounds, I will be forever grateful to those who . . . will succeed in rendering this instrument capable of expression." Couperin probably did not know that such an instrument had already been invented—the piano.

Italian letters dating from 1598 mention a keyboard instrument called the *piano e forte*, but the instrument they describe was merely an improved harpsichord with a mechanism to provide dynamics. The invention of the first true piano was undoubtedly the work of an Italian genius named Bartolomeo Cristofori, harpsichord maker and tender of musical instruments for Florentine Prince Ferdinand dei Medici.

Sometime between 1693 and 1700, Cristofori removed the plectra from the harpsichord's upright jacks and instead attached the jacks to leather-tipped hammers. When a key was depressed, the jack rose and threw the hammer against the string. The key also lifted a damper from the string to be sounded, allowing the string to resonate until the key was released.

In *piano e forte* models built in 1720 and 1726, Cristofori added a device that prevented the hammer from falling back to its original place immediately after striking the string, allowing for quick repetition of a note. But what was more significant about Cristofori's invention, the touch on the key determined the force with was that the hammer struck the string—the harder the touch, the louder the sound. In fact, Cristofori called his invention a *gravicembalo col piano e forte*—"harpsichord with soft and loud." Cristofori's 1720 piano is now on exhibit at the Metropolitan Museum of Art in New York.

Word of Cristofori's work soon reached Germany, inspiring organ builder Gottfried Silbermann to construct a piano of his own. In 1736, five years after Cristofori's death, Silbermann showed two of his pianos to Johann Bach, but the master did not find them to his liking, complaining that the touch was too heavy and the upper registers too weak. Ten years later, Silbermann demonstrated an improved piano to King Frederick the Great of Prussia, and the monarch ordered a number of them—three of which survive.

The harpsichord remained in common use through most of the 18th century, but the higher cost of maintaining the harpsichord's plectra made the piano a more attractive home instrument for most people. Although Voltaire called the piano "a boiler-maker's instrument," the piano gradually gained in popularity until it was recognized as a distinct new instrument rather than an improved harpsichord.

During the 1770s, Muzio Clementi became one of Europe's first pianists of renown, composing keyboard music in a new style suited to the piano. After 1790, Haydn abandoned the harpsichord in favor of the piano, and Mozart wrote almost all of his later keyboard music for the piano. But Mozart's piano pieces—as well as Beethoven's first piano sonatas—were composed for the then contemporary pianos which had only five octaves.

During the 1760s, a student of Silbermann named Johann Zumpe began making pianos in London, introducing the first English *square piano*—a piano in an oblong horizontal case, similar in shape to the earlier virginal. By 1800, the square piano had become the most popular keyboard instrument in middle-class parlors throughout Europe, and had even found its way to Mideastern harems, where its legs were shortened so that a player could reach the keys while sitting on a pillow.

By that time, harpsichord making had virtually ended. But most 19th-century pianos were far from perfectly dependable. Composer/pianist Franz Liszt often attacked his piano so violently that hammers would fly from the carriage, and strings would snap from the force of his blows. Audiences came to expect such accidents, and felt cheated if Liszt did not break at least one string during a concert performance.

Upright pianos and harpsichords had appeared during the 18th century, but the cases of these early instruments were extremely tall. Then, in 1800, John Hawkins, an Englishman who had emigrated to Philadelphia, patented the first upright "portable grand" similar to the shorter upright piano of today, with the vertical strings reaching to the floor. By 1900, the upright was by far the most popular home piano in the United States. In 1904, when the piano manufacturers' convention met in Atlantic City, New Jersey, the conferees symbolically ushered in the reign of the upright by burning a collection of old square pianos.

The upright piano may be smaller, cheaper, and more convenient to transport than the concert grand, but it cannot match the latter instrument in tone quality. With a concert grand, the floor underneath the horizontal strings acts as an additional sounding board, and the raised lid helps project the sound. Also, the concert grand employs gravity in part to return a hammer to place after it strikes the strings, while the hammer of an upright is returned by a spring mechanism. Thus the grand has slightly better action.

By 1900, the Pleyel firm of France, Bechstein of Germany, and Broadwood of England were virtually synonymous with the piano in those countries. The earliest pianos in America were imported from Europe; but by 1775, Americans had piano manufacturers of their own. The first U.S. piano was produced that year by a German immigrant in Philadelphia. Within a decade, piano factories were common in New York. By the end of the 19th century, the best American pianos were recognized as equal to any produced in Europe. American piano sales were climbing toward their peak year of 1909, when 364,500 new pianos were purchased there.

The firm that did the most to establish the quality of American pianos was founded in 1853, when a German immigrant named Heinrich Steinweg and four of his sons began manufacturing pianos in New York. By 1859, a huge factory was turning out pianos bearing the family name—changed by now to Steinway—that were to become the premier concert pianos in America. In 1867, Steinway pianos earned the plaudits of Europeans when displayed at a Paris exposition, with composer G.A. Rossini proclaiming the Steinway "as great as thunder and the storm, and sweet as the piping of the nightingale."

In 1903, the Steinway Company presented its 100,000th piano to the White House, where it resided until 1938, when it was replaced by the firm's 300,000th model. Today, the Steinway remains for most pianists the last word in fine American pianos, but in sheer numbers the largest piano producers in this country are Aeolian, Baldwin, Kimball, and Wurlitzer.

The standard concert grand piano is now almost nine feet long, with a compass of seven octaves plus a minor third, although some European pianos have a compass of eight full octaves. Ebony has long been used for the black keys—according to some, it

19th-century piano that could be turned into a table.

was originally adopted to better show off feminine white hands—but many pianos now use black plastic instead. Concert grands still employ ivory as a covering for their white keys, but most upright pianos substitute a white plastic substance. The modern piano, incredibly intricate in construction, contains close to 12,000 individual parts.

Even more intricate is the *player piano,* probably the only musical instrument in history that replaced the musician altogether. Patented in the United States in 1897, after an earlier English model, the player piano employs a spinning roll of perforated paper; the pattern of perforations governs the passage of air acting on a valve, which in turn sets the keys in motion. All the proud owner of a player piano has to do is preset the tempo for a particular piece of music. Some player pianos were self-contained units, while others were attached to a regular piano for automated playing. Though player pianos enjoyed a brief resurgence during the 1960s, they have, by and large, disappeared in the wake of radio and phonographic records.

Other piano novelties include a 1780 model with a circular keyboard, so constructed as to bring all keys perpendicular to the player. Pianos have been designed with all keys level and of the same color, or with a keyboard of alternating black and white keys.

In 1882, a Hungarian patented a piano that employed six keyboards, three tuned a half-tone higher than the other three. Designed to facilitate the fingering of certain chords and arpeggios, this piano enjoyed a brief vogue during the 1890s, when schools teaching the instrument's playing style were established in New York and Berlin.

Another piano constructed during the late 19th century contained a number of special-effects keyboards, including a "bassoon" pedal that brought a piece of parchment into contact with the lower strings to produce a buzzing sound reminiscent of the reed instrument; a pedal that activated a triangle and cymbal; and another that beat a drumstick against the underside of the soundboard.

Still another piano that enjoyed passing success during the 19th century was the pedal piano, which was equipped with a full pedal keyboard similar to that of the organ.

Most modern pianos are equipped with only two pedals— the *soft* pedal produces a softer sound by bringing the hammers closer to the strings, or by shifting the hammers so each strikes two instead of three strings; the *sustaining* pedal lifts the dampers from all the strings to sustain harmonies and allow each string to vibrate along with the sounded strings. American pianos sometimes contain a third pedal, the *Sostenuto,* which allows all sounded strings to continue resonating until the pedal is released.

The most recent arrival on the keyboard scene is the *electronic piano,* which first came into widespread use during the 1960s. These instruments electronically amplify tones most often produced by hammers striking metal bars. Though its sound lacks the overtones of a true stringed instrument, an electronic piano can be amplified to high volume for use in large jazz or rock bands, or attached to special-effects devices that alter the piano's timbre. Just as keyboard players gradually came to recognize the piano as an instrument distinct from the harpsichord, many pianists now regard an electronic piano as a distinct instrument rather than an amplified piano, with a playing style all its own.

If nothing else, the much lighter electronic piano could someday put the piano mover out of business. Another piano that might have driven even the brawniest piano mover to seek other employment was manufactured in 1935 by Challen of London, measuring 11 feet, eight inches in length, and weighing over one-and-a-third tons. The longest string of this piano, the grandest grand of all times, was nearly 10 feet long!

But the most astounding superlatives associated with the piano are related not to size, but to endurance. In 1894, an Englishman set the first recorded mark for long-term piano playing by tickling the ivories for 48 consecutive hours—without repeating a single song!

An even more impressive endurance record was established in 1967, when 67-year-old Heinz Arntz played continually—except for two hours of sleep daily—for 1,056 hours. Beginning his stint in Germany, Arntz was carried in a van to a seaport, traveled by steamship to the United States, and finished his performance at Roosevelt, Long Island, 44 tuneful days later!

Alas, Arntz's transatlantic marathon remained a world's record for only three years. In 1970, James Crowley of Scranton, Pennsylvania, played consecutively for almost 45½ days—except for the allowed two hours of sleep daily. We're not sure if Crowley was paid for his feat, but if so, his fee probably did not approach the $138,000 that American pianist Liberace once earned for a single New York performance. Adjusting for inflation, however, the highest paid classical pianist of all time was probably I.J. Paderewski, Prime Minister of Poland around

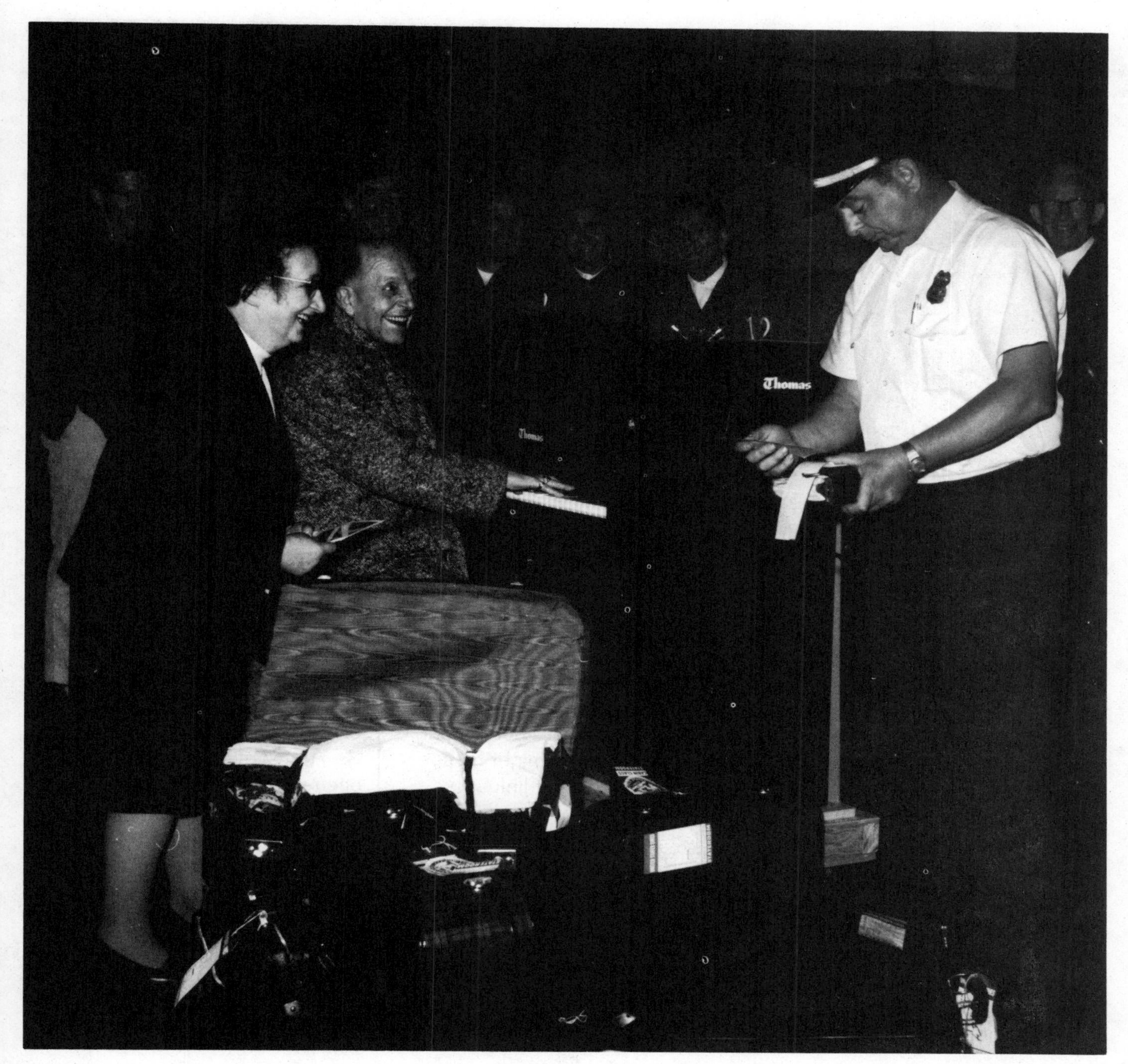

Heinz Arntz, aged 67, establishes a record of continuous nonstop piano playing. As his wife watches, he continues to pound the piano which he took aboard the S.S. United States from Bremerhaven, Germany on September 15, 1966. At the time of this photo, he had played nonstop for 816 hours. He is shown here as a Customs Inspector in New York checks his baggage.
Wide World Photos.

1920, who amassed a fortune of some five million dollars for displaying his keyboard wizardry in concert.

Record-setting piano performances are also within the reach of those not fortunate enough to play the instrument. The sport of piano smashing has been a popular pastime in the British Isles for some time. In 1968, six Irishmen in Merton, England—well, smashed all previous records in their sport, by demolishing an upright piano and passing the pieces of wreckage through a circle nine inches in diameter in just two minutes, 26 seconds!

If you're wondering how the sport of piano smashing developed, you've never tried to discard an old piano.

In an age when amusement arcades offer their patrons electronic tennis, basketball, baseball, hockey, auto racing, tank, airplane, or rocket warfare, and an unlimited array of other video-screen games, an older, simpler pastime still holds center stage in most modern arcades: the venerable pinball machine.

Despite the allure of competing video games, pinball buffs in unprecedented numbers are now feeding coins into their favorite machine for a chance to test their reflexes against a flashing, ringing device that offers neither a cash reward, prize, nor congratulatory acknowledgment. Pinball is, quite simply, man versus machine. And though the machine is almost always the winner, man has been undauntedly accepting the challenge for close to 50 years—with no sign of surrender.

Games in which round objects are propelled into holes or against pegs probably predate written history. But the most immediate precursor of pinball may be the game of *bagatelle*. Popular during the 19th century, bagatelle was played on an oblong slate or cloth-covered board, with players using a cue stick to shoot balls into nine numbered scoring cups. Obviously, bagatelle was much more like billiards than modern pinball.

In 1871, a Cincinnati man named Montague Redgrave patented a game that might be considered the "missing link" between bagatelle and pinball. Called *Improvements in Bagatelle*, Redgrave's game employed a spring plunger rather than a cue stick to propel the balls onto the playfield, pins to alter a ball's direction, and bells to indicate a high score—all familiar elements of modern pinball. Redgrave's invention spawned many imitators, including the *Log Cabin* of the 1880s, a table-top game with pins that many people mistakenly call the first pinball game. Gradually, bagatelle-type games began to resemble pinball, but it wasn't until the 1920s that games similar to modern pinball really caught on in the United States.

Amusement arcades had been popular here since the turn of the century. But games of skill or chance usually took a back seat in the arcades to fortune-telling machines, mechanical peep shows, and strength-testing devices. As coin-operated amusement machines found their way into drugstores, bars, candy stores, tobacco shops, and other establishments, the demand for new types of mechanical games increased.

In 1928, one manufacturer produced *Billiard Skill*, the first

A political cartoon from 1863 showing American President Abraham Lincoln playing a game of bagatelle, an early forerunner of present-day pinball.

game in which steel balls were propelled by a plunger onto a horizontal playfield. Two years later, a Chicago firm turned out *Whoopee,* a game similar to *Improvements in Bagatelle* played on a 24-by-48-inch board. In arcades, a nickel bought a play of 10 balls. Neither of these games bore a strong resemblance to pinball. But 1930 also saw the appearance of *Little Whirl-Wind*, the game most often credited for the surge in pinball popularity that occurred during the next few years.

Though *Little Whirl-Wind* was to provide an impetus for the subsequent growth of the pinball industry, the game actually resembled modern pinball a good deal less than some of its predecessors. Invented by one Howard Peo of Rochester, New York, *Little Whirl-Wind* was an upright game small enough for a countertop. For one penny, a player could propel five balls around a spiral maze and into scoring holes; the farther through the maze the ball traveled, the higher in value the scoring holes. The game was easy to maintain, inexpensive to purchase, and challenging enough to attract players by the droves. Advertisers billed it as the "Greatest Legal Penny Amusement Machine Ever Put on the Market." The pinball boom had begun.

One of the first entrepreneurs to move into the pinball industry was David Gottlieb, a Chicago-based film distributor and arcade machine manufacturer. In 1931, Gottlieb produced a counter top game called *Baffle Ball,* the first widely successful horizontal pinball game. *Baffle Ball* was a simple game by modern standards: for one penny, players attempted to shoot seven balls into four circular scoring areas, or into lower-scoring slots at the bottom of the playfield. A ball shot into a cup called the "Baffle Point" doubled the score of the entire table, provided it was not knocked off by a subsequent ball. The added challenge of the Baffle Point struck the fancy of pinball players from coast to coast. Within a year, Gottlieb was producing 400 *Baffle Ball* machines a day.

One of Gottlieb's West Coast jobbers was Harry Williams, considered by many the true father of the modern pinball industry. At a 1929 convention, Williams was intrigued by a coin-operated game called *Jai Alai,* in which players attempted to flip balls into scoring hoops mounted on an upright playfield. Williams immediately took out a franchise for *Jai Alai;* then founded a manufacturing company in Los Angeles and began turning out his own coin-operated games.

At first, Williams bought and modernized old bagatelle-type machines, designing new playfields and installing them in the old bagatelle cabinets. Later, he began to invent entirely new games, devising many of the features still common to pinball machines around the world. His first invention was called *Advance,* a 10-ball game whose intricate design demanded more skill of players than any previous game. More importantly, *Advance* was the game that spawned the familiar "tilt" mechanism so detested by avid pinballers.

Early pinball machines were vulnerable to sharp blows by players that could jar a ball into a desired hole, making pinball a game of brute force rather than finesse. When Williams observed a player smacking the bottom of an *Advance* machine to jar open mechanical gates that were supposed to be opened only by a well-aimed ball, he decided to devise a mechanism to prevent such rough treatment. His first attempt was crude: nails were hammered into the underside of the machine to provide a painful surprise to players attempting to slap the board from underneath.

Soon after this, Williams devised a more gentle deterrent. Called a "stool pigeon," the device consisted of a small ball set atop a pedestal, with a metal ring underneath. When the machine was lifted or pounded too heavily, the ball fell from the pedestal to the metal ring, stopping play. A player trying out the newly-equipped *Advance* game, surprised when his strong-arm tactics ended the game, exclaimed: "Look! It tilted!" And "stool pigeon" became "tilt" forevermore.

Williams was also the inventor of the electric "pendulum tilt" built into many modern machines. The device consists of a plumb bob hung by a wire, with a thin metal rod protruding from the bottom of the bob. If the machine is pushed too far in any direction, the rod makes contact with a metal ring, completing an electric circuit that stops the machine and illuminates the "tilt" light. Needless to say, this device is not overly popular among pinball fans, but it does increase the challenge of the game and limits wear and tear on the machines.

In 1933, Harry Williams broke new ground with the invention of the first electric pinball machine feature. Included in a game called *Contact,* the battery-powered device was the forerunner of the modern kick-out hole. A ball landing in a certain hole completed a circuit that triggered an electrically powered peg and ejected a ball placed in another hole. Shortly after, Williams added an electric doorbell to one of his games. Other electrical innovations followed, completely revolutionizing an industry that had heretofore been entirely mechanical.

Williams included his first electric tilt mechanism in *Multiple*, a game produced in association with the Bally Company, founded by Chicago manufacturer Ray Moloney. Moloney had been a coin machine distributor for Gottlieb and other firms until 1931, when he built his first pinball machine, *Ballyhoo*. The game included a "Bally Hole," similar in principle to the Baffle Point. At 10 balls for a penny, *Ballyhoo* was an immediate sensation, launching Moloney on a pinball-machine making career, and laying the groundwork for the Bally Manufacturing Company, today the world's largest producer of slot machines and other electric coin game equipment.

The back glass—the upright portion of the modern pinball machine—made its first appearance during the late 1930s. Originally intended to hold various electric features such as the point totalizers, the back glass was soon sporting the comic artwork so much a part of the modern pinball machine. Artwork quickly began to appear on the playfield itself. Attracted by the colorful illustrations, the electric buzzers and bells, and the continuing innovations of Williams, Gottlieb, Moloney, and others, gamesters began swarming around pinball machines in unprecedented numbers.

But at the same time that pinball manufacturers were turning out new electric games to challenge the growing number of players, pinball came under increased opposition from political and church groups opposed to gambling. During the early 1930s, slot machines and other pay-out games were still legal in many parts of the country. Since pinball was a novelty game played for fun only, many players began to turn their attention to games that offered cash as well as self-satisfaction for a skillfully played, or lucky, game. In 1933, Bally introduced *Rocket,* the first automatic pay-out pinball machine. Now a player reaching a certain score, or hitting a special target, received an immediate cash pay-out from the machine—a highly attractive feature to Americans of the Depression era.

Until then, pinball had suffered little from legal restraints. But once Bally, Williams, and other manufacturers began to produce pay-out games, opponents of gambling cast a suspicious eye toward pinball. Newspapers carried stories incorrectly linking pinball operators with organized crime. Politicians accused pinball makers of teaching and encouraging gambling among teenagers. In 1939, the city of Atlanta passed a bill stipulating a fine of $20 and imprisonment of up to 30 days for operating a pinball machine in the city. Other cities and states rushed onto the anti-pinball bandwagon, banning not only the pay-out games, but all novelty pinball games as well.

In 1941, the police commissioner of New York City took a stand against pinball, declaring that "children and minors who play these machines and frequent the establishments where they are located sometimes commit petty larceny in order to obtain funds, form bad associations, and are often led into juvenile delinquency and, eventually, into serious crime." In 1941, Mayor Fiorello La Guardia went on the campaign trail with a sledgehammer in hand, personally smashing pinball machines for the benefit of newspaper photographers. In December of 1941, pinball was declared illegal in New York.

As pinball machine factories were converted to other uses for the war effort, it appeared for a time that pinball was dead in the United States. But, after the war, those pinball manufacturers who survived began campaigning for a relaxation of the laws against machines without pay-outs, claiming that pinball was a game of skill rather than chance. In 1947, the Gottlieb Company brought out *Humpty Dumpty,* the first machine equipped with flippers. Flippers are the short arms near the bottom of the board activated by control buttons on the side of the game. By manipulating the flippers, a player can return a ball to play when it is about to drop through the outhole. Pinball makers could now claim that flipper pinball was completely a game of skill, and as such should not be outlawed along with gambling games of chance.

In 1956, a Federal court decision made a distinction between gambling devices and flipper games without a pay-out. Soon all pinball machines were fitted with flippers, and the pay-out pinball machine disappeared almost completely. To make the game more rewarding, manufac-

OPPOSITE:

Flipper buttons established pinball as a game of skill rather than a gambling device.

ADD-A-BALL
ADD-A-BALL
50 POINTS
10 POINTS
FLIPPER
FLIPPER
D. Gottlieb & Co.
10 POINTS
10 POINTS
50 POINTS
FLIPPERAMA
FLIPPER
BUTTONS
ON SIDE OF CABINET
D. Gottlieb & Co.

turers substituted free games or "add-a-ball" bonuses in place of cash pay-outs. Even today, pinball machines intended for use in different parts of the nation are manufactured differently to comply with local standards, since add-a-ball, free games, and automatic plungers are still illegal in some places.

Most anti-pinball legislation was erased from the books during the late 1960s. In 1972, pinball addicts could again exercise their reflexes legally in Los Angeles. In 1976, pinball again became legal in Chicago, the city of its birth. And the same year, the New York City Council voted to allow pinball machines in the Big Apple—though thousands of illegal machines were already in use there at the time. Pinball was once again respectable.

Today, few people think of pinball as anything but a harmless, fun game for players of all ages. Pinball machines are turning up in shopping malls, department stores, airports, college dormitories, and restaurants, as well as in the video game center, the modern version of the penny arcade. The success of the movie *Tommy*, which featured a "pinball wizard," did much to spur a new interest in the game. In 1975, after the release of the movie, Bally's *Wizard* became the fastest-selling pinball machine in the United States.

Along with Bally, D. Gottlieb and Company, Williams Electronics, and Chicago Coin are the major pinball manufacturers in the nation. To suggest the size of the pinball industry: the Gottlieb Company was recently sold to Columbia Pictures for the sum of $47 million!

Each of the four major manufacturers now brings out from six to 12 new games every year. It's a long road that takes a new machine from the designer's head to the arcade floor. After a new design is presented by one of the company's staff, a mock-up of the new playfield is constructed and tested. Care must be taken that the game is neither too easy nor too difficult—and most important, that an average game will be completed in about two-and-a-half minutes, considered the ideal time for a pinball game. Designers aim for a game that demands about 75 percent skill, but allows for 25 percent luck, so that unskilled players can enjoy playing, too.

After all features are in place in the final mock-up, from 50 to 200 complete test samples are constructed and shipped around the world for on-the-floor testing. If the game meets with the approval of its most demanding critics—pinball players—the game is placed in full production. The success of the test models in various countries will determine where most new models will be shipped.

A new pinball machine will cost over $1,000. But if a machine were kept in continual operation for, say, six hours a day, one machine could return close to $15,000 a year to its owner. If you'd like a pinball machine in your home, you might look at a used model. Machines from two to five years old, removed from an arcade to make room for new models, can be purchased for $500 to $800. Older, rebuilt machines cost under $500.

Surprisingly, over 60 percent of all pinball machines manufactured in the United States are exported, the majority to Western Europe. Americans first traveling to Europe are often stunned by the ubiquity of the "American" pinball game there. But Europe has enjoyed decades of uninterrupted pinball growth, while development of the game in the United States was hampered for 25 years by anti-pinball legislation.

In England, "pin tables" are a fixture in most pubs. Since pay-out devices are legal in that country, many pinball machines in Britain offer an immediate cash reward for the skillful pinballer.

The competitive Germans most often enjoy *Kampf Flipper* as a four-player game. In France, *les flippers* machines are everywhere—in cafés, restaurants, stores, and in *palaises des jeux*, or game arcades. In quieter cafés, the bells are sometimes removed from pinball machines so that players won't disturb other patrons. Spain, the only European nation that does not permit the importation of American machines, has nine pinball manufacturing companies of its own. The Spanish *maquinas del millon* are usually built with more of an incline than their American counterparts, providing a faster, more challenging game.

The popularity of pinball in Europe may be due, in part, to its price. In France or England, a player can enjoy two games for about 20 cents, while most American games cost 25 cents per play. Dutch and Spanish pinballers can battle their machines for just about seven cents a game. It's no wonder that many Americans who never play pinball in their own country become avid gamesters the moment they reach Europe.

Each European country has developed a pinball lingo all its own, but we don't have to delve into any foreign languages to find a colorful array of terms pertaining to America's most popular coin game. *Gunching,* for instance, is body English applied to the machine. *Kickers* are targets made with stretched rubber that send a ball rebounding quickly in the opposite direction, while *kick-out holes* are holes in the playfield that electrically propel a captured ball back onto the playfield. *Drop-targets* may be struck only once by each ball, falling below the playfield after contact.

Thumper-bumpers are the large circular targets, usually equipped with a bell and a light, that send a ball careening off rapidly after each score. Motion is imparted to the ball by a spring system that spins the thumper-bumper when a ball makes contact with it. Most thumper-bumpers bear the words "100 Points When Lit," or some such legend to explain the scoring provided by the target. A *free game* mechanism is just that—a player attaining a certain score, or hitting a certain target, moves a numbered drum inside the machine that allows him to push a button for a replay without inserting another coin.

The names of modern pinball machines are no less imaginative than their earlier counterparts. Old machines bore names such as *Wang Poo, Who's Goofy, Stop and Sock, Jiggilo,* and *Hell's Bells.* Newer games include *Cue Tease, Op-Pop-Pop, Rawhide, Hula-Hula,* and *Love Bug.* A list of all machine names, old and new, would include well over 1,500 entries, so only the most dedicated pinballer can claim to have played even half the games now in existence.

Now that most anti-pinball legislation has been removed from the books, the future of pinball looks bright, indeed. A small home pinball machine recently sold 50,000 models in its first week on the market. Manufacturers are now experimenting with games that can be played by two persons at once, games with multi-level playfields, and machines with video back screens.

Speaking of video screens, the first all-electronic video pinball machine was *Spirit of '76,* constructed in 1976 by Mirco Games. A pinballer can now battle wits with video pinball machines whose playfields change design every half-minute or so, or after a certain score has been attained. Video pinball games use blips instead of balls, and an entirely different range of sound effects. It's too early to tell whether pinball buffs will take kindly to these games. But the keenest players will likely remain loyal to the older electric games, for body English (twisting one's body to exert slight pressure against the machine in a particular direction), one of the most important elements in a good game of pinball, is completely useless against a video machine.

There is one trend in the pinball industry that is indeed disheartening to players of any ilk. Pinball machines must now compete in many arcades with a complete range of video games, most of which have a shorter playing time than their pinball neighbors. To discourage arcade managers from removing pinball machines in favor of the shorter-playing and therefore more lucrative video games, pinball manufacturers are now turning increasingly to games that offer just three balls per play, rather than the customary five.

Experienced players will undoubtedly cry "tilt!"

To suggest the size of the pinball industry: the Gottlieb Company was recently sold to Columbia Pictures for the sum of $47 million!

Playing Cards

Card parties are no novelty—this scene depicts a card party of the 15th century.

Ask even a hard core cardsharp about the origin of playing cards and, pointing to the king and queen in their Renaissance raiment, he may well answer smugly that, of course, cards originated in Europe during the 15th and 16th centuries. Well, the reply would be half correct; yes, the design of modern playing cards can be traced back to 15th- and 16th-century Europe. But the cards themselves are a good deal older than the paper money often used to wager on them.

The exact origin of playing cards remains uncertain, but most historians agree that China is their most probable birthplace. But no matter where they originated, cards—like their gaming counterparts, dice—were probably used, at first, exclusively for fortune telling.

In early times, cards were connected with various religious rites. Some ancient Hindu cards, for instance, were divided into 10 suits representing the 10 incantations of the god Vishnu. The four-suit deck may be symbolic of the four hands of the god, as represented in Hindu statuary.

No one seems quite certain how cards found their way to Europe. Marco Polo may have brought them back from China in the 13th century. Other theories credit—or blame—the gypsies with bringing cards from Arabia to Europe, or claim that the Arabs themselves introduced cards in Europe during their occupation of Sicily and Spain. Probably, all of these sources were, in some part, responsible.

The first reference to playing cards in Europe appears in an Italian manuscript of 1299, although cards did not become well known on the continent until the 14th century. A receipt, dating from 1392, shows that Charles VI of France purchased three decks of cards in "gold and diverse colors." By 1495, playing cards were so well established in Europe that card manufacturers in various nations petitioned their kings for protection against imports.

Many believe that Tarot cards are the forerunners of the modern deck. The fact is the two decks developed independently—Tarot cards were unknown in China, and playing cards were virtually unheard of in Europe before the 13th century.

The Tarot deck consists of 21 pictorial representations of material forces, elements, virtues, and vices, plus the Fool—the precursor of the joker that found its way into the playing card deck. For centuries gypsies have claimed the ability to foretell the future based on their interpretations of the Tarot cards, which show characters and dress strikingly similar to those of the Romany tribe.

Renaissance Venetians were probably the first to combine the 22-card Tarot deck with the then current 56-card playing deck. The playing deck of the time consisted of a king, a queen, a knight, a page, plus number cards from one through 10 in each of four suits—*cups, coins, swords,* and *wands.* Several games derived from the combined 78-card deck—22 Tarot plus 56 playing cards—are still played in some countries.

Further combinations of number and picture cards resulted in decks of 32 or 36 cards in Germany, 40 cards in Spain, and 52 cards in France. The English adopted the French deck, with its designs which originated in 15th-century Normandy. The picture cards were in royal dress from the period of Henry VII.

The English retained the French symbols for the four suits, but changed their names. If you want to call a spade a spade in France, you would say *pique,* literally "pike." The French *carreau* ("tile" or "square") became in England the diamond; the *trèfle* ("cloverleaf") became the club; and the *coeur* ("heart") remained the heart.

In Germany, the spade, diamond, club, and heart are known respectively as the *Grun* ("leaf"), *Schelle* ("bell"), *Eichel* ("acorn"), and *Herz* ("heart"). In Italy, it's *spada* ("sword"), *denaro* ("coin"), *bastone* ("rod"), and *coppa* ("cup").

In Soviet Russia, government officials once tried to replace the "corrupt" monarchy face cards with proletarian revolutionary figures, but the tradition of Russian card design was so well entrenched that the attempt had to be abandoned. The famous 19th-century poet Pushkin wrote a novel, *Queen of Spades,* in which card playing leads to the death of the three main characters, and then Tchaikovsky based a celebrated opera on Pushkin's novel.

The earliest European playing cards were laboriously hand painted. Later, they were printed with wood-block techniques. German card makers were perhaps the first wood-block engravers in Europe.

In 1832, Thomas de la Rue invented a typographic process for card manufacture, and institutionalized the design of "double-headed" cards, readable from either end.

Early mass-produced playing cards were printed on paste-

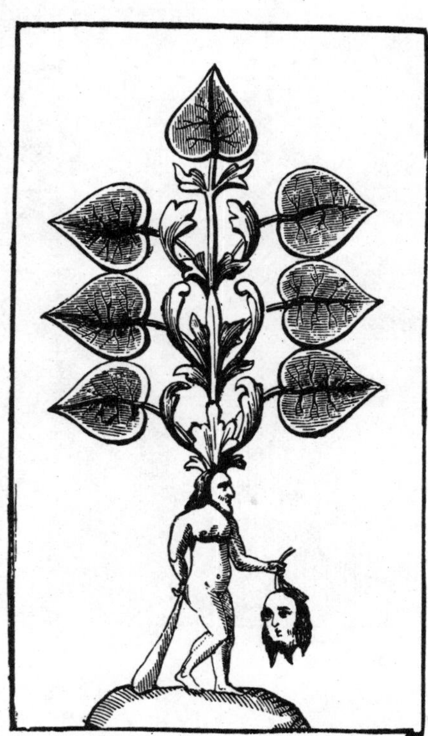

These old German tarot cards were used to tell fortunes. The top card is the seven of clubs; the bottom card is the seven of spades.

This engraving shows a Fench card factory in the era of Louis XIV.

board, with two sheets gummed together and lacquered.

At various times, card makers have tried to introduce different types of decks. One such effort was a deck with five suits.

Metal cards, intended for play on magnetized boards, have been manufactured, and these come into view occasionally on a windy day at the beach. But basically, card design has remained unchanged for centuries.

European governments have always found playing cards an ideal subject for heavy taxation. England began taxing card imports in 1615. By 1628, the tax on each deck had risen to a then exorbitant half-crown. Taxes on playing cards once became so high in Austria that card makers began selling oversized decks that

could be gradually trimmed as their edges became worn, thus lasting two or three times as long as a regular deck.

Did you ever wonder why the ace of spades in every pack is so distinctive, with the central spade by far the largest symbol in the deck? Well, the ace of spades was the card designated to bear the tax stamp. Even today, card makers use the ace of spades to carry their trademark or brand name.

More than 70 million editions of what the Puritans termed "The Devil's Picture Book" are now sold in this country each year— one deck for every three persons. The figure is misleading, though, since Las Vegas casino operators probably account for a large chunk of the total—owing to their practice of throwing away a deck after just a few rounds of blackjack.

The number of games that can be played with cards is virtually limitless. New games are invented continually. Yet, almost all games can be divided into one of two categories: rank games and combination games.

The earliest Chinese games were rank games, in which the player turning over the highest card won the round. Many modern games are based on that simple ideas with variations, such as the trump suit—designating which beats any card of the other three suits. Among the popular games in this category would be *loo, euchre, whist,* and *bridge*.

Combination games are those in which the winner of a round is determined by the entire hand held and the combinations formed by the cards—for example, *poker* and *gin rummy*. Games which are a combination of the two are: *pinochle* and *klobiash*.

Poker became popular in the United States in the 19th-century, especially among gold-digging forty-niners. The game was actually based on an older Spanish game called *primero* that included elements of betting and bluffing just like the modern game. According to Shakespeare, Henry VIII played *primero* the night Queen Elizabeth was born. The term *poker* comes to us from the German *pochen*, "to brag" or "to knock," or from a similar German game called *pochspiel*.

Reportedly, there are over 350 different versions of that great boon for a rainy day— *solitaire*.

The popularity of a card game varies greatly from country to

ODDS AT POKER

Hand	*Number Possible*	*Odds Against*
Royal Flush	4	649,739 to 1
Other Straight Flushes	36	72,192 to 1
Four of a Kind	624	4,164 to 1
Full House	3,744	693 to 1
Flush	5,108	508 to 1
Straight	10,200	254 to 1
Three of a Kind	54,912	46 to 1
Two Pairs	123,552	20 to 1
One Pair	1,098,240	4 to 3 (1.37 to 1)
Nothing	1,302,540	1 to 1
	2,598,960	

country, and from one era to the next. In the United States today, most people have at least heard of *canasta*—a Latin American invention—and also are familiar with *poker, rummy, bridge, gin, blackjack, war, go, cassino, keno, pinochle,* and *old maid.* In the past, such games as *faro, whist,* and *euchre* were more popular.

Blackjack is easily the most popular casino game in the United States today. Actually, all popular casino games—*baccarat, banque, chemin-de-fer,* and *blackjack*—date from the 15th and 16th centuries. All were extremely simple to play. In each of these games, the object is to reach a number close to—but not above—a predetermined limit. In blackjack, it's 21; in baccarat, it's nine.

You may have been confused in the casino, or in your reading, by the games of baccarat and chemin-de-fer. The rules of play are actually the same in both games, but the betting procedure is different in each. Baccarat is *the* big-money game in most American casinos, while chemin-de-fer remains more popular in Europe. In both games, six 52-card decks are used, shuffled together and placed in a wooden box known as the *sabot.*

Speaking of rules, Edmund Hoyle has been credited with formulating the rules of many popular card games. Actually, Hoyle wrote only two books on cards, and never heard of most of the games for which he is supposed to have formulated the rules. Among them is poker, which was not invented until almost 100 years after Hoyle's death.

If you're a real card freak, you may want to take a gander at some of the world's great playing card collections. The most notable are in the British Museum in London, the Morgan Library in New York, and the Cincinnati Art Museum, which includes a display donated by the U.S. Playing Card Corporation.

Morrisey's Gambling House at Saratoga, New York was a popular 19th-century casino.

And talking about card freaks: Carter Cummins holds the record for building the greatest number of stories in a house of cards—51 stories in a tower of 2,206 cards, 9½ feet high. Joe E. Whitlam of England built a house of 73 stories—a stupendous 13 feet, 10¼ inches—but Joe cheated a bit by bending some cards into angle supports.

We might also mention what must be the single largest loss in a game determined by the turn of one card. William Northmore of Okehampton, England, an inveterate gambler of the early 18th century, lost his entire fortune of $850,000 on the turn of an ace of diamonds!

Northmore's tale does have a happy ending, though. After the game, Northmore vowed never to gamble another penny. The townspeople of Okehampton, in sympathy for his plight, elected Northmore to Parliament, where he served for 19 years until his death.

Without doubt, the card game most widely played over the world today is *Contract Birdge,* a partnership game played by four persons. Bridge is derived from *Whist,* which can be traced back to 1529. The earliest treatise on Whist written by Edmund Hoyle in 1742, was a best-seller.

Duplicate Whist was played in London as early as 1857. The idea of Duplicate Whist was to eliminate luck and transform the game into a contest of skill.

In 1891, the American Whist League was established. My, how the game has grown! Today, bridge is played by over 30 million people in the United States, of whom 200,000 are dues-paying members of the American Contract Bridge League.

William Northmore gambled $850,000 on the ace of diamonds— and lost!

It is estimated that over 60 million people play bridge throughout the world. In Sweden, Holland, and Belgium, the game is even more of a rage than it is in the United States. Today, champions compete on television, and there are bridge columns in newspapers throughout the world.

During the 1930s, the big name in bridge was Ely Culbertson, who developed a system of bidding which took the bridge world by storm. With a host of bridge teachers under his tutelage, Culbertson turned the game into a multi-million dollar business. He wrote a number of books on the Culbertson System, which sold in the hundreds of thousands. Included in his hoopla were matches played by himself and his wife as partners against such topnotch bridge stars as Sidney Lenz and P. Hal Sims. These Culbertson matches became parlor chitchat throughout the country and turned the name of Culbertson into a household word.

During the 1940s, the ascendant star was Charles H. Goren, who ruled the world of bridge for some 20 years.

Apart from being played in tournaments, bridge is, of course, also played for money; sometimes, it is rumored, for fairly high stakes. In the early days of the game, Charles F. Schwab, the steel magnate, is reputed to have run a game where the stakes were a dollar a point. In today's clubs, the stakes run as high as 10 cents a point, which on a bad evening when Lady Luck frowns, might cost a player around $500.

SUIT DISTRIBUTION AT BRIDGE

The odds against finding the following distributions are:

Distribution	Odds	Distribution	Odds
4-4-3-2	4 to 1	7-4-1-1	about 249 to 1
5-4-3-1	9 to 1	8-4-1-0	about 2,499 to 1
6-4-2-1	about 20 to 1	13-0-0-0	158,755,357,992 to 1

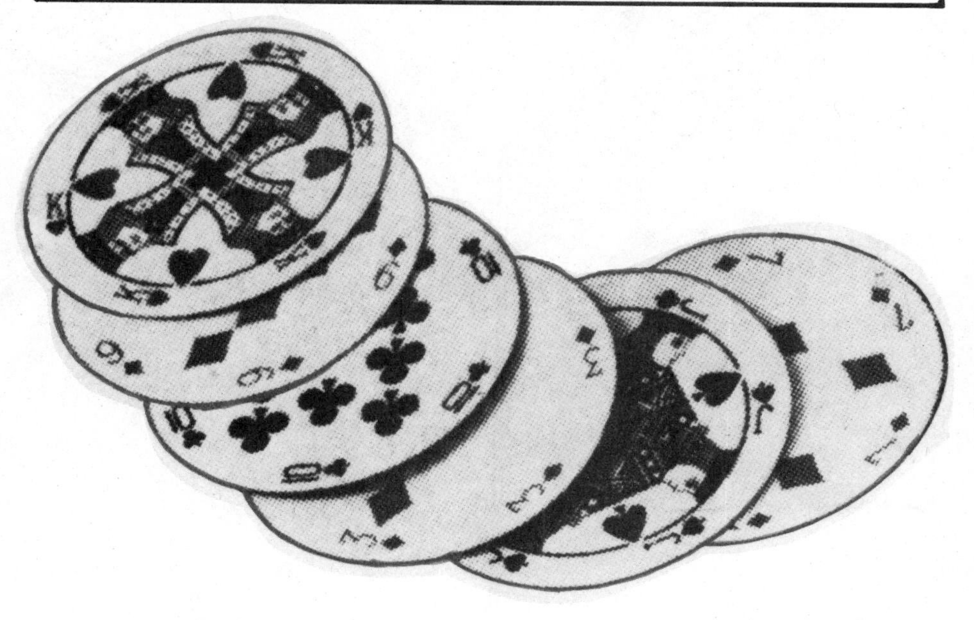

The well-rounded card player might like these round cards, which can be read no matter how you hold them.

Ely Culbertson was a critical figure in the history of bridge playing. Culbertson turned bridge into a multi-million dollar industry.

This 80-blade English pocketknife, inlaid with gold and mother of pearl, was exhibited at the Great Exhibition of 1851 in the Crystal Palace, in Hyde Park, London.

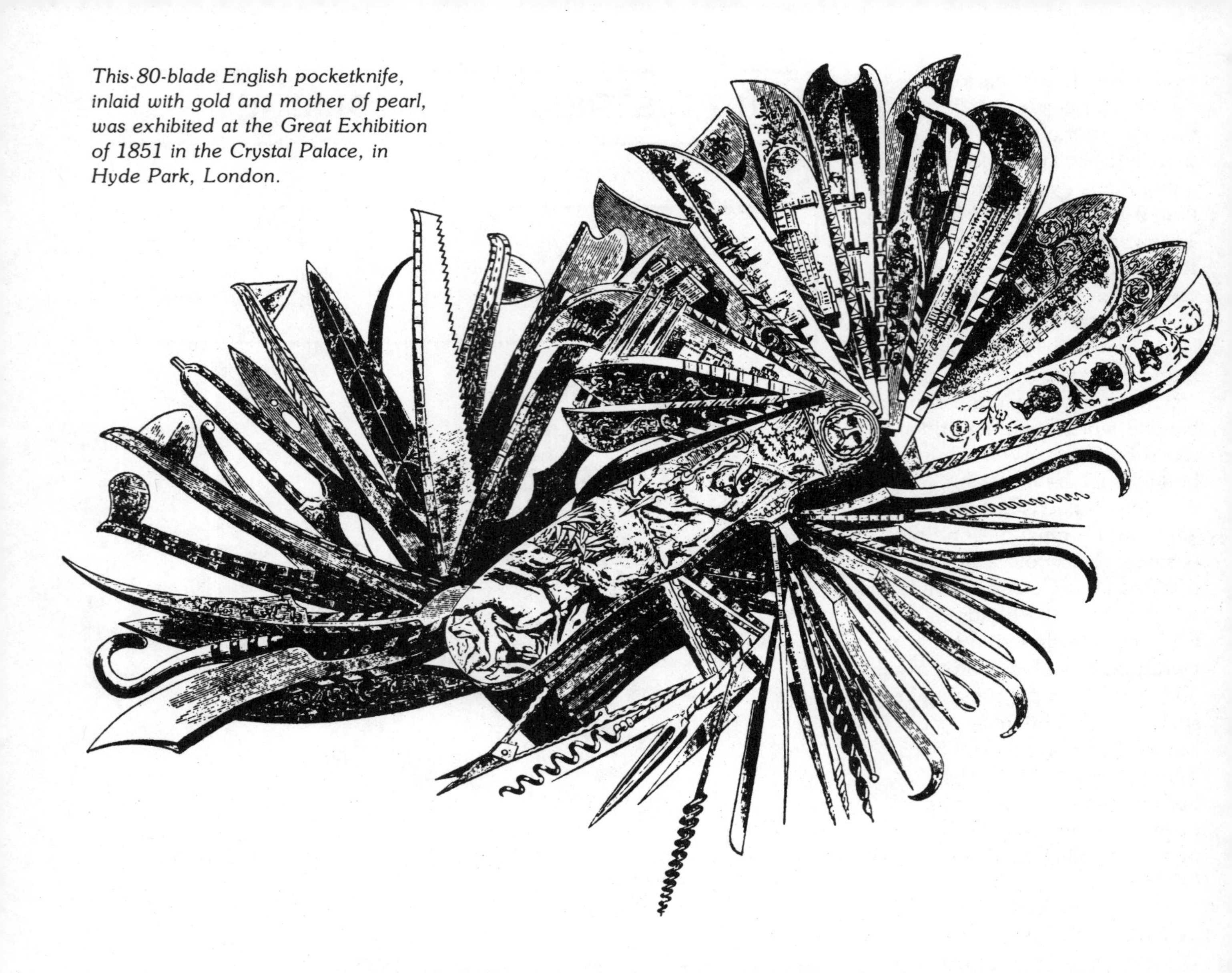

POCKETKNIVES

The pocketknife is obviously a recent invention, right? After all, the technological skill required to craft a workable fold-up knife must be a product of the industrial age. Besides, what need would men have had for a pocketknife in the days before pockets? Well, don't be surprised if you come across a rusty, time-worn pocketknife in the display cases of a museum—a tool, say, 2,000 years old!

Knives themselves, of course, have been with us since the Stone Age. Primitive man used cutting tools and weapons made from stone and flint, and later, from bronze and iron. The ancient Romans were skilled metalworkers, spreading their craft throughout their Empire—and the Romans left us the world's first known fold-up pocketknives.

The Roman implements were about three inches long when shut, fashioned without a spring or "nail nick"—the groove used to open the blade. The handles were often elaborately carved. One pocketknife surviving from the first century features an ivory handle skillfully carved into the shape of an armored gladiator. Another Roman knife, now in the British Museum, had the carver's name scratched into the handle.

Table knives did not exist in the Middle Ages—each diner was expected to bring his own knife which, between meals, doubled as a dagger. Nor did innkeepers provide table cutlery. Affluent travelers often carried sets of elegant tableware in their baggage. Obviously, the pocketknife would have been an ideal all-purpose tool for the medieval European, but few pocketknives were in existence at the time. Most men preferred an nonfolding knife in a scabbard to a pocketknife—owing either to lack of good spring knives or to the shortage of pockets.

Until the 18th century, the only kind of pocketknife generally available was the jackknife, a heavy tool with one blade that closed into a groove in the handle. Then cutlers began using springs to secure the blade in both the open and closed positions, providing a safer, firmer tool. From that time on, pocketknife manufacture became known as spring knife cutlery.

As the craft improved, multibladed tools began to appear—the penknife by far the most important. No, *penknife,* is not, strictly speaking, interchangeable with *pocketknife.* A penknife was a specialized pocketknife with one blade at each end of the handle. The smaller of the two blades was used to trim and sharpen quill pens.

Throughout the 18th and 19th centuries, anyone who wrote had to own a penknife, and spring knife cutlery became a major industry in Europe and the United States. The penknife was the premiere product of the cutler's craft, for the fitting of a spring knife demands highly skilled work. The blades were made from high-grade steel, tempered slightly harder than table knives. The more expensive models were finished by jewelers, with handles fashioned from silver, ivory, pearl, horn, ebony, and tortoise shell. An American cutlery catalogue from 1893 lists some 1,500 pocketknife models, which might suggest both the size of the industry and the variety of product available at the time.

Since at least the 14th century, English cutlery had been centered around the city of Sheffield, while German knife makers from Solingen have long excelled at their craft. It was 19th-century Sheffield cutlers who began fitting pocketknives with various other tools, among them buttonhooks, files, leather borers, tweezers, gimlets, saws, and implements curiously known as "castrating blades." One interesting Sheffield creation sported both a pistol and a dagger.

The jack-of-all-trades knife—often known as the sporting knife—is today the most popular kind of pocketknife, fitted with nail files, clippers, scissors, corkscrews, forks, spoons—you name it. Special sporting models have been designed for fishermen, engineers, and campers, some combining a toolchest of implements into one handy pocketknife.

The Norfolk Sportsman's Knife, manufactured in 1851, was fitted with 75 blades, and took two full years to manufacture. But the award for pocketknife-blade proliferation surely goes to the Year Knife, made—like the Norfolk—by the world's oldest cutlery firm, Joseph Rodgers and Sons Ltd. of Sheffield. This knife, introduced in 1822, contained 1,822 blades, and the firm has added one blade to the knife each year since. By now, of course, it's far from a "pocket" knife. In 1977, this one-of-a-kind tool was fitted with its 1,977th blade, and the number will continue to match the year until 2000 A.D., when there will be no further room for blades in this gargantuan tool.

Though we have little need for the penknife today, pocketknives are still widely manufactured. In the recent past, young boys often carried pocketknives for whittling, or for games like mumblypeg; but after the teenagers of the 50s took to carrying switchblade and push-button knives for less savory purposes, we no longer look kindly upon knife-wielding youths. Laws have been passed in some states stipulating the maximum length for a pocketknife blade—a longer blade is considered a deadly weapon.

If you number yourself among the ranks of pocketknife owners, take note: pocketknife manufacturers warn that their products demand constant attention. The spring joints of each blade should always be kept well oiled. And most important, a pocketknife blade should never be used as a screwdriver or lever. The blades are made from special steels tempered to maintain an edge, but not to withstand the strains of bending. If you need a screwdriver, you'll have no trouble finding a pocketknife fitted with one.

POSTAL SYSTEMS

"In snow or rain or sleet, the mail must go through," is an expression sometimes heard, in various forms, in compliment to the men and women whose task it is to deliver the mails. Is this a slogan coined recently in homage to the sure, speedy postal service of our modern world? Well, the Greek historian Herodotus used much the same words to describe a contemporary postal system, close to 2,000 years ago!

Herodotus was describing the mounted courier system of the Persians, a network of road stations, each a day's ride from the next. "These men will not be hindered from accomplishing at their best speeds the distance which they have to go," the historian wrote of the couriers, "either by snow or rain, or heat, or by darkness of night." Herodotus' words have been incorporated into the oath taken by a mail carrier in a number of countries, and stand chiseled in stone across the front of the General Post Office building in New York City.

But the history of the postal system actually begins long before Herodotus or the Persians.

Speedy courier service was not unknown in Biblical times, as evinced by Job's comment: "My days are swifter than a post." As early as 2000 B.C., an Egyptian courier system linked the royal government with local princes and military outposts, employing foot runners and boats plying the Nile. Assyrian couriers delivered three-inch-square clay tablets, inscribed with cuneiform and enclosed in clay envelopes. By the seventh century B.C., the well-developed Assyrian system was widely imitated by nations throughout the Mideast, including Persia.

By 1000 B.C., the Chinese had established an imperial postal system that included the use of homing pigeons. Confucius, like Job, used the post as a symbol for speed, declaring that "the influence of righteousness travels faster than royal orders by stage and couriers." After his journey to the East in the 13th century, Marco Polo declared the Chinese postal system superior to any in Europe, describing a network of 10,000 courier stations and a force of 300,000 post horses.

Postal service in India in 1858.

The Venetian traveler claimed that Chinese foot couriers running between stations three miles apart carried most of the mail. Urgent messages were carried by men on horseback, traveling up to 250 miles a day. Chinese foot couriers ran with bell-studded belts so that couriers waiting at the next station would be warned of their approach. At night, they carried torches. In return for their services, the couriers were exempted from taxation, and were presented with a badge that allowed them to requisition any horse needed for mail delivery. In China as well as Japan, the postal system was restricted to government use for many centuries, with private companies serving the public until the postal systems of both nations were modernized around the beginning of this century.

In Rome, the Emperor Augustus instituted the imperial post office, or *cursus publicus,* during the first century. The Roman system was initially restricted to government and military officials, but a bribe in the right place could avail a private citizen of the service. A pass called a *diploma* was issued to authorized users of the government service. Private mail and parcel companies also flourished. Imperial couriers transported the mails between stations from five to 12 miles apart, with local communities responsible for providing horses and food for the mailmen.

The Romans were the first to attach a postmark to letters, indicating the hour at which they were received, and the first to establish a system truly speedy by modern standards. In and around Rome, delivery was quick enough to enable the historian Pliny to write his wife twice each day. On the average, the mails moved through Italy at a rate of about five miles an hour, traveling 30 to 50 miles per day, although daily distances of up to 100 miles were not uncommon. At one point, letters could reach Reims from Rome in but nine days, more quickly than many letters sent between those cities today!

A French Post Office at the time of Louis XIV during the 1600s.

Mail delivery in Europe deteriorated with the end of the Roman Empire. Although sporadic attempts were made, usually by universities or guilds, to establish local delivery systems, it wasn't until the 13th century that fairly dependable postal networks began to appear. By that time, "clerks of the fair" carried mail between cities in France and Flanders, while mounted couriers traveled between castles in Germany and Italy carrying dispatches in waterproof, wax-lined leather bags. But deliveries were far from dependable. Letter writers often crossed their fingers and scribbled on their missives such exhortations to honesty as *Per postas cito cito et fidelis*—"By post haste, haste, and be faithful."

It is in Venice that we find the first effective European postal system since ancient Rome. In 1290, Amadeo Tasso established a postal network that within two decades had monopolized the delivery of all foreign mails within reach of Venice. At first, Tasso used foot couriers alone; later, horseback riders and post wagons were pressed into service. By 1460, the average daily delivery time between Venice and Rome was less than 10 days, and same-day service was available between many neighboring towns.

In the mid-15th century, Tasso's postal system merged with another company to form the Thurm and Taxis network that was to dominate the European mails for centuries. In 1505, the firm reached an agreement with the Holy Roman Empire for the delivery of all diplomatic mails between Germany, Italy, France, and Spain, cutting the delivery time between Venice and Paris to just 44 hours. At its peak, Thurm and Taxis employed 20,000 couriers throughout Europe. The French Revolution effectively ended the firm's monopoly on foreign mails, but remnants of the system survived until as late as 1867.

France, Spain, Portugal, and the German states depended upon Thurm and Taxis for foreign mails, while developing their own royal postal systems for domestic service. In 1464, a royal messenger service was begun in France, but it was Cardinal Richelieu who truly modernized the French mails in the 17th-century. Until 1627, the charge for mail delivery had to be agreed upon by the courier and the sender, but Richelieu established both rates and schedules for domestic delivery. By 1676, postal rates were determined by zones, the number of sheets of paper in the letter, and the use or nonuse of an envelope.

The French, incidentally, were the first to depend upon "airmail" delivery for any length of time. During the siege of Paris in the Franco-Prussian War of the 1870s, mail was sent out of the capital by balloon, as well as by hundreds of homing pigeons. Return letters were photo-reduced to one four-thousandth of their original size, then delivered to the capital by pigeon. Thirty-five pigeons carried the identical 30,000-message mail cannisters so that at least one was certain to survive Prussian pigeon snipers. In Paris, the messages were enlarged on a projection screen, copied by clerks, and delivered to addresses within the city.

In England, the first extensive postal system was established during the 15th century for the transport of diplomatic dispatches. The word *post* began to appear around this time, borrowed from the French *poste*, which was derived from the Latin *ponere*, "to place," since horses were "placed" along the routes for use by postal messengers.

After 1711, when Parliament declared that postal fees were to be considered a tax, the price of mail delivery in England rose steadily. But in 1840, Parliament began lowering prices, declaring that postal fees should be designed merely to cover the cost of delivery rather than to raise revenue for the crown. The changes were due in large part to the efforts of one of the major reformers in postal history, Rowland Hill.

In 1836, Hill published a pamphlet that was to profoundly change the postal systems of

Postman of old England.

England and many other nations. Among other things, Hill recommended that postal rates be lowered and be determined by the weight of the parcel, and that the fee be paid by the sender rather than the addressee, as had previously been the custom throughout Europe. Most importantly, Hill suggested the use of "pieces of paper just large enough to bear the stamp, attached to the letter with moist gum"—postage stamps as we know them.

By 1840, most of Hill's recommendations had been adopted by the English postal system. On May 1, 1840, the world's first adhesive postal stamps were placed on sale in England, selling for one or two pence and bearing the image of Queen Victoria. Hill had recommended using both stamps and prepaid envelopes, expecting the envelopes to become the more popular. To Hill's surprise, the public favored the stamps from the very beginning, quickly buying up the first printing of 68 million "penny blacks." The first perforated postage stamp appeared in England 14 years later. By 1870, over 30 nations had adopted stamps and stamped envelopes for their postal systems.

During the 19th century, most nations instituted government postal systems, taking the mails out of the hands of private companies and offering service to all citizens. In 1874, the International Postal Convention met in Bern, Switzerland, to arrange a unified system of mail delivery between nations. By 1914, almost all independent countries were parties to the agreement, and the modern postal system had arrived.

Parcel Post travels about Oxford in a red wicker pushcart in 1929.

The United States mail system had its humble beginnings in 1639, when the city of Boston declared that mail to or from England should be deposited and picked up at Richard Fairbanks' tavern. Previously, mail delivery across the Atlantic had to be arranged individually between the sender and a ship's captain, who would usually transport a letter for a penny. The first domestic mail service in the United States did not begin until 1673, when an overland postal route was established between Boston and New York along the Boston Post Road, which later became U.S. Route One.

In 1692, Thomas Neale obtained a 21-year patent for a colonial postal system in America, and appointed Andrew Hamilton as Postmaster. Neale, who never visited America, died in 1699, and Hamilton himself took over the system until 1707, when the English government bought the patent and instituted the official colonial post.

In 1753, Benjamin Franklin, who had served as Postmaster General of Philadelphia since 1737, became Co-Postmaster General of the American Colonies. At the time, riders traveled between New York and Philadelphia three times each week, making the journey in an average of 33 hours. The following decade saw the introduction of night riders. But still mail service was generally slow, undependable, and expensive, with couriers often carrying goods,

In 1873, the "One-Penny Magenta" was purchased from a schoolboy for 84 cents. In 1940, the stamp was bought for $35,000. In 1970, the stamp was sold for $280,000!

driving horses, and performing other jobs while on their rounds. Consequently, private postal companies began to flourish, though outlawed by the British crown. Reliance on the official postal system continued to dwindle until 1775, when all colonial mails were taken over by the Continental Congress.

Every schoolboy knows that the imposition of the Stamp Act on the American Colonies played a large part in fomenting the dissatisfaction that led to the American Revolution. In 1765, the bill was introduced in the British Parliament by Lord Grenville to help cover the expense of the French and Indian War. As extended to the Colonies, the act set duties on every "skin or piece of vellum or parchment," including legal documents, licenses, academic degrees, newspapers, and pamphlets. The outraged colonists immediately passed a resolution of protest, declaring at the Stamp Act Congress that thereafter no taxes would be accepted without the consent of the colonies themselves. Opposition to the tax was so great that the expense of collecting it exceeded the proceeds earned, and the tax was repealed the year after it was instituted.

During the Revolution, however, postal rates in America soared as never before. By 1780, the cost of the conflict had helped raise fees by 4,000 percent, though rates were lowered immediately after the war. In 1792, new rates were established along with the adoption of the Constitution, which allotted Congress alone the right to fix postal rates for first-class mail—a right that Congress surrendered early in the 1970s. Benjamin Franklin was the Postmaster General during the Revolution, but Samuel Osgood was actually the first man to be constitutionally appointed to that post.

In 1789, there were but 75 post offices and 1,875 miles of post roads in the United States. Within a decade, the network had grown to include more than 16,000 miles of post roads. But even then, mail delivery was neither inexpensive nor trustworthy. Delivery of a one-page letter more than 400 miles cost 25 cents, a goodly sum at the time, and most fees had to be collected from the addressee. It wasn't until 1845 that postal rates were determined by weight alone, and in 1855 all fees were paid by the sender rather than the addressee. And it was well into the 19th century before Americans began to trust the mails for the delivery of money or checks. A common device of the time—not unknown today—was to send half of a bill, await word of delivery from the receiver, and then send along the other half.

Home delivery was a rarity in the early days of the United States; letters had to be picked up at the post office everywhere but in Boston. But postal routes continued to expand, stretching westward to the territories. In 1806, stagecoaches came into use for mail transport, and by 1822, they were operating day and night between many American cities. Around that time, Congress declared all steamboat routes to be post roads, later extending that designation to all railroad lines. Today, the designated post roads in the United States exceed two million miles in length!

The first adhesive postage stamps printed in the United

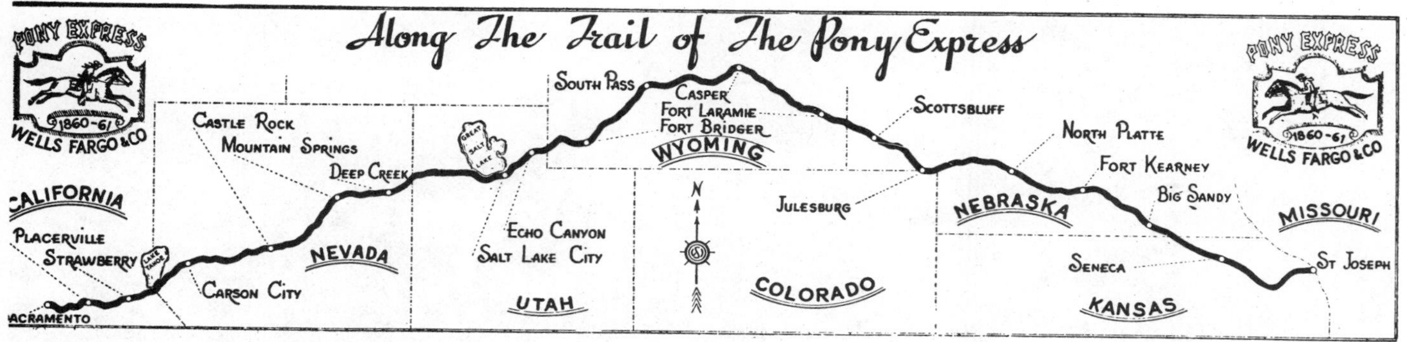

The route of the Pony Express.

States were placed on sale on February 1, 1842, by the City Despatch Post of New York, a private courier service. Five years later, the first government postage stamps appeared: a five-cent stamp bearing a picture of Benjamin Franklin, and a 10-cent stamp bearing George Washington's image. In 1851, the prices of those stamps were lowered to one and three cents, respectively. Early American stamps were printed by private companies until 1893, when the Bureau of Printing and Engraving took over the job.

Mail ships began to reach the West Coast in 1848, when the crew of the first mail steamer to arrive in San Francisco from the East deserted en masse to join the burgeoning California gold rush. The same year, the legendary Kit Carson helped deliver the first coast-to-coast mail shipment to Los Angeles. In 1857, a stagecoach relay network was established, transporting mail shipments between St. Louis and San Francisco in about 25 days.

The Pony Express in America was actually more renowned in legend than in deed, enjoying but a brief life before disappearing into the annals of Western lore. In 1860, a private company set up a network of relay stations, each 10 to 15 miles apart, to carry U.S. mail by horseback between California and St. Joseph, Missouri. The mail was transferred to a fresh horse at each station, and a courier rode three horses successively before passing the mail pouches to the next rider. Ponies were never used.

The scheduled delivery time was eight days, although the fastest trip was seven days, 17 hours, when Lincoln's first inaugural address was brought to California. The service was expensive, initially costing five dollars for delivery of a half-ounce parcel, but the rates were lowered sharply soon after. Soon indeed, for the Pony Express system survived but 18 months—having been made obsolete by the completion of the first transcontinental telegraph line.

The horse has long since given way to faster, more dependable means of mail transport. In 1864, the post office itself was placed on wheels with the appearance of the first railroad sorting car. Airmail delivery was instituted in 1918, on a flight between New York and Washington. Within six years, regular round-the-clock airmail routes crisscrossed the United States from coast to coast. Pneumatic tubes were employed for a time for intracity mail transport, beginning with a tube in Philadelphia that shortened travel time between two large post offices from 15 minutes to just two. And from the 1890s until 1953, mail was transported between two New York City post offices via a pneumatic tube stretching across the Brooklyn Bridge!

Special delivery was instituted in 1885, six years after the beginning of fourth-class delivery service, or parcel post. Today, there are four classes of mail: first-class for letters, postcards, and some printed matter; second-class for periodicals; third-class for circulars and miscellaneous printed matter up to one pound; and fourth-class for parcels.

By 1863, free doorstep mail delivery was available in 49 cities. Rural Free Delivery had its beginnings during the 1890s, starting with five routes in West Virginia. Previously, mail had to be picked up at the post office in most rural areas, as it still is today in many places. As Rural Free Delivery was extended throughout the United States, the number of post offices steadily declined, falling from a peak of 76,000 in 1901 to 52,000 by 1920 and about 40,000 today.

Doorstep delivery is now the rule in all American cities and suburbs and in many rural areas as well. Since 1909, mail boxes in front of the home have been

How Union soldiers got their mail. Taken outside Petersburg, August, 1864.

required by law. By the way, the first house numbers appeared in 1463, on the Pont Notre-Dame in Paris. The first street mailboxes appeared in England and the United States around the middle of the 19th century, due in part to the suggestions of Victorian novelist Anthony Trollope. The oldest continuously used mailbox location is on Guernsey, one of the Channel Islands, where a series of boxes have stood on the same spot since 1853.

The U.S. postal system is now by far the largest, handling close to one-half of the world's volume. Americans presently post some 80 billion items each year, or about 410 for each citizen, spending over one-and-a-half billion dollars annually in postal fees. The United States is also the nation with the largest discrepancy between mail import and export—we receive about one-and-a-half billion pieces of mail from abroad each year, while sending out only 887 million items.

A system of U.S. postal zones was first suggested in 1899, but not established here until 44 years later. That system has in turn been replaced by the ZIP Code system. By 1970, Zone Improvement Plan numbers were finding their way onto 85 percent of all U.S. mail. When usage reaches 100 percent, the postal service can begin to use OCR machines—optical character readers—on a larger scale. These machines, in use in selected cities since 1965, can sort letters automatically by scanning ZIP Code numbers.

Under the Postal Reorganization Act of 1970, the Post Office Department has become a government-owned corporation, the U.S. Postal Service, employing 700,000 persons—including 40,000 postmasters and 90,000 carriers. Congress no longer fixes postal rates and salaries, although it retains veto power over any changes in those figures. Originally, the new system was conceived as a self-supporting corporation, but so far increasing Federal subsidies have been necessary to cover the gap between revenue and expenses.

Unfortunately, additional subsidies have come from the pocket of the letter writer, who has endured five rises in first-class rates during the last decade. The latest increase, from 13 to 15 cents, saw the introduction of a nondenominational stamped marked with the letter *A* rather than a figure. These stamps were printed in 1975 and 1976, before the new first-class rate was determined, so that the letter *A* could represent 15 cents, 16 cents, or whatever fee was ultimately decided upon.

The use of postage stamps has spawned a new hobby, stamp collecting, or *philately*. The term was coined in 1865 by M.G. Herpin of France, who combined the Greek word *philos*, "love," with the negative *a* and a derivative of *telein*, "to tax," since stamp-bearing letters came "without tax" to the receiver. The first published reference to stamp collecting appeared in 1841, when a woman placed an ad in an English newspaper for cancelled postage stamps she planned to use to wallpaper her dressing room. The mania for stamp collecting spread so quickly in England that by 1842, the magazine *Punch* could declare that stamp collectors "betray more anxiety to treasure the Queen's heads than Harry the Eighth did to get rid of them!"

The first stamp catalog appeared in 1861; within five years, catalogs contained as many as 2,400 entries. A modern catalog can list well over 150,000, and single collections have been sold for as much as four million dollars. Two of the world's largest stamp collections can now be viewed in the British Museum and the Smithsonian Institution in Washington.

Stamps have ranged in size from a 1913 Express Delivery issue in China, nine-and-three-quarters inches long and two-and-three quarters inches wide, to midget stamps, issued in Colombia during the 1860s, that measured just eight by nine- and-a-half millimeters. The highest nominally valued stamp ever released was issued in Germany during the inflation of 1923—one stamp cost 50 billion marks! In true worth, the objects of the philatelist's eye have ranged from a 100-pound ($280) stamp issued in Kenya in the 1920s, to a 3,000-pengo stamp issued in Hungary in 1946, which due to inflation was worth less than one hundred-trillionth of a cent!

This famous 65¢ stamp, commemorating the flight of the Graf Zeppelin, has now become quite valuable.

This 24¢ air postage stamp, on which the plane was printed upside down, is now a collector's item of the first magnitude.

Rarity rather than size or denomination usually determines the worth of a collector's stamp. Postage stamps with printing errors are also highly prized, such as a 1848 Mauritius specimen bearing the word *penoe* instead of *pence*, and a U.S. stamp with an upside-down picture of an airplane. But the most valuable stamp in the world today is a nondescript one-cent stamp issued in 1856 by the colony of British Guiana. Only a single copy of the stamp exists today.

In 1873, the prize stamp—called "One-Penny Magenta"—was purchased from a schoolboy for 84 cents. In 1940, the stamp brought $35,000 when sold by Mrs. Arthur Hind, the wife of a noted philatelist. Insured for $560,000 when exhibited in 1965, the stamp was sold five years later in New York for $280,000!

Since the stamp's only claim to fame was its rarity, Mr. Hind took no chances with his investment. In 1938, the philatelist allegedly bought the only other surviving copy of the stamp—and burned it!

Potatoes

"Meat and potatoes" are the foundation of most American cooking, and of many European cuisines as well. The spud is so rooted in Western cooking that it's hard to believe the vegetable was totally unknown in Europe just a few hundred years ago.

In the mid-16th century, Spanish conquistadores in South America discovered that the Incas ate a white tuber they called "papa." (Perhaps it was the "father" of their diet.) The Incas used the plum-sized vegetables in hundreds of ways, baking them in hot ash, eating them raw or dried, and even pounding them into a flour.

The Spaniards thought the tuber was a form of truffle, since the Incas found them underground. Pedro Cieca, an officer of Juan Pizarro, shipped a load of the spuds back to Spain. From there, they were sent to the Pope for inspection, and eventually to a Belgian botanist for classification.

The botanist called the vegetable *taratoufli,* "little truffle," a word recognizable in the present German word for potato, *kartoffel.* But the Spaniards found the spud similar to the sweet potato, called *patata* after the African *batata,* and christened the new vegetable by the same name.

Within 20 years of their arrival, white potatoes were being grown, sold, and eaten in Spain, though far less than the sweet potato. After Sir Walter Raleigh planted potatoes on his Irish estate, spud farms began to sprout up all around the Emerald Isle. But in England and Scotland, the potato remained unpopular for 200 years—defamed as "Ireland's lazy root."

In the late 17th century, the German monarch Frederick William decided that the potato could solve his nation's food shortage, and he decreed that all peasants should plant spuds. Those who refused, would have their noses and ears cut off. It's unknown how many farmers lost their features because of the bog apple, but Frederick's decree may help explain why potatoes have become so popular in Germany.

The English did not become large-scale potato eaters until the latter half of the 18th century. The Scots, meanwhile, continued to resist the spud, with some Presbyterian clergymen declaring that since the vegetable was not mentioned in the Bible, it could not be fit for human consumption.

France was the last European nation to accept the potato. A soldier who had spent considerable time in Germany returned to his homeland to convince fellow Frenchmen that the potato was both edible and delicious, despite medical advice that the vegetable was "toxic and the cause of many illnesses."

The first potato to reach the shores of North America arrived around 1622, imported by Virginia colonists as a food. The first potato cultivation didn't begin in America until 1719, when Irish immigrants planted spud fields in New Hampshire. Thomas Jefferson, by the way, was the first American to serve french fries with beefsteak, a combination now as institutionalized in America as the Declaration of Independence. And it was the German immigrants you can either thank or blame for potato salad.

Of all the foodstuffs indigenous to the Americas, none is as useful as the potato. Potatoes are easy to cultivate and can be stored for long periods of time. To give you an idea of the fecundity of the potato, in 1968, an English farmer reported that just six seed potatoes had yielded a whopping 1,190 pounds of spuds.

The potato is also one of the most versatile vegetables. You can do almost anything to the spud and still it insists on remaining edible. Potatoes can be *home-fried, French-fried, deep-fried, mashed, hash-browned, baked, boiled, oven-roasted,* or made into *chips, sticks, salad,* or *pancakes.* They can be coal-roasted as *mickies,* or powdered into *instant potatoes*—well, you get the idea.

The well-known *Saratoga chips* were invented, not surprisingly, in Saratoga, New York, when a guest-house chef, appropriately named George Crumb, lost his patience with a guest who insisted on thin French fries.

Crumb cut a potato into paper-thin slices, dropped them in oil, and—presto!—another American institution was founded.

In 1969, Australian Paul Tully set a record for potato chip devouring by consuming 30 two-ounce bags in 24½ minutes—without a drink. And while we're on the subject, the record for potato gobbling is three pounds in one minute and 45 seconds, set in Worcestershire, England in 1976. We have no idea if the spuds were peeled or unpeeled—or served with or without Worcestershire sauce.

To settle an oft-heard dispute: no, the sweet potato and the yam are *not* the same vegetable. The yam is in fact almost never seen in this country—no matter what food packagers claim to the contrary!

More than one American tourist has been known to ask his confused French waiter for *French fries*. The French actually call them *pommes frites*—and the French word for potato is *pomme de terre,* literally "earth apple."

The French have also contributed *pommes soufflées,* or souffled potatoes, to our gastronomic repertoire. The delicacy was reportedly created by the personal chef of Louis XIV. In this case, necessity was definitely the mother of invention. One afternoon, the king left the palace to inspect his army, then engaged in warfare with the Dutch. On the return voyage to the palace, the Sun King's coach was delayed by a downpour that made the roads impassable. When his master did not appear at the expected hour, the Royal Chef began to panic. The Great Monarch was a most fastidious diner, who insisted that his repasts be served the instant he arrived at the royal dinner table. The cook had prepared a huge batch of the king's beloved *pommes frites,* but as the hours passed and still Louis failed to appear, the fries began to frazzle and turn cold and soggy.

Suddenly, a herald announced the entrance of the king. The agitated chef, in dismay, grabbed the deep-fat fryer and submerged the wilted French fries in sizzling oil, shaking the fryer madly from side to side. Et violà!—a dish fit for a king was born. The potatoes emerged from this second bath in deep hot oil all puffed up—golden brown and heavenly delicious.

To make *pommes soufflées* is a culinary feat. The heat of the oils must be perfect. Consult a good cookbook and try it. You, too, might achieve gastronomic immortality.

According to another tale, however, the origin of the souffled potatoes is considerably less regal. A 19th-century French chef was charged with preparing a banquet to celebrate the opening of a new railroad line. While preparing the repast at one of the new stations, the chef was notified that the train carrying a coachload of dignitaries to the banquet would be delayed. So he took his half-cooked French fries out of the oil and began preparing a fresh batch. Then he was notified that the train was pulling into the station, on time after all. Frantic, the chef plunged the half-cooked potatoes back into the fat, and the soggy fries puffed into crisp ovals—*pommes soufflées!*

Today, Americans consume literally billions of spuds each year—production usually hovers around 34 billion pounds—with the most well-known varieties hailing from Idaho, Maine, and Long Island.

Potatoes remain, pound for pound, one of the cheapest foodstuffs available, perhaps because they can be grown so easily. If you believe some mothers, they'll even grow behind the dirty ears of little boys.

This potato digger is a handy contraption for unearthing spuds from the soil.

A refrigerator is a place where you store leftovers until they are ready to be thrown out.

REFRIGERATION

A prominent encyclopedia has suggested that the invention with the greatest impact on worldwide economic life since the railroad is—no, you'd never guess—the refrigerator! Isn't the refrigerator more of a convenience item? Hardly. Refrigeration technology has completely revolutionized farming and has led to the rapid development of a world-wide food trade. It would be difficult, indeed, to find a person in the world today who has not benefited in some way from the introduction of refrigerated food preservation.

The growth of cities and suburbs in the last century has steadily moved most of us further and further away from our food source, the farm. Without food-preservation techniques, especially refrigeration, it's doubtful that this urban growth could have moved ahead so rapidly. And since the advent of refrigeration, a nation no longer has to feed itself—the abundant supply of one nation can balance the scarcity in another, allowing many nations to industrialize more quickly. Improved food preservation has also helped increase the world's food supply by eliminating much waste. Foods that would otherwise perish can remain in storage until needed.

Refrigeration may be a recent advance, but food preservation itself has engaged man's attention since the beginning of time. Cheese and butter may, in a sense, be regarded as preserved milk; wine, as preserved grapes. For thousands of years, meat and fish have been preserved by salting or drying, or more recently, by curing with sugar or nitrate compounds. Most of these early stratagems were discovered by chance—they worked, but no

This ice-house was used by George Washington at Mount Vernon to preserve food.

one knew why. Only when the existence of bacteria and their influence on foodstuffs became known, could man begin to deal adequately with food preservation.

Without bacteria, edibles would last almost indefinitely. All food-preservation techniques, then, are designed to kill or limit the growth of bacterial life. For instance, the process of drying works because bacteria cannot grow in the absence of moisture. Sterilization by heat—cooking—will completely destroy bacterial life, but the effects are temporary. Cooked food will spoil as rapidly as uncooked food if left untreated.

Cooling does not kill bacteria, but it does stop their growth. Once scientists learned that most bacteria cannot grow at temperatures below the freezing point of water, and also that long-term freezing or cooling of foods does not influence their nutritional content, they knew what was needed for the perfect food-preservation system—a refrigerator. It remained only to invent one.

It had long been known that low temperatures would, for some then unknown reason, preserve food. People in Arctic lands often stored their meat in snow and ice. But to preserve

TOP RIGHT:

A primitive icebox used in India in the 1870s.

BOTTOM RIGHT:

This Victorian precursor of the refrigerator had detachable parts that were easy to assemble and disassemble.

food, people in warmer climes needed man-made ice.

Ancient Indians made ice the simplest and least dependable way possible—leaving water in special outdoor receptacles overnight. The ancient Romans cooled their wine cellars with snow brought from nearby mountains. They also discovered, as did the Indians, that water could be cooled with the addition of saltpeter. The Romans sometimes chilled liquids by immersing bottles in vessels filled with water and saltpeter, and rotating the bottles rapidly.

Primitive cooling techniques could chill food and drink, but not freeze them; the beneficial effects were temporary. During the 18th century, many scientists developed an interest in mechanical refrigeration, but with neither electricity nor the means to manufacture large quantities of ice, the scientist's road to the new "ice age" was a long and difficult one.

The first "refrigerator" in the United States was invented in 1803 by Thomas Moore of Baltimore, but Moore's machine was really a "thermos" device—two boxes, one inside the other, with insulating material in-between. Food stored with ice in the inner box would remain cool for a long time, but not cool enough to inhibit bacterial growth for very long.

The next giant step toward successful refrigeration came in 1834, when Jacob Perkins, an American living in England, developed an ice-making machine functioning on the compression principle. Gases subjected to high pressures will remain in the liquid state at temperatures beyond their normal boiling point. Perkins showed that when these compressed liquids were used as refrigerants, they would absorb a great deal of heat before changing to the gaseous state.

The 1870s saw vast improvements in refrigeration techniques. A refrigerator car—really a rolling icebox—had made its earliest appearance in 1851, when several tons of butter made the journey by rail from Ogdensburg, New York to Boston. But the first application of refrigeration technology to marine food transportation came in 1880, when the steamer *Strathleven* carried a meat cargo from Australia to England. Oddly enough, the meat was meant to be cooled, not frozen—but freezing did take place, and the excellent results led to the subsequent freezing of all meat cargoes.

The domestic refrigerator was not to be used on any scale until this century. In the past, urban Europeans had often hung dairy products out the window to keep them cool for a time. The larder was also used throughout the West for temporary preservation. Earlier in this century, most American homes relied on the icebox for their victuals. The icebox, however, left much to be desired, especially when the iceman did not cometh.

The modern domestic refrigerator is based to a great extent on the work of the Frenchman Edmond Carre. In the 1830s, Carre perfected the first refrigerating machine to be widely adopted for individual use. Carre's machines were used in many Paris restaurants for the production of ice and ice cream products. The first household

This advertisement appeared in Century Magazine *in 1888.*

JOS. W. WAYNE, Manufacturer of the CELEBRATED

PATENT SELF-VENTILATING **AMERICAN REFRIGERATORS**

New and Improved BEER and ALE COOLERS, and all kinds of ICE CHESTS.

Ten First Premiums and Silver Medals Awarded at the Cincinnati Industrial Expositions.

Twenty-five Years' experience has shown that they are undoubtedly the best, cheapest, and most reliable Refrigerators in the market, and

These are the only Refrigerators that are packed or filled with GROUND CORK between the walls, the best non-conducting material known for the purpose, as it does not absorb and retain moisture, and, being light and elastic, will not settle or pack down in the walls as charcoal or sawdust does.

Unexcelled for **Simplicity, Efficiency, Economy** and **Durability.**

Send for Illustrated Price-lists to **JOS. W. WAYNE, Manuf'r,**

☞ Liberal Terms to Dealers. 124 Main Street, Cincinnati, O.

A walk-in freezer of the 19th century.

refrigerator patent in the United States was granted in 1899 to one Albert T. Marshall of Brockton, Massachusetts.

Modern refrigerators and freezers use a circulating refrigerant that continually changes from the gaseous to the liquid state. Most machines use dichlordifluoromethane and other refrigerants mercifully known under the trade name of Freon. The liquid refrigerant changes to a gas in the evaporator, then absorbs heat from the food chamber and carries it to the condensing coils, where the refrigerant is cooled by air passing over the coils, and is reconverted into liquid. The cycle is then repeated, spurred on periodically by a small electric motor. Incidentally, your refrigerator is probably your greatest electricity consumer—after your air conditioner.

Wartime restrictions limited the growth of the domestic refrigerator in this country, but after World War II the 'fridge found its way into almost every American home—and so did frozen foods. The American, Clarence Birdseye, is responsible for the development of methods for freezing foods in small packages for the retail trade. The General Foods Corporation introduced the now familiar Birds Eye commercial pack in 1929. Since then, the use of frozen foods has grown with the refrigerator. As early as 1944, Americans were consuming some three billion pounds of frozen meats, vegetables, fruits, fish, and dairy products each year.

During and after World War II, military and industrial research led to the development of the science of cryogenics, the study of matter at extremely low temperatures. Basically, cryogenics—from the Greek word *kryos*, "icy cold"—deals with the production of temperatures below that of liquid oxygen (-297 degrees F.). You hardly need such frigid temperatures to keep your eggs fresh, but cryogenic engineering has had an impact on many elements of modern life, from medicine to space travel.

Scientists are now freely discussing the ultimate cryogenic marvel, suspended animation. Living organisms, including man, can theoretically be kept in a deep freeze almost indefinitely, and resume normal life functions upon thawing. Persons with presently incurable diseases could be frozen before death in the hope of reviving them when cures are found. Intergalactic space travelers could be frozen and revived upon reaching their destination thousands of years later. And think of the possibility of a living time capsule, a human being frozen for thousands of years, to be resurrected by some future civilization to see how we lived in the 20th century!

Restaurants

The restaurant is such a seemingly natural and necessary institution that you'd suspect it's been with us for as long as man has lived in cities. But the restaurant, as we know it today, is a surprisingly recent development. That's not to say there weren't any commercial eating places before our time. But the menu, with its choice of dishes, is only about 200 years old. The fact is that the diner or the coffee shop in which you may have lunch today offers more of a menu selection than the best of restaurants of the world did just a few centuries back.

The earliest forerunners of the restaurant were the medieval tavern and cookshop. The tavern customarily provided a daily meal, or "ordinary," at a fixed hour and price, usually serving just one dish, much like a household cook providing dinner for a large family. Cookshops primarily sold cooked meat for carry-out, but some did, on occasion, serve food on the premises.

By the 16th century, Englishmen of all classes were in the habit of dining out often. Local taverns offered fixed price meals, wine, ale, and tobacco, and served as a meeting place and informal clubhouse to boot. Entry was generally restricted to men. Among the more famous Elizabethan taverns in London were *The Falcon,* a popular haunt of actors, and *The Mermaid,* oft frequented by William Shakespeare.

Beginning in England around 1650, the coffee house began taking over many of the tavern's social functions. At first, the coffee house served only coffee, tea, and chocolate—all new arrivals to Europe. Then, the coffee houses began providing wine, ale, and occasional hot meals. Another attraction was its supply of gazettes and newsletters regularly kept on hand for coffee swillers on their way to and from work. The clientele evidently was quite varied. An early 18th-century writer noted: "Some shops are a resort for learned scholars and wits; others are the resort of dandies, or of politicians, or again of professional newsmongers, and many are temples of Venus."

For the first real restaurant, we must naturally turn to France. In 1765, a soup vender named Boulanger opened a shop offering diners a choice of dishes rather than the then standard "ordinary" or "table d'hôte" dinner. The sign above Boulanger's door read *"Restaurants,"* meaning "restoratives," referring to the hot soups and broths available inside. The term restaurant or a derivative, was eventually adopted by many other nations and languages, although the word was not generally used in England until the late 19th century.

Hungry Parisians so enjoyed the new eating place that hundreds of similar establishments began springing up around the city, one offering close to 200 different meat dishes daily.

The first "luxury" restaurant to open its doors in Paris was *La Grande Taverne de Londres,* founded in 1782 by Antoine

The Old White Hart Tavern on Bishopsgate Street, London, a popular Renaissance establishment, was one of the precursors of the modern restaurant.

Beauvilliers. He was later to write a cookbook that became a standard work on French culinary art. According to the rotund gastronomist Brillat-Savarin, Beauvilliers' establishment was the first to offer the four essentials of a fine restaurant: "an elegant room, smart waiters, a choice cellar, and superb cooking."

Prior to the French Revolution, aristocrats maintained elaborate culinary staffs. When the aristocracy was driven from power, their cooks were likewise driven from the kitchen. Many sought work in restaurants or opened their own eating places. By 1804, there were well over 500 restaurants in Paris.

The great culinary establishments of 19th-century Paris included the *Very,* whose menu listed 12 soups. 24 fish dishes, 15 beef dishes, 20 mutton specialties, and scores of side dishes. In 1869, the *Very* was merged with a neighboring restaurant to form the *Le Grand Vefour,* which still ranks near the top among French restaurants. Another great restaurant of the era, the *Cafe Anglais,* had a chef, Adolphe Duglère, who created the famed "Three Emperors Dinner" in 1867 for

Waitresses with bloomers are used in a San Francisco restaurant to attract customers. The drawing is from a Police Gazette *of the 1890s.*

three well-heeled diners: Tsar Alexander II of Russia, his son, the future Alexander III, and William I, the future emperor of Germany.

Across the English Channel, by the end of the 19th century, the tavern had given way to the restaurant and the tea shop. The first teahouse opened in 1884, initially serving only teas. Later, it offered full meals. Teahouses became immediately popular among women, who, for the first time, had a place where they could eat in public without a male escort. Meanwhile, the lower classes turned to cheap eateries nicknamed "dives" due to their customary underground location.

In the United States, the earliest restaurants on record appeared in Philadelphia around 1680. The *Blue Anchor Tavern* was among the first. New York's *Fraunces Tavern*—the site of George Washington's farewell to his troops—was a popular watering hole in Revolutionary times, and still operates today.

The major American innovations in the field of eateries were the self-service restaurant and the automatic restaurant. The first self-service eatery in New York opened in 1885, but self-service establishments called *cafeterias* first became popular in San Francisco of the gold rush era.

The first automatic restaurant was opened by the Horn & Hardart Baking Company in Philadelphia in 1902, using mechanisms imported from Germany. Other American innovations were the specialty restaurant—the steak house and seafood restaurant, for example—the Pullman diner car, and the riverboat dining room.

By 1955, there were close to 200,000 eating places in the United States—one for every 800 persons—serving over 60 million meals a day with a staff of 1.3 million workers.

The dollar lunch was still a possibility at the posh restaurant, Rector's, *in 1894.*

Rector's Specialties

Onion Soup — *Lobster, Thermidor*
Chicken casserole, Catalane — *Sweetbread, Prince of Wales*
Boneless Squab en cocotte, Nerac — *Venice Peaches, Mephisto*

Luncheon

1894

OYSTERS 25 — CLAMS 25

Soups

Julienne, Pea or Tomato 25 40 — Chicken Gumbo 35 60
Mongole 25 40 — Consommé Brunoise 25 40 — Oyster Stew 50

Fish

Filets of Sole, Marguery 40 75 *9 minutes*
Aiguillette of Kingfish, Rector 50 90 *9 minutes*
Oysters and Oyster Crabs, Opera 75 *6 minutes*
Brook Trout, maître d'hôtel 45 80, *10 min.* — Bluefish au gratin 40 70, *12 min.*
Frogs' Legs, Poulette 60 1 10, *5 minutes* — Filet of Bass, Mornay 40 70, *7 minutes*

Hot

Roast Beef 40 60 — **Spring Lamb**
Braised Beef with noodles 35 60, *ready* — **Irish Lamb Stew 35 60**, *ready*
Shirred Eggs, chicken livers 50, *5 minutes* — Omelette à l'Espagnole 50, *5 minutes*
Emincé of Lamb, green peppers 40 70, *4 min.* — Lamb Fries, Béarnaise 40 70, *8 min.*
Pig's Feet, sauce moutarde 35 60, *6 min.* — Calf's Brains, brown butter 35 60, *4 min.*
Corned Beef Hash browned, poached eggs 40 70, *7 minutes*
Brochette of Chicken Livers, Madeira sauce 40 70, *9 minutes*
Tripe en casserole, nouvelle mode 40 70, *4 minutes*
Deerfoot Sausage, purée of peas 35 60, *6 minutes*
Ham and Spinach, demi-glace 40 70, *5 minutes*
Fresh Mushrooms on toast 60 1 00 *9 minutes.*

Vegetables

New Peas or Beans 50 — **New Asparagus 1 00**
Potatoes Sarah 20 30 — Oyster Plant 30 — Egg Plant 40 — Spinach with egg 25 40
Bouldin Island Asparagus 35 60 — Asparagus Tips au gratin 35 60
Céleri braisé au jus 30 50 — Macaroni, Spaghetti or Noodles 25 40

Game, Etc.

Ruddy Duck 2 00 — Squab Chicken 1 25 — Teal Duck 1 00
Squab, Plover, Snipe or Railbird 80 — Spring Chicken 1 50 75
Broiled Half Capon 1 25 — Half Spring Turkey 1 50

Salads

Hot House Tomato or Cucumber 35 60 — Chiffonade 40 70 — Rector 45 75
Lettuce, Chicory, Celery or Escarole 30 50 — Romaine 35 60
Fetticus with beets or dandelion 30 50 — Mayonnaise 10

Dessert

Fresh Strawberries with cream 75 — French Pastry [assorted] 25
Brandied: Figs, Peaches, Cherries or Plums 25 40

Ices

Fancy Ice: Plombière au kirsch 40 — Souveniers: Pin Cushion 50
All Plain Cream or Ices 25 mixed 30
Cheese — Fruits
COFFEE: French 15 Turkish 20 Special 25

HALF PORTIONS FOR ONE PERSON ONLY

Rector's

GRAND VÉF

LES POTAGES

Vichyssoise au Cerfeuil
Consommé Chaud ou en Gelée
Bisque de Homard
Germiny
Tortue Claire au Xérès
Saint-Germain aux Croutons

LES ENTRÉES FROIDES

Terrines Assorties
Assiette Landaise
Foie d'Oie Frais
Terrine Foie Canard Frais
Jambon de Parme
Salade Quimperloise

LES ENTRÉES CHAUDES

Œuf au Plat Louis Oliver
Œuf Brouillé Montensier
Soufflé de Grenouilles
Brochettes Langoustines et Mousseline
Croute Landaise
Toast à la Moelle

Au Salon Sainte-Beuve - Repas 8 à 12 Couverts (Sur Commande)

Carte du Jo

Salade de Fonds d'Artichauts
Feuilleté d'Huîtres Arcachon
Rouget Soufflé "Elisabeth
Filet de Saint Pierre aux Pet
Ragoût d'Ecrevisses et Broch
Coquilles Saint-Jacques au

Canard Sauvage au Porto (
Civet de Lièvre "Aust de Pr
Suprême de Faisan aux C
Perdreau Rotie sur Canapé
Grouse Rotie Grand Mère (
Côte de Veau aux Petits Lég

Salades Vertes (Assaisonnem
Plateau de Fromages

DESSERTS

Soufflé au Cointreau *Soufflé*
(A Commander Début Repas
Poire Grand Véfour *Gâteau*
Glace ou Sorbet *Salade*
Coupe Joséphine *Fruits*
Méringue Joinville *Crêpes*
Oranges Maspronne *Petits F*

½ Bt. de Vin de Saute

CAFÉ

R

LES POISSONS

Sole Véfour
Sole Foie d'Oie "René Lalou"
Timbale de Homard "Palais Royal"

LES VIANDES

Tournedos Belle Hélène
Filet au Poivre
Mignonnettes au Poivre Vert
Côte de Bœuf grillée à la Moelle (2 pers.)
Côte de Bœuf poêlée aux Echalotes (2 pers.)
Carré d'Agneau Cécilia (2 pers.)
Côtes d'Agneau Albarine
Rognon de Veau aux 3 Moutardes
Ris de Veau Yves Labrousse

LES VOLAILLES

Poulet Sauté au Vinaigre de Miel
Ballottine de Canard P. Henocq
Pigeon Prince Rainier III

LES LÉGUMES

Pommes Soufflées
Epinards
Haricots Verts

Service 15 % non compris
Pas de Carte de Crédit

THE FOOD STALLS OF SINGAPORE: *A series of restaurants open to the public under the aegis of the city-state. The interior may consist of 30 or so individual food emporiums. Stalls specialize in dishes. There is a stall that sells roast duck, another that sells roast pork, still another that sells fruit juice, another cake, etc.*

You walk around in these restaurant complexes, and you select the food you want. Each table is numbered. When ordering, you give the stall keeper the number of your table. A few minutes later, your order is delivered to you. The food is good, clean, and exceptionally well priced. These pictures show the food stalls on Tanglin Road.

Annual sales totaled about nine billion dollars, making the restaurant the third largest retail business in this country. About 20 percent of all restaurant sales are now rung up on the cash registers of large American chains. These include *Howard Johnson's*, *McDonald's*, and other various hamburger drive-ins.

Two men sat down in a restaurant and ordered their main dishes. Then they closed their menus. The waiter said, "Thank you, gentlemen, and would any of you wish a beverage with your meal?"

One man said, "Well, I usually have coffee, but today, I think I'll have a glass of milk."

The other man said, "That sounds good. I'll have milk, too. But make sure the glass is clean!"

"Very good," said the waiter, and he left.

Soon he came back with a tray and two glasses of milk, and said, "Here you are, gentlemen. Now which one of you asked for the clean glass?"

Today, the last word in gastronomic excellence is the guide published by the Michelin Corporation, a French tire firm. Michelin annually rates restaurants in thousands of towns and cities, awarding each from zero to three stars according to culinary quality. One star indicates good quality in its class; two stars suggests the restaurant is well worth a detour; and three ranks the establishment among the best in the world.

In a recent typical year, Michelin rated a total of 3,036 restaurants in France: 2,382 were rated as unstarred; 581 received one star; 62 received two stars; and only 11 restaurants earned the highest Michelin compliment of three stars. Five of these gastronomic palaces were in Paris, among them *Grand Véfour* and *La Tour D'Argent*, the oldest surviving restaurant in Paris.

Many culinary connoisseurs, however, maintain that for the best in *haute cuisine* you'll have to travel to Vienne, near Lyons, where you'll find the renowned *Pyramide*. Other gourmets would name Paul Bocuse's *Auberge Pont de Collonges*, near Lyons, as the world's premier restaurant, or perhaps the *Auberge de l'Ill* in Illhausen, Alsace, or the *Hotel Côte D'Or* in Saulieu, near Dijon.

France, of course, has no monopoly on fine food. (Modern French cuisine, by the way, is Italian in origin.) Many gourmets avow that Chinese cuisine is actually the world's finest, and excellent Oriental restaurants can be found in most cities of the world.

It's been estimated that a New Yorker can dine out every night of his life until age 65 without visiting any establishment twice!

Among New York's restaurants, *Lutèce* and *La Grenouille* have been given high marks by Michelin, and certainly rank among the finest restaurants on this side of the Atlantic. *Windows on the World*, located atop one the 110-story World Trade Center towers, has been lauded for its view more than its food. Reservations for dinner at the sky-high restaurant must sometimes be made weeks in advance. And any list of Gotham's posh restaurants must include *The Palace* where dinner prices are, at this writing, $75 per person—without drinks!

It's been estimated that a New Yorker can dine out every night of his life until age 65 without visiting any establishment twice!

ROSES

The Madame de Watteville Rose

The red rose whispers of passion
And the white rose breathes of love;
O, the red rose is a falcon,
And the white rose is a dove.

—John Boyle O'Reilly, *A White Rose*

Quick, name a flower. Well, you may not have said *rose,* but if you were to experiment with the question you'd probably find that, of the estimated 300,000 species of plants on earth, the rose is the first flower to pop into most minds.

Why? It's difficult to say. Many other flowers are larger, more colorful, more fragrant, or more valued. But no single flower is so universally known, so closely connected with the culture of many civilizations, so rich in poetic and mythologic significance as the rose. Symbol of beauty, romance, love, secrecy, perfection, elegance, and life itself, the rose has figured in legend, heraldry, and religion, and has served as the favorite of poets and artists from time immemorial.

Immortalized in songs, such as *The Last Rose of Summer, Sweet Rosie O'Grady,* and *My Wild Irish Rose,* the rose has been, and will likely forever remain, the queen of flowers.

The botanical family Rosaceae, which includes close to 200 species and thousands of hybrids, has flourished for millions of years. Indeed, roses have been cultivated for so long that it's impossible to determine where or when the flower was first domesticated. The Egyptians were familiar with cultivated roses by 3000 B.C., building rose gardens in their palaces and often burying roses in their tombs. By the time of Cleopatra's reign, the rose had replaced the lotus as Egypt's ceremonial flower.

The mythologies of various ancient cultures touched on the rose. Most agreed that the flower was created when the gods were still on earth. The Greeks called the rose, "the king of flowers" until the poet Sappho, in her *Ode to the Rose,* dubbed it as the "queen of flowers" forevermore. According to the Greeks, the rose first appeared with the birth of Aphrodite, the goddess of love and beauty. When Aphrodite (in Roman mythology, Venus) first emerged from the sea, the earth produced the rose to show that it could match the gods in the creation of perfect beauty. The well-known painting by Botticelli, *Birth of Venus,* depicts dozens of roses in a scene of the goddess emerging from the sea.

Another myth tells of a beautiful maiden named Rhodanthe (*rhodon* in Greek means "rose") who was tirelessly pursued by three suitors. To escape her pursuers, Rhodanthe fled to the temple of Artemis, where her attendants, convinced that Rhodanthe was even more beautiful than Artemis, flung a statue of the goddess from its pedestal and demanded that Rhodanthe be represented there instead. The god Apollo, angered by the insult to his twin sister, Artemis, turned Rhodanthe into a rose and her attendants into thorns. The three suitors were changed into the three courtiers of the rose: the bee, the worm, and the butterfly.

Yet another myth blames the god Eros, or Cupid, for the rose's thorny stem. According to the tale, the god of love was enjoying the aroma of the thornless rose when he was stung by a bee lurking in the petals. To punish the flower, Cupid shot the stem full of his arrows, and the rose forever after was cursed with arrowhead-shaped thorns. Yet, according to a Chinese proverb, "The rose has thorns only for those who gather it."

The word *rosary* comes to us from the Latin *rosarium,* meaning a "rose garden," and later the word came to mean "a garland of roses." Christian legend tells of a monk who made a garland of 150 roses each day as an offering to the Virgin Mary. Later, the monk substituted 150 prayers for the flowers.

Though various mythologies have explained the origin of the rose differently, almost all ancient cultures valued the rose for its beauty and fragrance. Roman aristocrats strewed roses around their banquet halls and served a wine made from roses. Moslem monarchs in India bathed in pools with rose petals floating on top of the water. According to the *Thousand and One Arabian Nights,* the Caliph of Baghdad served a jam made from roses that held captive anyone who ate it.

The use of the rose as a symbol of beauty, frailty, and love is quite understandable, but the flower has also symbolized creation, secrecy, the Church, and the risen Christ. The rose windows featured in most Gothic cathedrals are thought by some to represent life and creation, or hope radiating from faith and the Church.

A root in the right soil,
Sun, rain, and a man's toil;
That, as a wise man knows,
Is all there is to a rose.

—Orgill Mackenzie,
Whitegates

As a symbol of love and romance, the rose needs little introduction. As some are fond of noting, *rose* is an anagram of "Eros."

Robert Burns compared his "love" to a "red, red rose, that's newly sprung in June." And a German custom dictated that a groom send a silver rose to his bride before the marriage ceremony—a custom that forms the basis of the plot of Richard Strauss's opera *Der Rosenkavalier.*

Since classical times, the rose has been a symbol of secrecy. In 16th-century England, a rose was sometimes worn behind the ear by servants, tavern workers, and others to indicate that the wearer heard all and told nothing. In Germany, roses in a dining room suggested that diners could speak freely without fear that their secrets would travel beyond the

The Papa Gontier Rose

room. The expression *sub rosa*, which literally means "under the rose," actually means "secretly," and is thought to originate in the custom of carving a rose over the door of the confessional in a Catholic church.

Exactly why the rose came to be a symbol of secrecy is open to speculation. Perhaps the unopened rosebud suggests beauty or truth hidden by the closed petals. In any case, medieval alchemists used the rose as a symbol of the need for secrecy in their art, and as a representation of certain highly guarded scientific principles important in their work. The secret society of the Rosicrucians—from "red cross"— used a cross with a red rose as their symbol.

In medieval England, many families employed a representation of the rose in their coat of arms: the red rose of Lancaster and the white rose of York are two well-known examples. During the 15th century, these two houses fought for control of the English crown in a struggle that came to be known as the War of the Roses.

The rose has, of course, proved useful in more ways than the symbolic. Rose water was first distilled around the time of the Crusades. When the Moslem leader Saladin retook Jerusalem from the Crusaders, he refused to enter a mosque until all the walls and the objects had been purified with rose water. Over 50 camels were required to transport the aromatic cargo from Baghdad to Jerusalem.

Rose oil, used in perfumes and lotions, likewise originated in the Near East, and did not appear in Europe until 1612. A 17th-century German book lists 33 diseases that supposedly can be cured by rose water or oil.

During the 18th century, rose petals occasionally were included in English salads, and essence of roses was used to flavor ice cream.

Today, roses are grown extensively in many parts of the world, especially in France, India, and the Balkans, and attar of roses is used in perfumes, cosmetics, and flavoring syrups. Rose hips, the fruits of the rose plant, are used to make tea, or as a source of Vitamin C.

The Empress Josephine of

France, the wife of Napoleon, put the rose to a more singular use. Josephine built a huge rose garden at her estate at Malmaison, with over 250 varieties of the flower flourishing—every variety known at the time. The Empress often carried in hand a Malmaison rose that she could raise to her lips when smiling, since she was particularly sensitive about her imperfect teeth.

The rose has been cultivated and hybridized for so long that there are, strictly speaking, no species of purely wild rose left on earth. The flowers extant today range in size from just half an inch in diameter to varieties that spread to more than seven inches. Colors range from white through yellow, pink, red, and maroon.

Some roses smell like—well, roses, while others suggest green tea, hay, or various spices. Biologically, the rose's fragrance is quite important, since roses normally do not secrete nectar and depend mostly on aroma and color to attract pollinating insects.

There are about 35 species of rose thought to be native hybrids of North America. Various roses are the state flowers of Iowa, North Dakota, and New York. While the Greeks and Romans named their roses after gods, and the English after court figures, in America the preference is for descriptive or geographical names, such as the *pasture*, the *prairie*, the *smooth*, the *prickly*, or the *California rose*. The Chinese, meanwhile, have long used metaphoric names for the flower. The names of some Chinese rose varieties translate as *After Rain*, *Clear Shining*, *Tiny Jade Shoulders*, and *Three Rays of Dawn*.

Speaking of poetic descriptions, the prominent metaphoric use of the rose through the ages has left us with a considerable body of "rosy" verse. Robert Herrick wrote *Gather ye rosebuds while ye may*, William Blake gave us *The Sick Rose*, and W.B. Yates, *The Rose of the World*. But surely the simplest observation concerning the queen of flowers came from the pen of Gertrude Stein, whose poem, *Sacred Emily* includes the line, *"A rose is a rose is a rose is a rose."*

Roses are distilled to make perfume.

Rulers

Here's something to think about: a dry goods dealer has a five-yard piece of 32-inch wide material, and wishes to sell a customer one-and-a-half yards. But neither a yardstick, nor a tape measure, nor any other measuring device is available. Can the dealer complete the sale?

Yes, it can be done, as you'll discover later; but for now, take our word for it. Using a ruler or a tape measure would be a lot easier than figuring out this problem in your head. In fact, much of our commercial life would be next to impossible without implements for estimating length and distance. Why "estimate?" Well, if the American mission that landed a man on the moon had depended upon measuring devices only as accurate as the ruler in a schoolboy's briefcase, our astronauts would most likely have missed the moon altogether!

No ruler or measuring device is completely accurate; in fact, no measurement of any kind is ever *absolutely* correct. A measuring device is, in effect, only a reproduction of an arbitrary standard. While the standard itself is perfectly accurate, the reproduction *never* is. For instance, the standard of length measure in the United States is the yard. Theoretically, a yard is a yard is a yard, but no yardstick ever measures *exactly* 36 inches.

The first common unit of length was the *cubit,* used by the Egyptians and Babylonians thousands of years ago. Originally, the cubit was defined as the length of a man's arm from the elbow to the end of the middle finger (the word comes from the Latin word for "elbow"), but the actual length of the cubit varied from place to place and from time to time. Through most of Egyptian history, the cubit was equivalent to about 20.6 inches. One advantage of the cubit was that in the absence of a measuring device the unit could be easily—handily, you might say—approximated. Presumably, long-armed merchants were quite popular in Egypt.

In Egyptian, the cubit was called the *meh,* and divided into units called *sheps,* or "palms." There were seven *sheps* in a cubit, and the *shep* in turn was divided into four parts, called *zebos,* or "digits." "Let's see—I'll have two *mehs,* six *sheps,* three *zebos* of that linen..."

The ancient Greek cubit was about 20.7 inches, but another unit of measurement, the *foot,* was more widely used. The Greek foot was about 12.5 inches, divided into 25 digits. The Romans adopted a *pes,* or foot, of about 11.6 inches, divided into 16 digits.

Prior to the 19th century, each country in Europe had its own system of weights and measures. In medieval England, for instance, the foot was equivalent to 13.2 inches, with six feet to a *fathom,* 10 fathoms to a *chain,* 10 chains to a *furlong,* and 10 furlongs to an *old mile,* equivalent to about 6,600 feet. The English units of measure evolved from many origins, some as old as the Roman conquest.

By 1800, length measure standards were fixed in England at their present values. The unit of length measurement was the *yard* (from the Anglo-Saxon *gyrd,* "measure"), divided into feet and inches. English kings kept a bar known as *the standard yard* in London as the ultimate arbiter of the yard's exact length.

The idea of a physical standard is an old one. Physical standards are kept, not to settle every measurement dispute by direct reference to the standard, but to have a permanent—or so it was thought—record of each measuring standard. But even a physical standard can be inaccurate. It's been estimated that the new British standard yard has decreased by .0002 inches since it was cast a little over a hundred years ago.

The original standard yard was lost when the Houses of Parliament burned in 1834. Scientific studies followed to determine a new standard and to produce a unified system of weights and measures. In 1878, the British imperial yard was defined as the distance at a specified temperature between two lines engraved on gold studs sunk in a certain bronze bar.

Measurement systems from England, France, Spain, and Portugal were all brought to America by colonists, and all were used here briefly in various places. By the time of the American Revolution, standards of measurement here were identical to those current in England. In 1832, an American physical standard was adopted, defining the yard as the distance between the 27th and 63rd inch of a certain 82-inch brass bar kept in Washington, D.C. Since 1893, the U.S. standard yard has been defined in terms of the meter.

The yard is still the standard of length measurement in this country, of course; but most other nations, including England, have gone over to the metric system. Although a decimal system for measurement was first proposed as long ago as 1670, the essentials of today's metric system were embodied in a report made by the Paris Academy of Science in 1791.

The original plan for a metric system defined the meter as one ten-millionth part of a meridional quadrant of the earth Larger units were formed by the addition of Greek prefixes (deca-, hecto-, kilo-), and smaller units with Latin prefixes (deci-, centi-, milli-). A platinum bar was cast according to this definition for use as the physical standard, although few scientists at the time were satisfied with its accuracy.

The new measuring system did not catch on immediately. Many years passed before it was widely adopted in France and other countries. In 1875, a treaty was signed assuring international unification and improvement of the system. Four years later, the standard meter was newly defined with reference to a bar of platinum-iridium alloy. In 1927, a supplementary definition described the meter in terms of light waves, for while a platinum bar can be destroyed or altered, light wave measurement will always be available. With such a standard, a unit of measurement can be verified anywhere in the world without risking damage in transit to the physical standard.

Along with the United States, only Liberia, Southern Yemen, and a handful of other small nations still employ the so-called British system, and the metric system will soon be introduced in most of these countries as well. The exact date for total metric conversion here has not yet been fixed, but Canada began the switchover in 1977.

A number of other terms are sometimes used for length measurement. For instance, have you

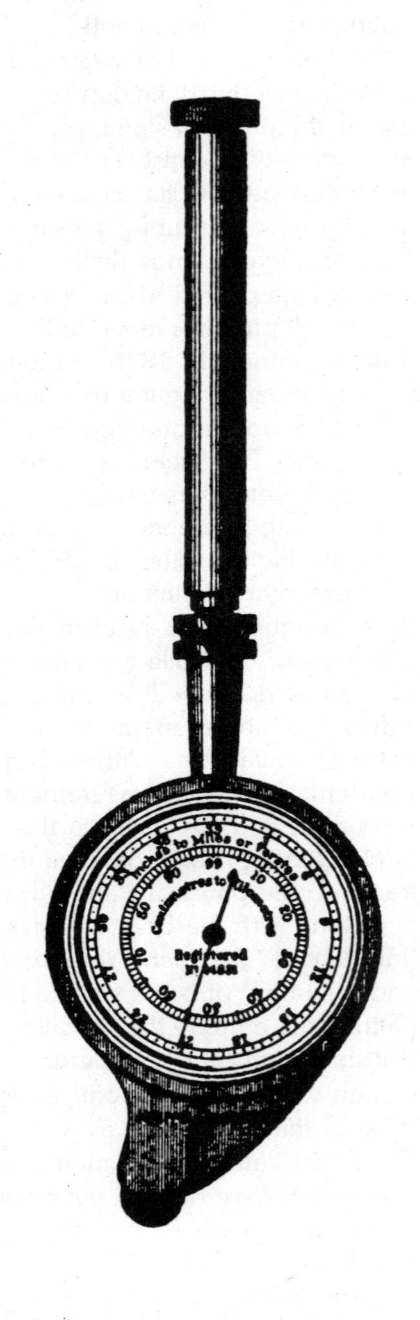

With this map-measure, you can calculate anything from centimeters to miles.

ever wondered what a *furlong* was? The term originated with the word "furrow," and at one time was thought to be the length most suitable for a plow furrow. The furlong is now defined as 220 yards.

The word *league* has varied in meaning in different times and countries. In England, the league was equivalent to about three miles. For centuries now, the word league has been used chiefly in a figurative sense.

The *knot* is not a measurement of length, so if you ever hear a sailor say "knots per hour" you'll know he's a landlubber in disguise. The knot is actually a measurement of speed, equivalent to one nautical mile per hour.

The *nautical mile* is defined three different ways, since navigators once regarded the nautical mile as the length of one minute of the meridian at the place where they were taking the reading. The U.S. nautical mile has been identical to the international unit since 1959, measuring 6,076 feet.

The *fathom* was originally thought to be the length to which a man can extend his arms—if you can fathom that. Today, the fathom is equivalent to six feet, and is used most often in reference to water depth and cable length.

The smallest unit of length measurement in the world is the *atto-meter,* equivalent to a mere quintillionth of a centimeter. Your pinky is probably about 7,000,000,000,000,000,000 atto-meters long!

For a measuring device, early man probably first used his arms or his foot—but even during the Egyptian era, when the cubit was the unit of length measurement, a ruler of some kind was more often used. There are two basic kinds of length-measuring devices: the end standard, and the line standard. With an end standard, the unit is defined as the length from one end of the device to the other; with a line standard, from one calibration on the device to another. Most modern rulers are end standards; that is, a foot ruler is one foot long from end to end, and a yardstick is one yard long.

How accurate is a modern ruler? Suppose you want to draw a two-inch line on a piece of paper. First of all, the calibrations on the ruler are a fraction of an inch thick. Thus, a dot that looks correctly placed to you, may appear off-center to another eye. The calibrations themselves are never absolutely precise, and the edges of most rulers are slightly warped. The chance of your line measuring precisely two inches, then, is slim, indeed.

Rulers come in many shapes and sizes, among them the three-edged or triangular ruler so often used by students—both for measuring and for launching rubber bands across the classroom.

A tape measure is used for very long measurement, or for the measurement of a bent surface. Calipers consist of two prongs joined by a pin; they are best for measuring thickness or the distance between two surfaces.

As any draftsman can tell you, there's a world of difference between a ruler and a straight edge. No draftsman worth his T-square would use a ruler for drawing an accurate straight line, since rulers are designed chiefly for measuring, not line drawing.

For a crisp, straight line, it's best to use a triangle or other device specifically designed for line drawing.

You remember our dry goods dealer and his measuring dilemma? Well, here's what you would have to go through to cut the material without a measuring device.

The customer wants one-and-a-half yards, or 54 inches. Without a ruler, this will have to be measured out along a strip of paper. First, fold the five-yard piece of fabric in half. It now measures 90 inches long. Overlap the material so that you divide it into three equal parts. Each part will be 30 inches. Lay this on the piece of paper and mark off the 30 inches. Now, unfold the material. This time fold the width in half; this will give you 16 inches. Mark off 16 inches next to your 30-inch mark on the paper. Now fold the width in half again, giving you eight inches. Mark off an additional eight inches along your piece of paper. You now have marked off a total of 54 inches. Lay your length of material along the marked paper and cut your customer the desired one-and-a-half yards.

And next time, get yourself a ruler or a tape measure!

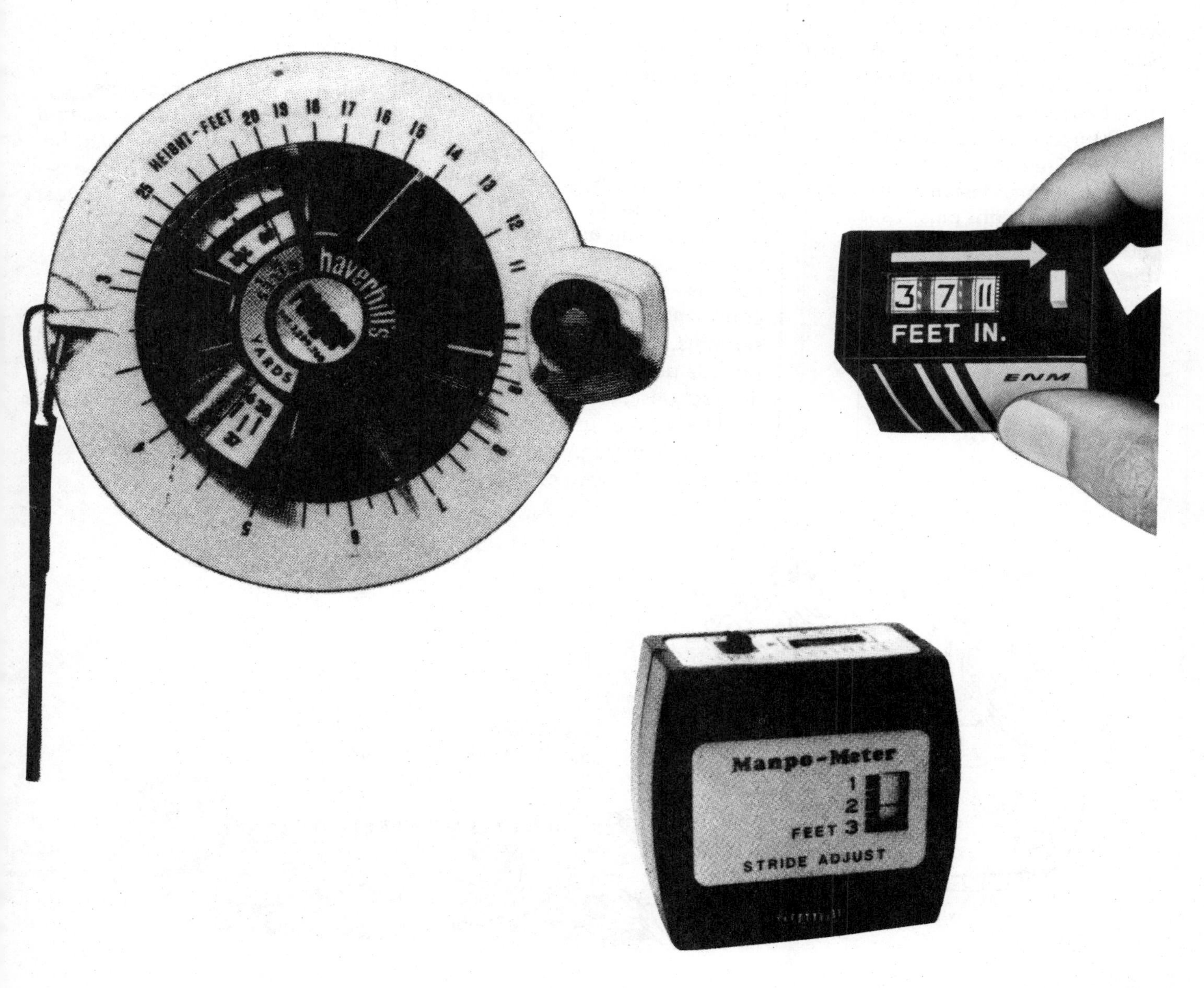

Measure for measure, these modern devices pictured below achieve maximum accuracy.

Left: The Disc Ranger measures distances from 6 feet to almost as far as the eye can see, in yards, nautical miles, and statute miles.

Right: The Tapeless Tape Measure is a skid-proof, mar-proof wheel that glides along surfaces and measures distances on a digital counter.

Bottom: The Manpo Measure Meter tells you at a glance how far you've walked.

Safety Pins

On April 10, 1849, a New Yorker by the name of Walter Hunt was granted patent Number 6,281 for a device he called the safety pin. Never heard of Walter Hunt, you say? Well, Hunt was not destined to be pinned with the tag "inventor of the safety pin" for one simple reason: the safety pin, or devices virtually identical to it, had been in use for more than 2,500 years—since the days of ancient Greece!

The earliest fasteners used by man were straight pins, usually simple thorns. Relics of prehistoric man 20,000 years old include bone needles with eyes, and pins with decorated heads. The art of pin making actually predates agriculture, pottery, and metalworking.

The Egyptians didn't use the safety pin or button, but they did fashion straight pins and needles from metal. Bronze pins eight inches long have been found in Egyptian tombs, many with decorated gold heads.

Every period of classical Greece and Rome had its own forms of safety pin and clasp. In fact, the forms of each period were so distinctive that a safety pin can frequently be used to accurately date an entire archaeological find. During some periods, safety pin heads commonly took the form of serpents, horses, and lutes; other periods produced heads with abstract designs.

Homer tells us that a dozen safety pins were presented to Penelope, the wife of Odysseus by her suitors, suggesting that the Greeks considered pins fitting gifts, even for royalty. Presumably, almost all early Greeks used safety pins to fasten their tunics, since the button wasn't to arrive from Asia Minor until considerably later.

Athenian women used long, daggerlike pins to fasten their chitons over their shoulders. According to Herodotus, when a group of angry women used the pins to stab to death an Athenian soldier, the city forbade the wearing of all but the Ionion tunic, which did not require pins. The law was later revoked; but by then, women were using buttons as well as safety pins.

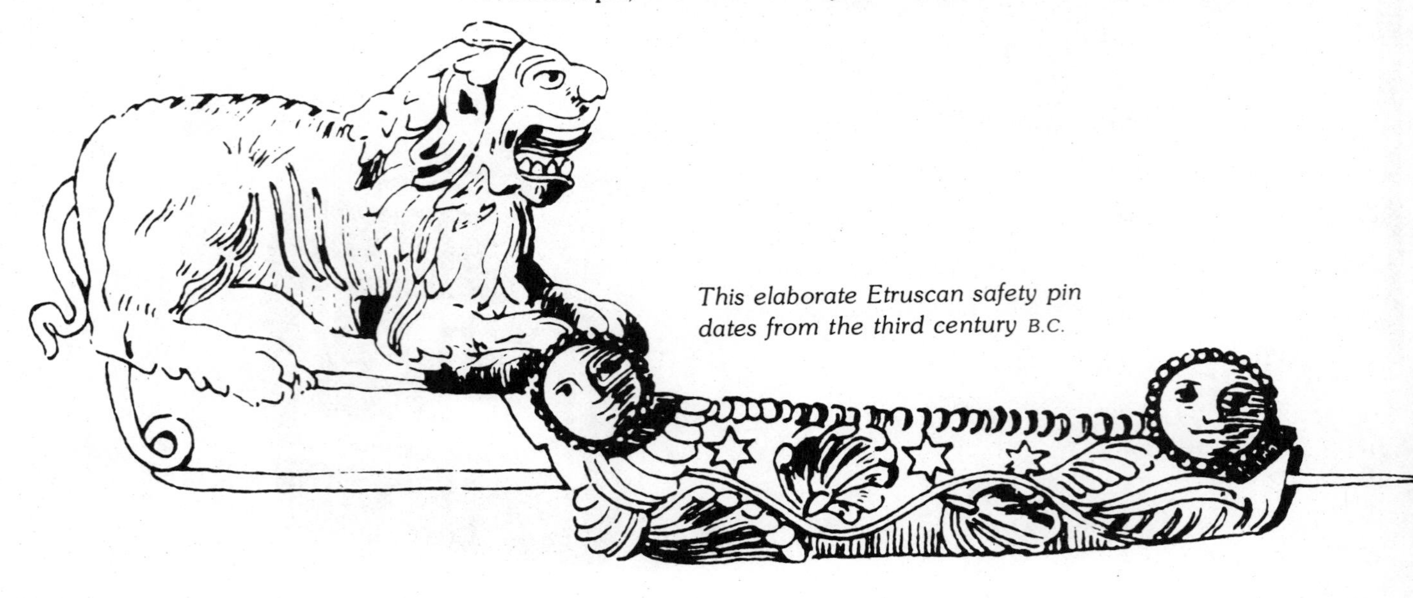

This elaborate Etruscan safety pin dates from the third century B.C.

This Roman fibula, or safety pin, dates from the seventh century B.C.

Courtesy, Museum of Fine Arts, Boston. Gift of Mrs. Edward Jackson Holmes.

The Romans called the safety pin *fibula,* a term still used for a clasp, and also for a certain leg bone. A bust from the late Empire shows a consul wearing a tunic fastened by two safety pins as long as his head, suggesting that in Rome the size of a *fibula* may have indicated rank.

In Medieval Europe, the wealthy used elaborately fashioned safety pins of ivory, brass, silver, and gold, while the poor had to make do with simple wood skewers. By the 15th century, pins were being manufactured from drawn iron wire, and a pin-making industry was well established in France.

But for centuries, metal pins remained rare and costly items reserved for the rich. You've heard the expression *pin money,* meaning a small sum allotted by a husband for his wife's use, or money for incidental items. Well, when the term originated in the 14th century, "pin money" was just that, for at that time, pins were expensive enough to be real items on the budget. By custom, a husband would present his wife on the first or second of January with enough money to buy her pins for the year. "Pin money" went by the boards in the 19th century, when mass-production made pins the inexpensive purchase they are today.

The father of the American pin industry was Samuel Slocum, who in 1838, founded a pin factory in Poughkeepsie, New York, capable of turning out 100,000 pins a day. Though Slocum was not the first to design a machine for manufacturing pins, his pins were the first to be mass-produced in America. Slocum's pins had solid heads, and came to be known as *Poughkeepsie pins.* Slocum was also the first to devise a machine for packaging pins in grooved paper boards.

There's another reason why Walter Hunt is forgotten as the "inventor" of the safety pin. The would-be pin magnate rather hastily conceived his idea, made a model, and sold his patent rights for the sum of $100—all within three hours! In any case, diaper-wearing babies have expressed their gratitude ever since, with hours of sob-free slumber.

This horse-shaped Etruscan safety pin dates from 700 B.C.

Courtesy, Museum of Fine Arts, Boston. Helen and Alice Colburn Fund.

The safety pin made a critical contribution to the wasp-waist look of the gay 90s.

The 19th century was the big era for fasteners of all kinds. Buttons are thousands of years old, but it wasn't until 1863 that Louis Hannart invented the *snap*.

And 1896 saw the first patent for a "slide fastener," a device invented five years earlier by Witcomb Judson as a "clasp locker and unlocker for shoes." The term we use today, *zipper*, originally referred only to a boot equipped with a slide fastener.

Judson, a Chicago inventor, became so tired of lacing and unlacing his high boots that he set out to devise a quicker, easier way of fastening them. At first, he peddled his invention door-to-door as the *C-Curity Placket Fastener*, using the slogan "Pull and It's Done." But Judson's zipper, a series of hooks and eyes, was crude by modern standards, and tended to open or stick.

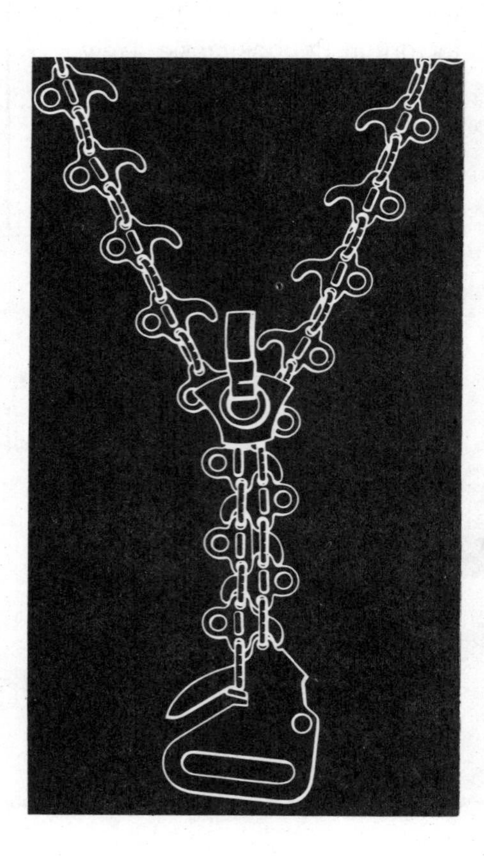

The first zipper was invented in 1891 by an engineer named Witcomb L. Judson.

Courtesy of Consumer and Educational Affairs, Coats and Clark, Inc.

Judson eventually sold his patent rights to Lewis Walker, who, with the aid of a Swede named Gideon Sundback, developed the first modern zipper in 1906. Zippers began to appear on tobacco pouches, mailbags, and galoshes around 1920; but by and large, the garment industry regarded the zipper as a passing fad. At the time, the only garments fitted with zippers were theatrical costumes for quick-change artists.

The 1930s saw the development of an improved zipper, with the metal teeth die cast directly onto the zipper tape fabric. Die cast teeth with rounded edges made the zipper completely dependable for the first time. Soon, everyone was using zippers.

Those of you who are presently struggling with torn, toothless, or unlockable zippers might be interested to know that modern zipper manufacturers claim their products can withstand 200,000 openings and closings without showing signs of wear. Tell it to the marines!

Interior of a salt mine.

When we eat and drink, we consume hundreds of chemicals combined in an appetizing form, and our bodies do the work of separating and distributing them. But there are two chemicals that we consume largely in their pure form, and these are two of the most important: H_2O and NaC1—water and salt.

Fortunately, these are also two of the most abundant chemicals on our planet. Two-thirds of the earth is covered with water, and the oceans are about three percent sodium chloride—that's the chemical term for ordinary table salt. Considering its abundance, it might seem odd that salt has been so highly valued by man throughout the ages—salt not only *costs* money, in some places it has been used *as* money!

Salt occurs in crystals of various sizes, made up of any number of individual molecules, each of which contains one atom of the element sodium, and one atom of the element chlorine. In the body, salt bathes all living tissues and helps flush out wastes. Unfortunately, it will also flush out water from our cells. For if a man could drink salt water, there would be no need for many of the extensive water-carrying systems we've constructed through history to bring water to our cities. And there would be little need for a salt trade.

But salt water, instead of replenishing living cells with water, has the opposite effect: Salt water, denser than pure water, draws water out of the cells through osmosis. Thus, even a man dying of thirst dares not drink salt water, as Coleridge's Ancient Mariner bemoaned in the oft-misquoted lines:

> *Water, water, everywhere,*
> *Nor any drop to drink.*

As you might expect, the use of salt dates back to the oldest of man's civilizations, though there are still peoples today who do not use it. Before the beginnings of agriculture, nomadic man subsisted on milk and roasted meats, which retain their natural salt, and therefore he did not need additional salt in his diet. But the rise of agricultural societies, with their vegetable and cereal diets, created the need for salt supplements.

We know that the ancient Sumerians ate salted meat and used salt to preserve food as long ago as 3500 B.C. According to a Mesopotamian legend, the benefits of salt were discovered when a wounded pig ran into the ocean and drowned. The pork thus soaked in brine was found to taste better than unsalted meat. The value of salt as a preservative and purifier was well known by Biblical times, for Job said: "Can nothing which is unsavory be eaten without salt?" Salt trade routes connected Mesopotamia, Egypt, and India at a very early date.

Because the habitual use of salt accompanied man's transition from nomadic to agricultural society, salt has long been esteemed as an object of religious significance and a gift of the gods. According to a Finnish myth, the god of the sky struck fire in the heavens, and the sparks fell to the ocean and turned into salt. Another ancient myth held that our salt water oceans are made up of all the tears ever cried. Early man often included salt in his sacrificial offerings to the gods, and used salt-filled pendants to ward off evil.

Salt was also used to seal covenants among ancient men, for its preservative qualities made it a fitting symbol for an enduring agreement. The Arab expression "there is salt between us" means a binding agreement has been reached, while the Persian "untrue to salt" refers to a broken covenant. The Biblical phrase "salt of the earth" still implies "elite."

Homer called salt divine, and mentioned its use at feasts. The ancient Greeks ate salted fish, and sometimes used salt in bartering for slaves and other items. The expression "worth his salt" may have first been uttered by a satisfied slave buyer who'd made his purchase with a quantity of salt.

Salt was a major commodity in ancient Rome. The *Via Salaria,* or salt route, was one of the oldest roads in Italy, the route by which salt was transported from salt pans near Ostia to other parts of the peninsula. By Imperial times, the salt oases of Northern Africa were linked by caravan routes, and other trade routes brought salt to Italy from salt pans around the Black Sea. Roman soldiers were given a ration of salt, called a *salarium,* which later became an allowance of money with which to buy salt—thus the origin of our word "salary."

The phrase "with a grain of salt" also dates back to Roman times. The Triumvir Pompey was known to add a grain of salt to his drinks as a supposed antidote to poison. Therefore to take something *cum grano salis* is to regard it with suspicion, or accept it with reservations.

Salt was used as currency in Tibet, Ethiopia, and other parts of Africa, in some cases until relatively recent times. During an invasion of Ethiopia in the late 19th century, Italian soldiers found blocks of salt stored in bank vaults along with more familiar forms of currency. Tribal Africans have been known to prefer salt to cash as payment for their wares, explaining "you can't eat dollars." And when salt has not been used by governments as official currency, it's often been used to *raise* money. European monarchs at various times taxed salt so heavily that it became affordable only on the black market.

The first American colonists had their salt shipped across the ocean from England. But a salt factory was established in Virginia as early as 1630, just a few years after the arrival of the colonists at Jamestown, and was probably one of the first factories of any kind on this side of the Atlantic. Americans continued to rely largely on imported salt until the War of 1812 cut off English shipments, at which time an American salt industry began to flourish in the area around Syracuse, New York.

In 1848, the company that was to become Morton Salt, the largest salt producer in the United States, was founded in Chicago. Morton now maintains salt processing plants in a number of states, and works almost every large salt field in the nation, with major deposits in New York, Pennsylvania, Ohio, West Virginia, Michigan, and the Great Salt Lake area of Utah. The Morton girl, with her umbrella and salt cannister, has graced packages of the firm's salt since 1914, though she's been redesigned a number of times since then.

Salt is found on earth in three basic forms: salt water, brine deposits, and rock salt crystal. The oceans hold by far the largest supply. Each gallon of sea water contains about four ounces of salt. It's been estimated that all the seas of the world contain some 4.5 billion cubic miles of salt, an amount equal to over 14 times the bulk of Europe!

Sea water close to the polar regions contains slightly less salt than water near the equator. The salt content of enclosed seas such as the Red Sea and the Mediterranean is also higher than ocean water. The most saline of all water, the Dead Sea, covers only about 350 square miles, yet contains some 11.6 billion tons of salt. The highly saline River Jordan pours six million tons of water into the Dead Sea daily, which after evaporation leaves behind about 850,000 tons of salt each year, much of it sodium chloride. The peculiar taste and smell of the salty Dead Sea water moved ancient Arab writers to call it "the stinking sea."

Rock salt deposits are almost entirely the result of sea water evaporation in areas once covered by the oceans. In Utah, salt can literally be scooped up off the ground, but in other places salt domes may be found more than 1,000 feet below ground. The Wieliczka mine near Cracow, Poland, is one of the world's most famous, with almost 70 miles of multi-leveled tunnels, a restaurant and two chapels with rock-salt walls and statues hewn from salt, and an underground salt lake that tourists can row across.

About 45 percent of the salt mined today comes directly from sea water. But in the United States, the largest supply comes from the evaporation of natural and artificial brines. In an artificial brine, water is pumped into a salt dome and then brought back to the surface, where the water can be evaporated and the salt collected.

The brine is first placed in settling tanks to remove impurities, then fed to a vacuum pan evaporator to eliminate the water. Invented in 1886 by the American Joseph Duncan, the vacuum pan evaporator allows salt producers to turn out the uniformly-sized cubic grains of salt we're likely to see in our salt shakers. Before the vacuum pan, salt was packaged in crystals of varying shapes and sizes.

After the salt is removed from the pans, it's filtered again, dried by heat, and passed through screens to produce grains of the desired size. Chem-

Russian convicts at work in the salt quarry at Iletsk, in Siberia, in the 1880s.

icals such as magnesium silicate and tricalcium phosphate are then added to table salt to make it free flowing. Since 1924, potassium iodide has also been added to some table salt to assure that Americans living inland receive an adequate supply of iodine, normally supplied by fresh seafood.

The United States is presently the world's largest producer of salt, turning out about 45 million tons each year. Other large salt-producing nations include the U.S.S.R., China, India, France, West Germany, and the United Kingdom. Annual worldwide production stands at around 160 million tons.

That may seem like a lot of salt for the salt shakers of the world. But the fact is, less than 10 percent of the salt produced in the United States is used in food industries, and only about three percent as table salt. Salt is now produced predominantly for use in the manufacture of major chemicals and household products such as bleaches, glass, soap, cement, paints and dyes, plastics, and water softeners. On the farm, salt is fed to livestock in large blocks. And since salt lowers the melting point of snow, it's often strewn over icy roads to speed up melting.

Once one of the most highly prized materials on earth, salt is now one of the cheapest products available in the supermarket—it costs only about 15¢ per pound. In fact, salt is so cheap and plentiful that the overuse of salt has become a bigger health problem than salt deficiency. The sodium in salt can contribute to high blood pressure and other ailments. Nutritionists have begun to petition the food industry to remove some of the salt now added to almost all prepared foods.

But convincing Americans to forsake salt may be a difficult task. After all, salt cellars will be found on the tables of every restaurant, diner, and coffee shop in the nation. Salt is still one of the very few things that you can get for free!

Sewers

Concrete proof that what goes on beneath the surface is of vital consequence may be more certainly demonstrated by sanitation engineers than by psychiatrists. We may not find looking at sewers any more agreeable than we find examining our own subconscious terrains, but their salutary effects cannot be denied. It's been a long time since mankind was assailed by such killers as cholera and plague, and the hero in the tale of horror is the sewage system.

In 1842, a British Royal Commission was appointed to suggest various means of improving the sanitation system of London. For their model, the commissioners chose neither the contemporary systems of other European cities, nor to the facilities then in use in large American cities. Rather, they chose to emulate a sanitary system employed nearly 2,000 years earlier—the sewers of Imperial Rome.

The Roman system was simply superior to anything London could boast at the time, better in fact than anything that had been seen in Europe since the decline of the Roman Empire. Although the Romans generally shunned the construction of grandiose temples and tombs, they were justly proud of their magnificent achievements in civil engineering: bridges, roads, baths, aqueducts, and sewers. Frontinus, the water commissioner of the Imperial City for part of the first century A.D., went so far as to boast: "With such an array of indispensable structures . . . compare, if you will, the idle Pyramids or the useless, though famous, works of the Greeks."

A look at the ancient Cloaca Maxima, *a sewer which still functions today in Rome. The sewer empties into the Tiber.*

In fact, the Romans were not the first people to devise a means to carry off waste materials from an urban area. Street drains have been found in an ancient Mesopotamian ruin near Nimrud, Iraq. In the Assyrian palace at Dur Sharrukin, water for flushing was provided by a jar and dipper beside each latrine, and drains carried waste away. Some ancient cities of the Indus Valley could boast brick-lined ditches that carried waste off from the home to larger masonry drains.

But, for the most part, the sewers of ancient pre-Roman cities were not waste drains, but storm drains intended to get rid of water from the streets after a heavy rain. The derivation of our word *sewer* suggests the original function of most early drains. The Latin words *ex,* "out," and *aqua,* "water," were combined to form the Vulgar Latin *exaquare,* which developed into the Middle French *essever,* "to drain off." The Middle French *esseweur,* and our word *sewer,* were both derived from this term.

The palace at Knossos, Crete, constructed around 1600 B.C., offers the finest surviving example of pre-Roman domestic drainage. Each quarter of the palace was served by a separate drainage network. The ceramic latrine drains were completely separated from water-supply and storm drains, to prevent sewer gases from entering the palace.

If the Romans were not the first to install sewers, they were surely the first to devise a well-maintained sanitation system for a large city—Imperial Rome was the largest city the world had seen up until that time. The

Roman sewer system had its humble beginnings in the sixth century B.C., when Tarquinian kings ordered the construction of a ditch to drain the swampy land below the Seven Hills, which later became the Roman Forum and cattle market. The ditch, an open channel lined with masonry, followed the path of an old stream and emptied into the Tiber.

The ditch was covered by a stone vault early in the Republic, and later enlarged and connected with smaller subsidiary drains. Marcus Agrippa, the first-century engineer and statesman responsible for many of Rome's fountains and aqueducts, personally rode a boat through the giant main to direct its renovation. Though the oldest surviving parts of the *Cloaca Maxima* ditch were constructed during the third century B.C., the sewer continued to serve as a storm drain right into the 20th century!

To say that all Romans enjoyed the benefits of a modern water-supply and drainage system would be far from the truth. While the wealthy brought water through sewer mains to their homes, the poor often had to make do with an inadequate supply of public latrines flushed by waste water from the public baths. For many people, an open window was far more convenient, and the only thing available. Water-supply pipes rarely reached above the ground floor of the poor Romans' *insulae,* or tenements, and most poorer folk had to rely on public fountains. The privileged few, meanwhile, paid fees or bribes to connect their homes with public water mains.

At its peak, the aqueduct system of Rome brought 300 million gallons of fresh water daily to the capital. Compare this figure with that of modern New York. With a population close to eight times that of ancient Rome, New York City brings only five times the amount of water in each day—one-and-a-half billion gallons.

In the smaller cities of medieval Europe, sanitation systems were poor or non-existent. Monasteries generally boasted the best facilities. Monks frequently diverted a nearby stream so that it ran under the *rere-dorter,* or sanitary wing, as well as under the kitchen and under the infirmary. The "secret passage" that often connected a monastery and neighboring convent—to shatter some fantasies cherished by the profane—actually was a sewer connecting the two structures with the main watercourse.

In Kohln, a town of monks
and bones,
And pavements fang'd with
murderous stones
And rags, and hags, and
hideous wenches;
I counted two and seventy stenches,
All well defined, and several stinks!
Ye Nymphs that reign o'er sewers
and sinks,
The river Rhine, it is well known,
Doth wash your city of Cologne;
But tell me, Nymphs, what power
divine
Shall henceforth wash the river
Rhine?

—Samuel Taylor Coleridge,
Cologne

Leonardo da Vinci, in his plan for "Ten New Towns," proposed the use of the *vie sotterane,* or sewer, to carry waste, garbage, and rainwater to nearby rivers. But even in Paris and London, sewer systems as "modern" as the one Leonardo designed in the 15th century were not to appear until the 19th century.

As the city of Paris grew during the Middle Ages, most people disposed of their waste directly into a nearby stream, or into the Seine. When open ditches were constructed solely to carry off rainwater, many citizens began dumping their waste and garbage into the nearest ditch. Flushed only by an occasional downpour, the ditches quickly became noxious cesspits. During the 13th century, the stench moved Philip Augustus to order that all citizens transport their refuse outside the city walls. However, few citizens heeded the royal decree.

The sewer system of Paris was gradually improved. By 1663, there were only one-and-a-half miles of underground drainage mains and five miles of open canals serving the city, most of them emptying directly into the Seine. By 1800, Paris could boast 16 miles of underground drains, but much of the effluent was delivered to nearby swamps and ponds. An outbreak of cholera around the middle of the 19th century convinced city officials that, at last, something had to be done to improve the sanitation system. Parisians called on Georges Haussman, who was to oversee the construction of vast public works in 19th-century Paris.

Films such as *Phantom of the Opera* may have contributed to the popular misconception that the city of Paris is built over a vast maze of ancient sewers and catacombs. While it is true that a network of caverns lies under Paris, these caverns are neither ancient nor catacombs. Most of the present sewer system was constructed during the mid-19th century by Haussman.

The sewers Haussman constructed were large underground channels roofed by a masonry vault. Porcelain plaques along the walls indicated the street directly above.

By 1878, the Paris sewer network stretched for 385 miles, and the Seine was at last freed from sewer duties. By the middle of this century, the system contained over 800 miles of underground mains. Visitors to Paris can still tour the city's sewer system, entering at the Place de la Concorde, where several lesser mains converge to carry sewage to treatment plants.

Medieval Londoners, like their Parisian contemporaries, traditionally directed their waste to the nearest stream or storm drain. At first, the accumulated sludge was carted off to nearby farms for use as manure. But as the city grew and the surrounding farmland moved further away, almost all waste found its way to the Thames. Medieval monks complained that the stench of the river overcame their incense and "caused the death of many brethren."

Covered public sewers connected to London mansions became common during the 18th century, but sanitation in the poorer quarters remained primitive. In 1841, the Fleet River in London, or the Fleet Sewer as it could more aptly have been termed, was replaced by a sewer main in a massive construction project that entailed, in the words of one contemporary, the "diversion of a miniature Styx...from a bed of half-rotten bricks to an iron tunnel...without spilling one drop of Christian sewerage."

By the 1850s, the Thames was sufficiently rank to prompt talk of moving Parliament—whose windows had not been opened in years—from its building on the river. Large-scale renovation and enlargement of the city's sewer system was finally inaugurated. Many of the sewers had already backed up to the houses they served, sending foul gases and rats into even the finest homes. An old clogged main in Westminster yielded 400 cartloads of sludge. Gases in some sewers were so thick that lanterns carried by workers caused explosions.

By 1870, an overhauled sanitation system, including 83 miles of new sewers, carried 420 million gallons of waste from the city each day. Equally important, the sewers were now cleaned regularly. One of the brave band of workers who toiled in the depths preferred this job because he "didn't like the confinement or the close air in the factories." Londoners were delighted. "Nothing can be more satisfactory," one contemporary proudly wrote, "than a good water closet apparatus, properly connected with a well-ventilated sewer." The Prince of Wales himself declared that if he could not be prince, he would choose to be a plumber. Across the Atlantic, most American cities were young enough to profit from the 19th-century advances in Europe, and to build sewers continually as they grew. But not all American cities were without sanitation problems. In Chicago, waste carried directly to Lake Michigan had by 1870 sullied the lake up to four miles from shore. During the 1890s, a system of drainage canals was constructed to flush the city's sewers with lake water at the rate of up to 600,000 cubic feet per minute!

Today, cities in America, Europe, and increasingly, in the

22 billion gallons of waste must be collected nationwide *each day* in the United States—about 100 gallons for each person!

rest of the world, employ two unconnected drainage systems to carry off their waste. Rainwater and street sweepings collected in storm drains are rarely treated, while domestic drainage usually undergoes some kind of purification before it is deposited in a body of water. The job of managing the sewerage is a big one, for 22 billion gallons of waste must be collected nationwide *each day* in the United States—about 100 gallons for each person!

Everywhere, the aim of sewage treatment is to eliminate disease germs—from the soil, the air, or from your intestines—and to decompose organic matter into a chemically stable product. Sewage is first brought to preliminary settling tanks, where the solid matter collects as sludge. Anaerobic bacteria—bacteria that cannot live in the presence of oxygen—break down proteins and other organic matter. Then the remains are aerated, so that aerobic bacteria can continue the decomposition process. Aeration produces innocuous gases and liquids. Some of the resultant substances are high in nitrogen content, and can be used for fertilizer or irrigation. Water produced by the treatment system of Cairo, Egypt, for instance, is 30 times as valuable for irrigation as water drawn directly from the Nile. The most modern of today's sewage treatment plants are so effective in purifying waste that the water they extract can be used for drinking! Despite this, most of us would, apparently, prefer beer, wine, or Perrier.

A section of the great Paris sewer system.

Scissors

Scissors are one of those ubiquitous everyday objects so common and useful today that it's hard to imagine a time when they weren't around. You don't have to—scissors of one kind or another have existed for almost as long as man has had something to cut!

Scissors are probably as old as the loom, but the oldest pair still in existence is a bronze tool from Egypt, dating from the third century B.C. These scissors were richly decorated with figures of metal inlay, and the blades could be detached for separate sharpening. But they probably belonged to a wealthy family, and were not typical of the kinds customarily used by ancient people.

Most early Egyptian and Greek scissors resembled the Roman *forfex,* which consisted of two blades connected by a curved bowspring handle. There was no pivot screw, and the tool was forged usually from one piece of iron. The scissors were worked by finger pressure against the handle or the blades themselves. A pair of *forfices* from Pompeii with crude iron blades and a bronze spring, along with comments by contemporary authors, suggest that a trip to the Roman *tonsor* for a haircut or shave could indeed be an uncomfortable experience.

Used for clipping wool, trimming plants, and a host of other tasks, as well as for cutting hair and thread, scissors of the Roman type remained in widespread use into the Middle Ages. These primitive shears were still being made as late as the 16th century—and in the Far East, the 19th century.

But pivoted shears, with a pivot pin of some kind connecting the blades, were in occasional use as early as the first century, and perhaps earlier. Most of these ancient shears looked more like a pair of modern pliers than the scissors we're familiar with today. By the fifth century, shears with pivot pins were in common use by the tailors of Seville—and yes, by the barbers too. Steel blades were already replacing iron blades before the end of the Roman Empire, due in part to the metalsmiths of Damascus and their work with hard "Damascus" steel.

Scissors managed to find their way into the mythology of the ancient world, too. The Three Fates of Greek myth were Lachesis, who determined the length of the thread of life; Clotho, who spun the thread;

These three ornate scissors were exhibited at the Crystal Palace in London during the 19th century.

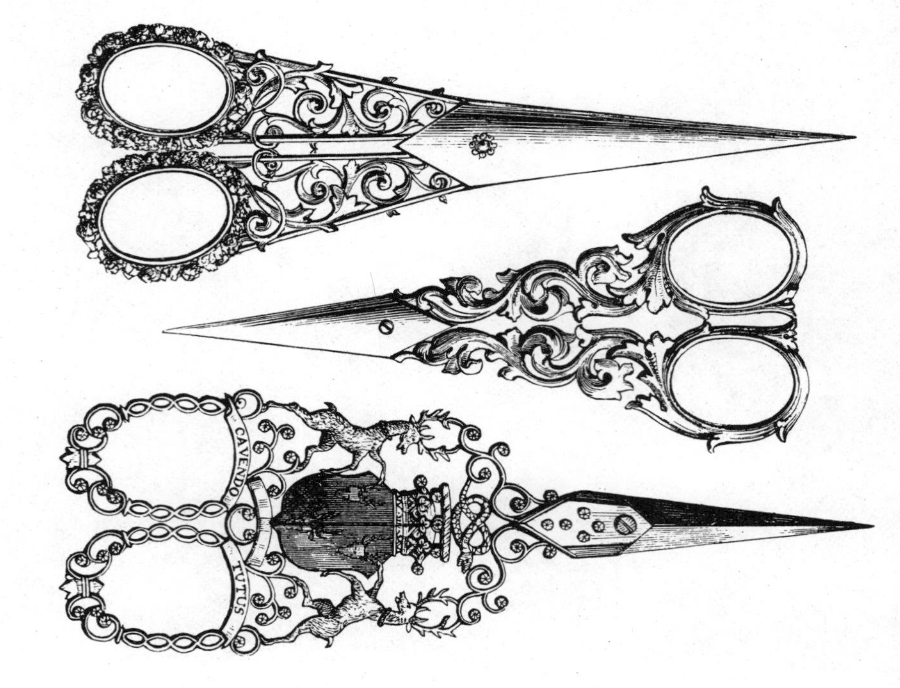

and Atropos, who used shears to snip the thread. And while we're on the subject of legend and superstition, an old belief of Northern Europeans held that the giving of cutlery as a gift would lead to the severing of a friendship—unless the receiver of the gift gave a penny to the donor.

The Roman word for scissors, *forfex,* has given us "forficate," an adjective meaning "forked." But our word "scissors" actually came from two other Latin words. One was *cisoria,* the plural of the word for a cutting instrument. The other was *scissus,* a form of *scindere,* a verb meaning "to cut," which spawned the Latin *scissor,* "one who cuts." *Cisoria* led to the Old French *cisoires* (the modern French is *ciseaux),* and in turn to the Middle English *cysowres,* while the Latin *scissor* produced *sisours.* The latter word and *cysowres* together became the modern "scissors."

The production of scissors and cutlery of all sorts has long been centered in the European cities of Thiers, France, and Solingen, Germany. In England, Sheffield was already noted for its cutlery by the time of Chaucer. All three cities are situated near mountain streams that turn waterwheels to produce the power needed for grinding and sharpening blades.

From earliest times, New England was the center of the cutlery industry in the United States. But the man who was largely responsible for the development of the American cutlery industry, Jacob Wiss, plied his trade instead in Newark, New Jersey. In 1847, Wiss immigrated to the United States from Switzerland and joined the old cutlery firm of Rochus Heinisch. A year later, Wiss founded his own company—with his power initially provided by a dog running on a treadmill!

Wiss and his descendants found a way of utilizing two metal alloys together to produce the sturdiest, longest-lasting scissors. By 1914, Jacob Wiss & Sons was the largest producer of fine shears in the world. Wiss's firm was also responsible for introducing pinking shears on a national scale—pinking shears have notched blades that produce a saw-toothed cut—and for popularizing scissors whose handle can double as a bottle opener.

The manufacture of a pair of scissors or shears from raw metal may require as many as 175 individual steps. Formerly, the blades were sharpened by grinding on a natural stone, and polished with a wooden wheel. Today, the blades are die cast, then forged, trimmed, ground, heat-treated, polished, and finished. That leaves only about 165 other steps.

Modern scissors usually have steel blades, while the handle section may be made from aluminum or other light metals. The pivot screw is made of hard steel, and firmly riveted to one blade; the other blade turns on the pivot screw. The blades are slightly bent toward each other to produce a close contact along the cutting edge.

Modern scissors are plain, utilitarian tools, but in past centuries shears sporting fanciful shapes and designs abounded. During the 18th century, scissors with shanks in the shape of women's legs—called *Jambes des Princesses*— were the rage in France. The 19th century saw scissors in

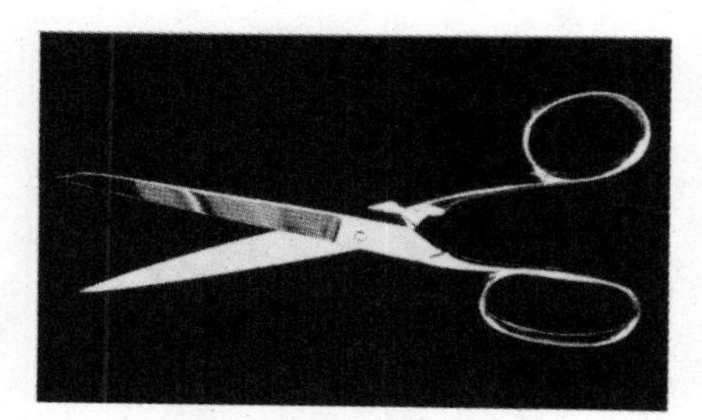

A pair of left-handed scissors.

the shape of castles, butterflies, and birds, with the blades forming a bird's bill. Today, there are scores of specialized shears, scissors, nippers, and snips, from barbers' to bankers', surgical to cuticle, ranging in size from tiny scissors fitted to pocketknives to huge tailors' shears up to 16 inches in length.

Have you ever wondered what the precise difference is between "scissors" and "shears"? The use of the two words is fairly arbitrary. Generally, the former is used for a pair of blades less than six inches in length, with usually two small matching finger holes in the handle. "Shears" is generally applied to a tool longer than six inches, with one small hole in the handle for the thumb and one larger hole for a finger.

And haven't you ever wondered if the word "scissors" is singular or plural? The dictionary tells us that "scissor" is much less preferred than "scissors," but that the latter word may take either a plural or singular verb. To avoid the question completely, you might opt for "pair of scissors"—for what's one "scissor" without the other? As Charles Dickens wrote in *Martin Chuzzlewit:* "We are but the two halves of a pair of scissors, when apart . . . but together we are something."

Shoes

An Egyptian silver sandal.

Roman sandals.

Step into a modern shoe store and take a look around. High-heeled and platform shoes, boots, sandals, moccasins, wooden-heeled clogs—quite a variety for today's shopper. Recent fashions? Well, not one of the footwear styles you see today is less than 400 years old!

The loftiest high-heeled and platform shoes you can find today are flat pumps compared with some of the shoes in fashion during earlier European eras. No, our ancestors didn't don stiltlike monsters to raise themselves above muddy streets, or for any other utilitarian reason. In former times, as today, shoe style was dictated by fashion—among the upper classes, at least. Class distinction via footwear? Yes—differentiation of shoe styles to indicate social rank is as old as Western civilization.

In ancient Egypt, the sandal demonstrated a person's rank in society. Slaves either went barefoot or wore crude sandals made from palm leaves. Common citizens wore sandals of woven papyrus, consisting of a flat sole tied to the foot by a thong between the toes. But sandals with pointed toes were reserved only for the higher stations of society, and the colors red and yellow were taboo for anyone below the aristocratic rank.

Shoes have been regarded as a sign of dignity since well before the Christian era. Going barefoot has often demonstrated humility and piety in the presence of God. Hindu documents, thousands of years old, warn worshippers to remove their footwear before entering a shrine; and Moslem tradition demands that shoes be removed before entering a place of worship. In the book of Exodus, 3:5, when God appears to Moses in the burning bush, His first command was "Put off thy shoes from off thy feet, for the ground whereon thou standest is holy ground."

In the days of ancient Greece, aristocratic women owned as many as 20 pairs of shoes, with a style to match every occasion. Slaves were employed solely to carry a supply of their lady's shoes when she left home, assuring that she would be appropriately shod throughout her travels.

The Chinese custom of binding women's feet to keep them small is many centuries old. Originally, the practice owed little to pedal aesthetics—bound feet were thought to insure faithfulness, since with such deformed feet the wife would supposedly find it difficult to travel very far on her own.

In the West, shoes have had a place in marriage ceremonies for many centuries. In some cultures, the bride's father threw his shoes at the newlyweds to signify the transfer of authority from father to husband. In Anglo-Saxon ceremonies, shoes were as indispensable as the wedding ring is today. Instead of exchanging rings with her betrothed, the bride customarily passed her shoes to her husband, who then tapped her on the head with a shoe.

During the Middle Ages, in the colder climes, the sandal gave way to more protective footwear. Often, a single piece of untanned hide was wrapped around the foot and tied with a leather thong. Beginning in the 12th century, the sabot, a shoe cut roughly from a single piece of wood, was the predominant

LEFT:
Chinese women bandaged their feet and wore dainty, embroidered shoes.

RIGHT:
Poulaines, or crakows, were long, pointed-toe shoes popular in Europe in the 14th and 15th centuries. The shoes were named for Crakow, Poland, where the fashion originated.

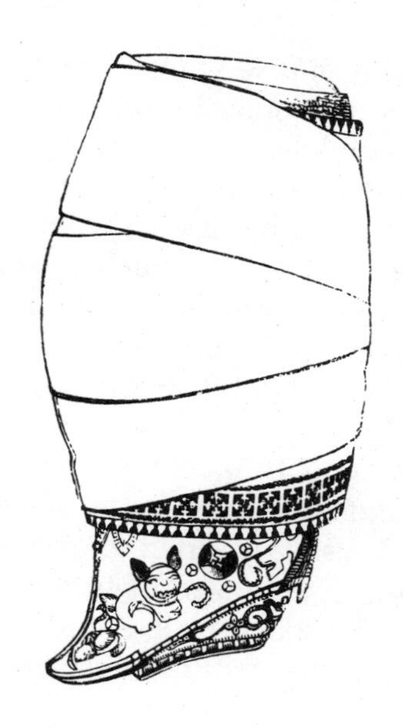

footwear of the European peasant. In those times, the Dutch were not unusual in their use of the wooden shoe. In England, the sabot took the form of the clog, a fabric mounted on a wooden platform. In Japan, wooden shoes mounted on thin blocks three or four inches high have been worn for centuries. The Japanese traditionally selected their wooden shoes with an ear for the sound made by the wooden blocks, for a discordant pair of clod-hoppers were considered the epitome of poor taste.

The long journeys undertaken by European crusaders made stronger, longer-lasting shoes a necessity, but medieval aristocrats still took their cue from fancy. The wearing of elaborate, unwieldy footwear was an indication of lordly rank, demonstrating that the wearer did not—and could not—perform manual labor. Such shoes were genuine "loafers."

Pointed shoes became the vogue in France, reportedly because of a Count of Anjou who wished to hide his deformed hooves. To assure that the peasantry did not ape the aristocrats, the 12th-century French king Philip Augustus decreed that the points of his subjects' *souliers* should be between six and 12 inches long, depending upon one's station.

But the rush toward outlandishly long shoes went on unabated. Fashionable shoes were soon so long that their toes had to be stuffed to prevent the wearer from constantly tripping over the ends. In the 14th century, the points of shoes grew to such monstrous lengths that some had to be fastened to the wearer's leg just below the knee. The clergy objected vehemently to the fashion, claiming that the long-pointed shoes prevented the faithful from kneeling in church. In many communities, shoe-point length was eventually limited by law to about two inches.

In the 16th century, aristocratic French women began wearing high-heeled shoes so steep that the—er, well-heeled wearer was literally standing on her toes when she wore them. Later, stiltlike wooden platform shoes became the rage in Venice. The heels eventually became so high that women could not walk

Among 16th-century Venetian prostitutes, the vogue for stiltlike shoes was carried to absurd lengths. Eventually, high heels were prohibited by law, because of the high death rate resulting from ladies of the night tripping and falling to their deaths.

It wasn't until the invention, in 1818, of the left-shoe last and the right-shoe last that the left shoe was constructed differently from the right shoe. Prior to that, either shoe could be worn on either foot with equal discomfort!

in them, and servants were hired to help the ladies in and out of their gondolas. The fashion reportedly owed much to the Venetian husband's desire to make sure his wife didn't travel far while he was away—the same concern that motivated the Chinese to bind their women's feet.

Among 16th-century Venetian prostitutes, the vogue for the stilt-like shoes was carried to absurd lengths. Eventually, high heels were proscribed by law, because of the high death rate resulting from ladies of the night tripping and falling to their deaths.

During the 16th century "elevator shoes" were worn by Venetian prostitutes.

Henry VIII initiated the vogue for wide-toed shoes in England, presumably to hide his gout-swollen feet. Shoes soon grew to such widths that Parliament passed a law limiting the width of a shoe to six inches.

That European lawmakers have historically taken such an oppressive interest in their subjects' footwear can be partly explained by the way in which fashion was dictated in earlier centuries. To a great extent, the king himself was often the trend-setter, the aristocracy was expected to follow suit, and the peasantry was forbidden to emulate their betters.

Many monarchs opted for shoes that would best veil their physical shortcomings. If the fashion didn't catch on naturally, well, laws could guarantee its implementation. For instance, the custom among men of wearing high-heeled shoes at the court of Louis XIV grew out of the Sun King's desire to mask his diminutive stature.

Compared to modern footgear, the shoes of earlier centuries were, for the most part, highly uncomfortable. It wasn't until the development of woven stockings in the 17th century that footwear could be made snug-fitting and shaped to the foot.

To give you an idea of the crudity of earlier shoes, it wasn't until the invention in 1818 of the left-shoe last and the right-shoe last that the left shoe was constructed differently from the right shoe. Prior to that, either shoe could be worn on either foot with equal discomfort!

Until the introduction of mass-produced footwear in the 19th century, shoes were usually handmade in the cobbler's shop, with nails or pegs used to bind the sole to the upper. As mechanization set in, machines were

In 1851, a shoe exhibition was held by one J. Sparkes Hall of London.

TOP LEFT AND RIGHT:
14th century English slippers.

BOTTOM LEFT:
Blue satin slipper decorated with honiton lace for Queen Victoria.

BOTTOM RIGHT:
This shoe, worn by the Duchess of York in the early 19th century, was notable for its small size.

devised for sewing shoes together. By 1900, most footwear was being made, at least in part, by machine.

The first shoe manufactured in the United States was the handiwork of one Thomas Beard, a *Mayflower* pilgrim, who nailed together the first pair of American shoes in 1628. At that time, the colonists also learned how to make animal-hide moccasins from the Indians, and the moccasins became so popular in the mother country that the colonies began exporting moccasins to England as early as 1650. America's first factory for mechanized shoe production was established in Lynn, Massachusetts in 1760.

Tanned leather has been a favored material for footwear since the Arabs introduced fine leatherwork in Spain in the eighth century. The leather-making trade of the Spanish Arabs was centered around the city of Cordova—to which we owe the origin of the cordovan, a soft, fine-grained leather shoe.

By the way, the average American woman now buys about five pairs of shoes each year, and the average man, about two pairs—as a rule men's shoes last longer and remain in fashion longer than women's footwear.

Each model of a modern shoe is manufactured in some 150 sizes, with length designated by a number and width by a letter. But a size 10 shoe is not 10 inches long—so where does the number come from? Believe it or not, it stands for 10 barleycorns!

The English king Edward II decreed in 1324 that an inch was equal to three average-sized barleycorns laid end to end. The normal shoe was declared to measure 39 barleycorns, and this size, for some reason or other, was designated with the number 13. Other sizes were graded from this standard, with one barleycorn difference between each successive size.

Today, the foot-measuring system used in England is one size different from the American system in both length and width. In metric countries, one size indicates a difference of about two-thirds of a centimeter.

Speaking of shoe size, the largest pair of shoes ever sold—apart from those specially built for elephantiasis sufferers—were a colossal size 42, built for a Florida giant named Harley Davidson. (Yes, it's the name of a British motorcycle manufacturer.) Let's see—a size 42 equals 39 barleycorns plus 29 for a total length of some 22½ inches!

The average person has literally thousands of styles to choose from today, from the modern machine-stitched leather shoe, or the rubber-soled sneaker, to such ancient favorites as the sandal, the clog, the platform shoe, and the pump. The pump is thought to owe its name to the early use of the shoe for ceremonies of "pomp." Footwear ranges in price from rubber *thongs* selling for less than a dollar to mink-lined golf shoes—with 18-carat gold ornamentation and ruby-tipped gold spikes—selling in England for some $7,000 a pair.

The U.S. Patent Office has on file a design for boots with pockets—for use by nudists. A bit outlandish? Well, if the shoe fits, wear it!

SKATES

The people of the Netherlands have been associated with skating for so long that most of us would probably choose that canal-crossed land as the most likely birthplace of the ice skate. Roller skates? Invented by an American, you would say? Well, the Dutch did not invent the ice skate—but a Hollander did devise the first roller skate! And the roller skate's most recent incarnation, the skateboard, was invented not by a roller skating enthusiast, but by a surfer!

As you may imagine, ice skates are a good deal older than their wheeled cousins—older than the Dutch nation, in fact. The earliest written reference to ice skates comes from second-century Scandinavia, but archaeological evidence suggests that skates may be much older than that. The oldest surviving ice skate, made in Sweden sometime between the eighth and 10th centuries, consisted of a piece of cow rib fastened to the foot with leather thongs. The god Uller, of Icelandic mythology, surely must have had a fancier pair of ice skates, for he was exalted in literature for his "beauty, arrows, and skates."

A Description of London, written in 1180, shows that at that early date, ice skating was already a popular English pastime. Although the author was inspired to write "many young men play upon the ice; some, striding as wide as they may, do slide swiftly . . . some tie bones to their feet and under their heels, and shoving themselves by a little picked staff, do slide as swiftly as a bird flieth in the air," it's doubtful that those skaters flew with anything near avian speed, since most skates of the time were heavy and awkward.

During the 14th and 15th centuries, wooden runners faced with iron and fastened to wooden shoes began to appear in the Low Countries. Dutch illustrations of the period show skaters slipping across frozen canals on blades almost as wide as their shoes. A legend tells that the width of the skate runner was narrowed quite by chance. A Dutchman, visiting a country where the metal-plated skate was not yet known, commissioned a blacksmith to make him a pair. The blacksmith, misunderstanding the instructions, produced skates in which the narrow edge of the runner was left as the traveling edge, with the broad edge affixed to the shoe. When the thinner runner was found to provide much more stability, it was quickly copied by other skaters.

Ice skaters on the canal. An engraving by Bruegel, circa 1560.
The Bettmann Archive, Inc.

By 1648, the Dutch word *schaats* had become *skates* in England. Though the Dutch noun was singular, the English took it as a plural, and hence inferred *skate* as the singular. The word *skate* also became a slang word for *person,* a usage that has survived to this day, as in *good skate* and *cheapskate*—though some etymologists see a connection between the latter and *skite,* the Norse word for excrement.

During the 17th and 18th centuries, skating on metal-faced runners became a very popular pastime in many countries. In France, Marie Antoinette was particularly fond of skating. Samuel Pepys, describing mid-17th-century London, wrote of "people sliding with their skates, which is a very pretty art." The skates he saw were most likely attached with straps to a wood base. The blades were frequently curved in front, and shorter than the shoe in back to allow for braking.

Then, during the 19th century, a host of ice skate innovations appeared, most of them designed to attach the skate to the foot more securely. In the United States alone, over 200 patents were granted for improving ice skates. Most important was the work of E.W. Bushnell. In 1850, the Philadelphian designed the first all-metal skate. By the 1870s, Everett Barney of Springfield, Massachusetts, was marketing all-metal skates attached to the shoe with screw clamps. From there, ice skates evolved into the skating boots we're most accustomed to.

Ice skating has spawned a number of sports, but to purist skaters there are only two: speed-skating and figure skating. Speed-skating events began in the Netherlands at least 200 years ago. English speed-skating had its formal beginnings in 1814, and was dominated by the Smarts. William "Turkey" Smart won his first championship in 1854, and remained speed-skating champion for more than a decade. In 1878, "Turkey's" nephew, George "Fish" Smart, took the title, which he held until 1889, when his brother James took over. In the United States, the Donoghue family of Newburgh, New York, held a similar grip on speed-skating superiority. At various times, each of three members of the family was considered the fastest speed skater in the world.

The Dutch may not have invented ice skating, but today they are probably the world's best skaters. Of 13 million Netherlanders, an estimated 25 percent are speed-skaters—and rural women skaters are confident enough to carry egg baskets on their heads!

The biggest speed-skating event in the Netherlands is the *Elfstedentocht*—"Tour of the Eleven Towns"—which has been held annually since the 18th century. The route stretches over 124 miles of rivers, lakes, and canals in Friesland, in the northern Netherlands, and is the longest regularly held skating race in the world. In 1954, 26-year-old Jeen van den Berg established the all-time record for the race when he completed the course in seven hours, 35 minutes, besting the previous record by more than an hour.

In the United States, figure skating is a far more popular pastime than speed-skating for participant and viewer alike. Figure skating was first mentioned in London in 1772, but it's likely that skaters began to twist and twirl—or at least, attempted to—from the moment they first put on cow-rib skates. In 1876, with the construction of the first indoor rink with artificial ice, figure skating received a major boost. The London rink, called the *Glaciarium,* measured but 24 feet by 40 feet. Ice was mechanically produced from water and glycerine refrigerated with ether. Three years later, Americans had an indoor rink of their own, a 6,000-square-foot surface in New York's Madison Square Garden.

An even bigger spur was provided by Jackson Haines, an American ballet teacher who

This ornate skate was made of satinwood, enriched by plates of gilded metal work. London, circa 1850.

The world's most difficult winter sports course, laid out in the Netherlands. It is the circuit of the 11 villages of Friesland, a province in the northern part of Holland, a route of 200 kilometers over the frozen canals and lakes which link the villages. On the day of this race the temperature was 25 below zero, and a 100-kilometer wind was blowing. The race, now about 150 years old, is a Dutch tradition. Paris Match.

raised figure skating to the level of a fine art. Haines combined music with skating to transform the sport from an aimless series of random movements into a precise, rhythmic exercise. Haines's innovations were largely ignored in America, but the skating master captivated Europe during the middle of the 19th century, and was instrumental in evolving the international style of figure skating that now predominates the world over.

Figure skating was first included in the Olympic Games in 1908. Norwegian Sonja Henie was the most noted figure skater of the period, winning the Norwegian championship at age nine and the world title at age 13. She captured gold medals at the Winter Olympics in 1928, 1932, and 1936, then went to Hollywood to star in close to a dozen movies. Among her other innovations, Sonja was the first woman skater to wear the short skating skirt. Among Americans, Richard Button was was the outstanding figure skater of recent times, winning the Olympic gold medal in 1948, and again in 1952.

There are now an estimated 20 million ice skaters in the United States, and the U.S. Figure Skating Association can boast over 30,000 members. In

1950, there were but 120 indoor ice rinks in this country. Today, American ice skating rinks number over a thousand, logging about 20 million admissions annually. The best known ice skating rink in the United States is in Rockefeller Center, New York City, a small outdoor rink that has been opened to the public every winter since 1936.

But the largest artificial ice skating rink in North America can be found in Burnaby, British Columbia. The quadruple rink, completed in 1972, covers 68,000 square feet of ice surface. (Coincidentally, the largest roller skating rink in history, the Grand Hall in London, measured precisely 68,000 square feet—but it closed in 1912.) The largest outdoor ice skating rink now stands, surprisingly, in Japan. Completed in 1967, the colossal 165,750-square-foot ice palace cost close to a million dollars to construct.

People evidently enjoy watching others skate as much as they do skating themselves, for ice skating has acquired a definite place in the entertainment world. The first large skating spectacle in America took place in 1862, when 12,000 costumed skaters took part in a carnival in Prospect Park, Brooklyn. The first ice show with a large cast was a 1913 extravaganza in Berlin. The 65-member troupe's "Flirting in St. Moritz" was brought to the New York Hippodrome in 1915, and enjoyed a three-year run.

The year 1936 was a banner year for ice skating, marking the first appearance of Sonja Henie in a film, and the first Ice Follies spectacular, a stage show on ice. The Ice Capades have presented musicals and operettas on an ice-rink stage since 1940, when the show began in Atlantic City, New Jersey. Ice skaters have even made it to television—in 1952, an entire Arthur Godfrey show was presented on ice skates!

Hockey, by far the most popular team sport on ice, was enjoyed in some form by the Dutch as long ago as 1670, for a Dutch painting from that year shows a number of players with sticks in their hand batting a small object across the ice. The first record of an organized hockey game dates from 1855, and took place in Kingston, Ontario, with players using bent branches as sticks. The rules of the game were formalized 20 years later at McGill University, Montreal.

Ed Fitzgerald of the New York Chiefs hits the track with a thud at Madison Square Garden, New York on June 4, 1950 after a body block by Al Masiello of the Jersey Jolters.
Wide World Photos.

In 1917, the National Hockey League was founded and hockey has been flourishing ever since, on both sides of the Atlantic. In 1948, the game was virtually unknown in the Soviet Union, but it now ranks as one of that nation's most popular sports. In the 1950s, there were but 1,500 hockey players in Sweden, and only one arena with artificial ice. Since then, the number of registered Swedish players has soared to over 160,000.

Incidentally, the Zamboni machine, the mechanical ice resurfacer you may have marveled at during a hockey match or ice skating exhibition, was invented during the 1940s by a Californian named Frank J. Zamboni. The machine shaves the surface, scoops up loose snow, washes the ice, and squeezes out excess water in one fell swoop.

If you live in a warm climate, you may never have enjoyed the thrill of gliding over a glassy strip of ice, Zamboni-smoothed or otherwise. But who hasn't strapped, buckled, and clamped himself into a pair of roller skates, "skate key" dangling from belt or neck? This curious pastime actually originated during the 18th century, when an unknown Hollander strapped crude wooden wheels to his feet—perhaps hoping to keep his skating form well-honed during the iceless months. In 1760, an Englishman named Joseph Merlin placed the first skates on the market in Huy, Belgium. But for many years, roller skating remained too difficult and uncomfortable, and failed to achieve any kind of popularity.

A century later, the easily warped boxwood wheels of early skates gave way to metal wheels with wheel trucks, or frames that hold the axle and wheels. In 1863, an American named James Plimpton devised the first four-wheel skate with a cushioned truck, making roller skating a comfortable, easily-mastered pastime. Three years later, Plimpton opened the first public roller skating rink in the United States, in Newport, Rhode Island, beginning a skating craze that swept America and Europe alike during the end of the century.

Giacomo Meyerbeer's opera, *Le Prophète*, contained a skating scene which became famous—and promoted the growing interest in roller skates. Jackson Haines, of ice-skating renown, also contributed to the roller skate's rise to popularity by demonstrating his balletic skating style during an 1860s European tour. The ballet master had little idea that his graceful turns would help put drive-in waitresses on roller skates a century later!

How fast can a roller skater travel? Surprisingly or not, the official speed record achieved on roller skates is less than half the record speed for an ice skater. In 1963, an Italian named Giuseppe Cantarella averaged almost 26 miles per hour over a 440-yard course, setting an official world's record that may have been broken, unofficially, many times since then. An impressive record was achieved by Pat Barnett, a Londoner who at one time or another held every women's roller skating record from two miles to 201 miles. In 1962, Pat covered close to 21 miles in an hour on a London rink. Alas, Pat's record was topped by Marisa Danesi six years later in West Germany.

If roller skates have proved less than ideal for high speed skating, they have certainly fared

Surprisingly or not, the official speed record achieved on roller skates is less than half the record speed for an ice skater.

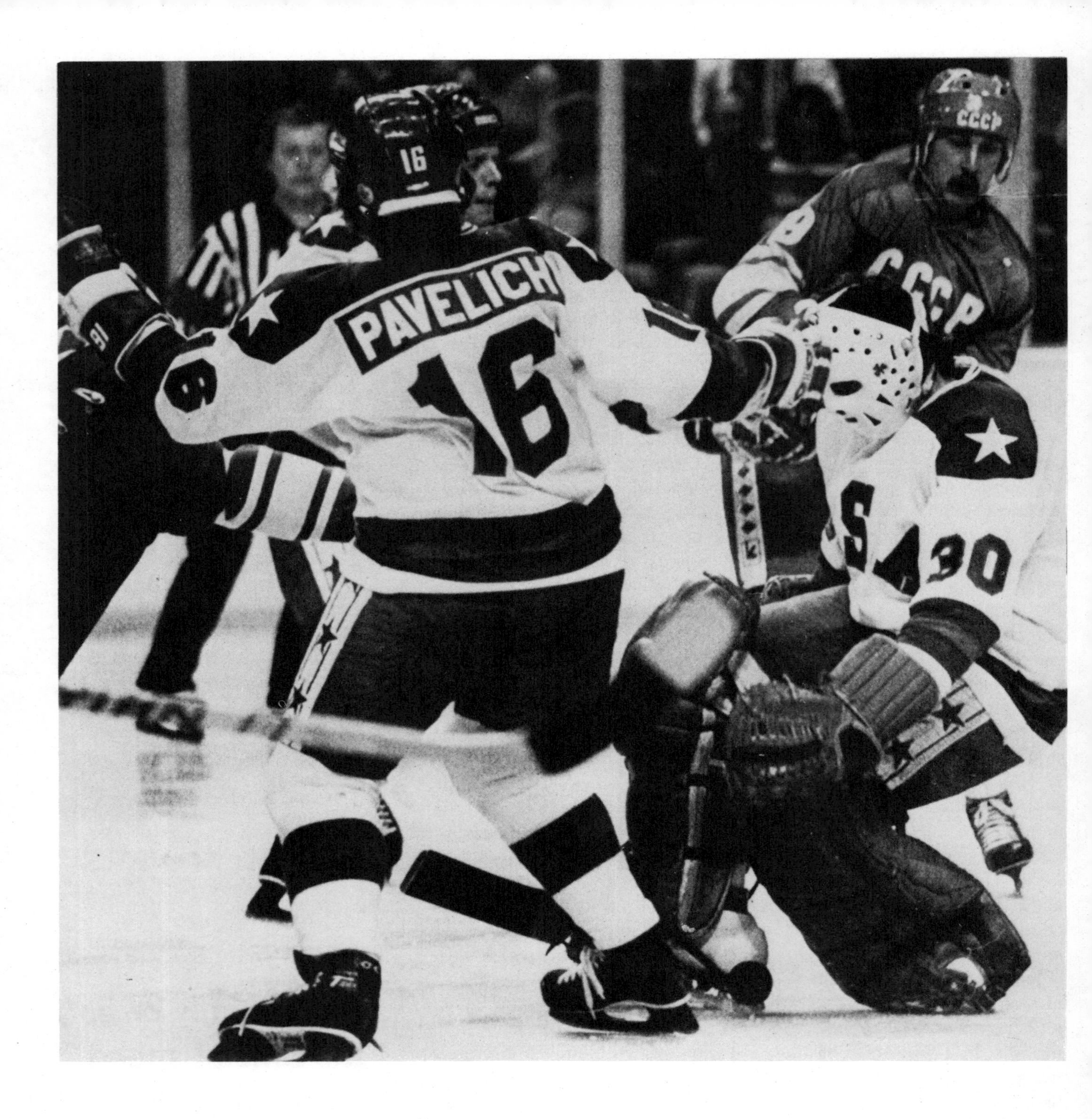

On February 23, 1980, in a surprise upset, the U.S. ice hockey team defeated the formidable champion Soviet team in the Winter Olympics at Lake Placid, N.Y.

better in endurance trials. In 1975, a Canadian named Clinton Shaw set the nonstop roller skating record when he remained atop his wheels for over 183 hours at a California rink. Before that, Shaw had already made his mark as a marathon skater, having covered 4,900 miles roller skating across Canada, and later, logging up to 106 miles per day from New York to California in just 78 days.

Roller hockey exists, but the game is far less popular than ice hockey. A more familiar roller skating sport is roller derby. Roller derby originated as a marathon relay race, when in 1935, 25 two-person teams met at the Chicago Coliseum to race a distance of 3,000 miles. Today, roller derby is predominantly an all-woman rough-and-tumble entertainment spectacle.

In 1937, after Fred Astaire and Ginger Rogers danced around on roller skates in the film *Shall We Dance,* roller skating briefly became a fad in the United States. Now, roller skating is again reaching the level of a craze— and so is roller dancing!

Americans are increasingly donning skates for a spin through the park or a trip to the store, and some devotees are even rolling to work. Roller skate dancing, or roller disco, is really taking off. In some cities, rinks are converted into discotheques complete with flashing lights and quadraphonic sound systems. Roller disco clubs have already sprung up in New York, with such picturesque names as the Roller Rockers and the Jigaboo Jammers.

The latest roller skating mania has been attributed to the new boot skates now on the market, with smoother, wider urethane wheels similar to those used on skateboards. Many skates are now fitted with a rubber toe stop—a skater simply tilts the toe of his skate forward, presses the stop against the ground, and slides to a quick halt. But the new skates will cost you a lot more than the clamp-on skates of yesteryear—from $50 to over $200 for a good pair.

There is no skateboard hockey, derby, or dancing just yet, but judging from the way the sport of skateboarding is catching on around this country, those pastimes won't be long in coming. Skateboarding did not reach the public eye until 1962, when the proprietors of the Val Surf Shop in North Hollywood, California, contracted with the Chicago Roller Skate Company to produce roller skate trucks for skateboards. The new skateboards sold quickly to surfers, who used the boards for equilibrium exercises to improve their surfing.

By 1965, many companies were manufacturing aluminum, wood, and fiberglass skateboards. But trouble was just around the bend. Skateboards were objected to as being noisy and dangerous. When the California Medical Association released a report announcing that the skateboard had replaced the bicycle as the chief source of childhood injuries, cities all across the country began to outlaw skateboards on public streets. The skateboard fad died, along with dozens of manufacturing companies and *Skateboarder* magazine.

Then, in 1973, a California surfer named Frank Nasworthy devised the first skateboard with urethane wheels, which provided more traction and a quieter ride than the earlier wheels. New fiberglass boards increased board control. Skateboarding became safe and acceptable, and the sport took off again.

Skateboards are now a familiar sight in almost every American city, and are gradually working their way into everyday American life—welcome or not. In 1975, Emery Air Freight announced that deliverymen in some cities had taken to the skateboard to shorten delivery time. And, in Sepulveda, California, two men held up a doughnut shop, making off with $125 aboard this unusual getaway vehicle.

Skateboarding speed records are significantly higher than those set by roller skaters, but most skateboard tracks, or skateparks, enjoy the advantage of a downhill incline. The record speed, achieved in 1976 by a 225-pound California longshoreman, stands at 54 miles per hour.

But skateboard tournaments often include competitions of finesse as well as speed. In 1976, a 25-year-old skateboard ace set the high jump record when he launched himself from a moving skateboard, cleared a bar four feet, five-and-a-half inches high, and landed atop the board again. The same year, a 17-year-old Californian set the barrel jumping record by leaping from a moving skateboard and landing atop a second skateboard 16 barrels away. This is just one barrel short of the best barrel jumping performance by an ice-skater—a 28-foot leap, in 1965, by Ken LeBel, in Liberty, New York.

As skateboarding popularity soars, auxiliary enterprises have been quick to follow. *Skateboarder* magazine is back. Manufacturing companies are doing a booming business in helmets and kneepads, and turning out exotic boards that sell for over $100. Skateboard tournaments, such as the New York Masters Contest, are flourishing from coast to coast. Skateboarding organizations proliferate and there is even an International Professional Skateboard Association. Yes, that's right: *professional* skateboarders!

SOCCER

To an American sports fan, soccer and football appear so dissimilar that it's hard to believe the games were once virtually identical. And even today, outside the United States, the names for the two sports are identical. The word *football* is used around the world to refer to the game Americans call "soccer." Only in America is the terminology confusing, because only in America is there a difference between the two games.

When it comes to football, America stands alone. Football is the only spectator sport that's played exclusively in the United States. Baseball has spread to Latin America and the Far East; basketball and hockey are played in many countries. The Irish play Gaelic football, but that game is a variation of soccer; Australian football is actually a good deal like rugby; and even Canadian football has some major differences from its American counterpart. Football remains strictly an American sport.

Soccer, relatively unknown in the United States until a decade or so ago, is now the most popular sport in the world. It's played in over 140 nations under uniform rules, and in most countries is either the only or the major professional sport. Soccer matches regularly draw the world's largest sports crowds, and soccer players are among the highest paid of all athletes.

Why is soccer so universally popular? Think of the amount of equipment and organization necessary for a simple high school football game—and think of the complex rules. A soccer game, on the other hand, requires little more than a ball, and can be played on a field of almost any size. The play is swift and continuous, involving both individual effort and teamwork—and the rules are simple enough to learn in a minute!

You'd probably guess that soccer is a good deal older than its American cousin, football. In a sense that's true; but surprisingly, organized soccer competitions played under uniform rules are less than a decade older than football.

The first soccer organization was formed in 1863, and the first intercollegiate football game took place just six years later. (Coincidentally, both football and baseball had beginnings of sorts in the year 1869, when the Cincinnati Red Stockings became the first professional baseball team.) But the origins of football undoubtedly go back to a much older game whose evolution has produced not only soccer and American football, but rugby as well.

Some historians believe that the true forerunner of football was a Greek game adopted by the Romans some time before the beginning of the Christian era. We don't know much about how the game was played, but its object was probably to drive a ball beyond a line drawn behind the opposing team. Most likely, the game was not played with the foot alone, since the name of the game, *harpastum,* was derived from a Greek word meaning "handball."

It's quite possible that Roman soldiers played *harpastum* during their occupation of Britain, the nation most often credited with the origin of football and its related sports. But according to a British tradition, football had its beginnings sometime during the 11th century, when workmen excavating the site of an earlier battle came upon the bones of a Danish soldier and began kicking around the skull of the hated invader. A group of young boys noticed the workmen's diversion, and dug up a skull of their own to kick around. Shortly after, an inflated cow bladder was substituted for the skull, and thus was born the game of "kicking the Dane's head" or "kicking the bladder."

The story may be fiction, for it was also reported that the first "football" was not the skull but the actual head of a slain Danish brigand. But in any case, the new sport gained popularity in Britain over the next century as football games were staged annually in various towns. For many years, the drapers of the town of Chester held a football match on Shrove Tuesday (the day before Ash Wednesday), using a leather ball. Derby claims that the first football matches were held there on Shrove Tuesday, in celebration of a victory over the Romans in 217. In one Scottish parish, an annual football match pitted the married women against the spinsters. It was reported that the married women almost always won handily.

Most of these early football games were really free-for-alls, violent melées between teams whose players could number in the hundreds. Matches were often held between adjacent towns, with the ball put in play midway between the towns and each team seeking to attain victory by driving the ball into the middle of the rival town. There were few rules, and many casualties, both to players and bystanders.

To limit the damage to town and player alike, English authorities began to restrict the matches to vacant areas that could be marked off to form a sort of playing field. But around the middle of the 12th century, when the game was already being called "futballe," English kings began to take a sterner view of the sport.

Henry II banned football for fear that Englishmen were spending too much time playing it, to the neglect of the more militarily useful sport of archery. King Edward II banned the game due to "great noise in the city caused by hustling over large balls from which many evils might arise which God forbid." Other monarchs, including Richard II, Henry VIII, and Elizabeth I, also tried to eradicate the sport, with little success.

During an Anglo-Scottish war late in the 12th century, English soldiers reportedly sought to settle the dispute on the football field instead of the battlefield—which suggests not only the popularity of the sport, but its violence. At the end of the 16th century, the game remained so violent that an English writer claimed it seemed more like "a bloody and murdering practise than a felowly sporte or pastime . . ." often involving "fighting, brawling, contention, quarrel picking, murther, homicide, and great effusion of blood."

In the 17th century, when archery was no longer important in warfare, James I lifted the official ban on football and the game quickly found its way into almost every town in the British Isles. Matches were still held between adjacent towns, with the "goal lines" as far as three or four miles apart. And the sport was still quite violent, with tripping, shin-kicking, and rough tackling an integral part of the game.

The game as played from the 11th century to the middle of the 19th century was basically a kicking game, much closer to modern soccer than to

The word *football* is used around the world to refer to the game Americans call "soccer." Only in America is the terminology confusing, because only in America is there a difference between the two games.

football or rugby. Rules varied from place to place and from school to school, but there was one universally observed rule: the ball could not be picked up with the hands. It was the flagrant violation of that rule that was to spawn the game of rugby, and in turn, American football.

In 1823, a student at the Rugby school by the name of William Webb Ellis, frustrated after failing to kick a bouncing ball, picked it up and dashed downfield. Ellis was severely criticized for his infraction, but word of his deed spread throughout England, and other players began to experiment with new rules. In 1838, players at Cambridge decided to try "the game at Rugby," and within 10 years the new game was being played at almost all English schools.

Gradually, the games of football and rugby began to diverge, with some clubs and schools adopting the new game and others staying with the older "feet-only" sport. In 1863, a group of football enthusiasts met in London and adopted a set of rules that forbade using the hands, publishing them under the title of *Rules of the London Football Association*. From the term *association football* came the modern word *soccer*. But many other players continued to enjoy "rugger."

During the 19th century, both rugby and soccer were played in the United States, especially at Eastern colleges. Football of any kind was banned for a time at Harvard and Yale, but in 1867, a set of rules was drawn up at Princeton. Two years later, a team from that school took on a squad from Rutgers University at New Brunswick, New Jersey, in a match often called the first intercollegiate football game in America. But the fact is, the game that day was soccer and not football: each team consisted of 25 men; a round ball was used; and running with the ball was not permitted.

A young student by the name of Irving Lane was a member of the Rutgers squad that won the match, 6-4. In 1938, Lane—the last survivor of the game—was in attendance when Rutgers again defeated Princeton, 20-18. That marked the first time in 69 years that Rutgers had beaten their old foes. Lane died a few days later.

Two years after the first Princeton-Rutgers meeting, students at Harvard adopted a sport, known as "the Boston Game," that like rugby permitted a player to run with the ball. So in 1873, when Princeton, Rutgers, Columbia, and Yale met in New York to draft a code of rules for football, Harvard refused to attend. The decision was momentous in the history of soccer and football. If Harvard had gone along with the four other colleges and adopted a set of rules forbidding players to run with the ball, the game of soccer would most likely have developed as the major academic sport in the United States, and American football may never have been born. Hereafter, the paths of what became soccer and American football would continue to diverge.

Other American colleges soon began to follow Harvard's lead, and abandoned the kicking game. In 1875, the first game of true "football," between American universities pitted Harvard against Yale. The Crimson won 4-0. The following year, a new set of rules based loosely on those of rugby was adopted by the newly formed Intercollegiate Football Association. Yet the administrations of many colleges remained less enthusiastic than their student players. When students at Cornell requested permission to travel to Cleveland to meet a squad from the University of Michigan, the Cornell president replied: "I will not permit 30 men to travel 400 miles to agitate a bag of wind."

Despite such protests, American football continued to evolve from a rugby-like game to the unique sport it is today. By 1888, football was being played in the United States on a field 110 yards long, with 11 players on a side and the familiar egg-shaped ball. By 1906, when the forward pass was legalized, football was the national academic game of America, played in a way recognizable to any modern fan.

Also easily recognizable by that time were the differences between the game and its earlier cousin, "association football," or soccer. While American football had evolved into a running and passing game incorporating elements of both soccer and rugby, football enthusiasts in England had stuck by the kicking game. The rules of English football had become codified at the 1863 meeting of the London Football Association (F.A.); by 1870, soccer was played in the British Isles with 11 men on a side, as it is today.

During the 1871-72 season, the F.A. organized a competition among member football clubs for a trophy, the F.A. Cup, which was soon to become the most highly regarded soccer prize in the world. The following year, a similar tournament was organized for a Scottish F.A. cup. As the level of competition rose, professional players quickly began to outnumber amateurs. So in 1894, another competition for amateurs only was established. The two trophies, the Association or Challenge Cup and the

League or Amateur Cup have been awarded almost every year since then—though in 1895, the original Association Cup was stolen from a Birmingham shop and never recovered.

If baseball is the American pastime, and the major leagues the premier baseball organization in the United States, then the British Football League is the "major league" of England. In 1889, this professional soccer league was formed with 12 teams, and a second division was added three years later. A rule was soon put into effect establishing that the two best teams from Division II would replace the two poorest teams from Division I each year, a rule that is still in effect. A Division III was established in 1921, and another section of Division III soon after, with a similar provision for dropping two Division II teams to Division III at the end of each season—surely an attractive idea to American supporters of perennial also-rans.

By the mid-1950s, the British Football League included 22 teams each in Divisions I and II, and 24 teams in each of the two sections of Division III—for a total of 92 teams! The teams that have won the Division I title the most times are Arsenal, Liverpool, and Manchester United. The Challenge Cup has been in the hands of the Aston Villa squad more than any other team.

As soccer grew in the British Isles, the game was continually spread around the Commonwealth by British soldiers, administrators, and travelers, until a football association of some kind existed in many countries. In 1904, these associations joined together to form an international governing body called, in a curious combination of languages, the Federation Internationale de Football Association, or F.I.C.A.

In 1930, the F.I.C.A. instituted the first world competition for the Jules Rimet Cup, or the World Cup, which is probably the most prized sports trophy in the world today. Uruguay won the first competition. Since then, the World Cup competition has been held every four years, except in 1942 and 1946, with Brazil the only team to win the Cup three times. Other winners include—in addition to Uruguay (twice)—West Germany (twice), Italy (twice), and Argentina. In 1928, the British Football Association left the F.I.C.A., but it rejoined the body in time for the 1950 competition. In 1966, England finally won the Cup.

Both professionals and amateurs are allowed to compete in the World Cup series. Amateurs may also exhibit their skills at the Olympic Games, which have included soccer matches since the turn of the century. Over the last 20 years, teams from Eastern

At the soccer stadium in Rio de Janeiro, the playing field is surrounded by a moat seven feet wide and five feet deep to keep overenthusiastic fans from the players—and the referees.

Europe have dominated the Olympic soccer competition.

But it's the professional soccer leagues in many countries that have made soccer the most popular sport in the world. The total attendance at all the games played each year is almost inestimable; it certainly outshadows the total attendance of hockey, basketball, and other worldwide sports. In 1937, an incredible 149,000 people packed into a stadium in Hampden, England, to watch a match between teams from Scotland and England, setting the all-time attendance record for that country. Today, crowds of 80,000 or more are not uncommon.

In 1950, the world record for soccer attendance was established at the World Cup finals in Rio de Janeiro, when 205,000 people tried to cheer their Brazilian team to victory—but Brazil lost to Uruguay. At the stadium in Rio, the playing field is surrounded by a moat seven feet wide and five feet deep to keep overenthusiastic fans from the players—and the referees.

Soccer in the United States is only now starting to catch on as a popular sport. Toward the end of the 19th century, when soccer was mushrooming in Britain, the game was played here chiefly by small groups of English, Scottish, and Irish immigrants. In 1913, a governing body for American soccer was formed, called the U.S.F.A., and an affiliation was established with the F.I.C.A. But there was still little interest here in the sport, due to most Americans' conception of soccer as a "foreign" sport, and the then growing popularity of baseball and American football. Even the shocking victory of the U.S. team over England in the 1950 World Cup series gained little notice in the United States; in 1953, the return match at Yankee Stadium drew only 7,271 people.

Today, professional soccer matches in the United States often attract five or more times that number—though attendance is far below the 58,000-per-game average of professional football and the 35 million annual total of college football. The soccer boom in America began slowly after World War II, when soldiers stationed overseas first learned the game, and has been spurred by the influx of European and South American immigrants. The biggest spur to American soccer development, however, was the formation of the professional North American Soccer League.

In 1968, the NASL began with 17 teams, but partially collapsed during the next two years. Then the steady upswing in soccer's fortunes began. Between 1970 and 1975, the league grew from five to 20 teams; by 1974, the game was attracting more than a million fans annually. The year 1975 was the key year for the league, due to a big rise in attendance and, most importantly, the signing by the New York Cosmos of a Brazilian player named Edson Arantes do Nascimento—better known as Pelé. During his 18-year career in Brazil, Pelé had scored 1,216 goals in 1,254 games—almost a goal a game—and had become the most famous athlete in the world.

The rules of soccer are fairly simple, and the game can be learned quickly by any novice—that's one of the major reasons for its widespread popularity. Soccer is played on a field from 100 to 120 yards long and from 55 to 75 yards wide. Goal posts at each end of the field are eight feet high and 24 feet apart, connected by a crossbar, with a net in the rear. Each team has 11 players, including a goalkeeper. Players advance the ball by kicking it or playing it with any part of the body except the arms and hands; the goalkeeper can use his hands. A team scores one point for each ball they play into their opponent's net. A game consists of two 45-minute halves, and the play is continuous, with a time-out called only for a serious injury.

Unlike football or basketball, the clock continues to run in a soccer match even if the ball is played out of bounds. Whenever a player drives the ball off the playing field, the ball goes over to the opposing team. If the ball goes beyond the side line, or "touch line," the opposing team throws it in with a two-handed toss. If the ball is driven beyond the end line, or "goal line," by the attacking team, the defenders are awarded a free kick, similar to the kick-off in football; if the defending team drives the ball beyond its own goal line, the attacking team is awarded a corner kick, playing the ball in from one corner of the field.

A penalty kick is awarded an attacking team for certain infractions committed by a defender within his own penalty area, which is 44 yards wide and extends 18 yards from the goal line; a penalty kick is taken from a spot 12 yards in front of the goal. Aside from a few other basic rules, that's about all there is to the game of soccer!

As soccer grows in the United States, there's sure to be a controversy about the relative merits of the game and its historical cousin, American football. There's already a debate as to which game is the more violent.

Football is surely more of a hard-hitting contact sport. As long ago as 1906, President Theodore

A picture of the Brazilian soccer star, Pelé, working his magic on the field. He is seen bouncing the ball on his knee.

Roosevelt threatened to abolish the game unless it was made less brutal, and the injury rate among football players has certainly not tailed off since then. In a recent season, professional football teams suffered an injury rate close to 50 percent—one reported injury for every two players. Among non-professionals, an estimated 35,000 college students and 375,000 high school players suffer football-related injuries each year!

But football players are protected by pounds of equipment to soften the blows. The soccer player, engaged in a rough and tumble contact sport, wears only knee guards and a pair of shorts. The action can get quite rough, at times approaching the free-for-all of the medieval game. To quote the remarks made by a Frenchman after witnessing an 18th-century game of football in England, "If this is what the English call playing, it's impossible to tell what they might call fighting."

SPICES

Some spices were even worth as much as gold and silver. One pound of ginger could buy a sheep; a pound of cloves, seven sheep. Spices were often included in wills, or given as part of a marriage dowry.

As any schoolboy can tell you, it was the desire of Europeans to find a faster, cheaper route to the spice supplies of the Far East that spurred the great explorations of the 15th and 16th centuries. Have you ever wondered why men were eager to undertake those long, dangerous journeys in pursuit of such lightly-regarded items as pepper, ginger, and cinnamon?

The answer is simple: spices were as valuable to contemporary Europeans as the gold so avidly sought by California prospectors a century ago. A shipload of spices could make a man rich for life, and the nation that controlled the spice trade to a great extent controlled the commerce of Europe.

Spices were highly prized at the time not only because of their rarity, but because of their extreme importance in daily life, and the wide variety of uses they served. In the days before refrigeration, spices were needed to preserve food, to disguise poor-tasting, often tainted dishes, and to salvage sour wine. Herbs and spices were also used for embalming, and to make incense, perfume oils, and medicines. In fact, the earliest known treatise on medicine was a 2700 B.C. Chinese work entitled *The Classic Herbal.*

As early as the seventh century B.C., the Assyrians of Mesopotamia were importing dozens of spices from India and Persia, including cinnamon. The ancient Egyptians used spices for embalming as well as food flavoring and preservation. Spices were valued so highly in Egypt that many monarchs, including Cleopatra, had supplies placed in their tombs along with jewels and precious metals.

Since Biblical times, caravans laden with spices had traveled from India and points east to the Mediterranean. There are four references to cinnamon in the Bible. The ancient route brought caravans through Mesopotamia to the Phoenician port of Tyre. After Alexander the Great captured Tyre in the fourth century B.C., the city of Alexandria in Egypt gradually became the center of the spice trade in the Mediterranean.

The ancient Romans used a wide variety of spices and imported them in large quantities. Spices were so valuable during Imperial times that a single sack of peppers could pay a man's ransom. In the fifth century, the Visigoth chieftain Alaric accepted 3,000 pounds of peppers as part of a tribute to lift the seige of Rome.

The barbarian invasions of the Empire killed much of the spice trade in Western Europe, but some shipments from the East continued to reach Europe via Constantinople. Throughout the Middle Ages, spices were far too costly for the average person.

Spice cabinet, a Jewish religious object, made in Nurnberg.

The nutmeg tree and its fruit.

Besides aristocrats, only monks, who used spices to make medicines, could afford them in any variety. Most commoners had to content themselves with onions. Oddly enough, saffron, one of the few affordable spices in medieval times, is now the most expensive spice in the world.

The long distances spices had to be transported to reach Europe only partly explains their great expense at the time. Until the 13th century, Arab merchants owned a virtual monopoly on the spice trade, and closely guarded the secrets of where they were obtained.

To justify their high prices, the Arabs maintained that they had brought back their wares from "paradise," or from barbarous lands frought with danger. Cinnamon, they claimed, grew only in deep glens infested with poisonous snakes. Since few Europeans had visited the Far East, the

In the days before refrigeration, spices were needed to preserve food, to disguise poor-tasting, often tainted dishes, and to salvage sour wine.

Produced from the dried inner bark of a small, bushy evergreen tree, cinnamon is one of the few spices made from the bark of a plant rather than from the leaf, root, flower, or seed.

general public was ready to believe almost anything.

The "secrets" of the Arab spice trade had been exposed by the time the Crusaders seized the ports used for spice export. The cost of spices fell quickly in Europe, and the demand increased. Gradually, merchants from Genoa, Pisa, and especially Venice, took control of the Mediterranean trade.

At the time, spice supplies were still brought overland by caravan from the East. The main route followed the Euphrates River and ended in Constantinople or the Levant. High custom duties imposed by kingdoms along the route forced many caravans to cross Arabia and the Red Sea and trek through Ethiopia and Egypt to the port of Alexandria. Venetian merchants then transported the cargo across the Mediterranean and sold their wares in French and Italian ports. From there, spices were shipped over the Alps or up the Rhone River to Northern France and Flanders, then on to England.

It was largely the demand for spices—and the great profits that could be made by selling them—that triggered the great discoveries of the era. The Portuguese explorer Vasco da Gama was searching for a cheaper, all-water route to the East when he rounded the Cape of Good Hope and sailed to India. In 1503, he returned to Portugal laden with supplies of cinnamon, nutmeg, ginger, pepper, and other spices from ports on the Malabar Coast. And it was Columbus' attempt to find a faster western route to the Far East that led to his discovery of America.

Without cargo ships suitable for ocean travel, the Venetians quickly lost their spice trade. Portuguese merchants soon owned a monopoly on much of Europe's Eastern imports. Then the Dutch, and later the English, began to roam the Eastern seas, seizing many of the lands where the Portuguese had carried on their trade. By the beginning of the 17th century, Portugal had a monopoly on only one spice: cinnamon.

At the time, cinnamon thrived along the Malabar Coast of India, which was still in the hands of the Portuguese. But in the mid-17th century, the Dutch deviously took control of cinnamon commerce, buying the rights from Malabar kings to destroy all cinnamon plantations in the area to enhance the value of the new Dutch plantations on the island of Ceylon. Thus, when the English seized Ceylon in 1795, they inherited the Dutch monopoly.

The spice trade was still quite lucrative at the time. In the 15th century, a pound of pepper cost an Englishman about six times the average daily wage of a laborer. As late as the 17th century, a load of spices bought in the East for 3,000 pounds could be resold in England for as much as six times that amount.

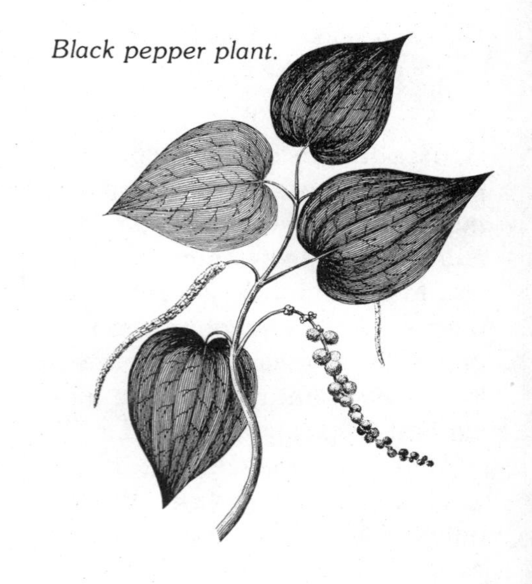

Black pepper plant.

Drying cardamom in Ceylon.

Understandably, many of the herbs and spices shipped to Europe found their way into the hands of the wealthy. One 15th-century German monarch insisted that his women bathe in tubfulls of expensive aromatic oils. French noblemen at the court of Louis XIV often enjoyed perfumed foods, such as meats sprinkled with rose water, eggs flavored with musk, or cream mixed with ambergris.

What's the difference between an herb and a spice? A spice is an aromatic vegetable used to season food. An herb is defined as a seed plant that does not develop woody tissue, but is more or less soft or succulent. An herb may have either a medicinal or culinary use, while a spice is always primarily a flavoring.

Cinnamon has been used in Europe longer than most other spices, since it is native to India rather than the more distant East Indies, where a majority of spices originate.

Biologically, the cinnamon plant is known as *Cinnamonum zeylanicum.* The second word is derived from the Portuguese name for Ceylon. *Cinnamon* itself comes from the Greek *kinnamon,* in turn derived from the Hebrew *qinnamon.* The Germans call the spice *Ceylonzimt,* while *cannelle* is cinnamon in France.

Produced from the dried inner bark of a small, bushy evergreen tree, cinnamon is one of the few spices made from the bark of a plant rather than the leaf, root, flower, or seed. Untended cinnamon trees will grow up to 40 feet high, but to facilitate harvesting they are usually pruned to about eight feet.

At the plantation, the bark is stripped from the trees, fermented, scraped, and dried. The yellow, rolled strips of bark are then inserted one within another for shipping, forming solid rods about three-eighths of an inch in diameter and three feet long. Some of the bark is instead pounded, macerated in sea water, and distilled to produce cinnamon oil.

Ceylon, now known as Sri Lanka, still produces the world's best cinnamon. Other supplies hail from India, Indonesia, Brazil, and the West Indies.

Cinnamon and other spices cost but a fraction of their worth just a few centuries ago, but international spice trade still totals over $200 million a year. Pepper accounts for about a quarter of the total.

Some 150 million pounds of herbs and spices are imported by the United States yearly, with a value of over $70 million. Cinnamon oil alone accounts for about 200,000 pounds of the total import figure.

Spanish saffron is presently the world's most expensive spice, selling in England for as much as $780 per pound. About 32,000 saffron flowers are required to produce just one pound of the powder.

At the other end of the scale, Portuguese rosemary and Canadian mustard are the cheapest spices available today, selling for as little as seven or eight cents a pound in the United States.

If the value of spices has dropped sharply over the last few centuries, so has our need for them. No longer employed on a large scale for food preservation or medicine, most spices are used today as simple flavorings. Cinnamon, with a warm, sweet flavor, is used mostly in confectionery and baked goods. Much European chocolate contains cinnamon, as do many liqueurs. Mincemeat spice, pumpkin pie, baked apples, and the coffee concoction known as *cappucino* all include cinnamon as an essential ingredient. And without cinnamon, could you hope to bake the grandmother of all American desserts, apple pie?

Streetcars

Imagine a vast network of streetcar lines connecting America's cities, with trolley cars whisking passengers between neighboring towns at speeds of seventy or eighty miles an hour. A prospect for the distant future? No, a fairly accurate description of American interurban travel around the turn of this century. Yes, that's right, we said *trolley cars!*

Today, most people would think of the streetcar as a creature of the big city. True, most American cities have operated trolley systems at one time or another. But before the country was laced with freeways and interstate highways, streetcar travel was the best means of transportation to and from the city, as well as within its boundaries. Trolley lines took salesmen to small towns to peddle their wares, and trolleys brought farmers and housewives into town to shop or deliver goods, and trolleys carried city dwellers to nearby beaches and resorts.

Interurban streetcar lines operated with heavy, individually powered cars, quite unlike the lighter, locomotive-drawn railroad cars. Trolleys ran more frequently than mainline trains, and they usually served areas inaccessible by railroad. It was common, too, for a streetcar company to construct an amusement park in an otherwise inaccessible suburban area along its trolley line in order to increase weekend and night travel on the line.

The first interurban streetcar line in this country connected the cities of Granville and Newark, Ohio, beginning in 1889, and the first high-speed interurban trolleys ran between Cleveland and Akron in 1895. Within a few decades, many of America's cities, large and small, were linked by streetcar lines, especially in Ohio, Indiana, Illinois, and Michigan. No burgeoning town was considered major league until it was connected by streetcar line with at least one neighboring city.

Early in this century, it was possible to ride by trolley from New York all the way to Boston for less than four dollars! Of course, there were frequent changes of line.

The longest continuous streetcar route—again with frequent changes of line—ran from Freeport, Illinois to Utica, New York, a distance of over 1,000 miles!

One Colorado line climbed over a 10,000-foot peak to reach the mining boomtown of Cripple Creek.

With even the fastest modern trains rarely exceeding 60 miles per hour, it now seems hard to believe that the normal operating speed of the interurban streetcar line was *80 miles per hour.*

Incredible as it seems, cars of the Crandic Line between Cedar Rapids and Iowa City in Iowa once claimed top speeds of 110 miles per hour!

Within the city, streetcars were the first motor-driven means of public transportation. Streetcars provided the first dependable intra-city travel in the days before the bus, auto, and subway. Dependable, yes; fast, often not. The first streetcar in this country, in fact, was powered by only a few horsepower—provided by, yes, a few horses!

This horse-drawn conveyance was constructed by John Stephenson in Philadepia, and placed in service in New York City in 1832 by the New York and Harlem Railway. Called the *John Mason* after a prominent banker who had organized the railroad company, the car seated 30 passengers in three unconnected compartments. It ran between Prince Street and 14th Street in Manhattan, with a later extension to uptown Manhattan. The fare was a then rather steep 12½ cents. No, we don't know what the conductor did for change of a penny if you didn't want a round- trip ticket.

The earliest electric trolleys were powered by storage batteries, which proved expensive and inefficient. The first electrified streetcar tracks, too, often short-circuited in the rain.

One of the world's first electric lines was constructed in London in 1860 by the American G.F. Train—that's right, Train—with two more tramlines following shortly after in that city. But it was the invention of the electric generator that led to the application of transmitted power to streetcar lines and fostered the proliferation of tramlines throughout Europe and the United States.

There are three kinds of electric streetcars. One is drawn by cable; another is powered by an electrified third rail; and the third is powered by overhead transmission lines, with the car connected to the power lines by a collapsible apparatus called the *trolley*. Strictly speaking, then, only a streetcar powered by overhead lines can be called a "trolley."

There are two varieties of trolley system, one utilizing two overhead wires—the European preference—and the second using one wire and one electrified track to complete the electric circuit. The later type is the overwhelming favorite of American lines.

Berlin got its first electric tramway in 1881, Budapest in

In the 1870s, steam-powered trams provided public transportation in Paris.

The Constantinople trolley was making its rounds in the 1870s.

1897, and Paris in 1901. A gas-powered streetcar was placed in operation in Providence, Rhode Island in 1872, while the first commercially owned electric streetcars in this country plied their course in Baltimore in 1885. The first "soundless, shockless" tracks were laid in New Orleans in 1930.

The famed San Francisco cable cars were the world's first cable-drawn cars. The Bay City's cable car was invented by Andrew Hallidie, and introduced in 1873 on Sacramento and Clay Streets.

Cable cars were drawn by an endless cable that runs in a slot between the rails. Cable cars are best suited for steeply inclined streets—thus, their early popularity in San Francisco and Seattle. But a cable car can run only at a constant speed, and a cable jam can stop every car on the line.

By the turn of the century, most cable car lines had been replaced by electric trackage, although Seattle retained its system until the 1930s.

The San Francisco cable car lines still operating today are maintained chiefly as tourist attractions, with most lines long-since replaced by buses or trolley-bus systems.

Streetcar lines in general began to rapidly disappear in the 1930s, in the face of competition from cars and buses. An intermediate step in the trolley-to-bus transition was the trackless trolley, a buslike vehicle that ran without tracks but was powered by electricity from overhead lines, like the trolley. The first trackless trolley began service in 1910 in

Los Angeles. Despite its present automobile mania, LA once boasted one of the nation's finest streetcar systems. Brooklyn, New York, maintained trackless trolleys as late as the 1950s.

London did away with its last trolley in the 50s; Paris had ripped up its streetcar tracks about 20 years earlier. Today, the streetcar is virtually extinct in America, but the trolley is still widely used in Germany, Austria, Switzerland, and Eastern Europe.

But trolley-lovers, take heart. You can still catch a glimpse of the ancient streetcar in various museums throughout the country. The museum in East Hartford, Connecticut, contains 92 trolleys, ranging from some 1880 relics to a New York model from the 1930s. In that museum, trolley buffs can ride an open-sided car—complete with bell—over a two-mile route.

Streetcars were inexpensive to construct and clean. Although dependable, they were not without disadvantages. Among these was the danger posed to idle strollers by a speeding trolley. The Brooklyn Dodgers of baseball fame were not so-named because of their agility on the playing field. Initially, the team was called the "Trolley Dodgers," in tribute to the maze of trolley lines crisscrossing Brooklyn at the height of the streetcar era.

The tram was a fixture of city life in Valparaiso, Chile, in 1890.

"PREPOSTEROUS!" scoffed American tycoon Russell Sage to the first proposal for an underground transit system in New York City. "The people of New York will never go into a hole in the ground to ride."

Well, as everyone knows, Russell's counsel turned out to be less than sage. By the time of his death in 1906, subway cars were already rattling through Manhattan's first tunnel, with work proceeding on new lines in three boroughs. And every years, close to *two billion* people "go into a hole to ride" in New York City.

Though New York's subway is today the world's most famous—or infamous—it was not, as many people believe, the first every constructed. Actually, it was the sixth to begin operation, and the second in this country. For the world's first underground rapid transit system we must journey to Londontown.

By the mid-19th century, a traveler could ride by train from London's raid terminals to almost any point in England. But travel within the city itself still relied chiefly on horse-drawn streetcars and carriages. The rail lines that brought travelers to London did not reach into the city's main business and commercial center, and since the railroads and terminals were for the most part constructed by rival rail companies, there was no convenient means of transit between one depot and another.

Shortly after the opening of Marc Bunel's Thames Tunnel in 1843 had demonstrated the viability of underground rail travel, London city solicitor Charles Pearson proposed an underground railway connecting some of the city's major railroad depots. After 10 years of talk, Parliament authorized the first line: a three-and-a-quarter-mile run between Peddington Station and Farringdon Road, by way of King's Cross Station.

Construction was of the "cut and cover" method still used for the great majority of lines: first, a trench is dug in the street; then tracks are laid at the bottom of the trench; and then the trench is covered by the reconstructed street.

After three years of construction, London's first line opened on January 10, 1863. It was powered by steam locomotives fueled by coke. Despite the sulfurous smoke spewed into the tunnel by the locomotives, the "underground" was an immediate success, attracting 30,000 riders on its first day of operation, and well over nine million during its first year.

Londoners stroll in the new high level Metropolitan railway station at the Crystal Palace in 1865.

To appreciate the English feat, remember that with a comparatively limited technology, the builders of the first subway had completed in less than three years a project that even today would require years of effort. And this despite a flood that at one point filled the excavation to a depth of 10 feet! Today, the London Underground is over 100 years old, but is still in excellent condition.

This line, called the "Metropolitan," was gradually lengthened over the following decades, and remained the only subway in the world for close to 30 years. But 1890 saw the opening of London's second underground line, and the first "tube tunnel" in the world. In a tube line, a tunnel is actually bored through the ground, under the building foundations.

The 1890 tube line was immediately popular, with electric power freeing the deep tunnels of noxious fumes. A trip on the three-mile line cost two pence, but the fare bought little in the way of the view. Subway cars of the time were built without windows, since in the opinion of their designers, there was simply nothing to look at in a tunnel.

On a tube line, the stations must be located far underground. The greatest depth of the London system is 221 feet, but no station is more than 100 feet underground. Thus dozens of elevators, or "lifts" as they're called in England, are needed to carry passengers between the street and the tube platform—not the most efficient way to keep people on the move, considering there might be a 10-minute wait for a rush-hour lift.

At one time, there were 240 lifts throughout the London underground system, but with the invention of a satisfactory escalator in 1911, the number of lifts began to dwindle. One escalator can do the work of five elevators, eliminating the waiting lines that plagued the earliest London tubes. Today, there are less than 10 lifts in operation in the London subway system.

On the other side of the Atlantic, the streetcar and the elevated railway were the favored forms of urban transportation until the turn of the century. The nation's first elevated Line, or "El," had opened on Manhattan's Ninth Avenue in 1867, with a cable-drive system. In 1871, there was a switch to steam locomotives. The nation's first electric El did not appear until 1895, in Chicago.

> *In a rush-hour subway train, a gentleman bent over and murmured to the young lady standing beside him, "I beg your pardon, but would you like me to find a strap for you?"*
>
> *"I have a strap," she retorted icily.*
>
> *"Then please let go of my necktie!"*

While New Yorkers were debating the pros and cons of an underground system like the one then operating in London, Boston rushed ahead with the nation's first subway. Completed in 1897, the Boston line intitially ran one-and-a-half miles under Tremont Street, with trolley cars the first vehicles to ride the subway tracks.

By that time, New York had an intricate system of elevated lines. An underground line was thought to be impractical for the Big Apple, because of the hard granite rock that forms most of Manhattan Island. As plans were put forward for the first underground line in the city, skeptics like Russell Sage warned that the project would prove a distaster. Property owners claimed that their buildings would collapse. The city's water board expressed fears that construction would destroy the underground water pipe system.

But the subway proponents held sway; and in 1904, the first New York subway began operation—without the collapse of anything at all. The line ran from City Hall in downtown Manhattan to the Grand Central Terminal in midtown, then west to Times Square and then north to 145th Street. Another line was added almost immediately, extending to 180th Street in the Bronx; but it took until 1908 for the subway to touch the shores of Brooklyn.

The London system was and still is called the *underground,* but American rapid transit pioneers had to search for an alternative term. "Underground Railroad" to most Americans suggested the network of secret way-stations that brought escaped slaves North before the Civil War, so the word *subway* was born of necessity.

The first New York subway lines, like their London counterparts, were built by competing companies, and remained privately owned until the city took over in 1940. The IRT (Interborough Rapid Transit) was the first rapid transit company in the city, operating the maiden line from City Hall and most of the Manhattan and Bronx elevated lines. The BMT (Brooklyn and Manhattan Transit) was constructed from 1913 to 1920, and included most of the Brooklyn elevated lines. Oddly enough, the Independent Line (IND) was the only line never to be independently owned, built by the city in 1930s.

We mentioned that the New York City system was the world's sixth underground railway, with London and Boston two of its predecessors. The other three? Well, the Glasgow subway was the second to be completed, opening in 1891. The Scottish line, still in operation, runs over a six-and-a-half mile oval that

Construction on New York City's Sixth Avenue subway line was begun in the 1930s. The Sixth Avenue line was completed on December 15, 1940.

Photo courtesy of the New York Board of Transit.

33RD ST.
AILROAD TUNNELS.
SECTION THROUGH 33RD STREE
AT SIXTH AVENUE AND BROADWA

Several French Metro station entrances are decorated with art nouveau fixtures.

Photo courtesy of the French Embassy Press and Information Division.

never reaches the surface. Only one other subway line in the world never reaches daylight: London's Waterloo and City. On both lines, cars have to lifted by elevator to repair shops and sidings.

In 1896, Budapest opened the first subway on the European continent, running single cars over a two-and-a-half-mile electric line. In 1900, Paris opened its first *metro,* the world's fifth, a six-and-a-quarter-mile line.

Philadelphia was the third American city to build a subway, opening its first line in 1907. Chicago, which already had a large el network, was to wait until 1943 for its first underground.

Subways were opened in Buenos Aires in 1913, in Tokyo in 1927, in Moscow in the 1930s, and in Toronto in 1954.

At present, there are 67 cities operating underground rail lines of some kind. In addition to those already mentioned, there are underground transit lines in Madrid, Barcelona, Oslo, Rotterdam, Stockholm, Hamburg, Berlin, Lisbon, Milan, Rome, Kiev, and Leningrad in Europe; Osaka, Kyoto, and Nagoya in Asia; Sydney in Australia; and

Washington D.C., have recently installed subways and Atlanta is to follow suit in the 1980s.

By the way, recent work on a new subway line in Rome had produced some unexpected benefits; excavators have discovered extensive underground ruins dating from the days of the Roman Empire. Most finds have

An advertisement of "The Tube" by the British Transport.

Mexico City and Montreal in North America.

Construction is now proceeding on subway lines in a number of cities, including additions to the New York, London, and Paris systems. New systems are planned for Prague, Munich, Cologne, Cairo, Helsinki, Kharkov, and other cities. In America, San Francisco and

New York subway riders are depicted in this drawing by David Levine.

been removed and placed on exhibit at the Terminal Station.

Among all underground systems in operation today, London's is the most exensive, with 252 miles of track (77 bored tunnel, 24 cut-and-cover, and 151 outdoor; and 279 stations. A 600-train fleet with over 4,000 cars carries some 600 million passengeres each year, with the one-day record standing at 2,073, 134 on VE Day, 1945.

The longest continuous subway tunnel in the world stretches over 17 miles from Morden to East Finchley in London. Compare that with the longest main-line railroad tunnel in the world—the Simplon, at just over 12 miles—and the longest road tunnel, the Mt. Blanc, which is just over seven miles.

The New York system is shorter in track mileage, but far and away the busiest in the world, serving about four-and-a-half million passengers on an average weekday and over two billion a year. This massive systems—one of the few to remain in operation around the clock—spans 230 miles, with 462 stations, and its 134 miles of tunnel form the largest underground netword in the world.

The Paris *Metro* is 105 miles long, less than half of the London system, yet the Paris system attracts nearly twice as many passengers—over a billion each year. Some 270 closely spaced stations leave no point in the central area of the city more than 600 yards from the *Metro!*

Modern subway cars have come a long way from the early English windowless models. Those being built in America are for the most part sleek and air-conditioned, and much quieter than their forerunners. Subway stations, too, are now more imaginatively designed. In the Montreal subway, for example, an artist was commissioned to design each station, while the stations of the Moscow subway are marvels, bedecked with marble columns and elegant chandeliers.

And speaking of modern innovations, the first subway line to operate automatically without conductor or motorman began operation in New York in 1962, running between Grand Central Station and Times Square. But the city's Transit Worker's Union won a demand to place a non-functional motorman in each train; and today, the line is run manually, like the city's other lines. Since 1963, an automatic line has been in operation in London, running four miles between Woodford and Hainault. The San Francisco system is largely automated.

Why not use the "L?" *Egg tempera on canvas by Reginald Marsh.*

Courtesy of Whitney Museum of American Art, New York.

But long after the last engineers and conductors have given way to automation, the underground enthusiast will still be around to pass along subway lore. One subway buff set a record in 1968 by visiting every station in the London system in just 15 hours! Five years later, two other determined individuals established the New York record by traveling to each of the 462 stations in just 21 hours, 8½ minutes. It takes some people almost as long just to decipher the New York system's maps!

Botanical drawing of the tea plant.

In 2737 B.C., the Chinese Emperor Shen Nung was boiling a pot of drinking water over a fire fueled by leaves, when one of the leaves wafted up from the fire and settled in the pot. The Emperor smelled the boiling broth, and liked it. Then he sipped the brew, and liked it even more. This was no ordinary leaf broth, you see—man had unwittingly enjoyed his first cup of tea!

The Emperor went on to proclaim the virtues of his find, declaring that the beverage "is better than wine for it leads not to intoxication, neither does it cause a man to say foolish things." The story is merely a legend, for Shen Nung himself is a mythical figure. But the discovery of a beverage brewed from tea leaves probably did take place long ago in China or the neighboring lands of Burma and Thailand. And the Emperor notwithstanding, in the centuries since then, many a foolish thing has indeed been uttered over cups of tea in every corner of the earth.

The Indians, who discovered tea at a later date, had a few legends of their own to explain its appearance. According to one, the Buddhist saint Daruma devoted seven years to sleepless contemplation, but after five years found himself drifting into slumber. He chewed the leaf of a nearby bush, and gained the strength to continue his meditation. Another tale explains that Daruma, having fallen asleep during his devotions, cut off his eyelids upon awakening. The discarded eyelids sprouted up as a bush whose leaves could banish sleep.

The origins of tea are shrouded in legends such as these. The first credible mention of the beverage comes from a Chinese dictionary written around the year 350. In 780, Chinese scholar Lu Yu wrote the first handbook of tea, the *Ch'a Ching*, a three-volume treatise describing the tending and preparation of "a thousand and ten thousand teas." The best teas, he maintained, should "unfold like mist rising out of a ravine, and soften gently like fine earth swept by rain."

Tea cultivation spread throughout China under the patronage of Buddhist monks, and reached Japan sometime after 600. The Chinese at first regarded tea as a medicine, until they learned how to roast the leaves to make the drink more palatable. Tea remained a medi-

A tea house at Tashkent in the Soviet Union, the men lounging at ease sipping their tea and smoking their long waterpipes while musicians strum their stringed instruments. Occasionally, one of the men dances to the rhythm of clapping hands and native songs.

It takes some 3,200 shoots to produce a single pound of tea!

TOP:
The opium smoker's teapot manufactured during the reign of Keen Lung 1736-1795. The origin of the two spouts is not certain, but reason would seem to suggest that their purpose was to facilitate the tea drinking of the befuddled devotee of the poppy.

BOTTOM:
Chinese rib teapot of purplish brown stoneware, mid-17th century.

cine in Japan until the 14th century, when the Japanese began to brew the green tea they favor today. The teapot, by the way, was originally adapted from the Chinese wine jug.

Enjoyed in the Far East for thousands of years, tea did not

reach Europe until just a few centuries ago. No reference to the drink appeared in Europe until 1559, when a Venetian book about Arab traders described a beverage that "removes fever, headache, stomach-ache, pain in the side or in the joints and . . . no end of other ailments."

In 1610, the Dutch became the first to actually ship tea to Europe, and with it came the word *tea* itself. The Dutch brought their first tea from a region where the Chinese ideogram for tea is pronounced *tay*. In Canton, it's pronounced *ch'a* or *chah*. The latter word found its way into the languages of India, Japan, Russia, and other nations, and was even used for a time in England. The first reference to tea in England, in 1598, called it *chaa*. But the English eventually

A street tea seller in Moscow, circa 1874.

adopted *tay*, and by the 18th century, pronounced it as we do today.

Tea reached England in 1650. It was served initially in coffee houses and sold by chemists as an herbal health aid. One writer of the time claimed that tea "vanquisheth heavy dreams, easeth the Brain, and strengtheneth the Memory." Though a doctor advised moderation—no one, he claimed, should drink more than 200 cups a day!—tea quickly took England by storm, replacing ale at the English breakfast and closing many an English tavern.

For a time, the Chinese forbade the export of tea. But in 1685, the Emperor relaxed the restrictions and opened Chinese ports to European tea traders. The British East India Company, which was granted a monopoly on tea earlier in the century, did much to popularize tea in Europe and America, and for many years handled almost all the world's tea shipments—legal shipments, that is. For tea was heavily taxed by the English since 1660, and by the Chinese since at least 780. By the 18th century, two-thirds of all the tea drunk in England had been smuggled into the country.

Tea smuggling was not unknown in England's American colonies, either, for the East India Company was also granted a monopoly on American tea imports. In 1773, the colonists showed exactly how they felt about the tea monopoly and tea taxes when they dressed as Indians, boarded English ships in Boston harbor, and sent some 300 crates of tea to Davy Jones' locker. The event became known as the Boston Tea Party, but there were actually seven "tea parties" celebrated in American ports before independence.

The East India Company, whose monopoly on tea survived until 1858, was in large part responsible for making England a nation of tea drinkers, and America the land of coffee lovers. Until the company began to push its tea in England, coffee was the more popular drink there. The Americans were tea drinkers until the company's monopoly and high taxes turned Americans off of tea and opened the door for coffee. Today, the average Englishman drinks five times as much tea as coffee; the average American, 25 times as much coffee as tea.

Until the 19th century, all the tea to reach Europe came from the Far East. But in 1823, the

A 17th-century doctor advised moderation—no one, he claimed, should drink more than 200 cups a day!

English ornate tea kettle of 1886.

Tea cultivation on terraces in Japan.

English found wild tea growing in India, and began cultivating it there about a decade later. By the 1880s, Indian tea production was already about one-third the size of the Chinese; India later surpassed China as a tea producer.

Around 1830, Dutch traders smuggled tea and tea cultivators out of China on the risk of death, and transplanted the tea in Java. But the project failed, as did an earlier attempt in 1684, for Chinese tea did not take a liking to Javanese soil and climate. Indian tea was later taken to the island, and flourished there.

Ceylon (now Sri Lanka), acre for acre the greatest tea producer in the world today, might not have produced tea at all if it weren't for an unfortunate intrusion of nature. Until 1869, coffee was the chief crop of Ceylon. That year, a terrible blight wiped out the coffee crop. The planters decided to start over with tea, and today tea is the principal crop of Ceylon.

Tea was once grown in England, with little success. The Russians also tried unsuccessfully to grow tea around the middle of the 19th century, and brick tea was used as a form of currency in some parts of that country. Attempts have been made to cultivate tea in the United States, too. From 1890 to 1915, an experimental farm raised tea in South Carolina, but the crop grew poorly and the project was abandoned.

The fragrant beverage that we call tea comes from the leaves of an evergreen shrub called *Camellia sinensis*. In its natural state, a tea shrub will grow 15 to 30 feet high, but on the plantation the shrubs are pruned to a height of three to five feet. Tea grows well at altitudes up to 7,000 feet, and especially flourishes in the higher altitudes of the tropics, such as the hilly regions of Assam, India.

Tea plants are grown in seed beds, then transplanted in rows on the plantation. After about three years, the tea leaves are ready for their first picking. A single tea bush may flourish for 25 to 30 years, but reaches its peak production after about 10 years, when it can yield a quarter-pound of tea during each of several yearly pickings. Most picking is still done by hand. A single tea picker can pick 30,000 shoots in a day—and it takes some 3,200 shoots to produce a single pound of tea!

Until 1843, black tea and green tea were thought to come from two different species of tea plant. We now know that black and green tea come from the same plant; the difference in the drinks comes from the manner in which the leaves are prepared. After harvest, black tea is fermented and roasted. Green tea is steamed and dried, but not fermented. A third type of tea, oolong, is partly fermented before roasting.

Similarly, *pekoe, orange pekoe,* and *Souchong* teas may come from the same plant, for these terms refer not to different types of tea, but to the size and appearance of the leaf fragments. Orange pekoe consists of the buds and finest leaves of the plant, while pekoe and pekoe Souchong are large-fragment grades that produce a mild tea favored in Europe. The word *pekoe* comes from the Chinese *pekho*, meaning "white hair" or "down." Other grades, such as broken pekoe, broken pekoe Souchong, fannings, and dust, come from smaller leaf fragments, and produce the strong,

***Pekoe, orange pekoe,* and *Souchong* teas may come from the same plant, for these terms refer not to different types of tea, but to the size and appearance of the leaf fragments.**

Professional English tea tasters, circa 1876.

dark beverage that the English prefer.

There are some 1,500 kinds of tea currently produced around the world, and over 2,000 blends. So-called "English breakfast" tea was originally a blend of black Chinese congou teas. Darjeeling is a black tea from the Assam area of India, close to the Himalayas. Oolong, a partly fermented tea, is grown in Taiwan and in parts of China. Green tea is produced chiefly in China and Japan. The bagged tea you find in your supermarket is probably a blend of 20 to 30 different teas.

The Chinese have long flavored their tea with jasmine and other spices, and in American stores today you'll find a long line

The tea plant.

There are some 1,500 kinds of tea currently produced around the world.

of herbal or spice-scented teas, from sarsparilla to spearmint, camomile to catnip. Unusual teas may cost well over six dollars a pound. One particular kind of Formosan oolong, the most expensive tea in the world, sells for over $13 a pound!

About 30 countries now produce tea. The world's 6,000 or so tea plantations cover an area of some 2.6 million acres! China was long the world's largest tea producer, but since 1941, India has taken over as the number-one tea grower. Tea production in India is now close to a billion pounds a year, while Sri Lanka produces about 470 million pounds and China about 445 million. The Caucasia area, which includes parts of Iran, Turkey, and the U.S.S.R., produces some 210 million pounds annually, and Africa a like amount.

Sri Lanka has recently passed India to become the number-one tea exporter, shippng almost its entire annual harvest, while the Indians export less than half of the tea they grow. China and Caucasia now export little of their tea, while Africa exports almost all of its tea crop. In all, about three billion pounds of tea are harvested around the world each year, a little less than half of which finds its way into the export market.

As you would probably guess, the people of the British Isles are the world's number-one tea drink-

ABOVE:
An old Knicker-bocker tea-table.

LEFT:
Tea basket, Assam, India.

ers. But you may be surprised to learn that the Irish have recently passed the English to become the greatest tea drinkers on earth. The average Irishman now swills about eight-and-a-half pounds of tea each year, compared to the Englishman's seven pounds. The United Kingdom alone accounts for almost half of world tea imports: some 500 million pounds a year. That translates to about 100 billion cups a year, or six cups a day for the average Englishman!

The United States, the world's second largest tea importer, consumes about 150 million pounds a year. But that translates to a paltry 11 ounces—or about 135 cups—a year per person. About 95 percent of the tea we drink is black Indian tea.

The earliest teas to arrive in

ABOVE:
Mongolian tea jug.

OPPOSITE:
Professional tea tasters, United States, 1932, with assistants who record the savors as they are announced.

The Irish have recently passed the English to become the greatest tea drinkers on earth.

the New World, brought in by Dutch settlers around 1650, cost over $30 a pound, a small fortune in those days. At that price, the Dutch were not content to simply brew tea—they sometimes flavored the leaves with salt and butter and ate them!

But as long ago as the 17th century, tea was being prepared the way many of us enjoy it today: with milk and sugar. The

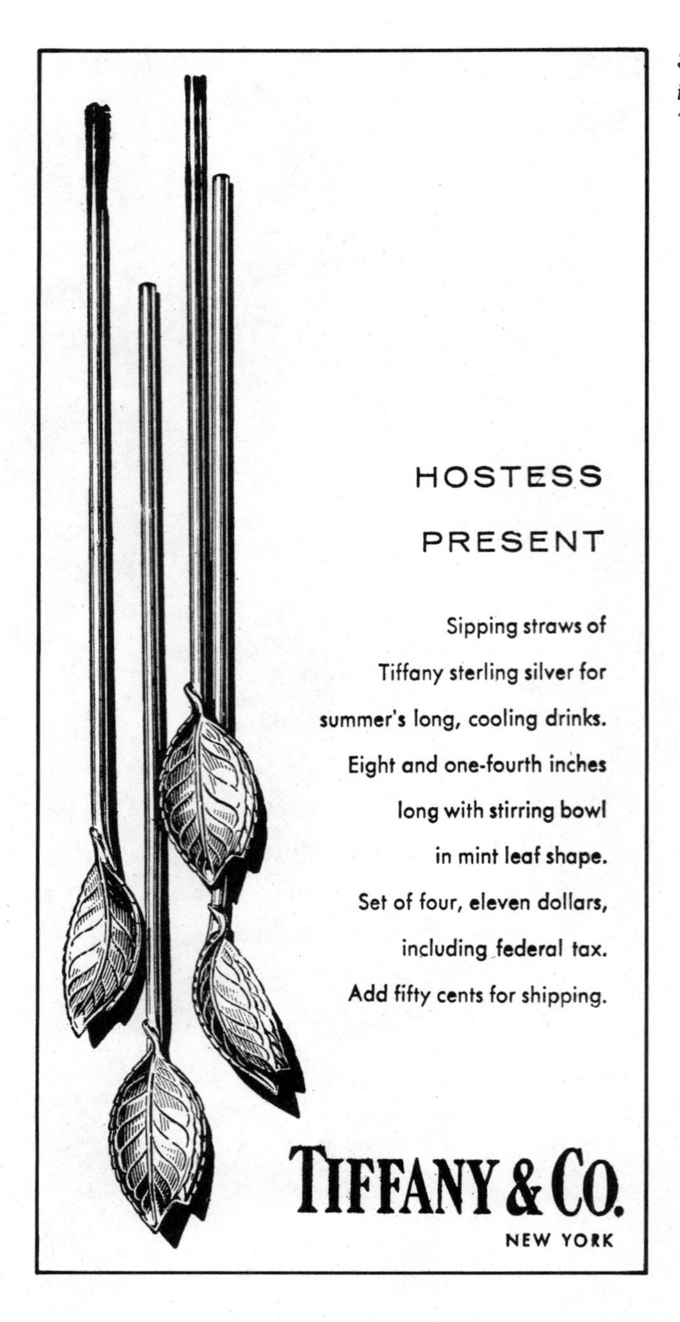

Silver straws for sipping iced tea, by Tiffany of New York.

Today, the average Englishman drinks five times as much tea as coffee; the average American, 25 times as much coffee as tea.

practice of adding milk to tea began in England or France, and was not unknown in China at the time. Tea bags, that distinctly American contribution to tea brewing, did not appear until early this century. In 1904, a New York merchant named Thomas Sullivan shipped tea in small silk bags instead of the usual tin containers. Customers found the tea easier to brew right in the bag.

That same year saw the invention of another American favorite, iced tea. An Englishman named Richard Blechynden has been credited with introducing the drink at the Louisiana Purchase Exposition in St. Louis. Incidentally, the first thing astronaut John Glenn requested after touching down from his earth orbit was a glass of iced tea!

Another American invention, instant tea, has been around only since 1948. Today, about 52 percent of the tea drunk in this country is brewed from tea bags, 34 percent from instant tea or iced tea mixes, and only 14 percent from loose tea.

Tea bags are considered anathema to the average Englishman, who has made tea drinking an institution and the four-o'clock tea a meal in itself. The custom of taking tea in the afternoon allegedly began with the Duchess of Bedford, who had tea and cakes served at five o'clock each day to combat what she called a "sinking feeling."

A nation that goes in for tea in such a big way is certain to have a host of tea legends and superstitions. You'll need a fortune teller to read your tea leaves, but you can be sure that to stir your tea while it's in the pot means to stir up trouble. Bubbles in your cup mean kisses are coming, while adding milk before sugar means you'll lose your sweetheart. Also approaching superstition is the Englishman's recipe for the "perfect cup of tea," of which there are probably as many recipes as there are Englishmen. A good rule of thumb, though, is to brew tea for three to four minutes if you plan to drink it plain, and four to five minutes if you plan to add milk.

A nation so fond of tea is also sure to have a considerable body of tea verse. In 1658, the first advertisement for tea appeared in England, and the first tea eulogy was penned four years later. The poet William Cowper praised "the cups that cheer but not inebriate," echoing a comment by George Berkeley and the ancient words of Shen Nung. The 18th-century writer and wit Samuel Johnson admitted to being a "hardened and shameless tea drinker." Poet Colley Cibber lauded "Tea! thou soft, thou sober, sage, and venerable liquid."

But not all Englishman have agreed on the merits of what another writer called "the sovereign drink of pleasure and health." In 1829, William Cobbett, in his *Advice to Young Men*, instructed the youth of England to "free yourselves from the slavery of tea and coffee and other slopkettle."

The beverage simply wasn't Cobbett's cup of tea.

An advertisement for Lipton's tea which appeared in 1897.

Telephones

"I believe," wrote Alexander Graham Bell in 1878, "that in the future wires will unite the head offices of the Telephone Company in different cities, and a man in one part of the country may communicate by word of mouth with another in a distant place. I am aware that such ideas may appear to you Utopian."

Well, if that's the case, we're now living in Utopia. Today, any American can pick up a phone and communicate not only with any other telephone in the country, but with almost any phone in the entire world—by direct dialing! The telephone has indeed brought the world to our fingertips and broadened the boundaries of our senses. Any temptation to underestimate the importance of the telephone in our lives can be quickly remedied by considering the efficiency of the modern postal system. In short, our lives would not be the same without that tool, toy, and infernal intruder, the telephone.

The man who wrote those prophetic words in 1878 is, of course, the individual most credited with the invention of the telephone. But Alexander Graham Bell was neither the first to conceptualize a voice-transmission device nor the first to design one. He was, quite simply, the first to patent one.

Before Bell began his work, other inventors in the United States and Europe had worked on systems for sound transmission to distant points. Philip Reis, laboring in Frankfurt in the 1860s, devised a crude voice-

This is the telephone into which Alexander Graham Bell uttered the historic words, "Mr. Watson, come here; I want you," on March 10, 1876. The receiver was constructed from a tuned reed.

transmission apparatus employing, at the transmitting end, a diaphragm structure that controlled an electric current. At the receiving end, the electric current governed a magnetized needle that vibrated a sounding board. But 20 years later, the German patent office decided that Reis's apparatus was not a true "speaking telephone."

Alexander Graham Bell was born in Scotland in 1847. He resided in England and Canada before moving at a young age to the United States. At 25, he became a teacher of the deaf at a Boston school; and the next year, a professor of vocal physiology at Boston University. At the time, Bell lived with the Sanders family in Boston, serving as a private tutor for the Sanders' deaf-mute child. He set up a workshop in the basement of the Sanders home for experiments that he hoped would lead to a "musical telegraph."

Bell worked mainly at night in his basement laboratory, alone and in secrecy, for he knew that many other inventors were then engaged in similar experimentation. To guard his work, he traveled around Boston to buy his supplies in various stores. "Often in the middle of the night," Sanders later wrote, "Bell would wake me up, his black eyes blazing with excitement."

The inventor eventually lost his professorship and most of his students due to his preoccupation with telephone experimentation. Most of his friends who were familiar with his work urged him to abandon it. "If I can make a deaf-mute talk," Bell countered, "surely I can make iron talk." With money from his father-in-law and Sanders, Bell moved into a shop in Boston and hired an assistant, Thomas Watson, to pursue his dream of a "musical telegraph."

On June 2, 1875, Bell first heard over a wire the twang of a clock spring operated by Watson in another room. He then knew he was close to harnessing undulating electric currents capable of transmitting speech. Bell's rudimentary apparatus did, in fact, transmit speech the following day.

In February, 1876, Bell filed a patent for his invention. Meanwhile, Bell kept at work to perfect the device. On March 10, 1876, the first complete sentence ever transmitted by telephone reached Bell's assistant in the basement: "Mr. Watson, come here; I want you." Bell received his patent soon after—at the age of 29!

In his patent application, Bell called his invention "an improvement of the telegraph." His wife suggested the name *telephone*, which had long been in use to describe many sound-transmitting devices, such as the "string telephone" invented by Robert Hooke in 1667. When his patent was filed, Bell probably had no idea how close others were to perfecting a similar device. Elisha Gray filed a caveat (notice of intent to file a patent) a *few hours* after Bell applied for his patent. And Thomas Edison had been on the verge of success with his own telephone, when distracted by other work. The stakes? Bell's patent had been called the most valuable ever issued anywhere!

Western Union, the telegraph company, offered Bell $100,000 for his patent in 1887, but Bell rejected the offer. Western Union went on to develop its own telephone system based on the work of Gray and Edison, but an 1878

The first commercial telephone, developed by Bell in 1876, was leased in 1877 by a Boston banker who wanted telephone service between his home and office.

In 1878, Francis Blake, Jr. invented this transmitter, which greatly improved telephone service. The instrument employed carbon to transmit sound with increased clarity.

This ancestor of the upright desk set was made in 1897, and was a refinement of earlier models.

"Number please?" was the standard greeting of Bell operators at the main office in Kansas City, Missouri in 1904.

court decision ruled that Bell had sole patent rights to the telephone. Litigation involving over 600 separate cases dragged on for years. Finally, the Supreme Court upheld Bell's claim for exclusive ownership.

By modern standards, the earliest telephones were crude, and conversations were barely intelligible. Many technological advances were necessary to produce the telephone we use today. In the beginning, phones were sold in pairs so that any telephone could connect with only one other.

The first commercial switchboard appeared in 1878 in New Haven, Connecticut, linking 21 phones.

Telephone lines were quickly strung throughout this country and Europe by Bell's company and others. By 1890, there were already 225,000 phones in use here, and there were 26,000 in Great Britain, and 22,000 in Germany. The first pay telephone reared its coin-snatching head in 1889, in Hartford, Connecticut.

The first telephone directory was in the hands of New Haven phone users in 1878—listing only 50 names.

At first, various telephone companies competed directly with one another in the United States, without provisions for link-ups. Mergers and acquisitions gradually unified the systems, so that by 1950, 82 percent of all American phones were served by the Bell System. Bell's parent corporation, American Telephone & Telegraph, today ranks as the firm with the greatest number of individual shareholders: 2,934,000 in early 1976—more than twice the number of its closest rival, General Motors. Altogether, the 582 million listed shares of AT&T stock now have a market value of almost $30 billion!

By 1900, long before the introduction of direct dialing, there were already 1.3 million phones in the United States. By 1910, the number had soared to 7.6 million; and by 1920, when "Number, please" was still the most common phrase heard through the telephone receiver, there were 13.3 million.

By the early 1950s, there were some 53 million phones in operation here, one for every three persons. By the mid-70s, 144 million phones were in use throughout the nation. American phones now register about 200 billion calls per year, or about 1,400 calls per phone.

Today, there are some 360 million telephones in use around the world, with the United States by far the leader in phone ownership. Japan has about 35 million phones in service, Britain 19 million. West Germany 16, Italy 11, France 10, and the Soviet Union an estimated 18 million. At the other end of the scale, the Pitcairn Islands in the South Pacific can boast only 29 telephones.

The nation with the highest per capita phone ownership is the tiny principality of Monaco, with 825 phones per 1,000 persons, compared with about 670 in the United States. The nation with the lowest per capita phone use is the Himalayan kingdom of Bhutan, with just one phone per 2,000 persons!

New York is far and away the world's top-ranking city in sheer numbers of phones, but the municipality with the most phones per capita is Washington, D.C., with 1,358 phones per 1,000 persons. Incidentally, the state with the least phones per capita is Mississippi, with about 500 phones per 1,000 persons—but the nation ranking second in telephone use, Japan, can claim only 320 phones per 1,000 persons.

Surely, you've often wondered where the world's busiest telephone might be found. Well, at last glance, that honor belongs to a phone in the Greyhound bus terminal in Chicago, whose bell ting-a-lings about 270 times each day!

The word *phony*, by the way, may or may not owe something to Bell's invention. A New York paper once reported that "phony implies that a thing so qualified has no more substance than a telephone talk with a supposititious friend." But most dictionaries trace the word to the expression *fawney rig*, British slang for a valueless ring.

The first commercial transatlantic telephone service was inaugurated between New York and London in 1927—with a charge of $75 for the first three minutes—but the first round-the-world telephone conversation did not take place until 1935. Round the world? Well, the call was placed in New York, routed via San Francisco, Java, Amsterdam, and London, and received in an office only 50 feet from the caller's!

Not surprisingly, there was only one person in the world capable of such telephone extravagance—the president of the American Telephone & Telegraph Corporation.

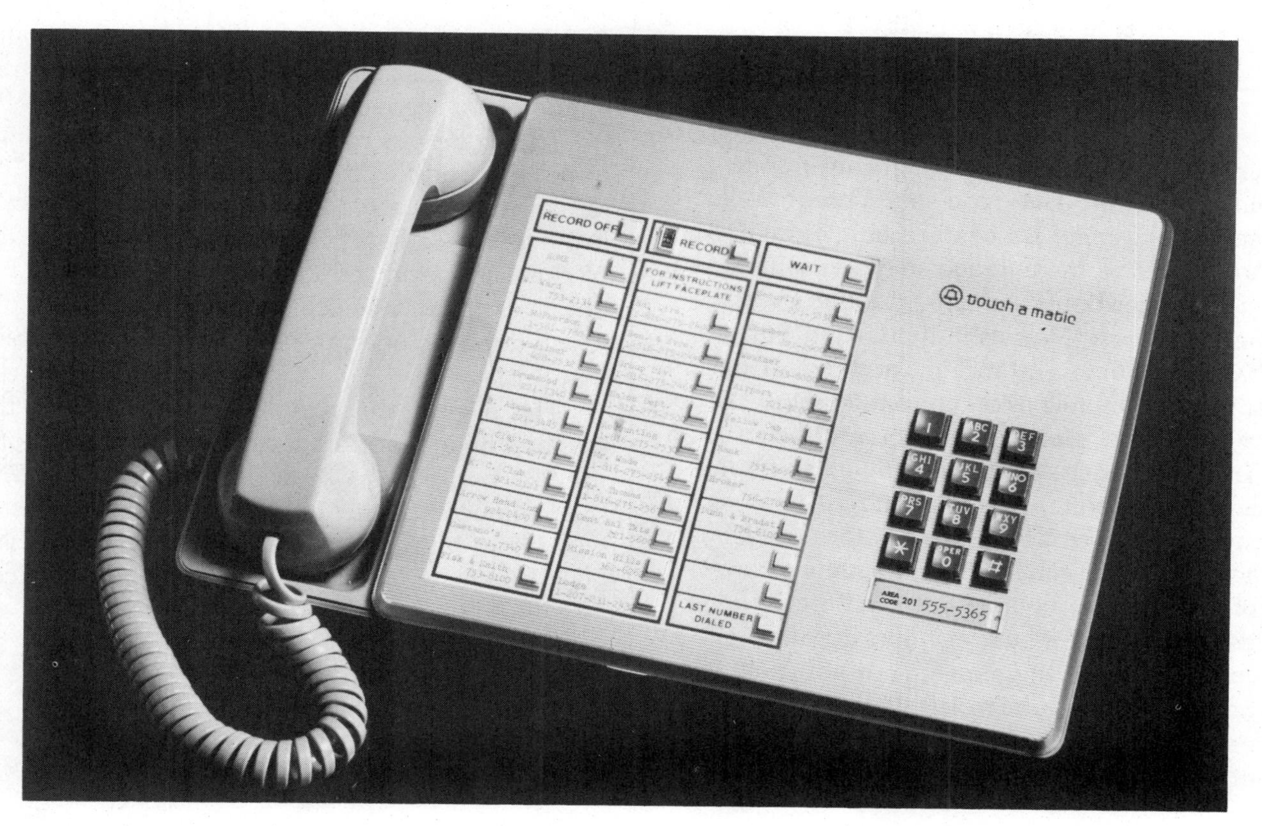

The latest word in telephones is the single-level Touch-a-matic telephone with Touch-Tone dialing.

TELEVISION

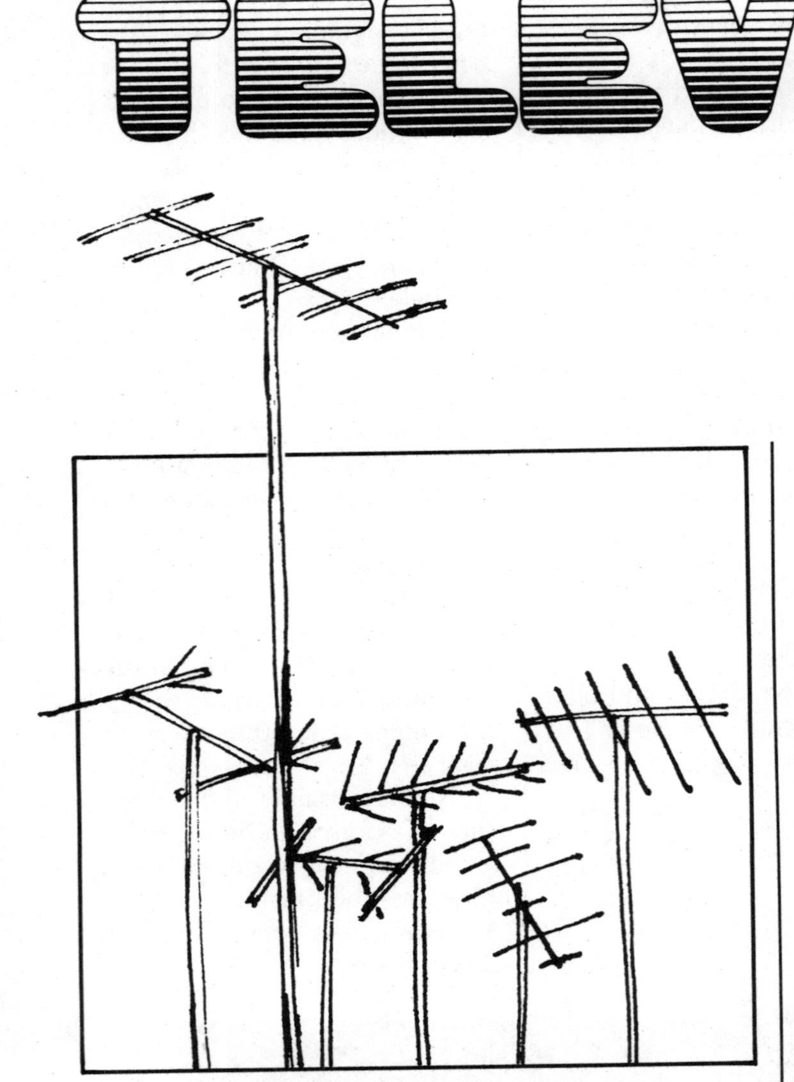

Would you care to venture a guess as to the number of hours per day the average American spends watching television? Two, you say? Three? Well, hold on to your chair: it's been reliably estimated that Americans on the average spend an outlandish six-and-a-quarter hours a day before the TV set!

There are more TV sets in the United States than bathtubs, some 120 million, and the 71 million homes reached by television constitute about 98 percent of the nation. But six-and-a-quarter hours a day? True, that figure is heavily influenced by the thousands of children and senior citizens who spend as many as 10 or 12 hours a day before the tube, and the majority of Americans certainly watch television for less than six hours a day. But the fact remains that six-and-a-quarter hours constitutes about one-quarter of the day—and if you subtract eight hours for sleep, you're left with the preposterous statistic that the average American spends 40 percent of his waking hours in front of the television set!

Of the thousands of hours you yourself have undoubtedly passed mesmerized by your TV screen, how much time have you spent wondering how that ubiquitous little box actually works? While almost all Americans watch TV, few of us are familiar with the complex electronic processes that bring the world into the living room.

Television is possible because of our visual sense persistence. When you watch TV, you're actually looking at a rapidly changing pattern of dots, with only one dot among thousands illuminated at any one time. But the brain retains the impression of illumination for about one tenth of a second after the light is removed. The eye is unaware that the picture is being assembled piecemeal in dots, and the whole surface of the viewing screen appears continuously illuminated. This pattern of dots changes much faster than once every tenth of a second—about four million individual details of an image are transmitted every second!

The entire process that translates a visual image to the electronic light pattern you see on your TV screen is rather complicated, but basically it works like this: the camera focuses the image onto a layer of chemicals arranged in about 350,000 dots. Each dot gives off an electrical charge, the strength of which depends upon the amount of light reaching that dot.

This mosaic of varying electrical charges is then scanned by a beam of electrons that moves along the 525 horizontal rows of dots, row by row. The scanning beam is trained first over each odd-numbered line, from top to bottom, then over each even-numbered line. This alternating process, called

All parts of everything we look at are seen by the eyes instantaneously. If the house shown above is being televised, each tiny detail of the image focussed on the "retina" or screen of the television camera must be dealt with separately in order to transmit the complete view.

The picture of the house above is shown here as being composed of 3,072 squares representing, on a very large scale, the myriads of photo-sensitive modules which are scanned by the electron gun of the television camera. The tones of the squares give a rough idea of how a televised scene is built up piecemeal.

interlacing, eliminates the flicker that would result if each line were scanned in order. The electron gun is quick, moving over all 525 horizontal lines 30 times each second!

The pattern of electrical impulses read by the scanner is eventually transmitted and reassembled in

The average American spends 40 percent of his waking hours in front of the television set.

the individual television set. Now the process is reversed: an electron gun shoots the video signal at the screen in a pattern of 525 horizontal rows of dots. Here's where visual sense persistence comes in—you see neither the lines nor the dots, but only the reassembled image.

Color television systems work basically the same way. The color image is scanned by three electron guns, one for each of the three primary colors.

Generally, there's an intermediate step between the camera and the transmitter: videotape recording. With a "live" show, the electrical impulse pattern is transmitted directly to the home receiver; with videotape, the pattern is first recorded on magnetic tape that can be edited and broadcast at a later date. Originally, much of television broadcasting was "live." Now, a "live" broadcast is virtually nonexistent except for news and special events.

Many of the television programs you watch today are film transfers. The original scene was recorded on film with a movie camera, edited, and then transferred to electronic tape for television transmission. Most television commercials, movies, and adventure, Western, police, and drama shows are shot on film, while news broadcasts, soap operas, and situation comedies are usually recorded directly on videotape. That's why the half-hour sitcom has a different "look" from, say, the hour-long police program.

Most of the technology we've just described has been perfected only in the past 20 years, but electronic media research is more than a hundred years old. In 1873, an Irish radio operator's accidental discovery of the light-sensitive properties of selenium first suggested that visual images could be translated into electrical impulses. George Carey of Boston proposed the idea of image transmission as early as 1875, and the concept of scanning we've described was first put forth in the 1880s by a number of inventors.

The first complete television system was patented in 1884 by Paul Nipkow, but Nipkow's invention was a far cry from the modern medium, employing a perforated disk for scanning. The perforations were arranged in spiral form and moved over the image as the disk rotated.

In 1911, A.A. Campbell-Swinton outlined a television system that is essentially the basis of modern TV. A lack of satisfactory amplifiers and other equipment kept the system an idea only, until the 1920s when V.K. Zworykin invented an electronic TV camera tube, called the iconoscope, that made practical picture transmission a reality. In 1926, J.L. Baird of England gave the first demonstration of true television—electrically transmitted moving pictures. The first person to appear on TV, by the way, was one William Tayton, an office boy in the building where Baird carried out his experiments. The youth was paid one crown (about 60¢) for his troubles.

Baird's scanning system moved over only 30 horizontal rows of dots, producing a flickering, silhouetted image. Television technologists quickly realized that for a satisfactory picture, any television system must reduce an image to at least 300 lines. It was 1932 before the RCA Corporation demonstrated the first all-electronic TV system, with 343 horizontal scanning lines.

In 1927, incidentally, the *New York Times* reported with front-page headlines the first public demonstration of long-distance TV transmission, commenting that the image was "like a photo come to life"—but adding that the "medium's commercial use is in doubt."

A regular broadcasting service was begun in Germany in 1935, with a low-definition picture, but the German transmitter burned out in less than five months. The first high-definition broadcasting service began in England the following year, with an interlaced scanning system of 405 lines. At the time, there were but 100 sets in the entire nation.

This 405-line system remained in use in England until 1964, when the 625-line international standard was adopted. Even today, European and American televisions operate with different scanning systems, the Europeans using the 625-line system, the Americans retaining a 525-line system.

Regular television broadcasting began in the United States in 1941, but wartime restrictions on the manufacture of TV receivers limited growth until 1946. When the lid came off, the rush to television was unstoppable. By 1949, there were a million television sets in use in America; by 1951, the figure had grown to 10 million; and by 1959, to 50 million.

Today, there are an estimated 363 million television sets in use throughout the world, with the United States the leader by far with 120 million sets. The Soviet Union can boast about 50 million receivers, Japan 25 million, and England 18 million—but there are still some countries, mainly in Africa, that have no television at all.

OPPOSITE:
Television apparatus of 1955.

To date, the record charge ever levied on an advertiser was $250,000 per minute, during the 1974 broadcast of the movie *The Godfather.*

Color television was not an afterthought—color technology progressed hand in hand with black-and-white during the early years of TV research. A German patented a color TV process as long ago as 1904, but the first practical demonstration of color transmission was the work of J.L. Baird in 1928. The British scientist used a Nipkow disk for his system, with one spiral of perforations for each of the three primary colors.

In 1929, H.E. Ives and others at the Bell Telephone Laboratories transmitted a 50-line color TV image between New York and Washington, D.C., using a mechanical scanning system with a separate channel for each of the primary colors. Among the objects shown in the first color broadcast were, prosaically enough, a watermelon, a bouquet of roses, and an American flag.

The Columbia Broadcasting System experimented with color broadcasting prior to World War II, but met with little success since their color programs could not be viewed on an ordinary black-and-white set. Then in 1953, the National Television Systems Committee designed a color TV system that was the first to tackle the problem of compatability. The NTSC system combined two image transmissions, one providing the TV receiver with brightness information, the other providing color information. Black-and-white sets could read only the brightness information, color sets could read both transmissions. Now color broadcasts could be viewed on every set.

Color televison took off in America in the 1960s, the number of color sets soaring from 200,000 in 1960 to about 57 million in 1977—about half of all sets. In the rest of the world, color TV is still a rarity, constituting fewer than 10 percent of all sets in most countries.

American television broadcasting today is dominated by the three major television networks. A network is a union of affiliated stations under the umbrella of a parent corporation—the networks do not own their stations. By law, each network is permitted only five owned-and-operated stations—called O & O's in the jargon of the trade. All other stations are merely individually owned affiliates. In each market area, there's likely to be one affiliate for each of the three networks, plus one or more independent, non-affiliated stations, and perhaps a Public Broadcasting Service station.

The groundwork for the first broadcasting network was laid by David Sarnoff, who in 1925 formed a network of radio stations that eventually became the National Broadcasting Company (NBC). Network radio quickly became so successful that the company was forced to split into two component networks, called the Blue and the Red after the colored lines that NBC engineers used to trace the separate network coverages on a map.

A third network grew out of an affiliation of radio stations called United Independent Broadcasters, formed in 1927, and later renamed the Columbia Broadcasting System after the Columbia Phonograph Company, a heavy advertiser on the network's early shows. The CBS network was barely off the ground, and floundering, when 26-year-old William Paley convinced his father and other owners of the Congress Cigar Company to purchase the ailing network. Paley moved to New York with only 16 employees, but he quickly built a broadcasting empire. By 1928, CBS had 53 affiliated radio stations. In 1930, CBS made over seven million dollars in sales—still peanuts compared to the profits of the older NBC.

In 1941, the Federal government forced NBC to divest itself of one of its two component networks. The Blue Network was sold in 1943 to Edward Noble of Lifesaver candy fame, and became the American Broadcasting Corporation—ABC. The network that Noble purchased for eight million dollars now boasts an annual TV advertising volume of well over a half-billion dollars!

A fourth television broadcasting network may be in the works. The prime movers behind the proposed network are the major advertising companies, who are finding it increasingly difficult to buy the time they need for television advertising—there's simply more demand for commercial minutes than there are minutes available! A fourth network, the advertisers say, would accommodate some of the overflow demand for prime-time minutes—and drive down the skyrocketing cost of all TV advertising.

How much does a minute of television advertising cost? That depends on the number of people who'll be watching the station at the time the commercial is aired. Advertisers pay according to CPM, or cost per thousand—they pay a certain amount of money for each one thousand viewers. Thus, advertising rates may vary from just a few hundred dollars for a late night spot on an independent station to over $100,000 for a prime-time network show. To date, the record charge ever levied on an advertiser was $250,000 per minute, during the 1974 broadcast of the movie *The Godfather*.

All told, advertisers now spend some five billion dollars a year on TV commercials. The Proctor & Gamble Company is the single leading TV advertiser, with a $261 million volume in 1975—almost twice the amount spent by its nearest rival, the General Foods Corporation.

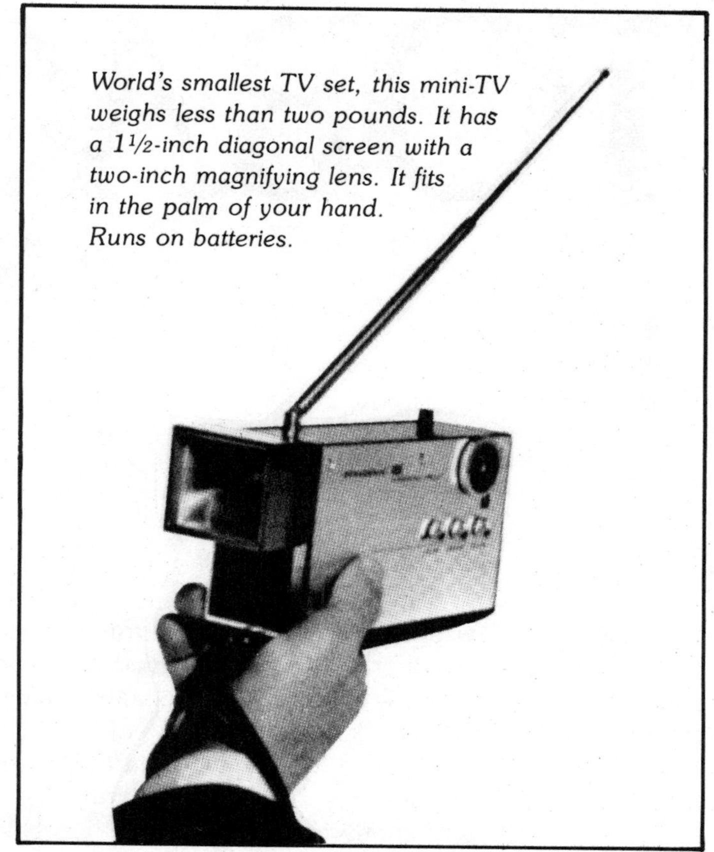

World's smallest TV set, this mini-TV weighs less than two pounds. It has a 1½-inch diagonal screen with a two-inch magnifying lens. It fits in the palm of your hand. Runs on batteries.

How do advertising agencies and television networks determine how many people are watching a given show? Ratings, of course. An independent firm called the A.C. Nielsen Company monitors TV viewing and assigns each show a rating. A rating of, let's say, 21.0 means that the program was viewed by 21 percent of all households available to watch the show. In prime time, that would translate to about 15 million households, or 33 million viewers. Let's see—at a CPM of four dollars, that's $60,000 per commercial spot!

The Neilsen ratings are determined by a continuing survey of about 1,170 homes, with viewing habits monitored by small black boxes attached to the set in each home. The poll can hardly be termed democratic: the 1,170 monitored sets constitute only .0016 percent of all television households in the United States; yet almost everything you see on the tube is influenced in some way by the viewing habits of those chosen few. As some television executives wryly note, never in history have so few influenced so many.

TOBACCO

"The pipe draws wisdom from the lips of the philosopher, and shuts up the mouth of the foolish," wrote W.M. Thackeray a hundred years ago; and to this day, pipe smoking retains a certain connotation of sophistication. The hoi polloi may take their tobacco by cigarette or cigar, but a true connoisseur of the brown leaf wouldn't think of any means of fumigation aside from the pipe. Perhaps the veneration of pipe smoking stems partly from its long popularity, for centuries in Europe, the pipe was virtually the only means of tobacco smoking.

The common myth about the introduction of tobacco in Europe credits Sir Walter Raleigh with bringing the leaf from Virginia to England in the late 16th-century. True, Raleigh's tobacco created an immediate sensation at the court of Elizabeth I, but tobacco smoking actually first came to Europe by quite another means, involving neither the English nor the North American Indian.

Christopher Columbus observed the Indians of the Caribbean smoking tobacco, writing of "men with half-burnt wood in their hands." According to one story, the first European to smoke was Rodrigo de Jerez, one of Columbus's crew members, who sampled tobacco in the West Indies and brought a pinch home with him to Spain. Jerez's wife, so the tale goes, later denounced him to the Inquisition as a man who "swallows fire, exhales smoke, and is surely possessed by the devil."

Spanish explorers in Mexico found the Aztecs smoking crushed tobacco leaves in corn husks. Tobacco reached the European continent at least as early as 1558, when a Spanish physician named Francisco Fernandes, sent to the New World by King Philip II to report on its products, brought back some plants and seeds. The following year, Jean Nicot, the French ambassador to Portugal, sent tobacco seeds to the French court of Catherine de Medici. The queen reported that tobacco cured her of crippling headaches, and she immortalized Nicot by proclaiming the new plant *Nicotiana*, a name recognizable in our word for tobacco's most baleful element, nicotine.

Sir Walter Raleigh may not have been the first to introduce tobacco in England. Some historians claim that one John Hawkins brought back the leaf in 1565 after a voyage to Florida. In any case, we know that Sir Walter had a large hand in popularizing tobacco smoking in Europe.

Raleigh sent Sir Francis Drake on an expedition to colonize Roanoke Island, North Carolina, in 1585. When the expedition failed, Drake returned to Europe. He brought some tobacco and smoking implements to Sir Walter, who soon became the most notorious smoker in Renaissance England. A die-hard smoker indeed, Raleigh even "tooke a pipe of tobacco a little before he went to the scaffolde."

By 1600, the "dry drink" was fashionable in much of Europe. Many pipe smokers of the time carried hand-carved tobacco rammers, used to press the shredded leaf into the pipe bowl.

Some of the more ornate rammers doubled as large finger rings. Smokers also had to carry ember tongs to hold the burning embers of juniper wood used to light their pipes.

Cigarettes were little known at the time. It was the beggars of Seville who get credit for creating the first paper-wrapped smokes.

Seventeenth-century doctors prescribed tobacco as a cure-all, fashioning the leaf into pills, plasters, poultices, oils, salts, tinctures, and balms. During the London plague of the 1660s, many people smoked tobacco as a preventive. Even in the later part of the century, doctors continued to prescribe the leaf for such disparate ailments as hiccoughs, imbecility, jaundice, corpulence, syphilis, and "general lousiness,"—for everything except a bad cough.

Some physicians even recommended a tobacco-smoke enema for various ailments. The enema—administered with a device known as the Clyster pipe—was said by one doctor to be "excellent good against colic." And James I of England proclaimed that the Clyster pipe was the only way to take one's tobacco. Well, different smokes for different folks.

It's odd that James would comment favorably on tobacco,

At Myrtle Grove, Sir Walter Raleigh was soothing his mind with the tobacco he had brought from Virginia, when his Irish servant, thinking his master was on fire, dashed water on him.

From the 1850s, tobacco connoisseurs have shopped at the original Philip Morris store on Bond Street, London.

in any form or guise, since the monarch had always been a bitter foe of the leaf. In his *Counter-blast to Tobacco,* James described smoking as "a custom loathsome to the eye, hateful to the nose, harmful to the brain, dangerous to the lungs, and the black stinking fume thereof nearest resembling the horrible Stygian smoke of the pit that is bottomless." And you thought the Surgeon General was harsh on tobacco!

Tobacco cultivation was important in the American colonies from their earliest history. In fact, before the Revolution, tobacco was legal tender in several Southern colonies with large plantations. Virginia enacted a law ordaining that taxes be paid in tobacco. George Washington, you'll remember, was reported to have written from Valley Forge: "If you can't send men, send tobacco."

American cigarette manufacture dates from the Civil War, when Greek and Turkish tobacconists in New York City began hand-rolling expensive imported tobaccos. By that time, the cigarette—from the Spanish *cigarito*—was already the favored tobacco product in some parts of Europe. It wasn't until the 1880s, when natural leaf cigarettes made from domestic tobaccos began to dominate the market and machine-rolled butts first replaced the hand-rolled varieties that cigarettes became affordable by all. Yet cigars and pipes remained more popular until 1920. By the 1950's, cigarettes accounted for over 80 percent of all American tobacco consumption.

In the early days of cigarette manufacture, a factory worker could hand-roll about 18,000 cigarettes per week. Crude machines for cigarette-rolling began to appear in the mid-1870s. In the following decade, the machines replaced hand-rollers almost completely, with one machine doing the job of 50 workers. A modern machine can turn out about 1,500 cigarettes per minute, or 36,000 packs in an eight-hour day.

In 1880, American cigarette production stood at a mere half

billion. By 1895, the figure had soared to four billion. A large increase following World War I pushed the figure up to 124 billion. Another big rise after World War II brought the total to 400 billion. In 1975, cancer not withstanding, American cigarette consumption passed the 600-billion mark for the first time.

Has the increased awareness of the dangers of tobacco smoking lowered cigarette use to any great extent? In 1964, the year of the Surgeon General's first warning regarding smoking, 52 percent of all men of presumed smoking age were regular smokers; by 1976, the figure stood at only 32 percent. But smoking among women showed an increase over the same period, and total consumption has risen since 1971. By 1975, there were an estimated 30 million former-smokers among the ranks of the non-smokers, with some 50 million persons still clinging to the habit.

Despite the Surgeon General's warning—repeated on every pack of American cigarettes—the United States still leads the world in per capita cigarette smoking. In 1973, the average American 15 years of age or older smoked 3,812 cigarettes—that's about a half pack daily for each person, and well over a pack for each smoker. Japan is close behind with 3,270 cigarettes per capita annually, the United Kingdom third with 3,190, and Italy fourth with 2,774. West Germany, Denmark, and Sweden round out the top seven.

Cigarettes today are sold in three basic sizes—regular non-filter, regular filter, and 100-mm. king size—but in the past, butts have been sold in a wide range of sizes. In the 1930s, when cigaettes were taxed individually in some places, to save tax, one manufacturer brought out "Head Plays," each cigarette 11 inches long.

One day, Dr. Creighton, Bishop of London, was riding on a train with a meek curate. The Bishop who ardently loved his tobacco, took out his cigar case, turned to his companion, and said with a smile, "You don't mind my smoking, do you?"

The curate bowed, and answered humbly, "Not if Your Lordship doesn't mind my being sick."

In 1933, a diminutive bellboy named Johnny immortalized Philip Morris cigarettes with his famous "Call for Phil-lip Mor-ress."

Philip Morris's "Marlboro" remains the most popular cigarette on earth, the 136 billion sold annually making the entire world "Marlboro Country."

In the early days of the tobacco industry, as today, manufacturers vied with each other in creating eye-catching advertisements.

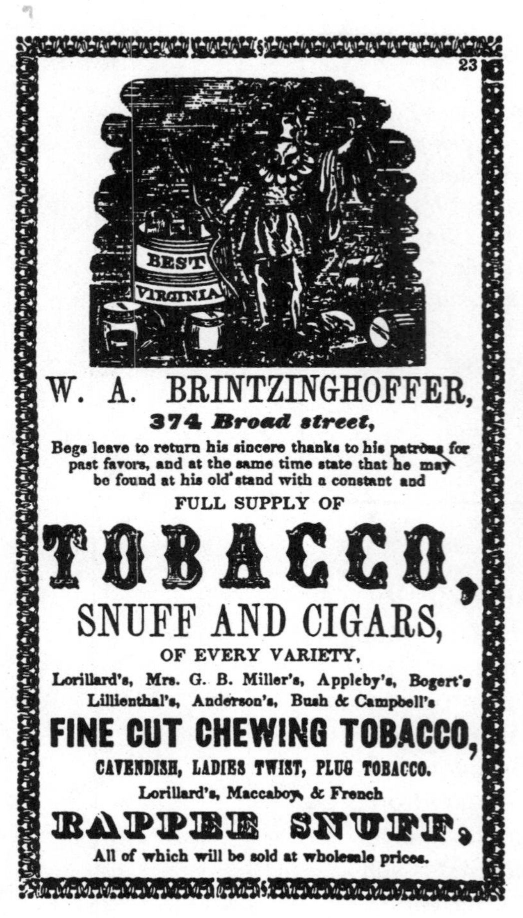

"Lilliput" cigarettes, only one-and-a-quarter inches long, appeared in England in the 1950s. And "English Ovals" are just that—oval in shape instead of round.

Philip Morris's *Marlboro* remains the most popular cigarette on earth, the 136 billion sold annually making the entire world "Marlboro Country."

Long before cigarettes became popular here, the pipe was well entrenched. Pipe smoking was common even among women for a time, and the wives of two American presidents—Andrew Jackson and Zachary Taylor—were wont to light up in the White House. Women pipe smokers are still numerous in China, where cigarettes are rarely encountered outside the major cities.

Speaking of female pipe smokers, perhaps you've heard the one about the young lady who retired to the cafeteria during her coffee break and lit up a pipe. "That's a despicable habit," remarked an elderly woman sitting nearby. "I would rather commit adultery than smoke!"

"So would I," answered the young lady, "but there just isn't enough time during a coffee break."

The first men—or women—to smoke probably managed without any implements at all, simply inhaling smoke billowing from a bonfire of burning leaves. The Greek historian Herodotus reported that certain Scythian tribes "drank smoke" from a fire, inhaling the fumes of what was most likely marijuana.

The first pipe fashioned by man was probably a tube pipe, a simple hollow cylinder of wood or bone. Tube pipes have been found in almost every cranny of civilization, some dating back as far as 200 B.C. And the use of a curled-up leaf as a makeshift tube pipe later led to the invention of the cigar.

In some cultures, the earliest pipe was the "mound pipe," a small mound of earth with a depression hollowed out on top to hold the tobacco, and hollow reeds protruding through the mound as rudimentary pipe stems. To make use of a mound pipe, the smoker had to lie on the ground on his belly and slip the reed through his lips. These primitive pipes were still being used by Indian soldiers in World War I.

The Indians of South America frequently built communal mound pipes, with as many as 150 people gathering around to share a smoke. When the first reed and clay pipes appeared among the Indian tribes, smoking was still regarded as a communal pastime. Thus arose the custom of passing the pipe around among the group.

Europeans exploring America in the 16th-century found some Indians smoking a kind of tube pipe shaped like the letter "Y"—the smoker inserted the two upper prongs of the pipe into his nostrils and aimed the lower tube at a mound of burning leaves. Archaelogists in Africa have found tube pipes made of clay or reed measuring up to six feet long.

Indians of the Central United States carved stone pipes with either straight or curved stems. They smoked a blend they called *kinnikinnik,* made of tobacco, sumac leaves, and the bark of the willow tree. The Indians, who considered tobacco a sacred herb and regarded smoking as a sacred art, frequently shaped their pipe bowls in the form of animals and other totems. Historians have been unable to explain why some pipes found in the ruins of ancient Indian settlements were carved in the form of elephants and sea cows, two creatures the Indians had presumably never seen.

The calumet, or peace pipe, was usually a long, slender pipe with a wooden stem and a shorter stone end-piece containing the bowl. The calumet was considered a token of peace and

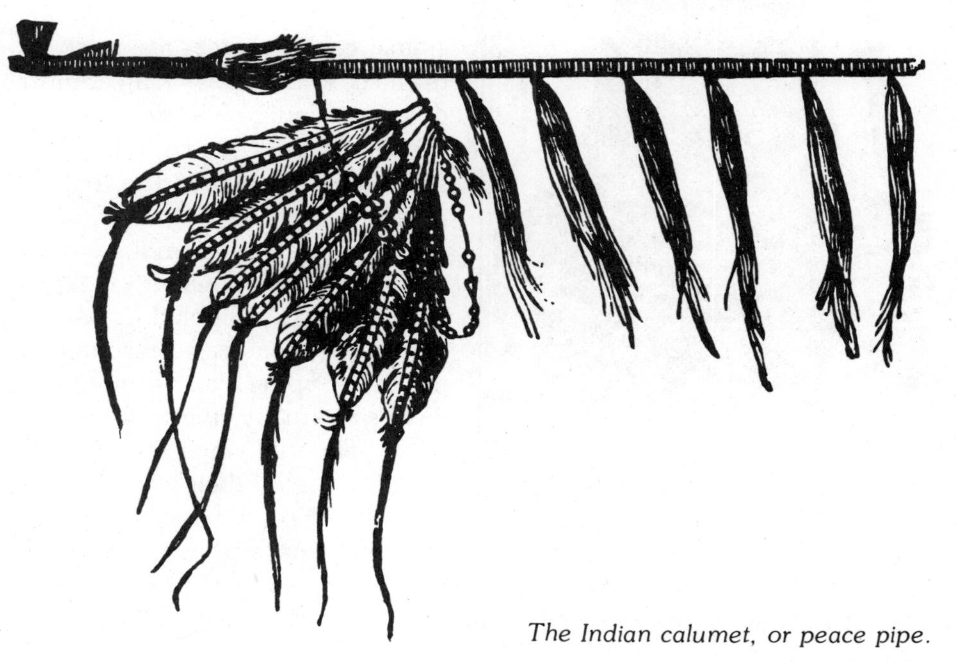

The Indian calumet, or peace pipe.

The hooka, an Oriental water pipe.

friendship, and pioneers exploring the American West often took along calumets in the event they ran into hostile Indians. No instance has ever been recorded of an Indian violating the peace-pipe compact.

Incidentally, the word *tobacco* comes from the Indian word for the tube of the calumet, not from their name for the plant. When East Coast Indians introduced smoking to the Europeans, they presented their pipe and repeated the word *tobacco* to urge the stranger to put the calumet tube in his lips. The Europeans naturally assumed the Indians were referring to the substance they were smoking, and the leaf was forever after known as tobacco.

The water pipe, a popular means of smoking in the Near East for centuries, was probably invented by the Persians for smoking hashish. The earliest water pipes were called *nargeelehs*, from the Arabic word for coconut, since the coconut was used as the base for the first hydro-cooled fumigators. Later, the Arabs fashioned more elaborate pipes from glass crystal.

The *hookah* is a kind of water pipe with a number of flexible stems, called *narbeeshes,* each from six to 30 inches long. British officers in India often employed servants called *burdars,* whose sole duty was to attend to their master's *hookah.*

In a water pipe, smoke is drawn from the bowl into the base, where it is cooled by water vapor and then drawn through the stem. Some Persian men were so partial to the taste of smoke-flavored water that they regularly forced their wives to smoke four or five bowlfuls of tobacco or hashish in succession to produce a well-flavored drink.

The earliest pipes popular in Europe were made from clay. Clay pipes with small bowls were favored in England, the story goes, because in the first days of tobacco smoking the Englishman's desire for the leaf far outpaced the supply; to indulge frequently, then, the Englishman had to content himself with a small pinch at each light-up.

The clay pipe had the distinct disadvantage of heating up rapidly, which might also explain why its bowl was so small. The French, true to form, developed clay-pipe making to a fine art, molding their pipe bowls to depict religious, military, and domestic scenes.

There were two basic types of clay pipe popular in 17th-century England, the cutty and the churchwarden. The small cutty, equipped with a stem of about three inches, was the more popular among the general populace, selling for as little as three for a penny. But the cutty stem was often so short that a pipe took on the nickname of "nose warmer."

The churchwarden was fitted with a stem of some eight to ten inches, and a more decorated bowl. As a rule, the wealthy opted for the churchwarden, and frequently bought elegant cases in which to carry their prize pipes. When the lower classes began smoking churchwardens to emulate the rich, the case was still beyond their means, so many an Englishman took to carrying his long pipe in a hole cut through his hat brim.

Washington Irving, in his *History of New York,* presents a tongue-in-cheek account of Dutch settlers in New Amsterdam who were ardent smokers of the long pipe until their leader, William the Testy, proclaimed smoking illegal. The furious populace refused to obey the edict, so William compromised by permitting smoking only from short-stemmed pipes. But the short pipes brought the bowl so close to the smoker's face that the fumes "befogged the cerebellum, dried up all the kindly moisture of the brain and rendered the people . . . as vaporish and testy as the governor himself."

The Churchwarden pipe, made of clay, has an ultra-long stem to cool the smoke.

The clay pipe is now but a curiosity piece. Only a handful of claypipe artisans remain to satisfy the smoker with a taste for the unusual.

Today, there are basically five kinds of pipe popular throughout the world. Many Alpine people prefer the porcelain pipe, usually fitted with a long, curving stem and two bowls, one for the tobacco and one for the residue of juices. Other smokers prefer cherrywood pipes. The most popular varieties by far are the meerschaum, briar, and corncob.

The odor-free Electra-Pipe reduces tar and nicotine and furnishes a cooler smoke.

Meerschaum is a magnesium silicate compound mined extensively in Asia Minor. The Germans thought the substance in its raw form resembled petrified sea foam, and dubbed it *meerschaum*—literally, "sea foam." Turkish craftsmen today still carve meerschaum pipe bowls by hand, favoring busts of Cleopatra, Bacchus, and other gods and notables.

The briar pipe owes its existence to a French smoker who journeyed to Corsica in the 1820s. Arriving on the island and discovering that his prized meerschaum pipe had been shattered in transit, the Frenchman asked a local artisan to carve a new pipe from the wood of the *bruyere,* or heath tree, which grows extensively on the island. The smoker was so delighted by the finished product that he sent heath wood and roots to France and began manufacturing the *bruyere,* or briar pipe. Today, the briar pipe is the most popular pipe in the world.

The corncob is an American invention. John Schranke, a Dutch immigrant farmer living in Washington, Missouri, first whittled pipes from corncobs as a hobby. In 1869, Schranke brought one of his creations to the shop of a friend, Henry Tibbe. Tibbe improved the pipe by filling in the uneven surfaces with plaster of paris, and then he began to market the pipes. A hundred years later, corncob pipe production stood at around 10 million per year. The president of the largest corncob pipe manufacturer in the world still uses Tibbe's workshop as his headquarters.

Corncob pipes have the overwhelming advantage of being dirt cheap. At the other end of the scale, the most expensive pipe in the world is the Charatan *Summa Cum Laude,* a straight-grain briar-root pipe that sells in the vicinity of $2,500!

But even such an expensive pipe won't guarantee a perfect smoke. To some tobacco connoisseurs, there's only one kind of pipe you can count on, as Henry Brown noted, in 1896, in a poem that begins:

There's clay pipes an' briar pipes
an' meerschaum pipes as well;
There's plain pipes an' fancy
pipes—things just made to sell:
But any pipe that can be bought
for marbles, chalk, or pelf,
Ain't ekal to the flavor of th' pipe
you make yourself.

Toilets

The earliest known indoor plumbing facilities in Europe were found in the palace of Knosses, Crete, which dates from about 2000 B.C.

Through all the films set in days gone by, and all the historical novels purporting to show how our ancestors lived during various eras, one particular element of daily life is forever conspicuous by its absence. You may have wondered, as Ramses, Nero, Sir Lancelot, or Marie Antoinette moved across the screen or page: how and where did they go to the toilet?

In a few areas of technology, civilization has regressed rather than progressed through the ages. Indoor plumbing is one such area. It's true that during some past eras the sanitation facilities of even the wealthiest households were far less convenient than the lowliest of modern American bathrooms. But if we go back far enough in time, we can find plumbing facilities superior to anything in the United States just a century or so ago!

The earliest known indoor plumbing facilities in Europe were found in the palace of Knossos, Crete, which dates from about 2000 B.C. Terra cotta pipes were ingeniously constructed of tapered sections and fitted together, narrow end into wide end, to give the water a shooting motion. One latrine at Knossos with a wooden seat over an earthenware pan evidently had a reservoir and piping for flush water. With a few scattered exceptions, no such sanitary device was to appear in England until the 18th century.

Around the time of Knossos's construction, people in the Indus Valley of present-day Pakistan were enjoying the luxury of indoor latrines flushed with stored water and connected by conduits to street drains. Some of the earthenware pipes and sewers installed in ancient Mesopotamian cities are still in workable order today. In Egypt, aristocrats relished the comfort of limestone seats on their latrines. But the vase positioned below the keyhole-shaped seat opening had to be removed for cleaning quite often.

The Romans were the first to construct water-supply and drainage systems on a large scale. Thirteen aqueducts brought water to the Imperial City from nearby mountains, though contrary to general belief, most of these aqueducts were underground. Of the 220-mile total length of Rome's eight main aqueducts, only 30 miles were constructed above ground. At its peak, the water-supply system of ancient Rome provided about 300 gallons of water per person daily. Today, the London water system provides only about 50 gallons per person each day.

By the fourth century, many private homes in Rome were equipped with flush toilets. Stone reservoirs stored flush water, and drains connected the latrines to outdoor sewers. Some homes found in ruined Pompeii were equipped with as many as 30 water taps. But most of the less fortunate Romans had to content themselves with public latrines, of which there were never more than 144 in the presumably odoriferous capital.

The Romans evidently brought the first flush toilets to England, for fortresses constructed along the Roman-built Hadrian's Wall included bathhouses and latrines with drains. Comfort was still at a premium: one latrine consisted of a 31-foot-long trough covered by wooden seats. Wooden seats were common in England right up to the 18th century, when Dr. Samuel Johnson expressed the view that "the plain board is best."

As the Roman Empire perished, so did plumbing in Europe. Monasteries could boast the best plumbing facilities of the later Middle Ages. Most monasteries included a sanitary wing, known as the *rere-dorter,* that contained all of the monastery's latrines. The schedule of the monk was so tightly regulated that most members of the monastery were required to use the latrine at the same time. Therefore, the rere-dorter was usually quite large—145 feet long at Canterbury.

A rere-dorter usually consisted of a long line of latrines partitioned from their neighbors, each with a seat set against the wall, and often, a window. Flush water was provided by stored rainwater or the waste water from lavatories or baths. A drain under the latrines carried off the waste, although frequently the rere-dorter was built over a diverted stream.

In England, Tintern Abbey employed the rising tide of the nearby Severn River to flush out its latrines. At Redburn Abbey, a private latrine for the Abbot was constructed after monks complained that they were "ashamed when they had to go to the necessary in his presence." At the abbey at St. Albans, latrines were positioned over a 25-foot ditch that, hundreds of years later, still contained some of the buckthorn seeds the monks used as a laxative. Also found in the ditch were pieces of cloth torn from old gowns that the monks used for toilet paper.

Chaise Percée. Unquestionably the snazziest john extant. Designed to fit over a water closet, this hand-carved, wooden cane seat, with cane back and cane sides, is finished in antique white and gold. This contraption is patterned after the chaise percée used by the French kings.

The first toilet paper manufactured in the United States, incidentally, was unbleached pearl-colored manilla hemp paper made in 1857 by a New Yorker named Joseph Gayetty. Gayetty's name was watermarked on each sheet. The paper, which sold for 50¢ per 500 sheets, was called "Gayetty's Medicated Paper," and billed as a "perfectly pure article for the toilet and for the prevention of piles."

Medieval monks usually referred to the latrine with the euphemism *necessarium.* But the most common name for the privy during the Middle Ages was *garderobe,* or "wardrobe," a term euphemistically comparable to the modern *rest room, water closet, comfort station,* or *john.*

The word *john* probably comes from an older term for the latrine, *jakes,* which in turn may be derived from the common French name Jacques. The word *privy,* of course, comes from "private." A score of jokes to the contrary, the latrine has absolutely nothing to do with the English position of Privy Councilor. Even our word *toilet* is a euphemism, adapted from the French *toilette,* a woman's dressing table or room, in turn derived from *toile,* a kind of cloth.

Garderobes were usually set within the thick stone walls of medieval castles, or in niches in turrets or buttresses. Each garderobe contained a wooden or stone seat, with either a shaft underneath to carry away the waste, or a pit that had to be cleaned out from time to time. Frequently, garderobes were mounted one above another on each floor of the castle, as is customary in modern apartment buildings. The drainage shafts usually emptied directly into the moat. Originally defensive, the moats must have quickly become rather offensive. Before you scoff, you might remember that even today most American cities channel their raw sewage directly into the nearest body of water.

A modern visitor to a medieval castle might find the garderobes rather cold, bleak places to spend one's precious time. Actually, many garderobes were quite cozy. Some were positioned beside chimney shafts to provide warmth, with wood paneling, matting, or papered walls, and even bookshelves! St. Gregory highly recommended the latrine as a place for reading and serious thought.

As the castle gave way to the city, public latrines began to appear over urban streams and watercourses. Like the moats performing similar duty, these watercourses quickly became foul-smelling cesspools. As early as 1307, the River Fleet in London was inaccessible to ships due to the accumulation of filth. During the 14th century, the London street Sherborne Lane became known as Shiteburn Lane in tribute to the pungent watercourse to which it ran parallel. Frequently, latrines were attached to the second or third story of a house, overhanging a street or alley. Streets and watercourses had to be cleaned out periodically by specialists known as *gongfermors.*

The London Bridge, which at the time carried over a hundred homes, could boast just one privy. Most bridge dwellers, therefore, opted for a more direct route to the River Thames, leading to a popular definition of London Bridge as a structure "wise men go over and fools go under."

Leonardo da Vinci designed a latrine with a flush toilet, ventilation shaft, and even a door that would close automatically in the event that the previous user was negligent. In 1499, a London man built a water closet with a flushing mechanism. But Leonardo's suggestions went unheeded, and the early water closet went unnoticed, resulting in a few more centuries of unnecessary olfactory offense.

During the 16th century, the garderobe was replaced by the *close stool,* a portable, lidded box. The user flipped the lid, sat down on the open seat, and made a contribution to a removable pot inside the box. European noblemen often had their close stools decorated with ribbons and gilt nails, and more importantly, velvet-padded seats. Some were even fitted with lockable lids to guard against unauthorized usage.

Of course, the close stool did not solve the problem of what to do with the collected waste. As cities continued to grow during the 17th and early 18th centuries, open fields and yards for dumping vanished. For the most part, close stool pots had to be emptied out the window. City residents customarily emptied their pots in the evening, shouting out "gardy-loo," a corruption of the French *gardez l'eau,* "watch the water," to warn passersby below. Since the streets were not cleaned until morning, a walk at night could be treacherous for more than one reason.

One enterprising Scot of the era may have invented the world's first pay toilet when he carried around a bucket and shielding cloth for any fastidious pedestrian who would not condescend to relieve himself in the nearest alleyway. Temporary rental of the bucket and cloth would set you back a mere halfpenny.

Members of royal households enjoyed considerably better accommodations. French monarch Louis XIV made use of a comfortable, highly decorated close stool euphemistically known as a *chaise percée* (open chair), *chaise d'affaires,* or *chaise necessaire.* His palace at Versailles at one time included 264 stools, but Louis' favorite was a black lacquered box with inlaid mother-of-pearl borders, a red lacquered interior, and a padded seat of green velour. The monarch's *chaise percée* sometimes served as a throne, and it was considered a high honor to be granted an audience with His Majesty while he was heeding the call of nature that all men, rich and poor, are similarly obliged to answer.

During the early 18th century, Europeans apparently became more self-conscious of their sanitary habits, for close stools began to appear hidden away inside pieces of furniture. A common custom of the time was to cover the lid of a close stool with a pile of dummy books. To correctly identify the apparatus they shielded, the dummy books always bore the title of *Voyage au Pays Bas* or *Mysteres de Paris. Journey to the Low Country* makes some sense—but *Mysteries of Paris?* The period may also have seen the first appearance of the "Men's" and "Ladies'" rooms. The host of a 1739 Parisian ball had the words inscribed on latrine doors to designate the sex for which each was reserved.

The *bidet,* that peculiarly Gallic instrument for feminine hygiene, also made its first appearance during the early 18th century. The device, first mentioned in 1710, must have been unfamiliar to many Frenchmen in 1739, when a dealer offered a bidet as a "porcelain violin-case with four legs." By 1750, portable metal bidets with removable legs were commonly secreted inside pieces of furniture.

Today, bidets are prominently displayed in almost all French hotels, and in many hotels in Italy, Greece, and Spain as well, though the device is rarely seen in any but the finest English or American hotels. The Ritz Carlton Hotel in New York was originally equipped with bidets, but the hotel was forced to remove them after a flood of complaints from outraged puritanical guests.

It was late in the 18th century that the water closet, or W.C., began to appear in Europe. Developed mainly by Englishmen Alexander Cummings and Joseph Bramah, the earliest W.C.'s consisted of a stool with an attached handle. When the handle was pulled, water from a reservoir mounted above the stool was channeled into the bowl, while a plug was opened to drain the latrine. Oddly enough, the English patent office had been opened for 158 years before it received its first application for a water closet patent, that of Cummings in 1775—almost 300 years after an unnamed genius built the first London W.C.

Early water closets were far from perfect, however, and the drains that carried waste to the sewer or cesspit frequently filled with muck that might remain undisturbed for up to 20 years. When the stench became unbearable, it was time to summon the *night men,* the descendants of the earlier gongfermors and the ancestors of the modern plumber.

Portable toilet in current use by campers. This contraption folds compactly, and uses disposable plastic bags.

By 1815, water closets were in general use in fashionable English homes. But the poor still had to content themselves with public privies, which were sorely lacking in both quality and quantity—many blocks had but one privy. At night, most people had to make use of the chamber pot, called *jerry pot* in England. The jerry was descended from the medieval *orignal,* a wide-mouthed vase usually kept at the foot of the bed so that those in need might relieve themselves without surrendering the warmth of their blankets.

Nineteenth-century jerries often bore humorous drawings or poems, both inside and outside. Popular thunder-mug ditties included this gem:

Use me well and keep me clean,
And I'll not tell what I have seen.

One jerry-maker with a sense of humor devised a pot with a concealed music box that chimed into song when the pot was lifted.

"Carriage pots" were often placed under the seats of carriages for those in too much of a hurry to duck into the bushes. A woman could lift the seat cushion, then sit down on the open board below, and shielded by her wide hoop skirt, relieve herself in broad daylight as her coach rattled through a crowded city street.

In case you were wondering, "jerry-built" most likely has nothing to do with the jerry. The term, which means cheaply, shabbily constructed, is usually traced to either the city of Jericho, jelly, the French word *jour* (day), or a presumably disreputable Liverpool contracting firm known as Jerry Brothers. But it may be related to the gypsy term for excrement.

By the mid-19th century, the waste deposited in privies, water closets, and jerries still found its way to the nearest cesspit or stream, a practice that was both odious to the nose and dangerous to the health of the populace. It wasn't until the 1860s, when a cholera outbreak in England was traced to poor sanitary facilities, that modern drainage systems began to appear in English cities. Around that time, London's most offensive stream, the already bridged-over Fleet Ditch, was finally recognized for what it had become—a sewer—and replaced with a large sewer main.

In 1889, D.T. Bostel of Brighton invented the washdown water closet, the basic prototype of the modern toilet. In the washdown W.C., a tube attached to an overhead reservoir sprayed water over the sides of the bowl after each use. An S-shaped drain allowed clean water from the last flush to remain in the bottom of the bowl between uses.

In 1889, D.T. Bostel of Brighton invented the washdown water closet, the basic prototype of the modern toilet.

By the 1890s, water closets for the most part resembled rather elaborate versions of the modern toilet. Some bowls were hidden by sinks that could be swung away when the bowl was needed. Other bowls were placed inside chairs, or fitted with elaborately styled supports in the shape of lions and other animals.

By the way, you can still buy a similar chair to conceal your home's least savory accoutrement. For about $550, a New York firm will send the man or woman who has everything a hand-carved caned seat to fit over a toilet bowl.

People in some Oriental countries prefer to squat over a simple hole in the floor, fitted with a drain, of course. In many parts of the world the outhouse or public privy are still the rule, but in most developed nations the trusty flush toilet bowl is the device found in almost all bathrooms. Toilet bowls are made of white glazed stoneware, glazed porcelain, or vitreous china, with or without a reservoir. A toilet with a reservoir employs a float to shut off the entering water when the reservoir is filled. Toilets without reservoirs draw their water directly from the water-supply pipes, and can be flushed again and again without waiting for the reservoir to fill up—an advantage that has made this kind of toilet unpopular among water-supply officials in some cities. Although the overhead reservoir has virtually disappeared in new American homes, we still call the handle on a modern toilet a "chain" in memory of its dangling predecessor.

Among the many names now applied to the toilet, *pissoir* and *crapper* are probably considered two of the more vulgar. Actually, *pissoir* is the accepted term for the enclosed public urinals that still appear on the sidewalks of Paris and other French cities. And the term *crapper* is derived, in the most curiously coincidental linking of an inventor with his invention, from Thomas Crapper, a 19th-century English sanitary engineer.

At the tender age of 11, Crapper left his home in Thorne, Yorkshire, and walked 165 miles to London, where he began work as a plumber's assistant. In 1861, he founded his own sanitation business. On the strength of a number of Crapper's inventions, the firm was soon installing the world's most advanced W.C.'s in English homes.

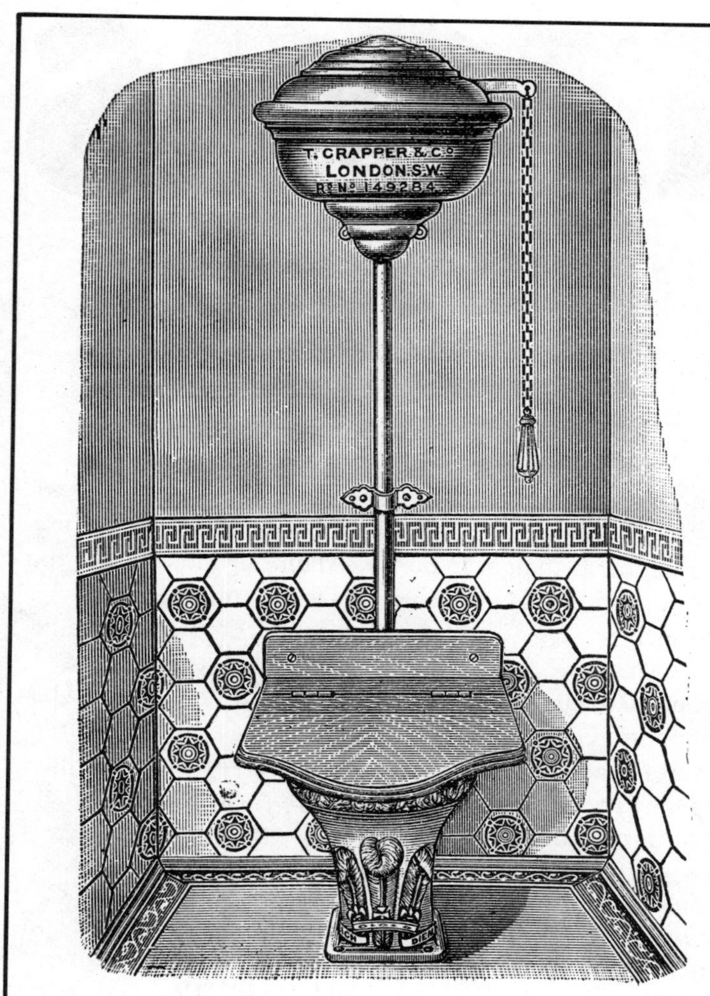

CRAPPER'S

Improved

Registered Ornamental

Flush-down W.C.

With New Design Cast-iron Syphon Water Waste Preventer.

No 518.

Improved Ornamental Flush-down W.C. Basin (Registered No. 145,823), Polished Mahogany Seat with flap, New Pattern 3-gallon Cast-iron Syphon Cistern (Rd. No. 149,284), Brass Flushing Pipe and Clips, and Pendant Pull, complete as shown £6 15 0

The original crapper.

Crapper's major innovation was a mechanism that shut off the flow of clean water when the reservoir was filled. Previously, the supply of clean water had to be turned on and off by the user, and many fastidious Victorians preferred to leave the water running continually to assure cleanliness.

In Crapper's W.C., the user pulled the chain to raise a plate inside the reservoir that propelled water up a tube and into the pipe leading to the bowl. As the water level in the reservoir went down, a float sank until it opened the attached intake valve. The same float closed the valve when the reservoir was filled again. Since the clean water valve could not open unless the chain was pulled, the saving of water with Crapper's W.C. was considerable.

The ingenious sanitary engineer advertised his product as "Crapper's Valveless Waste Preventer—Certain Flush with Easy Pull," although individual models later took on such names as Deluge, Cascade, and Niagara. In the 1880s, Crapper's firm installed the sanitary facilities in Queen Victoria's Sandringham House—including 30 toilets and a bathroom with side-by-side sinks labelled *Head & Face, Hands,* and *Teeth*. Expensive cedar wood was used for the toilet seats, since the wood, in the words of a Crapper official, "has the advantage of being warm . . . and subtlety aromatic."

The term *crapper,* little used in England, was introduced to the American idiom by GI's returning from World War I who found Thomas Crapper's name emblazoned on many English toilets. To those who remain skeptical, we might point out that the firm of "Thomas Crapper & Co., Merchants of Sanitary Equipment," has achieved four royal warrants, and operates "By Appointment to Her Majesty the Queen."

TOMATOES

The tomato is now such an integral part of many southern European cuisines, especially Italian and Spanish, that you'd surely surmise that the plant is a native of Mediterranean parts. But spaghetti sauce and Spanish omelette notwithstanding, the tomato was unknown in Europe until the 16th century—the fruit is actually indigenous to South and Central America.

Spanish explorers in the New World found the Mayans cultivating a plant they called *tomatl,* and brought back some seeds to Europe for experimentation. Tomatoes, it was found, would grow well in Iberia. At first, the Spanish didn't quite know what to do with them—the tomato was considered too tart to be enjoyed as a fruit. But an adventurous chef at the Spanish court combined tomatoes with olive oil and onions for Europe's first tomato sauce, creating a culinary sensation at the royal dinner table.

The English were at first skeptical of the new fruit—or is it a vegetable? A Briton named Gerard tasted the tomato during a visit to Spain in the 1590s and remained unimpressed. "In Spain and those hot regions," he wrote, "they eat the Apples of Love prepared and boiled with pepper, salt, and oyle; but they yield very little nourishment to the body . . . Likewise, they eat the Apples with oyle, vinegre, and pepper mixed together for sauce to their meat, even as we in these cold countries doe Mustard."

Well, it seems that the mustard-catsup controversey has rather ancient roots. Gerard brought some tomato seeds back to England for his garden, but found the plant "of ranke and stinking savour."

"Apples of Love?" Yes, that's what the tomato was called for hundreds of years after its introduction in Europe. The origin of the term is uncertain, but one doubtful tale suggests that Sir Walter Raleigh dubbed it thus when he presented a tomato plant to Queen Elizabeth and affectionately told her his gift was an "apple of love." Another story has it that love apple, or *pomme d'amour* in French, is derived from the Italian *pomo di mori*—"apple of the Moors," since Italians at the time called the Spanish *Mori.* And claims have been heard for the erstwhile belief that tomatoes, along with vanilla, cocoa, and many other New World novelties, were aphrodisiacs.

The French were introduced to the tomato via Spain, but the *pomme d'amour* didn't enter the classic cuisine until the 19th century, when Empress Eugenie brought Spanish dishes to the French court. In Italy, meanwhile, the plant made its first appearance around 1544, and quickly became a popular farm product in the southern regions.

Italy now produces some three-and-a-half million tons of tomatoes annually for home consumption and export throughout the world. Spain, Portugal, and Greece have become major exporters of the tomato as well.

Oddly enough, even while the tomato was being widely cultivated and eaten in southern Europe, many people in England and northern Europe considered the raw fruit poisonous until the early 19th century, and cultivated the tomato chiefly as a decorative plant. Though the tomato is a New World native, most Americans shied away from the presumably poisonous plant until Robert Gibbon Johnson stood on the steps of the Salem, New Jersey courthouse in 1830, and dared to eat a raw red tomato. Onlookers were horrified, and fully expected Johnson to die before the next morning!

Johnson did not, of course, suffer death by tomato; and by

1860, the plant was accepted by most Americans as versatile, delicious—and safe. By 1900, the tomato was a major farm crop in the United States. Today, tomato production tops the 40-million bushel mark each year. But that's not enough for the American appetite—another three or four million bushels are imported each year from Mexico and Europe.

The tomato is vine-ripened in warmer climes, but grown almost exclusively in hothouses in England, northern Europe, and some parts of the United States. The plant requires strong, steady sunshine. Hothouse tomatoes are usually picked when fully grown—but still green—and placed in cartons for the ride to market. Many American carton tomatoes are sprayed with dye to provide them with a "real" tomato color; but these carton tomatoes are, not surprisingly, far inferior to the vine-ripened variety in both flavor and nutritive value.

The "love apple" has become one of our most versatile plant foods, eaten raw, pickled, cooked, or pureed, and made into soups, sauces, pastes, preserves, juices, and dehydrated flakes. Tomato juice—the major weapon in the arsenal of many anti-hangover potions—was virtually unknown in America until 1929, when the first 230,000 cases were canned. Today, we gulp down some 35 million cases of juice each year.

And let's not forget catsup. The ubiquitous red condiment reportedly was based on an Oriental invention, called "kay-chup" in Malay, and was enjoyed in England for some 100 years before becoming popular in the United States. Some dictionaries, incidentally, will accept not only "catsup" and "ketchup," but "catchup" as well. The H.J. Heinz Company of Pittsburgh, packers of pickles and horseradish, began marketing their catsup in 1876. The Heinz name soon became virtually synonymous with the condiment—despite a reputed 56 other varieties of product.

There is no standard formula for ketchup, but most are made from various combinations of tomato pulp, sugar, salt, vinegar, spices, and sometimes, mustard. The U.S. Food and Drug Administration merely stipulates what optional ingredients may be added, and the maximum amounts of sugar and preservatives allowed.

The largest tomato on record, a proud 1974 product of the British Isles, tipped the scales at a whopping four-and-a-half pounds—that's a lot of catsup!

Let's settle once and for all that oft-echoed query: is the tomato a fruit or a vegetable? The question is difficult to answer. Botanically, the tomato is a fruit, the seed-bearing berry of the *Lycopersicon esculentum*. But in the United States, the tomato is classified as a vegetable for trade purposes, since it is most often eaten *with* the meal, rather than *after* it. In short, the "fruit" is used as a "vegetable." But to further cloud the issue, a U.S. ruling dating from 1893 defines the tomato as a fruit when it is eaten out of the hand or as an appetizer. Legally, then, the tomato in the juice you sip before dinner is a fruit, and the tomato in the salad that follows is a vegetable!

And one more thing: do you say "tom-A-to" or "tom-AH-to?"

Though the tomato is a New World native, most Americans shied away from the presumably poisonous plant until Robert Gibbon Johnson stood on the steps of the Salem, New Jersey courthouse in 1830, and dared to eat a raw red tomato. Onlookers were horrified, and fully expected Johnson to die before the next morning.

Toothpaste

Americans presently consume over one billion tubes of toothpaste each year, each tube a product of the very latest refinements in modern dental science. Yet caries, or tooth decay, is by far the most common disease in the United States today, afflicting about 90 percent of all people. Ancient peoples had neither effective toothbrushes nor toothpastes of any seeming worth, but we have no proof that they suffered from tooth decay any more than people do today!

Equally puzzling, many people who never put a brush to their teeth, go through life without a single cavity, while others who brush regularly spend considerable time in the dentist's chair. Diet certainly has an effect on dental health, for people sharing certain cuisines are conspicuously free from tooth decay. But the precise nature of tooth decay—and the way to prevent it—remain largely a mystery.

The science of decay prevention is relatively new. Early dentistry was entirely corrective—decayed teeth that became too painful to bear were unceremoniously removed with forceps, twine, or whatever else was handy. Medicinal remedies were often tried first, but most were of questionable value. One ancient remedy for toothache was to eat a mouse! Only since 1910 have dentists largely turned their attention to preventive dentistry, treating the teeth *before* they begin to decay.

The first tooth-cleaning device was undoubtedly the toothpick. Gold toothpicks dating from around 3500 B.C. have been found among ancient ruins in Mesopotamia, many of them encased in skillfully decorated gold boxes. It's doubtful that many people could have availed themselves of such luxury. The Greeks and Romans may have employed a brush or toothpick for cleaning their teeth, but a finger or a sponge were more the rule—perhaps dabbed in *dentifricium,* aromatic tooth powder. In India, sixth-century physician Susruta advised that "a man should leave his bed early in the morning and brush his teeth," promising that cleaning "removed bad smells from the mouth," and promoted "cheerfulness of mind."

Until modern times, two varieties of toothbrush were employed, the *fiber-pencil* and the *bristle-brush.* The *fiber-pencil* consisted of pieces of root or twig attached to the end of a thin handle, similar in design to the brush used for oil painting. Though the wood must have offered a rather rough brush, the substances most commonly used contain some of the very chemicals used in modern toothpastes. A fiber-pencil brush called a *misrak* was popular for a long time among Arabs, and Mohammed himself used the *misrak* as a religious symbol. Ancient Brahmins of India, who brushed their teeth with cherry wood while facing the sun, also considered the act of brushing to have religious significance. Natives of Ceylon, meanwhile, placed their pearly-whites on an altar when they had fallen out, beseeching the gods to spare those remaining—a custom not unlike the Western rite of placing a child's lost tooth under a pillow for the "tooth fairy."

In the *bristle-brush,* the toothbrush we're most familiar with, the fibers are attached at a right angle to the handle. In addition to cleaning food particles from between the teeth, a bristle-brush massages the gums. More teeth are lost to poor gums than to tooth decay.

By the 18th century, silk floss, the bristle-brush, and the fiber-pencil were all in use in Europe. The first toothbrush with synthetic bristles appeared in 1938, dubbed Dr. West's Miracle Tuft Toothbrush. The latest brushes on the market are equipped with two sets of bristles, one to remove food particles, and the other specially designed to massage the gums.

The earliest dentifrices used in conjunction with a toothbrush were made from natural oils, plant extracts, honey, or a wide range of herbal ingredients. While substances such as charcoal, chalk, baking soda, and pumice were genuinely effective, there may seem to be a touch of superstition associated with the use of "crab's eye" and "dragon's blood"—but both are curious names for plant extracts!

Late in the 19th century, American commercial dentifrices began to include heavy flavoring ingredients to overcome the often bitter, astringent taste of most tooth powders or pastes. But the "active" ingredients remained, as bizarre as hart's horn, cuttlefish bone, oyster shell, and myrrh. Most dentifrices were sold in the form of powder, which could then be mixed with honey to form a paste. One dentifrice advertised in the 1870s, billed as "Magic Tooth Paste," contained marble dust, pumice powder, rose-pink, and attar of roses. The paste was suggested as a "favorite nostrum for rapidly cleaning and whitening the teeth," though it was admittedly "one not adapted for free or frequent use."

Nineteenth-century mouthwashes were hardly less drastic—straight cologne was a favorite. Today, commercial mouthwash is basically an American phenomenon. So too, it seems, is an abundance of dentists. The United States can now boast over 125,000 registered dentists, more than any other country on earth—but two out of three Americans rarely or never call on their services.

During the 1880s, an American doctor named Willoughby Miller proved that caries was due in part to bacteria in the mouth. These microorganisms produce a substance known as dental

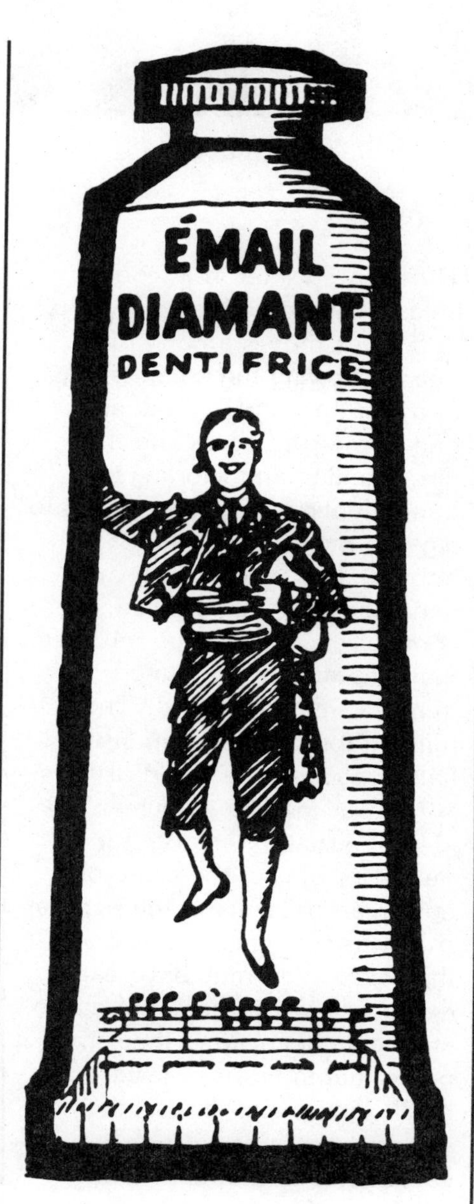

Gum-tinted toothpaste, manufactured in France, tints the gums pink, supposedly making the teeth look whiter by comparison.

plaque, which combines with carbohydrates to form organic acids. The acids then dissolve the calcium salts that make up most of the tooth.

Certain chemicals will retard the growth of oral bacteria or blunt their effects on the teeth, and these chemicals form the active ingredients in the toothpaste commonly used today. Most dentifrices contain an abrasive such as chalk or alumina; glycerine, which retains moisture and so improves taste; a gum to serve as a binder; and small amounts of detergent and flavoring. The formulas for commercial toothpastes are constantly changing, but the trusty collapsible toothpaste tube has been a familiar sight on the bathroom sink since early this century.

Within the last 40 years, scientists have learned that fluoride ions in water are especially effective in reducing caries. Most toothpastes now feature a fluoride compound as the chief preventer of decay. Fluoride was even administered for a time in the drinking water of some American communities.

Despite the recent advances in dental hygiene, tooth decay remains a problem, perhaps as serious as ever. The best advice a dental specialist can offer against tooth decay is still to brush and floss the teeth regularly, avoid sweets, and visit a dentist frequently. If all else fails, you might try a dentifrice, imported from France, that tints the gums pink to make the teeth look whiter by comparison!

Truffles

The white truffle of the Piedmont district of Italy presently sells for over $200 a pound, making it the most expensive food in the world.

The scene: winter in a wooded area of southern France. A group of farmers moves among the trees, following the meanderings of a half-dozen pigs. Suddenly, one of the pigs noses into the dirt, grunting and snorting in hungry anticipation, and begins to dig into the ground with its hooves. The farmers rush over and chase the animal, then complete the excavation job. Yes, they're searching for buried treasure—but what kind? They're hunting for the most expensive natural food in the world: truffles.

Caviar may be everyman's idea of gustatory luxury, but ounce for ounce, the acme of epicurean opulence is the peculiar subterranean fungus known as the truffle. You may have eaten a deliciously sweet morsel of dark and light chocolate of the same name, but in terms of taste, origin, and price, the candied imitation bears no relation whatsoever to the real McCoy.

The truffle is a fungus of the class *ascomycetes*, found mainly in the temperate zones. There are about 70 species of truffles, of which only seven are edible. Truffles are usually black with warty surfaces, ranging in size from a pea to an orange, with the average truffle about the size of a golf ball. Most truffles grow close to the roots of trees, from one to three feet below the surface, and seem especially partial to the roots of the oak.

Like the mushroom, also a fungus, the truffle has almost no nutritive value. But its taste, aroma, and ability to heavily flavor anything it comes in contact with have made it a prized edible since classical times. The Roman writers Juvenal and Plutarch both expressed the opinion that truffles were formed by lightning bolts that heated water and minerals in the ground where they struck.

After the fall of the Roman Empire, the truffle was virtually forgotten until the 14th century, but truffle hunting remained a hit-or-miss proposition until the 19th century. In 1810, a French peasant named Joseph Talon discovered a field of truffles in an area of Vaucluse heavily planted with acorns; he was the first to make the connection between the fungus and the oak. The enterprising Talon immediately went into the truffle business, and attempted to keep his discovery a secret, to no avail. But years of study have not revealed why the

A truffle hunter and his specially-trained rooting hog search for the precious mushrooms in Perigord, France.

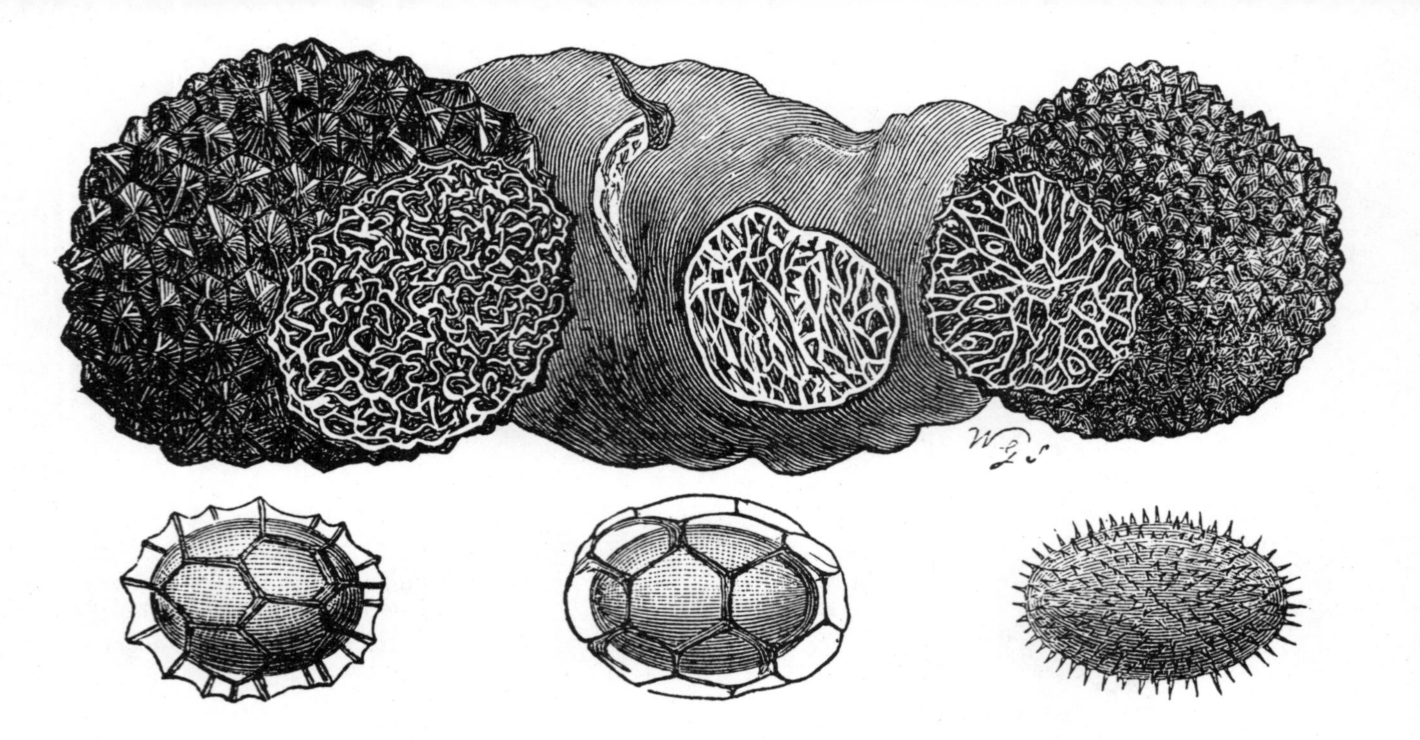

Three varieties of truffles are shown, with cross-sections.

truffle prefers to grow in proximity to the oak, or why the planting of acorns will not necessarily assure the growth of truffles.

Over the centuries, truffles have become an integral part of many French dishes. The French satirist Rabelais's favorite snack was oysters with hot truffle-flavored sausages. Gastronomist Brillat-Savarin—born, appropriately enough, in the town of Belley—was convinced that the truffle is an effective aphrodisiac, proclaiming that "whoever says *truffle* utters a grand word, which awakens erotic and gastronomic ideas."

Today, the most valuable truffle fields, or *truffieres,* are located in the Perigord district of France, near Bordeaux, and in the Vaucluse area north of Marseilles. The Perigord variety have been prized as the best since the 15th century. Truffles can be found in other areas, including North America, but are extremely rare outside of southern France.

Hunting the truffle is a difficult, delicate operation. Since the fungus grows underground, it's virtually impossible to tell where a crop of the delicacies might be found, but French farmers have developed a number of tricks. Some farmers with a nose for the truffle claim they can locate their catch by examining the ground around oak trees. Others maintain that columns of small yellow flies hovering over truffle patches lead them to the buried treasure.

Most truffle hunting, however, is carried out with the aid of specially trained pigs or "rooting hogs." The pigs are better at scenting out the truffles, but they present the farmer with an additional problem. Once a pig locates a truffle, he's likely to gobble it right up before the farmer can chase him off. The pig's palate, it seems, is as partial to the truffle as man's. Farmers can train pigs to search for truffles in a matter of days—but it may take two or three years to teach them not to eat their find!

France exports about one-third of its truffles, so the French government is eager to encourage their growth. The French recently undertook a massive reforestry project in certain barren areas of the south in the hopes of increasing production. To begin a *truffiere,* acorns or oak seedlings are planted with soil taken from truffle-growing areas. Truffles will appear, if at all, about five years after planting. But hunting for the fungus doesn't become profitable until about 10 years after planting; and in many cases, the maximum yield takes about 20 years to develop.

Sometimes even a 20 year wait will fail to turn up any truffles, and no one is quite sure why. It's known that the delicate Perigord variety requires drought in mid-summer, or the winter harvest will frequently be sparse. Recently, many French truffle farms have failed completely, and gastronomists predict that if the next 10 years doesn't see an increase in truffle finds, the delicacies may be priced right out of existence and disappear forever from our tables. But on the bright side, the attempt to encourage truffle growth has led to quite a boom in oak trees in some areas of France.

As you might imagine, thievery is a common problem in truffle-growing areas. A clever truffle-snatcher can become rich virtually overnight, since most varieties will sell for well above $100 a pound. The white truffle of the Piedmont district of Italy presently sells for over $200 a pound, making it the most expensive food in the world. On the streets of Milan, truffle vendors hawk this delicacy at the price of 5,000 lire (approximately $5.88) per truffle. An Italian law stipulating that any truffles found on leased property must be shared with the landlord has recently come under fire from Italian Communist politicians who have made the truffle law an important issue in the Piedmont area.

Truffles will probably be forevermore beyond the pocketbook of all but the rich. Gone are the days of the 1890s, when a Manhattan *bon vivant* could serve gallons of truffled ice cream at his dinner parties—leading to a custom that made that particular dessert *de rigueur* at fashionable New York parties for years.

The question in your mind might well be: could truffles possibly be worth their price? Well, the question can be answered only by your palate. For some gourmets, no price is too high for the pungent delicacy. For those who remain unconvinced, truffle fanciers propose a simple test. Taste any sauce requiring truffles, then sample the same sauce without the delicacy. The sauce without truffles, they're sure you'll agree, is simply not to be truffled with!

SAUMON AU SANCERRE

(Makes about 4 servings)

- 4 salmon steaks
- 1 carrot, shredded
- 1 small onion, chopped
- ½ cup chopped celery
- ¼ teaspoon thyme
- 1½ cup Sancerre, a dry white wine from the Loire Valley
- ¼ cup Armagnac
- ¼ cup butter
- ¼ cup flour
- 1 teaspoon grated lemon rind
- 2 tablespoons slivered French truffles
- 1 cup (½ pint) heavy cream
- Salt and pepper

1. *Place salmon steaks in large skillet. Add vegetables, thyme, Sancerre and Armagnac. Cover and simmer gently 20 to 25 minutes.*
2. *Remove salmon steaks with spatula and keep warm on serving platter. Boil pan juices until 1 cup is left in skillet.*
3. *In saucepan, heat butter and stir in flour. Stir in reserved pan juices, lemon rind, truffles, and heavy cream. Stir over low heat until sauce bubbles and thickens. Season to taste with salt and pepper.*
4. *Drain off any juice that has accumulated on serving platter and discard. Spoon hot sauce over salmon. Serve with boiled new potatoes that have been drained, and rolled in a mixture of melted butter and Herbes de Provence.*

Photo and recipe courtesy of Food and Wines from France.

TULIPS

To many minds, the tulip and the windmill are virtually synonymous with the Netherlands. Most historians would agree that the windmill in Europe made its first appearance in the Low Countries, sometime before the 12th century. But you may be surprised to learn that the tulip is not a native of Holland, and was totally unknown in that country until the 16th century.

The colorful, cup-shaped flower, long popular among gardeners, is actually a native of the western Mediterranean and the steppes of Central Asia, and some species can be found growing wild in northern Africa, southern Europe, and in Japan.

The empire of the Ottoman Turks once included much of the tulip's natural habitat, and it was through Turkey that most tulips reached western Europe and the Netherlands.

The Turks prized the tulip, and were cultivating that flower on a large scale by the mid-16th century when the Austrian ambassador to the Turkish empire brought some tulip bulbs from Constantinople to his garden in Vienna. From Austria, the flower found its way to the Low Countries. In 1562, the first large shipment of Turkish tulips reached Antwerp, then part of the Dutch nation.

The tulip quickly became a favorite among European gardeners and the Netherlands soon took the lead in producing prized specimens.

In the 1630s, a rage of tulip speculation, called tulipomania, gripped much of Holland, and farmers rich and poor began speculating in the tulip trade. Single bulbs of prized varieties sold for as much as $1,000—one particular bulb for $4,000, a small fortune at the time. Alas, the tulip rage tapered off within a few years, leaving thousands of Dutchmen penniless. The economic scars of the tulipomania were felt in Holland for decades.

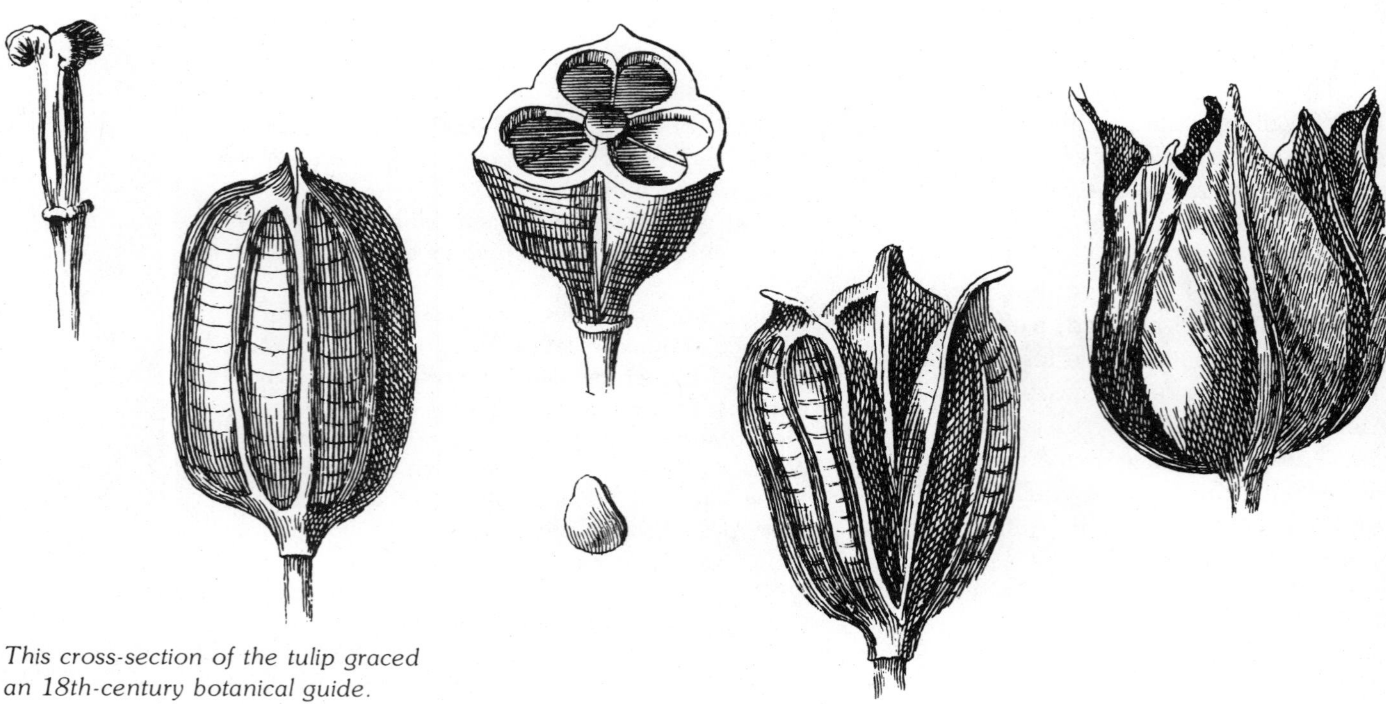

This cross-section of the tulip graced an 18th-century botanical guide.

Still, the Dutch continued to raise their favorite flower. Today, the Netherlands remains the chief source of tulip bulbs for much of the world, with millions cultivated each year. The total value of Dutch horticulture approaches a quarter-billion dollars annually!

Tulips are also grown on a large scale in Belgium, the Channel Islands, and in parts of England, Ireland, and the United States.

The Turks, meanwhile, endured a period of tulipomania all their own. During the 12 years between the defeat of the Empire by Austria and Venice in 1718 and the revolution of 1730, the cultivation of tulip gardens became a craze in Constantinople.

The origins of most modern tulip varieties are untraceable, due to frequent hybridization and the plant's peculiar power of variation. Tulips grown from a single parent flower can change so greatly over the course of two or three generations that the relationship between the later specimens and their parents can be scarcely recognizable. It is this property—and not hybridization—that produces the prized variegated tulip.

New tulip varieties are raised from seeds. They produce flowers after about seven years of meticulous cultivation. At that stage, all tulips have but one color throughout. After the poorer specimens are weeded out, the good plants are saved as "breeder" tulips. A breeder tulip and its offspring may then grow for years without producing anything but flowers of the same hue.

But then, suddenly and unpredictably, some of the flowers "break," producing flowers with variegated colors. The so-called "rectified" tulip is then graded according to its coloring. If it is yellow, with purple or red markings, it is called a *bizarre*. If it is white with purple markings, it is called a *bybloemen*. If it is white with rose markings, it is called a *rose*.

Most tulips are raised from the shoots of a parent plant, not from seed. A shoot will begin producing flowers of its own in about three years. Most bulbs require a period of darkness and a thorough winter chill to bloom in spring; thus, many commercially grown tulips are produced in darkened bulb cellars. If you plant tulips in your garden, you can expect most species to bear blossoms for several seasons.

Among the many thousands of tulip varieties, we might mention the colorfully named *Rising Sun, White Hawk, Couleur de Cardinal, Pride of Haarlem,* and *Prince of Austria.*

But the tulip tree is not related to the tulip. It owes its name to its tulip-like green-yellow flowers. This tree is also known as the canary whitewood in England and the yellow poplar in the United States. Tulipwood, a white or yellow wood prized by cabinet makers, is, as you might expect, not a product of the tulip, but rather of the tulip tree.

Tulips have been the subject of at least two popular songs: *Tiptoe Through the Tulips,* and *When I Wore a Tulip, and You Wore a Big Red Rose.*

The word *tulip* has a rather odd origin. When the tulip was introduced to Europe, many gardeners saw a resemblance between the flower's shape and Turkish headwear, and they dubbed the flower *tulipan,* from *tulbend,* a Turkish word for "turban." From *tulipan* came the French word *tulipe* and the English word *tulip*. There is, as you can see, only a whimsical connection between *tulips* and *two lips.*

Photo courtesy of Consulate General of the Netherlands.

Typewriters

The typewriter's first manufacturer predicted that the machine would "free the world from pen slavery and complete the economic emancipation of womankind."

At the 1876 Philadelphia Centennial Exposition, two recent American inventions were placed on public display for the first time. One, a certain voice-transmission apparatus invented by a man named Alexander Graham Bell attracted widespread attention among the fair-goers. The second, called the typewriter, attracted almost none. Yet by the time of the American Bicentennial Celebration, the typewriter had become such an integral part of American life that it's hard to imagine how business was carried on without it—just 100 years ago.

The fact is, more people are trained for the operation of the typewriter than for any other machine on earth—any machine requiring specialized training, that is. The typewriter has indeed come a long way. The early models resulted in machine writing being slower than handwriting. Today's modern machines are capable of speeds faster than speech, fulfilling the prediction of the Remington Company, the typewriter's first manufacturer, that the machine would "free the world from pen slavery and complete the economic emancipation of womankind."

The first recorded attempt to invent a typewriter actually took place in 1714, when an Englishman named Henry Mill filed a patent for what he rather long-windedly described as "An Artificial Machine or Method for the Impressing or Transcribing of Letters, Singly or Progessively one after another, as in Writing, whereby all Writing whatsoever may be Engrossed in Paper or Parchment so Neat and Exact as not to be distinguished from Print." If Mr. Mill was as verbose as this description suggests, it's no wonder he saw the advantages of a typewriting machine. In any case, Mill's typewriter was apparently never constructed, and no drawings of his project were ever found.

The earliest typewriting machines in America were crude attempts to mechanize the printing of Braille so that the blind could write as well as read. A machine called the "typographer," capable of printing ordinary letters, was patented in 1829. The type was set on a semicircular frame that had to be turned by hand, so that only one letter at a time could be shifted into position and printed. Needless to say, the machine was much slower than writing, as were most early typewriters. And many typewriting machines were as large as a piano, with keyboards resembling black and white ivories!

In the 1860s, two Milwaukee inventors were busy developing a machine for consecutively numbering the pages of a book. One of the men, Carlos Glidden, came across an article describing a new British machine capable of printing typed letters, and he brought the article to the attention of his partner, Christopher Latham Sholes. If our machine could print page numbers, Sholes wondered, why couldn't it also print regular letters? By 1867,

William Burt's "typographer," early typewriter of 1829.

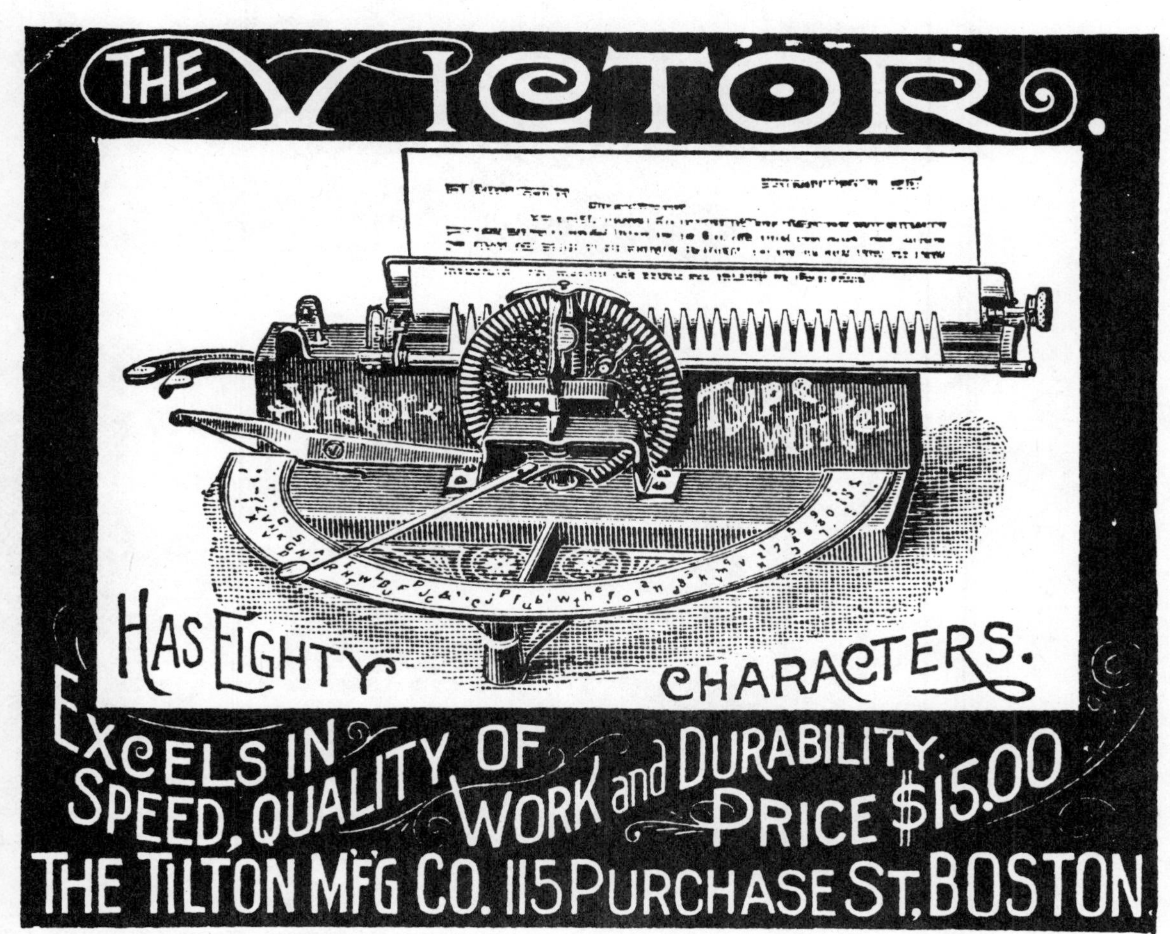

An advertisement for the Victor typewriter in Century Magazine *of 1890.*

TYPEWRITERS OF THE 19th CENTURY

Wheatstone's writing machine (1851).

Typewriter of 1890.

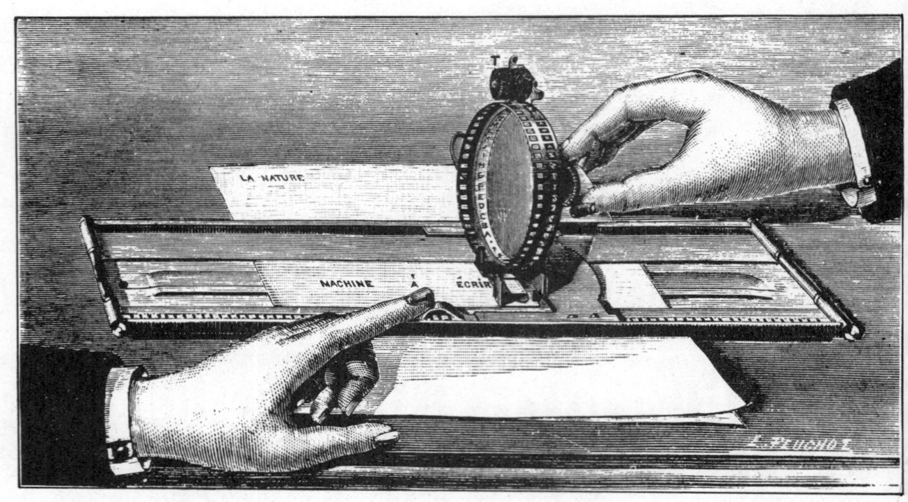

Herrington's typewriter (1891).

An 1865 typewriter made by John Pratt in 1866.

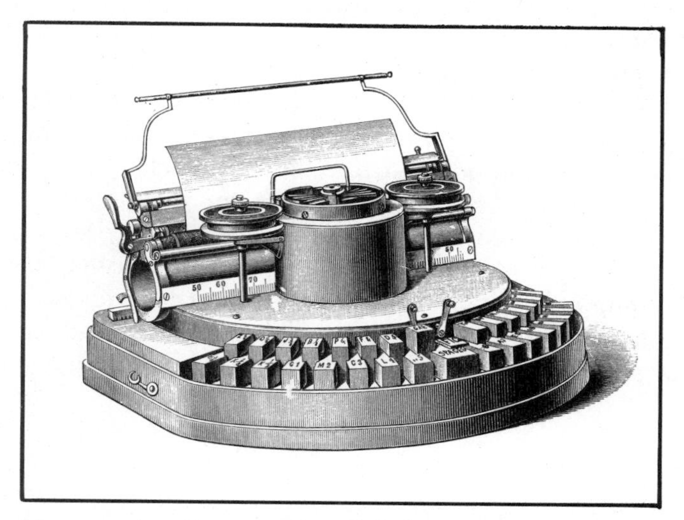

Hammond writing machine (1890).

An 1870 Schreibkugel of European manufacture.

Smith Premier No. 5 typewriter of Berlin (1890).

Sholes had constructed the first practical typewriter in his Milwaukee shop.

Sholes's first typewriter was a cumbersome machine with a piano keyboard, little improvement over other models then in existence. But in 1868, Sholes and Glidden turned out a second model, the first typewriter capable of printing faster than the pen.

Sholes's major innovation was an arrangement of keys that allowed two letters to be typed in rapid succession. With other early models, the typist had to wait until the type bar of the first letter had returned to the carriage before striking the second key, or risk locking the two bars together and bringing the machine to a halt. Thus, Sholes's keyboard, identical to today's except in minor details, was designed so that letters that combine frequently in our language would be separated on the keyboard—hardly the ideal arrangement for the typist, as proponents of the new Dvorak keyboard point out.

In 1873, Sholes signed a contract for the manufacture of his machine with E. Remington and Sons, gunsmiths of Ilion, New York, and the following year, the first model, called the "Remington," was placed on the market. You may imagine that the first Remingtons were scooped up by clever businessmen as fast as they could be manufactured. Not true. Most businessmen couldn't see the

Sholes typewriter of the late 19th century.

advantage of a machine only slightly faster than handwriting that cost, in the words of one, "a thousand times as much as a pen." As late as 1881, Remington was selling only 1,200 machines a year. It took almost a decade after the first Remington was manufactured for typewriter sales to begin a steady climb upwards.

One drawback of the early machines was their extremely slow speed. For one thing, upper and lower case letters were contained on separate keyboards, necessitating continual movement from one keyboard to the other; at the time, more words were capitalized than are today. It wasn't until 1878 that the first machine with a double keyboard (upper and lower cases on the same keyboard, with a shift key) was placed on the market, but even then the two systems remained in competition until 1888. In that year, a typing contest was held in Cincinnati between a Mr. Traub, one of the leading exponents of the separate keyboard system, and a Mr. McGurrin who'd taught himself touchtyping on a double keyboard machine. McGurrin won the speed contest easily, and the separate keyboard typewriter became a museum piece.

Typewriter, early 1900s.

The earliest typewriters were more cumbersome than today's models. This is the first commercial typewriter, developed by Chrsitopher Latham Sholes for Remington in 1873.

Another drawback presented by early machines was the inability of the typist to view the paper until it was removed from the typewriter. In 1883, the first typewriter with visible printing was marketed, and Correcto-Type became a practical though distant reality.

There were few inventions of the late 19th century that Thomas Edison didn't at least dabble with, and the typewriter was no exception. In fact, Edison constructed the first electric typewriter, which printed letters on a moving roll of paper. Edison's device eventually became the ticker-tape machine,with the first electric machine perfected by James Smathers in 1920.

The first portable typewriter had been manufactured in 1909. In 1956, the two inventions came together to form the electric portable, the term-paper writer's best friend.

The IBM Corporation broke new ground in 1959 with the

development of the Executive Electric, the first typewriter capable of line justification (the printing of lines flush with one another on the right sides as well as the left) and differential spacing. In machines without differential spacing, letters as narrow as an "i" and as wide as an "m" are allotted the same amount of space on the page. With differential spacing, letters are allotted space in accordance with their width, making possible line justification and a much neater, printlike page.

In 1961, IBM developed the first typewriter with a spherical type carrier, the "the type ball," eliminating the nuisance of interlocking type bars.

Today's typewriters can print in almost any language including computer code. A New York linguist claims he can, in one hour, adapt a typewriter to print in any of 146 languages.

There's a Chinese typewriter called the Hoang with 5,850 characters on a keyboard two feet long and 17 inches wide. Top speed on the Hoang is about 10 words per minute.

There's also a musical notation typewriter capable of printing 50 different notes and symbols. And a shorthand typewriter— invented in 1910— that can record up to 200 words per minute. Modern versions of the latter are used today by court stenographers.

If you've ever lived in an apartment next door to a budding writer, you might be pleased to learn that a noiseless typewriter was invented more than 50 years ago. The machine used heavier type bars that moved with lower velocity but carried the same momentum as regular bars. Alas, the model proved to be poor for producing carbon copies.

If you're a practitioner of the "hunt-and-peck" school of typing, you may be encouraged by the development of the Dvorak keyboard, patented in 1936. The Dvorak keyboard is arranged so that the letters most common in English are most easily and comfortably reached by the touch typist. The Dvorak keyboard looks much like the universal keyboard, with three rows of letter keys. But on the Dvorak, 70 percent of all letters in almost any given passage can be found on the middle row, with the most common letters placed under the strongest fingers.

Proponents of the new system claim that the increased speed of the Dvorak method and the lessening of typist fatigue could result in a savings of $20 million a year in business expenses throughout the country. However, the machine is a costly investment— an Olympia typewriter with a Dvorak keyboard costs an extra $300 above the regular price. It is not surprising then that as of April 1978, Olympia has sold no Dvorak keyboard machines for two years.

A cumbersome Japanese typewriter.

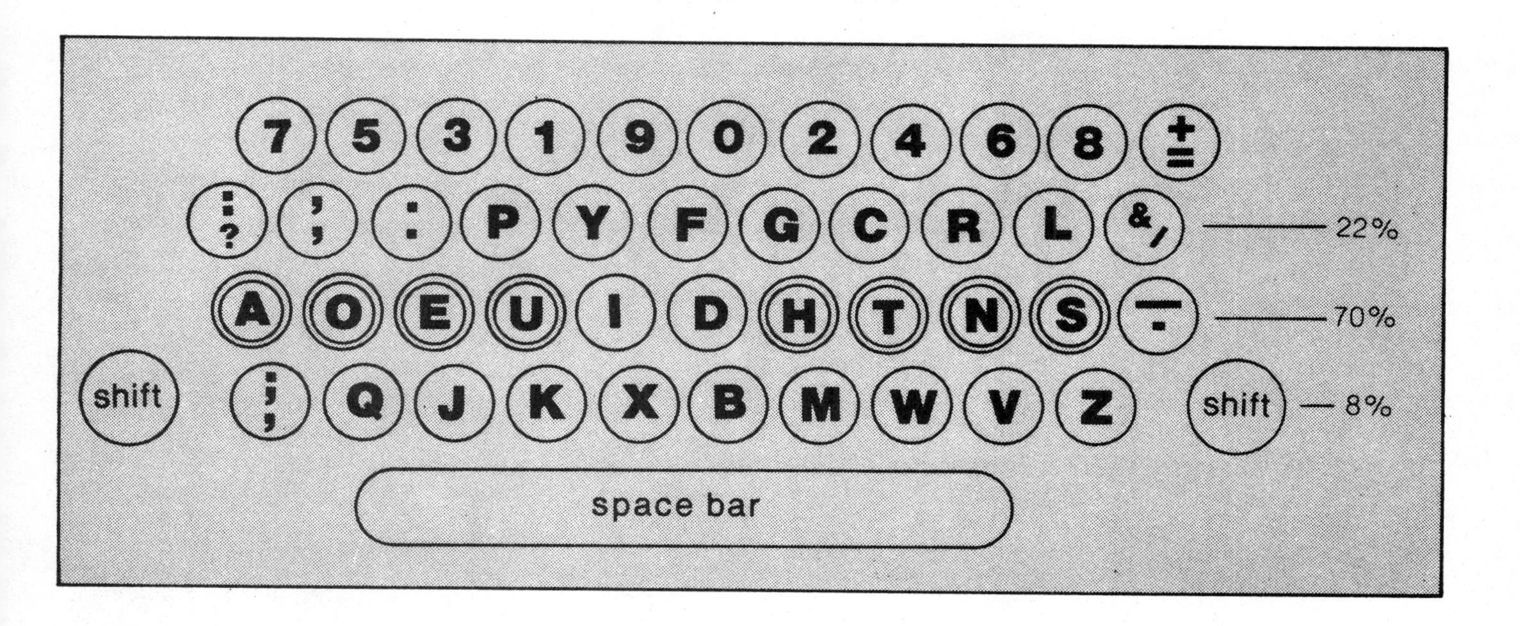

The Dvorak Simplified Keyboard, or DSK, attempts to combat the tyranny of QWERTY through a logical arrangement of keys. The DSK places the most frequently used letters (70%) on the middle line or "home row" of the typewriter. On the top line letters used 22% of the time; on the bottom row, letters used only 8% of the time.

The first touch typist in the world was, not surprisingly, Sholes's daughter, Lillian. In those days, incidentally, the typist as well as the machine was referred to as the "typewriter."

Candidates for typing instruction—both male and female—were chosen on the basis of physical strength rather than intelligence or dexterity, since operating the heavy keys of early typewriters was arduous work.

The first author to submit a typewritten manuscript was Mark Twain. But there's some disagreement as to which of Twain's manuscripts earned the honor. In his *Autobiography*, Twain maintained that *The Adventures of Tom Sawyer* was the first book he typed. But in a letter to a friend, Twain claimed that the earlier *Life on the Mississippi* was also submitted in typescript. In any case, Twain bought his Remington for $125. Later, when he attempted to give the machine away, he found it extremely difficult to find a taker.

In case you were wondering: Pope Pius XII was the first pontiff to use the typewriter. He was an excellent touch typist. And George Bernard Shaw was the first playwright to use a typewriter as a stage-prop—in *Candida* (1898).

What's the fastest typing speed ever recorded? The top speed ever achieved by a typist, 216 words per minute stands as the record, set by one Stella Pajunas in 1946 on an IBM electric. To give you an idea of her accomplishment, 60 words per minute is considered good professional speed. The record for top speed for over an hour of nonstop typing is 149 words per minute, also set on an IBM machine.

Perhaps the most remarkable typing record is held by Albert Tangora, who during a 1923 business show in New York, ran off a total of 8,840 correctly spelled words in one hour of nonstop typing, a rate of 147 words per minute. Incredibly, Tangora achieved his record on a cumbersome old *manual* typewriter that would seem crude in comparison with modern models. Judges estimated that Tangora executed an average of 12½ strokes per second!

The record for sustained speed on a Dvorak keyoard is 170 words per minute.

The longest nonstop typing stint was 162 hours, one minute, set by California high school teacher Robin Heil in 1976. A blind English office worker named Mike Howell holds the duration record for a manual machine: 120¼ hours.

But the world's greatest typing buff must certainly be Mrs. Marva Drew of Waterloo, Iowa. Over a six-year span, Marva exercised her skills by typing the numbers one to one million on a manual typewriter—a feat requiring 2,473 pages!

Umbrellas

The rain it raineth on the just
And also on the unjust fella:
But chiefly on the just because
The unjust steals the just's umbrella.

Bartine's Sunshade Hat was the rage in 1895.

Let us now turn to the subject of brolliology. What is brolliology? Why, it's the study of the brolly, of course—the gamp, the parasol, the parapluie, the bumbershoot, the bumbersoll—to you, the umbrella.

If you think the ribbed, collapsible umbrella was the invention of some clever 18th- or 19th-century Englishman determined to fight back against the soggy weather of London town—you're all wet. The fact is, the umbrella is one of the oldest artifacts in man's history, already a familiar item in many cultures by the time man began to write.

The umbrella is so old that brolliologists can't agree on its origin, or decide whether it was first used for protection from the rain or the sun. They do know that it was employed as an item of religious and ceremonial regalia from the earliest days of ancient Egypt. Egyptian mythology held that the visible sky was actually the underbelly of a god stretched from one end of the earth to the other like an immense umbrella. Hence, in contemporary art, priests and Pharoahs were often placed in the shade of an umbrella to symbolize royal and religious power.

Assyrian tablets dating from 1350 B.C. depict a king leading his retinue while servants shade the royal head with a long-handled parasol. In India, a religious group known as the Jains called their ultimate heaven of perfected souls by a name that translates as "The Slightly Tilted Umbrella."

The early Greeks used the umbrella as a symbol of productivity and sexual aggression, usually associated with the god Bacchus, and they carried umbrellas in many of their parades and festivals. In later centuries, the Greeks put the umbrella to a more utilitarian use as a sunshade, and developed sunshade hats similar to the sombrero.

The Romans, too, used parasols against the sun. Women attending chariot races in the amphitheatre sometimes dyed their parasols to denote their favorite chariot team. If you've ever attended a football game in drizzly weather and have been annoyed no end by umbrellas blocking your line of vision, you may find it comforting to know that the Romans had a similar problem at their games, with a hot dispute over parasol use finally decided by the emperor Domitian—in favor of the sunshade.

The use of the umbrella was well established in China at a very early date. Oiled paper or bamboo were the favored materials. A Korean tomb dating from 25 B.C. contained a collapsible umbrella complete with rib supports.

This bas-relief from the Palace of Persepolis shows Xerxes under the royal parasol.

Courtesy of Editions Albin Michel and Professor Laignel-Lavastine.

Europe was introduced to the bumbershoot through ancient Byzantium. In the eighth century, Pope Paul I gave Frankish King Pepin the Short a jewel-handled umbrella as a token of Papal support for his reign.

In the 15th century, Portuguese seamen bound for the East Indies brought along umbrellas as fit gifts for native royalty. Upon landing on a strange island, the seamen immediately opened an umbrella over their captain's head, to demonstrate his authority.

The Normans brought a 12-ribbed umbrella to England in the 11th century. But the first contextual use of the word "umbrella" (from *umbra,* Latin for "shade") does not appear in English literature until 1609, in the work of John Donne. The spelling was not finalized until much later, and *umbrellow, umbrello,* and *umbrillo* were common as late as the 19th century.

The man usually credited with popularizing the umbrella in London was one John Hanway, a 17th-

In the eighth century B.C., this substantial-looking brolly was in vogue.

century traveler who brought the brolly to England from Portugal. Hanway created quite a stir by strolling through London under the strange contraption. He perambulated about in all kinds of weather, and was often greeted by jokes from passersby. He was likely to suffer abuse from coachmen, who feared the popularity of such a device would cut into their trade.

Religious Londoners objected to the umbrella on moral grounds—after all, the purpose of heavenly rain was to make people wet. But despite these objectors, the use of the umbrella spread steadily in the showery city. For some time, they were called Hanways in honor of their eccentric pioneer. The word *gamp,* incidentally, comes from Charles Dickens's novel *Martin Chuzzlewit,* in which a large cotton umbrella is the trademark of one Sairy Gamp.

The English didn't invent the umbrella, but they did develop the first *practical* waterproof bumbershoot. This happened in the late 17th century. By 1700, umbrellas were in regular commercial production, with whalebone the favored material for the ribs.

Early English umbrellas were hardly perfect, though. They were large and cumbersome, frequently they leaked, and they broke easily in a strong wind. They were most in evidence in coffee houses, where a supply was kept by the door for patrons who might dash from the coffee house to a carriage. Like the ancient Romans, the English for many years considered the gamp too effeminate for use by men.

This Roman Fresco, "Woman With an Umbrella," is now in the Louvre, in Paris.

Photo courtesy of the Louvre and photographer M. Chuzeville.

This Greek vase depicts an original-looking parasol-bonnet—and the slave carrying it is an even greater original!

Some wily Londoners put the brolly to another curious employment: orators frequently held an umbrella above their head while addressing a crowd, to protect themselves from missiles tossed by less-than-approving listeners.

You may think that at least the fold-up or transparent umbrella is a recent invention. Not true! An enterprising gentleman by the name of Gosselin of Amiens constructed a fold-up "pocket" model with four interjoined steel tubes in 1785! In fact, the construction of the umbrella hasn't changed very much since 1760, when most bumbershoots were already being built with eight ribs, a sliding brace, and a curved handle.

Listen to this one: a group of British soldiers carried umbrellas into battle during the Napoleonic wars, until the British military decided the gamp was hardly a fitting implement for a fighting man. The Boers also used the umbrella on rain-drenched battlefields. Even the U.S. Cavalry carried brollies on occasion, particularly during the Indian wars in the rainy northern states.

By 1820, the umbrella had fallen out of fashion in Europe, and the parasol had arrived. Aristocratic English women imported from Paris fancy models made of silk or chantilly lace with elaborate enameled handles. Some handles were fitted to carry perfume or writing materials, or even a dagger. And believe it or not, there was a model designed with one protruding side to offer protection for the bustle that most women wore in those days.

The use of the umbrella in courtship dates back to the ancient Greeks. In the 18th and 19th centuries, young maidens frequently sat for their portrait with a delicate parasol in hand as a symbol of their class.

The umbrella or parasol has figured prominently in paintings by Degas, Monet, Goya, Delacroix, Seurat, and Renoir. In Brittany, custom still dictates that a young man can express his interest in a favored maiden by offering to carry her umbrella at the fair. Carrying her umbrella along the road is considered a sure sign of engagement.

Brolliologists are reluctant to estimate the number of umbrellas in use throughout the world, but the country with the highest per capita use of the gamp is definitely England. As late as 1954, 300,000 umbrellas were produced in the British Isles each *month!* Today, most umbrellas are imported from Hong Kong and Japan. During the 50s, the Japanese exported almost 12 million bumbershoots to us within a 12-month period.

Modern umbrella makers contend that today's models are so well constructed that the average person needn't go through more than two in his lifetime. But they make no mention of the phenomenon of the lost umbrella, which more often than not is the reason for a new purchase. To suggest the scope of this problem, it may help to know that close to 75,000 umbrellas are lost each year on the bus and subway systems of London alone!

And the number of yearly umbrella thefts is anyone's guess. Which brings to mind the one about the man who left his brolly in the umbrella stand in a London pub with the following note: *"This umbrella is owned by the champion boxer of England, and he's coming back in two minutes."* The man then went to the bar for a drink. When he returned, the umbrella stand was empty, and in place of his brolly, he found a note that read: *"This umbrella was taken by the champion runner of England, and he's never coming back."*

There's the widespread superstition that opening a bumbershoot indoors brings bad luck. Then, of course, there's the age-old belief that the easiest way to assure a rainy day is to leave your umbrella at home. Robert Louis Stevenson seemed aware of this peculiar meteorological wisdom when he wrote: "There is no act in meteorology better established . . . than that the carriage of the umbrella produces dessication of the air; while if it be left at home, aqueous vaper is largely produced, and is soon deposited in the form of rain."

This 100% windproof umbrella pops in and out in an instant from inside its walking stick.

Vanilla

Vanilla beans ripen on the vine over a period of six weeks.

The vast legions of American ice cream-lovers fall basically into two camps: those who favor chocolate, and those who champion its chromatic antithesis, vanilla. Although vanilla and chocolate—long the most popular ice cream flavors in the United States—may be diametrically opposed on the color scale, they share more in common than you might imagine. Both cocoa and vanilla come from a bean. Both are natives of Mexico and Central America. Both are used primarily as a confectionary flavoring. In fact, for many years *chocolate* and *vanilla* were not thought of as opposites at all—they were almost always used *together!*

When the Spanish explorer Cortes arrived at the court of the Aztec king Montezuma in 1519, the Aztecs offered their guests bowls of a frothy black liquid chilled with snow. Chocolate, which Cortes had already heard of, was the primary ingredient of the beverage; but Cortes learned through court gossip that the Aztecs sweetened their drink with a secret ingredient, an extract from a wild orchid called *thilxochitl.* The Spaniards dubbed the white bean of the orchid with a diminutive of the word *vaina*—*vainilla*—or "little pod."

When cocoa from the New World reached Spain, vanilla came with it, for the two beans do have one important difference: chocolate in its unadulterated form is bitter tasting; vanilla is sweet. Wealthy Spaniards began enjoying a chocolate beverage sweetened with vanilla decades before coffee and tea became popular in Europe. The Spaniards guarded the secrets of their preparation for years, and it was almost a century before the two beans were widely enjoyed elsewhere in Europe.

Vanilla and chocolate reached France in 1660, when Maria Theresa of Spain arrived at the French court, with her maids and cooks, to become the bride of Louis XIV. The new queen enjoyed a vanilla-flavored chocolate beverage prepared by a maid each morning, and other members of the court were soon clamoring for vanilla. The clergy then decried the beverage as "provocative of immorality"—it was rumored that vanilla, like chocolate, was an aphrodisiac.

Queen Elizabeth of England, the owner of a notorious sweet tooth, was wont to fill her pockets with candies; she would nibble on the sweets throughout the day. Many of the candies were made from chocolate or from vanilla, or from a mixture of both. English confectioners vied to create new specialties to delight the queen, and one apothecary struck on the idea of using the juice of the vanilla bean as a flavoring for *marchpane,* almond paste. The occasion marked the first time that vanilla was used to flavor anything but chocolate, and Elizabeth loved the results.

By the late 17th century, chocolate was popular as a beverage throughout much of Europe, and chocolate houses—the forerunners of coffee houses—were common in many cities. But sugar gradually replaced vanilla as a sweetener for chocolate, and vanilla struck out on its own as a flavoring.

It wasn't until 1836, however, that scientists found a way of growing vanilla outside Mexico. Charles Morren, a Belgian botanist, discovered that the vanilla plant was pollinated by the Melipone bee, a tiny insect that lives only in Mexico. Thus, the plant could not be naturally pollinated in other countries. Morren found a method for artificially pollinating the plant, and vanilla plantations soon began appearing in many of France's colonial possessions.

(LEFT)
In Madagascar, ripe vanilla beans are harvested primarily by women and children.

(RIGHT)
Green vanilla beans are sold in the marketplace, primarily for the production of vanilla extract.

Photos courtesy of The Vanilla Growers of Madagascar.

Rumor has it that Thomas Jefferson, credited with introducing spaghetti, french fries, and a number of other foods to America, was also the first to use vanilla as a flavoring agent. During the last 200 years, vanilla has become one of the most popular confectionary flavorings in the United States, and is now widely used in candies, baked goods, ice cream, carbonated beverages (cream soda is made from vanilla), sauces, and surprisingly, perfume.

The vanilla plant that the Aztecs harvested is the *Vanilla planifolia*, but another species native to Oceania is called, appropriately enough, *Vanilla tahitensis.* Vanilla is a climbing orchid that attaches itself to trees with aerial rootlets, though the plant does possess ordinary soil roots. The fruit, or pod, is long and thin, measuring from six to 10 inches in length and a half inch in diameter. The pods of the best varieties are, strangely enough, chocolate-colored, and are flecked with a crystalline substance called *givre,* or vanillin, a fragrant chemical secreted by the pod lining that gives vanilla its characteristic flavor. Vanilla is unique among the 20,000-odd species of orchid known throughout the world, for it is the only

Harvested beans are stored until the pods begin to shrivel; then immersed in hot water, drained, exposed to the hot sun, and boxed or covered with blankets at night. This process is called sweating.
Photo courtesy of the Vanilla Growers of Madagascar.

orchid that produces a commercially useful commodity.

Unripe vanilla is green; it turns yellow when ripe. Harvested vanilla beans are cured by immersion in hot water, stored for several months to develop the full bouquet. The beans are then shipped to factories for the production of vanilla extract. At the factory, the beans are first chopped, then steeped in a solvent to extract the vanilla essence. At some factories, the vanilla extract is aged for six months to a year before shipment to confectioners and retail stores.

Though a native of Mexico and Central America, and a favorite flavoring in Europe and the United States, vanilla is today almost entirely a product of various Indian Ocean islands, where it was brought for plantation cultivation by French colonists. The Malagasy Republic (formerly Madagascar), Reunion, and the Comoro Islands now account for about 75 percent of the world's vanilla supply. Quantities are also produced in Tahiti, Indonesia, Mexico, and the Seychelles Islands.

Artificial vanilla flavoring can be produced from the sapwood of fir trees; and vanilla flavoring, synthesized from chemicals, is becoming increasingly popular as the cost of the raw vanilla bean rises.

Now chocolate, too, is being synthetically produced; it's possible that the dish of vanilla and chocolate ice cream you just enjoyed owed nothing to either bean. The next time you buy a vanilla or chocolate product, check the list of ingredients to find out if you were given the real McCoy—you'll find it all printed there in black and white.

In many minds, the word "bacteria" suggests the scourge of disease, the threat of sinister microorganisms lying in wait for us and the plants and animals we rely on. But only a small percentage of all bacteria are in any way harmful to man. A great number are not only useful, but essential.

Without nitrogen-fixing bacteria in the soil, plant life would be impossible. Bacteria and other microorganisms aid in the digestive processes of most animals, including man, and play a vital part in the manufacture of cheese, the leavening of dough for baking, and the production of alcohol. Bacteria are also responsible for one of man's oldest and most useful culinary substances: vinegar.

Oddly enough, vinegar is both a product of bacterial life, and an inhibitor of bacterial growth. The specific bacteria that play a role in the production of vinegar are called *acetobacters*. In the presence of oxygen, these microorganisms convert alcohol into acetic acid, which can kill or limit the growth of other bacteria. When the strength of an acetic acid solution reaches a certain level, no bacteria, including the acetobacters themselves, can grow. Foods kept in an acetic acid solution will remain free of bacterial contamination for as long as the acid solution remains potent.

Vinegar is simply a dilute solution of acetic acid. The strength of the solution is usually between four and 12 percent, depending on the type of vinegar and its intended use. Household vinegar is low in acetic acid; vinegar used for pickling is usually of higher grain. *Grain* is the term used to measure the strength of vinegars: 10 grains are equal to one percent acid; thus "40 grain" vinegar is a four percent solution of acetic acid.

Vinegar can be manufactured from any saccharine, or sugar-containing, substance capable of converting to alcohol. Fruit juices that produce wine can also be used to produce vinegar, as can grains that are used to make beer and whiskey.

The process that turns this saccharine substance into vinegar consists of two chemical reactions. In the first, yeasts act upon sugar in the fruit or grain product and convert it into alcohol and carbon dioxide. In the second, acetobacters convert this alcohol along with oxygen into acetic acid and water—in other words, into vinegar. In most vinegar production, already fermented fruit juice or fruit mash is placed in an aerated container with a small quantity of bacteria, which convert the fermented material into an acetic acid solution.

Vinegar is used today as a food flavoring and a household cleaner, but by far its most important historical role lies in its use as a food preservative. Before refrigeration and chemical preservatives were developed, man had to rely on salting, drying, and pickling to keep food edible for any length of time. The most important pickling solution has always been vinegar.

Alcohol was the first pure organic compound made by man, and acetic acid produced by the natural souring of wine was man's first acid. The origin of vinegar's use is remote, but pickled meats and vegetables were important items in the diets of many ancient civilizations. Vinegar was mentioned in the Bible, and widely used among early peoples as a food, a preservative, and a medicine.

To the ancient Egyptians, Greeks, and Romans, vinegar was the only acid substance known. In the fourth century B.C., the Greek philosopher Theophrastus gave directions for the preparation of pigments from vinegar and lead, while the physician Hippocrates prescribed vinegar as a medicine. In the Roman Petronius' *Satyricon,* a character

A vinegar seller of old London, as depicted in a 19th-century publication.

who scratches his leg reaches for vinegar the way we might reach for a bottle of iodine.

In earlier times, most vinegar was produced from wine. The English word "vinegar," in fact, is derived from the French words *vin*, "wine," and *aigre*, "sour." France has long been noted for its fine vinegars, which have been exported since at least the 16th century. Frenchman Louis Pasteur used vinegar to a great extent in demonstrating the existence of bacteria.

There are two basic ways to manufacture vinegar: the slow barrel process and the quick generator process. The older slow barrel process is now used only for household production, while the quick generator process is used exclusively for commercial production.

In the *slow generator process*, a mixture of fermented matter—wine, fruit juice, mash, or whatever—is placed in a large aerated cask. The substance containing the acetobacters, called "mother of vinegar," is then added. Fermentation continues for about three to six months, when the vinegar is drawn off via a spigot at the bottom of the cask.

In the past 200 years, discoveries by a Dutchman named Boerhaave and another scientist named J.S. Schutzenbach determined that the rate of vinegar production will be greatly increased if both the surface area of the fermented matter and its oxygen supply are increased. The modern *quick generator process* is a result of these findings.

In this process, a tall vat or "generator" is packed with corncobs, pumice, coke, beechwood shavings, or other suitable materials, which are then covered with the bacteria-laden mother of vinegar. Alcohol trickles into the generator through the top, and comes in contact with the bacteria, in the presence of oxygen provided by air currents rising from the bottom of the vat. Thus more of the alcohol is exposed to bacteria and air at the same time, and vinegar production that once required months now requires as little as eight to 10 days.

The flavor of the vinegar produced by any process is determined by the kind of fermented materials used. In the United States, cider vinegar made from apples and apple cider is the favorite, while in France wine vinegar made from wine or grapes remains the most popular. Vinegar has also been made from fruits such as oranges and pineapples, and—believe it or not—from honey.

White vinegar, also called distilled vinegar, is a relatively tasteless substance made directly from a dilute alcohol solution. So-called wood vinegar is merely a dilute solution of acetic acid, and owes its name to the former practice of distilling acetic acid from wood. Some of the vinegars sold for household use are actually combinations of two or more kinds of vinegar, and many are flavored by the addition of spices such as garlic or tarragon.

The English favor malt vinegar, made from mixtures of barley, oats, and other grains. Malt vinegar is stronger than cider or wine vinegar, and is often used in food preservation. The first vinegar to be used in England, it originally was produced as a way of disposing of soured beer and ale.

Fortunately, most vinegar today has a less glorious origin.

Violins

An old vaudeville joke tells of a society hostess who thought it would be the height of elegance to play a few violin solos after a posh dinner. Accordingly, she had chairs set up in the living room, and invited the guests to be seated for her recital.

She began playing unevenly, and grew steadily worse. As the guests fidgeted, one music lover turned to his neighbor and politely asked: "What do you think of her execution?"

The second man replied instantly: "I'm in favor of it."

Probably no musician has been more ridiculed than the unskilled violinist, for there are few sounds more ear-piercingly offensive than the squeal of a bow scraping across the strings of an ill-played violin. But there are also few sounds more beautiful and evocative than the music of that same instrument in the hands of a master. That potential for lyric beauty has made the violin, though only a few centuries old, the most important instrument in Western orchestral music—and the violin virtuoso, along with the master pianist, the most admired of all concert soloists.

String instruments in general, including the ancient lyre and lute, originated in Asia. The bow, from Persia, was applied to early string instruments by the Arabs to produce the forbears of the modern violin family. In Europe, medieval bowed instruments included the *vielle*, with four fingered strings and a drone string, and the *rebec*, which probably had two or three strings. Of

Five-stringed waisted fiddle.

Ancient Hindu violin.

Some Stradivari violins have been valued at over $450,000.

these, not a single specimen survives. Both instruments were small, and rested on the shoulder when played.

The *viol,* which developed from these medieval fiddles, was the principal bowed instrument that was played from the 15th century until the 17th century. Normally, the viol had six strings, and a fingerboard with frets, like the guitar. The body sloped down obliquely from the neck, and bore sound holes in the shape of the letter *c.* The instrument was held downward on, or between, the legs when played.

In its earliest use, the viol doubled vocal parts, for through the Middle Ages vocal music had been more important than instrumental music. The viol family included three instruments, one for each of the three voice parts: a treble viol, a tenor, and a bass—and later, a double bass. Eventually, composers began to write instrumental pieces for the viol trio and the solo viol.

But the viol had a weak, delicate tone. Gradually, it was altered to increase its resonance, becoming lighter, with more lightly strung strings. The treble viol evolved into the violin, while the tenor viol became the viola. The new instruments featured fretless fingerboards, and four strings like the medieval fiddles, with sound holes in the shape of an *f* rather than a *c*. But the bass viol, or *viola da gamba,* survived into the 18th century, until supplanted by the cello. The double bass viol, or *violone,* is the ancestor of the modern double bass.

The viola was the first of the new instruments to emerge, taking its name directly from the viol. The word *violin* is a diminuitive form of *viola.* The cello was originally called the *violoncello,* which literally means "little violone' or "little big viol."

The violin family began to emerge around 1600, and superceded the viol during the 17th century. By 1750, the violin's form was fixed, and it has undergone only minor changes since then. The neck was made longer to increase the violin's range, and alterations were made to give the instrument a stronger tone suitable for playing in large concert halls. The violin eventually found its way back to Asia, and is now commonly used to play folk music in many nations.

The string quartet, the showpiece of the violin family, is an outgrowth of the old chamber ensemble. Until the 18th century,

Ancient Turkish violin.

this chamber group consisted of two violins along with a harpsichord and bass to play the *basso continuo,* or figured bass. But the harpsichord was an unwieldy instrument for traveling musicians or street performers. So the keyboard was replaced with the viola. By 1750, the cello had replaced the bass, and the string quartet was as it is today: two violins, a viola, and a cello.

By that time, the orchestra had still not reached its modern form. Though the Greeks were familiar with many instruments from the ancient world, they rarely used these instruments together. In medieval times, only

Sordino, an old type of fiddle.

The violin, though only a few centuries old, is the most important instrument in Western orchestral music.

vocal music was notated; and it's not until the 15th century that we find the earliest surviving piece of instrumental music. By the end of the next century, there was still no "orchestra" as we know it, but merely a collection of instruments—harpsichord, lutes, viols, flutes, trumpets, and drums, for instance—used in concert with little regard for balance or grouping.

The earliest music written for an instrumental group similar to the modern orchestra was Monteverdi's opera *Orfeo*, premiered in 1607. Monteverdi was the first composer to realize that a large string section was necessary to give the ensemble a balanced tone. The viol family or the newly developed violin was adopted for the orchestral string section, and all other unbowed stringed instruments were rejected, except the harp. Initially a back-up ensemble for vocal music, the orchestra gradually assumed an existence of its own, and composers began to write music for the unaccompanied orchestra.

The orchestra remained an aristocratic luxury until later that century, when orchestral music was first performed in theaters—and many German nobles boasted private orchestras well into the 18th century. In 1626, Louis XIII established a renowned orchestral group called "The Twenty-four Strings of the King," which featured, not surprisingly, 24 stringed instruments, plus horns.

A Bach piece, written about a century later, called for an orchestra of four trumpets, two flutes, five oboes, first and second violins, violas, cellos, and drums, plus an organ and four voices. Later, composers such as Haydn and Mozart helped shape a new orchestra, with clarinets, bassoons, French horns, and double basses. The modern orchestra usually contains a string section of 18 first violins, 16 second violins, 12 violas, 10 cellos, eight double basses, and two harps; a percussion section; a woodwind section with three flutes, clarinets, oboes, and bassoons, plus a double bassoon, piccolo, English horn, and bass clarinet; and a brass section with four trumpets and trombones, six French horns, and a tuba.

The violin, now the most important single instrument in the orchestra, is also regarded by many as the most beautiful, versatile, and expressive of all musical instruments. Some may opt for the piano, but when it comes to ease of transport, the violin has it all over its keyboard cousin. A violin is on the average just 23 inches from end to end, with a body 14 inches long, a neck with a fretless fingerboard, and four strings, tuned in fifths: g, d, a, e. The horsehair bow is pulled across the strings, whose vibrations are carried by the bridge through the body, where they resonate.

The viola, tuned a fifth lower than the violin, is usually 26 inches long. In the orchestra, the viola initially doubled the cello part, until composers such as Mozart and Haydn gave the instrument independence. But solo viola pieces are rare. Bartok did write a viola concerto, and Hindemith wrote a number of viola sonatas.

Similarly, the earliest cellos were used to reinforce the bass lines. But the cello took on an identity of its own during the 18th century, when it supplanted the viola de gamba. The instrument is generally 48 inches long, tuned an octave and a fifth lower than the violin. Unlike the viola, the cello is often featured as a solo instrument. Bach wrote six suites for an unaccompanied cello, and Beethoven wrote five sonatas for cello and piano.

Violin cello.

The double bass is about 72 inches from end to end, and is tuned two octaves and a third lower than the violin. The instrument originally had three strings, but it now has four, and sometimes five strings. One double bass constructed in the 19th century, called the octobass, stood more than 10 feet tall, and was played with foot levers!

At the other end of the scale, so to speak, we find a tiny violin of recent vintage, completely functional, that measured just two inches from end to end!

To the list of peculiar stringed instruments we might add the *violinista,* a sort of automated violin found in penny arcades in the 1920s. The machine was about three feet long and two feet high, and was electrically operated by air flowing through the perforations of a music roll. Then there was the *pantaleon,* the largest stringed instrument ever constructed for a single player, with 276 strings stretched over a soundboard 11 feet long. Built by an Englishman in the 1760s, the instrument was played with wooden mallets, like a xylophone.

These instruments may have been novel, but far more valuable are the simple violins produced by the greatest violin craftsmen, most of whom flourished in northern Italy between 1600 and 1750. All other musical instruments have reached the peak of their perfection during our century, but the greatest violins were undoubtedly produced during this earlier period.

Antonio and Geronimo Amati of Cremona were two of the early master violin makers who helped shape the instrument. Geronimo's son Nicholas Amati made further improvements on violin construction, but it was Nicholas' star pupil, Antonio Stradivari, who settled the design of the violin and constructed its finest specimens—though some violinists prefer the instruments of Giuseppe Guarnieri, another Cremona master of the time.

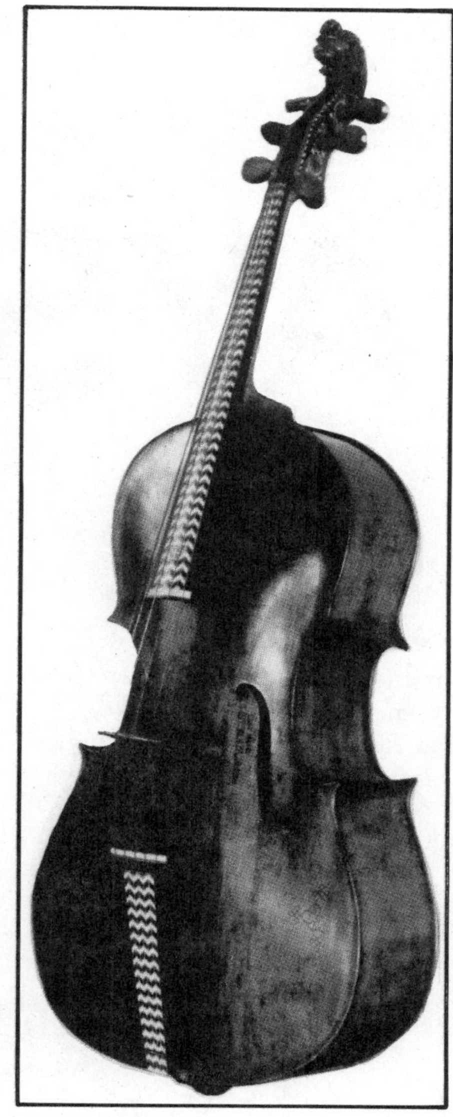

Bass viol (1662).

No one is quite sure what gave Stadivari's violins their exquisite tone. Some people have attributed their characteristic sound to the physical properties of the wood, or to the special pitch that Stradivari derived from the sap of trees then growing in Italy. Others credit his varnish, whose formula has never been discovered. But basically the "secret of Stradivari" is as much a mystery today as it was more than 250 years ago.

Stradivari fashioned about 700 violins, plus scores of violas and cellos; 540 of his violins still exist. One of these instruments, made in 1716, recently sold at auction for $250,000, and other Stradivari violins have been valued at over $450,000!

Among those who have profited most by the work of Stradivari and other violin makers are the great concert violinists, such as Austrian Fritz Kreisler, who reputedly earned more than three million dollars during his career. Another violinist who was amply repaid for his hours of practice was Nicolo Paganini, an eccentric 19th-century master considered by some the greatest violinist of all time. To demonstrate his virtuosity, Paganini occasionally played instruments with just one or two strings, or deliberately played with frayed strings so that when one broke, he could bedazzle his audience by continuing to play with three strings!

Among the most determined violinists, we must certainly mention Otto Funk, who at age 62 walked from New York to San Francisco, playing his violin continually.

But among the most fortunate violinists, we must point to Alexander Schneider, who once left his violin—a Guarnieri valued at over $200,000—in a New York City taxicab. The violin was found by the cab's next passengers, who happened to be sympathetic musicians, and returned it to its thankful owner!

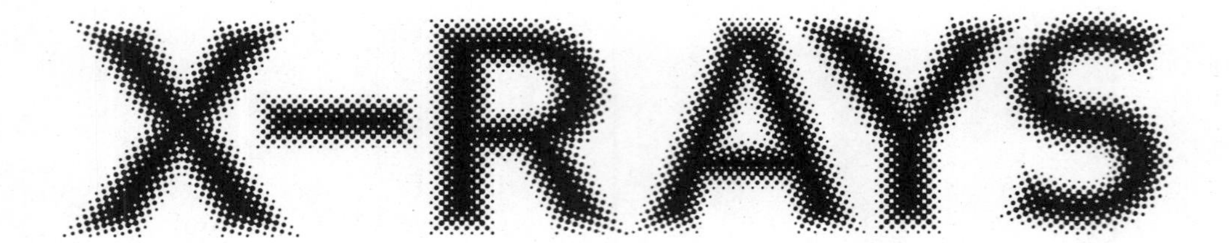

X-RAYS

On November 5, 1895, Wilhelm Konrad Roentgen, professor of physics at the University of Wurzburg, was carrying out some experiments with cathode rays. These rays are beams of electrons, produced by a high voltage current traveling between two electrodes within a closed glass tube. Roentgen covered the tube with black paper so that none of the light generated by the current could escape. But then something happened that was totally unexpected: when the current was turned on in the cathode-ray tube, a fluorescent screen lying nearby began to glow as if it were receiving light.

When the scientist turned off the current in the cathode-ray tube, the screen stopped glowing. Since the glass tube was completely covered, Roentgen knew that the cathode rays were emitting some invisible form of radiation capable of activating the fluorescent coating of the screen. He named the mysterious radiation *X-rays,* since *X* was the usual mathematical symbol for an unknown.

Roentgen immediately began research on X-rays—also called Roentgen rays for a time—and found they could pass through many substances that were opaque to ordinary light. He soon learned that different materirials would allow different

Wilhelm Conrad Rontgen (1845-1923), inventor of the X-ray.

amounts of the radiation to pass through. Since flesh absorbed less radiation than bone did, Roentgen discovered that he could view the shadows of the bones in his hand when he placed it between an X-ray source and a fluorescent screen. For the first time, man might be able to "see inside" a living human body!

Roentgen's findings caused great excitement in the scientific community. Hundreds of scientists began research on X-rays, and thousands of papers were published within just a year or two of Roentgen's initial discoveries. The X-ray research of one man, A.H. Becquerel, eventually led to the discovery of radioactivity. When the Nobel Prizes were instituted in 1901, Roentgen received the first award for physics—though at the time, neither Roentgen nor anyone else knew what X-rays really were.

We now recognize X-rays as a form of electromagnetic radiation, similar to both heat and light. All forms of radiant energy, or electromagnetic waves, are basically the same, differing mainly in the length of their waves, or their *wavelength*.

Electromagnetic rays with the longest wavelength are called *radio* waves. A radio wave may be miles in length, though the radio waves used to transmit sound to your radio are less than 1,800 feet long. The science of radio astronomy seeks to detect radiation of radio wavelength reaching the earth from distant stars and galaxies.

Becquerel develops plates exposed to uranium salts.

Moving down the electromagnetic spectrum toward shorter wavelengths, we next encounter *microwave* radiation, or radiant heat. Shorter still are the wavelengths of *infrared* rays, which are too long to show themselves as visible light, but can be felt as heat. The effects of infrared radiation will also appear on special infrared film.

What we call visible light is actually just one form of electromagnetic radiation, which we experience as color. But the range of visible light forms a very small part of the electro-magnetic spectrum, including only those rays with a wavelength of from 15 millionths of an inch, which we see as violet, to about 30 millionths of an inch, which we see as red.

Moving further down the spectrum, we find *ultraviolet* radiation just beyond the range of visible light. Shorter still are the wavelengths of X-rays. Any electromagnetic rays with a wavelength of from four millionths of an inch down to nearly a billionth of an inch are commonly called X-rays. And beyond X-rays, we find the radiation with the shortest wavelength of all, *gamma* radiation.

The shorter the wavelength of radiation, the greater its energy and the greater its ability to penetrate solid matter. Visible light cannot penetrate most substances, while the energetic gamma rays can penetrate deeply into almost all matter, including living tissue. X-rays have proved useful because of their ability to penetrate different substances according to the density and composition of the substances,

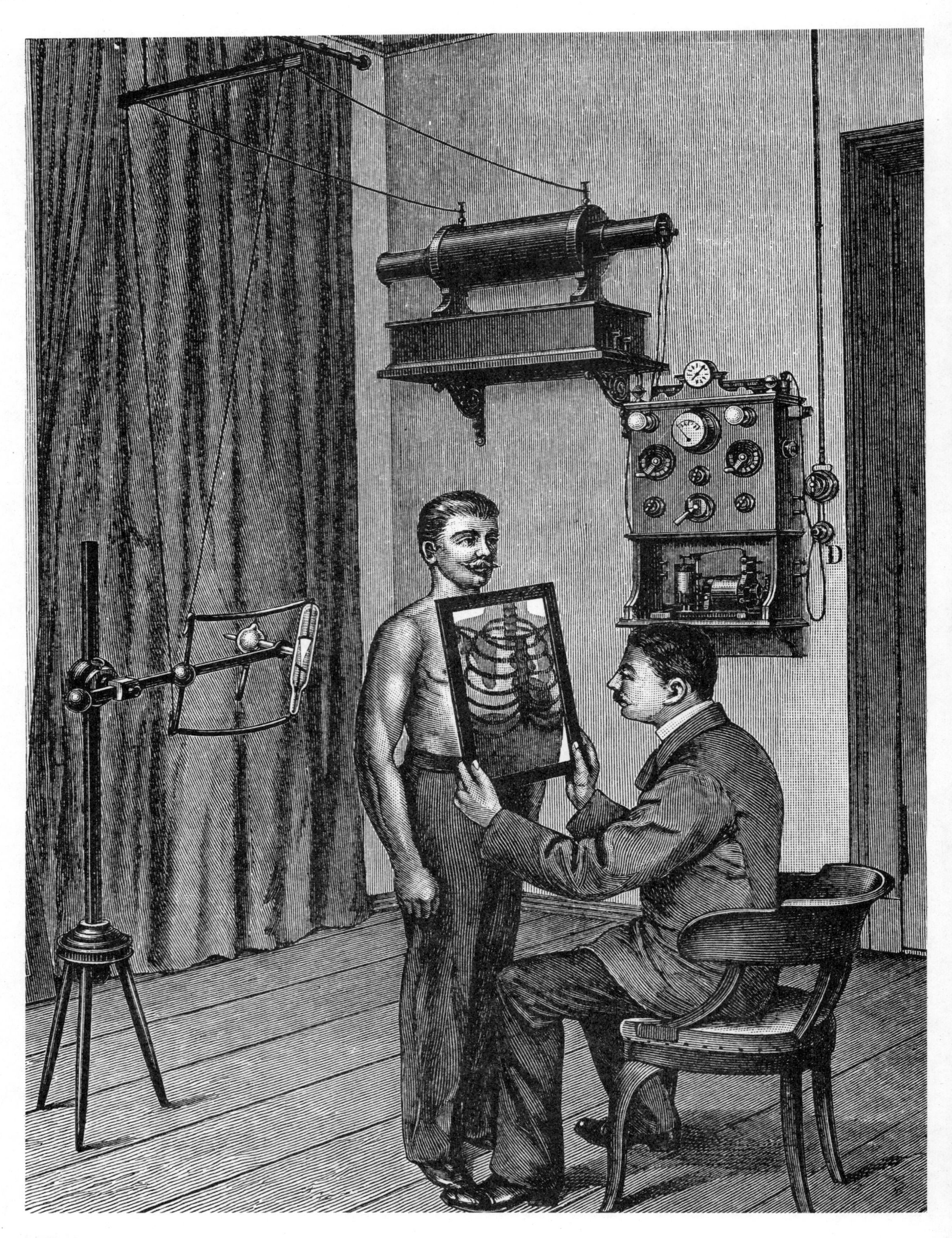

thereby allowing scientists to peer inside things as diverse as a ceiling beam or the human heart.

It wasn't until a few years after Roentgen had received his Nobel Prize that scientists following in Roentgen's footsteps proved X-rays were actually a form of electro-magnetic radiation. This discovery led to many others. In 1906, Charles Barkla was investigating the scattering of X-rays through carbon when he discovered the atomic structure of that element, and Barkla's discovery, in turn, led others to determine the atomic structure of all elements. Aside from their value in medicine, then, X-rays helped scientists unlock the secrets of atomic theory, the relationship between all elements, and the atomic structure of the crystal.

As early as 1896, an X-ray machine was exhibited at a New York amusement parlor, where for 25¢ the curious could view the "Parisian sensation." But X-ray machines were employed in medicine almost from the very beginning. The same year as the New York exhibit, a professor at Davidson College in North Carolina fired a bullet into the hand of a corpse, then used X-rays to locate the bullet. And in 1897, another doctor made the first American X-ray of the entire human body.

The cathode-ray generating device that Roentgen used was called the Crookes tube. In 1913, W.D. Coolidge of the General Electric Company invented an improved device for producing X-rays, the Coolidge X-ray tube. In the early 1920s, these and other X-ray machines became commercially available, and began to find their way into many areas of medicine and other sciences.

The Crookes tube, the Coolidge tube, and other X-ray generating devices employ basically the same principle. A negative-charged cathode made of tungsten is heated by an electric current until excited enough to emit electrons. (Tungsten is used because it has the highest melting point of all elements.) These electrons travel through a near vacuum to the tungsten anode, or positive-charged electrode. The anode stops the electrons, whose kinetic energy is changed to other forms of energy, including heat and X-rays. These X-rays are then channeled through a hole in the tube, and can be directed at any target.

For the most part, X-rays pass through the object to be examined, and show up on either a fluorescent screen or a sheet of special photographic film. But some X-rays are absorbed by the substances they pass through. Areas in which little radiation is absorbed show up lighter on a fluorescent screen, or darker on a photographic negative. Therefore bones or internal organs, which absorb more radiation than does flesh, show up darker, and their outline can be readily examined.

X-rays in higher concentrations will damage tissue cells, and these stronger X-rays have been used in cancer therapy. Radiologists try to kill cancer cells with concentrated beams of X-rays, without destroying the neighboring normal cells. But X-rays sometimes increase the growth of cancer cells, or trigger cancerous growth on their own by destroying cell structure.

X-rays have proved useful beyond medicine, too. Engineers use X-rays to examine the internal structure of building materials and to search for possible weaknesses in existing structures. For instance, an X-ray inspection of St. Peter's Cathedral in York, England, revealed damage to the roof beams from insect borings, and the beams were replaced before they could break. X-rays are also used to sterilize medical supplies that cannot be boiled, to inspect luggage at airports and customs entry points, and to distinguish diamonds from imitation gems.

Similarly, X-rays can verify the age and authenticity of a painting, or look underneath old paintings for traces of earlier works. An X-ray examination of the famous Gainsborough painting entitled "Blue Boy" revealed the figure of a man underneath, from an older canvas Gainsborough had cut down for his work.

Writers and entrepreneurs have put X-rays to a number of other imaginative uses. Among Superman's super powers was his "X-ray vision." A film called *The Man with the X-ray Eyes* hypothesized a man who could see through anything, even time. And shortly after the discovery of X-rays, a British firm was reportedly preparing to market X-ray eyeglasses that would allow the wearer to penetrate through clothing and view another person's body in native buff.

But an even cleverer London entrepreneur put the false report to his advantage, cleaning up on sales of "X-ray-proof" undergarments!

OPPOSITE:
An early X-ray machine.

INDEX

ACKNOWLEDGMENTS

Grateful acknowledgment is made to the following sources which have provided photographs for this work. The photos appear on the enumerated pages.

ALINANT BROTHERS, ROME
211

AMERICAN BANANA COMPANY
50

THE BETTMANN ARCHIVE, INC.
185, 109, 457

GENERAL FOODS CORPORATION
243

GENERAL MOTORS CORPORATION
35-a, 42-a, 42-b

HART PUBLISHING COMPANY, INC.
38, 40, 58, 63, 65, 67, 68, 69, 77, 100, 101, 102-a, 102-b, 103-b, 104, 105-b, 107, 108, 109, 110, 111, 113, 119, 122, 123, 130, 131, 147, 148, 149, 150, 160, 161, 163, 167, 173, 216, 220-a, 220-b, 221, 222, 227, 228, 231, 234, 237, 239, 243, 245, 246, 247, 249, 258, 260-a, 260-b, 260-c, 261-a, 261-b, 262-a, 263, 264-b, 264-c, 265, 267, 268, 269, 353-a, 353-b, 354, 357, 359, 360, 366, 370, 371-a, 371-b, 371-c, 373-b, 412, 416, 418, 419, 424, 435-a, 438, 443, 445, 446, 448, 449, 450, 451, 455, 461, 463, 464, 467, 473-b, 475, 477-a, 478-a, 478-b, 479, 493

HERSHEY CHOCOLATE COMPANY
152

HISTORICAL PICTURE SERVICES
472

HYATT REGENCY HOTEL, CHICAGO
231

MAC DONALD'S
252

MUSEUM OF FINE ARTS, BOSTON
373-a

NEW YORK PUBLIC LIBRARY
7-a, 10, 15-a, 23, 31-a, 31-b, 32-a, 33, 34-a, 35-b, 36, 39, 43, 45, 47, 49, 51, 52, 61-a, 61-b, 61-c, 62, 70, 73, 76, 79, 80, 85, 87, 88, 90, 91, 92, 93, 94, 95, 96, 97, 98, 99, 106, 109, 118, 125, 127, 133, 135, 137, 138, 139, 140, 141, 143, 145, 150, 153, 154, 157, 158, 175, 190, 203, 204, 206, 207, 209, 212, 219, 224, 226, 233, 235, 241, 248-a, 255, 256, 274, 275, 283, 284, 285, 293, 294, 295-a, 296-a, 296-c, 298, 303, 304, 305, 306, 307, 311-c, 318, 325, 326, 337, 342, 343, 348, 391, 405, 407, 409, 410, 411, 413, 415, 416, 417, 418, 420, 421, 422-a, 422-b, 423, 425, 427, 428, 429-a, 429-b, 430, 431, 432, 433, 435, 439-a, 439-b, 440, 447, 457, 469-b, 470-c, 471-d, 471-e, 471-f, 471-g, 480, 481-a, 481-b, 482, 484, 486, 487, 488, 489, 490, 491, 492

NEW YORK TELEPHONE COMPANY
434, 435-b, 436, 437, 453-c

PENNSYLVANIA ACADEMY OF FINE ARTS
270

PICTORIAL PARADE
403

SCHRAFFT'S ICE CREAM CO., LTD.
265

SHERLE WAGNER
453

SINGAPORE TOURIST PROMOTION BOARD
362-a, 362-b

WIDE WORLD PHOTO
378

WORLD OF CITIES AND PEOPLES, VOL. 6
53